The tiny room had become a geometric configuration of madness. The shadows of seven people and three guns flickered on the walls. The dread was palpable. Scientists have demonstrated that fear has its own scent. An ammonia odor. Brady could smell it. It was coming from him. That old boyhood bravado didn't exist anymore, no more than that boy still existed. That sense of exhilaration in the face of menace had been replaced by cold, stark fear. Something bad was about to happen and there was nothing he could do to stop it.

Et Tu Brady

Joseph Collum

Gulf Stream Press
Fort Lauderdale, Florida

Et Tu Brady
Copyright © 2013 by Joseph Collum
All rights reserved.

This is a work of fiction. Names, characters, places and incidents are products of the author's imagination and/or used fictitiously. Any similarities to actual events, locales, or persons living or dead, are purely coincidental.

ISBN – 13:978-1482601473 (paperback)
ISBN – 10: 1482601478 (e-book)
Library of Congress Control Number: 2013930845
CreateSpace Independent Publishing Platform
North Charleston, South Carolina.

Proudly written and manufactured in the United States of America.

Gulf Stream Press
Fort Lauderdale, Florida

Where the cool breeze blows and the warm sea flows.

Dedicated to my brothers,
John, Jim & Rick Collum

Prologue

From The Diary of Michael Fury
Slave, Pirate, Irishman

August 18, 1674 –

The end began at dawn with a cry from the crow's nest.

"Cap'n! Sails! Three leagues off larboard bow. Spanish galleons."

Ned Pike burst across the quarterdeck, a vision in white against an ominous purple sky. He cut through the wind, his frame lean and well above middle height, his billowy white shirt tuck'd haphazardly into tight white breeches. Black seaboots thudding the oak planks, he vaulted to the helm. His eyes was fiery lamps.

"Mr. Cobb!" he shouted to the First Mate in that Irish brogue I remember as if it be yesterday. "Rouse the bloody crew. Any man not on deck in thirty seconds will be strung from the yard!"

"Aye, cap'n."

"Mr. Fury!"

I be Michael Fury and on that fateful day I be'd Ned Pike's cabin boy, a wide-eyed urchin of but ten-and-three years.

"Wake Mr. Binns," the captain ordered me. "Tell him to stoke the galley fires and prepare breakfast. I want me crew fed before we engage."

"Aye, sorr," said I and rushed off to the trill shriek of the bo'sun's whistle piping the crew to their posts.

At that instant *The Nemesis* was plowing through whitecapped seas pushed by an angry south wind. The night constellations had but recently receded and the sky had morphed from black to purple to opalescent. Then I got me first glimpse of the ghostly silhouettes of the Spanish galleons on the ocean's rim. Ned Pike shouted at the barefoot men scrambling from the hold.

"Make haste, lads. They'll soon be upon us," He turned to a short, stocky, rugged man at the helm. "Mr. Folger, bear forty-five degrees southward."

Mr. Folger grappled the whipstaff and forced the tiller hard over and *The Nemesis* veered severe to starboard. But the ship was sluggish. She was riding low and I could see in the captain's eyes that he be savvy we would not outrun the square rigs, not with every rag of cloth on our yards.

For six months, Ned Pike had been leading *The Nemesis* on a rampage through the Caribbean. With our crew of fifty-five we stalked the coasts of Peru, Mexico, Barbados and Cuba. Harrying the Spanish treasure fleet and harvesting a vast hoard. But after the long incursion the schooner's underbelly was corrupt with barnacles and too foul for speed. That condition was embellished by the many tons of gold and silver bullion, chests of pieces-of-eight, doubloons and escudos, casks of pearls, and artifacts pillaged from Incan tombs. All of it stowed beneath our decks.

Irony is lost on no Irishman. Like Ned Pike, Irish blood runs through me own veins, and I fathomed the sad irony of our plight. With the ship's bowels gorged to the brim, our peregrination was nearing its end. Pike was the most notorious rascal in the Caribbean and a handsome price had been put upon his head. The captain told me so hisself in a reflective moment whilst taking breakfast in his cabin not three days prior.

2

"Laddie, the dice has fallen our way longer than any mortal men dare expect. The hour has come to abandon these piratical ways or we'll all find ourselves dancin' the devil's jig at the end of hempen neckcloths."

Captain Pike had a plan. We was to sail *The Nemesis* east to the Isle of Bimini where we would beach her in Tyree's Lagoon. There we'd scrape her bottom and tar and pitch her. Thereafter the captain would divvy the trove. Double share for him. Share-and-a-half for First Mate Phineas Cobb. One share-and-a-quarter to the other officers. And a full share to each crew member. Any man who'd lost an arm or leg during our sojourn would receive an extra thousand pieces-of-eight. Even I, a lowly cabin boy, was promised a half-share. For most of the men that meant the equivalent of fifty bowls of gold coin, a vast and generous fortune. Ned Pike intended to abandon the Caribbean and sail to Polynesia.

"Live out me days in unruffled tranquility on a pristine beach surrounded by languorous beauties in grass skirts. If ye like, lad, I will take ye with me."

The first breath of sizzling sowmeat was rising from the ship's belly and mingling with the briny wind when Captain Pike's steely gaze veered from the Spanish vessels larboard to the cockcrow sky. There appeared to be a long cloud hanging low over the western horizon.

"The Floridas," said he.

"'Tis sanctuary, cap'n?"

He cast benevolent eyes down on me. "Ney, lad. The natives is not a peaceable race. I have heard many a tale. They be hardy warriors, but they be cannybals. We shall take our chances with the Spaniards. We have dispatched plenty enough of 'em to know their measure."

Pike's eyes shifted to the southward sky. It looked like Dante's nightmare. Hideous black thunderheads was rolling toward us like a raging herd of African elephants.

"We be in for a storm, sorr," said I.

"Quite a tempest, lad." He turned his attention to the enemy warships looming ever larger to the east. "Crowd the canvas, Mr.

Folger," he hollered. "Point her sou-by-souwest. We will hug the land and search for safe harbor. If'n that fails mayhaps we can lose 'em in the weather."

"Aye, cap'n."

As morning lapsed, the enemy drew inexorably nearer. By noon the wind had grew to a fierce gale. *The Nemesis* heaved through ever more furious black swells. Mountains of sea crashed over our gunwales and we was deluged by impenetrable sheets of rain. The decks flooded and the bilge pumps was got to work.

Tall and steadfast, Ned Pike remained at his post on the quarterdeck, his shirt pasted like whitewash to his broad shoulders, holding tight to the carved taffrail, reading the sails, barking orders, measuring the progress of the approaching galleons. A faint eerie smile curled on his lips as his eyes vacillated betwixt the Spanish and the endless shoreline a league west. But there was no trace of cove or lagoon suitable for retreat. The galleons pressed resolutely. Pike put his eye to the telescope and shouted into the wind.

"If'n we find no harbor, lad, or cannot vanish into the storm, them barks'll be athwart our hawse before next bell. When they commence to loosing broadsides, stick close to me side."

The wind and water grew to a ghastly state, as if Neptune hisself be scorning us. The deck was a fuddle of frenzy and confusion. Crewmen hurtled in every direction bellowing wildly over the gale. Bare-chested men strained furiously at the ropes trying to keep the crowd of canvas bellying to the fore. Sailors stretched sturdy nets over the waist to snare toppling spars. Gunners enflamed their matches.

All the while *The Nemesis* plunged through the angry black swells in desperate search of deliverance. Despite her full yards, though, the ship was listless. Our race was futile. In no time the first galleon was within a cable's length of our starboard. Eighteen brass cannons nosed from her flanks.

Mr. Folger hollered from the wheel. "I'm afeared we be checkmated, cap'n."

Ned Pike turned on the hatchet-faced helmsman with Hades in his eyes.

Et Tu Brady

Chapter One

MORE THAN THREE centuries later, Benjamin Chance knelt before a full-length mirror. He was naked and his hands were bound behind him. His neck was swiveling like a bobblehead doll as he gazed bleary-eyed at his own grotesque reflection. He looked up at a dark figure standing behind him.

"Why are you doing this to me?"

The shadow was holding a long white electrical cord with the rubber coating shaved from its end. The bare metal had been fashioned into a shiny copper noose. Chance watched the mirror as the umbral silhouette slipped the loop over his head and tightened it around his throat. The fat man shivered at the touch of the chill metal on his pasty white skin.

"Because, Benjamin, it is your destiny."

Chance's body quaked and he began to weep.

"But I never hurt you."

"I'm gratified to hear that, Benjamin. But you have opened a grave. You have unleashed demons. You should have let the dead lie. That was your mistake. I'm genuinely sorry."

The dark figure wrapped a wet cloth around his neck over the exposed wire. Chance whimpered.

"Please don't hurt me."

The shadow stretched the plug-end of the wire to the nearest wall, leaned over and, with a gloved hand, inserted the prongs into a socket above the floor board.

"I want you to know, Benjamin, this will not be painful. I'm afraid, though, it is the only way. You understand."

"No, I don't."

Ben Chance fell back onto his haunches. His chin sank to his chest and a plaintive high-pitched wail came from somewhere deep inside him. The intruder reached out to a light switch on the wall. He flipped it upward and one hundred twenty volts of electricity coursed through Chance's skin, hair, and muscles. He bolted upright and his mouth opened in a silent scream. His body convulsed and his heart twitched wildly. Black smoke wafted from beneath the cloth around his throat and the floor where his knees and feet were touching the carpet. The shuddering lasted thirty seconds before his aorta seized and his blood stopped flowing and Chance collapsed onto his side.

With the scent of cooked flesh tinging the air, the shadow let the electric current continue another minute before yanking the plug from the socket, then knelt beside the still body and pressed a finger to Chance's carotid artery. He was gone. The murderer pulled open a black satchel, extracted a needle-like device, and spoke to the lifeless mound.

"Now, Benjamin, for your epitaph."

8

Et Tu Brady

Chapter Two

"OCCULT."

"ORACLE."

"ORATORIO."

"Obligato."

Max Brady wondered how he'd gotten to this place, stretched out in front of this fire, laying on this blanket, outside this tent, next to this woman…

"Oscillate," he volleyed.

"Oxymoron," she countered.

…both of them in their birthday suits, blissful, content, engaged in a war of *O*'s.

"Oligarchy."

"Onomatopoeia."

"Good one."

Their only cover was a radiant canopy of stars dappling the night sky over Fort Lauderdale. She lay on her left side, head propped on one hand, orange flames dancing in her pupils, her lips crimpled at the corners in the barest hint of a smile.

"Tell me again, Brady. This game is supposed to prove what exactly?"

"Vocabulary. Multiply all the *O* words you know by one hundred and that's the size of your vocabulary."

"Oh."

"That doesn't count."

"What's good?"

"Somebody like you, with degrees in French literature and zoology? Fifty thousand words."

"That's a lot of words."

"Five hundred *O* words. It's good mental exercise, too. Fends off J.A."

"J.A.?"

"Junior Alzheimer's."

"How's that going?"

"How's what going?"

"Brady, you're such a knucklehead. Oeuvre."

"No French words."

"Says who?"

"Moi."

"You're making the rules up as you go. Okay, how about octothorpe?"

"Now you're throwing words against the wall hoping they stick like SpaghettiOs. You have to know the definition, Miss Smartypants."

"In case you hadn't noticed, I'm not wearing any pants."

He looked at her with agitated eyes. "Stop trying to distract me? Definition?"

"Octothorpe – that hash mark thingy. Looks like a tic-tac-toe board. The pound key."

"Hmmm. You think you're pretty clever, don't you?"

"Clever, *oui*. Pretty, *peut-être*."

"There's no *maybe* about it, mon amour."

"Merci, monsieur."

"Organdy."

"Definition."

"Fabric."

"Not very precise, but I'll accept it. Obdurate."

"Orgasm."

"Oh, no," she said.

"Don't 'oh, no' me, lady. I know you know that one."

"Oh, no. My telephone. It's vibrating."

"Oy vey!"

A silver moon was smiling down from its perch in the stars. In the light her face looked like finely carved ivory. She stretched her arm inside the tent flap and felt around until her hand came out clutching a thin white rectangle with a pulsating neon screen. She arched her brow apologetically.

"Sorry, Brady. That's what you get for canoodling a public servant."

"Just doing my civic duty."

She smirked at him and spoke into the device.

"Hello, this is Commissioner Rose Becker."

They'd been together for months. Ever since a stormy October night when she saved his life and he, in turn, saved hers. Not together as in married. Closer than that. So close sometimes it was as if they were no longer Max and Rose, but a single being. Reading each other's thoughts, feeling each other's emotions, only happy when they were together, talking, laughing, touching, kissing.

They'd made an art of long languorous trysts that often lasted entire days and nights – miles out at sea on the deck of his schooner, lingering between the sheets of her pink canopy bed, camping in his tent. Or fast, furious assignations. Brady running upstairs to the Papillon, Rose's rooftop gym, and pulling her into the shower room. Rose slipping downstairs to the Sea Shanty, Brady's beach bar, and luring him into the cramped galley. They were carefree as a couple of kites.

One lazy day they were dawdling down the beach, splashing each other, jumping in and out of the turquoise surf, when the yearning overtook them. They dashed across the beach road into one of the new luxury hotels and searched about until they found a room on the third floor left open by a cleaning crew. They hung a *Do Not Disturb* sign on the door knob and didn't come out for two hours. Another night, after an evening drinking French champagne and gliding around a dance floor, they snuck into Rose's office at City Hall. The next morning they were sprawled on the floor, still in a state of communion, when they were awakened by a cleaning lady pounding on the door. Brady was as rapturous as a love-struck teenager. It was the first time he'd felt true bliss since the death of his wife Victoria in the terrorist attack on 9/11.

"Oh, yes, captain," Rose said. "He's right here. Let me put him on."

She pressed the phone against the white flesh of her right breast.

"It's Captain Register from the police department. He wants to talk to you."

"About?"

"I didn't ask."

"Tell him I'm in front of a campfire, canoodling my City Commissioner."

"Brady, that's no campfire."

"Tell Register I didn't do it. I swear. I'm innocent."

"Innocent?" Her face wore a dubious expression. She put the phone to her ear. "Captain, I'm sorry. Mr. Brady is canoo…"

Brady snatched the telephone from her hand and crushed it against his thigh.

"Are you crazy? Think of my reputation." He raised the phone. "Hello, captain. No, no, don't apologize. No, nothing important." Rose stuck out her tongue. "What can I do for you? What's that?" Brady listened for several seconds. "No, captain, there's some mistake. I'm not a lawyer. Not anymore. I haven't practiced in years."

He shrugged at Rose. They were *camping* on the rooftop of the Papillon Gym. Brady had set up his red Adirondack pup tent and ignited three Quik-Start faux logs in a cast iron firepot with stars and crescent moons cut into the sides. He'd brought up fruit, cheese, and two bottles of good Beaujolais from the Sea Shanty. As sparks from the fire drifted into the black sky, they had spent three magnificent hours enjoying each other. Brady intended to stretch that as far into the night as possible.

"Mrs. Cross?" he said. "Sorry, captain. Name doesn't ring a bell. She's got me confused with someone else." Then his eyes widened. "Delray Cross? Are you sure?"

Brady listened for a moment then shot upright.

"Ben? When? Where? Yes, I know it. I'll be right there."

Et Tu Brady

Chapter Three

RED AND BLUE light ricocheted off the oak boughs arching over Rio Vista Boulevard. A fire truck, an ambulance, and a dozen police cars were parked at all angles in the road and grassy margins next to the sidewalks. Neighbors in bathrobes clustered behind yellow crime scene ribbon, hands-to-mouths, speaking in hushed tones, heads shaking, like early Christians contemplating the Pharisees. They didn't seem mournful so much as horrified that the strobe lights might further diminish the battered property values in their elegant enclave. Rio Vista was a street without joy.

Brady had reluctantly – very reluctantly – left Rose on the rooftop next to the fire. She'd wrapped herself in a thin blanket and watched him dress. Ever the fashionista, he threw on a pair of tattered khaki shorts, a Sea Shanty T-shirt with its skull-and-crossbones logo, and black high-top sneakers. He planted a wet kiss on her lips and promised to return soon. She opened the blanket.

"You better, Brady, if you want more of this tonight."

He moaned involuntary and walked away, but the image remained lodged in his brain during the ten minute drive. He steered his old red Jeep Wrangler south on the beach road then west over the

17th Street Causeway Bridge. He turned right on Cordova Road and wended his way to Rio Vista.

Brady hadn't been to the Chance home in nearly three decades. The graceful white Spanish-style house he remembered from childhood was gone. Now a rambling modern structure with lots of glass and metal and sharp edges sat on the site. It was so large he had to look twice to make sure it wasn't two separate homes. Ben Chance was either very rich, he thought, or in a metric shitload of debt.

Human shadows swarmed in the artificial light outside the house. Brady parked on the roadside swale, ducked under the yellow tape, and made his way to the end of the cul-de-sac.

Captain Ron Register was conferring with three uniformed officers outside the front door. Register was Chief of Homicide, a tall, lean, ramrod-straight man who looked like a two-by-four was strapped to his spine. He saw Brady and raised a forefinger for him to wait. A young officer carrying a clipboard marched up like a tin soldier and asked Brady to autograph the security log documenting everyone entering the crime scene.

Register met him at a spiked black wrought-iron gate at the mouth of the driveway. The police captain was a couple of inches taller than Brady's six-feet-three-inches and at least a decade older than his forty two years. He was impeccably dressed in a charcoal gray gabardine suit, crisp white shirt, and yellow-and-white striped tie that made Brady nostalgic for cops in leisure suits.

"Thanks for coming, Brady," the policeman said with starched formality. "I hope I didn't interrupt anything."

"Where's Delray?"

"Mrs. Cross is with paramedics in the study. She fainted while we were questioning her. I thought we'd let her rest until you arrived."

Brady followed Register through the gate and across a cobblestone drive and they stamped up the front steps into the house. The foyer was large and grand, the floor black marble with an ornate *BC* inlaid in red. A magnificent crystal chandelier showered light on a spiral staircase made of glass. It was very *Architectural Digest*.

At the top of the stairs Register turned right. Brady was distracted by a flash at the opposite end of the hallway, like heat-lightning from an unseen source. A knot of police officers and crime scene technicians stood in muted consultation outside a doorway. Beyond them a floor-to-ceiling window looked out over an expansive patio and swimming pool.

The house was built on a bend of New River, hence Rio Vista, español for River View. Clever. Branding was everything. Fort Lauderdale – with three hundred miles of inland waterways – had long ago branded itself the *Venice of America*. New River was its Grand Canal. A sizable white Hatteras yacht was moored to the dock behind the house. Beyond it a polychromatic reflection of downtown skyscrapers shimmered upside-down on the glassy black water.

Heat-lightning flared again at the corner of Brady's eye. Cameras were at work in a room overlooking the river. He felt a rush of melancholy. A three-decade old image of Ben Chance sprang from his memory bank. He shook it away and followed Captain Register in the opposite direction. They entered a darkened room illumined by a single green-shaded lamp on a broad mahogany desk. A female police detective wearing white latex gloves was rifling through the drawers, holding a small Kel-lite flashlight and scribbling on an inventory list. Another officer was searching a bookshelf that covered the wall behind her.

A woman in a feather-print black V-neck dress sat in a high-backed green leather chair beside the desk. Her face was thinner and more acutely boned than he remembered, but the basic geometry hadn't changed. The long palomino locks were shorter now and the color of freshly minted gold, accentuating a long white throat as graceful as a swan. The girl frozen in his recollection had grown into an elegant woman. At that instant, though, she looked meek and fragile, like a lost child. She glanced up and raised a hand to her throat.

"Max? Is that you?"

"It's me."

"Oh, Max."

Delray Chance's face crumpled and tears streamed down her cheeks. Brady stepped to the chair, dropped to one knee, and wrapped his arms around her shoulders. She buried her face against him and sobbed. He felt her fingernails dig into his back.

"It's okay, Del. I'm here."

It had been twenty nine years since Brady last saw her. Any feelings he'd once harbored for her had long-since turned to dust. Yet, the sensation of holding her in his arms again was like an out-of-body experience.

"Max," she said, "Benjamin's dead."

"I know, Del. I'm so sorry."

"The police think I murdered him."

Ron Register stood on the opposite side of the desk, hands in pockets, watchful, shrewd, kneading something in his mouth.

"That's not exactly the case, Mrs. Cross," he said.

"Then why did you read me my rights?"

"At this moment we have no preconceptions. We're simply trying to piece together what led to your brother's death."

Brady separated himself from Delray, regained his feet and gently squeezed her right shoulder. She tilted her tear-streaked face up to him. Her wet eyes were blue as cornflowers, as vivid as he recalled from childhood.

"Captain Register's just doing his job, Del. I'm sure he doesn't consider you a suspect."

He reached into his back pocket and extracted a handkerchief. She sniffled and tried to smile.

"You never were without a handkerchief, were you Max?"

She dabbed her eyes with trembling hands, brittle to the point of breaking. He motioned toward a green leather couch against the book-lined wall.

"Why don't you lie down and rest while I have a word with the captain."

Delray swiped the cloth across her cheeks and nodded. "Okay, Max, whatever you say."

Her voice caught and more tears cascaded. Brady helped her to the couch.

"It's so good to see you, Max. You look wonderful."

"You too, Del. Sorry it has to be under these circumstances."

18

Et Tu Brady

Chapter Four

BRADY STEPPED INTO the hallway behind Register. They turned right and proceeded toward the flashing lights. The walls on either side were adorned with pieces of art. They looked expensive.

"You two were friends?" said the homicide chief.

"Long time ago. What's the story, captain?"

"Nine-one-one got a call just before twenty-one hundred hours."

"From?"

"Mrs. Cross. I haven't heard the tape yet. I'm told she sounded frantic. Screaming that her brother was unconscious and needed immediate help. By the time EMS arrived he was ten-fifty-five. Coroner's case. Body's still here."

They rounded the corner and were about to enter a sprawling room when a female crime scene tech stopped them and handed Register and Brady blue surgical booties.

"Gentlemen," she said with curt professionalism, "please put these on over your shoes, thank you."

Brady did as asked and entered the room. To his right French doors were opened onto a balcony that overlooked the river. A fragile breeze coming off the water rustled floral-print silk curtains on either side of the doors. At the opposite end of the room two chairs and a loveseat were arranged into a sitting area. On a raised platform in between sat a king-sized bed covered by a lush comforter and skirt identical to the curtains. More paintings garnished the walls, all of them modernistic. They looked to be originals. He thought of his late wife and all the art museums she used to drag him to. The Met, the MoMA, the Guggenheim. Ben Chance had made his home into a museum. Hanging on the wall over the bed was an avant-garde image of a woman whose face was fractured into a dozen pieces. He recognized it as a Picasso. Cubism Period. Brady whistled silently between his teeth. Ben *had* been loaded.

Blue-shod police and crime scene techs were picking over the room like a flock of birds pecking for worms. One was inside a large walk-in closet, his fingers methodically testing each garment for suggestive lumps, ears alert for the suspicious crinkling of hidden paper. Through an open bathroom door, Brady watched an investigator lift the ceramic lid off the toilet's water tank and stare inside. Beside him a woman was nosing around in the medicine chest, like a guest at a house party. A young male technician was on hands and knees with a flashlight searching beneath every stick of furniture while a fingerprint man dusted black powder onto a door jamb. Another tech was stretching a tape measure from wall to bed and relaying numbers to an artist drawing a detailed sketch of the room. Yet another investigator was documenting what everyone else was doing and cataloguing items being confiscated for evidence. Brady had gone through the same drill hundreds of times in his past life as an NYPD detective and had to fight off a Pavlovian instinct to join in on the fun.

At the foot of the bed, a photographer was snapping photos of an obese body lying on the floor. The dead man's back was facing the door and his hands were lashed behind him with silver duct tape. An electrical cord with the rubber insulation stripped off one end was wrapped around his neck like a dog's leash. The wire snaked to the nearest wall, its plug on the floor below an electrical outlet. A tall floor lamp shaped like a coconut tree lay on its side in the corner of the room.

"Hello, Max."

A slim, well-constructed woman in a white laboratory smock was standing beside him with her hand extended. She had dark eyes, long lashes, and a black ponytail. *Broward County Medical Examiner's Office* was stitched in blue over her left pocket. Brady took her hand and gave it a small squeeze.

"Hello, Belinda. We've got to stop meeting like this."

Belinda Boulanos regarded him with a tiny smile. They'd met months before at the murder scene of Brady's friend Jonas Bigelow.

"I guess I'm not exactly the neighborhood Welcome Wagon, am I?"

"Not for the breathing."

"I take it Mr. Chance was a friend of yours."

"Once upon a time."

"My condolences."

Brady's eyes strayed to the large form on the floor.

"Thanks, but I haven't seen him in many, many years. How'd this happen?"

Boulanos' handsome face twisted in thought and she referred to a clipboard wedged into the crook of her elbow. Brady wondered why such an attractive woman had chosen to dedicate her life to the science of death.

"Electrocution," she said, scanning her notepad. "Electrical execution to be more precise. Initial indications are the perpetrator slipped Mr. Chance a Mickey Finn. Corpus delicti shows no signs of resistance. We found a glass containing a few drops of whiskey and a white residue. I gave it a sniff test. Seems to be some type of opiate. Won't know exactly what until the labs come back. His hands and ankles were bound and the killer knelt him in front of that standing mirror. He…"

"Or she," Ron Register interjected.

"Correct," agreed Belinda. "The bad guy could be a bad girl. At this point we don't know Mr. Chance's sexual proclivities. The fact he's naked introduces the possibility he was engaged in some kind of sexual activity. Perhaps fetishistic or sadomasochistic, consider-ing the bound hands and legs. Possible bondage or domination. If he was sufficiently drugged, a woman could have done this. So far we've got nothing either way."

"Maybe there were two perps," Brady said.

"Possibly. So far, though, I see no signs of an accomplice. He, eh, or she, ripped the cord from that palm tree lamp over there, shaved a length of rubber coating off the end, and wrapped the bare copper wire around Mr. Chance's throat. A wet cloth was placed over the wire, probably to enhance electrical conductivity. Then the cord was plugged into the wall socket."

Brady grimaced. "Jesus!"

"The skin around his neck is red and blistered and his knees and toes have some charring." The coroner approached the corpse and, with the blue toe of her right booty, pointed out two black patches on the camel-colored carpet. "He was hit with one hundred twenty volts of alternating current. The electricity shot through his body and exited through his knees and toes, thus the burn marks on the rug."

Brady shook his head. "Sounds gruesome."

"But not necessarily painful. My guess is the actual cause of death will be cardiac arrhythmia brought on by V-fib."

"V-fib?"

"Ventricular fibrillation. A violent twitching of the vascular muscles. Sudden shock, even at low voltage, can disrupt the heart's electrical rhythm and bring on sudden cardiac death. Electrocution fatalities are typically instantaneous."

"What is the estimated time of death?"

Boulanos looked at her watch and absently tapped the face with one finger.

"Body temp is ninety two degrees Fahrenheit. Cadavers lose about a degree-and-a-half of heat per hour. So he died approximately four hours ago. Around nineteen hundred hours."

Brady gazed down at Ben Chance's corpse. The skin of his back was already gray with necrosis. The police photographer had finished taking pictures and the Medical Examiner's body removal team was unfolding a black plastic bag on the floor. Ron Register stepped up, the perpendicular creases between his eyebrows crinkled into a *W*.

"There's something else," he said with grave solemnity.

Brady studied his face. He wasn't sure he wanted to hear anymore. "Don't keep me in suspense, captain."

Register moved to the far side of the body and waved him forward like a cop directing traffic. Brady went to his side and looked down at his old friend's face. He gasped.

Ben's eyes bulged from their sockets, as blank and inanimate as a pair of glass marbles. His fat face was petrified in a death grin and the swollen tongue protruding from his rictus mouth was black as Brady's sneakers. The grotesque sight reminded him of strangulations he'd responded to at NYPD.

But the real shock was the three words tattooed across Ben Chance's forehead.

Et Tu Brady

Chapter Five

MAX BRADY AND Ben Chance became friends on a blue spring day in eighth grade. They were classmates at Our Lady of Perpetual Sorrow, an elementary school run by a gaggle of Roman Catholic nuns who ruled their young charges with a witches brew of iron discipline, abject fear, and God's good love.

It was an exciting time. School was about to recess for summer. Next year Max would enter high school and be rid of the sisters, especially the ruthless Irish principal Sister Mary Aloysius, known to a generation of students as *Attila the Nun*.

On that day his thoughts were as far as they could possibly be from pencils and books and Sister Attila's bloodcurdling looks. Max was ensconced at his desk, third seat from the front in the far right-hand row. Across the classroom sat Richard Strong, his best friend, a freckle-faced boy with rust-colored hair. Strong was six inches taller than Max, who had thus nicknamed him *Peanut*. They'd met one day in second grade – when Max cajoled him into swapping his chocolate milk for a bag of Oreos – and had been inseparable ever since. Frick and Frack. Butch and Sundance. Batman and Robin. The nuns had spent the better part of their elementary years trying to keep them as far apart as possible in a doomed crusade to sabotage their endless laughing, whispering, and spitball fights.

At the front of the classroom, a prehistoric vestal named Sister Margaret Mary was droning on about Mortal Sin. Mortal sins were the capital felonies of Catholicism. A one way ticket to Hell. No *Get Out Free* cards. The landmines were everywhere. Skip Sunday Mass – eternal damnation. Commit blasphemy – permanent perdition. Eat meat on Friday – your soul shall be toast. The way the nuns told it, though, the nuclear bomb of all sin was *sex*. Sister Margaret Mary had dropped that unwelcome tidbit on the class of thirteen-and-fourteen-year-olds like the pilot of the Enola Gay unleashing Little Boy on Hiroshima.

"Deliberately stimulating your private organs for sexual pleasure is a Mortal Sin!" she announced. "Punishment is the everlasting fires of Hell."

The words were barely out of her mouth when Skinny Wentworth fell out of his desk onto the floor. Ginger Brennan burst into tears. Scotty Knoll raised his hand and asked if he could go make a Confession. About half the class began to sweat visibly.

Max rarely paid attention anymore. The nuns and priests had lectured, browbeat, and bullied him for eight years, indoctrinating him with their rules on how he must live his life. For most of his time at Our Lady of Perpetual Sorrow he'd accepted their teachings without question. But somewhere along the line he'd stopped listening. It was his life and he would live it the way he saw fit.

"Water is life," his grandfather was fond of telling him. That suited the boy fine, because water was *his* life, or at least the best part of it. So when Sister Margaret Mary went into her fire-and-brimstone routine, he began daydreaming about the coming summer and spending every waking hour on or in or under the water. Skiing on New River. Mango wars at Whiskey Creek. Scuba diving on Three Mile Reef. And every scene included a tall yellow-haired girl with sapphire eyes and the face of an angel.

Brady had worshipped Delray Chance since third grade. She was so exquisite she seemed to give off her own light. He dreamed of floating through the sky with her on a cottony cloud. Riding dolphins with her in the sea. Kissing her at The Cove. Tragically, though, Delray barely knew he existed. It wasn't her fault. Over all their years in school together Max had never actually spoken to her. He'd tried. More times than he could count. But, invariably, he became so hopelessly tongue-tied that his normally fertile mind went blank.

Once, as an altar boy, he was assisting Father O'Brien serve Holy Communion during a student Mass. They made their way around the altar rail until they came upon Delray, kneeling, eyes closed, hands steepled in prayer, head tilted back, tongue out, waiting to receive the sacred host. She may as well have been wearing a halo. Max melted inside. This was his chance to get her attention. On impulse he rubbed the sole of his shoe on the carpet and touched the gold server's plate to her long white throat, sending a short jolt of static electricity through her. Delray started, then stiffened, then glared up at him like he was a zit on the end of her nose. As far as he knew he was less than nothing in her eyes. Even so, to his eye Delray Chance was the prettiest girl in school and he vowed to finally break the ice at next week's Eighth Grade Cotillion by asking her to dance.

Max was still stargazing when the loud speaker crackled to life and Sister Mary Aloysius's harsh brogue rushed into the classroom like an arctic zephyr.

"All students into the courtyard – *at once!*"

He looked across the room. Peanut raised his eyebrows and shrugged. Chairs scraped, feet shuffled, and the class filed out into the warm May day. Five hundred uniformed kids. Boys in white shirts, black ties, and khaki pants; girls in green plaid skirts and white blouses. Cherubic six-year-old first graders to grizzled eighth grade teenagers. They lined up on the sidewalk surrounding the Great Lawn where the student body recited the Our Father every morning then the Pledge of Allegiance as the flag was raised.

Peanut squeezed through the pack to Max, a complicit smile painted on his bespeckled face.

"Holy surprise assembly, Batman," he said. "What's happening?"

"They're renaming the school."

"Really? But Our Lady of Perpetual Sorrow is so appropriate."

"They've decided to name it after the greatest student in school history."

Peanut regarded him with a scornful squint. "And who might that be – as if I didn't know?"

"I can't reveal my sources, however I have it on good authority that henceforth Our Lady of Perpetual Sorrow will be known as the Maximus Brady School for the Very Cool."

"Brady, you're such a peckerhead," Peanut said and frogged his arm. Max's knees buckled.

"Retard!" he said, rubbing a knot welling up on his forearm. "Do that again and you're screwed, dude."

"Mister Brady," Sister Margaret Mary's stern voice called out. "Any more of that, young man, and you'll be scraping chewing gum off the bottom of desks after school?"

He waited for the inevitable slap to the back of his head, but the blow didn't come. Sister Margaret had apparently grown too old to inflict corporal punishment. *Figures,* he thought. *Two weeks before I graduate.*

"Yes, sister," he said with sing-songy Eddie Haskell sincerity.

When she walked off Peanut broke out laughing.

"Brady, you got so busted."

"Zip it, spaz," Max said and laughed too.

They looked up in time to see Attila the Nun marching to the center of the courtyard. She looked like an imperious penguin in her black-and-white robes billowing in the breeze. A long string of black wooden prayer beads clacked at her side. She was holding a bullhorn. Coach Howard Pickens, the school's physical education instructor, was at her heels. He was dragging two students by the wrists. Junior Ball and Ben Chance. Neither looked happy. For that matter, Max noticed, neither did Pickens.

"What's your uncle doing, Brady?" said Peanut.

"He's not really my uncle."

"Why do you call him Uncle Howard?"

"He was my dad's best friend."

"That's why he treats you like your farts don't stink?"

"They grew up together. They were like brothers. Dad died saving his life in Vietnam. My grandmother says he and Aunt Mo

28

consider me the son they never had. They're at our house every Thanksgiving and Christmas. Buy me birthday presents."

"Wish I had an uncle in the police department. Why's he even working here?"

"Grandpa called it moonlighting. He and Aunt Mo don't have much money."

They watched the quartet reach the center of the yard.

"What is this?" Peanut said.

"No idea. Chance looks like he's about to pee in his pants, though."

Max glanced down the sidewalk. Delray was standing about thirty feet away, surrounded by Ginger Brennan and a group of girls. Her face was frozen in a mystified expression.

Junior Ball was the biggest kid in school, a man-child taller than Peanut and way stronger. He was also the school bully. His hair was trimmed close on the sides and flat on top and his upper lip had a permanent surly curl.

Ben Chance was another case. Max couldn't fathom how he Delray were related, let alone twins. She was lithe and graceful and an honor student. Ben was fat and slovenly and always in trouble. Not for anything serious. Stupid stuff, like chewing gum, talking in class, and generally being a pain in the ass. Just like Max, but minus the straight 'A' report cards. Chance was an outcast who didn't have any real friends. Max had spoken to him little more than he had to Delray. He knew Uncle Howard wasn't particularly fond of Ben. Athletically the kid was a disaster. Chickens could fly further than he could run.

Attila raised the bullhorn to her mouth and the hum of five hundred murmuring children hushed as her dissonant voice exploded over the gathering like shrapnel from the Army of God.

"Our Lady of Perpetual Sorrow cannot function without proper deportment," she blared. "When a student is continually disruptive, and when that student refuses to behave, he or she will either be expelled or severely disciplined. I've tried everything to get Mr. Benjamin Chance's attention, yet he persists in his misbehavior. This is the last straw. Coach Pickens."

29

The principal stalked off the lawn and left Uncle Howard standing with the two boys. At age fourteen, Junior was taller even than Pickens and possessed the strength of a grown man. He'd been tyrannizing kids since he enrolled at the school in fifth grade. For some reason he'd kept his distance from Max, who wasn't sure why. Neither had shown any inclination to tangle with the other.

"I want a fair fight," the coach said. "No biting, no kicking, no low blows."

Junior Ball raised his arms in a pre-fight victory pose and then took a boxer's stance, clench-fisted, feet spread, bouncing on his toes like Muhammad Ali ready to take on Smokin' Joe Frazier.

"What the hell's going on?" Peanut said, no longer whispering.

"I don't know. I don't like it, though."

Chance stood motionless as a wax figure, his head down and arms at his sides. Something about his submissiveness reminded Max of paintings he'd seen in his grandmother's Bible of St. Ignatius of Antioch as he waited to be devoured by lions. Pickens swept his arms together, a silent bell signaling the fighters to begin. Ben was obviously no fighter. He immediately extended his arms in supplication toward the larger boy.

"Don't hit me, Junior," he sniveled. "I don't wanna fight."

"Stand up to him, Chance," Pickens said. "Be a man."

Junior moved in fast. Ben backed away and gave no sign of defending himself. Junior hesitated. His face was painted with confusion. He normally relished beating up kids too afraid to fight back. Apparently not with the entire student body as witness, though.

"Take it to him, Ball," the coach bellowed. "He'll fight."

Junior glided forward and threw a straight right fist that caught Ben square on his left cheek. A couple of hundred kids gasped. Ben fell down and landed on the grass in sitting position. He touched his fingers to his face and began to cry.

"I don't believe this," Peanut said.

"Get up, Chance," Howard Pickens said.

When Ben failed to respond the coach rushed forward, grabbed him under his arms, and lifted him to his feet. Max watched his uncle's face. He looked as unhappy to be there as Chance. Junior moved in again and peppered Ben's pudgy face with jabs. The heavyset boy kept retreating, making no effort to defend himself.

Brady looked around. A few kids were snickering, but the faces of most students were transfixed in horror. Several girls were weeping. Even Sister Mary Margaret's mouth was agape. Delray Chance was sobbing while Ginger Brennan tried to console her.

Junior threw another punch. It landed on Ben's chin and he went down on his knees at Ball's feet. He clawed at the larger boy's legs, begging not to be hit. Pickens pulled him off the grass. A red welt covered his left cheek. Snot dripped from his nose and mingled with his tears.

"Please, no."

Chance was a stationary target. Junior's next punch landed on his nose. Blood gushed out. Ben tripped backwards, barely keeping his feet.

"This is unbelievable," Peanut said. "Why are they doing this to the kid?"

Ball moved in again, feeding off the fear of his retreating opponent, eager now to punish Ben.

"Come on, Chance," the coach yelled, "Defend yourself."

Junior reached back and was about to inflict another blow when something snapped in Max and he found himself sprinting onto the lawn.

"Stop!" he hollered.

Junior froze mid-punch and turned toward the voice. Like a moth to the flame, Max bolted to the center of the courtyard and squared himself between Junior and Ben. His lungs were working hard and he wondered what he was doing there.

"No more," he said. "Chance has had enough."

Ball looked at him like he was crazy.

"Get away from him, Brady. This is none of your business. Fat boy ain't even your friend."

"You're killing the kid. It's not fair. It's not right."

Max turned to Ben. His face was a muddle of blood, tears, and nasal mucus. He seemed as shocked by Max's intervention as Ball.

"It's over, Chance. He's not going to hit you anymore."

Pickens ran up and grabbed Max's arm. A hank of dark hair fell across the boy's brow and he brushed it back with his free hand.

"What are you doing, Max? Get back in line before you get in trouble."

Brady yanked his arm free. "I'm not moving, Uncle Howard. If there's gonna be more fighting, Junior can fight me."

Uncle Howard lowered his head and whispered. "Just walk away, my boy, before Attila expels you from school."

Max almost laughed. "You know about Attila?"

"Forget that old bag," Ball said. He was still bouncing on his toes, hands in a boxer's pose, straining like a bulldog on a leash. "Come on, Brady. I'll kick your skinny ass too."

"Don't bet on it, Junior."

Max tried to sound defiant, but his knees were jelly. He raised his fists with all the bravado he could muster and attempted to puff himself up. At one hundred ten pounds, though, there wasn't much to puff up. *What am I doing?* he thought. A good question, for which he had no answer. He told himself to be positive. *Be Ali!*

Junior advanced, reared back and threw a right.

Float like a butterfly!

Max feinted left and parried the blow with his forearm. He felt a flutter of air on the tip of his nose from the draft of Junior's fist. The bigger boy lunged wildly past him. Max's jitters vanished and he experienced a rush of exhilaration.

Now sting like a bee!

He turned and pivoted on his right foot, coiled his arm, and launched his right fist like a piston. His knuckles caught the left side of Junior's face just below his eye socket. The student body erupted in cheers.

Max felt a surge of elation. He imagined himself Muhammad Ali standing over a fallen Sonny Liston. He considered raising his arms and shouting *I am the greatest*. The sensation lasted approximately two seconds before it occurred to him that Junior Ball was still standing and would now beat him to a pulp. But to his astonishment the air seemed to go out of Junior. He dropped his hands and stepped back rubbing his cheek, his eyes crowded with confusion. Kids had been afraid of Ball for so long he'd convinced himself he was tough. Max remembered his grandfather telling him once that bullies don't like to fight people who actually fight back. As usual, grandpa was right. One punch and Junior's bluster had fractured like Humpty Dumpty's eggshell.

His plight, however, had only just begun. He looked up and saw Sister Mary Aloysius hurrying onto the lawn coming straight toward him. Max was keenly aware that Attila possessed a diverse arsenal of tortures. Most of them salvaged, he guessed, from the Spanish Inquisition Handbook. She was fond of paddling, forcing students to kneel on concrete for hours at a time, and locking kids in coat closets. Her favorite cruelty, though, was known to every boy in the school, and a fair number of girls. She seized his right ear between her thumb and forefinger and gave it a savage twist. Max grimaced in agony.

"Mr. Brady," she shouted into his captive ear, "you are in deep trouble. Now march yourself to my office this minute."

She wrenched the ear again, but he refused to budge, keeping a buffer between Junior and Ben.

"Please, sister," he said, his voice quivering. "Do what you want to me, but Chance has had enough. Don't hurt the kid anymore."

The principal looked at him like he'd questioned the Virgin Mary's virginity. Hot tears welled in his eyes and he fought desperately to keep from crying in front of the entire student body. Max knew he was, to paraphrase Attila, in deep doo-doo. He would surely be expelled from school. And probably excommunicated from the church. His grandparents would be incensed. His boat would be dry-docked. And he would be banned from the river and the ocean. Life as he knew it was over.

The Irish nun kept wringing his ear, pulling his face so near hers that he was given an appallingly microscopic view of the small crooked teeth in her cruel mouth, her prune-wrinkled lips, and her twitching red cheeks. Behind the rimless spectacles, her black eyes were burning like hot coals.

"Mr. Pickens," she said finally, "take Mr. Brady and Mr. Chance to my office." She released him then swung around and raised the bullhorn to the gathered students. "Let this be a lesson to all of you. I will not tolerate students who misbehave. Now everyone back to class. And I want *SILENCE!*"

Uncle Howard was leading Max and Ben toward the principal's office when Delray Chance jostled through the pack. Her eyes were red and her pretty face was splashed with tears. She threw her arms around her brother.

"Are you okay, Benjamin?"

Max wilted. Chance sniffled while Delray examined him. Then she turned fierce eyes on Pickens.

"My father is going to be furious. The mayor and police chief are friends of his. You are going to be very sorry."

Uncle Howard looked down at her. Max could see contrition in his eyes.

"Delray," he said, "your father knew about this. Sister Mary Aloysius spoke to him this morning. He approved. He thought it would be in Benjamin's best interest. It was the only reason I agreed to go along with it."

Dismay filled Ben's face and a sob escaped him. Delray's mouth opened, but no sound came out. She turned to Max and they communicated for the first time, conversing not with words, but their eyes. A faint smile lit her face and he thought he'd never seen anything so beautiful. Then she whispered.

"Thank you."

Max's brain told him what to say. *"Don't mention it. Not a problem. Happy to be of service. Oh, and by the way, I have been madly in love with you my entire life."* As usual, though, he stood feebly before her, mute and imbecilic, until she gave up waiting and walked away.

Uncle Howard led them to the Principal's Office. Before they entered, Max turned and looked at Ben. His white shirt was covered with green grass stains and red blood spots and his face looked like it had been scrubbed with sandpaper. Max pulled a handkerchief from his back pocket.

"My grandmother makes me carry one," he explained, almost apologetic. "Wipe your nose, Ben."

"Thanks, Max."

They were the first words to pass between Max Brady and Ben Chance.

Et Tu Brady

Chapter Six

TWENTY NINE YEARS later Brady stared down at Ben Chance's bloated corpse, with its swollen black tongue and wide eyes frozen in terror. Brady's knees were as marmalade as they'd been that day on the Great Lawn. Holding Delray in his arms had been surreal. Now to have Ben dead at his feet was downright ghoulish. Making the scene even more macabre was the primitive tattoo scrawled across Ben's forehead, like graffiti on a gravestone.

Et Tu Brady

Brady looked up and saw Captain Register calculating him, his brows arched now in inverted V's.

"What do you think?" he said.

Brady shook his head wordlessly.

"Don't you find it strange?"

"That's a good word for it."

"Can you explain why your name is inscribed on a murder victim's forehead?"

Brady felt a shiver run through him, as if the policeman's words certified the tattoo was not some outlandish fluke. His heart was thudding inside his chest. He filled his lungs with air and exhaled slowly, trying not to betray his flabbergast.

"You don't know that tattoo is meant to be my name?" he said, refusing to say aloud what he knew the instant he saw Chance's face. The inscription *was* his name. The killer *had* been thinking of him.

"How many Brady's are there?"

"A bunch."

He'd repeated the quip a million times and was always amazed at how many people didn't get it. Register stared at him without a trace of a smile.

"You haven't seen Benjamin Chance in how many years?"

Brady did the arithmetic one more time, just to be certain.

"Twenty nine."

"Now all of a sudden…"

"Twenty nine years ain't exactly all of a sudden."

"Even so, your childhood friend is murdered, in ritualistic fashion, and your name is engraved on his face? Brady *is* your name."

"It's stenciled on my boxer shorts, if you want to see."

Register didn't smile again. He looked back down at the body.

"I assume," he said after a moment, "whoever did this knew both you and Mr. Chance?"

Brady shrugged.

"And if you haven't been in contact with the victim for twenty nine years, the killer must have known you both when you were kids."

"A lot of people knew us then."

Now it was Register's turn to shrug. "Including Delray Chance Cross."

The Medical Examiner's body removal team was composed of two men, one black, one white, both husky. They gazed down on Ben Chance's adipose form like furniture movers assessing a grand piano.

"Shoulda brought a block and tackle," the white guy mumbled.

Rigor mortis had set in and the cadaver was stiff as a department store mannequin. They knelt on the floor and began straining to shoehorn Chance's mass into the black plastic body bag. The white man grunted while his partner growled obscenities. They finally pulled up the zipper and Brady watched Ben's death mask and its gruesome eulogy disappear.

He turned and looked around the bedroom. Ron Register was gone. So was the police photographer. Other than the two men lifting the body onto a gurney, he was alone. The coconut tree floor lamp and electrical cord had also vanished. Crime scene techs had littered the floor with small pieces of numbered red paper folded like tents. Brady remembered his own red tent. Rose was probably asleep inside it now. He could still taste her on his lips and wished he was still with her in front of the fire.

He exited the bedroom and removed the blue booties. Register was down the hallway talking to Belinda Boulanos. She peeled a white Latex glove off her left hand. Brady noticed she was not wearing a ring. He was surprised no one had snapped-up such a smart and eye-pleasing woman and decided it must have something to do with her fondness for cadavers. Brady interrupted their conversation.

"You're out of your mind if you think Delray murdered her brother."

The Assistant Medical Examiner apparently thought he was addressing her and shook her head. "Determining culpability is above my pay grade."

Register leaned toward him and spoke in a conspiratorial tone.

"I'm not saying she did, Brady. So far, though, the arrows in my quiver point toward your girlfriend."

"She's not my girlfriend. We haven't seen each other since we were kids."

Boulanos walked away and the captain jerked his head at Brady to follow him. They walked to the top of the spiral staircase.

"Mrs. Cross told us she and her brother were estranged. Barely spoken in years. Phone calls occasionally on Christmas and birthdays. Then two days ago she was in Dublin – you know, Ireland – giving a speech at an international conference. She's apparently a big shot economist. PhD professor at Duke University. She checks her hotel voicemail and finds a frantic message from her brother."

Register paused and patted his belly. His face wore the look of a man in the throes of a gastro-intestinal disturbance. He reached into his pants pocket and fished out a small tin of *Tums* and popped an orange tablet into his mouth.

"When the call came tonight I was dining at Anthony's Runway 84. The sausage-and-peppers are a little slice of heaven, but the heartburn's hell."

"Do you know Americans consume forty percent of all indigestion remedies in the world?"

Register sucked on his Tums and fixed him with a blank stare.

"Why would you know that?"

"No idea."

The detective offered him the tin. He declined.

"What did Ben say on this recording?"

"He begged her to come to Fort Lauderdale immediately. Something about *'that night'*."

Brady felt a thump inside his chest, followed by momentary breathlessness, but fought to suppress any outward display of revulsion.

"That night?"

"Mrs. Cross said she didn't know what he was talking about, but the tone of his voice scared her. Said he sounded suicidal. She rushed here on the first flight. Air Lingus direct from Dublin. Flew into Lauderdale shortly before five this evening. Airline confirms. Mrs. Cross checked into the Yankee Clipper. Hotel says she registered at six-thirty. According to their phone records she called her brother's house at seven thirty. It didn't go through. Called again an hour later. Same thing. Then at eight forty five. Still no answer."

"I'm guessing because he's dead. Belinda put time of death at around seven."

"Mrs. Cross says she took a cab from the Clipper and got here about ten after nine. We're trying to locate the cabbie now. She rings the doorbell but gets no answer. Lights are on so she tries the handle. Front door opens. She calls out. No response. She hears a radio or stereo or television and follows the sound upstairs. Finds him on the bedroom floor wearing the copper necktie. The cord had been unplugged."

Brady mulled Register's words for a good half-minute before speaking, visualizing Delray move from the hotel to the house to her brother's body. He could only imagine how traumatized she was. He looked at Register.

"That's what you've got? Those are your arrows? It'll take me about five minutes to win a directed verdict."

"I thought you didn't practice law anymore."

"I won't need any practice. Your case is dog vomit."

It was one of those lines that could evoke a punch in the nose or a smile. Register smiled, though not in a friendly way.

"There's more," he said.

"Horsefeathers."

"Horses don't have feathers."

"Birds don't fly backwards, either. And you don't have a case. Maybe it'll take me ten minutes. Do you plan to file charges against Delray tonight?"

Register sucked on his Tums for a few seconds. "No rush. I do want her to come to the station and give a full statement."

Brady shook his head. "Sorry, captain. Mum's the word. I ain't Clarence Darrow, but it's as clear as the stripes on your pretty yellow tie you're gonna try to pin Ben's murder on his sister. As her attorney, I'd be derelict to let you talk to her before we've had a chance to confer."

"So you *are* her lawyer?"

"For now."

"I could bring her in anyway. Ask the questions."

"Not without me. And I'll tell her to say nothing. Besides, Register, that's a bullshit way to do business. Remember, I've got friends in high places."

"You're not playing that card on me, are you Brady?"

He smiled. "Nah. Just like the sound of it rolling off my tongue." Brady reached out and put his left hand on Register's right shoulder. "Look, Ron, I guarantee you Delray did not kill her brother. Give me time to talk to her. I'm sure she'll want to cooperate in any way possible."

A sour look crossed the detective's face. Brady wondered if it was the sausage-and-peppers, or the hand on his shoulder. Register popped another Tums and considered his options.

"Okay, Brady. I'll give you tonight. But I want her in my office at noon tomorrow or I'll have her picked up and brought in wearing handcuffs."

"She'll be there."

Brady watched Register descend the corkscrew staircase. Ben Chance's house was equipped with an elevator, he guessed because of Ben's weight. He looked to have tipped the scales at three hundred pounds plus. The stairs might have killed him long before his killer. The elevator door was across from the staircase. Belinda Boulanos and her removal team used it to take out the body. When the door slid closed Brady returned to the library.

A uniformed policewoman was sitting on a chair beside Delray, who was still stretched out on the green leather couch with a wet washcloth folded across her forehead.

"Officer, do you mind if I speak to Mrs. Cross alone?"

The policewoman left the room and closed the door behind her. Brady took her seat and rested his elbows on his knees. Delray removed the cloth and looked at him with reminiscent eyes. She tried to smile. A tear squeezed out from beneath her lashes and slid down the fine line between her nose and cheek. He cupped her hand in his, gentle as a newborn kitten.

"Delray, what did Ben say in the telephone message that scared you?" She grazed her tongue over her lips, but didn't respond. "Captain Register said you told him Ben was frantic. That he sounded suicidal. That he said something about *that night.*"

She blinked several times, took a deep breath, and turned her eyes toward the ceiling.

"Max, I'd never heard Benjamin so distraught. He sounded deranged. Like he was trapped in a terrible nightmare. I thought he might harm himself. That's why I rushed here."

Another tear spilled, this one from the outer corner of her right eye, and trickled down the side of her face.

"Why, Del? Why was Ben so scared?"

"*That night.* He kept saying *that night.*"

"What did he mean?"

She looked up at him. "Please don't pretend, Max."

Brady didn't want to ask the next question, but he couldn't help himself. He gave her hand a small squeeze. "How do you know he was talking about *that night?*"

"Because Benjamin said…"

She hesitated and raised her right hand to her mouth. She pinched her lower lip, like she was trying to decide whether to speak.

"What did he say?"

She shifted on the couch, wrestling with some inner voice. The longer she vacillated, the less Brady wanted to hear the answer.

"What, Delray?"

"Benjamin said…he said… '*Duke Manyon is back.*'"

Brady dropped her hand and fell back against the chair. He felt himself plummeting down a rabbit hole. He was thirteen years old again. Bobbing unseen in a riotous black sea. Raindrops pelting his face like stones. A boat seesawing above him. An anguished scream. A savage curse. A plea for mercy. *Max, where are you?* Launching himself into the air. Pulling the trigger. The primal sneer. Ben and Peanut's terrorized faces. Delray fetal. Bloody. Naked. The memory still raw as an open wound, even after so many years.

"Max?" Her voice jolted him back to the present. "I didn't… I didn't mention…him…his name…to Captain Register, I mean. I wouldn't do that."

He looked down at her. His eyes were hard and cold and she shrank from him.

"Duke Manyon is not back," he said. His voice was harsh. "It's impossible."

"Why are you so certain?"

"You know why, Delray. You were there. You saw what happened."

Et Tu Brady

Chapter Seven

THE YANKEE CLIPPER was the most venerable hotel on Lauderdale Beach. Designed to look like a 1860s era clipper ship, it had once been the spring training headquarters of the New York Yankees. Mickey Mantle recounted walking out of the hotel one evening for a night on the town with his teammate, Yogi Berra. The legendary catcher was dressed in white pants and a flowered shirt. A woman hollered at him.

"Hey Yogi, you look cool."

"Thanks lady," replied the inimitable Berra. *"You don't look so hot yourself."*

Brady jockeyed the Jeep up to the hotel's front door, left the keys with a valet, and accompanied Delray inside.

"I need a drink," she said.

"The Wreck Bar's downstairs. It should be quiet this time of night."

It was almost midnight, but the place was alive with revelers. Many in tuxedoes and evening gowns who appeared to be in the rowdy final stages of a wedding celebration. Others wore football regalia. Brady remembered it was Super Bowl Week. The big game was being staged in South Florida. Steelers versus Packers. The town was in for a wild week. Plenty of disorganized confusion. Or organized debauchery. Or both.

Brady and Delray retreated to the far end of the room and slid into a booth out of earshot of the party animals. A giant aquarium stocked with brilliantly colored exotic fish lined one wall. Behind the bar, big glass windows gave a fish-eye's view into the underwater of the hotel swimming pool. Even at that hour, a dozen people were frolicking in the water, visible from their necks down. A few wore bathing suits. Most were in formal attire and could have been in a commercial for a snooty cognac. To the delight of the merrymakers in the bar, the silver gown of one woman had floated up around her waist, revealing a lacy garter belt and thong panties that left little to the imagination. Every few minutes a swimmer pushed his or her bare bottom up to the glass and mooned the wedding party, which erupted in cheers.

A redheaded barmaid who looked like she was working the tail end of a double shift placed napkins on the table.

"What'll it be folks?"

She looked at Delray, who looked at Brady.

"Something strong," she said.

He ordered two Johnny Walker Reds on the rocks. The waitress left and no words passed between them for several minutes. Delray sat with downcast eyes, fidgeting with her napkin, tearing off a corner and balling the paper between her trembling thumb and forefinger with obsessive concentration. Then her shoulders quaked and she was wracked by a spasm of sobs and her face crumpled into pieces, reminding Brady of the Picasso over Ben's bed. She covered the fragments with her hands. Big tears leaked between her fingers. Brady noticed an older man watching her two tables away. Leaning back in his chair, with his prominent belly, crossed legs, and drink in hand, he looked like a human ampersand.

Brady slid around the booth and draped an arm over Delray's shoulders. "Just let it out, Del. Let it go"

She continued for some time. Gradually the cadence of her tremors subsided and she was quiet again. The tears had left jagged trails on her cheeks, like skis make in fresh snow. She was swabbing the wetness away with a napkin when the barmaid returned and looked at her with concern, then at Brady with an accusatory expression.

"Are you okay, honey? Can I do anything for you?"

Delray shook her head. Brady gave the woman silent kudos, one bartender to another. She placed the scotches on the table and walked off with an empty tray in her hand and suspicious eyes aimed at Brady.

"Feel better?"

Delray nodded. She wiped her nose, raised her face, and made a short unhappy stab at a smile.

"Forgive me, Max." She tossed down an ample portion of her drink. "This hit me out of the blue. I wasn't prepared."

"Ben was your brother. No one is prepared to find someone they love like that."

She looked at him, studying his face for several seconds. "I'm sorry to invade your life like this. It's so unreal seeing you after all these years." Her face cracked again and new tears spilled. "They ripped me away from you too. I never even got to say goodbye."

He released her hand and picked up his tumbler and downed the amber liquid in a single slug then raised two fingers in the barmaid's direction.

"That was eons ago, Del. We've got more immediate things to think about."

She finished her scotch and her pale complexion began to take on color. The waitress returned with fresh glasses. She took a sideways peek at Delray and aimed another disapproving scowl in Brady's direction. When she was gone Delray took more than a sip of the scotch and fixed him with searching blue eyes. He read her thoughts.

"Duke Manyon's gone, Delray. He's not coming back. You have nothing to fear."

"Tell that to Benjamin. Yesterday he told me the monster had returned. Today he's dead. Murdered. With your name scrawled on his face." Her voice was climbing the hysteria meter. "I can't help it. I'm scared. If Manyon didn't do that vile thing to Benjamin, who did? Who killed my brother?"

Ampersand Man was still watching them. So was the Good Samaritan behind the bar. Delray took another quaff, scanning the room with wary eyes. Brady knew she was searching the crowd for Manyon's face. Reflexively he did the same, knowing he would not be there. Could not be there. The bar was too loud for eavesdroppers to overhear them. Even so, Delray was pensive.

"Max, I need to run upstairs to check my messages and get out of these clothes. Will you come up?"

Brady frowned. He wanted to get back to Rose. He didn't wear a watch. He looked around for a clock. There were none in sight.

"It's getting late, Delray. You should get some sleep. I want you alert when we talk to Register tomorrow."

She put a hand over his on the table.

"I've got something to show you. You should see it."

Reluctantly he nodded, threw some bills on the table, and they headed for the door while the overworked redhead stared at them from behind the bar.

Et Tu Brady

Chapter Eight

THEY TOOK THE elevator to the fifth floor. Delray turned left and Brady followed her down a long corridor. He wondered if Joe DiMaggio – the *Yankee Clipper* himself – had ever walked this same hallway. Or, more intriguing, if he and his wife, Marilyn Monroe, had slept together here.

Delray's suite was the last door on the right. She flipped a light switch and crossed the room and slid open a glass door. The balcony looked out over a black beach. The room was invaded by the babble of night ocean and the briny bouquet of a soft February breeze.

"Drinks are in the icebox," she said. "I could use another whiskey. Can you pour?"

"It's what I do."

Delray gave him a quizzical glance and retreated into the bedroom. Brady husked the cellophane off a pair of short glasses, plopped in ice cubes, and decanted airline-sized bottles of Canadian Club into each. He deposited himself onto a supremely uncomfortable merlot settee slightly softer than a center field bleacher seat. *Home of the Yankees!*

He thought of Rose again asleep in the tent and had a sudden craving to be with her. Wishing he'd never left her. Wishing he hadn't seen what he'd seen tonight. Wondering who had committed such an atrocious act. And what Delray wanted to show him.

He'd finished his drink, poured another, and was back on the sofa when she emerged from the bedroom wrapped in a white silk robe that clung to her like moving water. She found her drink on the kitchenette counter and joined him on the calcified couch. Her blonde hair was wet and combed and just long enough to dampen the collar of her robe. She smelled as fresh as rain. Brady held up his glass.

"I'm one ahead of you."

Delray swirled hers and took a sip. She crossed her legs and the white silk slid to one side, exposing toned thighs only a shade darker than the robe. Brady looked away.

"Why did you have Register call me, Del?"

She inhaled deeply and exhaled with a sigh. "I was in a state of shock. Finding Ben like that. Then to see that terrible tattoo on his forehead. Your name. It was horrible. I didn't know what to think. When the police read me my rights and told me I could call a lawyer, you were the only person I could think of. I'd heard you'd moved away and become an attorney."

"Prosecutor. Federal. Assistant D.A."

"New York?"

"Brooklyn. Came back a few years ago. Needed to breathe salt air again."

"Captain Register said he knew you." She started to say something, hesitated for an instant, then continued. "He said you're friendly with a City Commissioner? A woman?"

He nodded. "We can catch up later. But I don't practice law anymore."

She looked surprised. "What do you do?"

"Nothing to brag about. Got a little bar up the beach."

She held up the drink. "'It's what I do?' I was wondering what you meant."

"Don't worry. I'll help you find a good lawyer tomorrow."

Delray grabbed his hand from the couch and squeezed, her eyes brimming with urgency.

"No, Max. Please. Stay with me."

"Trust me, Delray. You'll be better off with a member of the local bar."

"No one would be better than you, Max. You're a winner. You always were. I'd bet on you any day."

"Be careful what you wish for. The favored horse at Gulfstream loses seven-out-of-ten races."

Delray leaned forward and placed her glass on the onyx coffee table. For a fleet second her robe fell open and a milk-white breast fell out. He averted his eyes again. She pulled the gown together with casual indifference and turned to Brady, gazing at him with the same blue eyes that had rendered him speechless as a boy. Her face had been scrubbed of cosmetics but, for a woman entering the wrinkled phase of life, she showed little trace of aging. She was as beautiful a woman as she'd been a girl.

"What did you want to show me, Delray?"

She took another long breath. "Max, I didn't tell Captain Register everything."

"You mean besides about Duke Manyon?"

"Ben did call yesterday and leave the message about Manyon. But we spoke twice before that. He found out from my office at the university that I was in Dublin staying at The Hibernian Hotel. He called me there Tuesday. I was shocked to hear his voice. My first reaction was that it had to be bad news, but I couldn't imagine what. Both of our parents are dead. Mother passed away two years ago. Ben didn't even attend her funeral."

"That's hard to believe."

Delray looked away momentarily, as if reluctant to go on, then seemed to make a decision. "Our parents split up a long time ago. Benjamin took it very hard. Harder even than me. Mother took me away and left him with father. He never forgave her for abandoning him."

"Why did she do that?"

She waved a dismissive hand. "It's very complicated." It was clear she didn't want to elaborate and he didn't pry. "Anyway, my initial alarm was quickly dispelled. Benjamin sounded great. No, better than that. Elated. He seemed genuinely happy to hear my voice. And it was wonderful to hear his. With mom and dad gone, I guess I thought this might be the icebreaker. A chance to reconnect with my brother."

"And?"

"We exchanged pleasantries for a few minutes. Both of us tentative, like intimate strangers. Then Benjamin told me about his research."

"Research? I thought you were the academic in the family."

She looked at him and raised an eyebrow. "In a very real way, Max, it involved you."

"Me?" He was taken aback. "I haven't seen or heard from Ben since…well, since the last time I saw you. What was he researching? How did it involve me?"

"Not you directly. He was investigating treasure. Sunken treasure."

"Why would he do that?"

Delray raised her feet to the coffee table. She had delicate arches and perfectly aligned toes, which she flexed against the sharp black edge. "Benjamin never got over what happened that night."

He frowned and looked away. "That was a lifetime ago, Del."

"Yes, but I know you remember."

Brady nodded. "Of course."

"He was haunted by what happened. It was like a black shadow that followed him everywhere. Contaminated his entire adult life. Benjamin took over our father's electrical contracting business and was very successful. He built the company and far surpassed dad in terms of monetary wealth. But he never married. Never had a family. To be blunt, he was a dysfunctional human being."

"What's that got to do with me and sunken treasure?"

"We spoke twice on the telephone. He called me the next day and opened up about himself. It was the first time I'd heard him speak so intimately since we were kids. Benjamin had gotten it into his head that the only way to exorcise his demons was to go back in time. Go back to the days when we were all together. Go back and find the gold."

Brady stared at her. A light was burning in her eyes that hadn't been there before.

"The gold?"

"Yes."

"Our gold?"

"He called it his salvation. His Holy Grail." They looked at each other and neither spoke for a brief moment, then she continued. "I knew he'd been looking. After mom took me away, Benjamin and I only saw each other a few times. We rarely spoke on the telephone and only occasionally traded cards or letters. A couple of years ago, though, he began sending me e-mails. He made reference once or twice about spending time out on the reef."

"The reef?"

"Yes."

"Our reef?"

"Your reef."

"And?"

"Benjamin said he was hunting for the motherlode. He'd found more gold coins and thought he was getting close." She sipped her drink. "When he called me at The Hibernian he was absolutely gushing. *'Delray,'* he said, *'there's a billion dollars under that sand.'* He asked me to do him a favor. I agreed. I was willing to do anything to get my brother back."

"What kind of favor?"

"He said he'd been researching gold ships that sank off the southeastern coast of Florida centuries ago. He had a name."

"What name?"

"Michael Fury."

"The pirate?"

"You've heard of him?"

"Blackbeard. Henry Morgan. Ned Pike. Michael Fury. The real pirates of the Caribbean. Plundered billions from the Spanish gold fleets. What about Fury?"

"Benjamin said he'd learned about some papers Michael Fury donated to Trinity College upon his death in seventeen-something-or-other. He had planned to travel to Ireland himself. When he found out I was in Dublin he asked me to investigate."

"And?"

"Stop saying that," Delray said and smiled. The first smile he'd seen on her face since they were thirteen. Brady felt something warm inside. He quickly ascribed it to the whiskey. "I was there to deliver a speech to the Society of International Economists. *Intertemporal Tradeoffs In Macroeconomic Policy*."

"Sounds fascinating. Sorry I missed it."

She smiled again. "I love your insincerity. Anyway, I had some spare time. I'd planned to do a little sightseeing. You know, Dublin Castle, Davy Byrnes Pub where Joyce and Keats drank. But Trinity was at the top of my list anyway, so I ended up spending two days sifting through the stacks of its research collections. The school is more than four hundred years old. The library contains thousands of very old, very dusty scrolls. The really good stuff's off limits to the public. So I pulled my Duke University faculty card."

"And?"

"You hot shot lawyers with your machine gun interrogation style. *'And? And? And? And? And?'* Wear down your witness until she breaks. Brilliant."

"Johnnie Cochran Light. And?"

Delray reached over and grabbed a soft black leather Gucci bag from the merlot chair beside the couch.

"And so I found it." She extracted a manila envelope. "It was in a leather pouch bound tightly with heavy thread. Max, its over three hundred years old and I don't think it had ever been opened. I felt like I was breaking into Tutankhamen's tomb. The library refused to let me check it out, or make a copy, or even take notes."

"And?"

"Oh, for heaven's sake," she said with mock exasperation. "I batted my eyes at a handsome young clerk named Padraig O'Toole."

"Shameless."

She batted her eyes and he felt her seductive power.

"Then I paid him fifty euros to Xerox it for me."

"You bribed him?"

"Arrest me."

"I'm trying to prevent that."

Delray handed him the envelope. She drew her knees up beneath her chin and hugged her legs while she watched him weigh the package in his fingers. Brady pinched the brass wing clasp at the back, lifted the flap, and extracted a two-inch thick sheaf of paper. He examined the legend.

The Diary of Michael Fury
Slave, Pirate, Irishman
1709 A.D.

Et Tu Brady

Chapter Nine

VICTOR GRUBER LOOKED like a big woolly lab rat. He was sitting in his wheelchair in the exercise room of his waterfront hacienda, an oxygen mask strapped over his face, blood pressure cuff wrapped around his arm, and more wires affixed to his chest than a telephone switchboard. His furry arms were pumping like locomotive pistons, spinning the wheels of his chair, which was sitting in place on a raised platform.

"Victor, you look like you're trying to escape from a mad proctologist."

After he left Delray at the Yankee Clipper, Brady called his friend and landlord and recounted the night's events. Despite being well past midnight, Victor told him to come over right away. He stopped spinning and pulled off the mask.

"I'm doing research, Max," he said, breathless.

"Did you know research causes cancer in laboratory animals?"

Victor ignored him. "I've been asked to run some tests by WHO."

"Who?"

"Not who. WHO."

"Yes, but *who* are you doing the tests *for*?"

"WHO."

"I asked first."

"WHO."

"That's what I'm asking. Who?"

"Silly man. W.H.O. The World Health Organization."

"Oh! That WHO."

Victor regarded him with bemused resignation, then turned to a monitor attached to the contraption he was sitting on. It was a treadmill for wheelchairs. A short ramp led up to the platform, which was equipped with twin rollers. The chair wheels sat on the rollers and turned in place. Sweat was drizzling off Victor's nose, chin, and earlobes. He ignored it and, with the concentration of a chess master, consulted the screen, jotting notes and numbers on a yellow pad.

"I'm writing a report for my dear friend Dr. Jay Glasser at WHO. We used to participate together every year in the Ironman Triathlon in Hawaii. Before, well, you know."

Brady knew well. Victor was talking about the random shooting on the streets of Manhattan fifteen years before that left him a paraplegic. Brady was a cop on the beat and happened by in time to save his life, but not his legs. They'd been friends ever since. Before that terrible day, though, Victor had been a robust athlete.

"I thought it was time I got back into shape," he said, still scribbling.

"You're healthy as an ox."

"I wish that were true, my friend. In case you hadn't noticed, my boyish figure is slowly going to seed. I'm fifteen pounds over my fighting weight."

Brady waved a hand at him. "That's nothing, Victor. Did you know Earth gains a hundred tons every day just from falling space dust? That's seventy three million pounds a year."

"I feel much better knowing that, but I don't think space dust is my problem. The A1A Marathon is two weeks away. While I've been training I've developed this new treadmill for wheelchairs. I plan to sell it for less than three hundred dollars per machine."

"Victor, I know it's none of my business…"

"Why do I sense a 'but' coming?"

"…but that makes about as much sense as a nap before bedtime. You've already got more money than God." That was only a slight exaggeration. Victor had made a vast fortune developing sophisticated financial software for Wall Street. "Why do you want to sell treadmills – even at three hundred dollars?"

"Because, my dear friend, the current market price for similar devices is twice that amount. I estimate that worldwide two million more people with spinal cord injuries will have access to upper body exercise. That will lead to a dramatic decrease among paralytics in coronary disease, diabetes, hypertension, and obesity."

"Two million? At three hundred dollars each? That's what? Sixty million dollars?"

"Actually, six hundred million. I do hope you have a good bookkeeper watching your ledger at the Sea Shanty?"

"Did you know *bookkeeper* is the only word in the English language with three back-to-back double letter combinations?"

His friend raised his bushy eyebrows.

"Max, you are an endless font of fascinating yet utterly useless information."

"Seriously, Victor, what's up with the Midas syndrome? Everything you touch turns to gold."

"For the record, I won't make a penny. All profits will go to The Buoniconti Fund to Cure Paralysis. Getting back to your original question, I informed Dr. Jay what I've been doing. He asked me to monitor my heart rate and VO2 *max*."

"Why ask me? I don't even know what VO2 is?"

Victor looked at him and shook his head.

"You are silly, aren't you? VO2 *max* is maximal oxygen consumption – aerobic capacity. That's why my treadmill is equipped with an ergometer."

"Okay. And that is?"

"Simply a device that measures the amount and rate of a person's physical work. Derived from *ergon*, the Greek word for *work*."

"Don't tell me you're fluent in Greek, too."

"How else does one read Homer's *Iliad* or Plato's *Republic*?"

"Ever hear of *CliffsNotes*? How's your Latin? And what do you know about pirates?"

"Two of my favorite things."

Victor detached the electrodes from his chest, yanked a release lever, and rolled down the short ramp. He toweled off his hirsute torso and pulled a sweatshirt over his bushy head.

Brady followed him into the adjacent library. Victor's manservant, Charles, had gone to bed and the house was hushed as a chapel. A large bay window overlooked a wide canal behind the house. In the distance, lost in the darkness, was the Intracoastal Waterway. Brady's home was moored beneath a spotlight at Victor's dock, a sixty-foot schooner named the *Victoria II*. His twenty one-foot Sea Ray power boat was tied up alongside.

The library was an intimate room. Sedate, masculine, with muted lighting, dark wood-beamed ceiling, and plush brown leather furniture. The carpet was a rich burgundy pile adorned with gold diamonds. On the mantle above the fireplace sat a brass 19th Century brick mill clock complete with a working waterwheel. Low black bookshelves filled with thousands of leather-bound volumes lined three walls. Victor being a polyglot, they were in a half-dozen languages. Brady scanned the spines. Tolstoy's *Anna Karenina* in Russian; Thucydides' *History of the Peloponnesian War* and Euripides' *Medea*, both in Greek; Cicero's *Catiline Orations* in their original Latin; Darwin's *On the Origin of Species;* Newton's *Mathematical Principles of Natural Philosophy;* Boswell's *The Life of Samuel Johnson;* Byron's *Don Juan;* Faulkner's *Light In August*; Einstein's *The Evolution of Physics;* More's *Utopia;* Chandler's *The Big Sleep;* Kant's *Critique of Pure Reason;* Twain's *The Adventures of Huckleberry Finn;* Dostoyevsky's *The Brothers Karamazov;* John D. MacDonald's *The Quick Red Fox*.

Brady stared at the wall of words.

"Have you read all these?"

Victor wheeled himself to a shelf marked *Classics*. "Perish the thought. I just chew on the covers."

Brady looked at him wide eyed. His friend's virtuoso repertoire of talents did not typically include zingers. He snorted out a laugh. "Victor made a funny."

"I'm so pleased you noticed," he said with a straight face.

He pulled down a heavy black volume and pushed himself behind his desk. Brady moved to an étagère at the far end of the room and lifted the stopper off a Baccarat decanter.

"*Huck Finn's* my favorite book," he said. "I really relate to it, having grown up on the river. New River, that is. And MacDonald is required reading around Bahia Mar. *The Quick Red Fox* is a fine book, but *Darker Than Amber* is the definitive John D. *'You can be at ease only with those people to whom you can say any damn fool thing that comes into your head.'* I'll take philosopher Travis McGee over Cicero or Kant every time."

He splashed two inches of Asbach Uralt into a brandy snifter and collapsed into a cozy chair facing the desk. Victor was studying the black book, a pair of steel-rimmed bifocals balanced at the apex of his bulbous nose.

"*Julius Caesar* by William Shakespeare," he said, his sonorous voice all the more resonant with the book-lined walls acting as bass traps. "Act Three, Scene One. It is the Ides of March in the year 44 B.C. Gaius Julius Caesar is the Roman Republic's *Dictator in Perpetuity*. He is at the height of his power, but that power has gone to his head. In an imperious and vainglorious assertion for the leader of a democracy, Caesar has declared himself both king and a god. The Roman Senate rebels. A cabal is hatched, led by Caesar's closest friend, Marcus Junius Brutus. Brutus beckons Caesar to the Forum, allegedly to read a proclamation calling on Caesar to return power to the Senate. General Marcus Antonius, Caesar's cousin and trusted commander of the Army of Rome, has learned of the plot, but too late. Before he can warn Caesar the conspirators attack with daggers. Sixty six senators take part. Caesar resists until he sees among his assassins his dear friend Brutus. Whereupon he utters the three most famous words in literature: *'Et tú, Brute?'* "

"You too, Brutus?" echoed Brady.

The room was quiet. With a sense of moment, Victor slammed the volume shut, pushed his spectacles to the top of his head, and regarded his friend. "Of course there is no historical proof Caesar actually spoke those words. Shakespeare was a supreme dramatist, however he tended to play fast and loose with the particulars."

"Never let facts get in the way of a good story?"

"Most of his Roman plays – including *Antony and Cleopatra* and *Coriolanus* – were based on the English translation of *Lives* by Plutarch, the Greek historian. Plutarch wrote that Caesar died silently, uttering not a word as he was slain, merely covering his face with his toga when he saw Brutus among his executioners. Another account reported that Caesar did cry out *'Kai su, teknon?'* Greek for *'You too, child?'*"

Victor wheeled himself to the bookshelf and returned the volume. He moved down the wall to a section labeled *Histories* and grabbed a brown leather-bound book. Brady leaned forward, elbows on thighs, marveling at his friend. He could almost hear his brain go thwickety-thwack inside that shaggy, oversized, grotesque, magnificent cranium. Victor was like a human Google. The entire content of the World Wide Web seemed to be stored inside his brain, which he could nimbly retrieve at supercomputer speed.

"Victor, if *'Et Tu Brady'* means *'You too Brady?'* someone is trying to make it sound like I played a role in Ben's murder?"

"Perhaps." His friend stared at him, absently squeezing his bottom lip between finger and thumb. "Although we must consider another possibility."

"Such as?"

"Mr. Chance's slayer hijacked an interpretation others have attributed to Caesar's final words."

"Which is?"

"*'Your turn is next, Brutus.'* No question mark. In that construal Caesar isn't lamenting that his friend has become his assassin. Rather he is telling Brutus he would die next. Which, of course, foreshadowed Brutus' death by suicide two years later after his army was defeated by Marcus Antonius at the Second Battle of Phillipi."

Brady drained the dregs of his drink and crunched the remaining ice between his teeth. "Meaning Ben's killer may be predicting my death, not implicating me in his murder?"

"That would seem to be a possibility."

"Well, that's a relief."

"My dear friend," Victor said judiciously, "I don't think this is a joking matter. You must be extremely cautious."

They sat in silence for a time. Brady pondered the probability that he knew Ben's killer. At the very least, the slayer knew him, or of him. He looked up at the waterwheel clock babbling softly on the mantle. It was two in the morning.

"I don't want to keep you from your beauty sleep," he said, "but…"

The man in the wheelchair raised a hand. As usual he was a step ahead. Brady had mentioned the Michael Fury diary over the telephone. Victor held up the leather volume.

"What do you know about Michael Fury?"

"I think he was born a slave. Somewhere in the Caribbean."

Victor layed the book against his chest and removed his reading glasses.

"Fury's father was a wellborn Irishman named Lochlan Fury. Captured by Cromwell at Drogheda during the Irish rebellion of 1649, Lochlan lost everything and was lucky not to be hanged. His younger brother Fergus was the smart one. Sided with the Brits and ended up with the family estate while his brother was shipped in irons to Barbados where he was sold at auction in the Bridgetown marketplace. Bought by a Colonel Nelson Howell, Lord of Somersetshire, at the time the largest sugar plantation in the New World." Victor placed the volume on the desk. "In 1661, Lochlan Fury and a slave girl, Fiona Higgins, also Irish, had a son, Michael. Seven years later Lochlan and Fiona died in a yellow fever epidemic. Their boy was left an orphan. However young Michael Fury had been blessed with a beautiful singing voice and the Howell's kept him as a house slave to entertain their guests. At age thirteen he was caught in a compromising situation with the Howell's niece, Lady Arianna Hightower. She was the boy's age and they reportedly were quite enamored with one another. Michael was put under the lash. A short time later he escaped by stowing away aboard *The Nemesis.*"

"Ned Pike's ship."

"Very good, Max. You know your pirate history. Captain Ned Pike – *Scourge of the Caribbean.* Pike had been on a rampage, attacking Spanish treasure ships and making off with an incalculable fortune in gold, silver, pearls, and artifacts. According to lore, the pirates found the boy hiding on the ship and Pike was about to maroon him on an uninhabited island off the coast of Jamaica when he discovered Fury's beautiful voice. The captain kept him on as his cabin boy and to sing to the crew at night. Nine months later *The Nemesis* vanished in a hurricane off the lower coast of eastern Florida. Pike went down with his ship. Only a handful of his crew made it to shore. Among them, Michael Fury. Nothing more was heard of him until 1680 when, at the still tender age of nineteen, he turned up as captain of his own vessel."

"The Scourge."

"In honor of Ned Pike. Fury and *The Scourge* took up where his mentor left off. Ravaging the Spanish gold fleet and making off with a fortune before he retired from piracy. Legend has it he returned to Barbados and absconded with the beautiful Lady Arianna Hightower and returned to Ireland where he took retribution on his uncle and reclaimed his father's estate. Fury died of unknown causes at age forty nine."

Brady rose from the chair, reached into his right pocket and removed a coin about the size of a United States quarter.

"When we were kids my friends and I found this and a few others like it out on Three Mile Reef."

With a sense of moment, he placed the coin in Victor's palm. Gruber lowered the spectacles down onto his nose again and stared into his hand.

"It's old. Very old."

"For once, Victor, you're telling me something I already know. According to Delray, her brother Ben believed this was part of the treasure that went down with Ned Pike and *The Nemesis.*"

Victor gave no indication he'd heard. "It's odd shaped. Round but not perfectly so like a modern coin. More irregular, like a skimming stone you'd find on a beach."

"I assumed that was caused by corrosion?"

Victor lapsed into silence and Brady looked to make sure he hadn't fallen asleep. He was simply lost in thought. He removed his glasses and nibbled at the black-tipped right stem while he held the coin up to his reading lamp.

"In the sixteen hundreds Spanish currency was minted by hand. Mined gold was melted and poured into a die. As it cooled a minter stamped the front and back of each coin. The head and tail. If it was too heavy, little bits and pieces were clipped off, giving this irregular shape."

Brady shook his head. "Victor, do you just know this stuff off the top of your head?"

"As a boy I was fascinated by all things pirate. Those old black-and white films. Errol Flynn as *Captain Blood.* Tyrone Power in *The Black Swan.*" He picked a magnifying glass off the desk and studied the coin closely. "The cross on the face is beautifully struck. Above it and to the right I make out some numbers. It looks like a *one*, a *six*, a *seven*, and the lower half of what could be a *three,* indicating it was minted in the year 1673." He flipped over the coin. "This side has a shield or coat of arms with the letters *'NR'* on one side and *'A'* on the other."

Victor pointed at the bookshelf and asked Brady to retrieve another volume. *Flota de Tierra Firme* was on the third shelf. It was written in Spanish. He handed it to him then went to the credenza and poured himself another measure of brandy. For the next five minutes he sat alternately sipping and scrutinizing the brown liquid sloshing in his snifter while his friend leafed through the pages and compared the gold coin to photographs in the book.

"Ah," he said. Then nothing for several minutes, his dark eyes darting back and forth between page and coin. "During the Sixteenth and Seventeenth Centuries, South and Central America was Spanish domain. Thanks to the fabulous bonanza of gold, silver, emeralds, and pearls she took from the New World, Spain was the richest country on the planet." He raised the coin toward Max. "This, my dear friend, is a *pistole*, at the time the equivalent of two *escudos*, or one-quarter of a *doubloon*." Victor's eyes returned to the book. "According to this text, the gold was mined in the fall of 1673 in *Cerro Rico*, or Rich Mountain, which overlooked Potosi, the capital of present day Bolivia which, at the time, was still part of Upper Peru. It was smelted into ingots and coins in Potosi and transported to Havana in an armada called *Flota de Tierra Firme* which met up in Cuba with another Spanish flotilla from Mexico."

"I love this stuff," Brady said. "Got any popcorn?"

"I can call Charles. I'm sure he'd happily to get out of bed and pop some for you."

"Better not. The question is how did that gold coin end up on Three Mile Reef?"

"Every year an enormous treasure fleet sailed from Cuba bound for Spain. In order to avoid the summer storm season it usually set sail in late spring. In 1674, however, there were delays and the convoy didn't depart until August. It was a massive squadron, more than one hundred ships strong. Man-of-war, frigates, corsairs, galleons. But, alas, the Spanish had tempted Mother Nature and she wreaked her vengeance. Before they crossed the Straits of Florida the flotilla was hit by a terrible hurricane. Dozens of ships went down and vessels were scattered far and wide. Many of them alone and disabled. Easy prey for vulturous buccaneers."

"Ned Pike?"

"Ned Pike, Red Legs Roberts, and Henry Morgan were among the most prominent feasting on Spanish gold. *The Nemesis* appears to have intercepted at least three galleons and made off with what today would amount to a billion or more dollars in treasure."

Brady whistled through his teeth. "Holy!"

"Unfortunately for Ned Pike and his crew, *The Nemesis* soon crossed the path of a Spanish man-of-war, the *Barborosa*, and two support vessels, which chased down the pirate ship and attacked. It is unclear whether Captain Pike succumbed to the Spanish guns or a storm that struck simultaneous to the onslaught. Whatever the cause, *The Nemesis,* its crew, and its swashbuckling captain were dispatched to the bottom of Davy Jones' Locker somewhere off the southern coast of Florida." Victor slammed the book closed. "That's all we know. The exact location was never recorded."

Et Tu Brady

Chapter Ten

MORNING'S FIRST LIGHT spilled across the wall of the red tent like a puddle of blood. Brady had returned from Victor's around three, a different man than the one who left hours before. He tried to restoke last night's fire. The few remaining cinders peered up from the pit like scarlet eyes from the underworld, all but expired.

There was no restoking Rose, either. Wrapped in a light blanket, she had kissed him with eyes closed, mumbled something about the scent of alcohol, where had he been, with whom, doing what, and was snoozing again before he could answer. Her head was resting on the sturdy pillow of his right bicep and her angelic face was inches from his, so near he was breathing in her delicate exhalations. Rose was a sound sleeper. No demons in her dreams. Brady wished he could be as lucky.

Instead he lay there, eyes wide, sleep impossible, jousting with black remembrances he had long thought entombed beneath the strata of time, like the mummies of Pompeii. He'd spent most of his life trying to forget a single night from childhood, but his Vesuvius was erupting again and decades-old sounds and images were flooding over him like a river of molten magma. The bodies. The blood.

The terror. The guilt. As animate again as a beating heart. In the time it took to whisper a simple sentence.

"Duke Manyon is back."

Brady knew more than anyone that that was impossible. Manyon was not back. Could not be back. Yet, when he closed his eyes the visions came to life. He considered trying to rouse Rose and decided that might not be the best idea, considering where he'd been, and with whom. Then he remembered the diary Delray had found for her brother. *What was Ben up to?* Was he actually hunting for treasure? *Our treasure?* Was he murdered because of the gold? The possibility seemed so farfetched as to be laughable, if not for Ben's corpse. He slid the sheaf of pages from the envelope. Maybe they contained some answers.

The Diary of Michael Fury
Slave, Pirate, Irishman
1709 A.D.

The document was written in an elegant hand. A notation on the initial page noted that Michael Fury had dictated the contents to *Shamus Butterfield, Scrivener* at his estate *Nitcrosis* in County Cork, Ireland, just three months before his death, March 19, 1709. Brady licked his thumb and began reading.

The first section detailed the death of the pirate Captain Ned Pike and the sinking of his ship *The Nemesis*. Fury's account jibed with what Victor had read to him. Pike had amassed a vast fortune in Spanish gold and treasure, so much that it actually precipitated his demise by weighing down *The Nemesis,* allowing Spanish gunships to catch him. Michael Fury watched Pike's throat ripped open by enemy gunshot before he was thrown into the ocean, where he watched *The Nemesis* sink. Brady kept reading.

I awakened in the black of night on a white beach surrounded by dark creatures swarming in the sand as far as me eyes could see. Me first thought was that they be me crewmates crawling out of the sea. But on closer inspection I saw many of the shadows was creeping not out of the water but into it which further confused me addled senses.

Being too exhausted to move I lay watching until, after some time, it dawned on me the creatures wasn't human at all. They be too low to the ground and moved in slow motion like enormous rolling stones.

One plodded closer and closer until I recognized it to be a giant tortose. I was familiar with the species, having accompanied Lady Arianna Hightower on turtle egg expeditions on the beaches of Barbados. This was a Loggerhead and I surmised she had just layed a nest on the beach and was returning to the sea destined never to know her own progeny.

Some things hadn't changed in three centuries. Approximately sixty thousand loggerhead, leatherback, and green turtles still pilgrimaged thousands of miles every year to lay their eggs on Florida beaches. As a boy Brady had spent many nights patrolling Lauderdale Beach in search of newly hatched baby turtles. Attracted by automobile lights, the tiny creatures would crawl toward A1A rather than the ocean. Every hatching season the beach road was strewn with thousands of silver dollar-sized reptiles flattened by car tires.

I knew not where I be, recalling only Captain Pike's words during our doomed escape from the Spanish. Standing on the quarterdeck of The Nemesis, spy-glass trained on the long low cloud along the westerly horizon. "The Floridas," said he.

Only five of *The Nemesis's* fifty five man crew survived and, as night turned to day, the full degree of their tragedy became wretchedly clear. The beach was littered with planks, sailcloth, barrels, and all manner of flotsam from the sunken vessel. They found the bodies of Simeon Folger and Thomas Comstock washed up in the surf. Comstock was the man they could least afford to lose – the ship's navigator.

"If by chance a wherry from The Nemesis washed ashore, or we succeeded in fashioning a piragua from the detritus, our hopes of reaching hospitable port was dashed without our pilot to decipher the higher mysteries of the trackless sea."

They were marooned in a hostile land without food or water. Their only weapon was a dagger they found in the sheath on Simeon Folger's hip. One of the survivors, Phineas Binns, was *The Nemesis's* cook, who employed the dirk to butcher a terrapin.

"She possessed as much flesh as a cow," Fury wrote. *"The bushel of eggs in her belly was tastee as Hens eggs, this I can assure you, as well as a great store of oyle as sweet as the finest butter. We gathered drift wood and started a fire. Mr. Binns used the creature's enormous shell as a cauldron to produce a savory stew composed of Sea kelp, fresh eggs, and Tortose meat boiled in its own oyle."*

Emboldened by their sated stomachs, their next task was to find fresh water. They ventured inland toward a long dark stand of trees several hundred yards from the water line. It wasn't long before they were rewarded with good fortune. Beyond the vegetation, in a sparsely wooded area, a freshwater creek ran parallel to the shore as far as the eye could see.

The description reminded Brady of Whiskey Creek, the long, serpentine ribbon of water between the Atlantic and the Intracoastal Waterway where he and his friends played as kids. The creek had been the scene of some of his most sublime memories – and some of his most horrific. He wondered if Whiskey Creek could be the same stream where Michael Fury and his crewmates slaked their thirst three centuries before.

When the shipwrecked sailors had drunk their fill they looked up and found themselves surrounded by a band of natives more than four times their number. They were naked. The men were tall and powerfully built, with straight black hair to their hips, sharp features, and hawk-shaped noses. They brandished bows, arrows, long spears, and shields fashioned from the shells of sea turtles. Among them were three females, including a maiden no older than Fury.

The men broke into three groups and surrounded the castaways. They were a disciplined group and moved in military formation, dark eyes never leaving their prey. Ned Pike's words echoed in Fury's ears. *'The natives is not a peaceable race...They be cannybals.'* Zachary Cobb was *The Nemesis's* First Mate and senior ranking man among the survivors.

"What do we do, sorr?" I asked Mr. Cobb.

"I fear we have but one hope, lad. Our only chance be to seize their women and use them as shields."

The tallest of the natives stepped forth and commenced to bellow at us in a strange tongue. I looked to Mr. Cobb. He held Simeon Folger's knife and spoke in a hushed voice.

"On me count, rush the females. Keep 'em 'twixt us and the savages. At the ready, lads."

They caught the warriors off guard. The two elder squaws fled, but Cobb seized the maiden and put the dagger to her throat. The Indians charged and were about to strike when the tall leader shouted and they came to a standstill. Cobb made a slashing motion beneath the girl's chin and screamed.

"Stay back ye dirty barbarians or on me oath I'll fillet her."

Fury pleaded with Cobb not to harm the maiden, who had done nothing to harm them. But the sailor's eyes were wild and his breathing erratic. Fury saw blood drip from the girl's throat where the knife blade was pressed.

Mr. Cobb had the look of a rabid dog.

"If'n they attack," he said, panting hard, "I will take the lasses head before the cannybals take ours."

"No," I shouted.

I could not stand by while an innocent was slayed. I threw meself at him. Mr. Cobb fell back and I got me hands on the maiden. I pulled her away and placed meself betwixt she and me crew mates. The natives rushed us and it was over in seconds.

The girl was torn from Fury's arms and the Indians fell upon the sailors. Cobb and the others resisted and were quickly dispatched at the sharp ends of the native spears. Fury was the last remaining alive. He lay on his back in the sand, at the mercy of the brutes. The tall leader raised a war club over his head and was about to bring it down when the maiden dove atop him and cried out. Fury couldn't understand what she was saying, but surmised she was pleading for his life, begging that he be spared in return for saving her. After much back and forth, the tall warrior relented. Fury's wrists were tied with strips of rough hide and, at the point of the native spears, he was forced to his feet and prodded along the stream bank toward a fate he dared not contemplate.

Despite not having slept, Brady kept reading into the small hours. He finally tucked the pages of Michael Fury's diary back into the envelope and closed his eyes. Weary as he was, though, sleep would not come. His mind was reeling. He felt like he'd fallen into a time tunnel and been transported back three hundred years. Could Michael Fury have been captured at Whiskey Creek? Were the coins he and his friends found on Three Mile Reef from the belly of *The Nemesis*? Was Ben Chance murdered because of Ned Pike's gold?

Et Tu Brady

Chapter Eleven

THEY DISCOVERED THE gold on a sundrenched midsummer morn. The day began with a needle-nosed yacht slashing through the Intracoastal Waterway cutting a handsome figure as it bore down on the 17th Street Causeway Bridge. Three women in bathing suits were stretched out on the bow laughing and sipping drinks, the star attraction being a curvaceous blonde in a pink polka dot bikini. At the stern a small throng of bare-chested men wearing shorts and Ray-Bans stood with the wind blowing through their hair enjoying the shimmering July day. The yacht captain sounded his airhorn for the bridgetender to raise the span.

At the same moment a small flat-bottom boat puttered up from the opposite side of the bridge and coasted to a stop in the span's shadow. Max Brady leaped from his Boston Whaler onto a wood piling. Summer had baked his rawboned frame brown as brick. He mounted a steel ladder and scampered barefoot thirty feet to the top, adroit as a trapeze artist.

Rubber tires droned across the drawbridge's steel grating. Just as he reached it, an alarm sounded. Gates descended blocking the road and traffic stopped. Max crouched low and locked his arms around the rail, outside the bridgetender's sightline.

Drawbridges have been around more than four thousand years. The Egyptians built the first ones. The 17th Street Bridge was a *bascule* design, operating like a seesaw with a counterweight below attached to the two spans, or leafs. Max was hanging onto the east leaf. He heard a powerful growl beneath him – the motor that moved the counterweight – then felt a sudden jolt and the span began to rise.

Thirty seconds later the grates were pointing at the sky. Max was seven stories above the channel. The Intracoastal sparkled below like a thousand eyes winking at him. The yacht closed in on the gap. He looked down. Peanut Strong was gazing up from the wheel of his boat, his face obscured by a big pink gum bubble. Ben Chance occupied the middle bench, or at least most of it. His sister Delray was stretched across the square bow in a one piece yellow bathing suit, looking like a golden mermaid. Max laughed and waved at them. Then he pushed off into thin air.

"Geronimo!"

He arched his back, pointed his fingers at the water and his toes at the sky, just like Johnny Weissmuller in *Tarzan the Magnificent*. It was a great dive, he decided. *A perfect 10.* Halfway down he changed his grade to *A big mistake*. He'd miscalculated. The yacht was moving faster than he realized. He was going to hit the bow. The blonde in pink polka dots saw it too. She pointed and screamed. Max told himself to remain cool. He even tried to crack a smile. Milliseconds from death, though, his face refused to cooperate. Then he remembered a maneuver he'd pulled a hundred times on the rope swing at Whiskey Creek. He tucked his knees into his chest and flipped backwards. The gambit bought him a few precious inches and he whooshed past the nose of the yacht and knifed into blackness.

"Yeeeooowww!" he screamed underwater, a jet of bubbles rushing from his mouth.

His momentum took him straight down. He stretched out his arms and didn't stop until his hands touched the slimy channel bottom. He stopped and waited, got his bearings, then pushed off from the goo and swam blindly in long strokes until he bumped into a wooden bridge spile. He felt for an opening and slipped through. By the time he came to the surface beside the Whaler, he'd been under-water well over a minute. The first thing he saw was Delray's face.

"Hello," he said, trying to sound nonchalant.

"Oh, my God," she yelped. "You're safe?"

He sprang into the boat. Ben shouted.

"That was incredible!"

Peanut smirked at him, his freckled face as red as the tangled nest on top of his head.

"Spaz," he said. "I thought you were a dead man."

Max waved a hand with false bravado. "I missed by three inches."

Ben pointed. The yacht had stopped and was backing up under the bridge.

"You scared the crap out of them."

The passengers and crew were hanging over the rails searching frantically for the jumper.

"Holy pink polka dots, Batman," Peanut blurted. "Look at them knockers."

"Shut up," Max said. "There's a lady on board."

"That's no lady," said Ben. "That's my sister."

Max looked at Delray and shook his head. She shrugged her shoulders and smiled a dimpled smile at him and he felt a tremor inside.

The spans were still skyward and dozens of people were lining both sides of the bridge peering down at the water. There was a lot of arm flapping and finger pointing. A bare-chested man dove off the yacht while the other passengers waved to a small Coast Guard cutter for help.

"Let's get out of here," Max said. He pushed the Whaler away from the bridge, hopped onto the bow and grabbed the rope. "Hit it."

Ben had taken the wheel. He gunned the engine and the small boat surged. The front end rose and Max bounced up and down, using his one hundred ten pounds to force it down. The propeller on the fifty horsepower Evinrude gained traction and the boat raced from beneath the bridge into the open waters of Port Everglades. Behind them, the bridgetender had climbed out of his shack on top of the span and was shaking his fist in the air. Laughing, they waved back and sprinted toward the Atlantic.

The Whaler skimmed past the granite jetties that lined the inlet and into the indigo sea, dancing over whitecaps, crashing from wave to wave. With each concussion Max's friends lifted their bottoms off the hard wood seats while he stood, rope in hand, like a rodeo cowboy riding a bucking bronco.

They turned sharp left and dashed north along the beach, a salty wind lashing their faces. The water was clear as glass. Peanut pointed to a cluster of starfish, bone-white against the sandy bottom. Schools of angel fish darted this way and that. A pod of slick gray porpoises glistened in the lemon light. Bathers waved from the shallows while red-suited lifeguards, their noses slathered white with zinc-oxide, blew whistles from their stands, signaling them away from the beach.

It had been two months since Max ran into the schoolyard to save Ben from Junior Ball. Had his Uncle Howard not intervened, Attila the Nun would surely have expelled him from Our Lady of Perpetual Sorrow. Max heard it all that morning from a hardback chair in the principal's outer office. Ben was sitting beside him, wiping away blood and tears with Max's handkerchief. Mrs. Hopkins, the grandmotherly white-haired school secretary, watched them from behind the counter. Max liked to brag that his ears were so acute he could hear a dog whistle. "*Your full of crap, Brady,*" was Peanut's routine response. *"Dogs can't whistle."* He did have good ears, though, and that day he sat there pretending not to listen to the heated debate over his fate.

Attila railed in her thick brogue. "Maximus Brady must pay the price."

Howard Pickens was just as adamant. "Max is your best student, Sister Mary Aloysius. He's from a fine family. His father was my closest friend. He died saving my life. The boy is my godson."

"That is no excuse. Mister Brady spit in my face in front of the entire student body. What he did was an abomination. I will not tolerate it."

Pickens refused to back down from the domineering Irishwoman. "Let me ask you a question, sister." His voice was firm, resolute. "What if this got into the newspapers?"

A stony silence ensued. Then Max heard the nun's voice. It was dripping with venom.

"What are you implying, Mr. Pickens?"

"What do you think the bishop would say if he read that you recruited one student to beat up another student in front of five hundred children?"

The nun hissed like a scalded cat. "Are you threatening me?"

"It's not a threat, sister. I've got half-a-mind to report you to the prosecutor's office. A good case could be made you committed child abuse today."

Max could almost see Sister Mary Aloysius's fleshy cheeks trembling with rage.

"And you, Mr. Pickens? A police officer? You oversaw that *child abuse*. Refereed it, in fact."

"I made a grave mistake. I told you I wanted nothing to do with this. I let you browbeat me. I'm ashamed it took a thirteen-year-old boy to make me see."

In the end, Uncle Howard saved Max from expulsion. The normally unbending Sister Mary Aloysius folded like a poker player holding a bad hand. He was suspended from school the rest of the term, but was allowed to graduate with his class. That was okay with Max. Even his grandparents understood.

"Maximus, you're as unpredictable as a hurricane in May," his grandfather told him at the dinner table that night. "It takes a strong character to confront harshness. Someday you'll relish what you did today. I'm proud of you."

His real penance was being banned from the Eighth Grade Cotillion, thereby foiling his plot to dance with Delray Chance. Things had worked out, though. Standing up for Ben became the seed that had flowered into a secret society of four. Since school ended Max, Delray, Ben, and Peanut had been inseparable. Water skiing on New River. Splashing in Whiskey Creek. Scuba diving in the Atlantic. It had been the best summer of Max's life. The days were dawdling by at tortoise pace and their conspiracy of fun still had weeks to go before it was back to school again.

From the wheel, Ben shouted over the engine blare.

"Where to?"

Max leaned back, still standing at the bow riding the waves.

"Three Mile Reef."

He stole a glance at Delray. She was watching him too, her long flaxen hair whipping in the wind, a wispy smile gracing her perfect face. They raced along the beach for another mile. Flying fish skipped alongside the boat like scaly racing pigeons. A small plane flew low overhead towing a banner advertising the Surf, Sun & Fun Surfboard Shop. When they were perpendicular to Sunrise Boulevard, Max waved at Ben to turn hard to starboard and they headed out into open water.

Fort Lauderdale was named after a 1830s-era general who built a fort near the present-day Bahia Mar to guard against Seminole attacks. The militant Indians were long gone, as were the old fort's walls. The biggest threat nowadays came from Mother Nature, which had also provided Lauderdale with its own natural walls of defense. Three coral ridges stretched along the sea bottom the length of the beach which served as oceanic speed bumps, dashing giant storm waves before they reached the coast. The nearest was just a few hundred yards offshore, the farthest barely a mile out. The reefs teemed with undersea life, making them magnets for fishermen and scuba divers. Too crowded for Max's liking. He waved Ben past the third rock formation and pointed toward his secret spot.

Nobody knew Three Mile Reef like Max Brady, except perhaps his grandfather, the legendary fishing guide Captain Zack Brady, who introduced Max to the exquisite pink coral outcrop when he was only five years old. Even at that age the boy understood the reverence his grandfather held for the reef.

"An undersea cathedral," Grandpa Zack called it. "Finest shoal 'tween here and Abaco."

Max had spent countless hours floating over or diving on the reef and had developed the same veneration for the spot as his grandfather. Three miles out and forty feet down, it was a prismatic extravaganza of fish and sea flora. The reef sat smack in the middle of the Gulf Stream, the extraordinary thermal river embedded in the Atlantic Ocean. The stream never dipped below seventy seven degrees Fahrenheit and was the reason Fort Lauderdale's ocean tides remained temperate year round.

When they reached the reef Max raised his arm. Ben yanked back the throttle and Peanut tossed a small anchor overboard. The rope unraveled fast and Ben trolled in a slow circle until it hooked on a rock.

Max strapped a knife to his calf and, without mask or fins, dove over the side and plunged straight down. The boy couldn't remember not knowing how to swim. Grandpa Zack swore he was half fish and teased that he'd caught him off Lighthouse Point *"on nine-pound test line with a bucktail jig."* Max did feel part fish. He loved being underwater. It was two minutes before he burst back to the surface.

"I can't believe you stayed down so long," Delray gushed.

"Who needs a tank when you have gills? Did you know crocodiles swallow rocks to stay underwater?"

Delray gave a good impression of looking impressed, then stretched her arm out and helped him into the boat. Peanut watched, peeling flakes of skin from his perpetually sunburned nose.

"Brady's showing off again," he said in a sing-song voice.

Peanut's father was an airline pilot. A few months earlier he'd come home with a dozen air bottles he'd found in an airport hangar.

"You boys should have these tested?" he told his son and Max. "If they're clean have them fitted with valves, get some regulators, and learn to scuba dive. There's a whole world down there you two have no idea about."

For Max it was like being baptized into a new religion. Suddenly he could remain underwater for an hour or more at a time, like a real fish. He discovered an enchanted wonderland filled with mysterious creatures, luminous colors, and a true sense of adventure. Enthralled, he and Peanut explored caves and hunted lobster until their tanks ran dry. Then Ben and Delray began joining them. Delray refused to scuba dive, pleading claustrophobia, but she enjoyed coming along anyway. Max didn't complain.

When the three boys were finally arrayed in their tanks, flippers, and masks, Max tucked a pillow case into his weight belt to hold the lobsters he planned to capture. They grabbed their spearguns, sat on the gunwale, placed hands over their masks, and fell backwards.

They descended in slow motion through diaphanous turquoise water to an opulent promontory. Three Mile Reef was a seven thousand year old living thing composed of billions of tiny polyps that had coalesced over the millennia to form an intricate coral skeleton. It was a subaquatic kaleidoscope populated by giant grouper, snapper, parrotfish, moray eel, manta ray, leatherback turtle, urchin, squid, sponge, sea spiders, crustaceans, and all manner of flora.

A gentle current pushed the boys along the top of the spiny ledge. A giant jellyfish drifted beside them like a gelatinous blue gum bubble, the umbrella of its bell-shaped veil expanding and contracting as it pulsated along, followed by a trail of toxic tentacles. The boys kept a wary distance.

They came to a large hole in the rocks the size of a circus ring. Max floated out over a vertical cave. Its walls were steep and its sandy floor snow white. He pointed his speargun and they drifted down into the cistern. Barbed tentacles waved from a dozen recesses. *Panulirus Argus*, Caribbean spiny lobster, their tails composed of sweet white meat that the cantankerous crustaceans were loath to surrender without spirited resistance.

Catching them was tricky business. They didn't have powerful claws like cold water lobster from Maine or Denmark, yet their ten thorny legs and spiked hinds were capable of inflicting harsh pain on careless hunters. Ben and Peanut preferred to keep their distance, prodding them from their sanctuaries and impaling them with spears. Max considered it more sporting to reach into the dark notches bare handed – man versus decapod.

There were so many to choose from. He glided lazily around the chamber, taking slow shallow breaths to stretch his air supply, until he spotted a particularly thick pair of antennas protruding from under a rock. He swam to it and put his face up to the hole. A pair of beady black eyestalks stared back at him. They were attached to a creature about the size of a Chihuahua and may have weighed three pounds; tiny for a dog, huge for a lobster. *Hello, Leroy.* Max liked to name his lobsters. They were always Leroy. Tonight Leroy would be guest of honor at his grandparent's dinner table. *I hope you like drawn butter, Leroy*, he thought and began the game of cat-and-mouse. He stretched his right hand into the cubbyhole and taunted his quarry. *Come and get me, Leroy.* The shellfish lunged at his fingers and Max pulled back. He reached in again, trying to lure Leroy out far enough to get a grip on his reddish-brown carapace. Leroy snapped his tail like a cranky castanet dancer, determined to snare one of Max's digits.

On the opposite side of the cave, Peanut was searching the wall for an easy mark. Ben was a few feet away using the tip of his speargun to goose a small spidery critter from its sanctuary. Suddenly the lobster bolted from the hole and scurried between his legs. Startled, Ben pushed off the bottom and smashed headfirst into a rock mantle a few feet above.

Max turned just in time to see it happen and burst out laughing, trying not to swallow salt water. In a matter of seconds, though, a red plume engulfed Ben's head. He dropped his speargun and began swimming, blind and erratic.

Forgetting about Leroy, Max dropped his own sling and raced to Ben. He got a grip on his friend's shoulders and tried to calm him. Behind the mask Ben's eyes were wild and unfocused. He was in full panic. Max knew panic was the mortal enemy of every scuba diver. The heavyset boy kicked and thrashed and broke loose from his grasp. Then he swam straight into the same wall again, bashing the crown of his skull on the coral. His mouthpiece came out and his airhose convulsed like an untended fire hose. Max circled behind him this time and wrapped his friend in a bear hug. Peanut saw what was happening. He grabbed the regulator and shoved it back in his mouth and Ben calmed.

Blood kept pouring from his head wound and the cave water was turning crimson. Max pointed his index finger upward, signaling them to surface. Ben didn't seem to notice, but Peanut nodded. He clutched Ben's wrist and led him up toward the mouth of the hole. Max followed. When they reached the top, Peanut stopped cold. Ben began swinging his arms and kicking his legs like a madman.

Max swam up past them to the cave entrance and saw what they were reacting to.

A large gray-brown fish was circling fifteen feet directly above them. It had a freakish head shaped like a skateboard, barren black eyes at either end staring at him like unearthly gunbarrels, and jagged teeth frozen in a hideous smile. *Hammerhead!* Max knew about hammerheads from Grandpa Zack. They were among the most dangerous sharks in the sea, and quite plentiful in these waters. Judging by its white underbelly he estimated this one was twelve feet long or more.

Something grabbed him from behind. It was Ben. His eyes were the size of silver dollars. Blood was wafting from his head like hickory smoke from a barbecue pit. Max knew the shark smelled it. He looked up. The fish was getting closer with every revolution, its desolate eyes watching them like a savory lunch waiting to be eaten. He could almost see it licking its lips.

He raised his palms and signaled Ben and Peanut to stay put and rushed down to the cave floor. He retrieved his speargun and kicked back to the top just as the shark attacked. It went straight for Ben, who must have looked like the most appetizing of the three boys. Max stabbed his spear tip into its flat, broad face and the big fish veered off. Ben lost his mouthpiece again and was on the verge of another bout of hysteria.

Max pushed it back into his mouth. While he was trying to calm him, Peanut shot out of the hole toward the surface. Max watched him ascend and vanish into the boat. The shark was apparently so enthralled by the scent of blood it didn't notice Peanut's escape. It began circling again, closing in for a second go at the humanoid smorgasbord. Max maneuvered himself in front of Ben, just like he'd done that day in the schoolyard, wishing Junior Ball was still his nemesis.

With its gruesome trigonal teeth smiling, the fish charged straight at them a second time. Max aimed his speargun at the center of its flat head. *Wait*, he told himself. *Wait. Wait.* When the shark was three feet away he pulled the trigger. The taut rubber sling snapped and the speargun recoiled. The shark rammed straight into his chest.

He felt like he'd been hit by a Volkswagen. The impact knocked him backward. He smashed into Ben and they tumbled head-over-heels in a cloud of blood and bubbles. Max's mask was ripped off. He reached out blindly, groping for Ben. He got a hand on his arm and dragged him down into the cave. Ben's air hose was out again and he replaced it once more.

Max's heart was racing and he was sucking air fast. Despite his rapid respiration, though, he noticed he was still calm. Not just calm. Almost euphoric. It was the same feeling he'd had diving off the bridge an hour before. The same rush he'd felt facing Junior in the schoolyard. A killing machine wanted to eat him, and he liked it. It occurred to Max that something might be wrong with him.

When the water cleared, he wheeled around. Despite his muzzy vision the predator was nowhere in sight. He did a quick inventory and determined neither he nor Ben had been cut or bitten. In the chaos of the collision, Max had no idea if his spear had hit its mark. He grabbed Ben by the straps of his backpack and patted his chest with an open palm and nodded that they were okay. He found his mask in the sand, slipped it on, tilted back his head, and blew a jet of air through his nostrils, forcing the water out. Then he took Ben by the arm and they swam to the top of the hole.

Max pulled his knife from its sheath and poked his head up out of the cave, wary, ready for the hammerhead to charge. Nothing. The fish could be lurking anywhere. Most likely on the other side of the reef. He gestured at Ben to wait and slipped out of the hole. Hugging the coral, he scanned the ridge. Still nothing. He hung his head over the side, prepared to jump back. The shark was nowhere to be seen. *Is he dead? Did I get him?*

Max returned to the cave and retrieved his spearless speargun. He gave Ben a thumb up and pointed at the boat. Ben watched him with big eyes. He nodded and bolted toward the top. Max took chase and managed to get a hand on his ankle and pull him back. A rapid ascent was like shaking a soda bottle before opening. Air bubbles could be released into the blood stream, triggering a case of the bends. A bubble reaching the heart or brain could be as lethal as the deadliest shark.

He motioned to Ben to rise slowly and they ascended at the speed of their own bubbles, Max below his friend, spinning in slow circles, knife in one hand, empty speargun in the other, searching for the predator. The shark might be dead, but if it was only wounded it would be even more menacing.

Peanut and Delray were leaning over the side when they broke the surface. While they pulled Ben from of the water, Max sank back down a few feet and kept lookout. Then he removed his weight belt and handed it to Peanut, followed by his tank and speargun. He re-sheathed his knife and climbed aboard.

Ben was prostrate on the boat floor, a dazed expression on his face. A small red pool had already formed on the mottled blue fiberglass beneath his head. Delray pressed a towel to the wound and whispered in his ear.

"You're safe now, Benjamin. You're going to be alright."

"Your brother's got more blood than a bloodbank," Peanut said. "Do you think he's in shock?"

Max examined his eyes. They were clear and his pupils were not dilated, nor was his skin cold or clammy, signs he was not in shock. Nonetheless, they raised his feet and covered him with towels. Ben looked up.

"My speargun! Where's my speargun?"

Two spearguns were on the floor of the boat. One was Max's, the other Peanut's.

"Must still be in the cave," Peanut said.

"My dad's gonna kill me. It's brand new. A Nemrod. He paid fifty bucks."

"Forget it," said Delray. "You're not going back down there today."

"I will," said Max.

"No," she cried.

Before she could stop him he filled his lungs and plunged over the side without mask or fins. He was pretty sure the hammerhead was dead. He'd speared it in the head from point blank range. Even so, his eyes scanned the water while he hurried to the reef. He entered the cave and surveyed the white floor. The speargun was nowhere in sight. His lungs still had a good ninety seconds of air left and he decided to use it sifting the sand with his bare fingers. He concentrated on the area where Ben had rammed his head into the rocks. After forty-five seconds, he had not found the Nemrod and was about to give up. The weapon wasn't going anywhere. They could find it tomorrow. Then his fingers grazed something. It felt metallic. He kept probing, massaging the sand like a baker kneading dough. He felt it again. Whatever it was, though, it was small. Way too small to be a speargun. He wrapped his fist around the object and pulled it out in a fog of sand.

When the water cleared he opened his palm. The object was round and about the size of a bottle cap. Despite being fifty feet under water, with no air tank, he nonchalantly examined the piece. It looked like some kind of coin. The shape was round, but not perfectly so. Rubbing his right thumb over its surface, he felt a raised impression and held the tarnished face close to his eyes. It looked like a cross. He scraped the surface with his right thumbnail and a jolt of exhilaration rushed through him. The claw mark was golden.

Max's mind raced. He couldn't wait to show the others. He felt his oxygen beginning to sap. Time to get back to the boat. He tucked the coin in his pocket and pushed off the bottom toward the mouth of the cave. Before he reached the opening, though, something caught his eye. The shiny tip of Ben's speargun was poking out of the sand ten feet from the spot he'd been searching. Despite his constricting lungs, he swam back to the bottom, grabbed the gun and rushed toward the top of the hole.

He was halfway out when the hammerhead struck. Max's spear was protruding from its right eye, followed by a trail of blood. But its left eye was trained on him and its teeth bared. A one-eyed fish looking for retribution. This time it didn't bother to circle and came right at him. Max didn't have time to aim. He extended the speargun in front of him with both hands like a shield. The hammerhead swam straight into it. The blow knocked the weapon out of his grip and he tumbled backward down into the cave.

The attack depleted what little oxygen he had left. His lungs were screaming. He had only seconds left. He considered his options.

Only two choices came to him, neither good. He could stay in the cave and drown. Or make a mad dash for the boat and risk becoming fish food. He felt as vulnerable as a conch without its shell. Yet, for a reason he couldn't explain, he wasn't afraid. Grandpa Zack's words came to him. *'Water is life.'* Somehow he knew he was not going to die here. He pulled out his knife and kicked for the boat.

Peanut and Delray were hanging over the side, their arms extended, the rippling water distorting their features like a carnival mirror. He was almost to the top when he saw Delray's mouth open in a soundless scream. She pointed at something. From the corner of his right eye he saw the hammerhead coming at him fast. He kicked harder, heart pounding, lungs pleading for relief. He felt himself start to black out, but resisted like he was fighting off sleep, waiting to feel the shark's teeth tear into him. Delray waved frantically, as if trying to will him to safety. Max surged to the surface and shot into the Whaler in a single bound as the fish vanished beneath the boat. He landed on top of Ben and gasped for air like it was God's own breath. Ben stared at him, their noses inches apart.

"Did you find my speargun?"

Et Tu Brady

Chapter Twelve

BRADY HAD GIVEN up on sleep. Too much adrenalin was gushing through his veins. Too many questions were swirling through his brain. So he lay in the red tent trying to reconcile his memory of Ben's face that day with the image of him hours ago with the copper noose around his throat and *Et Tu Brady* tattooed across his forehead. A sad end to a sad life. He pondered whether Chance's murder had been preordained that exquisite summer day.

It was near dawn. A new day. Enough of the past. His present was breathing softly at his side, her eyes closed. He loved to watch Rose sleep. He gingerly lifted the thin blanket covering her, as if disrobing Lady Godiva herself, and let his eyes roam. Her skin was pale but had a healthy tint of tan lines. The sight of her long lithe legs, firm tummy, full breasts, and puffy pink nipples swept the cobwebs from his head.

Women had always been his salvation. His mother, Mary. His grandmother, Kate. His wife, Victoria. Even Delray when he was a boy. Yet his time with them had been no more enduring than a haiku written in the sand. Each had been wrenched from him too soon. Now, gazing at Rose, he made a silent vow to protect her as long as an atom of life remained in him.

He brushed a fingertip across her bare left hip, as gently as the wings of one of her butterflies.

"Hey!" she murmured without opening her eyes. "Is that an ogler?"

"Good *O* word. Definition?"

"Scopophiliac."

"Whatta-butta-butta?"

She smothered a yawn with the back of her hand. "Peeping Tom."

"Drat! Caught red-handed. Wasn't Tom caught peeping on Lady Godiva? What are you, some kind of oracle?"

"Definition?"

"You know, like a seer."

"I think you're stretching it, *old* boy."

"Ouch! Bad *O* word."

He slid the wispy wrap off her altogether. Eyes still closed, she stretched her arms above her head and arched her back like a languorous cat on a plush carpet.

"What, sir, are your intentions?"

"I assure you, madame, nothing honorable."

"Do you plan to keep me captive in this tent?"

"Good plan."

"Ravaging me over and over?"

"Better plan."

Rose combed her fingers through long black Medusa tresses as wild as a nest of raw nerves. She opened one eye. It looked like a violet floating in a bowl of milk.

"Well, buster, you best not dilly-dally. I've got a city to save. And the gym opens soon."

"Did you know the word *gymnasium* in Greek means to *exercise naked*?"

"Did you know you're like a talking encyclopedia."

"Oh, but there's more. Did you know that South Floridians have sex twenty percent more often than New Yorkers?"

"I'm sensing a theme here."

"Did you know there are one hundred fourteen acts of sexual intercourse taking place between humans on Earth every second of every day?"

She rolled onto her side and threw a bare leg over him.

"I hope you plan on taking more than a second, Brady."

Thirty minutes later he threw back the tent flap and stumbled into the morning. He staggered to the waist-high wall that bounded Rose's rooftop Papillon Gym and gazed across the beach road at the Atlantic. An orange band stretched like a racing stripe above the curved wheel of the horizon, but the sun had not yet winked at Fort Lauderdale. Rose came up behind him wrapped in the flimsy blanket. She nuzzled her cheek against the staunch slope of his shoulder and they watched the surf lap gently ashore at nine second intervals.

"Ever wonder if fish get thirsty?" he said.

"Hmmm."

"Ever wonder if you can cry underwater?"

"Never."

"Ever wonder who'll be the last person you think of before you die?"

"What is this? Deep Thoughts by Max Brady?"

"Somebody's gotta think deep."

"Ever wonder how you got to be such a lucky *freaking* duck?"

"Pray tell."

"You leave me stretched out in front of a cozy fire, bare-assed and tipsy, and run off to see an old girlfriend. You don't get back until three in the morning. Reeking of booze. And I still let you have your way with me."

Brady thought deeply on that for a time. Finally he draped an arm over her shoulder and drew her close.

"Don't you mean lucky *fucking* duck?"

"Good girls don't talk like that."

"Do you know what they say about good girls?"

"Pray tell."

"They're just bad girls who haven't been caught."

A drowsy breeze whispered off the sea. Fronds rustled on the long belt of spindly tufted palms that lined the beach. The sun peeked over the brink of the world. Rose turned her face up and indulged him with a kiss. He looked her in the eyes and whispered.

"You're the only woman I care about. You know that, don't you?"

"Somehow, Brady, I get the feeling there's a lot about you I don't know."

His eyes widened. Rose was being way too astute for such an early hour.

"I am an open book. You can check me out at the library. Ask me anything."

A mischievous glint lit her eyes. "Okay. Tell me about this old flame you hurried off to last night."

"She's hardly an old flame. I haven't seen her since we were kids."

He told her about Ben Chance's murder. The copper noose. The tattoo on his forehead. And that Captain Register suspected Delray.

"Maybe she did murder her brother, knowing she could count on you to save her skin."

Brady stared out at the powdery pink dawn, watching something too distant for Rose to see. He loved her more than anyone in the world. But he had secrets he could never share, with her or anyone.

"I'm afraid Delray knows from experience not to count on me."

Rose frowned up at him. "Very cryptic, Brady. Very cryptic."

She stepped back and punched him hard in the arm.

"Ow!" He rubbed his bicep. "What was that for?"

"Maybe you forgot. We said no secrets. I don't like secrets."

Rose turned and did a saucy strut to the locker room door, letting the blanket fall to the ground behind her. She vanished without a backward glance, like Godiva without her steed.

Et Tu Brady

Chapter Thirteen

A JUMBO JET screamed in low overhead, so low it almost clipped the tree tops. The shriek was ear-splitting. The tremor rattled the dilapidated dock where a wiry, bare-chested man was crouched. Dismas Benvenuti didn't notice a thing. He was too busy dangling a string over a small pond with a Kentucky Fried Chicken drumstick hooked to the end. At the center of the little lake two black eyes watched him from just above the waterline. They were attached to a six-foot long alligator. Dismas jiggled the string.

"Come an' git it, ya wallet wannabe."

The reptile swished its tail beneath the surface and the coffee-black water rippled as it glided toward the bait. It swam right up to the dock, raised its head and opened its hinged lower jaw, exposing its white maw and picket fence of serrated yellow teeth. Dismas let go of the string and dropped the chicken neck into the void. The animal clamped down and began to sink into the water when Dismas dove off the dock onto its armor-plated back.

The gator exploded with savage fury, its studded tail whipping the water like a dervish. Dismas held on like a bull wrangler with no rope. The animal bucked him off for an instant, but he clambered back on and wrapped his left arm around what there was of its neck.

He stretched his right hand up and tried to get a grip on the gator's long snout. It opened its mouth and his hand slipped. The powerful jaws snapped like a bear trap, narrowly missing a five finger snack. After several aborted attempts, Dismas managed to slam the alligator's lower mandible against its upper jaw and shut the mouth like the hood of a car. He rolled off the wild beast and stood in chest-deep water then flipped it onto its back and began rubbing its soft white underbelly. Within seconds the fight went out of the gator and it appeared to fall asleep. A voice called out from the opposite side of the pond.

"Dismas, what the hell you doin'?" A frowzy little bag-of-bones was standing unsteadily on the weedy bank. "You goddamn crazy?"

Dismas looked across the water at Jimmy Jonas and responded in a strange tongue.

"What's that yer sayin', Diz? What the hell language you talkin'?"

"Injun."

Dismas released the creature. It sank beneath the surface and disappeared for several seconds then jerked awake and swirled away from its antagonist. Dismas slogged out of the pond up onto the bank. He was a nondescript man with one of those faces you wouldn't notice if you'd just seen it on a wanted poster.

"Injun?" Jimmy Jonas said. "What kinda damn injun?"

"My ancestral tongue."

"Ancestral? What's ancestral?"

"The language of my forefathers. The unconquered people. The only native tribe never to sign a peace treaty with the blood-thirsty interlopers from across the big water."

"The hell you talkin'?"

"The great Seminole people."

"Dismas ain't no Seminole name."

"It ain't nothin'. Dismas was the Good Thief they crucified next to Jesus."

"Well, then, what 'bout Benvenuti? Ain't that eye-tal-yun."

Dismas was wearing cut-off blue jeans. He picked a white V-neck T-shirt off the rickety dock and toweled beads of pond water from his torso then responded again in the mysterious argot.

"Talk American, Diz," said Jimmy. "Why you wrestlin' gators and speakin' funny?"

"My grandmother was a Seminole. I'm reclaiming my heritage."

"Why the hell would you wanna do that?"

"Hundred twenty grand a year."

"What?"

"That's what tribe members get every year just for bein' Seminole. From all that Hard Rock Casino money they get down in Hollywood. All I gotta do is prove my grandma was pure blood Seminole. That makes me quarter-blood. That makes me rich."

"Who was your grandma?"

"Matilda Cataldo."

"Cataldo ain't no more Seminole than Benvenuti."

Dismas said something again in Seminole.

"What'd you say?"

"You don't wanna know. By the way, Jimmy, wanna make five grand?"

Jimmy Jonas was a young-old man who reminded Dismas of the mangy mongrels that foraged around the garbage dumpster. He had a thinning head of hair the color of a nicotine stain, a scraggily beard salted with white whiskers that sparkled like broken glass, and hollow, deathbed eyes that lit up like beacons at the mention of five grand.

Another giant jet screamed overhead, its wheels spinning just above the trees. Both men ducked reflexively.

"Goddamned things never stop," Jimmy groused.

Dismas and Jimmy lived in the Cloud Nine Trailer Park, a flop-house on wheels hidden in an oak grove directly beneath the glide path to the Fort Lauderdale-Hollywood International Airport. Every three minutes of every day, park denizens were assaulted by a blitz-krieg of commercial airliners thundering in so low they could see the pilot's faces.

Temperance was a scarce commodity here. Cloud Nine was a community of burn-outs and derelicts, mostly white men and women who had started at the bottom and gone downhill from there. Jimmy Jonas was an addict. The substance didn't matter. Anything that helped him forget his wretched life. When he had money, which was rare, he spent it on whatever mind-altering agent he could get his hands on: crack, smack, mushrooms, acid, weed, cheap wine, malt liquor. When he was broke, which was the norm, he'd find a car, jump up and down on the bumper, and inhale fumes from the gas tank. He and his neighbors mostly sat in the shade drinking beer all day, half-hoping somebody would come by and offer them work, half-hoping they wouldn't. If Jimmy got real desperate he'd walk down to the Hi-Lo Gas Station on State Road 84 where roofers and yard services came to hire day laborers on the cheap. Dismas – who was Cloud Nine's manager – wondered how Jimmy ever got hired. He was emaciated, missing most of his teeth, and chain-smoked unfiltered Camels. The very act of breathing was an endeavor. But that just made it easy for Dismas to hire him and the others here for his *special jobs.*

"Five thousand bucks?"

"Pretty much guaranteed."

"Hell, yes. What I gotta do?"

"Follow me."

Dismas walked barefoot out of the woods, Jimmy tagging behind like an eager dog. Cloud Nine consisted of a couple dozen rusty mobile homes lined up on a rutted dirt path strewn with broken beer bottles, a mangled bicycle, and the fly-strewn carcass of a decomposing black cat.

Being park manager had its perks. Dismas got to live rent-free in a thirty-foot silver Slipstream, circa 1963, that sat at the far end of the path just beyond a thicket of scrub brush. He could see the pond from his window. The joy of waterfront living!

They climbed three shaky metal steps and entered a dark interior littered with empty bottles, dirty dishes, and old pizza boxes. The stagnant air reeked of cat piss and stale cigarette smoke. Neither man seemed to notice. Dismas's nose was inured to the stink and Jimmy's olfactory sense had deserted him years ago.

"Ain't smelt nothin' since the Nixon Administration," he was fond of repeating. Dismas had heard him say it a hundred times.

"You wanna beer before we do this?" Dismas said.

94

Jimmy's eyes brightened. "Sure. Beers healthy, ya know. Got all thirteen minerals ya need to sustain human life."

Dismas wondered how, or why, Jimmy would know that. He was tempted to ask him what the thirteen minerals were. Instead, he pulled a Coors from the fridge and motioned him to a small table in the cramped kitchenette.

"What're we doin'?"

Dismas dropped a hard-leather black briefcase on the table, snapped it open, and stuffed three thick telephone books inside.

"What hand do ya write with?"

Jimmy tilted his head and stared up at him with mud puddle eyes. "I don't really write."

Dismas shut the case and clicked the lock and thought that one over for a minute. Calling Jimmy a moron would have done a disservice to morons. His brain didn't have enough candlepower to light a birthday cupcake.

"What hand ya jerk off with?"

Jimmy ruminated for a time, his mind moving slower than the Earth's crust. He finally lifted his right arm.

"Okay, lay yer left arm on the table and count to three." Dismas held up three fingers. "You *can* count, can't you?"

"I can count to three," Jimmy said with a trace of pride. "One…"

Before he reached two Dismas swung the briefcase up over his head and slammed the front edge down on Jimmy's forearm. He heard bone break like a tree limb snapping.

"Shit!" Jimmy screamed. He fell off the chair onto the floor and writhed in agony, cradling his shattered arm like it was an injured cat. Tears streamed from his closed eyes. "Shit! Oh, shit! Ohhhh! That hurts so bad. Shit! What the hell'd ya do that for, Dismas?"

"Quit cryin'. Ya sound like a little girl. Ya just made five grand."

Et Tu Brady

Chapter Fourteen

THE SQUAT-AND-GOBBLE CROWD had yet to descend on the Sea Shanty, but the bar was already filled with the savory aroma of baked chicken wings and seafood gumbo bubbling in the cauldron. Brady prepared the fare before Gordy Cockroft staggered in looking like a one man slum. Gordy was a big, lumbering man with bushy brown hair and a two-day stubble. He wore a rumpled red-checked shirt and khaki pants that looked like they'd been lifted from a Salvation Army clothing bin. Brady stared at his own double reflection in the other man's mirrored sunglasses, Siamese twins connected at the nose bridge.

"You look like you've been breathing bad air," he said.

Gordy was Brady's relief bartender. He debated calling in someone else before he left.

"Sorry, Max," he croaked, sounding like his tongue was coated with lint. "My brain feels about five sizes too big for my skull"

"Firewater'll do that. Tequila?"

"Rum shooters."

"Ugh! Rum hangovers are the worst."

"I can vouch for that." Gordy removed the shades and squinted like an inmate just sprung from six months in solitary. His eyes were red roadmaps surrounded by more rings than an archery target. He massaged his temples with trembling fingers. "My brain hurts."

"Actually, Gordy, the human brain is insensate to pain. You're in a state of metabolic shock. The rum dehydrated you. Flushed the vitamins and nutrients from your system. That's why you're hands are shaking."

Gordy examined his fingers while Brady pulled a cocktail shaker from beneath the bar. Like a mad scientist, he shook in a dollop of olive oil, swished it around and dumped it out, then measured a tablespoon of ketchup, cracked an egg and plopped in the yolk, added salt, pepper, and several dashes of Tabasco and Worcestershire Sauce."

"Did you know Worcestershire Sauce is actually anchovy ketchup?"

Gordy almost retched. Brady almost laughed. He poured in a shot of vodka and spritzed it with something fizzy.

"Did you know the word vodka in Russian means *little water*?"

Gordy grunted. Brady poured the contents into a blender and flipped it on for ten seconds then tipped the potion into a glass and added a lime wedge.

"Nostrovia," he said and slammed the glass on the bar.

Gordy winced. "Please, Max. Not so loud. Is that Hair of the Dog?"

"Hair of the Dog that Bit You is the correct name. I don't know what's in that. This is a Prairie Oyster."

Again, Gordy looked like he was going to puke.

"Ain't that bulls balls?"

"Bulls balls is a Rocky Mountain Oyster. This is a Prairie Oyster. It'll replace the electrolytes you lost. Works ridiculously well. Better than you deserve."

Brady felt a twinge of regret as the words were leaving his mouth. Gordy deserved better. He was a sad case with a likeable face, one of the too-many-to-count victims of South Florida's economic implosion. Because of his size, some assumed he was simple-minded, Brady among them. But Gordy had once been a better man, earning a six figure income selling real estate before the crash. When the market capsized his fortunes plummeted like nuclear fallout. He lost his job, his home, his wife, and his two kids.

Gordy became so down-and-out he pawned his dentures to buy a little aluminum flatboat and became a wharf rat, puttering around Bahia Mar Marina doing odd jobs on yachts, scraping barnacles, cleaning bilges, varnishing teak decks. Brady got to know him when he began stopping into the Sea Shanty every morning to drink his breakfast. Gordy would be waiting at the door when he opened. He'd glug two Coronas then go back to the marina reeking of beer and desperation. Brady sensed he was trying to drink himself into a hasty grave. Even so, he took a liking to him. Gordy had a good brain and the cheerful exuberance of a born salesman.

Brady gave him money to get his teeth out of hock and began using him as his back-up bartender. He proved to be a good hire. The thing about Gordy was he was honest. And a hard worker. And loyal as a good dog. And, most important, he gave Brady time to be with Rose.

With a jittery hand, Gordy reached for the glass. He raised the Prairie Oyster to his lips and drank it down in a single breath. His forehead wrinkled and his top lip fluttered and he looked again like he might barf. He belched instead and, within seconds, he didn't look quite so green about the gills. The tightness in his face soon turned into a crooked grin. Brady smiled back.

"You gonna be okay?"

"Sure, boss. Sure. No problem."

"Good. If Rose calls, tell her I'm out playing lawyer."

Et Tu Brady

Chapter Fifteen

RON REGISTER TORE open a yellow packet of artificial sweetener and was pouring it into a steaming coffee cup when Police Chief Donald Begley walked into Homicide. Register looked up and feigned a smile. He didn't particularly like or respect his boss. Register had made his bones as a street cop working the city's toughest neighborhoods, like Boulevard Gardens and Washington Park. He graduated to plainclothes, first as a Burglary detective, then Narcotics, then Homicide. Now he was Homicide commander. By comparison, Begley rose through the ranks investigating traffic accidents; analyzing skid marks, measuring drag factors, assessing structural damage. As far as Register was concerned, he was no more than a glorified meter maid.

Yet, Begley *was* Chief of Police. He'd been handpicked by David Grand, the former mayor. Unfortunately for Begley, Grand was now serving seven years at the federal penitentiary in Atlanta. Thanks in large part to one Max Brady. A few months before, Brady uncovered an arson-murder-bribery conspiracy orchestrated by a wealthy and politically powerful resort developer named Sherwood Steele. Steele died a violent death, as did several of his co-conspirators. Brady and Rose Becker came very close to joining them. When Grand went bye-bye, Begley managed to survive the storm by announcing his retirement at the end of the calendar year. Ron Register wanted very badly to succeed him and needed to curry Begley's favor to do that. So, despite his disdain, when the Police Chief walked in he put on a happy face. Begley did not.

"I don't need this shit right now," he growled, scratching a hairless scalp baked brown by too many hours on the golf course.

The homicide captain's face wore a bemused expression. He stirred his coffee, took a sip, and smacked his lips.

"Don't worry, Don. We're gonna wrap this up quick."

"We better. Half the goddamned world's watching. We don't need a sensational murder case blowing up Super Bowl Week."

"The sister did it. I'd bet my pension on it. We'll be going to the grand jury in a day or two, unless her lawyer mucks up the waters."

"Who's that?"

"Max Brady."

The Police Chief cringed like he'd swallowed pink slime. Register considered offering him a Tums, then thought better of it.

"That cocksucker bar owner?"

Register smiled. "Don't know about the cocksucker part. Girlfriend is Rose Becker, the new city commissioner." Begley frowned. "Used to be a hotshot federal prosecutor in New York. Put a shitload of mob boys behind bars."

"Is he licensed to practice law in Florida?"

"Not sure about that. Until she's indicted, though, she can use anyone she wants. Apparently they were childhood sweethearts."

"Well, I don't like that guy. Watch him. He's trouble. And he's close with Howard Pickens. Which reminds me. That damned dedication ceremony's this week."

Register rolled his eyes. "Jeez, I still can't believe they're naming the entire bleeping detective bureau after that sonofabitch."

Register was less fond of Howard Pickens than he was of Don Begley. And Begley hated few people more. The reason boiled down mainly to Pickens being a department legend and them not so much. He had been Register's predecessor as Homicide boss and Begley's primary rival for Police Chief. If the rank-and-file had had a vote,

Pickens would have been a shoo-in. But Begley was Mayor Grand's lap dog. After he took command he forced Pickens into retirement.

"I thought I'd seen the last of that piece of shit," the Police Chief groused. "Now I have to get up on a stage and say nice things about him? If you covet my job, Register, you better be up there with me."

Knuckles rapped lightly on the door. "Sorry, boss," a female voice said.

Detective Pixie Davenport was standing in the doorway. Behind her loomed a massive black man, her partner, Detective Perry James. They were an odd pair. She was a smallish woman with short brown hair and dark intelligent eyes. James had been an All-American defensive end at the University of Miami during the schools glory days. He spoke in a rich, deep baritone over the top of Davenport's head.

"We got something you're gonna be interested in, captain."

Register waved them into his office. "Chief, you know Detective James."

"Sure do," Begley said examining the big man's hands. "I see you still wear your championship rings."

James held up hands the size of catcher's mitts. Both were adorned with diamond encrusted college football national championship rings. "Can't tell you how many cases flashing these babies in the hood have helped me crack."

"And Pixie Davenport is my techno whiz," Register said. "An absolute artist on the computer."

Begley's eyes strayed to Davenport's fingers. They bore no rings, championship or otherwise. Everyone in the department had known she was lesbian since she came out of the closet and moved in with a female Broward County Sheriff's deputy two years ago. She saw Begley look and the suggestion of a smile lit her handsome face, then vanished like a strand of hair brushed away. Davenport was all business.

"Captain, I ran that check on Benjamin Chance's probate records. Found a forensic accountant's audit attached to his Last Will and Testament. When he died Mr. Chance was worth approximately forty million dollars, which I believe is a gross underestimation."

103

"Why's that?" Register said.

"The Picasso on the wall over his bed is probably worth forty mil all by itself. Add the house, the yacht, and a bank account larger than the GDP of some small countries. He had to be worth a lot more."

Register glanced at Begley then back at Davenport. "What's your point, Pixie?"

"Mrs. Cross said last night she and her brother had been estranged since childhood."

"So?"

"So guess the name of his sole beneficiary."

"Delray Chance Cross?"

Davenport answered with a tight-lipped smile that didn't go away this time. Register leaned back in his chair and whistled in Begley's direction.

"That qualifies as motive to me," the Police Chief said. "That cocksucker Brady is gonna have a hard time explaining that away."

"It gets better, chief," Perry James said. He reached inside his jacket, pulled out a sheaf of papers and held it in the air. "It gets much better."

Et Tu Brady

Chapter Sixteen

EVERYTHING ABOUT DEMONIKA Ball was black except her milky white skin. That and the blue smock and yellow rubber boots she wore when she was hosing dog and cat excreta from the kennel runways at the animal shelter.

"Get over here little pussy," Demonika said.

She opened a grated metal gate and pulled out a black Siamese and shoved the cat into a smaller carry cage.

Judging by looks alone, Demonika was nineteen going on twelve. Her face was puerile and fine-boned and her slim figure was encased in a short black denim skirt and a tight black T-shirt that made no secret of her small, pointed pubescent breasts. Her spiky hair was jet black, as was her mascara, lipstick, nail polish, and studded leather choker around her throat. She opened the next cage, removed an orange Hemingway, and stuffed it in with the black cat. The felines hissed at each other.

"Stop that you little spitfires. You're getting out on furlough. A week's vacation with a rich bitch. Behave and maybe the old bag'll adopt you."

Demonika had been working at the shelter for six months. Not because she loved animals. The truth was she hated the barking, bleating, stench, and hauling euthanized carcasses to the incinerator every Thursday. At eight bucks an hour, the job would have been too foul for the money – if not for the cottage industry.

The enterprise had been the brainstroke of her boyfriend, Lazarus. *Temporal Pets – Cat and Dog Rentals.* As most South Floridians can attest, every winter millions upon millions of northerners make winter pilgrimages to the Sunshine State, many expecting to roost free of charge in the extra bedrooms of friends or family for days, weeks, or, God forbid, months at a time.

"Half of America is allergic to pet dander," Lazarus explained to Demonika. "You rent dogs and, particularly, cats to locals and when the freeloaders realize they'll be sniffling and sneezing their vacations away they'll pony-up for a hotel room. Do you know how many people would pay for a service like that?"

Demonika was raking in a small fortune. She'd even had business cards printed. This week alone she'd leased out a dozen cats at one hundred dollars per animal per week. And as word spread, demand had grown exponentially. Even so, Demonika thought as she loaded the animal cage into her lime green Honda Civic, she should not have been reduced to this in the first place. She cursed her sorry excuse for a father, as she did several times every day, for cutting off her allowance. Thank God for Lazarus.

The morning had a bright, tinny quality. Demonika steered east over the 17th Street Causeway Bridge into the seaside ghetto of Harbor Beach. This was the really good side of town; that being anyplace on the narrow band of sand between the Atlantic Ocean and the Intracoastal Waterway. The alcove was chock-a-block with multi-million-dollar homes where the one-percenters sequestered themselves from the riff-raff. She found the street and pulled up in front of a whitewashed two-story Mediterranean that yearned to be a mansion, but was a relative runt in a land of giants. An older woman greeted her at the door.

"Cat girl?"

She had the sandpaper rasp of a three-pack-a-day smoker, which explained the clear plastic oxygen tube plugged in her nose. She was wearing a bright floral-print apron. Beneath the apron, Demonika was startled to realize, the woman was stark naked.

"Mrs. Desmond?"

"Judy. Call me Nudey Judy. Everybody does. I'm a naturist. I hope nudity doesn't offend you."

"Uh, not really," Demonika mumbled.

"Clothing stifles me. It's actually quite liberating when the only thing you're wearing is a smile," she said and smiled.

Not quite sure how to respond, Demonika held up the cage. "I brought your cats."

"Just in the nick of time."

Mrs. Desmond turned and led her through the house, pulling a green oxygen bottle on wheels behind her. Demonika couldn't avoid noticing substantial breasts flopping from the sides of her apron, or a wrinkled brown bottom that looked like it could use a good pressing. They crossed a large high-ceiling living room appointed with expensive black-and-white furniture in a Far East motif. Demonika's mother had been an interior designer and she had a practiced eye for such things. There was a Borneo chaise and a Malacca rattan sofa with matching wing back chairs. Against the far wall a seven-foot Bombay armoire was stocked with Asian curios, mostly small objects of ceramic pottery, carved teak, and jade amulets. A large portrait of Judy Desmond hung over the fireplace – much younger and, thankfully, fully clothed. If the painting was to be believed, she had once been quite striking.

Judy led her to a big modern kitchen, also in black-and-white. Demonika looked out the back window to see if any zebras were grazing on the lawn.

"My loathsome cousin Alice and her vile husband Bert are arriving from Philadelphia today," Judy said. "They're taking a Caribbean cruise out of Port Everglades on that new ocean liner, the *Oasis of the* whatever. Supposed to be the world's biggest boat. They don't sail for two days and Alice and Bert invited themselves to stay here until then, and another three days when they get back. Lotta goddamn nerve, you ask me. This'll fix 'em. Cats make Bert gag like *he's* got furballs. Alice isn't much better."

Judy stopped and turned to Demonika.

"Will you have a nice glass of iced tea, dear?"

"Water would be wonderful, thanks."

Judy stepped to a cabinet with her bare backside facing Demonika. Her skin was brown as a Macadamia nut. No tan lines. Naturists! She stretched on tippy toes and pulled a black-and-white tumbler from the top shelf and pressed it against the water dispenser on a glass-doored refrigerator.

Demonika guessed Judy was about the same age as her grandmother – sixty-something – and had to suppress a rogue image of granny traipsing around *au naturel.*

Judy placed the drink on the kitchen counter. She yanked the air tube from her nostrils, pulled out a long white Virginia Slim, and flicked an ornate gold lighter under the tip. Her left ring finger was adorned with a white diamond the size of a gobstopper.

"I don't really like cats," Judy said in her braided voice and blew a slender blue jet into the air that lost propulsion and drifted weightlessly toward the ceiling. "Too independent. Too aloof."

Demonika set the cage on the black marble counter and removed the Siamese. The cat began sniffing at a bowl of fruit. Judy stepped back to the refrigerator, fetched a saucer of milk, and placed it on the counter. The kitten lapped at the dish.

"She's pretty. What's her name?"

"We call her Midnight. You can call her whatever you like. Cats don't really answer to their names anyway."

"Exactly my point. Like they don't need people. Like they think they're better than us."

Demonika pulled out the orange cat. "This is Ernestine. I guess because she's a Hemingway. You know, after that old writer guy? Used to have a bunch around his house in Key West. They're called polydactyls or something. See? Six toes."

"Would you look at that? Looks like its wearing mittens. How long can I have them?"

"Long as you want. It sounds like you might need them two weeks."

"I guess I will." Judy put the black cat down on the floor. She lifted the hem of her apron and wiped her hands, exposing her genitalia without a trace of inhibition. She had no pubic hair, save for a tiny gray heart-shaped patch. "What do I owe you, dear?"

"A hundred per cat per week. Two cats for two weeks is four hundred. Cash, if you don't mind."

Nudey Judy waved a dismissive hand. "Not a problem, dear. I've got paper money coming out my tookis. It's all over the house."

Demonika's ears perked up. "Why's that?"

"My husband's business is all cash. Vending machines. You know, soda, candy, and those silly cranes you see in the supermarkets, the ones kids badger their mothers into pumping five dollars into to snag a fifty cent teddy bear. What else he's got going, I don't wanna know."

Demonika looked out the window again. The backyard hosted a large swimming pool and patio. The manicured lawn ran down to a wide canal that looked out on the Port Everglades inlet. A very prime piece of real estate. Tall ficus hedges lined either side of the yard, providing total seclusion for a woman who preferred to air her privates in public. Demonika wondered if Judy planned to be out there when her cousin Alice and vile, hyper-allergic Bert set sail. That would be a bodacious bon voyage.

She turned back in time to see Judy open the top drawer of her kitchen counter. The sight took her breath away. It was stuffed with cash. Judy grabbed a fistful and counted out ten twenty dollar bills then reached back in and rummaged around until she fished out two more bills bearing Benjamin Franklin's face.

"Here you go, honey. Four hundred. If this works out I've got some friends who might want to avail themselves of your service. Can they reach you at the shelter?"

Demonika shook her head and handed Judy a black business card with white lettering.

"I like the colors," Judy said.

> *Temporal Pets*
> *Cat & Dog Rentals*
> *Demonika*
> *954-666-5151*

"Have them call that number." She closed the carrier door. "Feed them each a can of cat food every day and leave out a bowl of dry Kibbles 'N Bits. I'll call you later to make sure everything's okay."

Nudey Judy ejected another vapor trail, stubbed out her cigarette in an onyx stone ashtray, and grabbed the oxygen hose off the counter.

"You gonna finish that water, honey?" Before Demonika could respond, Judy dipped the nose prongs in her glass. Air bubbles burbled to the surface. Demonika suppressed an urge to upchuck. "Damned thing gets clogged. Seems to be working now. Want a refill?"

"No thanks."

Judy gazed at her for several seconds. Demonika was sitting on a kitchen stool with her legs parted slightly. The older woman reached down and stroked the inside of her left thigh. Demonika jerked away and pulled the short black skirt toward her knees.

"Oh, I'm sorry, dear. I'm not being fresh. I'm not one of them girls from the Planet Lesbos, if ya know what I mean." Judy smiled and winked. "I was just admiring that tattoo on your leg. What's it say?"

Demonika looked down at the inscription on her inner thigh. A single line of script that began just above her knee and disappeared beneath her skirt.

"It's Latin. My boyfriend gave it to me. He's got one too. We're the only ones who know what it means."

"How romantic," Nudey Judy rasped. "Listen, honey, I gotta tell you, you're a pretty girl, but you're skinny as a mopstick." She reached under her apron and squeezed her large left breast. "Men like a little meat on their women. And get some sun. You look like a goddamned corpse."

Et Tu Brady

Chapter Seventeen

BRADY ESCORTED DELRAY Chance Cross into the Fort Lauderdale Police Department a few minutes before noon. He had donned a natty navy blue Hart Schaffner Marx herringbone suit. Jacket pressed. Pants creased. Shoes polished. For a man accustomed to shorts, T-shirts, and black hightops, it was like putting out the Wedgewood china. He felt like he was strapped in a straightjacket.

Delray wore stylish black slacks and a black cotton top with white piping along the collar and lapels. The outfit looked hand-tailored.

The lobby reception desk was enclosed in thick glass with a cluster of small perforations at mouth level. It might have been a cash window at a liquor store on the seedy side of town. A uniformed woman without a badge sat inside the cage. Brady told her they had an appointment with Captain Register in Homicide. She picked up a telephone and punched four numbers.

"A Mr. Brady and Mrs. Cross for the captain." She listened then hung up and pointed to a row of green plastic chairs against a wall by the elevator. "Please have a seat. Someone will come for you shortly."

They sat without speaking. An awkward silence had hung over them on the drive over. After the emotion of the previous night it seemed to dawn on both that they were strangers, albeit with a primal bond. And that their once-feverish captivation with each other had happened in another life and was no longer thermal. Brady kept crossing and uncrossing his legs.

"Nice shoes," Delray said, noticing his black Cesare Paciottis. "They look expensive."

He jiggled his foot. He noticed a smudge on the left toe and polished it with his thumb. "I was a cop for eight years. When you walk a beat you understand the importance of good shoes."

More silence. Delray was blinking and sighing deeply. Brady patted her hand.

"Relax, Delray. We're going to be waiting for a while."

She glanced at a crepe-thin gold watch on her left wrist. "The captain insisted we be here by noon."

"Cops don't adhere to U.S. Naval Observatory time. It's part of the game. Make the suspect wait. Increase the tension. Inflate the importance of the interrogator."

"Max, do you really think Captain Register believes I murdered Benjamin?"

"Listen, Delray, you need to understand something going in. This isn't tiddlywinks. Interrogation is not a friendly game. It's a guilt-presumptive process. Register is going to do everything he can to force you to confess. Lie. Confuse. Intimidate. Try to make you so excruciatingly uncomfortable you'll admit to murder just to end the agony."

"Can he do that with you there?"

Delray was fidgeting with a tiny gold crucifix hanging on a delicate gold chain around her neck. Her fingers were long and slim and manicured, her nails painted a pale pink that matched her lipstick. Brady looked at her and tried to envision the girl who had once beguiled him. In the light of day he saw what an exquisite beauty she'd grown into. Fine narrow features. Nose straight and perfect. Crystalline blue eyes framed by silky blonde hair cut boyishly-short.

"We're here voluntarily. Sort of. We can get up and walk out any time. I doubt he's got enough to arrest you, but if Register wants to go goon squad he could play the material witness card."

"You mean lock me up?"

"Detain you, for a reasonable period of time."

"What's reasonable?"

"Used to be forty-eight hours. Since nine-eleven that's been stretched like the national debt."

"This is a nightmare." Her voice cracked. "My only blood relative is murdered and they want to put me through more hell? I don't deserve this. It's cruel."

"Just tell the truth, Del. You have nothing to hide. If I think you're straying onto dangerous turf, I'll step in."

Delray cleared her throat and crossed her arms. "Max, you know there are things I can't talk about."

"Like what?"

"Like Duke Manyon."

The mention of the name sent a tremor through him. Brady stood and walked away. He paced to the far wall and absently perused a glass-covered display. FBI's Ten Most Wanted List. Osama still #1, but with a red X stamped across his face. Brady flashed back to Ground Zero that hateful day. His wife lost forever in the rubble, his life imploded, like the towers. He was glad Bin Laden was dead. His only regret was that he hadn't been the one to put a bullet in his brain.

Beside the Most Wanted List was a tribute to the Fort Lauderdale Police Department's Fallen Heroes. Brady was surprised the list was only fourteen names long. NYPD, where he'd served, had more than seven hundred on its roster of line-of-duty deaths. No matter. They were all brothers-in-arms. He studied the faces with hushed reverence. Johnston, O'Neil, Kirby, Illyankoff, Conners, Petersen, Alexander, Bruce, Eddy, Dunlop, Mastrangelo, Brower, Peney, Diaz.

Another face kept intruding on his thoughts, though. The same face that had been imprinted on his hippocampus for three decades. His look of shock that night. His ruthless sneer. Brady strode back across the lobby.

"Who else knows?"

Delray stared up at him. A far away expression came into her eyes and red patches appeared on the white skin of her slender throat.

"Knows what, Max?"

"You know. Duke Manyon. Everything that happened. Who knew besides you and me and Ben?"

Delray swallowed and took a deep breath. "Peanut?"

Of course. Brady saw the freckled face and curly red hair of his boyhood friend. "Who else? Did you tell your parents?"

Her face flushed and she raised a hand to her temple. "No, no, of course not."

"You're lying. You told them."

Before she could answer the elevator door opened and Ron Register stepped into the lobby, impeccably attired, as usual, in a khaki wool blend suit which, like Delray's ensemble, looked hand-tailored. Brady wondered how a cop could afford his wardrobe.

"Sorry, Brady, Mrs. Cross," he said with false contrition. "Super Bowl Week. Too many meetings, too little time. Please follow me."

They rode the elevator in uncomfortable silence. When the doors opened on the second floor Register turned right. Brady and Delray followed him down a long terrazzo hallway with glass walls on either side, past tall blue doors marked Auto Theft, Burglary, and Narcotics. Homicide was at the far end of the corridor.

With the gravity of a pallbearer, Register led them through an expansive office. The walls were lined with black and beige metal file cabinets. The center of the room was occupied by the kind of cubicles typical in any workplace, strewn papers, grimy coffee cups, family photographs, crayon stick figure drawings. Several detectives, male and female, were at their desks. Brady recognized a petite woman and large black guy from Ben's house last night. They followed the captain into a small windowless room containing a gray metal table and mirrored wall that, Brady knew, had audio and video recording devices secreted on the other side. There were three chairs – one padded leather, the others hard wood. Register took the soft leather and motioned them to the seats opposite him. Delray took the chair on the right. Her body language was pensive.

"You know," Register said, "that piece of furniture is made from bitterroot. The same wood Ol' Sparky is made from."

"Ol' Sparky?" she said with a confused expression.

"Florida's electric chair. Of course, we dispatch our murderers by lethal injection nowadays. They say it's much more humane. Personally, I'm a traditionalist. I believe in an eye-for-an-eye. Cold-blooded killers deserve to die as barbarically as their victims."

Register was as subtle as a sumo wrestler in a tea room. Brady and Delray exchanged glances. Her eyes were wide and frightened. The policeman made a show of unstrapping his festive-looking red-white-and-blue nylon watchband and placing it in his pocket. Brady recognized the move. Another trick of the trade. Telling Delray the interrogation would be long. And unpleasant.

Register sat for a moment, mute, staring straight at Delray, his eyes stony and dispassionate, his tongue massaging something. Brady guessed a Tums. Under the glare of his gaze, Delray began fussing with her black leather Gucci bag. Register reached across the desk and snatched it from her.

"You won't be needing that, Mrs. Cross," he said and deposited it under the table.

Brady decided it was time to speak up. "Delray wants to help you find her brother's killer, captain. You have to appreciate, though, that she's suffered a terrible trauma. Ben was her last living relative. She'd like to get this over so she can deal with her grief."

Register's eyes remained locked on Delray. With her purse gone and nothing to occupy her hands, her fingers were twisting in her lap like restless octopus tentacles. The policeman spoke in a low, flat tone devoid of congeniality.

"I'll be blunt, Mrs. Cross. I believe *you* murdered your brother."

Her face pinkened and then reddened and she gulped in air before finding her voice. When she spoke it was with a defiant edge.

"Please stop saying that. You are wrong. I did not kill Benjamin."

Register held up a hand like a cop stopping traffic. "I'm not interested in denials." He paused and smiled with bland frigidity, his eyes flicking back and forth between Delray and Brady. The little room percolated with a charged silence. It was broken by Register. "I have no doubt you did it. The best thing for you is to get it off your chest. I'd like to understand why..."

Brady cut him off. "That's outrageous. Mrs. Cross is a world renowned economist..."

"Spare me the curriculum vitae."

"Look, Register, I know what you're doing. I used to pull the same shit. Even so, you have no grounds to accuse Delray of murder. It's preposterous."

The detective's eyes locked on her.

"Mrs. Cross, why did you lie to me last night?"

"Lie?" The red rash returned on her throat. "What lie?"

"How many did you tell?"

"I didn't tell any."

"No? You sure left out a lot of truth."

"What do you mean?"

"My goodness, I hardly know where to begin." *This does not sound promising*, Brady thought and braced himself. "Let's start with your brother's frantic message. The one you say made you fear he might be suicidal. He left it on your hotel voicemail at The Hibernian in Dublin. Nice place?"

"Yes," she said, wary.

"I can only imagine. Five stars. First class. You stayed in room four-thirteen. Luxury suite. Three hundred euros per night. Paid for, I'm guessing, by the Society of International Economists? Did I tell you my grandmother was born in Dublin? Love to visit there some day. Doubt I could afford The Hibernian, though."

"Really?" Brady said. "You'd never know by your wardrobe."

Register smiled. "Counselor, I'm Homicide chief of the second largest police department in Florida. I take pride in my position and dress accordingly."

"Sounds like you've had to explain the apparel thing before."

"Let's keep it professional, Max."

"Show me the way. Ron."

They stared at each other for a moment, two roosters with their feathers up. Register turned back to Delray. Her eyes had grown distant, fixed on the wall beyond the detective, the manicured pink fingernails of her right hand clawing absently at the palm of her left.

"One of my men, Perry James, contacted The Hibernian. The Irish are so cordial. So eager to assist. Especially Americans. Don't you find them a lovely people?"

"Wonderful," Delray said. "I'm Irish on my mother's side."

"My family's Irish, too," said Brady. "Maybe when we're finished here we can slip on down to the Blue Martini and sip a Guinness. Don't keep us in suspense, captain."

Register's crows-feet deepened into a lattice of pleats and a glint of malice flared in his eyes.

"At the request of Detective James, the manager examined your records. A Mr. Fintan O'Rourke. Irish, I'm guessing." Smug smile. "Mr. O'Rourke says you did indeed receive a telephone message from your brother's number in Fort Lauderdale."

"You mean Delray told the truth?"

"To a point, Brady, to a point." Register's stare was now approximately as warm as a polar icecap. "Every good lie contains a molecule of truth. You said your brother was making irrational statements about *'that night.'* Something that happened *'that night.'* But you didn't tell me the rest."

Here it comes, Brady thought.

"The rest?" said Delray.

"Fortunately, the voicemail from your room had not been deleted. Mr. O'Rourke was able to retrieve it and was gracious enough to share it with us. Would you like to hear it?"

Register reached inside his jacket and removed a miniature tape recorder and layed it on the desk. Delray stared at it for several seconds then turned her head away.

"No, please, I'd rather not."

"Maybe you should. I think it will refresh your recollection."

He poked the play button. A series of clicks and white noise came out, then a man's voice.

"Sis, you've got to come home. Please, I need you. Get here as fast as you can." They hadn't spoken since childhood, but Brady was surprised to recognize the nuances and inflections of Ben Chance's voice. He sounded agitated and his breathing was labored, like he'd run up several flights of stairs. *"He's back. He didn't die that night.*

117

*He's back. He's going to kill me, Delray. I know it. He's going to fin-
ish the job. I'm scared. Come home, please. Duke Manyon is back!
DUKE MANYON IS BACK!"*

By the end of the message Ben was whimpering like a kicked
dog. Brady couldn't believe his ears. The police had Manyon's
name. He looked at Delray. She was weeping. He reached into his
pocket, pulled out a handkerchief, and handed it to her. She dabbed
the corners of her eyes. Register clicked off the recorder and rocked
back in the leather chair, his face inscrutable.

"Hard to believe that slipped your mind."

"I was too upset last night to remember every detail."

The detective looked back and forth between them. Delray sniffled into the hanky. Brady plucked a piece of lint from his pants leg.
Register cleared his throat.

"I get the sense the name is familiar to both of you." No reaction. "We have record of a man named Manyon who once lived
in Lauderdale." Neither looked at him. "Wayne Peter Manyon, aka
Duke Manyon, beach boy type, lived on a boat at Bahia Mar, had
a water ski school, ran the Polynesian Room parking concession,
suspect in a major jewel theft, vanished into thin air, left everything
behind, including his sixty-foot schooner, hasn't been seen or heard
from since. What do you think of that?"

"I think *you're* the guilty one here, Register."

"Of what?"

"A run-on sentence."

He didn't react. "Here's the interesting part."

"You mean it gets better?"

"Much. Manyon disappeared twenty nine years ago. Exactly the
same time you two last saw each other. The same time, Mrs. Cross,
your parents split up and you moved away with your mother."

Brady and Delray stared at him with blank eyes.

"Did you know Mr. Manyon?"

Delray reached up and stroked her hair. Her eyes strayed briefly
to Brady, then back to Register. "Not that I recall."

"Your brother knew him. That's crystal clear. Why did he think
Manyon was dead?"

She blinked several times. Brady had read somewhere that women blink twice as often as men. "How would I know?" she said.

"I'm told Manyon was quite the ladies' man. Maybe he knew your mother. Maybe your father found out. Maybe that was the reason they separated. Maybe that's the reason Duke Manyon vanished?"

Delray's face flushed and took on an indignant cast. "How dare you imply my mother was some kind of floozy," she said, taking the offensive. "How dare you imply my father was a murderer."

"Why did your parents divorce?"

Her features froze and her blue eyes vacillated behind her long, lush lashes.

"I was too young to understand what happened between them," she said, sounding defensive now. "Besides, a lot gets forgotten in three decades. Especially things you remember to forget."

"Why was your brother upset that Duke Manyon was back? To the point you were afraid he might kill himself?"

She shook her head. "I don't know."

Brady had a sudden thought and jumped in. "Don't erase that recording."

"Why not?"

"You're making our case. Charge Mrs. Cross and I'll use it to take you apart."

The detective stared at him with hard eyes. "How are you going to do that?"

"Really? You don't get it, Register? Ben told you his killer's name. You've got it right there on tape. This Duke Manyon character, whoever he is. *'He's going to kill me!'* He said it the day before his murder. He sounded scared to death of the guy. Any jury worth a hill of beans is gonna wonder what the hell you're smoking. Why are you wasting your time trying to pin Ben's murder on Delray? Why aren't you out looking for this Manyon?"

Brady finally had the upper hand. Register had hamstrung himself. Manyon was the killer. It didn't matter that he'd been dead almost thirty years. If Delray *was* indicted, Brady would dangle the specter of the missing mystery man in front of the jury. Ben's phone message would create about a ton of reasonable doubt.

Register didn't seem moved. He listened, implacable, like he was the most cunning detective in the western world. *Like he's Sherlock fucking Holmes!* thought Brady.

"You might be right, if that was all we had," Register said with a smile. One of those supercilious smiles that said: *But there's more.* "But there's more."

"Isn't there always?" Brady muttered and steeled himself for a haymaker.

"Your brother's Last Will and Testament." Brady glanced at Delray. She didn't look back. Very unpromising. "Last night I asked Pixie Davenport, another one of my detectives, to check probate. Pixie's amazing. I don't know how she does it. She was back to me this morning. Mr. Chance is, was, a very wealthy man. No surprise. Chance Electric is the largest electrical contractor in town. Just look at that swanky house. And that yacht. And that artwork. I noticed you notice it last night, Brady. Am I wrong or is that Picasso an original?"

"So?"

"Probate lists Benjamin Chance's net worth at about forty million dollars. That's probably conservative."

"So?" Brady said again, bracing for what he knew was coming next.

Register looked at Delray. "Do you know who the sole beneficiary is to your brother's estate? Be careful how you answer."

"I have no idea."

"Wrong answer."

This wasn't going well. Brady contemplated pulling the plug and getting Delray out of there. "What's the right answer?" he said.

"Your girlfriend, er, client. She gets everything."

"I didn't know," Delray said.

"Pixie spoke with your brother's attorney this morning. Timothy Duncan, a well-respected member of the local bar. Mr. Duncan said he sent a copy of the Will to you two years ago by certified post. Says he's got a receipt with your signature on it."

Brady decided it was time to tap dance. "Pretty flimsy, Register. Delray could have forgotten. She could have signed and thrown the letter in a drawer. There's no proof she read the papers."

The detective's eyes narrowed and he regarded Brady with professional distrust. "Come on, counselor. Who are you trying to fool? Juries aren't stupid. Forty million bucks buys a lot of motive. The fact that she lied to me about it only reinforces that impression."

This was going no place good. Brady blamed himself. Register was determined to pin Ben's murder on Delray. He shouldn't have exposed her to an interrogation. The policeman didn't let up.

"I'm afraid this is going to come to a bad end for you, Mrs. Cross."

"Sorry, Ron, but your premise doesn't hold water. Delray had no motive to kill her brother for money. She's already wealthy. She came here to help him."

Register's eyes were still on her. "Is that true Mrs. Cross? Is that what you told your beloved brother last night? That you'd come to help him? Was that before or after you drugged him and tied a copper noose around his throat?"

Brady jumped from his seat. "Don't say another word," he said to Delray. He looked down at Register. "I'm not going to let my client help you frame her. Let me know when you want to get serious about solving Ben's murder. Come on, Del." She stood and he took her by the hand. "We're outa here."

Et Tu Brady

Chapter Eighteen

BRADY SPIRITED DELRAY out of the police station before Register could clap her in irons, either as a material witness or for first degree murder. She was fair game either way. The interrogation had been a disaster. Ben naming his sister as his sole heir was bad enough. Her denying that she knew only made it worse. The one consolation had been Ben's hysterical rant about Duke Manyon. The upside was that Register would be forced to sniff around about Manyon. Unfortunately, that was also the downside.

The Jeep screeched out of the parking lot and Brady didn't breathe easy until he'd steered east onto Broward Boulevard. The road was the economic equator of the town. Dividing line between the haves and have nots. Rich and poor. Super-rich and wretchedly poor. He crossed railroad tracks that ran through downtown and turned right at Brickell – in the direction of the haves – then took a left on Las Olas Boulevard.

Las Olas was Fort Lauderdale's version of Rodeo Drive. Chic boutiques, art galleries, upscale restaurants. The street was packed with Super Bowl visitors and the town had put on its best face. Flowers everywhere. Game banners ruffling from lightposts. Every palm tree swathed in colorful lights. The embellishments could not hide the harsh reality, though. Tourists strolling down the sidewalks were checking their reflections in the whitewashed windows of too many vacant storefronts.

Brady continued through the commercial district to Las Olas Isles and turned left at Siesta Lane. He drove past one waterfront mansion after another to the end of the cul-de-sac and parked in the driveway of Victor Gruber's home.

Victor and his manservant, Charles, were out. Training for the marathon, he guessed. Probably at Lauderdale Beach doing a wheel-chair version of Brady's own *bikini run*, the jaunt up and down the beach he took every morning, today being an exception. It was based on the unscientific, but absolutely valid, theorem that the string of pretty girls lining the beach in scant bathing suits was motivation enough to complete the six mile peregrination. The farther you ran the more pretty girls you'd see. Victor, he knew, liked pretty girls.

They circled around to the back of the house. Brady unlashed the Sea Ray, cranked up its two hundred sixty horsepower Mercury inboard engine, and chugged down the canal to the Intracoastal. Fifteen minutes later they reached the mouth of New River and headed inland. It was a trail they'd taken many times as kids. Before long they reached Ben Chance's house. Brady coasted up behind the white Hatteras yacht. The name on the back said *Kill-O-Watt.* Appropriate for an electrical contractor. Eerie considering how he died.

He helped Delray onto the dock. She walked straight to the swimming pool. It was rectangular with a large *BC* set in black tile at the bottom of the deep end. Four ceramic pots containing lush red, green and yellow Exotica crotons sat at each corner. She tipped the planter at the shallow end nearest the house, reached under it and pulled out a silver key.

"Some things never change," she said.

The key fit the lock to a stained glass door at the back of the house. They entered a kitchen big enough to prepare a banquet for both Super Bowl teams. Brady made his way through the dining room, a sitting room, and into the living room and peeked out the front window. Yellow crime scene tape was still strung across the black spiked wrought iron gate at the driveway. A police squad car was parked in the street. A uniformed cop sat in the driver's seat facing away from the house. He looked like he might be sleeping. Brady tested the front door. It was locked.

The house had been sealed. Technically, they were trespassing. Technically, though, it was Delray's house now. Ron Register said so himself. Even so, if they were caught they'd be arrested. Brady was trying to keep her out of jail. She met him at the bottom of the staircase and they made their way to the second floor.

The walls and ceiling of Ben's study were shimmering with yellow light reflecting off the river. Brady checked the desk drawers. Empty. Register's people had cleaned them out. A tall dark wood file cabinet with brass handles stood in a recessed alcove in the right corner of the room. Its drawers were vacant too. They moved to the bookshelves lining the wall behind the desk. Unlike Victor Gruber's eclectic collection, these volumes fit two categories. Popular fiction. John Grisham, Dan Brown, Carl Hiaasen. Most looked like they'd never been read. Then there was a shelf lined with books on treasure salvaging. They were well-thumbed.

They found it on the top ledge to the far right side, hidden behind the complete works of Clive Cussler. That seemed apropos, considering Cussler was a serious treasure trover. It was a manila file two inches thick. The police had missed it. Brady pulled it down and layed it on Ben's big mahogany desk. He took a seat in the green leather chair while Delray perched herself on the arm and rested a hand on his shoulder.

Inside they found a sheaf of paper bound by one of those black metal clips shaped like an isosceles triangle with handles that fold up and down. Brady flipped them up and squeezed, releasing the pages. The first few were blow-up photographs of old Spanish coins. Doubloons. Escudos. Pieces-of-eight. There were pictures of cannons, cap-and-ball pistols, sketches of galleons and corsairs, and nautical maps of the Caribbean. One was adorned by a maze of lines marking the routes traveled by Seventeenth Century Spanish treasure fleets. Another purported to show the path Captain Ned Pike and his ship *The Nemesis* took on its ill-fated final voyage. It ended at a hand-scrawled red X just off the coast of Fort Lauderdale.

"Your brother was certainly doing his homework," Brady said over his shoulder. "The question is whether it cost him his life."

"Max, do you think Benjamin was murdered because of the gold?"

"Ben was searching for the treasure. He was also freaked out about Duke Manyon being back. We don't know why he believed that. But Duke knew about the gold. And he'd been willing to kill for it once."

"But Duke's dead."

"You know that. I know that. Ben knew it, too. Something changed his mind."

"What?"

Brady shook his head. He didn't have an answer. The file contained a copy of Florida statutes on treasure salvaging. There were articles on Mel Fisher, the salvor who discovered hundreds of millions of dollars' worth of Spanish gold on the wreck of the *Nuestra Senora de Atocha* in the waters off the Marquesas. He held up an envelope stamped *El Archivo General de Indias, Sevilla, España.* It contained a typed letter from a *Sr. Juan Bautista Muñoz – Archivista Histórico* addressed to *Sr. Benjamin Chance.*

The letter dealt with the *Flota de Indias,* the annual flotilla of treasure ships from the New World to Spain during the Sixteenth and Seventeenth Centuries. The convoys had been the quarry of every brigand in the Caribbean. Ben had written to Senor Muñoz seeking information about the fate of the galleon *Urca de Salamanca.* Muñoz responded that the ship departed *Havanna* with the gold fleet on August 8, 1674. Two days out a devastating storm struck, almost certainly a Category Three or Four on today's Saffir-Simpson Hurricane Scale, meaning winds of one hundred ten-to-one hundred fifty miles per hour. Of the more than one hundred vessels that sailed from Cuba, twenty seven went down and the surviving ships were scattered from the Bahamian archipelago to present-day Dominican Republic.

"The Urca de Salamanca," wrote Senor Muñoz, *"was commanded by Capitan-General Miguel Antonio de Mijares y Escheverez. The galleon was severely damaged by the storm. Our*

126

records indicate its rudder was fractured and its mainmast snapped in half. On August 18th, ten days after departing Havanna, the Urca de Salamanca was languishing alone off the coast of Las Floridas when it was attacked by the pirate vessel The Nemesis captained by the notorious sea rover Ned Pike."

"Ben seemed convinced he was on the verge of solving the mystery of Ned Pike's gold," Brady said.

Delray squeezed his shoulder. "Could it be, Max? Could the treasure have ended up on Three Mile Reef?"

"Those gold coins we found got there somehow."

"During this period Captain Pike was particularly nettlesome to the Kingdom of Spain," Senor Muñoz wrote. *"He attacked, looted, and sank the Nuestra Senora Isabella and El Nombre de Dios which, like the Urca de Salamanca, were separated from the gold fleet during the storm. According to our records, the holds of the three ships were gorged with an estimated 51 tons of silver bullion, 4,250 gold bars and discs, 500,000 gold pistoles, 734 copper ingots, 90 brass cannon, 1,000 pounds of worked silverware, in addition to 450 chests of indigo and 1,600 bales of tobacco. Most of that ended up in the belly of The Nemesis. As you are aware, two days after attacking the Salamanca, The Nemesis sank during a powerful tempest as it was being assailed by the Spanish man-of-war Barborosa and two galleons.*

"Accounts from Capitan Ernesto Rosario Zapatero of the Barborosa indicate his encounter with Ned Pike occurred somewhere between latitude and longitude 25° 47'25" N / 80° 17'14" W and longitude 26° 21'29" N / 80° 5'0" W, or approximately between your present day Miami Beach north to Boca Raton, Florida. Capitan Zapatero reported his guns struck what he believed to be a mortal blow to The Nemesis. However, the capitan lost visual contact with the enemy at the apex of the squall. Due to the ferment and Capitan Zapatero's efforts to save his own vessel, I regret to inform you El Archivo General de Indias has never pinpointed the precise location of the marauder's final resting place.

"As to your query about the cargo stolen from the Urca de Salamanca, Nuestra Senora Isabella, and El Nombre de Dios, our

experts estimate the present day value at more than two billion dollars US."

"My God, Max."

"Mind-boggling."

Brady became aware for the first time of the heat from her hand on his shoulder.

A color photograph of a gold *pistole* was attached to the letter. It had a cross on its face identical to the coins Max, Ben and Peanut found so many years ago. The right margin contained a lengthy note scrawled in what Brady presumed was Senor Muñoz's hand.

"I forwarded the specimen you sent to the archive's forensic numismatist, Dr. Pablo Vargas. He analyzed the coin, which I have here returned to you, and apprised me of the following:

- *Weight: 6.8 grams.*
- *Diameter: 20.32 millimeters (.80 inches).*
- *Denomination: one pistole (equivalent to two escudos or one-fourth doubloon).*
- *Mint Date: '1-6-7' above the cross appears to be 1673.*
- *Source: 'NR' is reference to Nuevo Reino de Granada, the Spanish colonial region that included Bogotá, where the mint was located.*
- *Assayer: 'A' is the mark of a man named Anuncibay."*

Brady flipped over the photograph. There was more.

"We at the General Archive of the Indies are quite interested in discussing this coin with you further. In particular, identifying the location where this historic currency was retrieved. Dr. Vargas will soon be in the United States to attend a conference in Washington, D.C. He informs me he would most happily fly to Florida to speak with you in person. If you can generously afford him your valuable time, please apprise us so a meeting can be arranged.

With the very warmest regards,

Sr. Juan Bautista Muñoz – Archivista Históric"

The letter was dated February third. Two weeks before Ben's murder.

Brady felt Delray's hand squeeze his shoulder. "Could my brother have been murdered by a forensic numismatist?"

"I doubt a European coin expert would kill Ben and tattoo my name on his forehead."

A stylish modern yellow Sunseeker yacht was gliding through the inky waters of New River heading east toward the Intracoastal. Its bridge passed at eye-level to the study windows. Brady and Delray were so engrossed in the gold file they didn't notice the boat – or the front door – until a female voice crackled over a radio and they realized they had company.

"Unit five-seven-four, please respond."

Brady bolted from the chair to the study door. A uniformed police officer was ascending the spiral staircase.

"This is Five-seven-four. What's up, Wanda?"

"Please report your location, Collins."

"Babysitting a crime scene. Six-two-four Rio Vista. Posh digs. Come on over. I'll give you a guided tour."

"Hold your breath until I get there, Collins. Before you do that, though, call Captain Register via land line. Stat."

The cop was almost at the top of the staircase. The only escapes were the windows, the stairs, or the elevator. The windows were a sheer two story drop to what looked like very hard patio deck. The stairs and elevator weren't options either.

"What does Register want?" Officer Collins said.

"He didn't share that with me. If you want to make detective someday, though, I suggest you call him ASAP. He sounds antsy."

"Tell him to hold his water. I'll call from upstairs."

Brady tiptoed to the desk and scooped up Ben Chance's treasure file. Delray pointed to a door in the left corner of the room. A small bathroom. They slipped inside and pulled the door behind them. Seconds later they heard a voice.

"Patrolman Collins calling for Captain Register." Thirty seconds of silence. "Captain? Collins here. You needed to talk to me?"

For the next minute the only sound was Collins grunting "yes, sir" and "no, sir" and "okay, sir." Then they heard the clack of the telephone being returned to its cradle on Ben's desk. A chair scraped against hardwood and footsteps came straight toward them. Just as the door opened they ducked into a narrow shower stall. The curtain was black and they pulled it closed and squeezed into the corner. Brady wrapped his arms around Delray. She pressed her face to his chest and they held their breath.

Et Tu Brady

Chapter Nineteen

SINCE HER APPOINTMENT to the Fort Lauderdale City Commission, Rose Becker had become as efficient with her time as a short order cook. After leaving Brady on the rooftop that morning, she opened the Papillon Gym and led a seven o'clock Pilates class. Afterwards she left the gym in the hands of Jenny Jarvis, one of her fitness instructors, shucked her Reeboks, spandex shorts and Madame Butterfly T-shirt and jumped under a shower. She brushed her teeth, gathered her long black hair at the back of her head and restrained it with a red clasp, then threw on a smart black pantsuit with cream pinstripes. By nine she was at City Hall for another in an endless succession of ever-more gloomy budget meetings.

The mood change in Fort Lauderdale was stark. Rose felt as if she'd stepped into a Dorothea Lange photograph from the Great Depression. The world that had always felt shiny and golden to her now seemed dismal and bleak. She almost felt guilty to be so happy.

The bean counters delivered the grim numbers. The economy had turned to Kryptonite. A town conspicuous for its glitzy hotels, fabulous yachts, and waterfront mansions was as broke as a sailor after Fleet Week. Collapsing home prices. Plummeting tourism. Skyrocketing unemployment. Bankruptcies at a twenty-year high.

Foreclosure signs sprouting like crabgrass. Banks that only loaned money to people who didn't need it. The tropical paradise had the feel of a Rust Belt factory town.

Rose and her fellow commissioners had been torturing their brains trying to make ends meet, but somebody kept moving the ends. The City Budget Manager, an officious little man with round glasses and the complexion of buttermilk, spent a mind-numbing hour expounding on shortfalls, millage rates, lagging indicators, credit ratings, declining revenues, restricted revenues, revenue transfers, and loan defaults.

"I'm glad you don't work for the suicide hotline," Rose said when he finished.

"That *was* depressing," agreed Mayor Liz Donnelly. "And confusing."

"Well, commissioners," explained the budget man, "confusing problems demand confusing explanations."

Commissioners shot confused looks at each other. One drooled slightly. The bottom line, though, was unmistakable. They needed to pinch the city's pennies until they cried uncle.

When Rose finally exited the dreary deliberations, Seymour Tate was waiting for her. He opened the conference room door and she gave him a grateful nod.

"And they said chivalry was dead."

"Chivalry is one crime I will never be convicted of," he said. "Are you wondering yet why you got into politics?"

"You must be clairvoyant, Seymour."

"I read the opinion polls."

Rose sighed: "And?"

"Voters want to tar-and-feather the lot of you."

"So my political career will come and go faster than cold fusion?"

"I wouldn't worry. We're screwed anyway. The honey bees are dying."

She wrinkled her nose. Seymour's toilet water smelled like *Eau de Ashtray*. Tate was City Hall reporter for *The Lauderdale News*. He reminded Rose of Poppin' Fresh, the Pillsbury Doughboy. Mid-thirties, roly-poly, shaggy white-blond hair. His shirt was a wrinkled

Tommy Bahama knock-off tucked haphazardly into blue jeans. A pen was wedged behind his ear and a thin reporter's notebook jutted from his shirt pocket.

"We need to talk," he said.

Rose studied him. Seymour had subversive gray eyes. *Anarchist's eyes,* she thought. They peered out from under white, almost invisible brows. Inside City Hall few were feared or loathed more than Tate. He rooted out scandal like a truffle pig foraging for fungi. Even Liz Donnelly was scared of him and, as far as Rose knew, the mayor was honest.

"Talk about…?"

"Listen, Rose…May I call you Rose?"

"Depends." She inserted the key into her office door. "Are you here to expose me?"

"Hmmm!"

Rose turned in time to catch his eyes strolling over her back side. His butterball face was painted with a salacious smile.

"Call me Commissioner Becker?"

"You should know something about me, Rose. I inherently distrust authority."

"That's pretty jaded, Seymour."

"*Power corrupts* is more than an adage with me. It's the rule. But I sense something different about you."

Rose threw her briefcase on a small couch against the wall and fixed him with a dubious glare.

"Who was it who said: *'When someone criticizes me I can defend myself, but against praise I am defenseless.'*"

"Dr. Freud, I presume?"

"Not bad, Seymour. For a reporter."

"Ten years in therapy will do that. But Lincoln said it best."

"Give it to me."

"*'Everyone loves a compliment.'* Seriously, though, you appear to be one of those rare public servants – honest, sincere, naïve."

"*'Ask not what your country can do for you…'*"

"Perfect example of a dishonest politician."

"JFK?"

"The bastard stole that line."

"That's blasphemy."

" *'Are you a politician asking what your country can do for you, or a zealous one asking what you can do for your country?'* Khalil Gibran. *The New Frontier*, 1920-something. Look it up."

"Wow, Seymour! I'm impressed." Rose reached back and released the red clasp holding her hair and a forest of black curls spilled over her shoulders. "Didn't Gibran also ask: *'Are you a newspaperman who sells his principle in the slave market like a buzzard which descends only upon a decaying carcass?'* "

"Wow backatcha, Commissioner Becker."

"Call me Rose."

She picked up a bottle of disinfectant, spritzed the top of her desk, and wiped it with a paper towel. Tate flopped into a black vinyl guest chair and watched with distaste.

"Neat freak?"

"For your information, desk tops have four hundred times more bacteria than toilet seats."

"You haven't been in many men's rooms, have you?"

"What's up, Seymour?"

"So, you are aware that Fort Lauderdale's three major industries are tourists, yachts, and flimflams."

"You stole that off our public relations brochure, didn't you?"

"More shell games are being played in the office buildings and strip malls of this town than Three Card Monty games in Manhattan. Ponzi schemes, pill mills, Medicare scams, money laundering, insurance fraud. You name it. With the possible exception of Wall Street, we are hands down the white collar crime capital of America."

"Next thing you know we'll be inventing the wheel. But it's great to be number one. Now tell me something I don't know."

He shrugged and continued. "It's all in my story."

"What story is that?"

"You know I'm an award winning reporter."

"Congratulations."

He held up his palms in false modesty.

"No need. We journalists love to give ourselves awards. Maybe to compensate for the long hours, shitty pay, and public disdain. But I've exposed a lot of wrong-doing in my time. I'm not proud of many things, but I'm proud of that."

Rose glanced at her wristwatch.

"Where are we going here, Seymour? I've got a city to save." As soon as she said it she made a mental note not to use the line again, at least today.

"Okay. So sometimes to amuse myself I go over to the court-house and read lawsuits."

"Whatever curls your toes, big fella."

"You'd be amazed at all the dirt hidden between the flaps of those innocuous buff-colored files. The most intimate secrets of the high and mighty. Business betrayals. Drug addictions. Adulterous affairs. Sexual peccadilloes. It's like my own private gold mine."

"Sounds more like a cesspool."

"Digging up shit *is* my business."

"Everybody's gotta pay the bills."

"So a few of weeks ago, just for fun, I started pulling files on litigations against the city. Went back five years and damn if I didn't find thousands of lawsuits. Everything from breach of contracts to zoning appeals to property tax disputes."

"I'm about to fall off the edge of my seat."

Tate ignored her sarcasm and forged onward.

"My editor's a first-class prick. No flair. No imagination. Always trying to keep me on a tight leash. But I was intrigued. I started stealing an hour here, an hour there, lunch breaks, even days off."

"I know there's a point to this, Seymour."

"I began to notice something. A pattern."

"You don't say."

"P.I. cases."

"Like in private eye?"

"Like in personal injury."

"Like in bad doctors?"

"Like in slip-and-falls. People tripping over cracked sidewalks and breaking their arm. Hitting potholes and slipping their disks.

Car wrecks caused by bad signage. Nothing big. But gobs and gobs of lawsuits."

"So what's the problem? On any given day a couple million people pass through our town. A lot of them are lawyers. Lawyers file lawsuits."

"True, but the sheer volume caught my attention. I did a spread sheet and started collating the data on hundreds of cases."

"Okay. Give me the bottom line."

"The city's paying out millions of dollars a year. Many millions."

"So? If that's what juries are awarding."

He shrugged. "That's the point. There are no juries."

"Say that again."

"No juries. No trials. Not one trail. Not one award. Everything's being done behind closed doors. Settled out of court."

"What kind of money are we talking about?"

"Under the radar. No more than twenty-five to thirty-five grand per case. So low nobody notices. Last year alone they added up to almost eighteen million dollars."

"Really?" *Really* was the word Seymour had been waiting to hear. It meant he'd hooked her. "How long has this been going on?"

"Five years, at the least. That's as far back as I looked. And here's the best part. Ninety percent of the cases were handled by one attorney."

Rose sat up for a moment and digested what she was hearing. "Did you talk to Walter Dean? What's he say about this?"

Tate laughed. "Pitched a hissy fit. *'I'm the City Attorney.'* Screaming at me. *'I'm saving taxpayer's money. Going to trial costs more than settling. Blah, blah, blah.'* His face four shades of red. Accusing me of questioning his integrity. Bastard kicked me out of his office."

"Well, God knows, we need to save money. What is it you want from me, Seymour?"

"The story was supposed to be in today's paper. To coin a phrase, though, my editor is a pussy. Pardon my French."

"*Pussy* isn't a French word. That would be *minet*. Don't worry, though. I'm a big girl. Why are they spiking your story? I thought you were a big shot award-winning reporter."

"Every newsroom has a food chain. In mine, my editor is the whale and I'm plankton. Perhaps you've heard, newspapers are bleeding red faster than a hemophiliac. Journalism these days is about truth, justice, and price-to-earnings ratios. When I called the attorney filing these suits he told me to screw off. Hung up on me and called my publisher screaming bloody murder. Threatening to sue his ass off if he printed a word of my scurrilous story. Last thing the suits upstairs want is some big shot lawyer who's friendly with every judge in the courthouse claiming he's going to own the paper. That's where you come in."

"Me? What can I do?"

Tate threw a blue file folder on the desk. "Read it. See what you think. If you decide to bring it up at the Commission meeting this afternoon, you have my permission. Unlike me, you are immune from being sued. Walter Dean's got some serious 'splainin' to do. Put him on the hot seat. He's gotta answer you. That opens the door for me to get my story in print. Names and all."

"Who's this private attorney?"

"Pompous asshole. King of the ambulance chasers. Has spotters in every E.R. in town. People come in with broken bones they got tripping over their Pekinese and by the time he's done with 'em they've stumbled on a broken curb on Davie Boulevard and the city's being hit with a lawsuit. Name's Austin Ball, Jr. Everybody calls him Junior."

Et Tu Brady

Chapter Twenty

THE TITTY ROOM was packed with housewives doing their weekly shopping when Dismas Benvenuti arrived. He promptly began flapping his arms around his torso.

"Dang, Junior, it's freezin' in here. Why the hell we meetin' in this ice house?"

Austin Ball, Jr. didn't answer at first. His eyes were glued on a woman in her early thirties pushing a Costco shopping cart past the Romaine lettuce bin while a litter of kids trailed her like frisky puppies.

"There's a reason they keep the produce section so cold. Check those out."

"Those what?"

"Not those." Junior nodded at the young mother. "*T-H-O's*. Titty-hard-ons. How'd you like to wrap your lips around them baubles? Hard enough to cut glass."

Dismas shivered. He quit flapping and just hugged himself.

"That's why you call this the Titty Room?"

Junior looked at Dismas and shook his head. He reminded himself he wasn't conversing with Albert Einstein. More like Forrest Gump. That didn't matter. Dismas had made Ball a ton of money and he planned to milk him for much more in the future. Junior displayed a mouthful of teeth that would have made a Paraguayan piranha jealous.

"I can see subtlety is not lost on you, Dismas. The answer is yes. I call it the Titty Room because it makes women's nipples hard. But that's not why we're here."

"It ain't? Why are we meetin' here?"

"Privacy, not protrusions."

"Privacy?"

"Look around. See anybody who looks like FBI? FDLE? Lauderdale PD? Broward SO? Starsky and Hutch?" He nodded toward the woman. She had stopped to squeeze the tomatoes while her children huddled close to her legs, presumably seeking their mother's warmth. "Those snipers poking out of mommy's funbags ain't microphones. Nobody's gonna hear us here. Now talk to me."

"About?"

Ball rolled his eyes. "Gosh, Dismas, I don't know. Okra? Cauliflower? The price of fresh-picked cucumbers? Or maybe nitwit trailer trash with busted arms? It's up to you."

Dismas flapped his arms again and bounced on his tippy toes, trying to fend off the cold. "Oh, yeah. Sorry, Junior. Ya kinda threw me with all that titty talk. I did like you said. I took Jimmy to that broken sidewalk on Andrews and had him lay down on the ground. Then I went and called nine-one-one."

"You didn't use your cell phone?"

"Payphone at 7-Eleven."

"You didn't give them your name?"

"Said I was a good Samarian."

"Samaritan – with a t."

"Really?" Dismas squinted. "Anyways, a few minutes later a cop shows up. Then a ambulance come and took Jimmy to Broward General. They did a x-ray. Said he busted his vulva."

Ball tore his eyes off a middle-aged woman whose nipples were standing at attention over by the Brussels sprouts. "Vulva, you say? Dismas, I hate to be the one to break this to you, but men don't have vulvas."

"They don't?"

"Vulva's a vagina."

"Really?"

"You mean ulna. For forearm."

"Ulna. That's it. Ulna. Anyways, Jimmy told the cop he tripped on the bad concrete and the cop gave him this."

Dismas handed Ball a copy of the incident report.

"Perfect. Did you bring him to Dr. Johnson?"

"Just like you said. He looked at the report. Said everything's good to go."

"Excellent. I'll file the papers tomorrow."

"Jimmy wants to know when he gets his five grand."

"Tell him to hold his water. It'll be a couple of months. My guy at City Hall can't just write a check."

"I need money too, Junior. My *tayke's* all over my ass."

"What the hell's a *tayke*?"

"That's Seminole for woman. She says if this lawsuit money don't start comin' in soon she's gonna split. Unless I start collecting my tribal loot first."

Ball was eyeballing a plumpish woman wearing a T-shirt with no bra whose mammillae were poking straight out.

"See those babies? Like buds on a prickly pear. If your *tayke* leaves, now you know where to come for a new one." He dismissed Dismas with the sweep of an arm. "Gotta go. Tee time in an hour."

Et Tu Brady

Chapter Twenty-One

BRADY AND DELRAY held their breath – and their embrace – in the tiny shower stall off Ben Chance's second-floor study. Standing no more than three feet away was Patrolman Collins. They heard the sound of the toilet seat being raised, a zipper being lowered, then Niagara Falls. It seemed to go on forever.

Cops and coffee, Brady thought. This was a three cup wizz, minimum. After thirty seconds he felt Delray's body begin to shake. His first thought was that she was crying, but he quickly realized she was laughing. He pressed her face into his chest to muffle the sound. Then the cop broke wind and Brady felt himself losing it too. He buried his face in her throat and prayed Collins couldn't hear them. Fortunately the policeman's cascade was strong and steady and drowned out whatever sound was eeking from them. Finally the toilet flushed and the officer walked out, without washing his hands.

A minute later Brady heard the front door slam downstairs. He removed his arms from around Delray, but she kept her face pressed against his chest. Her fingers had a death grip on his shirt.

"We're safe, Del. Let's get out of here."

She looked up and her celestial blue eyes burned into him like hot ice. Their lips were inches apart.

"I'd forgotten how nice it feels to be close to you," she said.

Brady had no response. Ben's treasure file was pressed between them. He stepped back and it fell onto the tile shower floor. Papers and photographs scattered. He bent down to gather the material. An embossed blue business card slipped from one of the stapled sheaves.

Francis U. "Fuzzy" Furbush – Private Security. There was an address in Plantation and a telephone number with a 954 area code. He handed Delray the card.

"Ever hear of this guy?"

They stepped out of the shower and returned to the study. He opened the file on the desk again and sat back down in the green leather chair. Delray resumed her post on the armrest. She leaned forward, her mouth almost touching his ear.

"Fuzzy Furbush?" she whispered. The way she said it gave him goosebumps. "No."

Brady held the card in his fingers and flapped it in the air, like he was drying wet ink. He detected a scent and held it under his nose.

"That's not Old Spice."

He riffled through the binder and removed a thin stack of stapled pages the card had fallen from. It was mostly articles downloaded off the internet. Almost all of them about Michael Fury. He found two notations scrawled at the bottom of the last page. One was written in a dainty, almost effeminate hand. He held it up to Delray.

"Is this Ben's handwriting?"

She leaned in so close he could feel her body heat. She shook her head.

"Benjamin and I didn't see each other or speak much, but sometimes we exchanged cards on birthdays or Christmas. His penmanship was essentially illegible. He printed everything."

The first line was a neat cursive written in red ink, like the Palmer Method the nun's taught at Our Lady of Perpetual Sorrow.

"2/9 – Hallelujah! MF journal. Trinity, Dublin."

"Whoever wrote this," Brady said, "connected Michael Fury to the gold."

"From the way Benjamin spoke on the telephone he'd been looking for the Fury diary for quite a while. Maybe he hired this Fuzzy guy to find it. After he discovered its location Benjamin found out I was in Dublin and asked me to track it down."

Delray's right breast was pressing against Brady's left tricep. Her right hand slid down his back and he felt her fingertips drumming the ridge of his spine. He tried to ignore it and flipped through the pages.

"Two nine. February ninth. What day did you say Ben called you? The first time?"

"That would have been Tuesday. The tenth."

"And the last call? When he was so frantic. Talking about Duke Manyon?"

"Two days later. Thursday the twelfth. Why?"

"Look at this."

He pointed to the second entry.

"That's Ben's hand. No question," Delray said and read aloud. *"2/11 – DM!"*

"DM? As in Duke Manyon?"

Three more words were scribbled below it.

"My nightmare lives!"

Melodramatic, but to the point. On February eleventh, the day before he left the voicemail for Delray in Dublin, Ben must have received information that Manyon was alive. Did he see him? *Impossible.* Did someone tell him? Fuzzy the private investigator? *Possible.* Or had he lost his mind? *Very possible.*

Brady rose from the green chair and looked down at Delray. "I just don't get why Ben believed Manyon was back? He was there that night. He knew what happened. He saw it with his own eyes."

Delray read the note again. *"My nightmare lives!"* Tears welled in her eyes. She reached up threw her arms around Brady's neck. "Oh, God! Poor, Benjamin, Poor, poor, Benjamin. He must have been paralyzed with fear."

She buried her face in his throat and sobbed. After a moment, she turned her wet eyes up to Brady and kissed him. He didn't resist. Quite the contrary. He found himself pressing his lips against her

145

soft pink mouth. It was ten seconds before he heard a voice in his head telling him to stop. He pulled away and fell back into the chair like a prizefighter collapsing onto his corner stool. *What the hell are you doing, Brady?*

Et Tu Brady

Chapter Twenty-Two

MAX BRADY'S FIRST encounter with Duke Manyon came the day after he discovered the gold coin on Three Mile Reef. As usual, his day began at five in the morning when he felt a gentle nudge in his back. He opened his eyes to a bedroom as black as India ink. He turned his head on the pillow. A barely perceptible silhouette was standing over him.

"Them newspapers ain't gonna deliver theirselves, Maximus."

"Morning, grandpa."

"Waffles on the griddle. Need something in your stomach."

"Thanks, grandpa."

Max rubbed sleepy sand from the corners of his eyes and climbed out of bed. He pulled on a stretched-out red sweatshirt and a pair of cut-off blue jeans. When he shuffled into the kitchen a short stack of waffles bathed in *Mrs. Butterworth's* was waiting for him. He wolfed it down with half-closed eyes and a grumpy face while his grandfather sipped from a steaming mug of black coffee.

"As W.C. Fields once told me: 'Start every day with a smile – and get it over with.'"

Max contrived a lethargic smile. "Who's W.C. Fields?"

The old man scratched his thick shock of white hair. "Fella I used to take fishin' on *The Summit*."

When Max was finished with breakfast he slung a canvas saddlebag over his shoulder and was heading out the door when Grandpa Zack called after him.

"Careful out there. Still an hour till daybreak. Don't expect them cars to see ya."

The last stars were evaporating in the western sky and every surface was bathed in predawn summer dew. Max used the sleeve of his sweatshirt to dry the banana seat on his red Schwinn bicycle and peddled barefoot into the lightless July morning. He hadn't worn shoes since school ended and his soles were leathery as a firewalker's. He could traipse across hot blacktop at noon without feeling a thing.

The birds were still sleeping and there were no cars in sight. He steered down the middle of Riverland Road, gliding in and out of random bowls of streetlamp light, breathing in the scent of night-blooming jasmine that sweetened the balmy air. He reached State Road 7 and turned right into the Piggly Wiggly where two bundles of *The Miami Herald* were waiting for him. He sat alone on the supermarket sidewalk and commenced the rhythmic routine of folding newspapers. *Left-right-rubberband. Left-right-rubberband.* His paper route consisted of sixty or so waterfront homes on Lauderdale Isles, a stretch of long cul-de-sacs that dead-ended at New River. The job earned enough money to buy gasoline for his boat tank and air for his scuba tank. In the pewter light of morning's edge, Max scanned the headlines while he snapped bands around his papers.

NIXON IN FIGHT OVER TAPES
BOMB KILLS 12 IN ULSTER
CONGRESS LIMITS VIET SPENDING

Vietnam! His stomach clenched every time he thought about the war that, in his mind, had destroyed his family. He remembered his father, John, and their last day together. Just the two of them. Trolling for marlin in the Gulf Stream. His dad's tanned face smiling down at him from the helm of Grandpa Zack's boat *The Summit*. Max too young to fully comprehend he was shipping out for Southeast Asia the next day. Not even considering he might never return. They spent the entire day out there and late into the night, father and son, laughing, singing, talking, treasuring what would be their final hours together.

"Maximus, it's not going to be easy for your mother while I'm away. Promise me you'll take good care of her."

"I promise, dad."

But Max had broken his promise. He hadn't taken good care of her. At least not good enough. He hadn't saved her. Hadn't saved either of his parents. The dark images still followed him like his own shadow. His father's uniform, caked in red mud, dodging Viet Cong fire, dragging his best friend, Uncle Howard, wounded and bleeding, through the hot jungle, surrounded by smoke and screams and death, until an enemy bullet found him. Months later, standing beside his mother at the White House, her skin yellow now, her body emaciated, her eyes italicized by dark half-circles. Accepting the Congressional Medal of Honor from the President of the United States. *"Marine Corporal John Maximus Brady, Bravo Company, 1st Battalion, 26th Marines, for conspicuous gallantry and intrepidity at the risk of his own life above and beyond the call of duty."* One month later he stood over an oblong box and placed a rose on his mother's breast as she lay waxen and still. His dad and mom dead in the same year. Him by gunfire, her by cancer. Both gone before his eighth birthday.

Max shook away the memory and, while he folded his newspapers, tried to think more pleasant thoughts. Despite the tragedy in his life, he knew he'd been lucky. His grandparents had showered him with love. They'd raised him to be a good person. He'd been blessed with a fine mind and was an above average athlete. He was growing up in paradise, surrounded by good friends, especially Delray. *Delray.* He thought about her smiling face and sky-colored eyes and made a silent vow to protect her better than he had protected his parents. In his daydreams he imagined saving her life, like the heroes in his favorite movies. From burning buildings. From sinking ships. From cutthroat pirates. And every fantasy ended with him kissing her lips. He'd never kissed a girl. Never really wanted to. But he wanted to kiss Delray Chance.

First, though, he had newspapers to deliver. *Left-right-rubberband. Left-right-rubberband.* A small headline at the lower right corner of the front page caught his eye.

COPS CLOSING IN ON DIAMOND THIEVES

Fort Lauderdale police say the jewel theft this week at the opulent home of a wealthy citrus magnate is the work of professional cat burglars.

"These guys know what they're doing," Detective Howard Pickens told The Herald.

"Uncle Howard!" Max said aloud, thrilled to see his name, thinking maybe he'd like to be a policeman someday, too.

Tuesday night two armed men wearing ski masks broke into SunSplash, the oceanfront home of Jonathan Osgood Kimble III, known throughout Florida as "King Orange." At the time of the robbery Kimble, 80, and his wife, former showgirl Mandy Binghamton Kimble, 32, were vacationing in southern France. Police say the thieves beat and bound a security guard then cracked open a floor safe and made off with several hundred thousand dollars in precious stones and gold coins.

Gold coins! Max reached into the pocket of his shorts and pulled out the coin he'd found the day before. He wondered if Jonathan Osgood Kimble III's coins were anything like his. He rubbed his thumb over the cross on one side of the odd-shaped disk. A vision of the hammerhead rushed back at him. Its freakish head and monster teeth smiling as it attacked. Fending it off twice. His spear impaling its eye. Swimming for his life. Vaulting into the boat an instant before the shark struck.

Detective Pickens said the thieves dismantled a security alarm and entered the home through a second story window.

"We're closing in on them," the detective said. "I expect arrests soon."

Two hours later Max was racing down New River in his Boston Whaler thinking about Delray again. She seemed to be at the surface of his consciousness every minute of every day. He throttled back and coasted to a rickety wooden dock beside a shady grove at the end of Flamingo Lane. She was there, Ben and Peanut by her side. They were leaning over the wall of the Alligator Pit. Peanut was growling.

"Goddamn Junior Ball."

The pit was a circular concrete enclosure about the size of a back-yard swimming pool. An open air jail for six big gators. Primordial prisoners for tourists on the sightseeing boats to gawk at. The reptiles didn't put on much of a show. They mostly just slept, their saw-toothed bodies half-in-half-out of a shallow basin of slimy green water. They couldn't do much else. They were blind. What was left of their eyes was bleeding.

"Poor things," Delray said, looking down at them near tears.

"Scotty Noll told me Junior and his wanker buddies were throwing rocks at them and laughing," said Peanut.

"Fucker," grunted Ben.

The others weren't certain if he was cursing Junior for what he'd done to the gators, or to him.

"What's a wanker?" Delray said.

"Gadzooks!" Max blurted. "It's getting late. To the Batboat."

Et Tu Brady

Chapter Twenty-Three

BEFORE THE MORNING dew evaporated they were back on top of Three Mile Reef. The sky was blue from brink to brink and the ocean was placid as a pond. Max felt frisky as a spring-hatched bird. He strapped his knife to his leg and picked up his speargun.

Delray wagged a finger at him. "Max Brady, don't you dare dive into that water all by yourself."

Her pretty face was resolute, as if she really cared about him. He smiled.

"Don't worry. Did you know that falling coconuts kill more people than sharks do."

"That's comforting," she said without returning his smile, "but there aren't any coconut trees out here. There is a killer shark, though."

Despite his bravado, Max kept a constant vigil for *Left Eye*, as he'd dubbed the hammerhead he'd shot in its right eye. There was no sign of the big fish that day and Max assumed *Left Eye* was dead.

While Delray remained in the boat, the boys foraged in the cave and surrounding reef searching for more gold coins. Ben and Peanut winnowed the sandy bottom with their fingers. Max brought a perforated bait bucket from his grandfather's boat and sifted until the water grew murky as a London fog. The morning wore on and, one-by-one, their tanks ran dry. Ben, a nervous swimmer, sucked up air fast as a sprinter and surfaced after just forty-five minutes. Peanut lasted fifteen minutes longer. Max, with his remarkable respiration rate, stayed down almost two hours. Between them they found four more pieces of gold identical to the one yesterday. Max unearthed two, Peanut and Ben one each.

"This is incredible," Ben said when Max finally climbed back into the boat. "We've found a sunken treasure."

"We're gonna be rich," said Peanut.

They jumped up and down, clapping and cheering and slapping each other's hands until Max found himself embracing Delray, not sure which of them initiated the contact. His face flushed and he released her. He stepped back, tripped over a scuba tank, and fell butt-first onto the bow seat. Ben and Peanut erupted in laughter. Delray put a hand to her mouth and tried without success to smother a giggle. Max had never been so mortified. He rolled over the side of the boat and tumbled into the water without tank, mask, or fins and shot down forty feet to the reef. Two minutes later he surfaced clutching a pair of wriggling red lobsters, one in each hand.

"Wow, they're huge," Ben said.

"Dinner for Zack and Kate tonight."

Triumphant, he dropped the crustaceans into the boat, his embarrassment forgotten. They stowed them in the bait well on the bow, filled it with water, and headed toward Port Everglades Inlet. When they reached the Intracoastal Waterway, Max stopped the boat and had Peanut take the wheel. He threw a long yellow nylon rope off the back, picked up his *Dick Pope* slalom ski, and dove into the water. Peanut and Ben looked at each other and shook their heads. Max was in hot-dog mode, and they knew it was not for their benefit.

He skimmed on the narrow slat through the port and under the 17th Street Causeway Bridge. The bridgetender recognized the boat and came out of his shack shaking his fist at them. Max waved to him. Delray laughed. They continued past Pier 66 Hotel, Lauderdale Yacht Club, Bahia Mar Marina, and beneath the Las Olas Boulevard Bridge, Max streaking back and forth, hurdling the wake, slapping the water with his ski, Delray applauding gleefully with every loud smack.

Just past the Las Olas Bridge he spotted a yellow Donzi speedboat with a big black Mercury engine idling near the east sea wall. A man and woman were floating in the water wearing skis and holding ropes, waiting to be pulled up. Two men were in the Donzi. The sign on its side said *Duke Manyon Ski School*. Max had a sudden impulse. He leaned left and swung out almost parallel to the Whaler then cut hard right and flew across the wake just as the Donzi started to take off.

"Yeeehawww," he screeched and unleashed a rooster tail onto the skiers, then drenched the boat with another plume.

He looked at Delray, euphoric, expecting to see her applaud his prank. Instead, her mouth was open and her eyes wide. She pointed at something behind him. He turned and thought: *Oops!* The Donzi had planed and was rushing straight at him. The driver was standing behind the wheel. Black-haired, muscular, tattoos covering his arms and chest. Everything about him screamed danger. He yelled something indecipherable and hurled a beer can. Max ducked and the can sailed inches from his head.

They were moving at thirty five miles an hour. Max pumped his thumb in the air, signaling Peanut to go faster, but the Whaler was no match for the Donzi. The yellow speedboat pushed up close behind him. He cut left to dodge it. The boat kept coming. He slashed hard right, but the driver cut him off. He was boxed in with no lane of escape. Max waved at the driver to back away. Instead, he pushed the throttle. The boat shot forward and its needle-nose stabbed him in the lower back. He felt like he'd been poked with a cattle prod. He lost his balance and nearly fell, but managed to right himself. He knew if he went down he'd be sucked under the boat and sliced to pieces by its propeller. He looked at Delray. Her face was a portrait of horror. Then a voice rang out from behind.

"You're screwed, Brady!"

The Donzi had backed off a few feet. He looked back. The passenger yelling at him was Junior Ball. The yellow boat surged again and poked Max in the hip. This time it was like a sword going into him. The tattooed driver fell back then thrust forward once more. The boat caught Max's left leg and he lost equilibrium. He was falling. He released the rope and dove head-first, cutting into the water like a knife. With his feet still in the ski shoes, he straightened his legs. The Donzi ran straight over him. The Mercury's lower housing kicked into the air with a roar, spewing blue smoke, its prop spinning like the meat slicer at Piggly Wiggly. The next seconds were a mad rush of sound and bubbles. Max somersaulted underwater, not knowing if he'd been lacerated, waiting to feel pain. He descended into the blackness and stayed there until he heard skis slice through the water above him and surfaced warily.

His ski had snapped like a matchstick, its pieces floating twenty feet away. The Whaler was making a wide arch and circling back. The Donzi was close behind, its skiers still upright. Delray leaned over the bow, her face washed in anguish.

"Are you hurt, Max?"

He coughed water while his hands felt beneath the surface. He didn't find any open wounds and nothing seemed to hurt.

"I don't think so," he said.

The Donzi coasted to a stop and picked up its skiers then glided to the Whaler. A second man was standing at the stern next to a woman with flaming red hair. She had a voluptuous figure and was wearing a white bikini. Junior's eyes were riveted on her.

"What the hell's Ball doing with them?" Peanut said.

Max pulled himself aboard and stood uncertainly on trembling knees as it sank in how near he'd come to being killed. Somehow this brush with death wasn't quite as exhilarating as his shark encounter the day before. That might have had something to do with the black-haired driver leaping onto the bow of the yellow boat. He was built like a lumberjack. His face was mean and pitted and dominated by a nose that resembled a carpenter's thumb.

He pointed a tattooed arm at Max. "You're lucky I didn't kill you, punk."

Fat cords bulged in his throat. Even his veins had muscles. Before Max could respond, Delray jumped in front of him and screamed.

"You big bastard!"

The three boys looked at her in disbelief. They'd never heard an obscenity cross her lips. The Donzi driver squared himself to her. His arms were rippling. A tattoo of a bucking bronco covered his broad chest. His eyes were thin and cruel and leering at Delray as though he was burning her image into his brain. He was wearing a salacious smile.

"A little sweet tart, are you? I like a girl with a filthy mouth. You look scrumptious in that yellow bathing suit. Like a lemon drop waiting to be eaten. Makes me wanna come over there and take a taste. Or have these faggots beat me to it?"

Delray shot right back. "I guess they wouldn't be faggots then, would they, Mr. Musclehead?"

The boys watched her, stunned. Junior was at the back of the Donzi patting the redhead's back with a towel.

"They are faggots," he called out.

"Well, then," the big man said, "maybe I will take that taste."

"Shut up, Buck." It was the second man. "You too, Austin."

He was different from the one he called Buck. There was something about him. Max wasn't sure what. A magnetism that drew the eye. Longish straw-blond hair. Square-cut face. Golden tan. Taller than Buck. And leaner. With broader shoulders. He reminded Max of the movie star Clint Eastwood. He had a military countenance that reminded him of his father. Buck regarded him with deference.

"Hell, Duke, you can't let a little tadpole like this go around thinking he's a goddamn barracuda."

"I said shut up." Duke's voice was calm, almost soft. He glared at Buck, who scowled back, but said nothing. Duke turned to Max. "You okay, kid?"

He was still shaking. He took a hasty draught of air and regained control of his nerves.

"Yes, sir. I think so."

"What's your name?"

"Max. Max Brady."

The boy detected a glint of something in Duke's eyes. Recognition? The man studied him for several seconds.

"Is that so? What's your father do, Max Brady?"

157

"He's dead."

"Sorry to hear that. How'd he die?"

"Vietnam."

Peanut interrupted. "His dad was awarded the Medal of Honor posthumously."

Duke nodded and kept staring for an uncomfortable moment. Finally his face broke into a laconic smile that gave Max a warm feeling.

"A word of advice, young Mr. Brady." He nodded at Buck. "Don't taunt a junkyard dog unless you're willing to get bit."

Max stared back at him without response. Junior laughed. Buck sneered.

"You pussies better hope I never see you again."

Duke glanced at Delray then turned to Buck. "Watch your mouth in front of the ladies," he said. "Let's go."

Buck climbed back behind the wheel and gunned the throttle and the Donzi roared off toward Las Olas Bridge. For the next five minutes Max and his friends sat adrift in the middle of the Intracoastal, silent, shaken. Then Ben snarled his lips and held his arms out wide like a muscleman and punched his left palm with his right fist.

"You pussies better hope I never see you again or I'm gonna bite your heads off, cause I'm a junkyard dog." He waved a hand at the receding Donzi. "Prick!"

"You heard the man," said Max. "Watch your language in front of the lady."

"Lady!" Peanut shouted. "Tell Delray to mind her tongue in front of us."

The four collapsed in laughter.

Et Tu Brady

Chapter Twenty-Four

ROSE BECKER SAT coiled and ready. She was poised at the end of the Fort Lauderdale City Commission table. The meeting was almost over. Most of the crowd had escaped for lunch. Seymour Tate was ensconced alone in the front row of the spectator gallery. His eyelids had drooped to half-staff and his head was propped in his right hand as he succumbed to the trance-inducing tedium of government in inaction.

"Before we adjourn, Madame Mayor," Rose said, "I'd like to ask one question."

Seymour bolted upright and his ears cocked like a Doberman hearing a silent whistle.

"Chair recognizes Commissioner Becker," said Mayor Liz Donnelly.

"This is for the City Attorney," said Rose.

At the opposite end of the table Walter Dean was shuffling files into his briefcase. When he heard his name he stiffened.

Dean was a wide-set, sedentary-looking man with a nearly bald head, which he'd cleverly concealed by stretching the few hairs he had left from one ear to the other. It was like hiding an elephant under a Kleenex. After twenty years as City Attorney, Dean was a

Fort Lauderdale institution, even if he was not exactly beloved. He had the personal charm of a trout and a reputation for eviscerating anyone who dared question his pronouncements of law, including at times members of the City Commission. He looked down the table and arched his eyebrows over the rims of tortoise-shell glasses.

"Yes, commissioner?"

"Mr. Dean it has come to my attention that the city is routinely settling personal injury lawsuits for slip-and-fall accidents. Is that so?"

Something twitched in Dean's fleshy face. The question startled him. He removed his glasses with his left hand and reached up and patted his comb-over with his right. Something seemed to occur to him. He looked down and shot a sour glance at Seymour Tate. Seymour had his reporter's notebook on his knee and a red pen poised. His eyes were swinging back and forth between Dean and Rose, like contestants in a ping pong match.

"I'm not sure what you mean by *routinely*, commissioner," said Dean. His voice was pregnant with scorn. "The city has several hundred legal actions in progress at any given moment. We settle cases all the time."

"I'm talking about lawsuits by people claiming they've broken bones tripping over cracked sidewalks or slipped disks driving into potholes. Those kinds of cases."

Dean shifted in his seat, poker-faced, except for a fat blue vein that had emerged at the center of his forehead.

"Yes, Miss Becker, unfortunately we've got some cases like that. So does every town in America. We live in a litigious society. Sadly the kneejerk reaction today when the least little accident happens is to file a lawsuit. Especially when they happen on city property."

"Isn't it a fact that your office never goes to trial on these cases. That you've been settling them instead. Hundreds per year. At a cost of millions to taxpayers."

Heads tilted inward and a babble of whispers could be heard among the sparse audience that remained. After hours of torpor, Rose's fellow commissioners seemed suddenly energized. Their attractive young colleague was putting Dean's feet to the fire, something they'd rarely witnessed. Sweat beaded on Seymour Tate's flaccid face as he scribbled furiously.

Rose zeroed her eyes on the City Attorney, who glowered back at her from the other end of the table.

"I can't tell you off the top of my head, commissioner." His words had a prickly edge. "I can research the matter and get back to you."

She tapped her pen on the table. "Come on, Walter. You settled one hundred eighty seven of these cases last year alone." Dean blanched at the precision of her numbers. "The city paid out over five-and-a-half million dollars. Most in small increments. Twenty-five or thirty thousand a pop. Not enough to get much notice. But not one dollar was awarded by a judge or jury. All settlements were between you and the plaintiffs' lawyers."

Crimson rose in Dean's cheeks. He hunched his shoulders like a cornered cat.

"What's your point, commissioner?"

"My point is this city's broke and we're giving away millions of dollars without a fight? This has apparently been going on for years. By now lawyers must know all they have to do to be guaranteed a nice payday is file a lawsuit against us."

Her words hung in the air like the echo of church bells. Seymour cast a fleeting glance at the City Attorney. He was bristling, his composure frayed. Seymour knew that Dean knew his story had been spiked. He didn't have to be Albert *freaking* Brainstein to figure out who had fed Rose Becker the information. The lawyer took a deep breath, regained his poise, and shaped a response.

"Commissioner, I don't settle a case unless it's in the best interest of the citizens of Fort Lauderdale." He spoke like Rose was a small child. Seymour balled his hand into a fist and sneezed into it. His *'achoo'* sounded suspiciously like *'bullshit!'* Rose suppressed a smile. Dean threw a vinegary scowl in the reporter's direction. "Sometimes it comes down to the lesser of two evils. Someone files a claim that he or she was injured on public property due to city negligence. Every case we've settled has been substantive."

"Define substantive, Walter?" she said, thinking of Brady and his war of *O's*.

Dean appeared to be incensed. Rose was half his age, and not even a lawyer, and here she was cross-examining *him* on the law?

"Substantive means the evidence showed an accident did occur on city property and was demonstrably caused by negligence on our part."

"So you protect taxpayer dollars by just handing them thirty thousand dollars?"

"I can go to trial and fight everything, Miss Becker. And maybe in some cases we don't pay a penny." He paused, picked up his water glass, and took a long swallow. Rose noticed a tremor in his hand. He replaced the glass and swept his right forefinger across his lips. "However, every time we try a lawsuit it costs taxpayers a minimum of fifty thousand dollars. That includes the salary of my lawyers, investigative expenses, expert witnesses, court costs, etcetera. That's fifty thousand – if we win. If we lose the sky's the limit. So we pay fifty thousand dollars plus whatever a jury awards. Thus, if we settle at a much lower figure we save taxpayers a substantial amount of money."

Dean leaned back with a satisfied countenance. He glanced at Seymour scratching away on his reporter's pad, then at Rose. Her face had adopted a skeptical cast.

"Just one more thing, Walter. It has also come to my attention that the vast majority of these slip-and-fall lawsuits are being filed by one attorney. Do you know who I'm talking about?"

Dean's nostrils flared like a bull preparing to attack. He looked down at Tate with fresh loathing and turned sourly to Rose. "I have no idea what you're talking about, Commissioner Becker."

"Not what. Whom. I believe his name is Austin Ball, Jr. Suing the city seems to be his specialty. Mr. Ball filed all but twenty of those one hundred eighty seven cases settled last year. His clients collected four point seven million dollars. It was a similar story the year before. And the year before that."

Dean snorted. "Mr. Ball is a respected member of the local bar. I know him and consider him an honorable attorney. I'm not sure what you're implying."

Rose took a quick peek at Seymour Tate. He gave her an almost imperceptible nod and smiled into his note pad. She looked back at Dean.

"Just curious, Walter. These are lean times. I want to be sure the public's money isn't being frittered away."

"Do we need a committee?" the mayor asked.

"Five people to do the work of one?" Rose said. "Mr. Dean is perfectly capable of preparing an analysis on slip-and-falls the city has settled with Mr. Ball."

"Is that a motion?" Mayor Donnelly said.

"Yes."

"Second," said Commissioner Allen Cutler.

"All in favor? Unanimous. Mr. Dean?"

The lawyer gave a placatory shrug. "I'll try to get something together, Madame Mayor. When do you need it?"

Liz Donnelly looked at Rose. "Commissioner Becker?"

"Yesterday would have been perfect. Today is better. Tomorrow's good."

"Have it for our next meeting, Walter," the mayor said and banged her gavel. "We are adjourned."

Chapter Twenty-Five

A YOUNG GIRL dressed in black stretched provocatively in the reclining chair. Slim as a sparrow, she had an angular face, high cheekbones, and enormous dark button eyes that followed Lazarus's every motion.

"Open wide, my pretty," he ordered.

His fingers were kneading a lump of sloppy green goop, massaging the blob into the shape of a crescent moon. He placed it gently between her teeth.

"Now, Pandora, bite down." She obeyed. "Not too hard."

Lazarus was tall and lean and also arrayed in black. Black jeans. Black T-shirt. Black top hat. Twists of tawny hair jutted out from beneath the brim like straw from a scarecrow. His face was square-cut and narrow, yet somehow soft, his physiognomy delicate, almost feminine, as though he'd been sculpted by Michelangelo. He leaned close to the girl and smiled. Sensuous. Sardonic. His lips drawn back, revealing long, sharp spiked eyeteeth.

"Now open wide again."

He removed the mold and handed her a paper towel.

"Yuck!"

"Don't be a baby. It ain't gonna kill you. Dental algenate, same stuff dentists use. I buy it on eBay."

Pandora spit into the towel and wiped her mouth, her dark eyes never straying from him. Lazarus poured white powder into a stone bowl, added water, and ground it like an apothecary with pestle and mortar. When it gained the consistency of wall spackle, he poured it into the mold he'd just made of her dental impression and tapped out the bubbles. The substance soon hardened until it resembled a bar of Ivory soap. Lazarus stepped to a work bench in the corner of the room and flipped a switch. A small skill saw buzzed to life and he used it to carve off the excess material. When the cast was complete he pulled on a pair of latex gloves and began mixing another concoction.

"Powdered acrylic with a liquid monomer to activate it. How manicurists make fake fingernails."

"Ugh. Smelly."

"When I'm finished you're gonna be the sweetest little blood-sucker at the Slimelight."

Pandora watched him with worshipful eyes. Lazarus slathered putty onto the model teeth and molded it with his fingers. Within minutes it was rock hard. He switched on another power tool, a grinding wheel, and shaved down the stony acrylic. Before long he'd fashion what looked like two miniature teepees. He pulled out a small roll of tape and tore off two tiny strips.

"Poly-Grip. Just like grandma uses." He applied the tape to the hollow interiors of the teepees. "Alright, my pet. Open that beautiful mouth and let me in."

She obliged and he fitted the implants over Pandora's incisors. He held up a mirror and she ran her tongue over her new fangs.

"They're beautiful. And so sharp."

"As daggers. Be careful who you bite."

She extended her arms.

"Come to me, Lazarus. Be my first. Let me taste your blood."

Lazarus looked down on her. It was a tempting invitation. He preferred cash. If every little Goth girl paid him with sexual favors he'd starve to death. But he knew Pandora didn't have any money.

And she was so young, and tender, and luscious, and willing. He'd be doing her a favor. He climbed into the chair and they entwined themselves. One thing led to another and, for the next half hour, they writhed and twisted like contortionists. Touching. Biting. Tasting each other's blood. Her face buried in his throat. His hands busy beneath her clothing. She breathless. He moaning. She snapping open his jeans. He unbuttoning her blouse. It went on that way until his pants were around his knees and her skirt was around her waist. Then a voice rang out.

"Who's this little troll whore?"

Lazarus bolted upright and gawked at a thin spectral form silhouetted against the doorway. Pandora fell back, gasping for air, lips smeared in scarlet, shirt open, skirt hiked. Demonika had a bird's eye view of her genitalia. The second time that had happened in two hours. Not that the sight shocked her. This time a year ago she was taking showers with her high school classmates in physical education class. The big difference was that the girls in the locker room hadn't been undressed by her boyfriend.

Lazarus climbed out of the chair, pulled up his pants, and buckled his belt. A trickle of blood dribbled down his chin. He wiped it with the sleeve of his black T-shirt, removed his top hat, and bowed slightly with a nonchalant sweep of his arm.

"Demonika meet Pandora. I made her a new set of fangs. She was giving them a trial run. Pandora this is Demonika."

Demonika gave him a withering look. "Why is she testing them on you?"

Pandora hastily pulled the skirt down to the top of her thighs and buttoned her blouse. A fat teardrop spilled from her big eyes and rolled down her cheek.

"She called me a troll whore," she whimpered. "What's a troll whore?"

"It means you're a little tramp," Demonika said.

Pandora burst into a full sob. She looked up at Lazarus. "Who is this bitch? Why are you letting her say mean things to me?"

Demonika stamped to the chair and glared down at her. She pushed Pandora's legs open and pointed to the inside of her left thigh. A line of script was tattooed on her milky skin. Eyes ablaze, Demonika turned on Lazarus.

"I see you did more than make fangs. What the hell is that? Our secret vow? The exact same maxim?"

An amused expression crossed Lazarus's thin face. He scratched his curly blond nest and replaced the top hat.

"No biggie," he shrugged. "She saw mine and wanted one too."

Demonika faced him, hands on hips, defiant.

"So, she's seen you with your pants down before now."

It wasn't a question. Lazarus's eyes got big. He hemmed-and-hawed for a moment then looked at her with a sheepish smile.

"Awkward!"

Demonika jerked her thumb at Pandora. "Get rid of the tramp. We've gotta talk."

Pandora pulled on her panties and pushed her skirt back down.

"You better go," Lazarus said. "Don't worry about the fangs. Or the tattoo. No charge."

She stared at him. Thunderclouds filled her brown eyes. She bared her new implants and hissed, like she was auditioning for a bit part in a *Twilight* film.

"No charge?" She was almost screaming. "Did you think that handjob was for my health?"

Demonika lunged at Pandora. Lazarus caught her by the shoulders inches before her fingernails reached the other girl's face. Pandora sprang from the chair and rushed to a blanket that doubled as a door and vanished beneath it while Demonika bellowed after her.

"You better get that skinny ass outa here. Troll whore!"

"Why do you say such things?" Lazarus said.

She turned on him. "Hand job?"

He raised his palms defensively. "That was her idea. She's broke. It would have been rude to refuse."

"Oh, I forgot!" Demonika said with a solicitous nod. "Lazarus. The wolf of warlocks. *Romeo of the Night.*"

"Don't make fun. That persona makes us a lot of money."

"Let me tell you something, *Romeo*," she said, spitting the name. "If those Goth bitches ever wise up to you, playing them for every dollar and carnal indulgence you can, the only handjobs you'll be getting are the ones you administer yourself."

Lazarus's face lit in an impish smile. "But you'll still be my wicked little witch."

He opened his arms and moved to wrap them around her. She pushed him away. "Don't be too sure. But that's not important now."

Demonika's mood changed in the time it took to snap a finger. Her anger subsided and her face grew serious. Almost stern. Lazarus moved to embrace her again. She stopped him with a finger in his face. "Not now."

Lazarus looked crushed. Girls didn't talk to him like that. Not Goth girls. And Demonika was all Goth. Very dark, very sexy, in her own very pale, very skinny kind of way. It hurt to hear her say no.

"You got me all worked up, baby. Climb into my chair and let me take care of your needs."

"Shut up," she snapped. "Listen to me."

Demonika told Lazarus about Nudey Judy. Her bare wrinkled ass. Her loathsome relatives Alice and Bert. Dipping her nose-hose in Demonika's water glass.

"That's disgusting," Lazarus said. "But what's it got to do with me?"

Her severe expression softened into a cunning smile and her dark eyes danced on her creamy white face.

"She's got cash coming out the wazoo. The stuff's all over the house. A fortune. And here's the best part."

Demonika held up a key.

Et Tu Brady

Chapter Twenty-Six

FIVE CENTURIES AGO a game was invented in Scotland. It's very first rule gave it its name. "Gentlemen Only…Ladies Forbidden." Since then men around the globe have been escaping their women by playing the ancient game of golf.

Junior Ball and his three playing partners – all men – were waiting on the tee of the 8th hole at Fort Lauderdale Country Club's South Course while the group ahead of them finished putting. The hole was a one hundred forty five-yard par three over a large lake to an undulating green surrounded by sand traps and grassy berms. A sporty silver Mercedes Benz CLK convertible was sitting on a raised platform at the center of the lake. A placard on its window announced its retail price at $56,900. The car was the prize for the lucky golfer who scored a hole-in-one on number eight at the annual Our Lady of Perpetual Sorrow Golf Tournament.

While Ball and his group stood on the tee, Howard Pickens, clutching a hand-held radio, watched the golfers putt from his perch on a lawn chair atop the knoll behind the green. His job was to watch every shot, in the remote case someone got incredibly lucky and aced the hole, the odds of which happening were approximately twenty five thousand-to-one.

The foursome finished putting, removed three golf balls from the cup, replaced the flagstick, and walked over to Pickens. All of them were former Our Lady of Perpetual Sorrow students.

"Coach!" Pat Graziano shouted and threw his arms around his old phys-ed teacher. "How's retirement?"

Pickens regarded them with a welcome light on his face. "Well, Patrick, I've become more active in the church since my wife passed away. I'm a deacon now."

"Saver of lost souls, are you, coach?

"Six o'clock Mass every morning. Love to see you there some day."

"God bless you, coach, but my soul doesn't wake up that early."

"As I recall, Patrick, any hour was way too early for you."

Graziano and his playing partners surrounded their old gym teacher, laughing, slapping shoulders, making a concerted effort to block his view of the putting green. While the others stood shoulder-to-shoulder in front of Pickens, John Simon wrapped him in an affectionate bear hug.

"You're a picture of health, coach." He picked up the older man's cane leaning against the chair and swung it like a golf club. "What's this about?"

"I'm afraid arthritis has gotten the best of my hip, boys."

"That's what you get for all that running and jumping jacks you made us do," Mark Bailey said.

Pickens patted his former pupil's prominent belly.

"Mr. Bailey it looks like you could use some jumping jacks. Are you still pulling the pigtails on that pretty little girl? What was her name?"

"You mean Anita?"

He looked confused. "I thought it was Mary Ann."

"It was. Then we got married and had two kids. Now she's living with her girlfriend. The only time I hear from her its *'Anitacheck. Anitamoremoney. Anitayouwatchthekids'*. I'm having her name legally changed."

"Coach!" Pat Graziano was pointing. "Look."

On the tee one hundred forty five yards away, Junior Ball and his team were jumping up and down and high-fiving each other. Junior started running toward the green, waving a golf club in the air, kicking his heels as he ran. Pickens and the others looked at the putting green. Three golf balls sat on the verdant, undulatory turf, none closer than twenty feet from the flagstick.

"Holy Saint Andrew, coach!" shouted Mark Bailey. "Did somebody just jar one?"

The golfers helped Pickens to his feet and escorted him down the knoll.

"Check the cup, coach," Graziano said. "Is a ball in there?"

With the help of his cane, Pickens hobbled to the hole and looked down.

"Mr. Graziano, will you please remove the flag and retrieve that ball?"

Graziano did as asked and handed the ball to Pickens. He examined it. There was a name imprinted on the cover. *Ball's Ball.* The coach held it over his head as Junior reached the green.

"By gosh, Mr. Ball," he announced, "you must be saying your prayers. You have just won a Mercedes-Benz."

Junior threw his arms around Pickens while the others crowded in laughing and cheering. Pickens clicked the radio key and held it to his mouth.

"Father O'Brien," he said, slightly breathless, his voice trembling, "we've got a winner."

Minutes later a procession of golf carts arrived at the green led by Father Michael O'Brien, Our Lady of Perpetual Sorrow's pastor. Jack Phelps, another OLPS alum, was beside him. Phelps owned Phelps Mercedes and had donated the car to the tournament.

"Sorry, Jack," said Ball. "Hope this isn't coming out of your pocket."

Phelps laughed and shook his hand. "Nonsense, Junior. I bought hole-in-one insurance. IRS lets me write it off." Then, in a stage whisper: "Plus, I collect a fat sales commission. You just made me about five grand. Thanks, pal."

Father O'Brien handed Junior the keys to the car and everyone shook hands. The celebration broke up and Ball and the others proceeded to the next hole. On the tee, Junior passed out celebratory Cuban cigars to the other golfers, who gathered around him like vassals around the lord of the manor. He trimmed one end of a golden brown Montecristo, set it afire, and waved his friends into a huddle. A veil of smoke curled in the air above them like blue dollar signs.

"Thanks fellas. That was better than a wet dream. Just like I drew it up."

"Best part is nobody loses," Pat Graziano shouted.

"Except the insurance company," said John Simon.

"Screw the insurance companies," Mark Bailey said. "Bastards just tripled my hurricane premium."

"Hell, even that asshole Phelps made five grand on the deal," Graziano said.

Junior smiled. "He's not the only one. Soon as I sell the car I'll cut you each a check for five thousand dollars."

He didn't mention his cut would be twenty thousand. They all high-fived and went back to golf. The ninth hole was a narrow par five with a driving range to the left and a coppice of Australian pines and black olive trees to the right. Graziano was in the middle of his backswing when the Led Zeppelin song *Communication Breakdown* began blaring. He jerked his tee shot into the driving range.

"Out-of-bounds," John Simon shouted.

Graziano turned and glared. "Which one of you sons-a-bitches' cell phone was that?"

Junior held up his iPhone. "Sorry, Pat. Forgot."

Graziano looked at him and shrugged. "It's *all good*, buddy. Five grand worth of *all good*."

Junior smiled and stepped away from the tee. He checked the telephone screen. Walter Dean was calling.

"Walter," he shouted, still euphoric over his phantom hole-in-one. "Talk to me."

He listened for a moment, while his face turned the color of a pomegranate.

Et Tu Brady

Chapter Twenty-Seven

RON REGISTER STOOD behind his desk in Homicide sucking a Tums and staring at his detectives, Pixie Davenport and Perry James. The ex-gridiron hero was smoothing his green-and-orange University of Miami tie over the front of a crisp white shirt. Like his boss, James was meticulous about his vestments. Also like Register, his goal was to someday be Chief of Police. He was already dressing the part. Davenport was a trim, plain-featured, but not unattractive woman of thirty years. She tended more toward blue jeans and a blue FLPD polo shirt. Register figured it had something to do with her being a lesbian, which didn't bother him a whit. Pixie was the smartest cop in Homicide. As long as she made him look good, he didn't care who she slept with.

"You're gonna love this, captain," said James. "We know Delray Chance Cross is sole beneficiary to her brother's estate. I dug deeper into her history. Turns out this isn't first windfall Mrs. Cross has collected from the mysterious death of a loved-one."

Register had always liked James. Originally it was the prestige of having a celebrated All-American athlete on his squad. But he'd had grown to respect James's professionalism and work ethic. He was a fine lawman who approached his job with the discipline of a trained athlete. Register liked the idea of one of his protégés becoming Police Chief and planned to help James reach the top someday – after he had his turn.

"You've got my attention, Perry."

"Mrs. Cross's husband, Charles Cross, died three years ago under suspicious circumstances. Mr. Cross was an economist, like his wife, although I gather much more high profile. A regular guest on those television business shows. Wrote scads of articles in business journals. Quoted in scads more. Predicted the crash years before it happened. A go-to guy on the economy. And loaded."

Register pulled the chair out from his desk and sat. "Let's hear it."

"Just got off the phone with a Luitenant Kolonel Willy Roozendaal. Ministry of Security and Justice on the island of Bonaire. They spell lieutenant funny down there. And colonel is with a K. Guess he'd be your counterpart."

"Bonaire? Isn't that part of Venezuela?"

"Fifty miles off the Venezuelan coast. Part of the Netherlands Antilles. It's actually a municipality of the Dutch Kingdom."

"Hmmm. Seems like a long way from Amsterdam."

"Four thousand eight hundred fifty three miles, as the crow flies." He noticed Register and Davenport give him curious looks. "Google. Anyway, Luitenant Kolonel Roozendaal told me Cross and his wife were vacationing on the island when it happened."

"How'd he die?"

"The kolonel said Mr. and Mrs. Cross rented a boat and were scuba diving. Mrs. Cross was evidently a strong swimmer and an accomplished diver. Her husband wasn't nearly as adept. Mrs. Cross told Roozendaal he'd only been certified by something called patty a few months before."

"Patty?" said Register.

"P-A-D-I," interjected Davenport. "Professional Association of Diving Instructors."

"That makes sense," James said. "Anyway, according to the kolonel, Cross had only scuba dived a handful of times. Mrs. Cross collects rare tropical fish. She was trying to capture something called a Flaming Prawn Goby." James held his big fingers a half-inch apart.

176

"Some kind of extremely exotic, extremely tiny fish. She claimed she was so absorbed trying to net one that she forgot about her husband for a few minutes. When she turned around he was gone. Told Bonaire police she searched frantically for him until her air ran out, but he had vanished. His body was found the next day. Drowned. The kolonel said Mrs. Cross appeared to be distraught and blamed herself."

"So she admitted being responsible for her husband's death?"

"To a point. She insisted it was an accident, though. The coroner, however, discovered drugs in his system." James paused for dramatic effect. "Oxy."

He didn't have to explain. In addition to being the *Yachting Capital of the World* and the *White Collar Crime Capital of America*, Fort Lauderdale had also become the nation's *Oxycodone Capital*. The town was teeming with *pill mills*. Addicts flocked in from around the country to buy the powerful painkiller, prescribed by a legion of unscrupulous doctors making millions from the trade. The annual death toll from oxy overdoses ran in the thousands. James continued.

"Mrs. Cross told Bonaire authorities he'd taken it for seasickness. Coroner ruled that he blacked out underwater and drowned."

Register mulled his words for several seconds, silent, sphinxlike. "And that helps us how?"

"The authorities down there smelled something rotten. For one thing, oxycodone isn't considered a common or effective treatment for motion sickness. In fact, it's been blamed for *causing* nausea."

"Doesn't mean doctors don't prescribe it for seasickness," Pixie Davenport said. "Those pill mill quacks will order it for dandruff."

"Second," James said, "the Crosses were only diving in about twenty feet of water just a couple hundred yards off the beach. The kolonel said there was barely a current and the sea was clear as glass. I'm no scuba diver, but that sounds like as non-threatening an environment as you could ask for. People don't get seasick in those conditions."

Register leaned back in his chair and popped another Tums. "So why didn't Bonaire prosecute?"

"Luitenant Kolonel Roozendaal said they are convinced something sinister happened. They just can't prove it. Even so, they've still got Charles Cross's death listed as *suspicious*."

"Good work, Perry."

"That's not all, cap," James said and turned to Davenport. "Pixie?"

"I ran a probate check on Charles Cross, sir. Delray Chance Cross inherited her husband's entire estate. Sole beneficiary. Just like with her brother."

"How much?"

"Five million."

"Is that so?"

"That's so." Davenport was all business. No preening, no smile, no emotion. She was almost robotic. "This is just me talking, sir. I think a jury will find it interesting that Mrs. Cross's brother and husband both died mysteriously after they'd been drugged."

"And that she was the only person around when they bought the farm," James added.

"And that she inherited their substantial fortunes," said Davenport.

Register rubbed his hands together and smiled at his young detectives.

"I think you're right, Pixie. I think a jury will find that extremely interesting."

Et Tu Brady

Chapter Twenty-Eight

AN ILL WIND blew through Fort Lauderdale that afternoon. Men wearing toupees were sent fleeing for cover as galloping gray thunderheads doused the town with a rare February cloudburst. One of those biblical drenchings that came and went in minutes.

Such storms were normally welcome purifying ablutions during the arid winter season. Unfortunately for Brady, the ragtop on his Jeep had more holes in it than a box of Krispy Kremes. Rainwater percolated through the canvas and soaked him from T-shirt to hightops.

Cars are status symbols for many men, their Porsches or Ferraris or BMWs essential elements of their personal image – or the image they want the world to see – their flashy wheels a palpable demonstration that they are smarter, or richer, or have bigger cocks than the average man in his Ford or Honda or Chrysler. Brady had never been big on status symbols. His car proved it. The Jeep's odometer had long-since passed the hundred thousand mile mark and its faded red coat was in dire need of fresh paint. It wasn't air-conditioned and its floors were bare metal. But it started every time he turned the key, and that was all he cared about. His only regret was not replacing the canvas top months ago and he mumbled curses to himself for the dereliction.

The drenching only deepened the melancholy that had descended on him like a fog. After he and Delray slipped out of Ben Chance's house, Brady navigated the Sea Ray to Bahia Mar Marina and dropped her off across the beach road from the Yankee Clipper. He returned to Victor Gruber's house, traded his Hart Schaffner Marx suit for shorts and a T-shirt, and drove the Jeep back to the beach. But the scald of Delray's lips was still burning on his. The kiss had not been planned, at least not by him. She initiated it. He wasn't sure why.

Was she still in love with him after all these years? Was she trying to curry his favor so he'd save her from prison? Or was she just plain crazy? Delray was a smart, beautiful, successful woman, but Brady was noticing cracks in her veneer. Not that he was surprised, considering all she'd been through. That didn't explain the kiss, though. Or his lack of resistance. He suspected his funk was a product of post-kiss guilt. *Guilt! You can take the boy out of the Catholic Church, but you can't take the guilt out of...*

Brady felt an urgent need to see Rose. He parked the Jeep in the lot catty-corner to the Swimming Hall of Fame, plugged the meter, sprinted across the street, past the Sea Shanty, and up the stairs to the Papillon Gym. She was wearing one of those black sports bras that accentuated her flat midriff. A skinny middle-aged woman wearing leather gloves was curling a barbell while Rose urged her on.

Without a word, Brady took her by the wrist and led her to the rooftop greenhouse. Rose was a card-carrying lepidopterist and had turned her arboretum into a butterfly garden. It was an opulent, enchanted wonderland teeming with a rainbow of botanic delights. Purple peonies. Pink gerbera daisies. Yellow dendrobium orchids. Exotic red ginger. The air was perfumed by the ambrosial incense of hundreds of flowers being tended to by a riot of butterflies dancing from blossom to blossom. For Brady it was a sacred garden. The place he and Rose first made love. He thumbed the amethyst petal of a gloxinia.

"Did you know flowers are the sexual organs of plants?"

180

Rose crossed her arms and gave him a long look. "Brady, sometimes I get the impression that all you think about is sex."

"What can I say? I'm a health nut. Did you know that sex is a natural antihistamine? Better for you than chicken soup. Unblocks stuffy noses. Relieves asthma and hay fever. Don't even get me started on stress. If Americans had more sex we wouldn't need Obamacare. Of course, sex can kill too. But if you gotta go. Do you know how Genghis Khan died?"

"I don't think I want to."

"Take a wild guess."

"I don't care."

"Come on, guess."

"Brady, why are you always asking me questions about useless information?"

"Did you know four-year-old kids ask an average of four hundred thirty seven questions a day?"

"You're starting to annoy me."

"I'm just reporting the facts, Rose. Genghis Khan died in bed making love to his beautiful girlfriend. You'll be fascinated to learn she ran a health club in Mongolia. Upper, of course. The Black Yak Spa, as I recall."

"And you know that how?"

"Trust me. I'm a doctor."

"Of what?"

"Jurisprudence, but that's beside the point. Back to flowers as sex organs. That, my sweet, is pure scientific fact. Do you know what the human equivalent is of the stamen and pistil?"

"I'm afraid to ask."

Brady whispered. "Penis and vagina?"

"How did you become such an authority?"

"As I recall, you share a healthy interest in the subject too."

"I've lost track. Which subject would that be?"

"That would be sex."

Rose pursed her lips and nodded. "I don't deny it. But I also have a business to run."

"And a city to save?"

"I didn't say that."

"Not since this morning. But I've got a business too. On top of that, I'm trying to save a client from Death Row."

He wanted to suck the words back into his mouth as he was saying them.

"You mean your old girl…"

Before she could finish he pulled her into his arms and planted a long, hard kiss on her mouth. Butterflies fluttered, daisies swayed, and Brady could have sworn he heard the orchids singing *So This Is Love*. It felt like a Disney cartoon. He held the kiss thirty seconds. Long enough, he hoped, to erase Delray from Rose's mind, like when Superman kissed Lois Lane.

"Thanks," he said when they broke. "I needed that."

"Glad to be of service," she said, breathless and slightly dazed.

"Did you know that during a French kiss couples transmit forty thousand parasites?"

"Oh, for heaven's sake!"

He left her amidst the pretty flowers and beautiful bugs and descended the stairwell three flights to street level, trying to recall the last time he'd kissed two women like that in the same day. Not since his spin-the-bottle days, he decided. Brady wasn't exactly a swinger.

Now, though, he had a murder to solve. The lady's man metamorphed into human blodhound. He'd been racking his brain since last night trying to get inside the twisted mind of Ben Chance's killer. *What was he thinking? Why so ritualistic? Why scrawl my name across Ben's forehead?*

The most conspicuous piece of evidence was the tattoo. It was a ham-handed job, more chicken scratch than art. The work of a seriously warped human being? Or an artist in too big a rush to be artful? Or both? Too many questions. Not enough answers.

Brady decided to spend the afternoon checking-out tattoo parlors. The beach was the best place to start, where they were more plentiful than pelicans. He sauntered down A1A. After the rain, the day had become South Florida perfect. Seventy-five degrees. Sky and sea a blizzard of blue. Sun smiling down. Astrophysicists say four-and-a-half pounds of sunlight falls on Earth every day. How they weighed sunshine Brady had no clue, but he estimated Fort Lauderdale was being buried under a couple of pounds of it today. That was the law this time of year.

As a kid he'd always hated winters, when the town was over-run and the roads and beaches were besieged by all those annoy-ing interlopers from the north. After all, it *was* tourist *season*. Locals should have had the right to shoot some of them. Thin out the herd. But his estimation had evolved. These days too many people were desperate for work. Tourists meant jobs, so the more the merrier.

Despite the lousy economy the beach was packed. The invasion was as much a product of the Super Bowl as the super weather. It was a ritual journey for a hallowed purpose. Muslims pilgrimage to Mecca. Tree Druids flock to the Yew Forest. Americans beat a path to the Big Game, fiscal doldrums be damned.

The air was redolent with the pungent scent of sunscreen slath-ered on a bumper crop of barely-clad damsels lined up on the sand like a golden field of summer corn. The sight was normally enough to put Brady in a whistling mood. Today, though, he was hunting a sadistic killer.

When he came upon a tattoo parlor he ducked inside and asked about Latin inscriptions. Whether they'd done any. Whether they knew anyone who did. Whether they'd even seen one. So far, none had. But Brady quickly discovered that the tattoo world was an intriguing subculture. Before long he knew more about *tats* than he ever imagined – including that they were called *tats*. Much of his education came courtesy of Penelope Peacock.

The Peacock Parlor was located in a narrow alley a block off the beach, squeezed between a dark, dank dive bar and a pirate para-phernalia shop. *I wonder if they stock Ned Pike stuff,* Brady thought. Penelope turned out to be no ordinary woman. She was more rooster than peacock, with granite arms, cinder block legs, six-pack abs, and bodybuilder-breasts, rock-hard plateaus rather than soft hillocks. Her hands were thick-veined and big-knuckled with short unpainted nails cut to the nub. Brady would not have wanted to tangle with her. Penelope's most prominent feature, though, were the peacock feather tattoos festooning her Terminator body.

When he walked in she was engraving Chinese characters on the lower back of a middle-aged woman lying face down on a table.

"Yum," he said with feigned sincerity. "Number forty seven."

Penelope frowned up at him. "What are you jabbering about, mister?"

He pointed at the tattoo. "Number forty seven on the menu at Beijing Gardens. General Tso's Chicken. To die for. I highly recommend it. Tell Wu Fat that Max Brady sent you."

The woman on the table turned and scowled at him through vexed eyes beneath penciled brows. "It says *Faith Hope* and *Love*. Jerk!" she snarled.

"Are you sure? I could have sworn…"

Penelope smirked at him and went back to work. Like every other salon he'd visited, *The Peacock Parlor* was spic-and-span. The room was well lit and the walls were papered with stencils of tattoo art. After the General Tso's woman left – in a huff – Penelope peeled off a pair of latex gloves and turned her formidable attention to Brady.

"Does she really think it says *Faith Hope* and *Love*?" he asked.

Penelope looked like she was about two seconds from pounding him back to the Twentieth Century.

"You are a wise ass, aren't you, mister…?"

"Brady," he said, extending his hand. She shook it like a man. "I just hope she doesn't run into a pack of hungry cats."

"Brady have you ever had that cute little tush of yours kicked by a girl?"

"I'm going to take that as a compliment, Penelope."

He flashed a smile. His razzle-dazzle smile. The one that exposed every chopper back to his third molars. Debonair incarnate. It really wasn't fair. Penelope turned to instant pudding and for the next hour gave him a primer on body art. It was fascinating stuff. Particularly some of the reasons people decorate – or defile – their bodies, depending on your point of view. Love. Religion. Vanity.

Membership in everything from the Hell's Angels to the Navy Seals to the Kiwanis Club.

"Then there are the clowns who screw up and come back the next day crying, begging me to remove it. That's why I don't do drunks anymore."

Brady was surprised to learn one-in-four Americans between ages eighteen and fifty have been *inked*. Penelope's clients were more likely to be high school girls and business executives than bikers or gang-bangers. Butterflies, hearts, and crucifixes had replaced skulls, demons, and naked women as the most popular tattoos. Tats, she said, were drawn not with ink but pigments composed of metal salts suspended in a carrier solution, often vodka, which inhibited the spread of pathogens.

Prices ranged from fifty to one hundred dollars, plus tip, for something simple, like barbed wire or a star, versus up to three hundred for a custom design, which was Penelope's specialty. She considered herself a serious artist. She did a thousand procedures a year and earned more than a hundred grand.

"Ever tattoo anybody with a Latin phrase?"

"No, but I could. How would Cicero have spelled General Tso?"

Et Tu Brady

Chapter Twenty-Nine

THE LATE AFTERNOON sky was iridescent as Mother of Pearl as he crawled westward through rush hour traffic on Sunrise Boulevard. The Jeep maintained a turtle's pace until it reached Fort Lauderdale's city limits at State Road 7. Just across the highway was the town of Lauderhill. When Brady was a kid he and his friends used to go camping there. Back then it was mainly cow pastures. Today it was a sprawling suburb populated largely by Caribbean immigrants. The town's biggest claim to fame was being home of America's largest stadium for cricket – the sport, not the bug.

Brady had come not for games, but food. He hadn't eaten a bite all day and his stomach was begging to be sated. He pulled into the Lauderhill Mall and headed straight for *Alice's Kitchen*. Alice made the best Caribbean beef patties he'd ever tasted, better even than he used to get walking his beat in the Jamaican neighborhoods of Flatbush, Brooklyn. He bought a Ting soda and a patty, doused it with Pickapeppa Red Hot Sauce, and stepped outside.

The parking lot was alive with car and foot traffic. Reggae and hip-hop music saturated the air. Brady was the only white face within eyeshot. A cluster of young black men walked past him speaking a language he didn't understand. Then they roared with laughter, a language he did. He leaned against the Jeep munching his patty and let his eyes feast on the vast stained glass explosion taking place over the Everglades, the daily clash between the titans of darkness and light that inevitably would soon be won by the nocturne.

His eyes strayed to the strip of storefronts that lined the mall's exterior. A hair salon, children's clothing store, and discount shoe shop. The window next to Alice's featured a large poster of Bob Marley's happy, smiling face. The sign said *Busyman's Tattoo Emporium*. Beyond the poster, dim lights glowed inside. Brady could see a large dreadlocked man working on the arm of a heavyset woman sitting in a chair. Him talking, her laughing, silent as mimes from where Brady stood. They were puffing on a fat cigarette that did not appear to be store-bought, passing it back and forth, and blowing out thick brumes of vapor like a pair of theatrical fog machines.

The stout woman eventually exited *Busyman's* and shuffled past the Jeep sporting a bright red rose on her massive right bicep. Still sipping his Ting, Brady stepped inside and was instantly engulfed by the piquant scent of smoldering herb. The walls were covered with artwork of dragons, wolves, stars, and crescent moons. A long glass display counter was stocked with glass pipes, bongs, hookahs, scales, cigarette papers, and kits that professed to outfox drug tests.

The big man was at the epicenter of the room reclining in the same chair the woman had occupied. Brady saw it was a barber's chair. The man sat silent and stonefaced following the stranger's meanderings. His eyes were bloodshot and Brady suddenly remembered Gordy. He hadn't thought about the Shanty all day, barely glancing at it when he ran upstairs to kiss Rose. He hoped the bar was still in business.

"Wa can I do fo ya, offisa?"

Busyman's Caribbean patois was not congenial, but not churlish either. More flat, non-committal. Brady studied him for several seconds. He debated whether to correct Busyman's notion and decided to let him think what he wanted.

"How'd you know?"

"Who da cap fits, let 'im wear it. I gotta nose for smellin' *bah-bee-lons*."

Flatbush had taught him – in addition to the joy of beef patties – a lot of Jamaican slang. *Babylon* was a buzzword for *policeman*. He tilted his head and sniffed.

"Is that your cologne, Busyman, or you been smokin' a spliff? Wanna tell me sometin', mon?"

Busyman's big black face softened from stone to clay to flesh and a deep chortle rumbled up from inside him.

"Da fish dat keep 'is mout' shut neva get caught. Yu wanna tattoo offisa?"

Brady hoped the tattooist wouldn't ask to see his badge. "I want some information."

"People in hell wan' icewata, too. I ain't no infahma. Go away now, why don't ya?"

"Don't say no, Busyman. It just encourages me. Or we can go down to the station."

"Yu coppas is like spidas dat tink black peoples is flies. Best ting for da fly is ta stay away from da spida."

Brady laughed. "That's a good one, Busyman. You're a funny guy. But I ain't no babylon."

"You look like a coppa, even with dat bokkle a Ting."

"Ex-coppa."

"Lemme tell ya som'pn, mista. Ex-coppa jes as bad as coppa. One han' wash da otha."

Brady examined the paraphernalia counter. "Like I said, I need some information."

"I don' talk to bah-bee-lons. Even if dey be ex-bah-bee-lons."

"No harm in talking to me, Busyman. Tell me about Latin tattoos?"

He noticed the glassy eyes suddenly focus.

"My mamma tol' me if ya eat with da devil, give 'im a long spoon."

"I'm not the devil," Brady said and raised his Ting. "Besides, I just ate."

They kept going around and around like a couple of horses on a carousel until Busyman shut up and sat back in the chair, brooding, silent, watching him peruse his shop. Brady decided to change his tack.

"Look, Busyman, I'm trying to help a friend. The *real* babylons are trying to prove she committed a crime she didn't commit."

Another laugh rumbled out of him, sounding like a bowling ball rolling on waxed wood.

"Ohhh! Dat's it. I see now. A 'ooman. Yu get her off, she get yu off. Go unda da sheet an' swalla yu man-juice?"

Brady laughed and shook his head. "No, Busyman, it's not like that. She's just a friend. I'm trying to help her."

"You still da cops, wedder you got da badge oh no."

They were back to that. Busyman was the first tattooist who'd shown any hint of reaction when he mentioned Latin tattoos. Brady decided to press him. He pulled a cellphone from his back pocket and held it up.

"I'm no coppa, but I know one. Friend of mine at Lauderhill PD. Narc named Logan," said Brady, who knew no such person. "Got him on speed dial. I push the button and he's here in two minutes. How much ganja would he find?"

"By two minutes it would all be down da crappa."

Brady looked at him with a mournful expression and shook his head.

"Such a waste. Why not be sensible? Answer a couple of questions and keep your weed."

Busyman inspected him for a time then tilted his head back and closed his eyes. He looked like he'd fallen asleep. Brady guessed he was weighing his options. Maybe he only had a couple of joints on the premises. If so, he would flush them down the toilet and tell Brady to call the whole damned Lauderhill Police Department. Maybe, though, his ganja stash was an ounce, or a pound. That would cost him thousands. If so, Brady suspected Busyman would get real cooperative real fast. He gave him another push.

"Tell me what you know and nobody's the wiser, but you and me. You have my word on that."

The big man was silent for another minute before he made his decision.

"Okay, ex-coppa. I know dis girly. Lilly winji white gal."

"Winji?"

"Skinny. Pretty face, but real white, like ona dem vampires dat hates da sun. Met her in a bar down on Second Street. She come winen up to me in a short purple dress, dancin' 'roun me, rubbing herself up against me like I be Samson an she be Delilah. I like a white gal now and den, but beauty witout da grace like a rose witout da smell. Dis gal ha' no grace. Talkin' 'bout she gonna smoke my ganja and ride my wood and we gonna feel awright, like she singin' da TV commercial 'bout comin' to Jamaica an feelin' awright. I tell her she look like jail bait to me. Busyman got plenty a gals. Don't need no trouble with da bah-bee-lons. She say no, dat she be legal. I say prove it. She show me her drivin' license. Dat be good 'nuff fo' me."

"So what's that got to do with Latin tattoos?"

"Didn't see it till mornin'. Dis lilly girly gots one. She be layed out asleepin' on da bed."

"Whose bed?"

"I gotta crib by da flea market on Sunrise. Gotta booth der. Do tats and sell dis shit in da daytime." He motioned to his display case of drug accoutrements. "So she be asleepin' and I be layin' der wit nuttin to do. So I be lookin' at 'er nice little cupcakes an' nice shaved gash an' I see she got som'pn writin' inside 'er left tigh from da knee right up to da quiff. I look real close tryin' to read it, but it ain't no language I ever seen. She wake up wit my nose 'tween her legs and before I know it..." Busyman got a faraway look in his eyes and chuckled softly. "Later I say wat dat writin' on yu tigh. She say it some Latin sayin' by some old Roman. Catullus or some shit. I say 'Wat it say?' She say it secret. Dat 'er boyfrien' give it to 'er and he got one too. Same words. An' he tol' 'er don't tell nobody wat it say. Even 'er madda and dada."

"What was her name?"

"Dat funny. I tol' yu, she be a freaky lilly gal. Supa freak. Called 'erself Pandora. I seen her a coupla mo' times down der on Second Street wit a guy in a black top hat, but she pretend she don' even know me. I figa dat be her boyfrien'."

"Much obliged," Brady said. He pulled two twenties and a Sea Shanty card from his wallet and handed them to Busyman. "Call me if I can ever return the favor."

"Sure ting, mon. An' if a flea had money he could buy 'is own dog."

By the time Brady exited *Busyman's Tattoo Emporium* the thermometer had plunged fifteen degrees. All the way down to sixty. *Oh, the horror!* He shouldn't have been surprised. In South Florida, rare February rains typically heralded equally rare blasts of arctic air. *Okay*, he conceded to himself, *chilly*. Fort Lauderdale's mercury had sunk to as low as twenty eight degrees – once. It had even snowed – once. A half-inch in 1977. So it could have been worse. Brady's blood had thinned since he'd moved back to Florida. The Jeep didn't have an air-conditioner, but it did have a heater, which made no sense. He was grateful now, though, and cranked it on for the first time since he couldn't remember when.

There wasn't much daylight left and he headed vaguely toward the beach, his brain on autopilot. He drove without thinking and it was ten minutes before he realized he'd taken a circuitous route and was turning onto Riverland Road. A homing pigeon returning to its roost. He hadn't been out this way in some time and was disappointed to find the area slightly down-at-the-mouth. The Piggly Wiggly where he used to fold his newspapers was now a warehouse in bad need of a paint job. He continued east to the Lauderdale Isles, past Whale Harbor Lane, Tortugas and Sugar Loaf Lanes. Okeechobee, Nassau, Gulfstream, and Flamingo where the Alligator Pit had once been. Past Cat Cay, Bimini, and Andros. He passed New River Middle School and rounded a bend. Ski Beach used to be right across the river here, when skiing was still legal on the river. A couple more blocks and he had to restrain himself from turning into the entrance of what had once been Eden.

In the thickening light he thought of his grandmother. This was the time he remembered her best. The time of day Kate Brady became Queen of New River.

Et Tu Brady

Chapter Thirty

WHEN MAX COASTED into the lagoon in his Boston Whaler, Grandma Kate was on the dock behind the big house performing her nightly ritual. In her flowered sundress and floppy straw hat with a red ribbon tied beneath her chin, she was leaning over the water warbling in her high-pitched, sing-songy voice.

"Dinner time, my little friends! Eat up."

A red bucket hung from the crook of her arm filled with loaves of stale bread, donuts and other morsels she'd collected from the Piggly Wiggly. As always, the fish were waiting for her when she arrived. Hundreds of mullet, bass, tarpon, and trout, roiling the black water as she chummed the tidal pond, laughing all the while. Max could almost see the rapturous delight in their eyes as they swarmed for their dinner. To these gilled creatures she truly was queen of the river. Max secured the bow rope to a dock cleat, grabbed his spear-gun, and pointed it at the water.

"What do you want for dinner, grandma? A couple of trout? I see a big fat bass. What are you hungry for?"

The old woman clapped her hands to her face in mock horror.

"You better not, Maximus Brady, or I will tan your skinny hide."

Then she broke out in another big infectious laugh that never failed to lift the boy's spirits. He put down the speargun, reached both hands into the bait well, and pulled out the two lobsters he caught on Three Mile Reef. He waved them in the air like Olympic torches, tentacles twisting, tails snapping.

"Look what I brought you, grandma," he said, clearly delighted with himself.

She smiled her approval. "Nice plump ones. Two pounds each, I'd say. Makes 'em about ten years old. Sweet meat."

Kate Brady had once been a fire-haired beauty, judging by the old photograph of her posing on the beach in a 1930s-style bathing suit that sat on the mantle over the big limestone fireplace in the Great Room. Now in her seventies, she was white-haired, lower built, and fleshy, but still unconquered by time. Still strong as an ox. Her sky-blue eyes still lively. Still filled with more life than anyone Max had ever known. A formidable woman. Beaming, she put down her bucket and took the crustaceans from his hands.

"Supper in one hour."

After Max and his friends had their encounter with the two men, Duke and Buck, they navigated back up New River. Past Cooley Massacre Park – where a band of drunken Indians had once slaughtered a family of pioneers – through the dilapidated downtown waterfront, and beneath the low black railroad bridge. They made a hairpin turn around a finger of land jutting into the river shaped like the Florida peninsula. Then under the Davie Boulevard Bridge and past Uncle Howard and Aunt Mo's little house. Max wondered if Uncle Howard had caught the jewel thieves he'd read about in *The Miami Herald* that morning. A half-mile up river they passed the Florida Queen, a large double-deck paddleboat packed with sightseers.

Eventually the riverfront homes gave way to jungle and the small boat's onyx ribbon of wake rolled into the mangroves and cypress knees standing sentinel beside the meandering waterway. They passed *The Cove*, a dark, mysterious brook covered by a tunnel of trees where, according to river legend, older boys and girls snuck off in boats to do whatever it was older boys and girls did in secret. They rounded a sharp bend and came upon the Seminole Village. A short, stocky, square-shouldered man was sweeping the slats of the long wooden dock.

"Good," Billy Panther shouted. "We need some fresh scalps."

Max had known Billy longer than he could remember. The Seminole had once been first mate on his grandfather's fishing boat. Grandpa Zack trusted him more than anyone in the world, except Grandma Kate.

Billy taught Max to fish, trap snakes, and hunt alligators. Now he presided over this tiny village that catered to the sightseeing boats that sailed up the river every day purporting to give tourists a taste of Old Florida. The village was supposed to represent tribal life in the days of the great Seminole chiefs, Osceola and Billy Bowlegs. It was a collection of straw chickee huts and a small zoo with pink flamingos, miniature Key deer, a few sleepy panthers, and a tired old black bear. There was a food concession and a souvenir shop that hawked colorful beaded belts, moccasins, and coconuts carved in the shape of human heads. At the center of the village was the amphitheater where Billy wrestled alligators.

The Indian rested an elbow on a dock piling and watched Max drift up. The boy threw him a rope and smiled with great affection at his old friend, always glad to see his jet black hair, dark skin, high-boned cheeks, and distinctive hooked nose. Billy nodded at the air tanks in the boat.

"Been scuba diving?"

"Three Mile Reef," said Max. He reached into his pocket and retrieved one of the coins they'd found that morning and tossed it to him. "Look at this."

Billy flipped the disk between blunt, leathery fingers, eyes narrow, intelligent, intent. Max thought he detected a sign of recognition.

"Looks like gold," he said.

"Ever seen anything like it?"

"Matter of fact, I have. Long time ago."

"Really?" said Max. Surprised. Eager. "Where, Billy?"

"Matty Fitt."

"Matty Fitt?"

"Old friend of the captain. Used to have one almost identical to this."

"Grandpa Zack's friend?"

"Used to be. They grew up together. Bad blood between 'em now, but. Real bad."

"Bad blood why?"

"Can't say."

"Can't say because you don't know? Or because you don't want to tell me?"

"Can't say," Billy said again. "After Zack put *The Summit* up in drydock I started a little boat business. Buying, selling, fiberglassing, overhauling engines. Matty didn't do much, but he did know boats. He was a genius with motors. So I hired him. Turned out he loved firewater more than money. Was about as helpful as a birdshit sandwich."

"Where'd he get his coin?"

"Matty used to fancy hisself a treasure hunter. Always babbling about pirate gold. How he was gonna find the motherlode. Get rich. Never did hit the bonanza. Nothing except some coins and artifacts, was all I ever heard. But old Matty probably did know more about that stuff than anybody in these parts."

"Is he still around?"

"Last I heard he was living in an old shack down on Sailboat Bend." Billy stared at Max and his broad brown brow furrowed. "Listen here, young Maximus. There's something you need to know. Your granddad ain't gonna want you within ten miles of Matty Fitt. Do you hear what I'm telling you?"

Before Max could answer a boat whistle sounded and a voice called out.

"Ahoy!"

The Florida Queen was swinging up to the Seminole Village. The big boat tied off, a gangplank was dropped, and a long line of sunburned sightseers streamed out, most draped in garish outfits decorated with parrots and palm trees. A little boy stopped and pointed at Billy.

"Look, mom. Is that a real Indian?"

196

"He damned well better be." She had a thick accent that Max guessed to be New York. "Or I'm gonna want a goddamned refund."

"Where are the alligators?" another visitor demanded.

"Show starts in ten minutes," Billy said. "Meantime, we have a zoo, snack bar, and souvenir shop. Take a look around."

"Typical tourist trap," the man growled and stalked off.

The captain was Stone Rathburn, a big red-faced man in a starched white uniform, white hat, and full white beard. Max's grandfather had known him for years. He called him Cap'n Crunch. Rathburn had washed out of the U.S. Coast Guard due to chronic seasickness and been reduced to operating the Florida Queen, a paddleboat that never strayed into open water. He was the maritime equivalent of a jockey leading ponies around a circle at the carnival. Cap'n Crunch was standing by the amphitheater where Billy staged his wrestling shows. He didn't look happy.

"Where's Bruno?"

"Had to put him down," Billy said.

"Another one?" The captain glared at him. "That's the third bull this year. Are you redskins that hard up for food?"

Max expected Billy to pick Rathburn up and throw him in the river, but the Seminole had an unflappable disposition.

"We do eat the meat when we kill 'em," he said with a patient inflection. "We also make belts and shoes from their hides. But I'm having to destroy 'em because somebody's been sneaking in here at night and putting their eyes out."

"Who the hell would do that?"

"I think I know. Ain't gonna say until I catch 'em."

"Why don't you call the police?"

"Because they don't give two shits about *redskins*."

Billy cast a sideways glance at Max and rolled his eyes.

"Well you better do something," Rathburn growled. "I pay good money for you to wrestle bulls, not pups. If you can't deliver the goods, I'm gonna sail right past this mudhole. You and your tribe can sell your moccasins and beaded belts out on State Road 7."

The captain traipsed off. Max looked at Billy. Despite his placid nature, the Indian's eyes were stormy. His face was a muddle of suppressed rage.

"Why don't you toss that paleface bastard into the gator pen?"

Billy eyed the boy with disapproval. "You ain't old enough for that kinda language, Maximus. But to answer your question, the economic survival of my people depends on paleface bastards like that."

Max and Billy laughed. Peanut, Ben and Delray were in the zoo section feeding dried corn kernels to a fawn. A wry smile broke out on Billy's face.

"Pretty girl. Your sweetheart?"

Max blushed and shook his head. Then his face turned serious. "Who's blinding your gators, Billy?"

The Seminole shrugged. "Can't prove it but I'm pretty sure it's that big kid who races up and down the river in a red Glasspar."

Max had already guessed as much. "Junior Ball. Him and his friends blinded the gators down at the Pit."

"Coupla times they came in here all high and mighty, runnin' around hootin' and howlin' and woo-wooin' like they was doin' an Indian war dance. I kicked 'em out and told the big one…"

"Junior."

"…told him don't come back. He's sitting in his boat about twenty feet off the dock, outa reach, and he yells he's gonna burn down the village some night when we're all sleepin'. I didn't take him serious. Then the other night, me and the squaw's cuddled up in bed when I hear a boat. I could tell by the sound it was the Merc on that Glasspar. By the time I run outside its gone. I find old Bruno. His eyes was both bleedin'."

"What'd you do?"

"Part of him's hangin' on the belt rack in the souvenir shop. The rest is gettin' grilled over at the snack stand. Gator burgers is popular with the touristas."

Max dropped his friends off at the Alligator Pit and returned to Eden. He and his mother had moved in with Grandpa Zack and Grandma Kate when his dad shipped out to Vietnam. After she died,

Max's grandmother swore it was a broken heart over her husband's death, and not the cancer, that killed her. Since then it had been just Max and his grandparents on the sprawling five acres on a sharp bend of New River.

Zack Brady bought the property in 1927. Back then Eden was as remote as the far side of the moon, but civilization had crept west and Eden was now nearer the center of Fort Lauderdale. Nonetheless, it remained a singular tropical wonderland dotted with exotic orchids, fern, pink hibiscus, purple bougainvillea, coconut palms, and several strains of orange, grapefruit, and key lime trees. All products of Grandma Kate's loving care.

Grandpa Zack built the big house with his own hands. A two-story redwood structure in a cool grove of oaks. The house had lots of windows and a wide veranda where grandma's red ladderback rocking chair was a permanent fixture. Max and his friends played football on the long, lush carpet of grass out front. Behind the house was the small private lagoon where Max docked his boat in the shade of tall cypress trees tinseled with air plants and Spanish moss.

A big red barn sat beside the house. Inside, grandpa's vintage 42-foot Wheeler Playmate was propped on stilts. The boat had been a workhorse back in the day when the Gulf Stream teemed with monster fish. Zack Brady was a legendary fishing guide. Ernest Hemingway, Joe DiMaggio, and Clark Gable were among the host of immortals who flocked from around the globe to catch marlin with the celebrated Captain Zack. He had the boat built in 1933 at the Wheeler Boat Yard in Brooklyn, New York. He named it *The Southwind,* but rechristened her *The Summit* in honor of a singular day in January 1942.

"Finest day of my life," he often said, "besides the day your grandmother married me."

Franklin Delano Roosevelt and Winston Churchill had come to Florida for a secret war conference. They were staying just up the coast at the Hillsboro Beach estate of Edward R. Stettinius, Roosevelt's Secretary of State. The President had personally requested Captain Zack take him and Churchill fishing. Instead, they spent the day five miles off shore drinking Tanqueray gin while a small armada of military vessels stood guard. Just the three of them. Zack Brady and the two titans, who listened while Captain Zack lectured them on how to defeat Hitler. The next day he renamed his boat *The Summit.*

A quarter century later, after his son was killed in the Asian war, Zack drydocked *The Summit* in the barn and became a walking, talking perpetual flame to the memory of John Maximus Brady…and that gin-soaked day on the Atlantic with Churchill and Roosevelt. Max had heard the story so many times he could repeat it verbatim.

"Them two fellas was honest-to-God giants! Not like the midgets we got now with their senseless goddamn wars."

Grandma Kate had taken Max's two lobsters up to the house and returned to the lagoon to finish tending her subaqueous flock still in the throes of their dusky feeding frenzy.

"Storm brewin'," she said.

Max peered up through a hole in the mossy cypress dome above the black pool, past a blue jay skipping from branch to branch, out toward the setting sun. Lavender clouds drifted across a flaming copper sky. Dark was coming, but he saw no sign of inclement weather.

"Why do you say that, grandma?"

He already knew the answer. Kate Brady was an oracle. Everyone on the river knew it. She'd been born with some kind of crystal ball in her head and always forecast hurricanes long before *Weaver the Weatherman* did on TV. She could predict the sex of unborn babies. She could identify a cheating spouse at first glance. And she knew when people were going to die – though she always kept those visions to herself. Sometimes she'd write them down and show Zack and Max after her muted prophecies came to be. She was never wrong.

Grandma waved at Max to follow her. They trudged through the grass to a gardenia hedge that ringed the lagoon. It was exploding with white blossoms emitting the most voluptuous fragrance. The old woman got down on her knees and pointed.

"See there." A large silver web dripping with pearls of evening dew had been woven beneath the shrub, the design simple, yet exquisite. A single spider rested at the center of the hammock, like a proud artist displaying its elaborate masterpiece. "Silk spider. Spinning low down by the ground. Storm's comin'. Tomorrow mornin'."

An hour later Max and his grandparents were dipping succulent cubes of steamed white meat into drawn butter, enjoying the fruits of his day on the ocean.

"Eat up, pup," grandpa said, as he did every night at the dinner table. "You're so skinny you only got one side to ya."

"Grandpa," Max said between bites, "did you know we eat sixty thousand pounds of food during our lifetimes?"

"Is that a fact?"

"Yes it is."

"And how on God's green earth do you know such a thing?"

"National Geographic. That's the equivalent of consuming six elephants."

"My, my, my," he said with a proud twinkle. "You got your daddy's brains."

After his mother and father died, Zack and Kate had been Max's candles in the dark. The only real family he had left. And they lavished the boy with the same love and devotion they heaped on each other. He couldn't envision life without them.

"Maximus," grandma said out of the blue, "who's this girl you're so in love with?"

Max choked on his lobster. He felt like his face was on fire. He'd never spoken of Delray around his grandparents, even though she was on his mind every minute of every day. But Grandma Kate was a seer. He realized that, as long as she was there to read his mind, he'd never be able to keep his secrets secret.

"I am not in love," he said and turned to his grandfather with helpless eyes.

Zack Brady was a hard, hearty man with big rough-hewn hands and the sunbaked skin of a fisherman. His wrinkled face was like an old house that hadn't been painted in many years. He smelled like hot shaving cream, the kind Ray the barber used in his shop on Riverland Road. Grandpa's hearing was poor and the boy half-hoped he hadn't heard. The old man stabbed a chunk of lobster, inserted it into his mouth, and chewed thoughtfully. He put down his fork and, still chewing, brushed back an unruly thatch of white hair.

"Kate," he said, "why would you say something like that to the boy?"

Grandma erupted in a jolly, high-pitched body laugh. Her face flushed and her cheeks jiggled like her red raspberry preserves. She wagged her fork at her husband and shook her head. Max could see the love in her eyes.

"Zackary Brady, I will swear on a stack of Holy Bibles you are only as deaf as you care to be." She laughed hard again while crimson spread across Max's face. "Maybe you haven't noticed that your grandson's been quiet as a church mouse lately. That's the sign of a boy moonin' over a girl. Just like John used to moon over Mary. Just like you mooned over me when we was courtin'." She turned her clear blue eyes back to Max. "So, Maximus, who is she?"

The boy sat mute, his jaws grinding away at the lobster, his face incandescent. Grandpa answered for him. "Probably that long, yellow-haired girl he's been squirin' around all summer."

Max looked at his grandfather with an incredulous expression. His ally had taken up with his inquisitor. "How do you know about her?"

"I might be retired, but I still got my ear to the water. Not much happens on this river I don't know about. I hear tell she's a pretty one."

"Tomboy, ain't she?" said Grandma Kate.

"Why do you say that?"

"Came by here the other day in a boat with that other gal. The one with the boobies."

Max choked again on his lobster. "Ginger Brennan?"

"You wasn't here but they was in the lagoon and she was whistlin' like a sailor."

He tried to hide his smile. "She *can* whistle, better than any boy I know."

"Well, you know what they say, don't ya?" She didn't wait for an answer. "When a young girl whistles, the Virgin Mary weeps."

"Oh, grandma, that's an old wives tale!"

"Well, my darling, I am an old wife." She patted Zack's hand. "But that don't mean I can't learn new tricks."

"The trick ain't learning new ones," grandpa said. "It's remembering the old ones."

Max was eager to change the subject. He reached into his pocket. "Look what I found, grandpa."

His grandfather took the coin and examined it with tapered eyes, like Billy had two hours before.

"Spanish," he said, matter-of-fact.

"How can you tell?" Max said, eager to learn more about the gold piece.

"By the cross. Where'd ya find it?"

Max explained what he and his friends had been doing the past two days on the Three Mile Reef. He told him about the hammerhead shark.

"Damned scavengers," the old man grumbled. "That stretch's crawlin' with 'em."

"It was right in the sand. I've been down on that reef a hundred times and never saw a trace of sunken treasure."

"Storm last week probably stirred up the bottom. No telling what's under that sand. When I was a sprite like you, this woulda been right after the big hurricane of, I guess it was 1918, I was spear fishin' down around where Lauderdale-by-the-Sea is now. Wasn't nothin' there back then. Found a Spanish scabbard layin' right on top of the sand, plain as day, not ten yards off the beach. Musta been three hundred years old."

"I stopped at the village and showed it to Billy. He said Matty Fitt had one just like it. Who's Matty Fitt?"

He looked at Grandma Kate. Her face had gone white. Grandpa Zack's had done just the opposite. His features darkened like a storm cloud passing in front of the sun. His face trembled and his eyes filled with fury. He turned on Max.

"You listen to me, boy. You stay away from Matthew Fitt. That man is nothing but trouble."

"Billy said you and him were friends when you were kids."

"*Were!* That was a long time ago. Matty went bad. I'm telling you now to stay away from him. Do you hear me?"

Max had never seen his grandfather so angry.

"Yes, sir," he said with a quiet voice.

That night he dreamed he kissed Delray Chance at The Cove.

Et Tu Brady

Chapter Thirty-One

WALTER DEAN LOOKED like SpongeBob SquarePants pacing in his double-breasted suit, shoulders hunched, hands buried deep in his pockets, pallid face glowering at bags of peeled organic carrot sticks, packages of Portobello mushrooms, and boxes of English hothouse cucumbers.

At that moment *hothouse* seemed like an absurd concept to the City Attorney, considering this *icehouse* had shrunken his gonads to the size of salted peanuts. Or perhaps his private parts had shriveled at the thought of spending the next twenty years in prison.

It so happened that Florida was the most corrupt state in America. Politicians were so morally challenged they had trouble spelling the word *ethics*. *"Is it one x or two?"* Tallahassee was totally in the pockets of big money developers and insurance companies. State lawmakers dealt with their malfeasance problem by passing laws that basically made corruption legal. Nonetheless, the FBI was having a high time. The list of dirty *public servants* being locked behind bars was growing faster than a Chia Pet.

Dirty fit Dean like a second skin. Not that he didn't rationalize. After twenty years, he considered payoffs a perk of the job. They balanced the scales between public and private employment.

Without them he couldn't afford to devote his life to the people's business. Until now he'd lost exactly zero sleep over the million or so dollars he'd pocketed from Austin Ball, Jr.

The cash was safe and sound, tucked away in a numbered Panamanian bank account. But now, thanks to Rose Becker, he was having visions of being marched out of City Hall in shackles and joining the rogue's gallery of mayors, county commissioners, sheriffs, and school board members who'd been disgraced and destroyed.

Destroyed!

He wondered if he was being paranoid. Paranoia didn't explain Junior Ball's bizarre behavior. The word *schizophrenic* kept popping into Dean's head. He had called Ball an hour ago to recount his awkward confrontation with Becker at the City Commission meeting. Junior set up a rendezvous.

"Titty Room?" Dean repeated. "You want to meet at a strip club."

Now they were standing in the produce department at Costco. While Dean contemplated being violated by his future cellmate, Junior's eyes were riveted on a trio of coeds wearing Nova Southeastern University T-shirts.

"See that, Walter? College girls are going braless again. Just like the good old days."

"We've got more serious things to think about," Dean said, his shoulders hunched against the cold.

Ball reluctantly tore his eyes off the students and narrowed them on Dean. The City Attorney could see his rage. His disposition had shifted in the bat of an eye. *Classic schizoid.*

"You know that cocksucker from *The Lauderdale News* set us up," Junior said through clenched teeth. "Albino bastard lit the fuse on that bitches tampon and she put my name out at a public meeting. He knows I can't sue his newspaper now for yellow journalism. Goddamn press. Tate's gonna wish he never heard my name."

He pulled out his cell phone and pecked a number. Dean heard him say "Darnell" before he turned away and walked over by a pallet piled high with sacks of Vidalia onions. He spoke in a subdued tone for about sixty seconds. When he returned his mood was sanguine again.

"That'll stop the bitch from yapping about me like a little dog?"

"Rose Becker's more Pit Bull than Pekinese," Dean said, his tone laced with grudging admiration. "She's only been in office a few months, but she's very smart. Has a gym down on the beach. Quite a looker, too."

Junior was quiet for a moment. "Is there some way to stonewall her?"

"I can try to put her off, but she's extremely persistent."

"What if I go after her? File some paper."

Dean shook his head. "She's immune. Public servant doing her job. You'd be asking for trouble."

"Correct me if I'm wrong, Walter, but we wouldn't be here if we didn't already have trouble."

"Going after a city commissioner would be insane. Forget it or we're finished doing business."

Junior turned on Dean and raised a sudden hand, like an abusive father. Walter recoiled. Ball's lips drew back in a malevolent smile. Junior was as refined as a kick between the legs.

"What are you afraid of, counselor? Think I'm gonna hit you? Well, listen closely. You talk to me like that again and I'm gonna slap you silly. I don't give a flying fuck if your fat wife and two fat kids are standing there watching. You're in this all the way, Mr. City Attorney. I go down, you go with me. Understand?"

Walter lowered his eyes, a supplicant before his master. Junior was right. He knew now he was, in fact, at the mercy of a psychopath.

"I'm gonna put a hook in that fitness skank's mouth," Ball said.

Dean kept his eyes down. His face was red as the vine-ripened tomatoes in the bin on his left. He took several long breaths, deep in thought, a lawyer in dire need of a very large loop hole. Finally he spoke without looking up.

"Maybe we can do an end run."

"What do you have in mind, Walter?"

Junior's voice was neutral now, his wrath come and gone as swift as a summer storm. His eyes were back on the college girls, as if nothing had happened, further reinforcing Dean's opinion of his mental state.

"Ever file a Dram Shop lawsuit?"

"Dram shop? You mean like a bar or saloon?"

"Rose Becker's boyfriend owns a bar down on the beach."

Ball's eyes shifted from the coeds to Dean. A light seemed to go on inside him and a phosphorescent smile kindled on his face.

"That's brilliant, Walter. Sorry about what I said before. You are a genius. Remind me to sweeten your pudding. Who is this guy?"

"Name's Brady."

Junior's brow knitted and he stood mute for a long time. Dean dug his hands deeper in his pockets. His *salted peanuts* had withered to the size of raisins.

"Brady?" Junior said after a while, his voice reflective. "I used to know a kid named Brady. Cocky prick. Major pain in the ass. Thought he was smarter than everybody." He snorted out a laugh. "Nah! That's too farfetched. Guy's name was Max. Max Brady."

"That's him."

Ball let out a loud belly laugh, startling the braless coeds, who were now examining eggplant a few feet away. They jumped at his roar and their breasts jiggled. Junior laughed again.

Et Tu Brady

Chapter Thirty-Two

ROSE BECKER BREEZED into the Sea Shanty wearing a black camisole tank top and leggings that clung to her like latex. The eyes of every soggy dollar in the bar swiveled in her direction, appraising her toned arms, trim tummy, and curved hips.

Gordy was serving drinks to a crew of oversized men in baggy bathing suits. Their faces were red from the sun, their feet pink and flecked with sand. They looked to be in their mid-to-late twenties and athletic. All of them were heavily tattooed, wore their ball caps backwards, and draped with plenty of bling. Gordy guessed they were on a marathon pub crawl that wouldn't end until Super Bowl Sunday. The tallest of them seemed familiar, but he couldn't quite place him. An action film star, maybe.

Brady got back to the Shanty a few minutes after Rose came in. He was starting to feel the effects of too little sleep and too much sensory overload. This time last night he was stoking a fire and setting up his tent on the roof, looking forward to a long night doing bad things to Rose. Since then his life had taken a sharp turn in the wrong direction. He'd looked down on the corpse of his childhood friend. Been hired to defend his childhood sweetheart. Been kissed by her. Committed burglary. And spent more hours in tattoo parlors than he imagined possible. The only thing he had to show for it was a vague tip about some girl with a Latin phrase inscribed on her leg. Running his little beach bar and making love to Rose seemed like such simple pleasures now.

When Gordy saw him walk in his face broke out in a lopsided grin, like a dog wagging its tail when its master comes home. Brady smiled too, relieved to find his bar still open and doing brisk business. Compared to the trembling drunkard of that morning, Gordy looked like a new man. After a long day nursing tipplers, he appeared to be sound and sober. The Prairie Oyster had done its job.

Brady stepped behind the bar. He checked the galley and then the register. Everything seemed ship shape. The Shanty was crowded. Business was good. Even with an economy in the outhouse, alcohol remained the ether of the masses.

"Well done, Gordo," he said and noticed his bartender puff up. "Just keep an eye out for anybody too drunk to drive. Call a cab if you need to."

"Always, boss." Gordy nodded toward the far end of the bar. "By the way…"

She didn't have Penelope Peacock's rippling abs or baseball biceps, but Rose's ethereal face and hourglass physique never failed to stir him. And, unlike Penelope, he was pretty sure she couldn't beat him up.

He stepped down the bar. "Can I get you something, miss?"

"Whatcha got in mind, big boy?"

He slapped his palms and rubbed them together like an evil sorcerer conjuring his genie.

"Well, my dear, I can mix you the *perfect* martini. Or the world's *greatest* margarita. Or, if you prefer a religious experience, there's *always* Purple Jesus."

"Purple Jesus?"

"One part grape juice, one part ginger ale, one part vodka, three parts Everclear grain alcohol, add sliced fruit and stir. Drink a pitcher and you are guaranteed to see Jesus."

"Sounds heavenly.'

"Sounds sacrilegious," a voice slurred.

It was the tall soggy dollar with the action hero aura. A gold crucifix the size of an elephant's tooth hung from a thick gold chain around his neck. He looked like a guy accustomed to being fawned over by women. He plopped onto the stool next to Rose and did something with his face that might have been a leer.

"Darlin' you shouldn't make jokes about our Lord and savior Jesus Christ."

Rose took one glance at him then looked at Brady, who smiled at her.

"I just work here, lady," he said and plucked a bottle of water from the cooler. He set it on the bar and retreated to the cash register to help Gordy tabulate the day's receipts.

The big man leaned over close enough to lick Rose's ear, and whispered. "Where you been all my life, sexy thing?"

She uncapped the water bottle and took a sip, studiously ignoring him. Her admirer reached into his pocket, removed a sodden one hundred dollar bill, and slapped it down on the bar in front of her. Rose continued to disregard him. He smacked down two more Benjamins.

"If you're lookin' for a religious experience, I got one for ya," he persisted, pronouncing the *x* in *experience* like *sh.*

Rose wasn't one to blush, but her face did color. She spoke without returning his gaze. "You want a religious experience, have one of your pals drive you south on A1A to the Church of the Sea."

This time the big man threw down three hundreds. Even sitting, he seemed to swagger. "What's it gonna cost me to see what's under that leotard."

Rose finally looked at him. "You don't have enough money."

She glared down the bar at Brady, still counting cash at the register. He grinned and continued his calculations. The drunk was about Brady's height, wrapped in about forty pounds more muscle. His forearms were thick as tree limbs, one of which was embellished with an ornate tattoo – *WWJD.* He sported a gold band on his left ring finger. One of his posse staggered over and clapped the flat of his hand on the taller man's shoulder.

"Hey, honey, don't you recognize this dude?"

Rose looked at the *dude*, who ogled back at her through glassy, arrogant eyes.

"Should I?" She said it with a crispy glint, as if her hobby was busting the balls of narcissistic men. His comrade howled with false frivolity. He sounded like a dog barking.

"This girl's got snap, dude," he said and slapped the big man's back again. "Finally met a babe that don't know you. Smack down."

The rest of his crew *oooohhhed* at the dude, who smirked and took a pull on the Pabst Blue Ribbon he was strangling by its long-neck. Swaying on the stool, he pulled out more currency and spanked the bar with it.

"Don't be such a buzz kill, baby. Come on back to the St. Regis with me. I'll show you who the hell I am."

Rose looked at him and sighed. "Listen, *dude*, you could be a Kardashian for all I care. I came here for a bottle of water. Why don't you go drink your beer with your buddies – even though you do look like you've already exceeded the legal limit."

"Don't you watch television, sugar?" said another one of his friends. "Lance Jeffries? Mr. Quarterback? Alabama Crimson Tide? Heisman Trophy? Arizona Cardinals? MVP? Pro Bowl? Star of Gatorade, Nike, and Cadillac commercials."

If Rose was impressed she hid it well. "I hope you're proud of yourself, Lance. I understand the NFL kills three thousand cows a year just to make its footballs. By the way, can you get me Tim Tebow's autograph?"

"Tim Tebow wears Lance Jeffries pajamas," one of the pack chimed in.

"What's the usual procedure, Lance? Do I bow down or just laugh in your face."

The quarterback seemed at a loss for words. Girls didn't talk like that to star quarterbacks. Then he smiled and regained traction.

"Come on, honey. You're so fine it hurts just lookin' at ya. Let's get it started. I wanna play in your garden."

Rose stared at the football hero with an expression of disbelief. "Does that stuff really work?"

Lance winked. "Never fails."

212

"I cringe to think women actually fall for that crap. I don't get it. I guess some girls just want your notch on their belt so they can brag to their friends. 'I did Lance the quarterback.'"

"More than you can count, doll."

Rose pointed to the tattoo on his forearm. "Tell me, Lance, is that Latin?"

The quarterback let out a short laugh that might have been a hiccup. "You don't know much do you, sweet pea? *WWJD* means *What Would Jesus Do.*"

Rose giggled derisively. "You're joking, right?"

Lance's face suddenly turned stony. He massaged his big gold crucifix. "I never joke about Jesus."

"Well, Lance, I might not be as religious as you pretend to be, but I know one thing Jesus would *not* do. Especially if he was wearing a wedding ring. He wouldn't be in a bar trying to pick up *sweet peas.*"

A ribbon of Pabst shot from Lance Jeffries nostrils. He slammed his bottle on the bar, picked up one of the hundred dollars bills, and wiped his face with it.

"You got a sassy mouth, girl. What the hell do *you* do, anyway?"

Rose pointed down the bar at Brady. "See that tall guy? I do him."

Lance scoffed with bored disdain. "That old dog?"

"Don't laugh, *dude.* That old dog is twice the man you'll ever be."

Brady stepped down the bar and stood across the counter eye-to-eye with the NFL quarterback. Lance sneered at him.

"I could put you six feet under, old fella, with both hands tied behind my back."

"Four-and-a-half," Brady said.

"What?"

"Graves. Did you know they're actually only four-and-a-half feet deep."

A muscle the size of a golf ball twitched in Lance's jaw. "Then I'll put you four-and-a-half feet down."

"Why should I believe that? You were wrong about six feet."

"You're as big a wise ass as your girlfriend, mister?"

Brady reached out a hand. "Let me take your bottle."

Jeffries pulled back his beer. "I ain't finished."

"Lance, did you know that if a scorpion touches one drop of alcohol it will go crazy and sting itself to death? Give me that before you hurt yourself."

The football player let out a scornful laugh. Brady countered with an indulgent smile.

"Ever hear of Penelope Peacock?" he said.

"What are you goin' on about, old timer?"

"If you're not outa here in ten seconds, I'm gonna call Penelope and she is gonna come over here and beat you like a longshore-man, which I will record on my cell phone and have up on YouTube before you get to the emergency room. Whadya think about that, Mr. MVP?"

Lance Jeffries stared at Brady with red eyes then laughed again, this time with the falsetto shriek of a hyena. When no one else joined in he turned to his entourage.

"Come on, boys, let's get out of this hoe shack."

The group was stumbling toward the door when Brady called after them. "Hang on, Lance. Gordy, what do these boys owe?"

Gordy was still at the register. He did a quick tally. "Eighty-eight dollars, Max."

Lance stepped back to the bar and grabbed the stack of hundreds he'd slapped in front of Rose. He plucked out one greenback, threw it down, and stuffed the rest in his pocket.

"Keep the change. Twelve bucks oughta be enough to buy a blowjob from the tramp."

Jeffries drained his beer, cocked his right arm, positioned the Pabst bottle behind his right ear, and let it fly against the wall behind the bar. A perfect spiral. You could see why he was MVP. The bottle exploded like a gunshot. Shards of glass flew everywhere. He raised his arms triumphantly.

"Touchdown, Jeffries!"

Lance turned toward the door. Before he got to it, Brady vaulted over the counter and sprang toward the football player. Without slowing down he grabbed the back of his T-shirt with one hand and his right elbow with the other and rushed forward. Lance's forehead hit the door jamb with a dull thud and the star of SportsCenter, Monday Night Football, and Coca Cola commercials grunted and sank to his knees like he'd run into a goal post without his helmet. One of his buddies caught him before he keeled over.

"Hey, man, that's roughing the quarterback."

"More like intentional grounding," said Max.

"You just assaulted an NFL superstar," another posse member barked. He flipped open his cell phone. "I'm calling the cops."

"Be my guest."

Brady reached into his back pocket, extracted his own phone and snapped a photograph of Jeffries kneeling by the Shanty door. His senses seemed to be elsewhere. An egg the size of a shot glass was surfacing at the center of his forehead, like a volcano rising from the sea. He held the phone up to the others.

"This photograph will be in tomorrow's papers, complete with tweeting birds, spinning stars, and that molehill growing out of his head? Do you really want to turn it into a mountain? The headline will read *MVP Propositions Young Lady – KO'd By Old Timer.* Forget about *What Would Jesus Do?* The question's gonna be: *What Will Nike Do?* And *Cadillac?* And *Gatorade?*"

The group mulled Brady's words for several seconds. He pegged them as hangers-on, probably ex-college teammates. Lance's entourage. Not uncommon among sports superstars. Sycophants surrounding their luminary like minor planets orbiting a sun. Heaping praise and adulation on him in exchange for drinks, meals, airfare, hotel rooms, and women he discarded like table scraps.

One of them looked at Max. "You got some bark on you, mister. But you shouldn't have done that. Mark my words, you're gonna be sorry."

Two others pulled Lance to his feet. "Come on, tough guy. Let's get out of here."

When they'd gone, Rose slipped off her stool and reached up to squeeze Brady's face between her hands.

"You are so brave," she said with mock-veneration.

He swelled up a little. "My dear, you just have to know how to handle people," he said with mock-humility. "I find charm goes a long way."

"It certainly does. You are my knight in, er, raggedy short pants." She planted a passionate kiss on his lips then sniffed. For an instant he thought she might be detecting Delray's scent. "You smell good. What are you wearing?"

"Johnson and Johnson."

"Cologne?"

"Baby powder."

"I like it."

"Did you know baby powder was invented by Joyce Kilmer's father?"

"The NFL quarterback?"

"No, silly. The football player was Billy Kilmer. I'm talking about the poet. *I don't think that I will ever see a thing as lovely as a tree.*"

"I don't think that's exactly how it goes, but nice try, Brady." She kissed him again and headed for the door, blithely calling back over her shoulder. "Gotta go. Pilates class in five minutes."

Et Tu Brady

Chapter Thirty-Three

SEYMOUR TATE SMOKED a joint for lunch and spent the rest of the afternoon drinking gin gimlets and daydreaming about Rose Becker. The truth was he'd been spellbound by her for months. Ever since he first layed eyes on her at her swearing-in ceremony. He saw at once that she had come equipped with a few extra rungs in the double helix of her genetic code. She was clearly a thoroughbred. And wholesome as a bowl of Cheerios. With her finely etched features, feline grace, and an anatomy as supple as a vowel, she reminded him of Katy Perry, minus the outlandish garb and bowling ball breasts. Even her name was perfect. A majestic Rose at full blossom. She had become the secret object of Seymour's most ardent desires.

The attraction wasn't purely physical. Rose was also as rational as arithmetic. Her analytical skills were daunting. At City Commission hearings she cross-examined witnesses like a machine gunner, firing question after question until the most complex issues were reduced to their essence. Recalcitrant department heads learned fast that if they tried to evade or obfuscate, this Rose had thorns.

Her evisceration of Walter Dean was the most recent example. Watching Rose slash through the City Attorney's bullshit this morning had given him a bigger rush than a bowl of Afghan hash. She'd painted him into a corner and opened the door for Seymour to get his story published. By this time tomorrow anyone with half-a-brain – and there were more than a few of those in City Hall – would see Walter Dean and Austin Ball Jr. were in cahoots. No way they survived. They were screwed.

To celebrate he'd stoked-up a fat doobie and spent the post meridian tottering on a bar stool at the Downtowner, a cool, dark watering hole on New River in the shadows of the Andrews Avenue Bridge. He sipped gimlets – two parts Plymouth Gin, one part sweetened lime juice, *Rose's,* of course – while he hammered out the final version of his slip-and-fall exposé on a laptop. Just after six he e-mailed the piece to his editor at *The Lauderdale News.* If the paper's chickenshit lawyers gave it their imprimatur it would be the next morning's lead story.

Seymour shut down his computer, stuffed it in his backpack, and staggered out of the Downtowner. He should have been elated, but a bleakness hovered over him like tomorrow's hangover. He felt as zestless as a bowl of day old potato chips. He looked it, too, dressed in the same wrinkled jeans and yellow Hawaiian shirt he'd woken up in this morning. *And you wonder why you'll never get to first base with Rose Becker?* He made his way across the bridge and headed toward home on the footpath along New River. The sun was just down and the water was pretty in the early evening. Festive lights reflected off its black veneer. As he walked he listened to the gentle sound of boat wakes rippling against the seawall bank. He didn't get far.

America's High Holy Day – Super Bowl Sunday – was coming fast and the mood downtown was carnivalesque. An outdoor bash was in full swing at the Riverfront, an open-air collection of bars and restaurants overlooking the water. Several thousand celebrants had gathered. A flotilla of yachts glutted the river carrying stars from film, fashion, music and sports. Superstar quarterback Lance Jeffries was supposed to be the Grand Marshall, but Tate didn't see any sign of him. A giant fireworks display exploded over the procession and he stopped to watch the pyrotechnics.

Banjo Billy's Ragtime Bar was only a few paces from the water. Seymour ducked inside and replenished himself with another gimlet before lurching back onto the river path. Whistling *I'm Looking Over A Four-Leaf Clover,* he tripped along in a spasmodic gate, wafting through the crowd, aimless as a weather balloon. He stopped at two more bars along the way and downed gimlets in each, which by now he needed like a fish needed fresh air. He followed a bend in the river past the Performing Arts Center and then turned away from the waterfront and entered the seedy neighborhood he called home.

All the while his gin-soaked brain fantasized about Rose and the things he wanted to do with her, or to her, or, if nothing else, just watch her do. Knowing he never would. He decided when he got home he'd call *Pretty Women*, the escort service on *Craigslist* he patronized occasionally. Maybe he'd get lucky and they'd send that sweet brunette again. The one with the nice firm body. She called herself B.J. and certainly lived up to the name.

Then he realized he had two major problems. First, B.J.'s last visit had cost him five hundred dollars. At the moment, his Visa card was tapped out. That may have been for the best. He doubted he'd be capable of getting his money's worth without a boost from one of those little blue pills. Unfortunately, his supply was as tapped out as his credit card. He'd been foiled by the dreaded double-ED – Economic *and* Erectile Dysfunction. The more he thought about Rose, though, the less it mattered. The prospect of working with her to bring down Walter Dean and Junior Ball was almost better than sex. Almost.

The sky was black by the time he reached Coontie Court. He lived in the Riverside Apartments, a rundown property as gloomy as a crematorium. Two brown one-story buildings, five-units each, separated by a crabgrass courtyard. Three coats of new paint would have made it look only dilapidated. Tenants here kept to themselves. Several windows were covered with tinfoil. The only neighbor Tate knew by name was Harvey next door, an overweight nerd who worked the graveyard shift at Blockbuster and spent his days holed-up in his apartment watching DVDs of *Star Wars* and *Lord of the Rings*.

Seymour careened off the street and zigzagged down the dregs of what had once been a concrete walkway, laughing to himself as he searched for his key. *If I fall and break my arm I can hire Junior Ball to sue the city.* He was still chuckling when he heard a trombone voice come from the shadows.

"Seymour."

Gloppy with gin, Tate thought it was Harvey doing his Darth Vader impersonation. He unleashed a dopey giggle and slurred the magic phrase.

"May th' forsh be with ya."

A silhouette emerged from the umbra and Tate realized it was not Harvey. The hulking shadow was as wide as a cement mixer and his head seemed to be attached directly to his shoulders.

"You fucked with the wrong people, Seymour."

"Who are you?"

"Do not fuck with them again."

It happened in slow motion. Tate watched the figure raise his right arm. His brain told him to spring backwards, but his body wasn't listening. The shadow was holding something in its hand. As it came down on him he realized what.

Blackjack!

He felt a crack on his forehead followed by instant searing pain. Then stars and pinwheels and roman candles flared. Then not anything.

Et Tu Brady

Chapter Thirty-Four

THE LIME GREEN Honda Civic was tucked into the dark end of the cul-de-sac facing the white-columned Colonial. Demonika was behind the wheel. Lazarus was beside her in the passenger seat.

"How much time do we have?" he said.

"I called Nudey Judy this afternoon. She said she greeted her cousin and her husband at the door holding Midnight in her arms."

"Was she naked?"

"She didn't say, but they apparently flipped when they saw her pussy."

Lazarus cackled. "You are such a freak."

"Alice and Bert started sneezing and immediately booked a room at the Harbor Beach Marriott. With the Super Bowl in town they had to pay a fortune. Judy said they were super pissed. She pretended to feel bad. To make up for it she and her husband are taking them to Martarano's for dinner."

"I hear that place is expensive."

"My father takes his bimbos there," Demonika said. "Martarano knows him by name. It impresses them."

"Why does he want to impress hookers?"

"He prefers to call them escorts."

"Why's he trying to impress paid escorts?"

"What can I tell you? The man's twisted. His idea of art is pasting thousand dollar bills in picture frames. His only complaint about Martarano's is it takes two hours to get served, but the tarts never have more than twenty minutes of conversation in them."

"That's good for us." Lazarus leaned over and draped his left arm around Demonika's seat back and started to slip his right hand under her short skirt. "It'll give us time to trade blood in their bed."

She slapped him away. "Maybe you should call you're little troll whore to come join you."

Lazarus raised an eyebrow and seemed to be entertaining the prospect when a pair of red lights backed out of the driveway of the Desmond home. They were attached to a black Lincoln Town Car. It pulled away and headed toward the beach road. When it disappeared around the corner, they climbed from the Honda. Lazarus tilted his seat forward and a big black Labrador Retriever sprang from the car. Demonika had borrowed it from the shelter. She called him Yank.

They had swapped their black Goth garb for attire more appropriate to chichi Harbor Beach. He sported khaki shorts and a red golf shirt with an alligator on the breast. She'd donned a green cotton halter top with a short yellow skirt. They sauntered up the street like a young neighborhood couple taking the family pooch for a stroll. When they reached Jake and Judy Desmond's house they let Yank sniff around and lift his leg on a couple of shrubs while Lazarus scanned the street for prying eyes.

"Clear," he said.

The driveway was guarded by a tall ficus hedge and they ducked behind it. Demonika used the key she'd palmed off the kitchen counter to unlock the front door. The big house was dark. Demonika followed the path she'd taken that morning, minus, thankfully, the sight of Nudey Judy's ripply brown ass. They entered the kitchen. The sweet scent of potpourri permeated the room. The only light came from a bulb burning beneath the black hood above a large modern stove. They heard a muffled crash.

Demonika lurched backwards toward the door. "What was that?"

"Relax," said Lazarus. "The refrigerator. Icemaker's dumping new ice."

She took a breath and returned to the center of the room. The kitchen chairs had spindletop backs and she looped the dog's leash over one of them.

"The cash is in that drawer on the right side of the island counter."

Lazarus went straight to the drawer, jerked it open, and laughed out loud.

"Bingo!" He reached in with both hands and pulled out a green ball of currency the size of a cabbage. "They stuff greenbacks in here like supermarket coupons."

"Do you think they're paying taxes on it."

He threw the loot onto the black granite countertop. "No way, baby. These people are criminals, like most of the bastards who live in houses like this. We're doing a public service. I'm like Robin Hood. You're Maid Marian. We steal from the rich and give to the poor."

"That would be us," Demonika said. She started sorting the bills into stacks according to denomination. "It's mostly tens and twenties."

"Here's some hundreds," said Lazarus. "Damn. There's thousands."

"From what Judy said, there's a lot more around here."

"We'll work our way through the house. First we check the ground floor, then we'll move upstairs."

Just then Ernestine, the red Hemingway cat Demonika rented to Nudey Judy, padded around the corner on her six-toed paws. She entered the kitchen and saw the big black dog and stopped cold. Yank saw her and growled. Demonika saw them both and cried out.

"Oh, shit!"

Ernestine arched her back and hissed. The black dog barked. The cat bolted. Demonika lunged for the leash, but too late. The dog took off in hot pursuit. The kitchen chair crashed to the ground and tumbled behind him like a wrecking ball. They vanished into the living room.

Demonika cringed. She remembered the expensive furniture and fixtures. By the time she and Lazarus reached the living room the place was a disaster. A three-foot tall Geisha had been demolished. A small end table was flipped upside down, its glass top shattered. The chair had caromed into a cabinet and exploded its glass door. Dozens of tchotchkes lay in pieces on the floor. The room was strewn with gold-leafed ceramic figures crumbled to bits. The black Lab chased Ernestine up a staircase to the second floor, leaving devastation in their wake.

"My God!" Lazarus said. "They're gonna know they've been hit the second they walk in the door. Get that mutt and tie him up in the garage. Let's scour this place and get the hell outa here."

After that they didn't even try to be discreet, rushing through the house like kids on an Easter egg hunt. Lazarus dumped the contents of an antique desk in an alcove off the kitchen and a cache of twenty dollar bills fell to the floor. Demonika found a clear plastic ziplock bag in the kitchen freezer containing several thousands in hundred dollar bills. A straw decorative basket sitting atop an étagère in the den hid a small fortune. A *Nordstrom* shopping bag in the foyer closet was crammed with currency.

Demonika screeched in delight. "We're rich."

She followed Lazarus up the staircase to the second floor. There were three bedrooms and an office. They began dumping out every drawer. Stacks of twenties and fifties fell out of the bottom right drawer of the office desk. A golf bag standing in the corner had bundles of cash wrapped with rubberbands stuffed in its zipper pockets. In a walk-in closet off the master bedroom Lazarus found a Bottega Veneta shoebox gorged with more hundred dollar bills, so many he couldn't begin to fathom how much it added up to. He tucked the shoebox under his arm.

"We just hit the lottery, baby. Let's go."

Demonika was standing on the far side of the room beside the Desmond's king-sized bed.

"Not so fast," she said, her voice seductive, bewitching, her dark eyes glistening, like she was channeling Morticia Addams. She reached behind her neck and her green halter top fell to the floor.

Then she slid out of her little yellow skirt and collapsed onto the big bed.

"Come to me," she purred and extended her arms, "my *Romeo of the Night*!"

Lazarus smiled, dropped the box of cash, and was out of his clothes in a jiffy.

"Call me Robin Hood."

Et Tu Brady

Chapter Thirty-Five

IT WAS WELL past midnight when Brady buttoned up the Sea Shanty, climbed into the Jeep, and took the five minute drive over the Las Olas Bridge to Siesta Lane. He turned right and proceeded down the long dead end street to Victor Gruber's sprawling home. The lights were out inside and he tramped through the dark dewy lawn back to the dock where his boat was moored.

The *Victoria II* was a graceful 1993 Hinckley Sou'wester Sloop, blue fiberglass hull, center cockpit, sixty one feet stem to stern, sixteen feet abeam, six foot draft with keel up, twelve with it down. The cabin had three staterooms – two forward and one aft – and two heads. It could sleep nine, though he'd never been at sea with more than one passenger – Rose Becker. The main salon was a warm space containing a lot of polished teak dominated by a U-shaped settee with Evergreen glove-leather upholstery and a drop-leaf table. The galley was rearward of the settee; a stainless steel gas stove, microwave oven, refrigerator/freezer, and custom dish and pantry cupboards.

Brady fished a jar of dry roasted almonds from the pantry, twisted the cap off a Budweiser, and retreated to his stateroom in the aft compartment. He'd bought the boat several years ago after his first sloop – the *Victoria* – sank in a storm off the windward coast of Little Exuma, an out-island in the eastern Bahamas. At the time he was still in a deep state of grief over the death of his wife, Victoria, in the World Trade Towers collapse. Victoria was always near the surface of his consciousness. But now, climbing into his bunk, it was Rose who monopolized his thoughts. He was gaga about her and he knew she harbored similar feelings for him. They'd been spending four or five nights a week together, on his boat or at her apartment. Neither had broached the idea of becoming fulltime roommates but, alone like this in the mute night, he felt hollow without her.

Then another face popped into his head. Delray! *Why did she kiss me? Why did I kiss her back?* He engaged in a short bout of self-flagellation before settling on an answer. *She's so fragile. She has no one else to lean on. I was protecting her.* If he'd rebuffed her, he reasoned, it would have been too devastating for her. *Keep telling yourself that, Brady. Maybe someday you'll believe it.* The truth was he had felt a throb of…what? He wasn't sure. He could not deny a spark of the childhood attraction between them remained. The sweet longings of youth may have gone into hibernation, but apparently had not died. Some people are just drawn to each other. Maybe it was chemical.

What about Rose, though? *Is it possible to be in love with two women at the same time?* He supposed it was. Then he remembered his grandmother's oft-repeated admonition about greed. *"He who coveteth all, shall loseth all."*

Brady lay there thinking about his grandparents and that black night long ago. *It was the gold that killed them.* Just as the gold may have killed Ben Chance last night? Just as it did kill the pirate Ned Pike. *Ned Pike.* He remembered Michael Fury's diary. It was still in the Jeep.

He hopped down from the bunk and took the stern companionway to the deck and ran barefoot through the wet lawn to fetch it. When he returned he switched on a blue-shaded reading lamp on the wall behind his pillow and extracted the sheaf of papers. He popped a roasted almond in his mouth, washed it down with a swig of beer, and began where he'd left off reading just before dawn in the tent on Rose's rooftop.

Fury's shipmates had been slaughtered by the native warriors but the boy's life was temporarily spared after he saved the young Indian maiden. The band of aboriginals marched him along the creek, prodding him with sharp spears and clubbing him without provocation. They traveled a league or more before reaching a small village at a fork where the creek veered into a bay or wide river.

Brady layed the manuscript on his chest. The creek Michael Fury described seemed eerily familiar. Several hundred yards from the ocean's edge, it ran parallel to the sea for a considerable distance. He was again staggered by the prospect that the Indian creek could be one and the same as his own Whiskey Creek. He picked up the diary.

The Indian village had been decimated by the storm. Women and children were weeping. Men were busy rebuilding small oval structures held together with mud and reeds and thatched with palm leaves. They looked to be family dwellings, perhaps three dozen in all, each approximately twenty five feet across with door openings about four feet high and three feet wide. At the center of the village, atop a mound of shells the height of a man, another group worked on a larger structure easily four times the size of the others. This seemed to be some sort of village hub.

The appearance of the young captive drew the instant attention of all inhabitants, who quit their work and surrounded him. Fury was forced into a low-roofed pen not ten feet in diameter constructed from thick bamboo stalks. Imprisoned like a caged animal, the villagers encircled the coop and peered at him through the bars. Fury sensed many of them had never seen a European before. A sobbing woman brandished a dead infant in her arms and looked at him with hateful eyes, as though she blamed him for the Devil Wind that had taken her child. He was paralyzed with fear, recalling Captain Ned Pike's warning about the natives. *"They be cannybals."*

As day turned to night, the entire population descended on the center of the storm ravaged encampment. A party of warriors opened the gate to the pen. Fury pushed back against the bamboo wall as far as he could squeeze. Two natives rushed in and grabbed him by his ankles. He kicked and cursed but resistance was futile. He was dragged out and hauled up onto the shell mound where the Indians lashed his arms over a platform the size of a tree stump.

A line of eight men stepped to the center of the mound and sat in a semicircle facing the prisoner, followed by four women carrying a large bowl fashioned from the shell of a sea tortoise. Steam was rising from it. The women placed the vessel on the ground in front of the eight and another man stepped forth whose face and body was painted with colourful dyes. He appeared to be some sort of priest or shaman. He ladled black liquid from the bowl and poured it into a smaller whelk shell from which each of the eight men took turns imbibing. Then, while Fury lay prostrate over the stump, they drank more. The villagers watched raptly, chanting gibberish which Fury took to be pagan prayer. Finally the men – who seemed to compose a tribal council of some sort – rose to their feet. Each began patting his stomach and shouting: *'Heemmmm!'* One by one they started vomiting projectiles of the black drink. The crowd flew into a frenzy, as though it was a sporting competition to see who could spew the farthest.

The natives cheered and danced, growing more maniacal as the exhibition continued. Men and women began dropping to the ground and fornicating in the dirt. When the villagers was at fever pitch the tall native that led the party that murdered me crew mates stepped forth and raised an ax. I knew at once that these was me final seconds. I thought of me mother and father and found succor in the knowledge I would be with them again this very day.

Then, in the blink of an eye, I felt an impact and waited for me head to tumble. But, to me great astonishment and confusion, it remained attached to me shoulders. The blow I felt had not been the blade on me neck, but a body. I heard a female voice, though I could not decipher her words. I soon deduced that it belonged to the maiden, the girl I had liberated from Mr. Cobb's dagger. It sounded like she was engaged in heated debate with the tall warrior. Her words were rushed to the point of frantic and I fathomed the girl was pleading for me life, just as she had earlier in the day when they seized me. The warrior's speech was harsh and unyielding, yet, after a series of exchanges, I detected the intensity of his tone abate. The girl remained stretched across me back while their deliberations went on. Then, suddenly, she was gone.

Fury surmised his execution was imminent. He stared at a patch of shells below him and acquiesced to his fate. Within seconds his head would land on that very spot. The natives would probably impale it on a spear and put it on display like some kind of trophy. Much to his surprise, he found himself quite calm. Resigned to his dark fortune, he pondered whether he would feel pain when the ax fell. Would he remain conscious until his soul passed into the next world? Would he meet his parents in Heaven? Or would the almighty Lord dispatch him to Hades? Those thoughts were swirling in his mind when he felt hands clutch his arms and pull him harshly off the stump. Two warriors dragged him down off the shell mound and threw him back inside to the pen.

I scrambled on me knees to the bamboo bars and scoured the throng of naked heathens, searching for the maiden. Me eyes found her standing alone beside the creek. Staring at the cage. Staring at me. A serene smile graced her lovely face, a face more bonny than any I'd ever set eyes upon. In that instant me heart was given over to the girl whose name, I would learn, was Princess Nitcrosis.

Brady thought about the letter he and Delray found that afternoon in Ben's library from the Archivo General de Indias. Señor Juan Bautista Muñoz wrote *The Nemesis* sank *"approximately between your present-day Miami Beach north to Boca Raton."* Brady did some quick calculations. That was about a forty mile stretch. Whiskey Creek sat smack in the middle of it. And Three Mile Reef was just three miles north of the creek. Michael Fury could easily have drifted that distance in the storm before he washed up onto the beach. If Señor Muñoz was correct, Ned Pike's ship may well have gone down on or near the reef. Carrying, by today's standards, two billion dollars in gold and treasure. *Was it possible?*

Questions bounced around Brady's brain looking for answers they could not find until fatigue overtook him and his eyes drooped and closed and he was thirteen years old again.

Et Tu Brady

Chapter Thirty-Six

MAX NAVIGATED THE Boston Whaler down New River with Peanut at his side. They tacked left at Sailboat Bend and cruised up the river's North Fork, beneath the old swinging bridge, and continued until they glided up behind a dilapidated shack. The building was almost invisible, hidden in a shaggy thicket of unshorn vegetation. The place felt sinister, guarded on three sides by stands of wild bamboo and covered in an umbrella of shade cast by a tall schefflera tree. The only remotely innocent thing about it was a single six-foot tall sunflower laughing up at the summer sky.

There was no dock and they tied up to a cleat on the seawall, then hesitated. The cabin looked uninhabited. If anyone did live here, Max wasn't sure he wanted to meet them. They walked in fits-and-starts through tall brown grass toward the gloom. Cockleburs lashed their ankles and they had to be careful to step over large volcano-shaped piles of sugar sand constructed by armies of fire ants. When they reached the bamboo wall they wedged through a narrow notch and came out the other side next to a cabin window. Max tiptoed up and peered inside. He saw nothing but blackness.

"This place gives me the willies," Peanut whispered.

"The willies? That's something my grandpa would say."

"I'm serious. I've got goose bumps. This was a bad idea. Let's get out of here."

Max didn't argue. He was creeped out too. They were squeezing back through the bamboo when a gruff voice came from the shadows.

"Hold it right there!"

The boys stopped cold and turned wary eyes on a rustling in the vegetation. A gaunt old man emerged from the darkness. He looked like a hermit, or hobo, dressed in dirty white pants and a grimy long-sleeved linen shirt with the breast pocket torn off. His scraggly gray beard had a brown streak running down the middle. And he was holding a double-barreled shotgun, which was pointed it at them.

"What're you rapscallions doin' sneakin' round my house?" His voice sounded of whiskey and cigarettes. He spit out a jet of brown juice and wiped the beard with his shirtsleeve.

Peanut blurted: "Listen, mister, we didn't do nothing!"

"I should shoot you trespassin' piss-ants where you stand. You better tell me what yer doin' here."

Max had never stared a gun in the eye before. He tried to keep his voice steady.

"We're looking for Matty Fitt."

"Who be you?"

"Billy Panther told us about you. This is Peanut Strong. I'm Max Brady."

"Brady?" He seemed startled at the name. He eyed Max with suspicion. "Not related to Zack Brady, are ya?"

"He's my grandfather."

"Is he now?" He leaned right and shot another spurt of tobacco juice. "Zack know you're here?"

Max shook his head. "He told me to stay away from you."

Matty Fitt cackled. "Ain't surprised."

He lowered the shotgun and cast a brown-toothed smile at them, then stepped closer and studied Max's face for a long moment.

"So you are," he said. "I see it now. Katy Doyle. Look just like her baby brother, Buddy."

"You know my grandmother?"

"Ain't seen nor talked to neither of 'em in…" He stopped and thought. "…hell, must be goin' on fifty years now. Where'd the time go? There was a day when me and Zack and Katy was tight as ticks."

"Why does my grandfather hate you so much?"

Matty coughed out a hacking laugh and Max detected the not so faint odor of drink.

"Me and Zack was like brothers when we was youngsters. Nary a day passed we wasn't together."

"What happened?"

"We did a little bootleggin' together back in the Volstead days."

"What's Volstead?" Peanut said.

"Volstead Act. Eighteenth Amendment. Prohibition. Ran Canada whiskey and Havana rum 'tween Bimini and Whiskey Creek."

"Whiskey Creek?" Peanut said. "We water ski there."

Matty Fitt spit another jet into the weeds, leaving a fresh brown track on his beard. "How ya think it got its name?"

"You're lying, mister," Max said. "My grandfather isn't a criminal."

"Hell, boy, bootleggin' weren't no crime, really. Goddamned sheriff was the biggest rumrunner in the county. Zack and me was small timers. Then we had a fallin' out. Ain't talked since."

"Falling out over what?"

Matty stared at them through watery, red-rimmed eyes. A cruel smile crept across his face.

"That'd be me and Zack's little secret, wouldn't it?"

Max reeled at what he was hearing. Grandpa Zack a bootlegger? Bootleggers were gangsters. Al Capone was a bootlegger. Grandpa was no gangster. He went to church every morning since Max was old enough to remember.

Matty Fitt turned and, stiff as a rusty gate, made his way through the overgrowth to a door at the back of the ramshackle little house and stepped inside. The boys looked at each other, shrugged, and followed him. Matty waited just inside the door.

"You scamps housebroke?"

"Paper trained," said Peanut.

Max laughed. Matty didn't. He looked up at Peanut who, even though a full head taller, took a step back. Matty wagged a finger in his face.

"Sass me again, boy, you'll find I ain't so old I can't teach you a lesson."

The shack was as dark as a cave, except for a vagrant mote of sunlight slanting through a crack in a curtained window. The air was stale and smelled like it had been piped in from a Roman catacomb. When Max's eyes adjusted to the dark, though, he was astonished at what he saw. Unlike the decrepit exterior, the interior was like a museum. The room was surprisingly large and filled with marine artifacts. Sitting on a table at the center of the room was an old cannon encrusted in coral. A large brass ship's bell hung from a wooden rafter. Fastened to the wall above the fireplace was a worm-eaten figurehead of a naked woman's torso that looked to be from the prow of a very old sailing ship. Another entire wall was blanketed with a huge ancient map of the Caribbean, the Bahamas and *The Floridas*. Dozens of red X's were slashed along the peninsula's southeastern coastline from Hobe Sound to Biscayne Bay.

The boys examined the objects with wide-eyed fascination while Matty watched them from the door, a shadow framed against a blinding oblong of light. He let them absorb the scene for a few minutes before he limped to the middle of the room.

"Now you whippersnappers are gonna tell me what yer doin' here."

"Billy says you know about pirate treasure," Max said.

A sparkle came into Matty's cloudy gray eyes and he waved an arm in the air.

"See for yerselves. Nobody knows more about shipwrecks in these parts than Matthew Fitt."

He crossed the room, opened another door, and crooked a finger at them. The new room was windowless and darker than the first and, from what Max could see, only half as large. Matty switched on a lamp and the boys stared with open mouths. The walls were adorned with relics. Daggers, cutlasses, flintlocks, shackles, gaffs, grappling hooks, belaying pins, a cat 'o nine tales. He pulled open a drawer on a long sideboard and lifted out a small weathered chest bound with leather straps. Max and Peanut stepped closer and watched him place it on a round table in the middle of the room. He unhitched the straps and lifted the lid. The box was brimming with pearls, silver jewels, and gold coins. Max plucked out one of the coins. It looked familiar. The face was engraved in Spanish. The other side was struck with a cross almost identical to the one on the coins they found on Three Mile Reef. It must have been the same one Billy Panther told him about. Matty watched him examine it, his eyes keen and alert.

"More'n three hundred years old, that one."

"Where'd you get it?"

"Not ten miles from this very spot. Found it on a shallow reef off Lauderdale-by-the-Sea."

"Grandpa said he found a scabbard there once. After a big hurricane in…"

"Nineteen eighteen. I was with him. We was about yer age."

Max considered the words. He tried to imagine Grandpa Zack and Matty Fitt as boys. All he saw, though, were wrinkled faces on young bodies. He held up the coin and looked at Matty.

"Do you think there are more like this down there?"

"There's a king's ransom sittin' a stone's throw off Lauderdale Beach." Matty reached into the chest and grabbed a fistful of coins and pearls and let them cascade through his fingers, a flimflam man stoking his prey. "These is just crumbs from a banquet waitin' to be found." Max was still studying the coin with the cross. "Why so taken by that piece, young Brady?"

He looked in the old eyes and saw eager anticipation. He reached into his pocket and pulled out one of the coins they'd found. Matty snatched it from his fingers and shuffled to the lamp. He held his coin under the light next to Max's. The boy noticed his boozy haze had vanished and his breathing accelerated.

"Where'd you say you found this?" he said, his voice suddenly urgent.

Grandpa Zack's words rang in his ears. *"Matthew Fitt is nothing but trouble."* Lying didn't come natural to Max, but he thought one up fast.

"Lighthouse Point. Crabbing on the beach after the storm last week. Found it in the sand at low tide."

Matty stared at him with cold calculation. Max felt like he was looking right through him.

"Me and your granddaddy built us a skiff when we was young. Used to sail it out to the reefs. No aqualungs in them days. No goggles neither. Just a coupla kids free divin' and havin' adventures. Zack and me found quite a few Spanish coins like these. Your granddad had lungs like one of them Japanese pearl divers. Never saw nobody that could swim underwater long as him."

"Max too," Peanut volunteered, looking at his friend with admiration. "Claims he's half fish."

"After me and Zack fell out, I guess he lost the taste for treasure trovin'. Bought that fishin' boat and that piece a property up the river and married your grandma." Matty's sharp eyes turned soft and distant. "'Bout broke my heart, they did."

The words snapped Max out of his reverie. "Why's that?"

"Katy Doyle was a spirited beauty," he said, still holding the coins to the light. "Sparkled like a chest full a gold. Everything about her was bright and shiny. Zack and me was both crazy about her. But she never had eyes for me. It was always gonna be Zack. I never blamed her, really. Goin' with him was the smart thing. And Katy was nothin' if she weren't smart." He shook his head and gazed at the coins. "But that's ancient history. After I lost her, this become my siren song. Never gave up on findin' the motherlode. Read all the books. Even traveled to Madrid and London coupla times. Went through ancient archives looking for clues." Matty turned Max's gold piece in his fingers, examining it closely. "This is quite a find. I think I know where ya found it."

"You do?" Peanut blurted. "Where?"

Matty looked at the boys like they were a couple of fish. He'd dangled his bait in front of them and they'd bitten. Now he set the hook.

"Can't say."

"I told you we found it off Lighthouse Point," Max said.

"Just cause I'm old don't mean I'm stupid. And if you're Zack and Katy's grandbaby, you ain't stupid neither. That means you ain't tellin' me the truth. That *would* be stupid."

Max tried to maintain an innocent face. "I don't know what you mean."

"I know where you live. You two is river boys. You ain't crabbin' way up at Lighthouse Point."

"It's not so far."

"Thirty miles."

"That's nothing. Light travels eight hundred thirty thousand miles per second."

Peanut and Matty stared at him, the boy's brow arched in approval, the man's pinched in animus.

"I seen them air tanks in yer boat. You didn't find this on no beach. You been out on the reefs. Which one?"

"I told you. We found it by the lighthouse."

Matty glared at him then cast covetous eyes on the coin, flipping it between his fingers one more time before he handed it back to Max.

"You got some sap in ya, boy, I'll give ya that. Come back when yer ready to deal square with ol' Matty. I can help ya's, but it's a two way street. Till then get yer skinny asses the hell off my property."

A few minutes later Max and Peanut were cruising back down Sailboat Bend. They'd just navigated under the swinging bridge and were turning into the South Fork of New River when they saw a yellow boat. It was the Donzi that had run over Max the day before. The man called Buck was at the wheel. He was alone this time, shirtless, one heavy-muscled gladiator arm slung over the boat wall, the bronco tattoo bucking on his brawny chest. He looked lethal as a cobra. The two boats passed. Buck appraised them with malevolent black eyes. Max had the sensation of being sized up for a rope. Buck pointed his left hand like a gun, pulled the trigger, and an imaginary bullet came at them. Buck flashed a switchblade grin.

Peanut shivered. "You think he practices that look in the mirror?"

"I don't think he has to."

"Call me a pussy, but that guy scares the shit out of me."

"Me too."

Et Tu Brady

Chapter Thirty-Seven

THE NEXT MORNING Brady left Gordy in charge of the Sea Shanty again and headed for Plantation, a shady suburb one ZIP code west of Fort Lauderdale. He had an appointment with Francis U. "Fuzzy" Furbush, the private investigator whose card he and Delray found in Ben's treasure file. He'd called the number on the card and a woman with a young voice identified herself as Lilia Rodriguez. She said she was Furbush's assistant and scheduled a meeting for ten o'clock in the morning. As he drove he called to confirm. A man answered.

"Brady? Furbush. Sorry I missed ya. Lot going on. Busy as hell. Lilia says you wanna talk. Wait 'til ya get an eyeful of her. My protégé. Cute don't do her justice. Too bad about Chance. Got my theories. Very fishy. Runs deep. Very deep. When it blows, watch out. Gonna rock this town to its core. See ya when ya get here."

The line went dead before Brady could say a word. He considered stopping at a Walgreens Drug Store and picking Fuzzy up some Ritalin.

Furbush's office was in a shopping center on Broward Boulevard. He drove into the parking lot past a Starbucks, Chicken Kitchen, Hallmark Cards, Pinch-A-Penny Pools, a UPS Store, an optometrist office, and an ice cream parlor and turned into a spot in front of the Naughty 'N Nice Lingerie Boutique. The door to Furbush Investigations was in a breezeway between a Publix Supermarket and a Century 21 Real Estate office that's front window was filled with yellowed photographs of houses that had obviously been on the market a very long time.

A black briefcase was sitting on the concrete walk outside Furbush's office. Brady knocked. Two seconds later the door jerked open. A thick man with a broad, dark face and high cheekbones stuck out his hand. Brady pointed to the satchel.

"That yours, or do we need to call the bomb squad?"

The man looked down. "There it is. Couldn't figure out where I left it." He grabbed the case and poked out his hand again. "Furbush, but people call me Fuzzy. Ever since I'm a kid. On account my name's Francis Urban. Used to be a cop. You too I hear. Lilia Googled you. How I knew you wore a badge. Clever girl, not just a looker. Teachin' her the ropes. Wants to be FBI. Tryin' to talk her into stayin' with me. Lots going on. Estates. Divorces. Polygraphs. Corporate security. Body guard. Background checks."

Fuzzy Furbush stopped talking to breath and Brady took the opportunity to jump in. He didn't know if he'd get another.

"What's your theory on Ben Chance's murder?"

Furbush put a hand to the side of his face and shot him an alarmed look.

"Sorry, Brady. Come in, come in."

The office was a single spartan room with no windows, two metal desks, some battered file cabinets, and a couple of visitor's chairs. The only adornments were memorabilia garnishing the wall behind his desk. A framed glass board with patches from police departments across the country. From Los Angeles to New York City to Suck Tooth, Texas to Two Egg, Florida. There were framed commendations from Interpol, Scotland Yard, and the FBI. Diplomas from Quantico and John Jay College of Criminal Justice. And photographs. Fuzzy arresting wise guys. Fuzzy firing an AK-47. Fuzzy standing in front of a table stacked with bricks of cocaine. Fuzzy dipping his finger in a drum of moonshine. Fuzzy at a press conference surrounded by stone-faced suits. A younger Howard Pickens was in one of them.

"Can I offer you an aperitif, Brady? Anything you want." He opened a desk drawer and pulled out a bottle of Chivas Regal. "Long as its Chivas. Client gave it to me. Rich old codger. Insurance guy. Tried to cheat the clock and married a babe young enough to be his grand-daughter. Smart old dog, though. Made her sign a pre-nup. If she got caught *in flagrante delicto* she'd be cut off without a penny. Snapped half a dozen shots of her outside Wild Things. Know the place?"

"Nope."

"Titty bar over on Powerline. She used to work there. Bimbo couldn't stay away. Caught her goin' down on some black dude in a car. That was one dumb cocksucker." Fuzzy brayed like a mule. "How about that drink?"

"I'll pass, thanks."

"Sit down, Brady."

Fuzzy returned the bottle to the drawer and began striding back-and-forth in a rapid gait in front of his trophy wall. Brady took a seat facing his desk.

"So tell me about Ben Chance."

The private detective stopped his ambulation midstride and leaned across the desk. "Look, Brady, I was a blue spook, okay. Criminal Intel. Lauderdale PD. Forgot more shit about wise guys this side of Palm Beach than the CIA will ever have on them cut-throat camel jockeys. Guns, dope, women, jewels. Nobody knew more shit than me."

Fuzzy seemed to be one of those archetypal cowboy cops, right down to his hand-tooled leather boots. Brady had seen enough of them to know the type. Big talk. Flair for the dramatic. Delusions of grandeur. Always the hero. Always the smartest guy in the room. At least in their own eyes. Most of them turned out to be more Barney Fife than Dirty Harry. But first impressions weren't always true. Maybe Fuzzy was more than that. His wall was impressive.

"So what about Ben?"

Furbush collapsed behind his desk into a squeaky brown Naugahyde chair. He opened another drawer and pulled out a blue rubber ball and began squeezing it, watching his forearm bulge with each compression.

"Here's the deal, Brady. Couple of weeks back your pal, Chance, calls me. Says he's getting phone calls in the middle of the night. Muffled voice telling him to leave it alone. I say *'Leave what alone?'* He says *'The gold.'* I say *'What gold?'* He says he don't want to talk about it. Says he wants to hire me to protect him from the voice."

"What voice?"

Fuzzy tilted back in the chair and frowned. "That's the thing. I ask, but he won't say." *Maybe because he couldn't get a word in edgewise,* Brady thought. "Real cryptic. Like he's got skeletons in his closet he don't want me to see. I press him, but I coulda been speaking Swahili. He gives me nothing. Finally I say *'Mr. Chance there ain't much I can do for you.'* Which I hate, cause I know he's loaded and, well, you know, with the economy these days. In my head I'm wavin' bye-bye to a sweet payday. But I don't bullshit my clients. If I can't help 'em I tell 'em straight up. So I forget about the guy."

"You mean that's it? That was all you did?"

Fuzzy sat forward and smiled. "A few days later he calls again. This time at three o'clock in the friggin' morning. Woke me out of a dead sleep. Almost hung up on him. But I heard something in his voice. Like he just seen Freddy friggin' Krueger. Thought he was gonna cry. Says he got another call. *'I told you to stop,'* the voice says. *'Now you're a dead man!'* I ask him again. *'Who could it be?'* He don't wanna say, so I lean harder. *'Listen, Mr. Chance, if you don't help me I can't help you,'* I say *'Goodnight.'* He shouts *'No, wait, please.'* Begging. *"Help me,"* he says. I say *'Give me something. A name. Address. Phone number. Whatever. Someplace to start.'* Finally he blurts out *'Duke Manyon.'* I almost fall outa my bed. Duke friggin' Manyon! Holy shit! Goddamned guy's still alive? I knew it."

Fuzzy popped out of his chair and was in motion again, prowling back and forth like a caged tiger. From one wall to the other. Snapping his fingers, bouncing the rubber ball, as if he was mainlining Red Bull. Brady noticed his boots had worn a path in the carpet, like a cow trail in a pasture. Fuzzy, he decided, had a terminal case of antsy-pants.

"How do you know about Duke?"

Furbush stopped in his tracks and turned on Brady. "Duke? Sounds like you know him too."

"Not really. Tell me what you know about Manyon."

"I told you, Brady." Fuzzy stuck his nose in the air and sniffed. "I'm a bloodhound. I can smell things. Got a sixth sense. Why I'm so good. Amaze myself sometimes."

"You said."

"Your boy Duke was doin' business around here before I ever pinned on a badge. I'm guessing you knew that. Long gone by the time I picked up his scent. Some people are addicted to crosswords. I'm a mystery freak. Get off on catching bad guys. Solving crimes. It's in my DNA. Lilia did one of them ancestry checks on my family tree. Turns out my great, great uncle on my mother's side was Wyatt friggin' Earp. True story. That girl's something."

"So what about Duke?"

"So when I was at the PD I used to sniff around the dust bin. Cold cases long before they had cold case squads. Shit people had forgotten. Where I came across Manyon."

Brady leaned forward, on full alert now. "What kind of cold case."

"Missing persons. Coupla bar girls. Strippers. Vanished. Gotta be twenty-five, thirty years now. Manyon was a real smooth operator. Beach boy. Movie star good looks. Oozed charisma. One of them guys women desire and men admire. Lived on a boat down at Bahia Mar. Ran a water ski school. Had the door at one of the big clubs. Polynesian Room on Federal. Anyways, Manyon had half the chicks in town dancin' on a string. But Duke had a secret life. Real dark side."

"What was that?"

"Cat burglar. Second story man. Specialized in fine jewels. Like Cary Grant in that Hitchcock flick. "

"*To Catch A Thief.*"

"That's it? The one with that blonde honey."

"Grace Kelly."

"You're good, Brady. Grace Kelly. Married some king or sheik, then drove off a cliff. What a waste. Ask me, though, she didn't hold a candle to my girl Lilia. Wait 'til you get a load of her." Fuzzy whistled and shook a hand in the air like he was drying fingernail polish. "Anyways, one day these strippers vanish. Gone! Poof! Into thin air. No bodies. No blood. No corpus delecti. No nothin'. Nobody gives two shits. Strip club owner they worked for filed a missing persons report but figured they found jobs in Vegas or someplace. Case raised about as many eyebrows as raindrops in August. But take it from me, them girls ended up worm sandwiches. And Duke did it. Snuffed 'em both. Bank on it."

Brady sat back and let Fuzzy's words sink in. *Two strippers vanish and Duke did it.* Furbush kept moving, ball bouncing, fingers snapping, eyes darting up and down, left and right.

"Why would Manyon kill a couple of strippers?"

"One of 'em was a snitch. Duke found out."

"How?"

Fuzzy stopped and pointed a finger at Max. "That, my friend, is the whack."

"Whack?

"UAQ."

"UAQ?"

"Unanswered question. You wanna know my opinion?"

"That's why I'm here."

"Duke had a snitch of his own. An insider at the PD who tipped him about the stripper. But that's a whole 'nother kettle a worms. Anyways, Duke had an accomplice. Buck somebody."

"Foxx."

Fuzzy stopped and stared at nothing for a moment, a man thinking important thoughts. Then he turned and his dark eyes zeroed in on him like lasers.

"Brady, you know more than you're lettin' on."

"You think? Keep going, Fuzzy."

Furbush started moving again, almost at a trot now, his fingers clacking like a Spanish dancer. The faster he walked the faster words tumbled out of him.

"Anyways, Duke and this Buck are suspected in some capers going down around the same time."

"Suspected why?"

"The doxy whispered it to a PD detective. Picked her up for hookin' and flipped her. She tells him her and her friend used to party on Duke's boat. Chug tequila. Snort coke. One night they go to Bahia Mar and Duke and Buck show up in a motor boat. They go inside and Buck pulls out a black velvet bag and pours a pile of stones on the table. Diamonds, emeralds, rubies. Light is shinin' through the baubles. Colors are dancin' on the walls, like one of them disco balls."

"How do you know all this?"

A smile ticked in Fuzzy's eyes then vanished. A cop smile. The kind that said *'I know all kinds of shit – and you don't.'* He stepped to the desk and circled his chair like a dog circling a soft spot on a carpet. He sat and opened the bottom right drawer and removed a manila folder. It was about three inches thick. He tossed it on the desk. It landed with a thud.

"Found it in a cabinet with a shitload of ancient cases. All unsolved. Made a copy before it got relegated to non-existent. Retrieved a coupla dozen. All of 'em real mind benders. Kept nibblin' away at 'em. Managed to close a few. Maybe now I'll use them to write detective stories. Funny stuff, ya know, like that Elmore Leonard. Guy cracks me up. Lilia says she'll help. I got the stories. She writes poetry. We make a good team." Fuzzy glanced at his wristwatch. "Hope she gets back before you go."

Brady cast greedy eyes on the folder. "So what do you have there on Duke and Buck?"

Furbush became very still. Brady guessed he was mulling whether to share his file. Information is currency for a cop. When Brady was an NYPD detective he guarded his intelligence like a jealous husband. Fuzzy finally reached his conclusion. He nodded, flipped open the file cover, pulled out a cover page, and read aloud.

"Wayne Peter Manyon, aka Duke Manyon. D.O.B. 12/12/46. Address Slip F-19, Bahia Mar Marina. No NCIC record. U.S. Marines. Honorable discharge. Suspected actor in series of jewel

thefts in Fort Lauderdale and surrounding area. Targets homes of wealthy residents. Two confidential informants have separately identified Manyon and associate, George David Foxx, aka Buck Foxx, D.O.B. 7/19/48. Last known address 2537 Rodeo Road, Davie, Florida. NCIC shows four felony convictions. Served two years at Indian River Correctional Institution for aggravated assault, three years at Florida State Prison at Starke for armed robbery. Manyon and Foxx at this time remain this affiants principal suspects."

Fuzzy returned the paper to the file, closed the cover and returned it to his desk drawer. Brady got the message. That was all he was getting, for now.

"Why did Ben believe Duke Manyon wanted to kill him?"

"You probably know better than me."

"Why would I?"

"Chance finally opened up about the gold. He told me about you, Brady. You and Richard Strong. Said when you three was boys you found some coins on a reef. He was convinced more was down there. Said he'd been researching it for years. Even hired us do some snooping. Said he thought the gold you kids found was from some pirate ship. I put Lilia on the case. Two days later she's got the name of the boat, *The Nemesis*, its captain, Ned Pike, and a kid that sailed with him."

"Michael Fury."

"You do know a lot, don't you Brady? I ain't no pirate buff. Never heard of Pike or this Fury, but Lilia's a natural born digger. She finds out Fury became a pirate in his own right. And that he mighta left a journal. Lilly thought it could have something in it about the gold." Fuzzy shook his head wistfully. "Girl's gonna make a hell of a FBI agent. Hate to lose her."

Brady recalled the whiff of perfume he smelled on Fuzzy's business card. "So it was Lilia who traced Michael Fury's diary to Trinity College in Dublin?"

"You heard about that?"

"I've got it."

Fuzzy's eyebrows shot up. He looked favorably impressed. "So tell me, Brady. Is the gold out there? Chance promised to cut us in if we helped him find it. I was hopin' Lilia would scotch her FBI plans. Told her we could move the shop to Tahiti. Track down coconut thieves. Just joking, of course. She wouldn't want to spend her life with an old burnout like me."

"Don't sell yourself short, Fuzzy. Some women appreciate men with, um, seasoning."

Furbish brightened. "Think so?"

"Hey, they've got oysters in the Caribbean that can climb trees."

Fuzzy's eyes narrowed. "What's your point?"

"My point is miracles happen. By the way, did Ben ever explain the connection to Duke Manyon?"

"He said Duke and Buck tried to steal your gold. Wouldn't say how. But I got a vibe that something happened. Something bad. Like I said, Chance was scared stupid at the mention of Manyon's name. Wanna tell me about it?"

"Keep going."

"That's about it," he said with a nod toward the drawer. "Whatever happened between you musta been around the time the jewels were stolen and the strippers vanished. Duke knew the heat was on. The hammer coulda come down any minute. I figure they X-out the whores and dump their bodies. Probably took 'em to the Glades and fed 'em to the gators. Maybe ran 'em through a wood chipper. Million ways to make a body go away. Then Duke and Buck vanish with a million bucks worth of hot rocks."

Fuzzy's deductive skills were impressive.

"Say you're right. Say Duke evaporates to some uncharted island. Think Fletcher Christian on Pitcairn."

"I know that one. *Mutiny on the Bounty*. Clark Gable."

"Marlon Brando, too. And Mel Gibson. Anyway, he's been gone thirty years. Why come back now. Why kill Ben?"

Fuzzy pondered the question for a minute. He glanced at his watch then at the door Lilia still had not walked through.

"Maybe the loot from the diamonds ran out. Maybe he got broke. Maybe he's desperate and comes back for the gold. Somehow he finds out Chance is after it too and decides to eliminate the competition. Like I say, though, I think you know more about Duke Manyon than me."

Brady smiled. A cop's smile. He rose from the chair. "Thanks for your time, Fuzzy."

Disappointment scrolled across Furbush's broad face.

"Too bad, Brady. Gonna miss Lilia."

Et Tu Brady

Chapter Thirty-Eight

CAPTAIN RON REGISTER was walking down the second floor hallway toward Homicide scanning the police department's Plan of Action for Super Bowl weekend when the elevator opened. Detective Pixie Davenport rushed out, her eyes glued to the screen of her iPhone. She collided with Register and the impact knocked him into a stepladder set up in the center of the corridor. A workman in white overalls was perched on the upper rung installing the new Detective Bureau sign for tomorrow's ceremony. The ladder pitched right and tottered on two legs. The worker's mouth opened in a silent scream and he tried to right himself by contorting his body like a Cirque du Soleil performer. Fortunately, another quick-thinking maintenance man rushed to the rescue. He got his hands on the ladder and saved his colleague from a long fall to the hard terrazzo floor.

The scene seemed to happen in slow motion, but actually played out in less than three seconds. Register knew a major calamity had been averted. Had the worker fallen on his head and cracked his skull and, God forbid, died, the blame would have been on him. Not that he was so concerned about the employee. He was thinking about his own career. His shot at being the next Chief of Police would have been as dead as the worker.

Register took a breath of relief and looked down at Davenport. He towered over the petite policewoman by more than a foot.

"You've got to be more careful, Pixie. You're going to kill someone." *Or something.*

Davenport looked up at him. Her eyes were bright. She seemed oblivious to the disaster she'd nearly caused, or the consternation in her boss's voice.

"I'm glad I ran into you, captain. You are not going to believe this."

Register saw her excitement. He shook his head and waved at her to follow him. When they reached his office he fell into his high-backed black leather swivel chair and motioned her to take the seat across the desk. She ignored the invitation, threw her bag onto the chair, and dropped a file in front of him.

"Delray Cross rented a car," she blurted.

"What?"

"The night of the murder. Mrs. Cross rented a car. She told us she checked into the Yankee Clipper at six thirty. The hotel confirmed that. She said she called her brother's house at six thirty five and got no answer. The Clipper's phone records verify that. She said she called again at eight. Confirmed. And again at eight-thirty. Confirmed. Then she said she took a taxi to Benjamin Chance's house. That was at nine o'clock. We found the cabbie who drove her. He backed her up."

"So?"

"So Mrs. Cross forgot, or intentionally ignored, to tell us she rented an automobile when she arrived. Hertz has a desk in the Clipper lobby. Looks like she rented it before she even checked into the hotel. A new BMW, two doors, color maroon, license AJC319."

Register reached into his pocket and retrieved his tin of Tums and popped one into his mouth, his eyes trained on Davenport. He liked his detective. He found her quite attractive, for a lesbian. And very smart. And even more enthusiastic. His only knock was that she sometimes wasted precious time chasing wild geese. Time was everything right now. The clock was ticking. He wanted the Chance murder closed fast before the media horde in town for the Super Bowl picked up on the juicy whodunit. His career didn't need the scrutiny any more than it needed a department employee's brains splattered on the floor.

"Okay, Pixie, she rented a car. So what? That doesn't prove anything. Where are you going with this?"

She smiled. She *was* pretty. Register wondered if the female deputy sheriff she lived with was as attractive. He knew from Davenport's personnel file the woman had been married to another deputy and they had a child before she and Davenport shacked up. So Pixie was a predator who turned straight women into lesbians. He imagined them in bed. Two women having sex made perfect sense to him. Two men made none. He wondered why and concluded it must be genetic predisposition. Those thoughts streaked through his mind in about one second before Davenport interrupted.

"I checked with the valet desk in front of the Yankee Clipper," she said. "They keep computer records of every car they park in the multi-level garage across the street. Hertz has a small fleet of about ten cars there at any given time. The BMW was checked out at six-forty-five the night of the murder, just minutes after Mrs. Cross rented it. It was returned an hour later. The attendant I spoke with wasn't on duty that night and they don't keep record of who actually takes out a car. I'm still trying to locate the valet who either fetched the vehicle or checked it back in when it was returned."

"So we can't put her in the car?"

Register saw a sparkle in her eyes and again imagined her naked and in the throes of passion with her female lover.

"Not yet, captain, but here's the good part. The valet desk keeps the keys. The BMW has not left the Clipper's parking lot since it was returned. That was just before eight o'clock the night of the murder. The Medical Examiner says Benjamin Chance died at about seven o'clock."

Register leaned back, folded his hands behind his head and rocked in the big chair. He realized the implication of Davenport's discovery and savored the moment.

"So," he said, "Delray Cross had time to drive to her brother's house, murder him, then get back to the hotel and take a cab to the house an hour later when she allegedly discovered his body."

Davenport smiled and nodded. Register sprang forward and reached a hand across the desk.

"Excellent job, Pixie. You're a fine detective."

"I'm not done, sir. It gets better."

"Don't keep me in suspense."

"Hertz records show that when Mrs. Cross rented the BMW it had two thousand three hundred and ten miles on its odometer. I checked about an hour ago. Now it's at two thousand three hundred and sixteen. So the night of the murder it was driven six miles."

"And the distance from the Yankee Clipper to Benjamin Chance's house?"

"Take a wild guess."

"Three miles. Six round trip."

Davenport beamed down at her boss, who beamed back up at her, wondering if there was a chance in hell he could ever arrange a ménage à trois with Pixie and her girlfriend. Maybe after they closed the case and he was chief. The Chance investigation was wrapping up faster than he'd expected. Delray Cross was going to prison. Perhaps even Death Row. And he was moving to the top floor. He decided to bring Davenport with him. He reached across the desk and took her hand.

"You *are* a good, detective," he said, holding onto her, feeling her soft skin, brushing his thumb over her knuckles. "Very good."

Chapter Thirty-Nine

AFTER BRADY LEFT Fuzzy Furbush's office he steered out of the shopping center and pointed the Jeep east on Broward Boulevard. Something was distracting him and he failed to see a road crew tamping asphalt into a pothole. He was inches from colliding with a hot tar truck when he swerved at the last second.

"Jeez, Brady," he murmured. "Wake up."

His attention deficit was the result of a bad case of *earworms*. That's what audiophiles call it when someone hears a song and it gets stuck in their head and they can't get it out. Mozart had *ohrwurms* so bad that when he heard someone play the piano and not finish the melody, he had to rush to a keyboard and complete the tune or be driven mad replaying it in his mind. Brady got earworms every time he heard Bruce Springsteen sing *I'm Goin' Down*. Springsteen repeats the word *"down"* about two hundred times. *"I'm goin' down, down, down, down, down, down, down, down, down..."* After hearing the song Brady invariably found himself singing it to himself for days afterwards.

He couldn't blame Springsteen for his earworms this time. Fuzzy Furbush was the culprit. His words kept repeating in his head.

Chance was scared stupid at Manyon's name...Something happened. Something bad...They X-out the whores...Wanna tell me about it?

The short answer was no. He had never told anyone. Not his grandparents. Not Uncle Howard. Not Victoria. Not Rose. He'd even fooled himself into believing he'd forgotten. Now he knew, though. It had always been there. In twenty nine years not a day had gone by that his subconscious hadn't replayed the events of that night like an endless film loop.

Brady had read somewhere that the suggested cure for *earworms* was to imagine a real worm crawling out of your ear and stomping on it. Either that or do what Mozart did. Play the tune all the way through. He knew he'd have to do something soon. Since Ben Chance's murder the *earworms* were taking over his thoughts.

Ben's bon voyage was held at Our Lady of Perpetual Sorrow Catholic Church. Brady detested funerals. Perhaps because he knew he'd be the guest of honor one day, stretched out in a box looking like a creature from a wax museum. Or maybe because he agreed with the Cantonese, who avoided interment ceremonies, seeing death as *sha-ch'i,* a plague that releases *killing airs* that steal energy and life from all who breathe them. Or possibly it was the tons of bullshit he'd heard during eulogies for the too-often-not-so-dearly departed.

Roman Catholic requiems were the worst. Black people know how to throw a funeral, sending off their dead in high style with lots of weeping, wailing, fainting, soaring oration, sprawling on caskets, and singing *Precious Lord.* Catholic solemnities were so bleak and grim they made Brady wish he was dead. A short Mass with a short sermon delivered by a priest who typically had never even met the stiff-in-the-box while he or she was still breathing.

Our Lady of Perpetual Sorrow wasn't as dead as Ben Chance, but it would be soon. Despite golf tournament fund-raisers, the parish was drowning in red ink and both church and school were on a lengthy hit-list to be closed by the Diocese of Miami. Even the Almighty, it seemed, was not immune to the bad economy.

Rose was waiting outside the church when Brady arrived. Before the ceremony they walked arm-in-arm through his old school. He pointed out the church door he used to enter when he served as an altar boy.

"Have you ever considered going back to the church?" she asked.

"Briefly. After the Pope admitted the Earth and the planets revolve around the Sun. That got the Catholic Church into the Seventeenth Century. Unfortunately, he didn't make the admission until 1992."

They strolled down the sidewalk he'd stood on the day Ben was thrashed by Junior Ball. *Junior the bully,* he thought, wondering whatever had happened to Ball. And to Sister Mary Aloysius, the bully in nun's clothing. Brady didn't believe in a place called Hell but, if there was one, Attila the Nun deserved a special place there. He considered whether that was too harsh. Before he reached a conclusion he heard Rose catch her breath.

The hearse had just pulled up to the church followed by a stretch limousine, like a black crepe procession. The limo door opened and Delray Cross climbed out, tall and svelte in a black mourning dress, black hat and black veil covering her face.

"Oh, Brady, she's stunning," said Rose. "So elegant and dignified, like the pictures of Jacqueline Kennedy at her husband's funeral."

Brady's heart sank. Delray had ridden to the church alone. He realized he should have been with her. He imagined how lonely she must have felt. Delray saw them approach and lifted her veil. She draped her arms around Brady's neck and kissed him on the mouth. He turned to Rose with a sheepish expression. She was staring at the ground.

"I apologize, Delray," he said. "I should have come with you."

"I'm fine, Max. You've done so much already. This must be…"

"Rose Becker." Rose extended her hand. "My deepest condolences, Mrs. Cross."

"Please, call me Delray. It's such a pleasure to meet you Rose. Max speaks very highly of you. Now I see why. Max, she's lovely. And so young. You are a lucky man."

"Very," Rose said and fired a fleeting glare in his direction.

Delray offered Brady her arm and they entered the church for the first time since childhood. Rose followed two steps behind. The fragrance of the cavernous nave flooded Brady's senses, as familiar after three decades as the scent of just-baked bread. The burning incense. The melting candlewax. The saccharine bouquet of flowers. The musky perfume of cedar confessionals. And the sounds. The chime of the Angelus bells. The drone of the ancient pipe organ. The austere chant of the Gregorian choir. A life-sized Jesus Christ hanging from the crucifix. Reds and greens and golds bathed in the rapturous light radiating through soaring stained glass.

A modest collection of mourners had come, which surprised Brady. Ben had spent his entire life in Fort Lauderdale and was a prominent businessman. Yet in death, as in life, he had few friends. Brady didn't see any familiar faces.

He joined Delray in the front pew, wanting to spare her the indignity of sitting alone. He was still plagued by the black memory of his grandparent's funeral, seated by himself that day, young and solitary, in the very row he and Delray now occupied. Never so lost or alone. Stricken not only by the grief of his grandparent's deaths, but by his own monstrous secret. The same flashbacks assailed him now. Duke Manyon and Buck Foxx chasing him like some hallucinogenic *dans macabre*.

Ben's send-off was a dry, dispassionate affair. Other than Delray dabbing her eyes, Brady didn't see or hear any weeping. The priest was a diminutive, dark-skinned Filipino. He seemed sincere, but his accent was so thick that his words were barely intelligible. The homily was a boilerplate pastoral delivered with all the passion of a stump speech by a candidate for the local water district. From what Brady could gather, the priest compared Ben to a metaphorical caterpillar he called *Carl*. Death had transformed him from a woolly worm into a beautiful butterfly that had flown off to its eternal reward in Heaven. It could have been written by Dr. Seuss. Rose seemed to be the only mourner who appreciated the simile.

After the service, Ben's casket was wheeled down the aisle. Delray and Brady followed hand-in-hand. Outside, she stood at the church door accepting ceremonious air kisses from mourners, mostly employees of Chance Electric. Word had spread that Delray was Ben's sole heir, which meant she was the new boss. The spigots had opened and copious tears were being shed to attest to their love for the old boss.

Off to the side of the churchyard, Brady noticed a solitary figure standing alone in the shade of a Royal Poinciana. He took Rose's hand.

"Come on. There's someone I want you to meet."

When they walked up the old man was wearing a wide smile.

"This must be Rose," he said.

The tall, thin man was leaning on a cane. His long, narrow face was wan and bloodless and lined with more wrinkles than a raisin. His full head of hair was as white as the Alps and his furry eyebrows – which reminded Brady of *Carl the Caterpillar* – sheltered alert blue eyes that were, at the moment, fixed on Rose.

"Rose, this is my Uncle Howard."

He offered her his hand and gave a slight bow. "You certainly weren't exaggerating, my boy. She is quite the beauty."

"Howard Pickens is the finest Chief of Detectives the Fort Lauderdale Police Department ever had."

"Until they sent me off to the elephant burial grounds," Pickens said. His words betrayed bitterness, but no trace of animosity was detectable in his smile. "But that's politics. And speaking of politics, I've still got contacts downtown, young lady. I'm hearing wonderful things about you. A rising star, they say. Young, smart, beautiful. Unlimited future, they say."

"*They* must have *me* confused with someone else. But thank you for the kind words."

Brady stepped forward and wrapped Pickens in a bear hug.

"Uncle Howard and my father grew up together," he said to Rose when they unclenched. "He was dad's best friend."

"You should also know, my dear, that I would not be here today if not for John Brady sacrificing his life to drag me out of a firefight at Khe Sanh."

Rose looked confused.

"Vietnam," Pickens said. "Long before you were born."

"Uncle Howard and his wife took me in after my grandparents passed away. And regretted it every day until I went off to college."

"Nonsense," said Pickens, draping an arm around Brady's shoulder. "I vowed to your father that if anything happened to him I'd watch over you like you were my own son. Besides, Mo would have insisted."

"Mo?" said Rose.

"Maureen. My wife. She and Mary, Max's mother, were the best of friends as well. We all grew up together. Unfortunately, I lost her to breast cancer last year."

"Of course. Max told me how wonderful you and Aunt Maureen were to him. He loves you very much."

Brady saw tears pool in Pickens's eyes. It dawned on him that, since Rose had come into his life, he'd been negligent about visiting and vowed to spend more time with him in the future.

"How are you, Uncle Howard?"

Pickens gave him a wry smile. "There oughta be a law against getting old, my boy. I keep telling myself that I'm going to feel as good as ever in a week or two. But I guess that's what old men do in their dotage. We lie to ourselves. Doctor says I need a new hip. One of those titanium deals. Either that or I'm gonna get hooked on all the pain pills he's been feeding me. A word of advice, my boy. Don't get old. You don't die all at once, but piece by piece."

An awkward silence ensued, considering the circumstances. Brady looked over at the church. Delray was still on the steps immersed in conversation with the wiry little Filipino priest.

"It's nice of you to come," he said. "Ben's sister will be grateful."

"I'm here a lot these days, helping Father O'Brien. I'm a deacon now, you know." He shook his head. "Terrible thing. Terrible. Talked to some people at the shop." He looked at Rose. "Cop shop. Doesn't sound like they've got much yet."

"Captain Register is fixated on Delray," Brady said.

"Poppycock," Pickens said with a disdainful wave of his hand. "Ron Register couldn't find the eye of a needle with a magnifying glass. After Don Begley forced me out he gave Homicide to that dunderhead. Which reminds me, my boy. Tomorrow they're having a small ceremony at the shop. Naming the Detective Bureau."

"Oh?"

"After some fellow named J. Howard something-or-other."

"J. Howard Pickens! That's fantastic, Uncle Howard."

"Just throwing an old dog a bone. After the way they ran me off, I was going to suggest they shove their *honor* up their collective arses." He glanced at Rose. "Pardon the coarse language, my dear. I wasn't going to mention it, but with Mo gone you're the closest I have to kin."

"Wouldn't miss it for the world."

Delray walked up. She took Brady's hand in hers. He glanced sideways. Rose was chewing her lip, her eyes fixed on the orange blossoms of the Royal Poinciana. The warm noon air chilled perceptibly.

"Delray, you remember Coach Pickens."

Rancor flared in her eyes and Brady felt her hand tighten around his.

"You're the last person I expected to see here," she said.

The day was becoming positively glacial. Brady was surprised icy vapor wasn't coming from her mouth.

Pickens sighed. "I debated coming, my dear. But I wanted to express my condolences. What happened with your brother way back when, well, I've regretted it since the day it happened. One of the few things in my life I'm truly ashamed of."

She stared at him with frigid eyes. "My brother never got over his shame after what you did to him that day. I suppose it's only fair you never got over yours."

Brady attempted to play mediator. "That was a long time ago, Del. Uncle Howard means what he says. He's told me the same thing many times."

"Did you ever tell Ben?"

Pickens would receive no absolution from Delray. He shook his head sadly and looked away. They stood like that for a time, no one making eye contact, the silence between them as frosty as the conversation.

"Well," Pickens said finally, "I'll be going. I just wanted to tell you I'm sorry. About then and now. If I can be of assistance, Max knows how to reach me." He turned to Rose. "It was a pleasure meeting you, my dear. Max is a lucky guy."

An appreciative smile flickered on her face. "So I hear."

"I hope you can make it tomorrow, my boy."

Brady hugged him. "I'll be there, Uncle Howard. I've got Heat tickets. Let's catch a game soon."

"You're on."

Pickens tottered off, hobbled by age, his cane supporting him like an extra leg.

Et Tu Brady

Chapter Forty

AS SOON AS Uncle Howard was gone, Rose bade Brady and Delray a curt farewell and left them standing outside the church. Minutes later she was barreling eastbound on Davie Boulevard in her little blue Miata, grinding gears, weaving through traffic, oblivious to the cars she was wheeling past like Danica Patrick chasing a checkered flag, too busy seething at the image of Delray Cross holding Brady's hand and kissing him on the lips.

What the hell's going on, Brady?

Rose Anne Becker had come a long way in her twenty seven years. The product of a broken home, she grew up in Ridgewood, New Jersey, a leafy, affluent suburb outside Manhattan, where, at an early age, she survived a war of wishes with her mother.

Mom wished her to be a beauty queen and Rose spent most of her formative years competing in, and winning, *Little Miss* crowns. *Little Miss Ridgewood. Little Miss Garden State. Little Miss Hudson Valley.* Her singing, dancing, and gymnastic performances were as compelling to judges as her porcelain skin, perfect face, and long black locks. The budding Rose, though, hated the plastic pretentiousness of childhood pageantry.

Her wish was to compete in the athletic arena. So, at the tender age of eight years, she abdicated her future claim to Miss America's tiara and set her sights on Olympic Gold. She loved vaulting, tumbling, aerobatics, and floor dancing and became a promising gymnast. But, alas, at age thirteen Rose sprouted like a beanstalk until she was a full foot taller than the girls she was competing against. Spindly, her teeth glittering with silver braces, the glam beauty queen had mutated into an ugly duckling. She gave up sports and buried her head in her school books.

Rose graduated valedictorian of her class at Ridgewood High. After two years at Rutgers, she won a scholarship to study French literature at the American University of Paris. During the spring of her second year in Europe she took a bicycle excursion through the Pyrenees and discovered a species of magnificent indigo creatures dancing and swooping and pairing off like acrobatic lovers amidst the buttercups and wild flowers that painted the mountains.

"Empereurs Violets," said her riding companion, Marcel. "Purple Emperors."

That was the moment Rose became enthralled by all things *papillon.* Just as the caterpillar transmuted into the glorious butterfly, she hoped one day to metamorphize from ugly duck to beautiful swan. After graduation she and Marcel moved into in an alcove studio in Montparnasse. She taught English to the children of wealthy Frenchmen. He was sous chef at La Table du Vin Vignon near Madeleine.

Marcel was a beautiful boy with vivacious green eyes and long luxurious black hair. Rose loved their bohemian life, picnicking beneath the Eiffel Tower, getting lost in the Louvre, listening to jazz at the Caveau de la Huchette, visiting Robespierre's bones in Les Catacombes. Rose liked Marcel but was not, after all, in love with him. After a year she returned to America and won another scholarship, this time to the University of Florida, where she entered the Master's Program for Zoological Science with a concentration in lepidoptery, the study of butterflies.

While she earned her degree she reacquainted herself with gymnastics, which led her to yoga, Pilates, and a full range of demanding but addictive exercise routines. By the time she graduated she had undergone her dreamed of transformation. The caterpillar had become a butterfly.

Rose left Gainesville and moved three hundred miles south to Fort Lauderdale to take a job at Butterfly World, the largest park of its kind in the world. But, to the surprise of everyone she knew, including herself, she quit that job after only three months, and with money she inherited from her maternal grandmother, opened the Papillon Gym on a rooftop overlooking Lauderdale Beach. During her first year there she dated a couple of guys, but nothing serious, nothing intimate.

All romances begin someplace, though, and Rose's began there. Max Brady owned a little beach bar on the ground floor of the same building as the Papillon and began coming upstairs every day to work out. Brady was tall and lean and heedlessly handsome, not one to stare at himself in the mirror when he exercised, a rare attribute in the narcissistic world of health clubs.

Yet, an air of mystery surrounded Brady. That first year he said little to Rose. A friendly nod, a polite hello, a shy smile. He seemed pleasant and she often heard other patrons laughing at things he said, but he remained aloof and showed no apparent interest in her or, for that matter, any other female at the gym. She concluded he was probably gay. Then someone told her Brady had been married and that his wife was killed in the World Trade Towers attack on 9/11. Realizing he must still be in grief, she left him alone. At some point, though, Rose noticed her spirits lift every time Brady walked through the door.

Not much of a drinker, she had little call to visit the Sea Shanty. But one day she stopped in to grab a bottled water and a quick bite. It was mid-afternoon, the quiet time between lunch and happy hour. The bar was empty and Brady was alone. He recommended the house specialty – gumbo.

"Does it contain meat?"

"Sausage, chicken, shrimp, fish."

"Sorry, I don't eat anything that used to have eyeballs."

"You don't eat potatoes?"

"Of course."

"Potatoes have eyes."

"But not balls."

"Don't tell that to Mr. Potato Head."

It was her first exposure to Brady's snappy repartee. From that moment on she didn't stand a chance.

By then Rose had become a hero to the local beach community. She'd founded *SOB – Save Our Beach –* a volunteer group to fight the proliferation of high rise condominiums and hotels that threatened to turn Lauderdale Beach into a concrete canyon. To the *SOBs* she was their Joan of Arc.

"Wasn't she Noah's wife?" Brady said that day, wiping the bar with a wet cloth.

For two hours they had the Sea Shanty to themselves. They nibbled French fries, laughed at each other's bad jokes, and flirted shamelessly. She discovered he was smart and gentle and had a quick, dry wit. She liked his clear green eyes. She liked his long, lean-muscled physique. She liked being alone with him. At forty two he was fifteen years her senior, but he seemed more like a teenager. By the time Rose left that day she didn't walk out of the Shanty so much as float. Max Brady, she suspected, was about to become a very bad habit.

Since then they'd saved each other's lives and become lovers. They began stealing passion whenever and wherever they could, be it for a night, a day, an hour, or five minutes. Their only disagreement had been about who occupied which side of the bed.

"I'm a left-handed lover," he said.

She coughed out a laugh. "Trust me, Brady, you're ambidextrous."

Rose was drawn to him more than she thought possible. He was a romantic, ardent, and generous paramour and she craved to feel him inside her when the morning light poured through her bedroom window. Or in the dozens of places they'd made love. Her bad habit fast became a hopeless addiction.

So what the hell's going on, Brady?

Rose careened along Davie Boulevard feeling as if her perfect world was spinning off its axis. Zigging. Zagging. Cursing at drivers.

Tears burning in her eyes. She remembered an adage she'd heard once: *They who love the fiercest, love the shortest.* She considered the possibility the white-hot fire between them had consumed itself. Was the dream she thought just beginning already at end? Rose didn't feel that way, but maybe Brady did. For the umpteenth time she saw Delray Cross kiss him on the lips. Watched them hold hands, like long lost lovers. Her heart sinking like a stone with each reiteration. Had Brady fallen in love again with his childhood sweetheart?

Her cell phone sounded. She punched talk.

"Brady?" Disappointment spooled across her face. It was Sandy, her secretary at City Hall. She listened for a moment and her let-down turned to shock.

"If Mr. Brady calls, tell him I've gone to Broward General."

When she reached Andrews Avenue, instead of turning left toward City Hall Rose swung the Miata right. Broward General Medical Center was four blocks down.

At the Information Desk she lied to the male attendant, who accepted her story without question. He took her photograph and a machine spit out an identification sticker. She stuck it to her blouse and followed the signs to Intensive Care.

ICU was on the third floor. A nurse at the station desk told her Seymour Tate had suffered cranial contusions and a concussion and would probably be released in a day or two. Seymour was awake when she entered a glass-walled space across from the nurses. His head was bandaged, his left eye was swollen to a mere slit, and his left cheek was purple as an eggplant. When he saw Rose he smiled and winced simultaneously.

"It's worth the pain just to have you visit," he mumbled, sounding like his mouth was stuffed with cotton.

Tate was probably ten years older than Rose, but something about him stirred her maternal instincts. She pulled a turquoise plastic chair up close to the bed and took his hand in hers.

"What happened, Seymour?"

"Fucked with the wrong people."

He told her what he could remember about the giant shadow with the deep voice and the blackjack.

"Seymour, who do you think the 'wrong people' are he was talking about?"

A half-hearted laugh slipped between his lips. "Gee, let me think about that and get back to you."

"Don't joke."

"Do you really need to ask, commissioner?"

"Call me Rose."

They agreed the timing was more than suspicious. The same day she publicly raised questions about the slip-and-fall lawsuits, the reporter who Walter Dean and Junior Ball both knew had fed her the whole thing is beaten and...

"And?" said Rose.

"And has drugs planted on him."

Rose bolted up in the chair. "Don't tell me that."

Tate closed his eyes. "Sad but true. An imaginary school of fish was swimming around inside my head when they brought me to the ER. When I opened my eyes a doctor was standing over me. Next to him was a cop. The doctor tells me I've got a Grade Four concussion. The cop tells me I'm under arrest for a First Degree Felony – possession of a quarter ounce of crystal meth."

"No way."

"I don't claim to be a saint, Rose. I drink gin and smoke reefers. But I've never touched meth or speed or any other hard narcotic. Whoever wacked me over the head planted that stuff on me."

"But why?"

"Two reasons come to mind. Destroy my credibility as a journalist. And make it look like the assault was over a drug deal, which is exactly what the police are calling it. I'm surprised they didn't charge me with attacking a blackjack with my face."

Tate closed his eyes again. Rose thought he might be on the verge of tears.

"I'm so sorry, Seymour. Is there anything I can do?"

He opened his eyes and stared up at the ceiling for a moment. Then he smiled. Then he grimaced. Then he looked at Rose.

"Have you ever committed burglary?"

Et Tu Brady

Chapter Forty-One

THE BRAWNY MAN stared at his reflection in the front door glass. The noonday sun was shimmering off his shaved head like a polished billiard ball. He took a final drag on his cigarette and flicked the butt into a bird feeder outside the whitewashed Mediterranean. He waited to hear it hiss then pressed the buzzer with a finger thick as bratwurst. He was brushing gray scurfs of ash from his thin black tie when the door swung open.

Judy Desmond stood in the solar eclipse of the big man's shadow wearing a wide smile and not much else – a flowery apron and an oxygen tube in her nose. Otherwise she was naked as a newborn, which she had not been in quite some time.

"You must be Detective Dent," she rasped.

He stared down at her from dark grottos that doubled as his eyes. He didn't smile so much as lift his upper lip and show her the sharp edges of nicotine-stained teeth. Cigarette vapor wafted from behind them. For an instant Judy thought he was trying to communicate by smoke signal.

"Retired detective," he croaked in bullfrog voice and handed her a card. "Darnell Dent. Private security consultant."

Judy didn't know why, but something about Dent stirred her inside. He had an air of animal menace about him. And his pitbull face moved her to wonder what he'd look like wearing a spiked collar. Whatever it was, her reaction was instant and primal. Beneath the apron she felt her nipples tingle and juices flow. She took a deep pull on her oxygen tube.

"We've been waiting for you, Mr. Dent," she said, slightly breathless. "This is terrible. I've never seen my husband so furious."

Dent followed her into a wood-floored foyer, keeping his eyes off her brown back, fleshy hips, and dimpled buttocks. She was so casual about her nakedness he assumed she was somehow deranged.

They entered a large room that looked like a tornado had cut a path through it. His dark eyes recorded the scene like surveillance cameras. Chairs and end tables lying sideways. Ceramic shards strewn everywhere. A tall étagère swept clean of bric-a-brac and crystal figurines. White walls blemished by squares of unfaded paint where artwork once hung.

At the center of the room a big ruddy man with a rain-barrel torso and conspicuous ears stood cracking his knuckles. His head was covered by an unruly shock of rust-colored hair that looked like he'd scalped someone to get.

"I want to know who did this," Jake Desmond growled, "and I want him to disappear."

Dent removed a small pad from his jacket pocket and scrawled something left-handed. Judy's eyes never left him.

"Can I offer you a nice beverage, detective?"

Dent looked at her. So did her husband.

"Goddamnit, Judy, put on a robe. Detective Dent doesn't want to look at your bare ass."

Nudey Judy's smoker's scowl took on a pained expression. "Does my nakedness offend you, detective? Would you prefer me to cover up?"

Dent stood stone-faced in police posture, straight-backed, feet shoulder wide, steadfast as an oak. His eyes darted between Jake and Judy Desmond with barely concealed contempt, as if they were some kind of deviants.

"I'm here to do a job, lady," he said in his baritone voice. "You can wear earmuffs and a pinwheel hat if it makes you happy."

Judy seemed pleased. Then her eyes strayed to the wreckage. "Look what they did to my house. This is a disgrace."

Dent fixed his gaze on Jake. "I understand a large sum of cash was stolen."

"You're a retired Fort Lauderdale police detective?" Jake said. "I'm told you were the mayor's personal body guard."

"Former mayor. He had some legal issues. Had to leave town for a while. I took my pension and went private. How much was stolen?"

"A shitload. Sixty grand. Seventy grand. Who knows? Probably more. I keep a lot of currency around. On account of my business."

"What's that?"

"Vending. Very cash intensive. You probably bought coffee or sodas from the machines I got down at the PD."

"Why contact me?"

"Do I have to spell it out?"

Dent already knew the answer. He wanted to hear Desmond say it. "Why not file a report with the police."

"I did. Chief Begley's a friend. Called him on his private line soon as we got home last night. He advised me to handle it privately. Said if I file an official report saying I got pinched for a pile of cash it'd be all over *The Lauderdale News.* Said the IRS would be after me like bloodhounds chasing a chain gang runaway. He recommended you. Said you're discreet."

"Did he tell you my fee?"

Desmond shook his head. "Look, I just want it handled. Quiet. Discreet. But handled."

Dent stared at him. Don Begley had explained everything over the phone this morning. The two went way back. Twenty years ago they rode a squad car together. That was before Begley became an accident investigator and Dent got his detective's shield. Dent was as surprised as anyone when Begley snatched the Police Chief's job. Everyone knew Howard Pickens was the best man for the job. But it paid off when Begley assigned Dent to head Mayor David Grand's security detail. The position came with fringe benefits that went away prematurely when Grand was carted off to prison. Afterwards, Begley greased the skids so Dent could retire without having to answer any inconvenient questions.

Dent's usual fee was five hundred dollars a day plus expenses. The Police Chief told him to raise it rate for this one. Desmond had deep pockets. And things to hide. Not just cash. He had ties to some unsavory characters he wouldn't want advertised. No surprise for a guy in the vending business.

"On top of that," said Begley, "the guy doesn't even know how much cash was stolen. Anything you recover over, say, seventy grand, is ours."

"Ours" echoed over the telephone line. The Chief of Police expected a generous finder's fee. Dent didn't respond. The second he heard cash had been stolen, he decided that if he tracked it down he was going to keep it all. Neither Begley nor the fool in the bad toupee would ever know.

"I get a grand a day," he told Jake Desmond. "Plus expenses."

Jake waved a hand in disdain. "I don't give a shit about money. Just find the moron who ripped me off."

Both men glanced across the room. Judy was bent over with her back to them picking debris off the floor. A puckered brown eye was staring straight at them. Jake groaned.

"Jesus, Judy. Put on a goddamn robe."

His wife straightened up and wheeled on him with unconcealed outrage. Without a word she thrust her chin in the air like a defiant concubine and stalked from the room pulling her green oxygen bottle behind her. She punished them with one more glimpse or her cottage cheese butt-cheeks and disappeared up the staircase. Desmond shrugged.

"Sorry, detective. My wife's one of them naturists. Not a bashful bone in her body."

"As long as she can cook."

Jake grimaced. "Trust me. If murdering meatloaf was a crime, she'd be doing life."

Dent steered the discussion away from Judy Desmond's naked body. "Exactly when did this happen?"

"Last night. We took my wife's cousin and her husband to dinner. They came to town to take a cruise. After dinner we took 'em to the top of Pier 66 so they could get a look at the tub they'd be sailing on. You can see it in the port. *Oasis* of the something or other. We dropped them at the Marriott and got home around midnight."

As if on cue, Midnight the black cat came into the room holding her feather-duster tail aloft. She tried to wrap herself around Dent's ankle. The detective didn't like cats, especially black cats, and nudged her with his foot until she scooted away. He stood rock-like and swept the house with shrewd eyes.

"Big place. Cousin's not staying with you?"

"Judy hates houseguests. Says it cramps her style. Can't walk around with her tits swinging in the breeze. Her cousin and her husband have allergies. She rented a couple of cats so they'd have to get a hotel room."

"Rented?"

Jake's scowl vanished and he smiled for the first time. "Craziest thing I ever heard. But it worked like a charm. When they saw them little fur balls they couldn't get outa here fast enough. After we walked in last night I thought maybe she rented one of them Pamplona bulls, too."

"Where was the cash?"

Jake swept an arm through the air.

"Stashed all over the house. Freezer, kitchen drawer, some in a basket up on that shelf. He found a shoebox in my closet upstairs stuffed with twenties."

"Cleaned out?"

"Dumb fuck missed the biggest bundle. I keep it stashed in a false bottom in my tool chest in the garage. I don't think he even went in there. I'm guessing he found the shoebox and thought he'd hit the lottery and got the hell out. The strangest thing was our bed."

"What about it."

"Looked slept in. Like the guy took a nap. Judy found spots on the sheets. She swore it was blood. Stripped the damned thing and put on new linens before we turned in. God only knows what he was doing."

"You keep saying *he*."

"He, she, it. Coulda been the goddamned U.S. Olympic Water Polo team for all I know. Listen, detective, I don't give a good goddamn about the cash. I got plenty more in places nobody'll ever find. But I want whoever did this. I want him found and finished."

Dent didn't ask Desmond what he meant by *finished*. He walked through the living room and into the kitchen and stood in the middle of the room. The drawers of an antique desk in a corner nook had been dumped upside down on the floor. So had the silver drawer. The contents of the refrigerator were scattered across the black marble tile. Dent noticed track marks on the floor that ran from the island counter into the living room.

"One of the kitchen counter chairs," Jake said. "Found it in my study on the other side of the living room. Looks like it was dragged there."

"You don't have a dog?"

"Hell, no. Just rental cats?"

"No security alarm?"

"Not in this neighborhood. Don't need one. At least I didn't think. Guess I was wrong."

"You should consider it, especially with all the cash. I can make arrangements."

Dent's black eyes scanned the room. He'd spent four years in Burglary and could feel his old muscles reawakening. Break-ins were among the least solved crimes. Desmond's insistence on secrecy meant he wouldn't be able to run fingerprints or footwear impressions, at least not through conventional channels. The odds of the perpetrator being *"found and finished"* were slim. But, for a grand a day, and maybe sixty or seventy thousand more if he got lucky and recovered the cash, Dent was willing to give it a try.

Point of entry was the routine starting point in burglary investigations.

"Damndest thing," Jake Desmond said, shaking his head. "We can't find any broken windows. No jimmy marks on the doors. Nothing suspicious. The guy musta picked a lock."

"Or had a key?"

"You'd think, but how's somebody gonna get a key to our house?"

Judy Desmond walked into the kitchen. Dent was relieved to see her wearing a wine-colored track suit. She pulled at the jacket and made it flutter, like she was trying to cool a menopausal hot flash.

"Funny you should mention a key," she said. "I can't find mine."

"You're always losing your keys. They're usually in that bottomless pit you call a hand bag."

"Not my keys. My key. My house key."

"When did you notice it missing?" Dent said.

"Yesterday. I was going down to the beach for a walk and dip in the ocean. I go in every day."

"Must be cold in February."

"Chilly but never colder than seventy seven degrees. That Gulf Stream thing. Good for the pores. This end of the beach is pretty deserted, so I can skinny dip. You should try it sometime," she said and smiled at Dent. His face retained its marbly cast. "Anyway, I was on my way out, looking for my key. I keep it right there." She pointed to a spot at the corner of the black stone countertop. "It was gone. I searched for ten minutes then gave up and used my spare."

"When was the last time you'd used it before that?"

Judy thought for a moment. "Yesterday morning. Went grocery shopping at the Publix Supermarket off the Causeway."

"Was anyone in the house between the time you got back from Publix and went to the beach?"

"No. I rarely have anyone inside." She lowered the zipper of her sweatsuit jacket and exposed a bare breast in Dent's direction. "Because of my wardrobe, or lack thereof."

"Jesus, Judy!" Jake barked.

"Oh, hush."

Dent acted as if nothing had happened. "Housekeeper? Pool boy? Lawn man?"

"No. Nobody. Except the cat girl."

"Cat girl?"

"The girl who rented me the cats. Delivered them about mid-morning. I'd only been back a few minutes. Just gotten out of my clothes."

"Did she come into the kitchen?"

"We sat right here at the counter. I got her a glass of water and we talked for a while. Nice girl, but dark."

"Black?"

"No, white. Too white. I told her so. Cute little thing, but her aura is very gloomy. Very bohemian. Black hair, black clothes, black nail polish. Tattoo on her leg. Silver stud in her tongue. They say kids wear those to enhance oral sex." Jake scowled. "The oddest thing was her teeth. She had two long sharp teeth. You know, like that vampire show on TV. *Bloodlust?*"

"What's her deal? Are the cats hers?"

"She works at the pound. Says it's a test program. They rent out animals hoping people will adopt them. Personally, I think she's got a side thing going. Some kind of scam." Judy rummaged through her hand bag until she found Demonika's card. She handed it to Dent. "Pretty girl, though. Just too white. And way too dark."

Et Tu Brady

Chapter Forty-Two

DISMAS BENVENUTI PULLED his beat-up white cargo van to a stop, his eyes on a big brown truck turning into a driveway two houses down the street. Kenny, the eight-year-old son of his girlfriend Betty Jane Marshall, was in the passenger seat playing *Grand Theft Auto* on the Xbox Dismas had given him.

"Okay, pipsqueak. Ready for action?"

Kenny glared up from the small screen. "I told you, don't call me pipsqueak," he said and returned to his game. "I'm about to beat my PR."

"PR?"

"Personal record."

Dismas had been following the UPS truck for the past hour, waiting for the right moment. He watched a strapping brown-skinned man in brown shirt and brown shorts carry a box to the doorstep of a split-level house on Avocado Lane on the Citrus Isles off New River. The driver knocked on the door and returned to his truck without waiting for an answer.

Dismas could hear a dog barking behind the back yard fence, but there were no cars in the driveway and no one opened the front door.

The UPS truck drove off. He waited a minute and eased the van up to the house.

"Okay, two bits. Showtime." He jerked the video game from Kenny's hands and pointed toward the doorstep. "You can have it back after you do this."

The boy glowered at him, his eyes crowded with contempt. But he opened the door and jumped out. He walked straight to the front door and picked up the box with the careless air of someone who'd done it before.

A minute later they were tooling down Ninth Avenue toward State Road 84. Kenny was spellbound by his carjack game again. Dismas turned right into the parking lot of a Winn-Dixie Supermarket. He steered to a far corner, stopped in the shade of a big ficus, and ducked into the back of the van. He lifted the leg of his jeans, reached inside his worn cowboy boot, and pulled out an ornate wood-handled knife with a silver pommel and an Indian in full headdress engraved on its honed blade. He slashed the tape and opened the box then wiped the dagger-edge across the image of another Indian silkscreened on the front of his T-shirt.

"Paydirt."

The box was packed with several smaller boxes, each wrapped in festive paper decorated with balloons and candles and cakes. Someone was having a birthday. Dismas tore one open. It contained an aqua-and-orange Miami Dolphins jersey, size small. Number thirteen was printed on the back, above it the name Marino. He tossed it to Kenny.

"Happy birthday, kid,"

"It ain't my birthday. Who's Marino?"

"Are you serious? Only the greatest quarterback in NFL history?"

Kenny shrugged. "I want a Lance Jeffries jersey."

Dismas shook his head and realized the boy hadn't even been born when Dan Marino retired from the Dolphins.

"I'm gonna have to learn you some things, kid."

His cell phone rang. He answered and heard a voice slur on the other end.

"Diz, it's Devo."

Devo was Devon Marshall, Betty Jane's brother and Kenny's uncle. He shared a rusted-out mobile home at the Cloud Nine Trailer Park with Jimmy Jonas, whose arm Dismas had broken the day before.

"What's the matter, Devo? Somethin' go wrong?"

"I'm at a pay phone at the Swimmin' Hall of Fame. Security guard's givin' me dirty looks."

"You don't sound sober, but you don't sound drunk neither."

"Bartender cut me off after three whiskeys."

"Why? What'd ya say to him, Devo?"

"Told him I'm dry as dust and need to quench my thirst. He kept sayin' I had enough. I told him to shut the fuck up and keep pouring. He tells me to get the fuck outa there."

Dismas groaned. *Junior's gonna be pissed*, he thought. Junior Ball had called the night before about "an emergency job." They met at the Titty Room. The lawyer explained while he ogled the erect nipples of a chilled housewife pawing escarole.

"Gravy train's been temporarily derailed," he said.

"The slip-and-falls? But we're making so much money, Junior."

"The shit's about to hit the fan. A reporter's been snooping around. I had him taken care of, but now a city commissioner named Rose Becker's raising hell. This morning the bitch read the riot act to my guy at City Hall. I gotta do something about her."

"What's the emergency job?"

"Dram shops."

"What's dram shops?"

"Bars. Saloons. I want you to send one of your guys into a bar. Have him drink until he can't see, then drive off and crash his car."

"Ain't that dangerous?"

"Nah. He doesn't have to get hurt. Tell him to wear his seatbelt and drive slow. Just wreck the car. My doctor will do the rest."

"How do we make money doin' that?"

"Bars carry tons of liability insurance, my friend. That means plenty of legal tender for our spending pleasure." Ball gave him the name and address of the Sea Shanty. "Tell your boy it's worth five grand, plus any damage to his car. I need it done tomorrow. And, remember, don't leave any rings in the tub."

There was a moment of silence. "Rings in the tub?"

Junior tore his eyes off the housewife's chest and turned to Dismas. "Stop playing dumb."

"I ain't playin'."

Junior sighed. "Don't do anything anybody can trace back to me."

Dismas immediately thought of Betty Jane's brother, mainly because Devo owed him two thousand dollars. He would skim that right off the top. When he got back to Cloud Nine Trailer Park he walked down the trash-strewn drive to the trailer Devo shared with Jimmy and entered without knocking. He was sitting on a dirty cloth couch staring at the screen with blank eyes. A cartoon was playing on a small television. Road Runner was foiling Wile E. Coyote yet again.

"Beep, beep."

Devo looked like he'd been spawned in a petri dish by an evil bacteriologist. Skinny and bald, his head had more furrows than a fresh-plowed field. Dismas assumed the grooves had wrinkled his brain, explaining why he was dumb as dirt. He started to say what he wanted when a jumbo jet almost landed on their heads.

Devo shouted over the din. "Ya ain't gonna bust my arm like ya did Jimmy, are ya?"

"All ya gotta do is get drunk," Dismas yelled back.

Devo's dead eyes came alive. "I can do that."

Dismas gave him five twenty dollar bills and directions to the bar. "Go in and drink till ya get shitfaced, then drive that jalopy a yours down Las Olas and steer into one of them Royal Palms in the medium."

"Medium?"

"Ya know, the middle of the road."

"You sure about that, Diz? I could get messed up."

"Just don't be drivin' like it's the Daytona stock car races. Don't go no faster'n fifteen or twenty. Ya ain't gonna get hurt. We got a doctor that'll say yer injured, even if ya ain't."

Devo scratched his ridged cranium with a pained expression. "I don't know, Diz."

"Ya get five grand, plus yer car fixed."

"What time ya want me there?"

Now Devo was calling from the Swimming Hall of Fame across the street from the bar.

"They got a big picture of Tarzan on the wall. I didn't know Tarzan's in the Swimmin' Hall a Fame."

"That ain't Tarzan. It's the guy used to play him in the movies. Johnny Wisenheimer or some shit. Used to be some Olympic swimmer. I heard when he got old and senile he used to break loose with that Tarzan yodel and scare the crap outa people."

"Cause they thought the elephants was gonna stampede?"

Dismas rolled his eyes. "Yeah, Devo. They was afraid of elephants."

"What ya want me to do, Diz?"

"Go back to your car and wait for me."

Dismas dropped off Kenny at Cloud Nine with his video game and Dan Marino jersey. Fifteen minutes later he pulled into a parking lot across from the Swimming Hall of Fame. Devo was sitting behind the wheel of his dilapidated 1960-something Buick Skylark. The car was pocked with dozens of tiny dents, like hail storms had been using it for target practice. He stumbled from the Skylark and blundered toward the van, a broken down, creaky-jointed wreck of a man. As a teenager he'd taken a high dive into a shallow pond and broken his neck, leaving it bent forward like a fish hook. He looked like he was perpetually counting cracks in a sidewalk. Dismas decided there was no way around it. Devo was an inferior life form.

"Get in," he said. As soon as the door closed Dismas's face puckered, like he'd bitten into one of those big sour pickles they sell at the movies. "Jeez, Devo. I know dead people that smell better'n you. No wonder they kicked you outa that bar."

Devo's stolid face was as enthusiastic as a flat tire. His nose looked like a shiny radish. He sniffed himself with it. "I don't smell nothin', Diz."

"You and Jimmy ain't got one good nose 'tween ya." Dismas handed him a bottle of Jack Daniels. "Wet yer whistle."

Devo snatched it and unscrewed the cap with quivering fingers. He took a long quaff and swished the whiskey in his mouth. His Adam's apple yo-yoed like a bobber on a fish line.

"What the hell ya think yer doin'?" Dismas said. "This ain't no fancy wine tastin'."

Devo swallowed with a grimace, as though he'd ingested napalm. He licked his lips and seconds later the bomb exploded and his eyes rolled back. He handed the bottle to Dismas, who refused it.

"That's all fer you. Finish it."

Devo stared at him like he was speaking a foreign tongue.

"Damn," he said finally and held up the bottle. "Lookout world, here I come."

Little men grow into big men fast when they're properly irrigated.

"Now yer gettin' the hang of it, Devo."

Et Tu Brady

Chapter Forty-Three

"WHAT THE HELL is going on, Brady?"

Rose Becker stalked back and forth across her City Hall office. Across the same rug she and Brady made love on just a couple of weeks before. Now there was only fury in her step, as if she desperately needed to be someplace, but didn't know where. Her eyes were wild and stormy and she seemed on the verge of tears.

Brady knew he was the reason and didn't like himself much at the moment. He felt like a walking, talking lipstick stain. First it had been Delray's sudden unsolicited kiss in her brother's library. Then today at her brother's funeral, holding his hand and kissing him on the lips while Rose stood by. Brady didn't know what to do about her displays of affection. He resolved to set her straight next time – if there was a next time.

He hadn't realized the extent of Rose's unhappiness until she abruptly marched away from him at the church. After she left, he filled Delray in on what he'd been digging up. Strictly lawyer to client. Then he drove straight to City Hall. Now he wished he hadn't. She ceased her perambulations and they stood face-to-face, staring at each other like they were from different planets. Brady couldn't remember if men were supposed to be from Mars or Venus.

"What is going on between you and that woman?" Rose demanded.

She was as accusatory as a courtroom prosecutor. Brady tried to look innocent.

"What are you talking about?" he said, rather lamely.

"Leave it to a man to overlook the obvious."

"Really? You're playing the *'leave it to a man'* card on me?"

He was trying to tap dance his way out of trouble, but Rose had the perceptive powers of a CAT scan. There was no hoodwinking her.

"Holding hands! Kissing her! On the lips!" Her eyes cut into him like scalpels. He wanted to glance down to see if he was bleeding. "Look, Brady, if you and I are gonna be together it's got to be all or nothing. I'm not playing second fiddle to anyone."

"Come on, Rose. Delray's brother was just murdered. The police want to put her on Death Row. She's alone. She needs someone to lean on."

"I'm not naïve. She wants to do more than lean on you. Would you rather be with her?"

"That's ridiculous," he protested, hoping his voice bore the timbre of truth, though he suspected she was right about Delray's intentions.

Nonetheless, Rose was showing a side of herself he hadn't seen before. She was a woman without shadows. Strong. Smart. Honest. Funny. Sensual. Everything he could ask for. After Victoria was killed he thought he'd never love a woman again the way he'd loved her. His passion for Rose, though, was at least as ardent. He hated to see her this way. Hurt. Angry. Uncertain of his fidelity. A tear escaped her. He'd never seen her cry.

"What was that between you two at the church?"

"There is zero between us. I haven't seen Delray since we were kids. There was barely anything back then."

"What exactly did happen with her – back then?"

He kicked himself for not shutting up when he had the chance.

"We were school classmates. We used to water ski. Sometimes she'd go out on the ocean with me and Ben and our friend Peanut when we went scuba diving."

"Come on, Brady. We promised each other. No secrets. Were you in love with her?"

"We were thirteen years old. You couldn't even call it puppy love."

"I was in love when I was thirteen."

That stopped him. "With who?"

"Raymond Ward."

"Who's Raymond Ward?"

"He's a doctor now."

Brady jumped at the chance to turn the tables. "Are you still in love with him?"

"I might be, if he wasn't bald and fat and living in Tacoma with a wife and three kids. Unlike Dr. Delray Cross, who's blonde and gorgeous and right here in town, holding your hand and kissing your lips."

"How do you know he's fat and bald?"

"Don't try to change the subject. Were you in love with her?"

"Jeez, Rose." He ran a hand through his hair. "We had a crush on each other when we were kids. You weren't even born yet. Then she moved away. I hadn't seen her again until two days ago. I hope you don't react like this every time I talk to a woman."

"Give me a break, Brady. Talk is one thing. Kissing is a whole nother thing. How many times have you heard about childhood sweethearts meeting late in life and picking up where they left off?"

He blanched. "I'm not late in life."

"Nobody knows where they are in life. We could all die tomorrow."

"You make it sound like I'm a member of AARP."

"Brady, I'm realizing more every day there are too many things I don't know about you."

The conversation had taken another twist, down a path he did not want to travel. There *was* a lot Rose didn't know. Secrets he dared not tell anyone. Secrets he wished he didn't know.

"Tell me what happened when you were kids, Brady?"

He glanced at his wrist. "I gotta go."

"What are you looking at? You don't wear a watch."

"Just practicing, in case I get one someday."

He turned toward the door.

"Something happened between you and her. I can feel it. Her brother was involved, too, wasn't he?"

For a split second he thought of his grandmother and considered whether Rose possessed the same oracular powers Kate Brady once had. That would be a problem.

"I'll see you later."

"Why won't you talk to me, Brady?"

"There's nothing to say."

He was at the door, his back to her, his hand on the knob.

"Brady, how did your grandparents die?"

He froze in his tracks and spun on her, his face taut and red. Jekyll become Hyde. Rose took a sharp breath and stepped backwards.

"Leave it alone," he growled. His voice had a cruel edge she'd never heard before.

"Why won't you tell me what happened to your grandparents?"

"I said let it be."

He opened the door and was halfway down the hallway when Rose yelled after him.

"Why won't you talk to me, Brady? What are you hiding? Why was that woman kissing you?"

Et Tu Brady

Chapter Forty-Four

FIRST KISSES CAN be more indelible than any that come after, maybe because first times only happen once. The first time Max Brady savored the taste of Delray Chance's lips they were hiding under a seagrape tree beside Whiskey Creek.

Max had spent the day on Three Mile Reef with Ben and Peanut hunting for more gold coins, though, his thoughts were on Delray. She'd gone to the creek that day with Ginger Brennan and a gang of river kids.

It was another blue July day, an armada of white cumulus clouds sailing over a sparkling sapphire sea. The boys brought extra scuba tanks and by day's end had found five more coins. Their discovery eclipsed imagination.

"We're like the Three Musketeers, lads," Max announced.

"More like the Three Stooges," Ben countered and they broke into laughter.

As they examined the booty, Peanut recounted to Ben their visit the day before to Matty Fitt's shack.

"Nasty old geezer." He held one of the coins up to the sun. "But he says there's tons more gold where this came from."

"Except he doesn't know where we found it and we need to keep it that way," Max said. He ran his fingers across his mouth. "Lips zipped. Tell no one. We're gonna be millionaires."

"Maybe if we live a hundred years," Ben said. "We've gone down three days now. Maybe ten hours under water between us. We've found ten coins. At this rate we're gonna have to live as long as that old guy in the Bible that Sister Margaret Mary used to go on about."

"Methuselah," said Peanut. "Nine hundred sixty nine years."

Max laughed. "You guys believe that crap? The Bible's half fiction. Do you really think the human race started with two people named Adam and Eve? Do you really believe Earth is only six thousand years old? I trust Carl Sagan." He did his imitation of Johnny Carson doing his imitation of the astronomer. *"It's billions and billions of years old."*

"You're gonna go to Hell," said Ben.

"I bet you still believe in Santa Claus," Max said.

Ben looked at him, confused. "What do you mean?"

"There's no Hell, Ben. They made it up to scare us. Keep us in line."

Ben and Peanut backed away from him, as if they expected lightning to strike at any second.

"Don't you believe in God?" Ben said.

"I believe in us. We've got to have faith in ourselves. We'll figure out how to raise the gold. Necessity's the mother of invention."

"Wow," Peanut said, his voice sodden with sarcasm. "Did you just make that up?"

"Did you know Thomas Edison invented the light bulb because he was afraid of the dark?"

"You sure about that?"

"Trust me. We'll find a way."

The afternoon was drawing on and Whiskey Creek was beckoning. Max hoped Delray was too. They hoisted anchor and he pointed the Boston Whaler toward Port Everglades.

The port inlet was the dividing line between Fort Lauderdale Beach to the north and Dania Beach to the south. Historically, Dania was a long, lonely stretch of sand that had once been the black beach. Lauderdale was off-limits to *Colored* bathers until 1961. Max had seen photographs of black people being arrested for swimming at the same beach he did.

Whiskey Creek was between the Atlantic and the Intracoastal Waterway. When they swung into the creek, the long curling green ribbon looked deserted. A pelican tilted toward them floating low on the wind, its wingtips dipping into the water as it flapped past. A large snook leapt three times in front of them. Snapping turtles were sunning themselves on fallen trees. Max recalled what Matty Fitt had said about him and Grandpa Zack smuggling bootleg liquor to this very spot. *"Why do you think they call it Whiskey Creek?"*

Halfway down the watercourse they came upon a line of boats pulled onto a narrow strand of white sand. Max recognized most of them from Ski Beach, their home base on New River. He throttled back and glided onto the bank. A radio was blaring *Crocodile Rock* while kids frolicked in the water. The scene was bursting with boisterous flirtations between pubescent teenagers reveling in the springtide of life. Shaggy Sam and Hot Lips Hogan were making out on a cypress limb. (The river gang had more nicknames than a Mafia meet-and-greet.) Scary Terry was dunking A-Bomb Adams in the middle of the creek. Scotty Noll and Rainbow Reynolds were in the water up to their necks with their faces pressed together.

"Those two have a serious case of lip lock," Peanut said.

"That's what Delray wants Max to do to her," said Ben.

Brady cringed and shot him a sour look. "Shut up, freak."

Ben laughed. "Don't you get it? My sister's madly in love with you."

"You're hallucinating."

Just hearing the words, though, made Max's insides churn.

"It's true. I heard her tell Ginger. She's been waiting for you to make a move. Ginger says you're too shy and that Delray should do it."

Ginger's boat was beached with the others, but Delray was nowhere in sight. Stinky Rinker raced past in his boat with Sally Kirtz's brother, Glenn, skiing off the back. Junior Ball and two of his thug buddies were smoking cigarettes in his red Glasspar, adrift in the middle of the creek. Three sides to the same coin. Snake Eyes Harper, a thick, bluntheaded kid with close-set eyes, was scraping wooden matches on the fiberglass hull, snapping the flares into the water, and laughing at the zilch sound they made. Skinny Wentworth, a frail, ferret-faced boy, stood on the bow with a Marlboro dangling from his lip, staring at Ben.

"Fatboy's here," he called out as Max beached the Whaler.

"Fatboy's gonna have to take showers in gym class next year," Snake Eyes said. "Everybody's gonna see his little willy."

"I bet he needs tweezers just to jack off," Junior added with an imbecilic laugh.

Moaning Lisa and Messy Jessie giggled on the beach. Max saw his friend's face redden and his shoulders sag. For a thirteen year old boy, being publicly indicted for having a *little willy* was the ultimate indignity. That Ben's jury was no nearer to manhood than him didn't diminish the degradation. He was saved from further humiliation by Skates Jameson calling out the battle cry.

"Mango war!"

That ignited a mad dash. Kids swam across the water to the mangrove island that separated Whiskey Creek from the Intracoastal. The miniature forest was thick with mango trees burdened with ripe fruit. Ammunition. Red and orange orbs began flying over the creek and were loaded into boats. Before long a dozen outboards were chasing up and down the tributary and kids began pelting each other with mangoes like medieval knights jousting on aquatic steeds.

Max set his sights on Junior. He and his friends had blinded the defenseless animals at the Alligator Pit. And Bruno, Billy Panther's bull gator, at the Seminole Village. He was going to make them pay. On their first pass he side-armed a squishy mango that caught Skinny Wentworth square in the chest and exploded in a hail of orange pulp. While Max laughed, A-Bomb Adams came up fast from behind and drilled him in the back, leaving a large red welt. Fruit bombs were flying everywhere. Hot Lips was whacked in the back of her head. Stinky Rinker took one in the gonads. Boats were soon bathed in ochreous mush. It went on like that until Max and his friends were down to their last mango. Ben was sitting at the bow. He turned back to Brady with a seditious grin.

"Get me a shot at Junior."

"Sure thing, pal."

He was more than happy to help his friend exact retribution. The red Glasspar was making a turn at the far end of the creek. Max gunned the Whaler. Junior saw him coming and cocked his arm ready to fire. Ben did the same in the Whaler. They closed in on each other at full speed. At the last second Max shouted.

"Hold on, Ben."

He spun the wheel and the Whaler cut hard left directly in front of the Glasspar. Junior dropped his mango and used both hands to jerk his own boat left to avoid a head-on collision. That gave Ben a wide open shot. He squeezed the fruit in his chubby right hand, reared back, and hurled a high, hard one. The blob caught Junior flush on the temple and detonated like an orange grenade. Junior's head snapped to the side and his hands flew off the wheel. The boat lurched left and Junior was catapulted into the creek. The Glasspar veered out of control and crashed into the mangrove, launching Skinny and Snake Eyes into the weeds.

Ben raised his arms in triumph while Max and Peanut cheered. Max turned and saw Junior in the middle of the creek. He was floating face down. He swung the Whaler around and raced back, threw the throttle into neutral and dove over the side. The water was about ten feet deep at the center of the channel. He grabbed Junior, flipped him onto his back, layed his arm across his chest, and side-stroked, scissor-kicking to the beach. Scotty Noll and Raggedy Bob helped him drag Junior onto the sand. They got him into a sitting position and Max thumped his back with the heel of his hand. After several whacks Junior vomited water and began to cough. He sat there for several minutes with his head between his legs, massaging his temple. Finally he lifted his eyes and grunted something in Max's direction that did not sound like a *thank you*. He staggered to his feet and dove back into the water and swam across the creek toward his boat, still nosed into the mangrove.

Peanut coasted up in the Whaler, laughing. "That kid's gotta learn to be a better loser."

Shaggy Sam jumped on Ben's back. "Big bad Benny. That was so bitchin'! Ain't revenge sweet?"

Soon everyone but Junior and his goons were congratulating Ben. There was a new gleam in his eyes. He looked as happy as a honey bear with a beehive. Max had never seen him so euphoric.

The sun was starting to sink in the western sky when Ned Thrift appeared on the dune separating the creek from the ocean. He waved them toward the beach and shouted.

"We're gonna play Firebase. You guys in?"

"Try to keep us out," Peanut called back.

They scaled the sand hill and high-stepped over feathery tufts of dune grass to the ocean side. Max's dive knife was still strapped to his calf. The beach was wide and deserted. No lifeguards or other signs of civilization, except the river kids. In the slanting rays of the late afternoon sun, he cast a long shadow that arrived at the waterline several seconds before he did. It startled a gull in the midst of cracking open a crab with its beak. The bird flew off with its snack and he saw Delray thirty feet beyond. She was floating in the surf with Ginger. Small waves were washing over them and tiptoeing onto the beach. Saffron light glistened on Delray's wet skin. Ben's words were still burning in his ears. *"Don't you get it? My sister is madly in love with you?"* He didn't *get it*, but he wanted to hear more and regretted telling Ben to shut up. He just couldn't bear the thought of everyone knowing how he felt about her. Who could handle that?

When the girls saw them, Ginger jumped to her feet and rushed from the water. Her wet blue Speedo did little to hide the lush curves of a much older girl. She could have been sixteen. Peanut gasped.

"Holy guacamole, Batman! Look at those babies. They're huge."

Max laughed. "Why don't you tell her you're hot for her?"

"Shut up, spaz," Peanut said and punched him in the arm. "Why don't you tell Delray?"

Before he could answer, Ginger ran straight to Peanut, threw her arms around him, and kissed him on the lips. Brady stared at them with his mouth open. He had not expected that. He knew Peanut

292

hadn't either. He walked into the water. Delray's eyes followed him like heliotropic flowers tracking toward the sun. She was wearing a wide smile.

"What's so funny?" he said.

"Peanut."

"I didn't know Ginger liked him."

"He owes me bigtime."

"Why?"

"He's been asking me to fix him up with her. I put a bug in her ear and..." She waved an arm at them still going at it on the sand. "*Abracadabra!*"

Max kept watching them, fascinated, while Delray watched him.

"How about you, Max? What girl do you work your magic on?"

The question caught him flat-footed. Flabbergasted, he felt a knot in his throat. He avoided her eyes.

"Me? I don't know. How about you?"

She laughed. "Oh, no! I asked first. You must have someone special."

Max felt like a cornered animal. He searched his brain, frantic for an escape, but it locked up on him, as it did so often around her. She wouldn't give up.

"Come on, spit it out. You must have a girl."

He cleared his throat and took a deep breath. "There is one girl."

"Really?" She watched him closely. "How long has that been going on?"

"Nothing's...going...on." He was barely able to get the words out. "I...just...kinda...like...her."

"Does she know?"

He shrugged.

A shocked expression lit her face. "You mean you haven't told her?"

He shrugged again and mumbled. "Not really."

"Why not, Max. You're the smartest boy in school. And the cutest. You stand up to bullies. You jump off bridges. You fight sharks. No one I know is as brave as you. And you're afraid to tell a girl you like her?"

His face flushed. Delray had called him *cute*. His grandmother told him he was *handsome*, but no girl had ever called him *cute*. He liked the ring of that. Much better than smart.

"Don't you know how many girls would give anything to be your girlfriend?"

"Me?" The question surprised him. He'd never thought about girls liking him, other than her. Then inspiration struck. "Name one."

Now she was at a loss for words. "Well," she stammered, "plenty of girls."

"How about you? Who is your boyfriend?"

"I don't have one."

"You? The prettiest girl in school?" He couldn't believe he'd just said that, but he saw her eyes twinkle. "You must have a boyfriend."

Her face twisted into a squint. "I really don't like boys much."

Something inside him buckled. *I really don't like boys!* Ben had been lying. If she didn't like boys, she couldn't be madly in love with him. He made a mental note to bash her brother with a big, fat mango.

Suddenly, Delray screamed and jumped into Max's arms, on the verge of hysteria.

"Something touched my foot! Get me out! Get me out of the water! Hurry!"

Max carried her to knee deep water and set her down and she sprinted onto the beach where Peanut and Ginger were still entwined. He remained where he'd put her down. In the next instant he fell off his feet and began flailing.

"Help!" he shouted.

He began moving away from the beach. He pulled his diving knife from its sheath and stabbed at something beneath the surface.

"Peanut!" Delray yelled. "Max needs help."

Peanut pulled his face away from Ginger's and looked at the water.

"Must be a shark," he said casually. "Big one too to pull him like that. I'm not going out there."

Ginger broke free of his arms and pushed away. "You jerk! A shark's got your best friend and you won't help?"

"Help!" Max screamed again. "Help!"

He kept slashing at the water. Whatever had him, though, was dragging him farther away from the beach. Fifty feet. One hundred feet. Then he vanished. Delray screamed.

Hot Lips ran up. "What's happening?"

"A shark got Max," Ginger said. She was in tears.

Within minutes all the kids were at water's edge. Delray pleaded. "Please. Somebody help him."

"No way," Scotty Noll said.

"Me neither," said Peacock Bill. "If there's one shark out there there's gotta be more."

"When they get you, you're gone," Glenn Kirtz said.

Delray started to sob. She looked up at a boy standing beside her. It was Junior.

"You're kidding, right," he said.

Ginger, Hot Lips, and Moaning Lisa huddled around her like maids of honor consoling a spurned bride. Minutes passed. The river kids stood staring at the ocean, mesmerized, searching for signs of Max, or the shark.

"Maybe somebody should go get help," said Raggedy Bob.

"Too late now," Stinky said. "I can't believe Brady was done in by a shark."

"I'm gonna miss that guy," Ben lamented.

"Me too," said Peanut. "He was a good friend."

A voice came from the back of the crowd. "What are you looking at?"

"Max got taken under by a shark," said Hot Lips.

"Why is everybody just standing here? We've gotta do something."

Heads turned. He was standing there with a horrified expression on his face. Delray broke through the throng and threw her arms around him. Then she pushed him away and slapped his arm.

"That wasn't funny!" Her voice was quivering and her face was streaked with tears. "I thought you were dead."

Max rubbed his arm and tried to look contrite, which wasn't easy considering Ben, Peanut, and Stinky were rolling on the sand in hysterics behind her.

Nicky Pickles started chanting. "Max's got a girlfriend! Max's got a girlfriend!"

"Guys are such jerks," Moaning Lisa said.

"That was cool, Max," said A-Bomb Adams.

"Thanks for trying to save me, you guys. I guess I know who my friends *aren't.*"

"I've seen you pull that stunt too many times," said Peanut. "You need some new material."

The chorus grew. "Max's got a girlfriend! Max's got a girlfriend!"

"Lisa's right," Max said. "Guys are such jerks."

Day collapsed into night. The kids stacked an enormous pile of driftwood on the beach and were ready for the game to begin. Firebase was hide-and-seek with a bonfire as base. Ned Thrift announced the boundaries. Whiskey Creek on one side, the ocean on the other, the Port Everglades Inlet jetties to the north and a tall Australian pine at the opposite end of the beach. They drew pine needles to determine who was IT. Ben pulled the short straw.

Jungle Boogie was blasting from a radio. Someone got a fuel tank from one of the boats and Ned poured gasoline on the driftwood. Snake Eyes Harper scraped one of his wooden matches on a log and threw it atop the pile and the pitch black night was emblazoned by a monstrous inferno. Smoke billowed into the sky while twenty kids danced around the pyre screaming like banshees. Ned switched off the radio and shouted over the crackle and hiss of the bonfire.

"Alright, Ben, ready, set, go!"

They scattered like a flock of seagulls being chased by small children. Peanut and Ginger ran to the creek and climbed a tree. Junior Ball and his punk buddies took off down the beach and began digging a foxhole in the shadows. Max saw Delray head toward Whiskey Creek and followed. He didn't hurry, knowing Ben moved at roughly the speed of Heinz Ketchup.

A bank of cumulus clouds rolled in and obscured the full moon so that the only illumination was coming from the fire. The light vanished when Max breasted the dune. He lurched down the steep bank and was swallowed by obsidian night. Delray had disappeared.

So had everything else. *This must be how Little Stevie Wonder feels*, he thought. He could hear kids giggling in the darkness as they scrambled for cover. Feeling the way with his bare feet, he skirted the creek, touching his toes to the water to keep his bearing. Then a voice called out from the blankness.

"Max."

He followed the sound, but could not find its source until a branch opened on a seagrape tree. It was Delray. He dove beneath the shroud of broad leaves and they huddled in the black velvet shadows listening to inexplicit whispers of disembodied voices.

After a few minutes they heard Ben stumble down the sand bank and plod past them. About twenty yards down the creek he shouted *"captured."* Someone cursed. It was Peanut. He and Ginger had been caught. Then Scotty Noll and Rainbow Reynolds. Max and Delray suppressed their laughs. The voices died and they were engulfed by the shrill stridulations from a choir of crickets. Brady turned and looked at her. It was too black to see much. He could barely decipher the profile of her turned-up nose and long curling lashes.

"I'm sorry I pulled that trick," he whispered. "I was trying to make you laugh, not cry."

They weren't wearing much. He was in cut-offs, she in her yellow Speedo. The bare skin of their arms and legs were touching. It was the closest he'd ever been to a girl, at least like this. And he liked it. He liked it very much.

"I guess it was pretty funny. But I was scared. I thought you were dead."

"You were scared for me?"

"Of course. Don't you know how I feel about you?"

"You said you don't like boys."

He heard a small laugh. "I might have exaggerated a little bit."

Max screwed up his courage and took a deep breath. "Delray, you know that girl I told you I like?"

"Yes."

He swallowed and just managed to get out the words. "I... meant...you."

"I know."

A stray cloud drifted past and the midsummer moon shone bright as the mantle of a gas lantern. A silver shaft slattered between the seagrape leaves and was captured by Delray's golden hair. He could see her face now. She was staring at him, so near he saw his reflection in her eyes. She reached up and brushed a forelock from his brow. Then, to his utter astonishment, she leaned forward and pressed her lips to his. It only lasted seconds, but he knew immediately it was the best thing that had ever happened to him. Better than scuba diving. Or water skiing. Or bridge diving.

An incandescent smile lit her face. "Better than fighting sharks, isn't it?"

"Shhhh!" he whispered and did to her what she'd done to him. This one longer. Savoring the sensation.

"You're a good kisser. You must've had a lot of practice."

"Me?"

"I bet you've made out with lots of girls at The Cove?"

Max almost laughed. "Not really. Have you?"

"Made out with girls at The Cove?"

"You know what I mean."

"You might not believe this, but that was my very first kiss."

"Ever?"

"Well, Scotty Noll kissed me on the playground in first grade. I ran away crying and Scotty got into trouble."

He kissed her again. "That's my third kiss. Ever."

"Our third kiss," Delray whispered and kissed him again. "Fourth!"

It was an awakening dappled in moonshadows. Virginal lovers cloaked by exquisite night. They went on like that as if they were the only two people on Earth. Kissing. Smiling. Laughing softly. Touching faces. Inhaling each other's breath. Smelling each other's scents. Cheeks flushed. Pulses racing. Respiration irregular. Powerful new chemicals firing through their brains. Billions of neurotransmitters shooting strange and extraordinary signals to all parts of their young bodies. Luxuriating in the deliciousness of their seminal moment. Max knew he would never forget the intimacy he felt with Delray beneath that seagrape tree.

"What do you think Attila the Nun would do if she caught us?" she said.

"Probably have us burned at the stake."

"Why?"

"Too much fun."

"Do you think kissing is a sin?"

"Most fun stuff is."

"Not all sins are fun. Not if they're hurtful."

"I prefer fun sins," he said and kissed her again. Then he pulled his dive knife from the sheath on his calf.

"What are you doing?"

"Watch."

He carved *MB + DC* into the trunk and dug a heart in the bark around it.

Delray kissed him once more. "You make me happy, Max. I wish I was you."

"Why would you wish that?"

"So I could be with you all the time."

She kissed him and he kissed her back.

"If you were with me all the time, you might not want to be me."

And then their lives changed, forever.

In the distance, they heard the drone of a boat motor. Max peeked out between the seagrape petals. They were a few feet from water's edge. The creek was smooth as black ice. He didn't see the boat for a minute, then it came fast. Without running lights. They retreated further into the shadows, wanting to maintain their luscious privacy. The boat noise drowned out the sounds of the crickets. Firebase was being played on the beach now and the creek was deserted. The Whaler and other boats were out of sight further upstream.

Another cloud drifted in and obstructed the moon just as the engine noise ceased. Max squinted, trying to see through half-eyes as the murky mirage of the new boat glided to a stop directly across the creek. The vessel was light-colored. Two shadows were moving on board. The silhouettes looked like men. They wore dark clothing and stood still for several minutes, seeming to survey the terrain.

Delray leaned closer to Max. He put a finger to her lips. His jungle instincts had gone on high alert. Something felt sinister.

The moon peeked out from behind the cloud and he saw them more clearly. One had light hair, the other darker. The dark man vaulted over the side and sank into chest deep water.

"Shit!" he blurted. He sounded surprised.

"Shut up!" the other man growled. He threw a rope in the water. "Pull!"

They seemed in a hurry. The man in the water dragged the boat to the mangrove island and lashed it to a branch. The blond man moved to the stern. He bent down and lifted something off the floor. It was white. It looked like a tarpaulin or rolled rug. He lowered the bundle over the side. The dark man stumbled and sank beneath the water. He surfaced and struggled to regain his footing. While he did, the bundle floated away.

"Fool," the man in the boat said with suppressed fury. "Can't you do anything right?"

"Shut the fuck up."

Max and Delray shook with silent laughter. They watched the dark man retrieve the bundle and wade to the bank. Slipping and sliding in the mud, he managed to haul it onto the island. Max thought it might be a tent or camping equipment, but something about these guys didn't fit. They didn't seem like campers. Besides, he'd explored the island many times. It was thick jungle with a lot of bugs and few clearings. If someone wanted to camp they'd do it on the beach side.

They kept watching, noiseless as the stars. The dark man slid back into the water and the blond lifted a second bundle identical to the first. He lowered it, picked up something, and jumped over the side. They dragged the second roll onto the island and vanished into the brush.

Max looked at Delray and leaned over and kissed her, holding his lips to hers longer this time.

"That's ten," he said. "Come on."

He took her hand and led her out from under the seagrape and they hastened back over the dune to the beach. The air was filled with the bittersweet scent of burning driftwood. He turned and looked at her in the firelight. Her face was flushed and her breath uneven, but her eyes were shining.

"Go get everybody together," he said. "Tell them to stay by the fire. Don't let anybody come down to the creek until I get back."

Delray grabbed his arm. Alarm had taken over of her face.

"What's going on, Max? What are you going to do?"

"I don't know. Something's strange. I just want to get a closer look. Go!"

She kissed him one last time and sprinted toward the fire. He watched her long, loping athletic form recede then returned to the dune and moved downstream. Keeping to the trees, he made his way about fifty yards, slid down the bank, and ran. His feet slapped the shallow water for another fifty before he slipped into its cool embrace and breast-stroked soundlessly.

Max reached the far shore and clawed his way up the embankment. Once on land he moved deliberately through dense vegetation, his bare feet sinking in the spongy mire. By the time he reached the blinding darkness of the island's interior he'd traveled what felt like at least one hundred yards. Breathless, he stopped and crouched and tasted the night air. The sky opened for a moment. A familiar constellation glittered in the celestial light. Orion – The Hunter. *Perfect.* A swarm of mosquitoes picked him up on their radar and attacked in a whirr. He was flapping his arms around his head trying to shoo them away when he heard a faint sound. It was coming from his left. Stealthy as a chameleon stalking a spider, he negotiated his way over gnarly roots and under low branches until the noise became more distinct. He couldn't make out what it was. Then he heard voices.

"Why am I doing all the digging?" a man said.

Another male voice responded. "Because if it was me digging you'd be rolled up in canvas, too."

Something touched Max's head and he gasped.

"Quiet!" one of the voices said. "What's that?"

Max pressed himself against a tree trunk, as close as a shadow.

"I didn't hear nothin'. You're getting paranoid."

The sound began again. Max brushed his fingers through his hair and discovered a leaf had floated down on him. He looked up and saw he was hugging a large mango tree. He found a foothold and, nimble as a monkey, scaled the trunk, scampering from branch to branch until he reached a nesting place in an elbow twenty feet up. He peered through the hanging fruit like they were cracks in a curtain. A lightbeam was flashing in a clearance between a stand of trees about fifty yards away. It illumined a shirtless man knee-deep in a hole stabbing a shovel savagely at the sand, like someone hacking the head off a rattlesnake. Something about him seemed familiar. A cowl of black hair cloaked his face, but his muscled chest and tattooed arms were unmistakable. A bolt of electricity shot down Max's spine.

Buck!

The two bundles lay on the ground beside him. Max couldn't make out who was holding the flashlight, but decided he'd seen enough. Scarcely hazarding a breath, he slid down the tree, quiet as a whisper. When he hit the ground, though, his foot snapped a dry twig. The shoveling stopped again.

"What was that?"

"I told you I heard a noise."

"Keep digging. I'll check."

Max heard rustling in the thicket. A flashlight flickered through the trees like a candle in a graveyard. He ducked low and moved catlike toward the creek. The light kept coming. He started to run, letting his feet feel the way through the brush. Then the lightbeam homed in on him.

"Hey! You! Stop!"

The voice was close. Max reached the bank. The sky had cleared and stars reflected off the black water like white nails. He lowered himself into the creek and dove to the bottom and swam as fast and far as his lungs would take him. He surfaced on the far side, crawled out, and sprinted over the dune straight to the bonfire. The other kids had gathered around the blaze. Max was panting hard through his open mouth.

"Everybody needs to get out of here." He pointed toward the far end of the creek. "Go out the south end. And be quiet."

"What is it?" Stinky Rinker said. "What's wrong?"

In the firelight, alarm showed on their faces. Max's friends had never seen him so serious. Or scared. They ran to the boats, even Junior Ball and his buddies. Peanut jumped into Ginger's boat. Delray and Ben went with Max in the Whaler. They tore out of the creek, turned into the Intracoastal and raced through Port Everglades. No one spoke. They made their way to the mouth of New River and navigated upstream until they reached the dock behind the Chance house. Ben and Delray climbed out and stared down on him.

"What was it?" Ben said finally. "What did you see?"

Max looked at him and then Delray. He shook his head and lied. "I don't know."

Et Tu Brady

Chapter Forty-Five

BRADY'S INSIDES WERE doing somersaults as he negotiated the Jeep east on Las Olas Boulevard. He'd stalked out of Rose's office minutes before, unsure what was rattling him more. Her suspicion about Delray. Or her sudden questions about the death of his grandparent's. What did she want to know? And why did she want to know it?

He was heading for the Sea Shanty. After two days playing lawyer he wanted to check up on things. He trusted Gordy, but the bar business was the butter on his bread.

As he approached the Las Olas Bridge, traffic screeched to a halt. He craned his neck out the window and saw a plume of black smoke rising in the sky. He opened the door and stood on the Jeep's side step. A line of about twenty cars had come to a stop ahead. Then he saw why. A black SUV was flipped over in the road. Smoke was pouring from its undercarriage. An older model car with its front end smashed in was in the east-bound lane facing west. A human form appeared to be stretched out on the pavement between the two vehicles.

He jumped down and began to run, then stopped abruptly. A black Mitsubishi Lancer was idling in front of the Jeep. A girl who looked to be high school age was at the wheel with a cell phone pressed to her ear. He rapped on the window and she jerked away. She looked up at him with an alarmed expression. He motioned to her to roll down the window. She hesitated, then complied.

"Call nine-one-one," he shouted. "Tell them there's been a bad accident on Las Olas just west of the bridge. Two cars. Do it now!"

When he reached the scene a heavyset woman was standing in the middle of the road. Tears were streaming down her face and she was flapping her arms like a semaphore flag waver. When she saw Brady she pointed toward the prone figure.

"Please, mister. That woman's hurt bad."

The upside down vehicle was a Cadillac Escalade. Its tires were still spinning and it was billowing smoke. He didn't see flames, but the sweet, stomach-turning stench of gasoline permeated the air. The woman lay face down on the blacktop, still as death. The other car was an old Skylark with faded blue paint. A man was slumped against the steering wheel. Drivers had exited their cars and were gathering. Brady hollered at no one in particular.

"Somebody check that guy."

He knelt beside the prostrate woman and pressed his right palm flat against her back. He didn't feel any pulse or respiration. He rolled her over and almost threw up. Her face looked like it had been smashed by a brick. She was young and blonde and, judging by her wardrobe and vehicle, well-to-do. Brady put his fingertips to her carotid artery. Nothing. Then the heavyset woman cried out.

"Oh, my God! There's a child in the car."

He left the woman and scrambled to the Escalade. Hanging upside down in the back seat was a little girl. She looked to be about three years old. Her little arms were hanging down limply over her head. So was her long hair, the same straw color as the woman on the road. The girl with the telephone ran up. She was tall and lanky and wore a green plaid skirt with a white blouse that marked her as a private school student.

"An ambulance is on the way," she said. She looked at the uncon-scious woman and let out a small whimper. "Is she alive?"

"I can't get a pulse." Brady's eyes were moving back and forth between woman and child. "What's your name, sweetheart?"

"Danielle," she said, her voice cracking.

"Do you know CPR?"

"I took a health class in school. They taught us artificial resuscitation."

Her knees were shaking and she looked like she was about to break down.

"Listen, Danielle, you need to be calm. See what you can do for her." Brady demonstrated. "Place the heels of your hands on the center of her chest and press down like this. Fast. A hundred compressions per minute. Don't worry about respiration. Just keep pumping her heart. Can you do that?"

"I'll try."

She knelt on bare knees beside the woman. He looked up at the growing group of bystanders.

"Please, somebody help her revive that lady."

He turned to the Escalade. The windows were closed and the interior was filling with smoke. He yanked on the back door handle. It wouldn't budge. The front door was locked too. A bystander shouted.

"Gas. It's leaking. Get back before it explodes."

Gasoline was splashing onto the road and forming an incendiary moat around the big car. Through the haze he could barely see the little girl. He tried the other doors but none would open. Brady crawled to the front of the SUV. The hood was crumpled but there was open space beneath. He lay on his belly and wedged himself into it headfirst and peered through the windshield.

At the center of the glass was a jagged hole the size of a large cannonball with edges like ghastly red Piranha teeth. The front seat was almost invisible in the smoke. The baby was completely lost. The driver's airbag had deployed and deflated, but hadn't stopped the woman from being jettisoned. Brady tried to envision what happened.

It appeared the Escalade had been traveling east, probably moving at or near the speed limit of thirty-five miles per hour. Maybe she'd been distracted. The baby was crying. Or her cell phone was ringing. She glanced at the rearview mirror. Or the phone screen. The other car came west over the bridge and crossed the center line. When she looked up she saw it coming straight at her. She might have had two seconds to react. Three at most. Her first response would have been utter terror. The hypothalamus of her brain instantly alerted her pituitary gland which pumped thirty different hormones into her bloodstream. Her heart rate and blood pressure shot up, her pupils dilated, her muscles tensed, and her veins constricted causing a chilly sensation and goose bumps to break out on her skin. One second gone. Maybe two more left to act.

Paralyzed by fright, she may have hesitated. Or maybe braced herself. Or jerked the steering wheel. Or turned to her baby. Whatever she did, she did it in the blink of an eye. Brady guessed her maternal instinct took charge and she acted to protect her child. She wasn't wearing a seatbelt. He suspected she unclipped the latch at the last instant and rotated her torso ninety degrees so that her chest faced the passenger door. Another second gone. One second to collision.

She twisted another ninety degrees and turned toward the back seat. She stretched her right arm toward the baby in a desperate attempt to stop her from flying out of her safety seat. At least another second gone. No more time.

The crash was head-on. The Skylark's right headlight struck the Escalade at the center of its front bumper directly below the distinctive hood ornament. For a reason he didn't understand, Brady remembered the emblem was the coat of arms of Le Sieur Antoine De La Mothe Cadillac, the Frenchman who founded Detroit in 1701. The new Escalade outweighed the old Skylark by more than a ton, but that didn't matter. Both cars would have stopped cold, as if they'd hit a brick wall. Without her safety belt, the woman kept moving. She shot through the windshield, a human projectile traveling thirty five miles per hour. She likely hit the other car's hood and bounced onto the street, face first judging by her ravaged visage. The Skylark spun off to the left and skidded to a stop one hundred feet away. The Escalade skidded sideways, rolled over, and landed bottom side up with its engine still running.

Smoke was pouring from the cannonball hole. If the girl was still alive, she was inhaling benzene, toluene, xylene, and about a jillion other vile toxins that would kill her respiratory system. Brady stretched out on his stomach. The pool of petroleum covering the pavement saturated the front of his shirt and trousers. One spark and he'd be immolated like a Tibetan monk.

Barely two feet of space separated the crushed hood from the road. He squeezed his shoulders and rolled onto his back with inches to spare then spun around on the slick asphalt until his feet faced the windshield. Brady reached up and braced himself on the hood and kicked with both feet. What remained of the windshield collapsed inward. But too late. Someone hollered.

"Fire."

Orange flames began following the gasoline down the doors and licking over the edge of the car frame seeking entry to the passenger compartment. Brady twisted back around and rolled onto his belly. He took a deep breath, hoping his lungs still had their boyhood capacity, and crawled in head first. The smoke was blacker than night. The fumes burned his eyes. He groped ahead, trying to see with his hands, and slithered over broken glass until he felt the front seat head rests. The girl had to be near. He flipped onto his back, lay against the SUV's ceiling, and shimmied inch-by-inch until he felt something soft brush against his face. The little girl's blonde locks. He looked up. An angelic face was hanging inches from his. Her eyes were closed but he didn't see cuts or bruises. He couldn't tell if she was breathing. His lungs were already starting to constrict and his eyes were on fire. He reached up and searched blindly for the baby seat's release. He pressed and squeezed everything his fingers touched. Nothing worked. He tried to roll the straps off her shoulders and pull her free. The harness was too tight.

Brady needed a tool. He lifted his head and looked toward his feet. He tried to call for help, but his oxygen was gone. Reflexively, he breathed and poisonous fumes invaded his lungs. He coughed and felt himself start to vomit. He turned his head to the side and retched, but nothing came out. He realized he hadn't eaten in almost twenty four hours. He steeled himself and shouted hoarsely through the smashed front window.

"Knife! Fast! I need a knife!"

A man's voice answered. "Here, mister."

Something touched his foot. He stretched his arm toward it until his fingers found a handle. A female voice rang out, frantic.

"Hurry, mister! It's gonna blow."

The saliva in Brady's mouth was boiling. His stomach heaved again. He turned his head and spit out bile, wasting precious seconds. He held his breath and raised the knife. He touched the little girl's head and worked his hands down her neck and shoulders until he found a strap and began to saw. The blade was razor sharp. It slit through the polyester webbing like butter, but the girl didn't release. The woman cried out again.

"Please, hurry!"

"Back up," another voice shouted. "Get away."

An explosion rocked the car. Flames poured down from the engine block through the front window. Brady's escape route was cut off. He curled his legs up away from the inferno and kept fumbling until he located another strap. He put the knife to it and sliced. The girl tumbled out of the chair and fell onto his face. He pulled her listless form to his chest and wrapped his arms around her. Everything was black. The heat was intolerable. Flames were crackling all around. With the girl on top of him he could barely move. He managed to slide on the glass shards and spin his body until his feet touched the surface of a side door window. He kicked hard and glass burst. The fresh oxygen fed the fire and the flames licked at his left side. He rolled to his right to protect the child.

"Pull me out," he hollered.

Brady felt something clamp his ankles like a pair of vises. In the next instant he was yanked outward. Gasoline rained down. He cupped his hands over the child's face as his spine raked over the broken glass and metal door ridge. He cried out in agony. Then he was in the street, coughing out smoke and sucking in precious oxygen. He opened his eyes. An Indian in full headdress was staring at him. It took him a second to realize it was a picture silkscreened on a T-shirt. Someone was standing over him. A man. His rescuer.

"Thanks," he managed to say.

The guy looked frantic.

"Move!"

Brady didn't react. The man reached down and tore the child from his chest then grabbed his wrist and jerked him to his feet.

"Run!"

Brady almost laughed. He could barely stand, let alone run. An ambulance screeched up with siren wailing and a paramedic sprang out. The man in the Indian T-shirt raced to him cradling the little girl in his arms. The SUV was popping like a July Fourth fireworks display. Brady started to stagger away, hacking like a tuberculosis victim. Danielle was still kneeling on the pavement pumping the woman's chest. She looked up. Her face was soaked with tears.

"She's not responding."

He pulled the girl to her feet and thrust her away from the burning vehicle, then leaned down and scooped up the stricken woman. He had taken two steps when he felt a flash of heat. An instant later he heard the Escalade explode. The concussion vaulted him through the air like he'd been shot from a circus cannon. Somehow he managed to twist his torso and land on his back with the woman sprawled on top of him. The back of his skull hit the road and his neocortex bounced off the inside of his skull like a basketball hitting a backboard. He lay there with his eyes pinched tight, paralyzed by an excruciating wave of pain. When it passed he tried to sit up but the woman was anchoring him down. Her body was slack and inanimate. She felt dead. He rolled over and gently flopped her onto her back and sat up blinking.

He could see, but he couldn't hear. It was eerie. Like he was trapped in a silent movie. The SUV was ablaze in the street burning like a funeral pyre. Ten seconds more inside the car and the funeral would have been his. And the child's. He took a quick inventory. His shirt and pants were charred and the hair on his arms was singed. His back was scraped up and a lump the size of a golf ball had grown from the back of his head. All in all, though, the damage wasn't too serious. He closed his eyes to let his mind clear. When he opened them an emergency medical worker was running up to him shouting something. Brady couldn't hear him.

The medic instantly triaged the woman and began performing CPR. Brady looked at her face and knew it was a lost cause. He suspected the EMT did, too.

He searched for Danielle. She was thirty feet away weeping on the sidewalk curb. Her hands and knees were scraped and bloody. He crawled to her.

"Are you okay?"

He heard his voice and her choke on a sob. His hearing was returning.

"I couldn't get her heart to start."

Fresh tears poured down her face. Brady reached over and squeezed her shoulder.

"You did everything you could, sweetheart. She was beyond help."

He regained his feet and stood swaying on the side of the road, still groggy, not sure if he was going to fall down. He looked over at the Skylark, an ancient Buick that looked like it had been painted with rust. The driver was slumped over the wheel. His door was open and bystanders were gathered around it.

The man in the Indian T-shirt was among them. He was staring at the driver with bewildered eyes, like a dog that had given birth to kittens and was trying to understand why. Brady realized he was still holding his knife. He examined it closer. The dagger was ornate, the handle wooden with a silver pommel, the blade engraved with an Indian in full headdress, like the silkscreen on his shirt.

He moved to the car and held out the knife. "Is this yours?" Brady saw he was weeping. "Do you know this guy?"

He shook his head numbly. "No, sir. No. I don't know him."

"Why are you crying?"

He quickly swiped away the tears with his fingers. "Smoke in my eyes, I guess."

A bald man with a small furry white dog in his arms was standing beside the Skylark. He nodded at the driver. "This guy's history."

"Good riddance," said a black man wearing a U.S. Postal Service uniform. He had his face up to the open window of the Skylark's back right door. "This car reeks of alcohol. He was drunk as a skunk."

"I saw it." It was the heavyset woman who beckoned Brady. Her face was flush and her eyes ferocious. "The bastard was driving on the wrong side of the road. He ran head-on into that poor woman. Didn't even slow down. It was like he was trying to kill himself. She didn't stand a chance. It was awful."

The driver's face was streaked with blood and his skin was gray as yesterday's grease. His eyes were open, staring through the steering wheel and into the distance. Brady reached in and touched his throat. He was gone. He moved his hand up and slid his lids down over eyes that would never see again.

He looked up and searched for the man in the Indian T-shirt. He wanted to thank him for saving his life. He was nowhere in sight.

Et Tu Brady

Chapter Forty-Six

BRADY SAT ON the tailgate of an Emergency Medical Service ambulance and sucked in several lungs full of oxygen. The EMT people wanted to take him to Broward General, but he declined further treatment. He gave a statement to a police investigator then spent a few moments consoling Danielle. Her family lived in one of the condominiums on the beach and her mother had come to bring her home. She was still distraught at not being able to save the young mother. Brady gave her a hug and assured her again she'd done everything possible then bade her farewell and headed on foot back up Las Olas.

He was eager to get out of there before the news media arrived and plastered his face on newspapers and television screens. He did not want to be trumpeted as South Florida's latest *hero de jour*. He certainly didn't feel like a hero.

His Jeep was still parked in the road where he left it. A parking ticket was wedged under the windshield wiper. Traffic was backed up as far as he could see. A police roadblock had been set up and eastbound vehicles were being diverted.

He looped around and made his way to Siesta Lane and drove to Victor Gruber's house. Around back he stripped down to his boxer shorts and stood on the dock under a shower nozzle protruding from one of the pilings. He still felt heat from the inferno on his skin and his back felt like it had been run over by a road grader. He rinsed off the soot and grime and blood. The cold water soothed his skin, but his ears were buzzing like a family of wasps had taken up residence in his skull.

Charles, Victor's manservant, came down to the schooner with bandages, alcohol, and Neosporin. Charles was very British, very circumspect, and very precise. During the early days of the Iraq War he'd been a battlefield medic in the Royal Army. He dressed Brady's cuts and scratches and dabbed his golf ball with peroxide. Charles examined his eyes and declared him free from concussion.

"It appears your head is harder than the tarmac, sir."

Brady tossed his scorched shirt and pants in the garbage – the pants representing one-half of his expensive Hart Schaffner Marx suit – and changed into a tattered but clean pair of shorts and a Sea Shanty T-shirt. A few minutes later he was back in the Jeep taking the two mile drive to Sunrise Key, an exclusive enclave in Victoria Park off Middle River. He crossed a small bridge onto the island, took a quick left and slammed on his brakes.

A four foot long iguana was crouched in the center of the street. The green reptile stared at Brady with sullen black eyes. He honked, but the creature just squatted there preening its spiny dewlap. The iguana population had erupted in southern Florida. Natives of South and Central America, the animals were relatively harmless vegetarians. Unfortunately, their favorite *vegetables* were flowers and shrubs and home landscaping and many local residents considered them nuisances.

Brady had always admired the lizards. They were direct descendants of the dinosaurs. Plus, male iguanas possessed not one, but two penises. He had to respect that. Now, man and reptile faced off, eye-to-eye, the smug varmint's expression seeming to say: *How many penises do you have, human?*

Talk about one-upmanship! Brady drove around him. As he passed he poked his head out the window. "I may only have one penis, but I've got a pair of boots that look just like your mother and father." Never give a lizard the last word.

Twilight was descending when he pulled up in front of a large salmon-toned house. The three-story structure was conspicuous for its dramatic angles and geometric windows in the shapes of triangles, octagons, and pentagons. A white Toyota pick-up was parked in the driveway. *Blue Water Pool Service* was painted on its doors. The bed was packed with white hoses, black brushes, and blue and yellow plastic jugs with *Chlorine* and *Acid* scrawled on them in black marker. Battered and bruised, in this neighborhood the truck stuck out like a warthog in a wedding dress.

Hip-hop music was blaring from behind the house. Brady couldn't hear it so much as feel the bass reverb pounding inside his chest. He followed a flagstone path around the side between the house and a high stone wall dripping with purple bougainvillea. A rather small backyard was dominated by a Mediterranean-style swimming pool with Jacuzzi and rock waterfall lit by versicolored underwater lamps. A dozen green slatted chaise lounges surrounded the pool.

Beyond the house was Middle River. The Intracoastal Waterway was a straight shot to the south and east. Past that big new beach towers were visible in the distance. Directly behind the house, a long dock ran the width of the seawall. A white Bayliner about thirty feet long was secured to it with mooring whips. It had a blue Bimini top and swim platform extension at the stern. Perfect for fishing and diving. *Nice tub*, he thought.

By contrast, the human scarecrow on the far side of the pool seemed totally out of place. He was wielding a long pole with a blue net attached, scooping bugs and leaves from the water like a chef ladling congealed fat from a soup. His bare chest and emaciated torso were covered with tattoos. A cigarette dangled from his mouth.

Brady padded around the pool perimeter. The scarecrow didn't notice he had company until he tapped him on the shoulder. He sprang backwards, dropped the pole, and covered his heart with his hands.

"Jesus Christ, mister, you scared the living shit out of me."

Brady was thunderstruck. The face was scorched and withered, the once-red hair was now a wooly green nest that reminded him of

317

a broccoli floret, and his eyes were the color of watermelon pulp. An imaginative chef could have made a healthy salad from his head alone.

"Sorry. I should have called. Didn't have your number, Peanut."

Peanut Strong squinted at him. He was surrounded by a pungent fog. Brady sniffed and realized the crooked cigarette between his lips was a marijuana joint. The music was coming from a boom box sitting on a small table beside the pool. Brady reached over and pressed the power button and his ribcage stopped palpitating. A glimmer of recognition finally came into the other man's eyes.

"Max? Brady? Is that you?"

"How are you, Peanut?"

Peanut coughed out a phlegmy laugh. "It's Richard."

"Richard?"

"People call me Richard. Not Dick. Or Peanut."

Brady couldn't count all the *Dick's* he'd known in his life who now went by *Richard*. He couldn't blame them. He supposed he'd do the same. Mostly he was trying to reconcile the sight of the man before him with his boyhood friend. The bright, happy, freckled face had faded like an old Polaroid left too long in the sun. He looked like one of the legion of vagabonds who populated Fort Lauderdale during winter, sleeping under bridges, panhandling at busy intersections, bathing at the public showers on the beach, fueling themselves on rotgut liquor, seeming to be twice as old as their years. Peanut was no exception.

"Nice digs," Brady said, trying to cover his shock. "Maybe I should start a pool service."

Peanut waved a hand at a small gray cabana about the size of a shower stall at the southeast corner of the patio. It had a flat-roof and the door and window were thin slats of white wood. He grinned.

"I stay in there, for now. Owner's only in town a month a year. Bastard's so rich he burns money for kicks."

He took a long drag on the joint and held his breath.

"Money's nice," Brady said, "but you still gotta die."

Peanut snorted out a laugh encased in a billow of blue smoke.

318

"Glad I'm broke then. Anyway, the guy lets me live here for taking care of the pool and maintaining the property. Gonna get me an apartment soon."

Brady heard a gurgling sound, like an empty stomach growling for food. It was the pool vacuum cleaner, a robotic device attached to a long corrugated hose racing helter-skelter back and forth across the bottom of the pool as if it was R2-D2 on acid.

"That's the fastest vacuum I've ever seen."

"Supercharged it," Peanut said, with a trace of pride. "Most pumps are three-quarter horse power. I installed a two horse motor. Cleanest pool in town."

He offered the joint to Brady, who shook his head.

"Trying to quit."

"Oh, shit man. I forgot. I heard you're a cop."

"Ex-cop."

"They say cops got the best dope," he mumbled and coughed out another cloud of smoke. "If you wanna know, I ain't ashamed of smoking dope. George friggin' Washington grew weed in his garden."

Peanut started to take a step and his gaunt legs wobbled. He did a barfly ballet along the edge of the pool. Brady was sure he was going to topple into the water. He reached out to brace him, but Peanut swept his arms out to his sides and righted himself. He looked at Brady. His bloodshot eyes were tearing up.

"I can't believe it's you, man. You're the best friend I ever had. I wish we hadn't grown apart. I know it was my fault. I'm sorry, man. I don't know what happened. Nothing was ever the same after that night. That one fucking night."

Brady felt profound sadness. The man teetering before him was a shell of the boy who'd once been like his brother. That night three decades ago changed everything between them. They hadn't spoken since.

"Let's sit down, Peanut."

He took him by the elbow and steered him toward a chaise beside the Jacuzzi. Peanut fell into the lounge chair with a grunt and Brady took the seat beside him.

"Thanks, pal. I'm so happy to see you." Peanut's head was bobbing as he looked at Brady. "You think we could be friends again?"

Brady shook his head. "No." He said it matter-of-fact, without animosity.

Peanut's head sagged. "I guess not. Why would you want anything to do with a loser like me?" His face was a portrait of pain. "My life ain't nothing but a bad joke without a punch line."

"You need to work on your self-esteem, Peanut. You could start by cleaning yourself up." He nodded at the joint smoldering between his fingers. "And cutting down on the ganja."

"You're right." His voice was filled with resignation. He reached over and touched Brady's arm. "I'm gonna do that. I just need my old friend to point me in the right direction."

Brady leaned forward and looked into eyes filled with the splintered remains of shattered illusions.

"Listen to me, Peanut. We used to be friends. That ended a long time ago. I'll never forgive you for what happened."

Peanut's head snapped away like he'd been slapped in the face. Then he recoiled.

"Ain't one to let go of a grudge, are you? I fucked up. I know. I've been living with it ever since. If I could take a knife and cut that night out of my memory I'd do it." Peanut's voice was getting loud and his words were coming fast. Brady sensed he was delivering a speech he'd been practicing most of his life. "You don't know what it's like to be ashamed. Not you. Not the golden boy. Not the great Maximus Brady."

The spasm of hostility dissipated and Peanut fell back, self-convicted of an unspoken crime. Snot and tears dribbled down his face like raindrops on a grimy window. Brady felt a pang of something. Pity? Disgust? He wasn't certain. Peanut was right about one thing. He was unforgiving. At least about some crimes. What he and Ben did that night was at the top of his list.

"Sorry to be blunt, Peanut. That's just how it is."

Peanut's head doddered on the gaunt fulcrum of his neck. He leaned toward Brady, groping for words. "Maybe you should look in the mirror, old buddy. I know I was weak. I was a coward. Ben too. We both knew it. But everybody's hands were dirty that night."

"Everybody but Delray's."

Peanut stiffened at the mention of her name, then nodded. "You're right. Delray didn't deserve that. But you were guilty too. Why did just me and Ben have to pay? Why didn't you take some blame?"

Brady's jaw muscles constricted. He had a sudden urge to hit Peanut. Hurt him. Purge the venom that had been running through his veins all these years. He sat in silence and let the compulsion pass.

"Let me tell you something, Peanut," he said finally. "I did take blame. I still do. Remember, I lost more than anybody that night. I just refused to let it destroy my life."

Peanut dragged a tattooed forearm across his messy face. A spiderweb of slime followed his hand back to his lap. Brady almost gagged. He reached into his back pocket and pulled out a handkerchief and thrust it at Peanut.

"Listen to me. I'm here because of Delray. Maybe you can do now what you were too chicken-shit to do that night."

"Like what?"

"Like help her. You heard about Ben?"

Peanut nodded. Brady watched him closely. He described the murder scene. All the gory details. Ben naked on the floor. The copper noose twisted around his neck. The burn marks on the carpet where the electricity shot through him. Peanut listened with a faraway look, as though he was watching it happen. He didn't wince or cringe or show any sign of shock or revulsion. Brady told him the police considered Delray their primary suspect. A trace of a smile materialized on Peanut's face.

"They think Delray did it?"

"You find that amusing?"

The smile vanished and he shook his head. A screw of chlorine-green hair fell down the side of his face. Brady told him about the treasure file he and Delray found in Ben's study.

"Ben told me about the gold," he said.

"You were in touch with Ben?"

"I clean his pool. And sell him weed. Coke sometimes, too. He showed me some of the shit he was digging up. Promised to cut me in if he ever found the gold. Ben didn't turn his back on me. Not like you. And Delray. And Ginger."

"Ginger? Ginger Brennan?"

"Ginger Ball now."

It took several seconds for the words to sink in. Brady wasn't sure he'd heard right. "Not Ball as in Junior Ball?" Peanut nodded. "No way."

"Hoity-toity bitch. They're divorced now. She kept the swanky house in Harbor Beach. I service her pool, too. She waves money in my face like she used wave them tits at me." Peanut's eyes took on a distant expression again and his bitterness gave way to a wistful smile. "Remember that blue Speedo?"

Brady couldn't help but smile too. When they were kids Ginger Brennan had been a conspicuous presence on New River. *Precocious puberty*, they call it today. Ginger had been blessed with a voluptuous anatomy while other girls her age still looked like, well, girls. She could cast a spell over boys and men. Sometimes she joined them on scuba diving forays to Three Mile Reef. On their way home they always stopped at Lauderdale Yacht Club, a snooty bastion of the town's upper crust that sat on the Intracoastal. The kids made a game of sneaking into its big freshwater swimming pool to rinse the sea salt off their skin. Not being members, they were habitually chased off – except when they brought Ginger. She was like a free pass. Sitting beside the pool, feet splashing in the water, flirting with the life guards, enticing them, bending over provocatively until her young flesh was spilling from the Speedo. Every male eye at the club riveted on her while Max, Peanut, Ben, and Delray splashed in the pool. Afterwards, Ginger laughing like a girl who'd discovered a magnificent new power. And loving it, like a Lauderdale Lolita.

"Ginger didn't come to Ben's funeral," Brady said. He didn't point out that Peanut hadn't either.

"No way she's going anywhere near Ben Chance, alive or dead."

"Why? What did Ben do to Ginger?"

"Plenty. They used to screw like rabbits."

"Are you serious?" Brady said, his tone incredulous.

Peanut sat up and ran a hand through his frizzy green hair. "They did it to torture me. I'd come to service Ben's pool, sweep, vacuum, throw in some chemicals. They'd be up in his bedroom with the French doors open. She'd be screaming in ecstasy at the top of her lungs, knowing damn well I was down there. Then she'd come out and stand on the balcony smoking a cigarette, them knockers swinging in the breeze, smiling down at me, reminding me what I never had and never will. Heartless bitch!"

He fell back in the chaise, lax as a wet towel, while Brady digested the image of Ben and Ginger together.

"If they were so intimate, why wouldn't Ginger go to Ben's funeral?"

"Junior found out." A sinister smile lit on Peanut's face. "Somebody sent him an anonymous letter. I doubt he cared that Ginger was cheating. Scumbag screwed everything in sight himself. He just couldn't stand it being with Ben. Ben told me he beat the shit out of her. Said if he caught them together they'd both wind up dead. Scared hell out of her. She knew he'd do it. He's a bigger bully now than he ever was when we were kids. After that she stayed away from Ben, even after the divorce."

Peanut's eyelids were drooping. Brady, on the other hand, was energized. Junior Ball was still around. And he'd threatened to kill Ben for sleeping with his wife. That made him a prime suspect. And Junior knew Max. That could explain the *Et Tu Brady* tattoo. He'd drop the name on the police. If he couldn't convince Captain Register he was wrong about Delray, at least maybe he could buy some time.

Peanut's head was see-sawing back and forth, his dazed eyes focused on something in middle space. Brady realized Peanut was also a potential suspect. For one thing, Ben was openly having an affair with the woman he lusted for.

"Where'd you get all those tattoos?"

Peanut looked down at his chest and arms. They were covered with green dragons, red devils, and barbed wire.

"Got some in the joint. Did three years at Okeechobee CC on a weed rap." He pointed to a black dagger on his left forearm with blood dripping from the blade. "Did this one myself. Not bad, huh?"

"Did you tattoo my name on Ben's forehead?"

"Huh?"

"*Et Tu Brady* was tattooed on Ben's forehead."

He gazed at Brady with befuddled eyes. It took a minute to process the information.

"No shit?"

"Whoever put it there murdered him. You know how to tattoo. Did you kill him?"

"Ben was my friend. We shared a bond. Remember? A pair of yellow-belly sap suckers. He carried half of my shame. Now it's all on me. Why would I kill him?"

"Maybe because he made Ginger scream in ecstasy and you didn't. Maybe to put your partner-in-disgrace out of his misery. Maybe for the gold."

Peanut didn't answer. His flickering pilot light had finally died. His head flopped forward and his chin cleaved his chest like a tomahawk. Within seconds a bumblebee buzz was coming from his nose. Brady reached over and gave his grizzled cheek a light slap.

"Wake up, Peanut."

He stirred midsnore and smiled.

"Peanut," he mumbled, his eyes still closed. "I miss that. I ain't no Dick. I ain't no Rick, or Richie, or Richard. I wanna be Peanut again. I wanna be friends again."

He rambled on like an ascetic monk chanting incantations. After a while he opened his eyes and refocused on Brady.

"Did you kill Ben, Peanut?"

"No."

"Who did?"

"Duke Manyon."

Brady shot to his feet and looked down at Peanut. He hadn't mentioned Manyon, or anything about him.

"Why do you say that?"

"I saw him."

"You saw Duke Manyon? When?"

"I don't know. Month ago. Maybe two months. Or weeks."

"Where?"

Peanut was fighting a losing battle to keep his eyes open.

"Not sure. Beach. Las Olas. Second Street maybe. Can't remember."

Peanut muttered something then his eyes rolled back. Brady left him there, sleeping as sound as a dead man.

Et Tu Brady

Chapter Forty-Seven

RON REGISTER POPPED a gin-soaked bleu cheese olive into his mouth and washed it down with the last dribs of his second Beefeater martini. He and Police Chief Don Begley were having their weekly dinner meeting at Shula's Steak House. They sat outside on the patio just a few feet from A1A. It was a Chamber of Commerce evening. Across the road palm trees rustled in the gentle breeze fluttering off the Atlantic. Sidewalks were crowded with celebrants in town for the Super Bowl. The restaurant was packed with football fans come to feast at the altar of the NFL's winningest coach. Begley sipped his own martini – vodka, Grey Goose – while Register updated him on the murder investigation.

"The noose is tightening around the sister's neck."

The chief shot him a quizzical look. Register realized why. The killer had wrapped the copper wire around Benjamin Chance's throat like a hangman's noose. "No pun intended," the Homicide captain added. A waiter came to the table carrying a small tray and set down Register's third silver bullet. "Delray Cross had motive – namely her brother's forty-plus million dollar estate. She had opportunity – a rental car she conveniently forgot to tell us about. She had an ample window of time to drive to Chance's house, kill him, and get back to the Yankee Clipper. Time to cover her tracks with telephone calls to the murder scene. Then she took a taxi to the Rio Vista house and tried to make it appear she found her brother's body. She also has a pattern."

He told Begley about Delray Cross's husband's drowning in Bonaire and that police on the island considered the death to be *suspicious*.

"Same modus operandi in both cases. The victims are drugged, they die of unnatural causes, and she's the only witness present." He paused for dramatic effect. "Oh! And she inherits all their millions."

Begley buttered a hot roll that wasn't quite hot enough to melt butter. He tore off a chunk with his teeth and chewed while he talked. "Can you make the arrest before Super Bowl Sunday?"

"I plan to do just that."

Register was acutely aware how momentous solving such a sensational case would be to his career. The national press was here in force. He would personally march the beautiful and renowned economist into the courthouse in shackles. Cameras would be rolling. The media clusterfuck would have a collective orgasm. He'd be the most famous cop in America. And it would virtually seal the deal for him to succeed Begley as Chief of Police.

In silent celebration, he polished off his third martini in a single swallow and wiped his mouth with the back of his hand.

"While you're arresting the sister," the chief said, "slap some cuffs on that sonofabitch bartender slash lawyer of hers."

Register knew Begley was still galled that Max Brady brought about the ruination of his political godfather. And that he was the reason Begley was being forced to retire. The Police Chief would love to get payback before he left office. Brady being Howard Pickens's godson would make revenge all the sweeter. Begley spoke as if he was reading Register's mind.

"I'm not putting on a happy face at the dedication tomorrow. I'm not pretending that I'm that bastard's friend."

The waiter came with their meals. Steak Mary Anne, the house specialty, for Register, sliced filet mignon swimming in brown sauce. He took a bite. After three martinis to whet his appetite, the sensation bordered on rapturous. He closed his eyes and was savoring the experience when his cell phone rang. He was inclined to not answer, but the caller ID said it was Detective Perry James.

"Excuse me, chief," he said and pressed the talk button. "What is it, Perry?"

"Another piece to the puzzle, boss," James said.

"What have you got?"

"Tox report on Benjamin Chance. Belinda Boulanos put a rush on it. She just sent it over."

Register stabbed another piece of steak and lifted it to his mouth. "What's it say," he said and wolfed down the meat.

"He was drugged with oxycodone hydrochloride."

"Belinda knew the night of the murder he'd been doped."

"But the oxycodone's significant. The coroner down in Bonaire said Delray Cross's husband was on oxy when he drowned scuba diving."

"All well and good, Perry, but I hope you've got more than that to interrupt my dinner with the Chief."

"Please give my regards to Chief Begley," James said. *Smart young man,* thought Register. *Chief someday, after I retire.* "Here's the kicker, cap. An old football buddy of mine is a guy named Delvin Hayes. Big old country boy from Lumberton. Nose tackle at UNC. We played in the Senior Bowl together. Even had a try-out with the Panthers. Got to be good friends. Delvin's with the North Carolina State Highway Patrol now. Raleigh-Durham area. Still owes me from last year when the Canes beat the Tar Heels. I called him to collect."

Register shoved another bite in his mouth. It may have been the best piece of meat he'd ever tasted. Across the table, Chief Begley was busy attacking something the size of a brontosaurus steak.

"And how, Perry, did your friend repay his debt?"

"North Carolina's got a serious prescription drug problem."

"Courtesy of our pill mills. They're flocking here by the busloads."

"Well, to get a grip on the problem Carolina initiated a strong prescription drug monitoring system. Almost unconstitutional, if you ask me. Wish we had it. Allows police to go into a pharmacy without a warrant and find out what prescriptions individuals are having filled, whose prescribing them, and whatnot. Delray Cross is a faculty member at Duke University. I had a hunch she gets her health care through the school medical center. I called Delvin and asked him to drop by the campus pharmacy."

"I'm guessing you found something or you wouldn't be interrupting my dinner."

"Consider this dessert, captain. Delvin faxed me a copy of Delray Cross's prescription history. One week ago she picked up sixty pills of OxyContin. That' the brand name for oxycodone hydrochloride. Same stuff her brother was drugged with. And the husband, too."

"Very impressive, Perry. You're right. No chocolate soufflé tonight."

He clocked off his cellphone.

"Good news?" said the Police Chief.

Register smiled. He raised an arm. Their waiter came over.

"Yes, sir."

"Two more martinis, please. We're going to the grand jury."

Et Tu Brady

Chapter Forty-Eight

"RICHARD," A VOICE said.

Peanut Strong was still snoring on the chaise lounge. His eyes opened into red slits.

"Huh?"

"Wake up. Drink this."

He looked up. Someone was standing over him, but the figure was too shadowy to identify. "Whoozat?"

A cup was placed to his lips.

"Drink it, Richard. You're going to love the buzz."

Peanut smiled vaguely. The shadow tilted the vessel and poured liquid into his mouth. Peanut didn't resist. It tasted like fine wine. He let it trickle down his throat.

"Tha's good," he mumbled and closed his eyes again. "Who are you, anyway?"

"A friend, Richard. A friend come to ease your pain."

Et Tu Brady

Chapter Forty-Nine

ROSE BECKER WAS as jumpy as a popcorn kernel in a microwave oven. Jumpy because in her entire life she'd never committed a crime. No crime. Never shop lifted. Never cheated on her taxes. Never even smoked pot. Now she was about to do something illegal. Rose wasn't sure exactly what the crime was called, but she was pretty certain it was a felony. Her emotions had mutated from the heebie-jeebies to the collywobbles to a terminal case of the tizzies.

She'd spent the evening at the Papillon trying to work off her angst. First leading a yoga class, then an hour of Pilates. But the arduous routine hadn't helped. All she could think of was getting caught and being sent to prison, another reprobate politician brought to justice.

Rose looked at the clock. It was past eleven. Normally she would have called it a night and gone home to bed. Or to Brady's boat. *Brady*. She desperately wanted to see him. Take back her harsh words from today. She'd behaved like a high school cheerleader who caught her boyfriend ogling another girl's pom-poms. She didn't blame him for running away. She wanted to coax him to her apartment and spend the night in his arms. She doubted it would take much cajoling. She'd calmed down since then. Despite Delray

Cross, she knew Brady loved her. And she loved him. Besides, it was going on two days since their last tryst. Or was it three. Too long either way. Instead, she was going to commit her first crime. If she could fight off the tizzies.

Rose locked the gym door and retreated to the women's locker room. She showered and dressed and then went into the tiny cubbyhole she called an office and grabbed a stack of files and the memory stick from her laptop. Despite her trepidation – or maybe because of it – she'd planned her incursion like a battle-field strategist.

City Hall was dark and deserted, except for Manny Gutierrez, a retired city cop who manned the night security desk. Gutierrez unlocked the lobby door and she breezed in with an exaggerated air of nonchalance. The guard ran his eyes over the bundle of folders cradled in her arms.

"Working late, commissioner?"

She lavished him with a dazzling smile. "Never too late for the people's business, Manny. How are you?"

"Just finished eleven o'clock rounds. Gonna sit here and watch *Law & Order* on my new iPad." He pointed to a small, flat screen propped up on the desk. "Amazing, ain't it? Christmas present from the wife. Then it's midnight rounds. Then again at one, then two…"

"Oh, Manny, I feel so safe with you in the building."

Rose seduced him with another smile and a soft kiss on the cheek, spreading the sugar like Martha Stewart frosting a spice cake. It seemed to work. Manny beamed.

"Don't you worry that pretty little head, commissioner. You're in good hands."

"I know that's right." Rose took two steps toward the elevator, then stopped and turned. "Oh, by the way, Manny, this morning I forgot a file in the City Attorney's office. I swear my mind's in twenty different places these days. I know right where I left it. Do you know if anybody's up there?"

"No, ma'am. Mr. Dean left hours ago."

"Gosh darn it."

334

Manny glanced at his iPad and sighed. *Law & Order* was just coming on. Nonetheless, he grabbed a big ring of keys off the security desk and clipped it to his belt.

"I'll come up and let you in, commissioner," he said and jangled toward the elevator.

"Oh, Manny." Rose pouted and pecked his cheek again. "You're so sweet. I'm so sorry." Then she snapped her fingers, as if she'd just had an idea. "Hey, I just had an idea. Give me the key, I'll grab my file, and you can get it when you do your midnight rounds."

Uncertainty clouded the security guard's face. He crossed his arms, raised his right hand to his chin, and kneaded it with his fingers.

"I don't know, Commissioner Becker."

"Rose."

"I'm not supposed to let anyone into a locked office, Rose, unless I'm with them."

She slapped the air with her hand. "Nonsense. We're all on the same team here. Do I look like some thief in the night?"

He smiled and shook his head. "Of course not."

"I'm a Fort Lauderdale City Commissioner. Besides, Manny, I will not let you miss your show." She'd gone from enchanting seductress to practical mom. "Now give me that key and go sit down right now."

Manny peeked at the screen. Jerry Orbach was running through Times Square over opening credits. He considered Rose's proposal for almost three seconds, smiled, and unclasped the clip from his belt. He sorted through the keys and removed one.

"Just lock the door when you leave. I should get to your office about ten after twelve."

"Perfect."

"And commissioner," he said with a grateful smile, "thanks."

She pointed a finger at him in mock accusation. "I told you, Manny. Call me Rose."

The lobby elevator dinged and she rode to the third floor. She unlocked her office door and dumped the stack of files on her desk. They were membership folders from the Papillon Gym. Her heart was pounding. Perspiration dampened the underarms of her blouse.

She couldn't remember the last time she'd been such a basket case. Then she did. Today. The funeral. Delray Cross kissing Brady. Anger. Cursing. Road rage. But that was passion. This was abject fear. Rose could feel her rock-hard resolve melting like hot fudge.

"Courage, girl," she said aloud and breathed deeply. "Okay, here we go."

Except there was no *we*. Only *she*. *She* was about to break the law. If *she* was caught *she* would go to jail. Rose took another long breath, plucked the memory stick from her shoulder bag and strode purposefully from the Commission offices. The hallway was dark and empty and smelled of floor wax. The lonely clack of her heels echoed like a tap dancer in a marble tomb. She chastised herself for not wearing her Reeboks. She made her way to the red exit sign at the end of the hallway, pushed open the heavy metal door, and descended the concrete stairwell to the second floor.

The City Attorney's office was on the east side of the building halfway down the corridor, past the Water Department and Building Inspector's office. She inserted the key into a tall brown wooden door and slowly pushed it open, as if she expected Walter Dean to pop out like a jack-in-the-box. The room was dark and silent. She slipped inside and the door closed behind her.

Dean lorded over a small team of lawyers and paralegals. The suite was a series of offices lining two long hallways to the left and right. Cubicles filled the open area at the center of the room. The walls were lined with black metal file cabinets. Dean's office was at the far end of the right corridor. The top half of the door was frosted glass bearing a legend painted in gold with black borders.

Walter J. Dean
City Attorney
Fort Lauderdale, Florida

Rose twisted the handle. The door was not locked. She entered, flipped on the light switch, and got to work with a minimum of fuss.

Dean's desk was a T-shaped monstrosity approximately the size of an aircraft carrier. Neat and orderly. Black leather pad, letter rack, pencil cup, paper tray holding a short stack of memos. A gold-framed photograph of a woman and two teenaged girls sat at the left-hand corner. A frumpy middle-aged woman in a pink suit with a string of fat pearls around a fat neck. The pearls looked like they'd make a sucking sound if they were pulled apart. The girls had been fated with their mother's genes.

Legal files were stacked like bales of hay on a long conference table attached to the desk. Rose wondered if any involved Austin Ball, Jr. There was no time for that now, though. According to Seymour Tate, the smoking gun she'd come to *"liberate,"* as he had couched it, was hidden inside the big, beige IBM computer on the left sidetable of Dean's desk.

"I got a guy at City Hall," Seymour whispered to her from his hospital bed this morning. "Can't reveal my source, but he's an I.T. geek. Real whiz. It so happens that every now and then he also likes to stoke up a doobie. You could say we're kindred spirits. Occasionally, I slip him a bag of choice buds. Strictly medicinal, of course."

"Of course," Rose said.

"Good for glaucoma."

"The geek's got glaucoma?"

"Not anymore."

"And the point of you telling me this is?"

"Most people get the munchies when they light up."

"I've heard."

"This guy gets diarrhea."

"Gross."

"Of the mouth. Talks and talks and talks. Can't shut him up. Not that I try."

"So that's how you reporters get your information? Isn't that a violation of journalistic ethics?"

He fixed her with an indulgent smile. "Journalistic ethics is more like a theory. Like fair and balanced. Besides, I have a loophole. The greater good and all that crap."

"How noble. So what kind of *good* things did your pothead I.T. geek tell you?"

"Walter Dean keeps encrypted files hidden on his hard drive. He tells my guy: 'Confidential. Top secret.' Like he's Director of the CIA. 'My eyes only. Don't touch them.' That's all my guy needed to hear. He thinks Walter's a douche. Took it as a dare."

Tate said his source cracked the encryption code in five minutes with deciphering software he downloaded free off the internet. The file contained a lot of numbers and letters, like codes or initials. One column looked like official case numbers, the kind assigned to court files for civil lawsuits. They went all the way back to 2005. For example, 05-2237. There was also a column of dates – month, day and year. And another with dollar amounts. He wasn't sure about the last column, but thought they might be bank account numbers.

"You mean like a Swiss bank account?"

"Or a Cayman Island account. Two trillion U.S. dollars are tucked inside the banks of that tiny country. Or Bermuda. Barbados. Dominica. Turks & Caicos. I could keep going. Switzerland's not the only place to hide money these days."

"Why don't you just have your guy print out the list?"

"What kind of reporter do I look like? You think I didn't try? He wouldn't do it. But he told me how."

"Seymour, there's just one problem," Rose said. "I am no computer hacker."

"Not a problem. You'll be in-and-out in ten minutes flat. Just don't break the Eleventh Commandment."

"What's that?"

"Don't get caught."

One consolation. Dean's computer was identical to the IBM desktop in Rose's office. That would save considerable time. She pushed the power button and the screen flashed to life. The machine was excruciatingly slow booting up. It felt like ages before all the applications and notices popped up. While she waited, Rose pulled the chain on a green shaded desk lamp. She stepped to the door, closed it, and switched off the overhead lights. Finally she was able to click on Dean's Microsoft Office.

She reached into her pocket and pulled out the notes she'd taken from Seymour's tutorial. It told her the keystrokes to unlock it, the decryption code, and how to download the data onto her flash drive. She plugged her memory stick into the UBS port of the hard drive tower beneath the desk and got to work.

With the lines of her mouth pursed in concentration, she followed the commands. Her lower back was damp with sweat and she had an overwhelming urge to pee. She noticed, though, that her hands were as steady as a surgeon's. She worked at a methodical pace, but locating the file took longer than she anticipated. It was labeled *Housekeeping.* Then another fifteen minutes fumbling around before she was able to open and unscramble it. Seymour had sorely underestimated. By the time she copied the information to her flash drive, clicked the file closed, and pushed the power button off, Tate's ten minutes had stretched to three-quarters of an hour. She checked her watch and breathed a sigh of relief. *Law & Order* still had another ten minutes to go before Manny came looking for his key. She pulled the chain on the green lamp and was stepping toward the door when she heard a sound. Her heart leapt.

Rose pressed her back against the door jamb and listened. Lights came on through the pebbled glass. Fluorescent overheads in the outer office. *Who could that be?* She had Manny's key. *The cleaning crew?* They'd nearly walked in on her and Brady a couple of weeks ago. Rose faced the door, twisted the handle gently, and pulled it open it a crack. She heard a voice. Male. Speaking English. *Not the cleaning crew.* Then a woman. Also English. The man said something. The female responded with a giddy laugh. Rose got a sense they were drunk. Very drunk. Considering all the Super Bowl celebrations around town this week, she wasn't surprised.

"That bitch must have found her file and gone," the woman said.

She was talking about Rose. Manny must have told them. She couldn't see their faces, but knew the voice belonged to Marci Bennett, one of Walter Dean's paralegals.

"Rose Becker's no bitch," the man said. "She's hot as a firecracker."

Well, thanks for that. Rose knew his voice too. Chief Assistant City Attorney Phil Stone, Dean's right-hand man.

"Do you think *I'm* hot as a firecracker, Philly Cheese Steak?"
Oh, lord! Really?

"You're my little cherry bomb," he said. Marci let loose another girlish giggle. "So hot, you know what I want to do to you?"

Marci and Phil came into view. Rose pushed the door to a sliver. Her nerves were tight as trip wires. Stone pressed Marci against a file cabinet and planted an ardent kiss on her lips while he frisked her upper torso, apparently searching for concealed weapons. Rose didn't know either of them well. She did know they were married, though not to each other. Their lips popped apart like a suction cup on a plumber's tool.

"What do you want to do to me, Philly Cream Cheese?"
Please!

"I want to make you scream with pleasure – on top of Walter's desk."
Shit!

Rose closed the door and dropped to her hands-and-knees below the glass. She reached up with her left hand and felt blindly until her fingers found the doorknob. It had a lock button. She pressed it in. Then a horrifying thought. *What if Philly Cream Cheese Steak has a key?* In the muted light she could barely see. She tried to remember if Dean's office had a back door. Or a bathroom. Or even a coat closet she could hide in. Then it was too late. The knob jiggled inches from her ear. She crouched lower to the floor.

"Damn," said Phil Stone. "Walter never locks his door. I don't get it. Something's going on with that guy. He's been acting strange."

"He is strange. You said so yourself."

"Stranger than usual, for Walter. That's very strange."

"Don't you have a key, Philly Tastykakes?" she said and they broke into hysterical laughter.

Tastykakes?

Rose heard lips smacking.

"No I don't have a key, Marci from Canarsie." More hilarity.

This has got to stop!

"Oh, baby," Marci purred. "Do me right here against the door. Then every time we walk into Walter's office we'll remember what happened on this very spot."

That sounded reasonable to Rose. They stopped talking and she heard muffled sounds on the other side of the door. She didn't have to imagine what was happening. A zipper was unzipped. A belt buckle clinked. Cloth rubbed against cloth. Then the door began to rattle. Rose froze, silent as a spider, her nose inches from Phil and Marci's feet. She hoped they were only kissing, or maybe petting, but the rattles quickly graduated to loud bangs. The bangs grew in seismic intensity. When they reached about six point nine on the Richter Scale, Rose started to worry. She was trapped at the epicenter of what was becoming a major earthquake. Phil was grunting something about torts while Marci begged him not to stop. He didn't. Philly Cheese Steak was the Energizer Bunny. He kept going and going while Rose prayed the smoked glass didn't shatter. Then Marci began unleashing a litany of ohs.

"Oh, oh, oh, oh, oh, oh, oh, oh…."

Rose thought of Brady and his *War of O's*. The absurdity of the situation hit her and she started to laugh. She slapped a hand over her own mouth, but couldn't stop. Her body began to shake. The lovebirds on the other side of the door were sure to notice. To distract herself she began playing the *O* game.

Oatmeal. Objectivism. Occult. Orthoscopic. Outlandish. Oscillate. Oeil-de-boeuf.`

"Definition," she heard Brady say.

"A small window, oval or round."

"Sounds French."

"Shut the fuck up, Brady."

"You said the F-word!"

"Don't be obtuse. Can't you see my outlandish ordeal with these oversexed oyster-eaters orgasming only inches away. If I'm overheard you'll be ogling my obituary. It's all so odious."

The *ohs* continued for some time, building in intensity until Marci reached her crescendo. She actually sang the last few notes and hit what sounded to Rose like a B-flat, an octave known to make alligators bark. She tapered off into tiny bird coos until, finally, there was silence. Rose had a sudden impulse to yank open the door and give them a big *ovation*.

Instead, she remained perfectly still, curled on her knees, nose pressed into the carpet, not daring to move a muscle. Eventually the pinstripe of light at the base of the door went black and she heard the outer door close. The blissfully promiscuous couple had gone, presumably back to their respective spouses. Just to be safe she waited five minutes. But Manny would be coming for his key soon. She got up and let herself out.

"Out?" a voice said in her ear. "Is that American?"

"Brady, shut the fuck up!"

"Ummm! You said it again!"

Et Tu Brady

Chapter Fifty

THE NOCTURNAL REVELRY was just cranking up when Brady got to Second Street. The three block stretch of bars, nightclubs, and restaurants was teeming with more life than pond water under a compound microscope. The place was a cavalcade of vernal flesh. In his own mind, Brady was still seventeen years old. In Second Street time, though, he was a fossil, old enough to have fathered most of the celebrants here. His only solace was the scattering of gray-haired, pot-bellied lechers standing on the street corners drooling at the procession of nymphets parading up and down the street, their pituitary glands in overdrive struggling to squeeze testosterone out their rapidly dwindling supplies. By comparison, he didn't feel quite so primordial.

Brady regretted that Second Street had not been here when he was a kid, at least not in its present incarnation. In those days the neighborhood, known as Himmarshee, was a tumble-down collection of flop houses and second-hand stores. Now music blared from every door – rock, blues, techno, Irish, salsa. He strolled past the Village Pie, Ebar, Tarpon Bend, Bourbon, Fat Cats and the Voodoo Lounge. He ducked inside Dicey Riley's and was greeted by a bad band, bad air, and bad vibes. The room was filled with more smoke than the burning car on Las Olas today. The throbbing beat made his ears want to bleed. The strobing lights revealed a room packed with dancing people half his age. Most ignored his presence, but some sneered at him like he was skulking outside a playground in a trenchcoat.

Brady exited the bar and walked diagonally across the intersection. Capone's was a loud bar with tables outside on the sidewalk. A group of college-aged kids was sitting beside the street. A tall, thin guy poured beer from a pitcher into a raised funnel. The brew shot through a long hose to the waiting mouth of a girl with her head tilted back, chugging it until it flooded out the corners of her mouth. The sight aroused ancient images of dorm parties at the University of Florida. Brady winced at the memory of straight tequila being squirted into his mouth from a wine sack. He could still feel the pain that followed. And still rued the decimation of so many brain cells. A stocky kid with close-cropped blond hair and a cigarette clenched between his teeth looked up.

"What can we do for you, pops?"

Beer shot from the nose of the girl sucking on the tube and they all burst out in laughter.

"I'm looking for help."

A mousy girl jerked a thumb over her shoulder.

"Nursing home's that-a-way."

More laughs. Brady laughed too.

"That's the funniest thing I've heard all day. Do I really look that old?"

"Not as old as my father?" said the blond kid.

"Goody gumdrops," Brady said with a smile, rewarding the boy's small attempt at wit.

"But older than my uncle." The jocularity just kept coming. "What kinda help?"

"I'm a doctor," he blurted. It just came out of his mouth. Technically, it was true. He was a doctor of the law. Brady realized the doctor thing could be a good cover. He only wished he'd worn scrubs. And white coat. And maybe a mirror strapped to his forehead.

The skinny kid stopped pouring beer into the funnel. "Doc, I got this major pain in my ass. What should I do?"

"Pull your head out."

The others howled. The thin boy's face turned crimson.

"We're looking for a young woman," he said, trying to look doctorish. "It's an emergency."

Some of the skepticism left their faces.

"What for?"

"I'm afraid that's confidential. However, I can tell you it is quite contagious. A matter of life-and-death. Her tests came back positive, but she's disappeared. We've got people looking all over town."

"What's her name?"

"That's normally confidential, as well, but we think it's a false identity. She called herself Pandora. We heard through the grapevine she hangs out around here. Petite. Very young looking. She's been known to wear a purple dress. Oh, and she's got an inscription tattooed on the inside of one of her thighs."

A brunette in a low-cut gingham blouse was sucking on the funnel hose. When she pulled the tube from her mouth beer dripped into the canyon of her bodice. She clamped a thumb over the aperture and pointed at another bar on the opposite corner.

"Bad Girls."

David Bowie blared from the speakers as a phalanx of eight young women in scant attire cavorted atop a long bar. High-stepping. Bumping. Humping. Convulsing. Pitching over so far that sixteen breasts threatened to dance free from their slender bonds, an eventuality being enthusiastically encouraged by the boisterous patrons packing the room.

When Brady walked in a buxom girl with pliant hips was gyrating at the end of the bar near the door. The hem of her denim miniskirt was riding high on a pair of formidable thighs and her lush figure was covered with a sheen of sweat. She looked like she was trying to win a wet dream contest. He stepped in close.

Behind the bar a hatched-faced bouncer watched him through a pair of flinty eyes. He had swollen arms and looked like he was eager to use them on any patron who dared get too close to the merchandise. Brady stared up between the girl's legs, feeling like a card-carrying ne'er-do-well. Her thighs bore no tattoos. Beside her a tall, thin girl with a boyish face was doing a spirited shimmy. Her red hair was braided into cornrows that could have been an alien crop formation. She had barbed wire tats on both biceps, but no inscription between her skinny legs.

At the center of the bar a very diminutive, very white girl was dancing at hyper-speed. She reminded him of Rose leading Zumba class at the Papillon. She looked too light to leave footprints in the sand. He'd seen older looking twelve year olds. Her dress was short and black and clung to her like wet cloth. Busyman's Pandora had worn purple, but Brady knew at once that this was his *"lilly winji white gal."* The legend started at the knee on the inside of her left thigh and disappeared under the black hem. He leaned in so close he half-expected to feel hatchet-face seize him by the scruff of his neck. She was moving at a breakneck pace and he couldn't decipher if the tattoo was Latin.

The Bowie song ended and the first strains of ABBA's *Dancing Queen* began vibrating over the sound system. The girl jumped down inside the bar and leaned forward, offering Brady a generous view of her *cupcakes*, as Busyman had so accurately portrayed them. She shot him a smile pregnant with possibility. A girl working hard for her tips. Breathless, she shouted over the din.

"What can I get you, mister?"

"Bud."

She reached down into the cooler, pulled out a dripping brown longneck and plunked it on the bar.

"Four bucks."

Brady threw down a twenty.

"Keep the change."

She looked pleased. Her *cupcakes* were obviously earning their keep.

"Thanks, mister."

"Interesting tattoo on your leg. Latin?"

She kept leaning toward him, maybe happy to give him his money's worth, maybe working him for another double-sawbuck.

"You a priest or something?"

"Doctor. We have to know Latin, too."

"Like what?"

He thought for a moment.

"Aegrescit medendo."

"What's that mean?"

"The cure is worse than the disease," he said, uncertain how or why he knew that, or if it was even true. "What does your tattoo say?"

"I thought you could read Latin?"

He nodded at the fist-faced bouncer. "Didn't want to get tossed."

"Oh, that's just Carmine. He's a pussycat." She cast him another smile, this one laden with even more possibility. He noticed her incisors were spiked. "Hope you liked what you saw."

"The tattoo? Ab imo pectore – from the bottom of my heart." He was speaking in tongues. It had to be a miracle. Either that, or a flashback to his altar boy days. "So what's it say?"

"Sorry. That's a secret."

Brady threw another twenty on the bar and ordered a second Bud.

"I've been thinking about getting a tat." He rubbed his right forefinger over his left forearm. "Maybe a seahorse here. Whadya think? Do girls really like them?"

"I don't know about older women." She said it with guileless candor. He flinched a little, inside. "Being a doctor, maybe you should get something in Latin too."

"Good idea. How about amor vincit omnia?"

"What's that?"

"Love conquers all."

"Perfect." Her eyes sharpened and her pretty young face turned almost bitter. "You should go to the bastard who did mine."

"Oh?"

"You can find him at the Slimelight. Name's Lazarus."

"Can I trust him?"

"Honey, he's so trustworthy you'll believe him even when you know he's lying. Tell him Pandora sent you. He'll give you a free tattoo – if you jerk him off."

Brady coughed out a mouthful of beer. Pandora handed him a napkin.

"Thanks," he said. "But I prefer to pay cash."

Et Tu Brady

Chapter Fifty-One

BETTY JANE MARSHALL was sitting on a threadbare pink couch in a dimly lit trailer holding a brush and a bottle of red nail polish.

"I should shove this up your ass and light a match to it," she said.

Dismas Benvenuti was stretched face down straddling her lap. His pants were pulled to his knees while she dabbed polish on an army of purple bumps that dotted his naked buttocks.

"These goddang chiggers is driving me crazy," he whimpered.

"Shut up. You kill my brother then have the balls to ask me to paint bug bites on your ass?"

Betty Jane was a slim woman with long, straight brown hair, delicate features, and hard eyes. Her temperament was as volatile as a sunspot and Dismas was never sure when she'd flare up at him. Right now her mood could best be described as fire-breathing dragon.

"You sure this'll kill 'em?"

"It don't kill 'em, fool. Chiggers is just mite larvae that attach to your skin and suck the juice outa ya. This'll keep the air off so they don't itch. Not that you deserve the relief."

"I hope it works fast. I cain't hardly sit."

"You wouldn't have no chiggers if you wasn't runnin' around half-naked in the woods all the time playin' Cochise."

"Cochise was Apache. I'm Seminole. Like my great-great-great granddaddy Billy Bowlegs. Besides, I'm doing it for us, B.J. Once I get into the tribe we'll have money. We'll be able to afford a double-wide. Maybe even a house. And you can stop bein' a whore."

"I ain't no whore."

"You turn tricks for money. That's bein' a whore."

"Whore's do it just for the money. I'm an escort. When I turn a trick it's cause I want to for my own pleasure. So I ain't no whore."

"Well, maybe I don't want you screwin' strange men no more."

"Maybe I don't want you usin' my son to steal FedEx packages off doorsteps no more neither."

A jet roared in overhead and the trailer rattled like a California earthquake. Dismas shouted over the ruckus.

"It was UPS. And wait till you see what I got ya for yer birthday."

She slapped his bottom hard. "Pretty sad when you gotta use my child to steal my birthday present."

"You'll think different when you see the jackpot we hit."

Dismas broke wind. Betty Jane screeched and shoved him off her lap onto the floor.

"You pig! You kill my brother then fart in my face? On the very same day!"

He pulled his dungarees up over his painted buttocks.

"Stop sayin' I killed Devo. It was a accident. Besides, you always said you hated him. Moochin' off you all the time. Eatin' yer food. Drinkin' yer beer. Stealin' yer money when you wasn't lookin'. You said yerself his brain was puny as an ant's asshole. Them tears yer cryin' fer him look pretty dry to me. Yer better off without him so don't go tryin' to make me feel bad."

The truth was, though, Dismas felt lower than he could ever remember. And that was plenty low. Not so much about Devo, who *was* dumb as a rock and a truly useless human being. But because never in his worst nightmare did he imagine an innocent mother being killed. The accident was supposed to be harmless. No one was going to get hurt. Now he couldn't get the image of the woman's ruined face out of his head. His only comfort was that he'd helped that guy save the little girl before the SUV exploded.

A hard knock on the door sent vibrations shooting through the thin-skinned mobile home. The door opened from the outside and Junior Ball stepped in. He was wearing a business suit and carrying a black leather attaché case. Dismas rose from the floor strapping his belt buckle.

"Hello, Junior."

"Dismas," he said. But his eyes were immediately drawn to the woman sitting on the couch. "And you must be Miss Marshall?"

"Junior, this is my girlfriend, Betty Jane."

"I ain't his girlfriend."

A pained look took over Dismas's face, as if his manhood had been mocked. "What are you talkin' about, Betty Jane?"

"Don't be lying to Mr. Ball." She turned her dark, vivid eyes up at Junior. "I live with him. He lets me and my son stay. For privileges."

"Privileges?"

"I let him diddle me once every week or so. That's as far as it goes."

Junior tried not to stare. He looked up at Dismas, but his eyes kept drifting back down to her, furtive, calculating. She was a little hard-bitten around the edges. Age-lines around young eyes. Tattoos on her ankle and shoulder. But she was slim and curvaceous and had waist-length brown hair. Dismas had let slip his girlfriend worked for an escort service, so he knew she was sexually indulgent. An angel with crumpled wings. Just the way Junior liked his women. Now that he'd seen her in the flesh he set about scheming how to make a date. The ticklish part would be Dismas. He couldn't afford to alienate a guy who made him so much money.

"I don't want to start trouble between you two, Miss Marshall."

She looked him straight in the eye. "Call me B.J."

Junior's eyes widened. "B.J.? Interesting name. How'd you get it?"

"I earned it," she said. Not amiably. More businesslike. Junior liked that in a woman.

"My condolences on your brother's passing," he said. "I came as soon as I heard."

"Cut the bullshit, Mr. Ball. I mighta been raised on rice and beans, but that don't mean I'm stupid." She shifted her glare to Dismas. "I know if it wasn't for you two, my brother'd still be alive."

"You're wrong, B.J.," Junior said. "Devon is dead because a bar let him drink until he was blind drunk, then get in his car and drive off."

"That don't bring back my brother."

"No, it doesn't bring him back. I'm sorry. There's nothing I can do about that. There is something we can do about the bar, though. "

"Like what?"

"We're gonna sue the owner and collect substantial damages."

B.J.'s frown turned upside down and she smiled at Junior like he'd just asked her to the high school prom. "How substantial?"

"Well, B.J., last week a jury in Jacksonville ordered a bar owner to pay four hundred fifty thousand dollars to the family of a man who drove off drunk and got killed in a crash."

"What's my cut?"

B.J. was all business. Junior's attraction was growing by the second. "My commission is thirty percent, plus expenses."

"What expenses?"

"Court costs, experts, investigators. You would be entitled to the rest. That is if you are Devo's sole living relative. Are you?"

"Yes. Our mamma's dead. He never knew his daddy. I don't know mine neither. How much is the rest?"

"Could be a quarter million dollars. Maybe more."

She got up from the couch and stood between the two men. Junior drew in a sharp breath. Her cut-off jeans were so short the firm white crescent moons of her bottom were on full display. Her flimsy white T-shirt looked like it had been washed a thousand times. He imagined her fondling butternut squash in the Titty Room.

"Dismas, you didn't tell me your, ah, girlfriend was such a knockout."

B.J. stepped close and stared straight up into Ball's eyes.

"I told you I ain't his girlfriend."

Her gaze was unflinching. A bystander would have been blind not to see the electricity between them, like lightning arcs on a Jacob's Ladder. Dismas was not blind. His shoulders sagged and his arms dangled loosely at his sides. He looked like a beaten man.

"I'm sorry, B.J." said Junior. His voice was intimate for someone who'd just met her. "I didn't mean to offend you."

Her face softened. She offered him her hand, almost like a gift. He lifted it to his lips.

"Now when do I get my money?" she said.

A jet blasted overhead and the trailer shook. Junior ducked reflexively and came eye-to-eye with B.J.'s breasts. They were jiggling like Jell-O beneath the flimsy fabric and he took the opportunity to gawk at them until the uproar passed, then straightened up.

"Jeez, does that happen often?"

"Only about every five minutes," B.J. said, matter-of-fact. "Soon as I get that money I'm outa this rattle trap before one of them tin birds lands on my head."

Junior opened his black leather briefcase and pulled out a sheaf of papers.

"First, I need your Jane Hancock on these documents. Standard attorney-client service contract. Sign where I've inserted the red arrows."

Dismas stood by watching her scribble, still deflated as a flapjack.

"Trust me, B.J." Junior said when she finished. He handed her his business card. "I'll take good care of you. Call me tomorrow."

Et Tu Brady

Chapter Fifty-Two

THE ALLEY OFF Second Street was black and sinister and Brady walked past it like a child scooting by a darkened bedroom. Then he realized it was the turn he'd been looking for and backtracked. He ducked into the narrow gloom, his boogeyman antenna fully extended. Halfway down he came upon a red velvet rope strung across the front of a steel-plated door studded with heavy bolts, just like every other dungeon he'd ever been in. No attendants were around so he pushed it open.

Apocalyptic music loud enough to puncture an eardrum throbbed from the walls of the Slimelight Lounge. It sounded like a symphony for the devil. Brady listened for a moment and gathered the song was about fire and death and zombie girls. The bar was one big shadow and he stood still while his eyes acclimated. When his vision adjusted he saw that the place was jammed with bodies. The dance floor was a riot of black-and-silver-clad figures. White fog wafted at knee-height, above it a sea of whitewashed faces with eyes outlined in charcoal jerked arrhythmically like spastic pandas.

A tall, burly guy walked up wearing sunglasses, a Mohawk hairdo, platform knee boots, red cape, and a black leather breast plate. Brady guessed he didn't vote a straight Republican ticket.

More likely he was a time traveler from the Praetorian Guard. He leaned in and growled over the opus of doom.

"What do you want?"

"I want to report a cultural collision."

Brady didn't notice a discernible reaction.

"What are you doing here, mister?"

"When does the sock hop start?"

The big man didn't crack a smile. Laughter seemed to be frowned upon in the Land of the Undead. He considered Brady for several seconds then walked away without another word.

Speaking of the undead, at the center of the room a black rectangular box was sitting on an altar-like platform with tall candles flickering at each corner. It was a nice touch, giving the scene the ghoulish air of a funereal orgy. Brady weaved through the dancers and looked down into the red silk-lined casket. Layed-out inside was the corpse of bountiful young woman with black lips and deathly white skin. Two teardrop tattoos were dripping from the corner of her right eye and the pink tops of her areolas were peeking out from a lacey black gown cut lower than the dancer's outfits at Bad Girls. Despite her cadaverous complexion, she was a surreal beauty. He leaned down to get a closer look at her face when her eyes opened. She bared a pair of stiletto fangs and hissed. He recoiled.

"Sorry, I thought you were dead, Miss..."

"Raven."

"Of course. Satan worshipper? Or just trying to piss off your parents?"

Raven sat up and examined him. Her tongue caressed her speartipped teeth.

"You don't look like you belong here, mister. This is a black garb zone."

"I'm a huge Johnny Cash fan."

"He's dead."

"Then I'm in the right place."

"You a cop?"

"Nope. Just looking for somebody. Tattooist named Lazarus?"

Raven bared her tusks again and raised a chipped black fingernail to her ebon lips. "The only Lazarus I know is that guy Jesus
raised from the dead."

"I thought you people were Satanists."

She smiled seductively. "Only on weekends."

Brady left Raven sitting in her funerary box and stepped to a
bar lined with angst-ridden young people in tortured poses. Some
with spiked haircuts. Some with shaved heads. Guys in frilly shirts.
An attractive damsel in a red leather bra and black skirt was being
tended to by an older woman with a ring in her nose who was nibbling on the girl's shoulder while she raked her bare arms with a
clawed glass device throwing off blue waves of electricity. Behind
the bar a tall anemic-looking man with a Lucifer goatee and Freddie
Krueger fingernails was mixing up dark offerings. His bushy eyebrows were twisted at the ends to look like demonic horns and his
hair was standing straight up, as though he'd been plugged into an
electrical socket.

"What can I get you?" he said.

"Whadya got?"

"Absinthe, Type-O Negative, Snakebite."

"Sorry, I'm not a member of the tribe. Snakebite?"

"Half pint cider, half pint lager. For an extra buck I add a shot of
blackcurrant cordial."

"Budweiser," Brady said, thinking maybe he should add
Snakebite to the Sea Shanty's drink menu, if he ever added a drink
menu.

A tall sturdy woman squeezed up to the bar. A dark angel in a
pair of feathery black wings. Black lipstick was smeared in the relative proximity of where her lips should have been.

"Absinthe martini, please," she said in a husky voice.

The bartender placed a stemmed cocktail glass on the bar and
banged a crystal sugar bowl down beside it. He pulled out a perforated spoon, scooped some sugar, and held it above the cone-shaped
receptacle. He reached beneath the bar and produced a bottle of emer-
ald green liquid and poured it over the spoon. As it streamed into the
glass it transposed into an opaque white beverage. He splashed in a

half shot of vermouth and stirred it with a glass swizzle stick as long as Harry Potter's wand. The large woman picked up the glass by its stalk, extending her pinky finger daintily. A true sophisticate. She lifted it to her lips and threw back her head and downed the concoction in a single swig and wiped her mouth with a forearm matted with black hair. She smacked her lips then shook a cigarette from a brown pack and turned to Brady.

"I'm Morbidia," she said with dreamy eyes.

"Why wouldn't you be? I'm Johnny Cash. Doctor Johnny Cash."

"Gotta light, doc?"

Her voice sounded like it had been dipped in testosterone and Brady realized that, in the strictest sense of the word, she was not officially female. He lifted a candle off the bar and let the flame flicker beneath the funny looking cigarette. Morbidia inhaled and expelled a spicy brume in his face.

"What is that?"

"Clove. It leaves such a sweet taste in your mouth." Morbidia banked toward him with puckered lips. "If you doubt my insincerity, take a taste."

"I'll take your word for it." He leaned back and raised his beer bottle to his mouth. Brady didn't consider himself particularly handsome, but he got the sense Morbidia might have accused him of such a crime. "By the way, do you know where I can find a guy named Lazarus?"

She fluttered long, lush eyelashes, the kind they sell at Party City.

"Our *Romeo of the Night.* We all worship Lazarus. He did my fangs. See?"

Morbidia smiled to reveal a pair of pincers.

"Sharp. Will they open a can of tuna?" Morbidia looked confused. "Where do I find *Romeo?*"

"This is his world headquarters." She pointed. "You should find him back there."

Brady gave her a slight bow and was rewarded with another flutter.

"Until we meet again."

He waded through a sea of disconsolate faces to the back of the Slimelight. The only entryway was covered by a hanging blanket. Brady saw a slash of red light on the floor beneath the cover. With no door to knock, he pulled it back and stepped inside and had the sensation of entering a photographer's dark room.

"Lazarus?"

It was a challenge to see through the muted glow, but he made out a tall man standing at the far end of the room. He seemed young and had the lean frame of a long distance runner. He was decked out in black tails, black cape, and black stovepipe hat.

"Bela Lugosi lives," said Brady.

The dark-attired figure turned and studied him for a moment before he spoke. "On your soul I shall dine."

"Sounds delish, but I gotta warn you I lead a dull life. You may need to spice me up. A pinch of parsley, smidge of sage, dash of rosemary, maybe some thyme."

Top hat didn't react. Maybe he was too young to get the Simon & Garfunkel reference. Or maybe it was true that laughing was a no-no at the Slimelight. Too bad. If they had a comedy night Brady could come back and do his Goth routine. *("I'm so Goth I make flowers wilt. I'm so Goth, when I smile people ask what's wrong. I'm so Goth the dark is scared of me.")*

"Who are you?" said the guy in black.

"Doctor Cash. Johnny Cash. I bet you're Lazarus. Or do you prefer *Romeo of the Night?*"

"What do you want?"

Brady anticipated the question and was ready with yet more clever repartee.

"My teeth are dull. I can barely bite the heads off small animals. I need a sharpening."

He noticed Lazarus had a barber's chair like the one in *Busyman's Tattoo Emporium.* At the moment it was occupied by a girl who looked only slightly older than Pandora. No more than fifteen. Dressed in black, of course. Stretched out on the recliner, her eyelids were half closed and she seemed slightly breathless. Brady got a sense he had interrupted a libidinous session of fang filing. He stepped further into the room and Lazarus retreated until his face was hidden in the shadows, like the blonde actress in that Hitchcock film Fuzzy Furbush mentioned, the one with Cary Grant playing a jewel thief. *What was her name?*

"You're lying," Lazarus said from the blackness.

"Grace Kelly," Brady blurted.

"What are you talking about?"

"You. You're standing in the shadow like Grace Kelly in that Hitchcock flick. Jeez, now I've forgotten the movie."

"*To Catch A Thief.*"

It was the girl in black on the chair.

"That's it. Say, you're good. You must be older than you look."

"You're lying," Lazarus said again.

"I am?"

"About the teeth."

"Oh, right. Actually, I'm here for a tattoo. A friend of yours sent me. Pandora?"

"That troll whore?"

It was the reclining girl again. Brady detected a heavy measure of green-eyed jealousy.

"Pandora told me you did the tattoo on her leg. The one in Latin. Being a doctor, I think I'd like one in Latin too. But not on my thigh. And, for the record, I pay cash."

"What are you looking for?" Lazarus said from the murk. Brady could hear suspicion in his voice.

"I was thinking something across my chest. *Matris,* maybe."

"What? Mattress? Are you some kind of bed doctor, or just a crank?"

"Hello-o-o? Not mattress. *Matris.* M-a-t-r-i-s. You know, *Mother* in Latin."

The girl in the chair sighed theatrically. "Lazarus, I'm waiting."

"Shut up, Demonika."

She bolted upright and turned on him. "Don't you dare talk to me like that."

Lazarus came out of the shadows with his fangs bared and hissed. The Slimelight had more hissing than a convention of cobras.

"Cope, bitch," he said.

His voice was cold and domineering. Then he turned toward Brady, who took one look and gasped.

"Holy!"

He tripped backwards and collided with a work bench against the wall. Tools clattered onto the floor, but he didn't seem to notice. He was too mesmerized by the face. It was narrower now, and whiter, and the eyes looked like they'd been marinated in blood. There was no mistaking it, though. It was the same face that had been lurking in the darkest recesses of his nightmares for as long as he could remember. *It can't be*, he thought. But it was.

Lazarus watched him, impassive. "What the hell is wrong with you, mister? Are you fruitbat?"

Brady shook his head and tried to speak. No words came out. Lazarus continued to stare at him until the girl filled the silence.

"Screw this!" she shouted and bounded out of the barber chair.

She stalked past Brady and disappeared under the blanket, leaving him to stare openmouthed at that face. Despite the dim light, the fanged eyeteeth, the macabre blood red pupils, the mustache and goatee, it was the same square jaw, straight nose, symmetrical face and athletic build. He was leaner and there was a diaphanous, almost feminine delicacy about him. Otherwise, Lazarus *was* Duke Manyon.

My nightmare lives!

Ben had written the words days before his murder. It wasn't just the way he looked. Lazarus radiated the same magnetism. An almost regal air. As if he'd been touched by the gods. *Or demons!* Had Manyon cut some kind of Faustian bargain and traded his soul for life and eternal youth?

Or maybe Lazarus was right. Maybe Brady was *fruitbat*, whatever that meant. Maybe the anemic bartender had spiked his beer with Snakebite or some witches' brew. Maybe the smoke Morbidia had blown in his face was a hallucinogen. Whatever was happening, Lazarus was Duke. *But Duke is dead.*

Then he remembered Peanut's words before he passed out tonight. He said he'd seen Manyon. He couldn't recall where, but it had been recently. And he mentioned Second Street as one possibility. He must have seen Lazarus. Peanut didn't seem so delusional anymore.

"You're no doctor," Lazarus said. "You're not Johnny Cash, either."

Brady finally found his tongue. "No."

"Who are you? What do you want?"

When it comes to human recall, smell and sight are the most powerful of the five senses, followed by hearing, taste, and touch. Brady still remembered *that night*. He remembered the scent of Coppertone on Duke Manyon. And he would never forget his face. But he had zero recollection of his voice.

"My name is Brady," he said, gathering himself. "Max Brady."

"You a cop?"

"Does wanting a tattoo make me a cop?"

"You've got a cop's aura."

"Tell me about it, Duke?"

"Duke? Who's Duke? My name's Lazarus."

Brady studied him for signs of deception. He had interrogated more murder suspects than he could count. He had a bloodhound's nose for sniffing out stone cold killers. He was having trouble picking up a scent from this guy. The hushed light didn't help. Nor did his crimson eyes. He was either taking some serious drugs or wearing blood red contact lenses. The effect was unearthly.

"I get it. Lazarus is Duke Manyon risen from the dead."

Lazarus removed his top hat, tossed it onto the barber's chair, and shook his curly blond locks.

"Mister, if you're not a cop you just got furloughed from the loony bin."

"Where were you Tuesday night?"

"You are a cop."

"A man was murdered. A Latin phrase was tattooed on his body."

"So?"

Even with the creepy red eyes, Brady did not detect surprise in Lazarus at the mention of a murder and a Latin tattoo.

"So you do Latin tattoos. I saw the slogan you wrote on your friend Pandora's leg."

"She's not my friend. We just trade blood sometimes."

"Romeo of the Night?"

A sardonic smile broke out on his handsome face. He could have been Duke that bygone day when young Max first encountered him on the boat.

"Goth girls love to role play. They've cast me as their Romeo. I'm their community Count Dracula. It's all in fun. Great for business. And I get pussy galore."

"Like that teeny-bopper who just walked out?"

"Don't worry, officer. She's street legal."

"You sure? Age of consent in Florida is eighteen."

"You're not here because of jailbait? Who's this Duke you're talking about? And what murder?"

"A man named Benjamin Chance was killed."

Lazarus's face twitched and he stepped back into the shadow.

"I don't know anything. Why are you even talking to me?"

"You're the only tattooist I've found who works in Latin. Where were you Tuesday night?"

Lazarus stood stock still. Brady could feel his scarlet eyes peering like lasers from the darkness.

"I was right here."

"Got any witnesses?"

"Only about a hundred."

Brady pulled a small notepad and pen from his back pocket and scribbled a couple of notations.

"By the way, what's your full name Duke?"

"What is this Duke shit?" he said, his voice laced with exasperation. "I told you my name's Lazarus."

"Your real name."

He seemed reluctant to answer, then spit it out. Lazarus was Lawrence B. Lazzara. B for Bradley. Age twenty eight. He lived in an apartment above the Slimelight.

"Who's your daddy, Lawrence?"

"Call me Lazarus. My father's name is Frank Lazzara. He was a plumber. Treated me like dog shit. I left home at sixteen and never went back."

"And home was?"

"Bethlehem."

"Like Jesus?"

"Pennsylvania. You're not here for a tattoo, are you mister?"

"Can't fool you, Duke? Or Lawrence? Or Lazarus? Now tell me about Duke Manyon. Is he your uncle? Cousin? Much older brother?"

"Listen officer, or detective, or whoever you are, I don't know why you keep asking me about this guy. I don't know anyone named Duke Manson."

"Manyon."

"Manyon. Banyon. Canyon. I don't know who you're talking about. And I'm done talking to pigs. So unless you have a warrant, please get the hell outa here."

"Does that mean you won't be dining on my soul tonight?"

Brady didn't wait for an answer. He brushed past the blanket and made his way out of the bar. He headed back up the alley toward the light, but stopped abruptly. His boogeyman detector was picking up something. A footstep? A whiff of cigarette smoke? He turned and studied the shadows for a moment. No movement. No sound. No smell. He shrugged and continued out of the alley, unable to shake an eerie feeling that he was being watched.

Et Tu Brady

Chapter Fifty-Three

LAZARUS EXITED THE Slimelight a minute after Brady. He rounded the building and took a creaky wooden staircase to a second floor apartment. The interior looked like a stereotypic college dormitory room. Floor littered with piles of crumpled clothing. Plastic cups and plates strewn about. Stink of stale cigarette smoke. Two fat brown cockroaches adorned the far wall.

A black duffel bag sat unzipped on the floor beside the door with a jumble of black clothes sticking out of it like dead weeds from an unkempt garden. Demonika was standing at the bed in jeans and a T-shirt. She'd dumped Nudey Judy's cash on top of the mattress and was splitting it into two green piles.

"What are you doing, Demonika?"

"Taking my share – forty eight grand – and getting the hell out of town. And don't call me Demonika anymore. My name's Elizabeth."

Lazarus listened with a stunned expression. "What brought this on? What happened to San Francisco? We were gonna to leave together. I thought you loved me."

Demonika slapped a stack of bills onto one pile. "Being *Romeo of the Night's* wicked little witch isn't quite as romantic as it used to be. You've got too many Pandora's in your coven. But the real reason is that guy. Dr. Johnny Cash. In case you didn't get it, he's a cop. That nutty nudist must have put two-and-two together and figured out I lifted her key and stole her money."

Lazarus crossed the room and tried to embrace her. She pushed him away.

"Listen to me, baby," he said. "He didn't mention the money. I swear. And his name's Brady, not Cash. I'm not sure he's even a cop. I don't know what the hell he is."

"What did he want?"

"I'm not even sure about that, Dem...You really want me to call you Elizabeth? How about Liz, or Liza, or Beth?" She continued dividing the cash without response. "Anyway, that guy was half crazy. He kept calling me Manson."

"Like Charles Manson?"

"Duke Manson."

"Who's Duke Manson?"

"That's what I'm saying, Demonika."

"Elizabeth."

"Elizabeth. I don't know what he wanted, but it wasn't the money."

Lazarus didn't mention the murder. She stopped divvying the loot and turned to him.

"Are you sure?"

He moved in close again and wrapped his arms around her. This time she didn't resist.

"Positive, baby. Now forget this crazy idea about leaving me. Let's do what we planned to do. Let's go to San Francisco – together."

"When?"

"Tonight. Five minutes." He picked up a stack of cash. "We won the lottery. Let's have fun. Get the frig outa Dodge tonight. Right after..."

Lazarus reached down and pinched the hem of Demonika's shirt and yanked it up fast over her head, then unbuttoned her jeans and let them drop to the floor so that she stood there only in black panties. He leaned over and spread the two piles of cash across the bed, pushed her down and layed on top of her.

366

"That cop, or whatever he is, Brady, was making noise about arresting me for having sex with a minor. He thought you were fifteen. Aren't you flattered?"

Before she could answer, the apartment door crashed open and a large man approximately the size of Humvee trudged in. He peered at them from eyes as dark as caves.

"Who the fuck are you?" Lazarus blurted.

The big man stepped swiftly to the bed and yanked him off Demonika. Lazarus was helpless against his strength. The behemoth rammed a fist the size of a bowling ball into his stomach. He went down in a heap and vomited on the floor. The intruder calmly leaned over and stamped his face with another short lollop from his big-knuckled left hand.

Demonika lay on the bed trying to cover her nakedness with paper money. He grabbed her by the hair, pulled her up off the bed and pushed her down on top of Lazarus. He stood over them and growled in a deep baritone.

"You two losers fucked up. Bigtime."

He kicked Lazarus hard in the ribs with the toe of a heavy black shoe.

"Stop hurting him you bastard," Demonika screamed and sprawled her panty-clad body across Lazarus like a protective shield.

"Sorry, Elvira. Some people don't take kindly to being robbed."

"Are you Judy's husband?"

The big man snorted. "Husband? I wouldn't touch that fruitcake with your boyfriend's dong."

"Please, mister, take the money and get out of here. It's all there. Just don't hurt him anymore."

He leered down at her trying to protect Lazarus, her arms crossed over tiny naked breasts.

"I got good news and bad news for you pagan bloodsuckers. The good news is you're not going to jail, at least not for this."

He reached down and picked up the black duffel bag. He dumped the clothes on the floor, threw the bag on the bed, and began stuffing it with cash. Demonika sniveled on the floor.

"You're not the police?"

"Not anymore." He finished filling the bag and zipped it shut. "Now for the bad news."

"But you said we don't have to go to jail."

"You don't."

He reached down and clenched Demonika's thin right arm in an iron claw grip and jerked her to her feet. She used her free hand to cover herself and tried to pull away, but it was useless. He pushed her face down on the bed. Lazarus remained on the floor, writhing, helpless. Demonika turned her head and looked back at the giant, her dark eyes filled with terror.

"Please, just take the money and go."

"Not yet," he growled. He reached for her panties and ripped them down. "You ain't going to jail, but you still gotta pay."

Et Tu Brady

Chapter Fifty-Four

BRADY JOCKEYED THE Jeep through bumper-to-bumper traffic down Second Street. Steering left-handed, he worked the stick shift with his right while his thumb punched numbers into his cellphone. After two rings a man answered.

"Homicide, Detective Perry James."

Not bad for two o'clock in the morning.

"I know it's late, detective. I'm trying to reach Captain Register. Is there a way to get a message to him?"

"About?"

About? Good question. Brady's head was swimming with more possibilities than a Greek diner menu. So many choices. The real answer was – *I've just seen a ghost.* Ron Register would send guys with butterfly nets for him.

Brady needed to buy time. Delay Register before he did something rash, like arrest Delray for murder. He'd already painted a bull's eye on her back. He did have some evidence, but it was circumstantial and would make for a weak case. Yet, he'd seen defendants convicted on less. And there was no telling what Register's people had dredged up since Delray's calamitous interview yesterday. He needed to slow things down. If she was formally charged the die would be cast. Cops are like anybody else. They hate to admit mistakes. Register in particular. Not with the Police Chief's job on the line. Better to introduce some new suspects before it was too late. Put some fresh arrows in Register's quiver. He'd already planted a bug in his ear about Duke Manyon. Now he gave Detective James the names of three more potential *persons of interest* in the Benjamin Chance murder: Richard "Peanut" Strong, Lawrence B. "Lazarus" Lazzara, and Austin Ball, Jr.

"The lawyer?" James said.

Brady heard surprise in his voice. He was surprised, too, to hear that Junior Ball was an attorney.

"I don't know what he does for a living. I have a witness who says Ball's wife had an affair with Benjamin Chance and Ball threatened violence against them."

Brady gave the detective some sketchy background on Peanut and Lazarus, but did not mention that Peanut was also his witness against Ball. James thanked him and promised to get the message to Register first thing in the morning.

His next thought was of Rose. He debated driving to her apartment. He still felt awful about their argument. He wanted to patch things up. He craved to see her face, smell her hair, touch her skin, hear her soft tremolos of passion. Brady counted backwards. They hadn't made love since yesterday morning in the tent. Almost two full days. It felt like an eternity.

So much had happened. Forty-eight hours ago life had been simple and carefree. Serving fruity drinks to soggy dollars at the Sea Shanty. Running with the wind at the helm of his sloop. And stealing as much time as the law allowed with Rose. Nothing else mattered. They existed in their own bubble. But the bubble had burst. Their dreamlike state had been poisoned by jealousy and suspicion.

Rose was asking uncomfortable questions. Brady was in no mood to discuss his character flaws. Or be cross-examined about things he'd spent his life trying to forget. Not tonight. Besides, it was late. Rose would be asleep. On top of that, he had wounds that needed healing. His head still throbbed and his back still stung from the car crash. He'd done enough damage – and been damaged enough – for one day.

He drove east over the Second Avenue railroad tracks, took a right on Brickell, a left at Las Olas, and ten minutes later pulled up to Victor Gruber's. He parked the Jeep in the garage. The house was dark and he retreated around back to the *Victoria II*. He popped a couple of Advil, unscrewed the cap on a Rolling Rock, and fell into his bunk, wincing in pain when his back hit the mattress.

Michael Fury's diary was still on the bedside stand, opened to the spot he'd left off last night. Fury had been saved from beheading by the beautiful Princess Nitcrosis. He did not give an exact location of the Indian village, but Brady couldn't help picturing the drama play out on the banks of Whiskey Creek. He picked up where Fury was thrown back into his bamboo pen.

That cage remained me prison for many days thereafter. At times I believed I would die there. Yet I was not ill-treated. I was fed twice every day. Nay with palatable Christian fare. The food was delivered in a pail made of Tortose-shell filled with savory fish, lobstars, berries, dates, grapes, and nuts. Sometimes fresh meat was included which tasted of venison. The meals was flavored with a spice reminiscent of garlic and was generally delicious, with the exception of an odious bread-like victual that made me retch. During the first week of me incarceration the food was brung by elder women. Then one morning the girl whose life I'd saved and who had saved me own from the headsmans ax came to the pen bearing me meal.

As I supped she sat outside the bamboo billet watching me with intent fascination, as though I was an untamed jungle beast in a zoologic menagerie. Until then I had caught only brief glimpses of her. Now I had time to study her face close and saw again how exquisite she be.

In the days to come Fury learned that Nitcrosis was the daughter of Solac, the tall warrior who had murdered his crew mates and nearly beheaded him. Solac was *Cacique* – or chief – of the *Loxahatchees*. (Loxahatchee, he later learned, was the native word for *'river of turtles'*.) The Loxahatchee was a small tribe of about two hundred members, one of many clans that populated the southeastern peninsula of the *Floridas*.

The boy taught Nitcrosis English words. She learned to say *Michael, food, fish, tree, boy, girl, arm, hand, head, village* and every other object they could see from the cage. She, in turn, tutored him on her tribal tongue. Before long they became friends.

A fortnight after the sinking of *The Nemesis*, Solac ordered Fury removed from the pen and brought out into the sea. By then Nitcrosis and he had developed a means of communication through words, gestures, and drawings in the dirt and the Cacique brought his daughter to translate.

The natives, he discovered, were fine boatmen. They navigated large canoes hollowed from cypress logs with shark's teeth. Sometimes two canoes were lashed together with poles and mats made from woven palm leaves stretched into a platform to form a vessel the natives called *kattumarams*.

They paddled in a small convoy of canoes and kattumarams along the shore one league north then east another league out into the sea. There they came upon several more vessels populated by natives who were diving into the water. Fury looked down into the crystal clear depths and saw why. *The Nemesis*, or at least part of her, was perched on a rocky shoal.

The masts was gone but the poop sat in pristine water barely three fathoms down. So near I could almost touch it. In truth, only half The Nemesis remained. The vessel had been severed at mid-beam and only the stern remained. The bow was nowhere in sight. It had apparently been swept away by the powerful Sea currents spawned by the whirlwind.

Brady took a deep breath. He could feel his heart pound. The Loxahatchee boats traveled one *league* north of their village on the creek. Three hundred years ago, the English considered a *league* to be approximately three miles – the distance a man or horse could walk in one hour. Sunrise Boulevard was about three miles north of Whiskey Creek. One *league*. The native boats paddled another *league* east out into the ocean. Three Mile Reef, as its name implied, was three miles east of Sunrise Boulevard. One *league*.

Ned Pike's ship was perched on a shoal, its poop deck three *fathoms* down, which meant the deck of *The Nemesis* was only fifteen feet below the surface. As a boy, Brady had been fascinated by the galleons favored by Caribbean pirates. He'd studied them in great detail and recalled that the distance between the deck and keel was generally about twenty five feet, give or take a few feet depending on the vessel. That meant the shoal *The Nemesis* sat on was roughly forty feet down. The same depth as the coral ridge that ran along the top of Three Mile Reef.

"My God," he said out loud. "It's true."

He read on.

Through Nitcrosis I explained to Solac that many chests of gold and jewels was stowed in the hold beneath the poop. For the purpose of ballast, other caches was kept below the forecastle and main deck at ship center approximately where The Nemesis was torn asunder.

The Loxahatchees was expert salvors. They set up an elaborate station comprised of canoes anchored to the wreckage and the shoal. The Indians could swim as strong as the Pearl divers I had encountered with Ned Pike along the Peru coast. The depth was nay challenge to them. I joined in the salvage, diving down with them to retrieve the treasure, and became quite an adept salvor meself, able to remain under the water for long periods.

Over the next months Fury and the Loxahatchees continued mining the bowels of *The Nemesis*. At the end of each day the booty was transported on kattumarams to *Tonista*, which Fury learned from Nitcrosis was what the Loxahatchees called their camp and which, roughly translated, meant *beloved village*. Once on land the treasure was dumped into casks and buried beside Solac's hut in pits *"no less in depth than a man's height."* The holes were like secret bank vaults. Several had to be dug to accommodate the vast prize the Loxahatchees were amassing.

Then, six months after the salvage began, another terrific storm struck and what remained of *The Nemesis* was swept away. By then, though, Fury estimated they had recovered the majority of Ned Pike's gold stored in the aft section of the ship.

Brady lay the pages on his chest again, stunned by what he'd read. He was certain now that Whiskey Creek, or a creek almost exactly where it now sat, had been the site of *Tonista*. And that Three Mile Reef had been *The Nemesis's* final resting place. The coins he and his friends found as kids had once been the ill-gotten property of Captain Ned Pike himself.

The Loxahatchees had salvaged, by today's accounting, approximately one billion dollars' in treasure. That meant another billion in gold and silver was still down there, someplace.

"How far could it have gotten?" Brady asked himself out loud, then answered his own question. "Not very."

Before he was able to wrap his mind around that possibility, though, his eyes closed and he drifted away.

Et Tu Brady

Chapter Fifty-Five

MAX FELT GRANDPA Zack's familiar nudge and awoke to a dark and blustery morning. It was five o'clock and rain was lashing at his bedroom window. Grandma Kate's forecast storm. Thirty minutes later he was sitting alone in the pre-dawn outside the Piggly Wiggly. A cool wet wind nibbled at his bare arms and legs as he folded his newspapers, stuffed them into waterproof plastic sleeves, and slid them into his canvas saddlebag. While he did that, his mind was occupied by the previous night's events.

Kissing Delray beside Whiskey Creek. Seeing Duke and Buck bury something on the island. His narrow escape. There were two things he knew with absolute certainty. He wanted to kiss Delray again, as soon as possible. And he did not want to see Duke or Buck, ever again.

Max threw the saddlebag over the back fender of his red Schwinn. A scant rain was falling and he could smell the earth's pores opening to receive it. Not a light shone in the low black sky as he peddled down dark, deserted Riverland Road and turned into Tortugas Lane. By the time he finished tossing papers up-and-down the long cul-de-sac the wind was stiff and the drizzle had turned to hard rain. It slanted into his face, forcing him to squint through the gauzy veil as he steered back onto Riverland, turned right, and headed toward Sugar Loaf Lane. He was halfway there when his bike skidded to a halt and he slammed into the handlebars. He turned and saw that the canvas saddlebag was entangled in the spokes of his back wheel.

At that instant, the downpour grew to monsoon force. Fat raindrops pelted his head and face, water invaded his eyes, nose, ears, and mouth. Breathing was difficult and sight almost impossible. Stuck in the middle of the road straddling the Schwinn's crossbar, he reached back and tugged at the canvas. It refused to dislodge. Then he looked up and something cold clutched at his entrails. Headlights. Coming straight at him. They were still in the distance, but there were no streetlights on this stretch of Riverland. In the dark and rain the driver would never see him in time to stop. He yanked the saddlebag again. It didn't budge. The bike wheel was frozen in place while the headlights drew inexorably nearer. He tried again with more urgency. Nothing. It was hopeless. Still straddling the crossbar, he began waddling like a duck trying to walk the bike off the street. His bare feet slipped on the wet pavement and the weight of the newspapers tipped the bike over. It fell onto its side and his papers were strewn across the road.

Max scrambled to his knees and began jamming them back into the sack. He looked up. The car beams were a block away. No more time. He grabbed the handlebar and dragged the bike toward the side of the road. Then, to his relief, the vehicle's bright lights flashed on. The driver had seen him. But, instead of slowing or swerving, the car accelerated and roared straight at him. It was only yards away when Max abandoned the bike and dove for his life.

He sailed over a low hedge that bordered the road and landed flat on his stomach on the soft cushion of someone's lawn. Brakes screeched and tires squealed and he heard the sound of metal being crushed. Heart racing, Max was about to jump up to see what had happened to his bike when something told him to stay down. He rolled onto his knees and peeked through a hole in the hedge. The Schwinn was lying in the street, twisted like a pretzel. A big white Bonneville with a black top had screeched to a halt twenty yards down the road. It sat there for several seconds, red brake lights shining, exhaust spilling from its tailpipe. Then its tires screeched on the slick asphalt and the car rushed backwards. To Max's horror it ran straight over his bicycle again.

The Bonneville braked a few feet from him and the driver's head poked from the window. It was a man. He climbed out into the deluge and walked to the rear of his car. What remained of the demolished bicycle was crumpled beneath it. He knelt on the pavement and stared at the damage for a moment. Then he raised his head and Max could see his face in the red glare of the taillights. The same mean, pitted face of the man who tried to run him down on the Intracoastal two days before. The same man wielding the shovel last night at Whiskey Creek.

"Goddamn tadpole," Buck growled over the thrum of heavy rain. He ripped the mangled frame out from under the Bonneville and threw it to the side of the street like a broken toy. Then he stood and hollered. "Where are you, kid?"

Max's hand slipped on the wet grass and he pitched forward into the hedge. Buck looked toward the sound. Max regained his balance and crouched motionless as a statue while Buck scanned the hedge. Suddenly he bolted in the boy's direction. Max sprang to his feet and ran but the wet grass was slippery as banana skins and he fell. He got traction just as Buck dove over the shrubbery. The man landed on his face while the boy dodged between two houses and disappeared. Buck called after him.

"Come back, kid. Are you okay? I'll buy you a new bike."

Max ran to the back yard of the home on his left. A shaft of light was coming from a window. A dog barked in the distance. He kept going until the yard dead-ended at a canal. He heard Buck coming in the black rain.

"Max Brady."

The clouds parted and last night's moon hung low in the predawn sky, not nearly as brilliant now, a speck of light just to its left. A planet. Max guessed Mercury. He realized he was trapped. A wooden fence ran down either side of the yard to the water's edge and a wooden dock. There was only one way out. He sat on the coral seawall to the right of the dock and lowered himself into the canal.

The water was less than knee-deep beside the wall, which made it easy to stand. But it also made docks popular spots for alligators to bed down. He hoped a reptile wasn't snoring under this one. He felt Buck closing in.

Why is he chasing me?

The nightwater was warm against his rain-chilled skin. He inched sideways toward the dock until his bare feet slipped on a hunk of algae-covered coral and he fell with a splash. He hoped his oscillations were drowned out by the downpour. Buck hollered.

"Show yourself, kid."

He was close. Another dog howled. Max couldn't tell from where.

"I ain't gonna to hurt you."

He knows I saw him last night!

He squatted in the water and waded out into the canal. It was deep there, but he had no cover and his head was visible. A cabin cruiser was moored behind the house to his right about fifty yards away. He set a bearing, submerged, and kicked blindly with arms extended until his fingers touched the boat's underbelly. He swam beneath the vessel and surfaced under the dock, wary again about waking a gator from its beauty sleep. Buck shouted from the distance.

"Come out, kid! I just want to talk."

You just want to kill me!

Max should have been paralyzed by fear. Yet, a strange sensation had taken grip of him. A grown man was hunting him with deadly intent while he hid in black water with cold rain pouring through the dock slats on him. And he was smiling. Something tingly was rushing through him. A primitive thrill. Like it was a game. The sensation was nearly as electric as kissing Delray. And standing up to Junior in the schoolyard. And diving off the bridge. And fending off the shark. He realized danger had become a perverse pleasure for him. Fear was fun.

Something's wrong with me!

Night was turning to day. He peeked around the boat and saw Buck's silhouette, black against the gathering dawn. He was perched on the seawall exactly where Max had slid into the canal. A porch lamp came on in the house behind him. Buck stood his ground, head turning back and forth, scanning the water. Max could see by his body language he was angry. The *tadpole* had slipped through his fingers. Another light came on and Buck finally made a hasty retreat. He ran back through the yard toward the road and, after a minute, Max heard tires squeal. He waited for a time, until he noticed he was shivering. He wasn't sure if the trembling was a result of the chill water or his brush with death, but the warm exhilaration had deserted him.

Rain was still coming hard when he got back to the road. The twisted remains of his bicycle lay crumpled beside the pavement. The sight saddened him. The Schwinn was the best bike he'd ever owned. He dragged the mangled carcass and leaned it against the hedge he'd dived over.

Three dozen copies of *The Miami Herald* were strewn across Riverland Road. Max stuffed them back into his saddlebag then draped the bag over his shoulders like a poncho. He had to finish his route. He couldn't afford to lose his subscribers. He'd need the money to buy a new bicycle. He delivered the newspapers on foot in the downpour, haunted every step of the way by a single thought.

What happened last night at Whiskey Creek?

Et Tu Brady

Chapter Fifty-Six

"WHAT THE…" Brady was wrenched from the black fathoms by a noise. His eyes bolted open and he found himself staring at a red *4:30* on the ceiling over his bunk. Projected by the clock Rose had bought him, for sleepers too lazy to actually turn their heads to see the time. It took him a moment to realize his cell phone was ringing.

"Who the hell…?" he said, his voice woolly with sleep.

He propped himself on his left elbow. Michael Fury's diary slid off his chest and scattered across the floor, like the newspapers in his fast-fading apparition. He reached over to the bedside table and his fingers fumbled in the darkness until they found the device. He fell back onto the pillow and massaged his forehead trying to rub away his exhaustion, then pushed the talk button.

"Hullo."

He listened for several seconds and sprang upright.

Brady relished few things more than a trip to the morgue. Impaling himself on a bamboo pole. Having moray eels invade his shorts. Diving head first into a sludge pit. Beyond those favorites, though, nothing lightened his mood more than the bone house.

Belinda Boulanos greeted him at the entrance to the Broward County Medical Examiner's Office. She was wearing no make-up, a weary smile, and looked like she'd been up all night. Brady was surprised to find the place smelled more like a department store than a portal of the dead. The atrium lobby was warm and cozy. Lots of wood and brick, plush carpet, earth tone furniture. The walls were adorned by murals of Old Florida. The Barefoot Mailman. An Indian village in the Everglades. Lobster boats in the Keys. All in all, quite homey, if you happened to be a cadaver.

Boulanos, tall and trim in her white lab coat, led him through a maze of hallways to an exit at the rear of the building. They went out through a covered breezeway and into a second building. The light was harsher here and the atmosphere bleaker. The décor was antiseptic. Stainless steel and white tile. The crushing presence of doom more palpable.

"This is the main morgue," Belinda said. They pushed through metal double-doors into a room with two long rows of gurneys. "We've got a dozen autopsy stations here. And another three in Decomp."

Decomp, he didn't have to be told, was the refrigerated room for bodies that had undergone extensive decomposition, or contained infectious diseases like tuberculosis and hepatitis. The deeper they moved into the bowels of the building the more his stomach clenched. At the far end of the autopsy room they came upon another metal door marked *Cooler*.

"We've got four coolers."

"Belinda, you are the consummate hostess," he said, trying to lighten the mood.

"Why, thank you, Max." She smiled brightly, ignoring his disingenuous tone. "Each cooler can hold one hundred twenty bodies. Decomp can handle another seventy five."

"Do you know something I don't?"

She looked at him with a confused expression. "What do you mean? Like what?"

"Like is Armageddon coming?"

"Don't be silly."

"Would you tell me if you knew?"

"No."

"I knew it. We're all going to die."

She frowned. "The numbers are based on the Seven Forty Seven."

"The jet?"

"Jumbo jet. Capacity five hundred fifty five. If one goes down, we should be able to accommodate everyone. If not, we go to refrigerated trucks."

"Please don't tell me Ben and Jerry's."

"Häagen-Dazs."

"Barump-bump-ching."

"Nice rimshot."

They entered the Cooler. Appropriately, it was the temperature of a meat locker. Brady suspected the bodies of the young mother and the drunk driver killed on Las Olas were in this room somewhere. Belinda moved to a gray metallic desk by the door and picked up a clipboard. She ran her right index finger halfway down the first page.

"Sixty three."

They stepped to a bank of bare metal rectangles that, also appropriately, resembled meat locker doors. Belinda yanked the handle on number sixty three and rolled out a narrow shelf. A white sheet was draped over a human form. Two bare feet protruded from one end. A yellow cardboard tag was attached to the right big toe. She peeled back the sheet.

"Do you know this man?"

The last time Brady saw Peanut Strong he was snoring beside a swimming pool. He wasn't snoring anymore. His soul, or spirit, or whatever it was that constituted the quintessence of life, had departed and he'd passed through that doorway all men and women eventually must, to a silent, perpetual, unsnoring sleep. From the looks of it, Peanut's crossing had not been serene. His glassy eyes were fixed in a ghastly death stare. His mouth was open wide, as if he'd turned to stone in the midst of a scream. He'd been dissected like a frog in biology class. A Y-shaped incision ran from his breastplate to his abdomen and another scar bisected the top of his skull. Topping that off, just below the autopsy scar a crude inscription was scrawled across his forehead.

Et Tu Brady

It was beyond bizarre staring down at the lifeless body of a man he'd spoken to only hours ago. Last evening he had shown Peanut no amity. He'd refused to forgive him for a mistake he'd made a lifetime ago. A mistake he'd made as a child. A mistake he'd paid for the remainder of his life.

Brady felt dirty. He wished he could talk to his old friend one more time. Show him some kindness. Take back his pitiless words. He knew as sure as he was standing there that he would regret what he'd said last night for the rest of his life.

"His name's Richard Strong. We were best friends once. I haven't seen him since we were kids. Not until last night."

A man's voice rang out. "He was found floating in a swimming pool on Sunrise Key."

Ron Register's lank frame came through the stainless steel double-doors. He moved down the row of autopsy tables, dressed impeccably, as usual, in a charcoal suit, white shirt, red tie, the heels of his black Oxfords clacking on the polished terrazzo.

"Peanut was living in the cabana behind the house," Brady said.

"Peanut?"

"His nickname. From when we were kids. He has, had, a swimming pool service. The owner let him live there in exchange for taking care of the property." Brady looked at Belinda. "Overdose?"

"Why do you say that?" Register asked.

Brady pinched his lower lip between his left thumb and forefinger. His eyes were locked on Peanut while his brain tried to reconcile the weathered gray face with the happy, smiling, freckled kid from childhood.

"Seeing him last night. I got the impression Peanut had become a bit of a stoner."

Register popped a Tums into his mouth and stared at Brady. "What prompted you to visit him after so many years? On the very night of his death?"

"I didn't know he was planning to die. We were all close friends once. Me, Peanut, Ben, Delray. I thought he might have some idea about who murdered Ben."

Register made a sucking sound, his tongue rolling the antacid around inside his mouth.

"It's *our* job to find the killer, Brady."

"Really? It seems like you've made your job proving Delray Cross murdered her brother. I'm trying to save you from embarrassing yourself."

The two men glared at each other for several seconds before Boulanos broke the silence.

"Your friend *was* stoned, Max. I sent samples of stomach content and ocular fluid to the lab. It'll be a while before toxicology is complete, but my preliminary blood tests indicate he was heavily drugged. Almost certainly too spaced-out to offer any resistance. I'm guessing he'd ingested an opioid analgesic similar to the narcotic we found in Benjamin Chance's blood. Oxycodone hydrochloride."

"Is that what killed Peanut?"

"It would have killed him, if he'd lived long enough. If he ingested, say, ten or more thirty milligram oxy pills, that's plenty enough to kill a man his weight, especially if the pills were crushed."

"Why does that matter?"

"Destroys the time release coating. The drug goes right into the blood. Causes respiratory failure. We'll know when the labs come back. Frankly, it would have been a much more pleasant way to go."

"How did he go?"

"Cerebral hypoxia prompted by obstructive or mechanical asphyxia."

"Strangulation?"

Boulanos directed Brady's eyes to Peanut's feet. She lifted his left ankle, then his right. The skin at the back of both heels was scraped raw, as though he'd been dragged over a roughened surface. Brady remembered the flagstone patio.

"It appears the killer pulled him into the pool, stuffed his nostrils with wads of tissue, then thrust the swimming pool vacuum hose down his throat. The killer literally sucked the life out of him."

"My God," Brady cringed. "This guy is medieval."

"Or gal," Register added with a sharp glance at Brady.

"The last time I saw Peanut he was unconscious, stoned out of his gourd on a chaise lounge beside the pool. Do you really think Delray could have lifted a six-foot-four-inch man and dragged him like that?"

"Mr. Strong was tall, but he didn't have much meat on his bones," Register said. "According to Dr. Boulanos he only weighed one hundred forty pounds. Not too heavy for a woman to drag a short distance. Mrs. Cross is certainly strong enough."

The two men turned to Belinda, waiting for her to take sides. She was having none of it.

"The vacuum pump was a fiendish touch, but a bit of overkill. Simply forcing the hose down his throat would have done the job. It was deep enough to occlude the passageway. Nor did the killer need to plug his nostrils. He would have succumbed anyway. Like choking on a piece of meat."

"Time?"

"Around midnight."

"That's about four hours after I left him. What can you decipher about the killer?"

"Like the captain said, the perpetrator could have been male or female." Belinda glanced at him, apologetic, knowing she was lending credence to Register's theory. "It appears he, or she, drugged your friend, dragged him to the pool, and placed him on a raft. The perp got behind him and pulled his hair, which forced his head back and opened his mouth. Then the hose was rammed down his throat. I found abrasions on the right inside wall of the trachea, which indicates the killer may be left handed."

"I believe Mrs. Cross is left handed, is she not?" Register said.

Brady ignored him. "What kind of sociopath does something like that?"

"The kind that wraps a copper noose around a man's throat and plugs it into a wall socket," the captain said.

"Maybe this is the work of some wacko copycat?"

Boulanos pointed to the tattoo on Peanut's forehead. "That wouldn't explain this."

"We didn't release any information to the press about the tattoo in the Chance homicide," Register said. "*Et Tu Brady* – You Too Brady. Whoever wrote that must be a mutual acquaintance of Ben Chance, Richard Strong, and you. Who fits that bill – besides Delray Cross?"

"Probably lots of people."

"Were you with Mrs. Cross last night?"

"Sorry, Ron, attorney-client privilege."

"I'll take that as a no. If you'd been with her you'd jump at the chance to provide her an alibi."

Brady refused to give him the satisfaction of admitting he was right. "Register, you're too certain about Delray. Be careful or you're gonna end up with a case of heartburn those Tums can't fix."

The policeman's expression tightened. He glowered at Brady with callous eyes.

"I'm confident we're going to be making an arrest soon. You'll be one of the first to know. By the way, I got the message you left with Detective James last night. You don't mind if I cross Richard Strong off my list of suspects, do you?"

Chapter Fifty-Seven

DAWN WAS BREAKING in the eastern sky when Brady climbed back aboard the *Victoria II* and collapsed into his bunk. Gordy was coming in early to open the Shanty so he had a couple of hours to get some of shut-eye. He'd barely slept in three days and his circadian rhythm was out of whack. Even so, sleep was impossible. Too much had happened too fast. His mind was racing to catch up.

First Ben murdered. Now Peanut. His name branded on both. Two people killed in the car crash. Duke Manyon back from the dead. Register determined to nail Delray. Delray intent on something else. *Seducing me?* He wasn't sure. Rose was, though, and she wanted to strangle him. Then there was the prospect of a billion dollars in gold on or near Three Mile Reef. Brady hated everything about the last three days, except the part about the gold.

He'd always believed there was more treasure. He and Ben and Peanut had unearthed ten Spanish coins in three days. No way that was all of it. Yet, after that night, he'd never returned to find it. Discovering the gold had unleashed a mummy's curse. The mummy in this case being Ned Pike. The sea rover had enticed them with a trail of ocher crumbs. He could almost envision Pike, after three centuries beneath the waves, beckoning them with a skeletal finger to his watery lair. But no bounty was worth the nightmare his treasure had spawned. No wealth could replace the blood that had been spilled. And was still being spilled. Nonetheless, after reading Michael Fury's diary, and the papers he and Delray found in Ben's house, his curiosity had been aroused.

Exhaustion finally overcame him. His mind began to drift like a blob of soft wax, a lava lamp in the time-space continuum. One minute he was squatting on his surfboard riding a tube at the Bonzai Pipeline. The next he was stretched out on the green lawn of Sheep's Meadow in Central Park. Victoria was lying in the grass reading a book, her head on his chest, her long blonde hair spread across him like a golden blanket. The radio was playing Sam and Dave singing *Soul Man*. Rose skated by on roller blades and waved to them. Then he was in the fuselage of a jetliner trying to reach the cockpit, his path blocked by an angry man with a boxcutter, shouting in a strange tongue. All of a sudden he was in a laboratory wearing a white coat celebrating his discovery of an antidote for cancer.

The next thing he knew he was jolted awake. Daylight streamed through the porthole. The red numbers projected onto the ceiling by his clock were no longer visible. He sat up and looked at the time. He'd slept two hours. His cell phone was ringing on the bedside table. *Not again.* He contemplated not answering.

"Hullo," he croaked.

"Sorry to call so early, boss."

"Gordy? What's up? Everything okay?"

"The pavoratti's are here."

Brady massaged his forehead. "Pavoratti's?"

"There's a mob of them outside."

He swung his legs over the side of the bunk and flattened his soles on the cool wood floor. He bent his head down between his knees, like a clam folding into its shell, and yawned mightily, expelling the last vestiges of sleep.

"A gang of opera singers is outside the Shanty?"

"No, Max. People with cameras. There's a half dozen of them."

"Paparazzi?"

"Two more are coming up now."

"What are they doing?"

"One of them told me it's something about that accident on Las Olas yesterday. Did you hear about it?"

Damn. The press had discovered his identity. They were going to make a big deal out of it. He could see it now. A giant *gang bang*, the media's crude euphemism for pack journalism. There would be interviews, inane questions, his face splashed all over the six o'clock news. Breathless reporters painting him as the hero who saved the little girl. He didn't need the distraction. Not right now. Too much was happening. Besides, it was unseemly being lionized after two people died, including a young mother.

"Tell them to go away, Gordy. I don't want to talk. Tell them I've got nothing to say."

There was a moment of silence at the other end of the line.

"I don't think they're here to talk to you, boss. One of them pavoratti's told me some lawyer's gonna hold a press conference. Something about a lawsuit."

Et Tu Brady

Chapter Fifty-Eight

TELEVISION SATELLITE TRUCKS were lined up on the street in front of the Sea Shanty when Brady pulled in. The sidewalk swarmed with reporters and camera people. He recognized one or two faces. Sylvia Sanchez from one of the local channels had a cell phone attached to her ear. A tall man stood beside her balancing a camera on his shoulder, his hairless cranium the size of a small watermelon, as though a voodoo priest tried to shrink it and goofed.

Brady had been on television many times during his days as a policeman and prosecutor. He'd seen his words twisted once too often and had no desire to go there again. Besides, he'd read somewhere that one-in-four Americans have appeared on TV. It was not an exclusive club. That didn't faze the covey of protesters who'd shown up and were getting plenty of face time, waving placards scrawled with incendiary catchphrases.

Killers Served Here!

Good Bars Don't Let Patrons Drive Drunk!

Drinking Here = Mourning After!

Brady wondered why incendiary catchphrases always ended with exclamation points! Gordy was standing in the doorway with his arms folded, guarding the Sea Shanty from the barbarian horde.

"I'm sorry, boss. I shoulda shooed them off the sidewalk, but there were so many all of a sudden."

"Sidewalks are public property. They have a right to be here."

The media crush began to scramble. A tall man in a blue vicuña suit, white shirt, and silver tie was making his way through the crowd, slapping backs and shaking hands with several reporters. They looked very chummy. Not a good sign.

Brady would have recognized him anywhere. The human face has approximately eighty landmarks, or nodal points. The experts have made a science of measuring them. Distance between eyes. Depth of eye sockets. Width of nose. Shape of cheekbones. Length of jaw lines. Facial recognition technology was based on the premise that these traits changed amazingly little between childhood and old age. His details had changed some. Puffy eyes. Two chins instead of one. Sprayed-on tan. Fleshy around the middle. The hair long now, swept forward and back in a Donald Trump double comb-over. But the basic architecture was the same. Right down to the surly curl of his lip, like a deformity he'd never outgrown.

On the surface, Junior Ball gave the impression of Rolls Royce respectability. Inside, though, Brady had always known him to be bankrupt. That kind of thing didn't change with time. He was surprised their orbits hadn't crossed since he moved back to town. He hadn't even heard Junior's name until Peanut mentioned it last night. A few hours later he was dead. *Coincidence?* Brady didn't believe in them. Now here he was, standing before a bank of cameras, cocky as a rooster. Brady stepped out onto the sidewalk and watched the circus unfold.

"Everybody ready?" Ball said.

"Good to go, Junior," said the watermelon-head cameraman.

"As you all know, my name is Austin C. Ball, Jr., attorney at law." Brady suddenly wasn't so proud to be a lawyer. Junior poked a hole in the air with his fingertip. "*C* for Churchill."

That's just wrong. Grandpa Zack's face flashed from his memory bank, drinking gin on *The Summit* and lecturing the two lions Churchill and Roosevelt on how to save the world.

"I have called you here to announce that I am filing a ten million dollar civil lawsuit this morning in the tragic deaths of Devon Marshall and Linda Bishop. Both were killed yesterday in a head-on collision on Las Olas Boulevard. I represent Miss Betty Jane Marshall, sister of the late Devon Marshall. The lawsuit alleges Mr. Marshall and Mrs. Bishop died as a direct result of the callous indifference and inexcusable neglect on the part of the owner and employees of the Sea Shanty Bar."

Junior was as strident as a provocateur fomenting a lynch mob. Brady half-expected someone to throw a noose over the nearest coconut tree. He turned and looked at Gordy propped in the doorway. His face wore a mystified expression.

"Mr. Marshall spent several hours inside this establishment yesterday immediately before the accident. According to the coroner's office, his blood alcohol level was zero-point-three-three. My friends, that is more than four times the State of Florida's legal limit. Based on Mr. Marshall's size – he was a diminutive man – we estimate he consumed the equivalent of twelve-to-fifteen shots of whiskey during the hours leading up to this needless tragedy. No tavern owner in his right mind would serve that much whiskey to one person then allow him to get behind the wheel of a car. It is tantamount to criminal neglect. Minutes after departing the Sea Shanty, Mr. Marshall was driving westbound on Las Olas Boulevard and crossed into on-coming traffic. His car collided head-on with Mrs. Bishop's. Both were killed instantly. Our only solace is that Mrs. Bishop's three-year-old daughter, Sarah, survived with only minor injuries."

Junior was *The People's Lawyer*. Defender of the downtrodden. Crusader for truth and justice. Brady was tempted to throw himself at the mercy of the media.

"Mr. Ball?" It was Sylvia Sanchez. With her long black hair, flawless face, and svelte physique she could have been a movie star, which seemed to be the primary requirement for a TV journalist these days.

Ball's face lit up in an unctuous smile. "We've been friends too long, Sylvia. Call me Junior."

395

Nice touch. Very smooth. Reporters love hearing their own names. Sanchez hesitated, though, slightly flustered. Being called a *friend* by the person you're covering is not the best advertisement for journalistic credibility, even if it was true. Sylvia compromised.

"Austin, wasn't Devon Marshall responsible for Mrs. Bishop's death?"

"I'm glad you asked that question, Sylvia. My client understands her brother does bear some liability. Nobody forced him to drink that whiskey. And no one forced him to get behind the wheel. But Mr. Marshall was a hardcore alcoholic. He'd been in and out of rehab. Florida's Dram Shop Law specifies that any establishment which knowingly serves liquor to someone habitually addicted to alcohol is liable for injury or damage caused by the recipient's intoxication. Mr. Marshall was a frequent patron here and his alcoholism was well-known to the owner and his employees. Nonetheless, they served him glass after glass after glass of whiskey. Their sole concern was profiteering. As a result, two people are dead."

"That's a lie."

All eyes turned toward Brady standing in front of the Shanty's open door.

"Excuse me, sir," Ball said, his voice petulant, like a true Donald Trump devotee. "This is my press conference."

"Yeah? And this is my bar. And you're a liar, Junior."

Ball's eyes narrowed to thin, cagey slits. He seemed to be gauging Brady's age, height, poundage, net worth, political affiliation, and maybe sexual preference. Then his face pinched, like he'd just swallowed pickling solution.

"Brady?"

"Ball?"

"I didn't recognize you."

"Did you know Charlie Chaplin once won third prize in a Charlie Chaplin look-alike contest?"

Ball's color changed. For a brief moment he seemed to lose some of his pluck. Then his top lip curled up over his teeth. *Same old Junior.* He pointed an accusatory finger at Brady and turned to the cameras.

"Ladies and gentlemen, this is Mr. Max Brady, owner of the Sea Shanty. This is the man I will prove in court is responsible for the terrible events of yesterday. It was this man's heartless disregard for human life in the pursuit of profits that led directly to the deaths of Linda Bishop and Devon Marshall."

Before Brady could respond a burly, bald-headed man exploded from the crowd and came at Brady like a suicide bomber. He was several inches shorter, but outweighed him by thirty pounds. His right fist came in a wide arc. Brady ducked a millisecond before it reached his face. The attacker plowed into him and they tumbled onto the concrete in the middle of the press corps. The crowd parted while photographers jockeyed to record the imbroglio. The assailant threw several wild punches. A few caught Brady's head and shoulders.

"You bastard!" he screamed. "You killed Linda! You killed my wife!"

Brady managed to free his arms and wrap the man in a bear hug while the dead woman's husband kept shouting.

"I'm gonna kill you, you bastard."

Gordy and someone else moved in, grabbed him by the shoulders, and pulled him to his feet. While he was being dragged off, he kicked Brady hard in the left ribcage. A strapping police officer finally restrained the man. Dan Mason patrolled the beach area. Brady had known him for years.

"Are you okay, Mr. Brady?" he said.

"I'm okay, Dan. Thanks."

He staggered to his feet, his chest expanding and contracting. Mason turned to the attacker.

"Sir, you are under arrest for aggravated assault. Please…"

Brady interrupted. "That's not necessary, Dan." His right hand was pressed to the side where he'd taken the kick. "This man's wife was killed by a drunk driver yesterday. He thinks it was my fault."

Sylvia Sanchez shoved a microphone at the attacker's chin.

"What is your name, sir?"

"Joe Bishop. Linda Bishop was my wife. She'd be alive now if this sonofabitch hadn't…" Bishop's voice quaked and he collapsed sobbing. Gordy and Mason propped him up.

The cameras recorded every second. This was news media nirvana. Sensationalism on steroids. A story with all the elements. Pathos. Violence. Outrage. A villain – in the person of Max Brady, the greedy whiskey merchant who put profit over people. Sordid details at six.

Brady fell back against the Shanty's door jamb and took inventory. He touched his face where Bishop's fists had fallen. No blood. Fingers and toes still in place. Dull pain in his left side, but no ribs broken. Half a dozen cameras were swinging back and forth between him and Joe Bishop. Brady knew he didn't look good. Hundreds of thousands would see what happened on TV. Millions more if the video went viral on YouTube. If viewers were a jury, he'd get the gallows. At the very least the Sea Shanty would be out of business and he'd be run out of town on a rail. He needed to defuse the situation. He held up his arms like he was announcing the winner of a free lunch on *Taco Tuesday*.

"Can I have your attention, please?"

It took a minute for the crowd to settle. Junior Ball was standing behind the press now, a satisfied smirk on his face. Dan Mason kept a hand clasped around Joe Bishop's arm. Finally the cameras were back on their tripods. Sylvia Sanchez and the other reporters extended their microphones toward Brady.

"The first thing you need to know," he said, "especially you Mr. Bishop, is that I have a strict policy against serving people who are obviously drunk. Second, and more to the point, the man who killed Mrs. Bishop was not a Sea Shanty patron. To the best of my knowledge he's never been in my bar."

Junior Ball bayed like he'd been sodomized by a cattle prod. He barged through the mob and stood face-to-face with Brady. He pulled out a snapshot and waved it in front of his eyes.

"You deny Devon Marshall was in your bar yesterday? You deny this man was drinking here?"

Brady examined the photograph. "I did see this man yesterday."

Junior turned and addressed the jury of cameras. "So now you say Devon Marshall *was* here, as I've alleged?"

"I saw him, but not in the Shanty."

398

His face still turned toward the press, Ball laughed derisively. "Stop changing your story, Mr. Brady. Which is it? You saw him, or you didn't?"

"I saw him. He was on Las Olas leaning on the steering wheel of his car. He didn't have a pulse."

Junior's head snapped back toward Brady. He stared blank-faced, as if his brain had gone on vacation and forgot to tell him it was leaving. Brady could see him trying to process what he'd just heard. Then he sputtered to life.

"If you were on Las Olas Boulevard yesterday afternoon, Mr. Brady…" He sounded uncertain, stretching out his words like he knew he had to say something, but had no idea what. He stopped for several seconds. Time stood still. Brady watched the reporters watch him, their mouths open, their heads nodding, as if trying to prod it out of him. Then Brady saw a light go on in Junior's eyes. An idea seemed to come to him. He raised his right arm and waved a forefinger in the air, a lawyer mustering his bluster. "If you were on Las Olas Boulevard yesterday afternoon, sir," he repeated, stentorious as Foghorn Leghorn, "how then can you claim Devon Marshall was *not* in your bar drinking whiskey?"

The media issued a collective sigh of relief. Brady sighed for a different reason. His was a sigh of surrender. He didn't want to do it. Did not want to play the hero card. But, at this point, it seemed like the only way to keep the Sea Shanty from being firebombed by enraged viewers.

"I was too busy to worry about Mr. Marshall," he said.

A triumphant grin spread across Junior's face. He'd painted Brady into a corner. Now for the kill. Foghorn attacked.

"Aha! Too busy, you say? Busy doing what exactly? Counting your money?"

Brady could no longer resist. It was that day on the Great Lawn all over again. Junior's punch had just breezed past his jaw. In his mind he stepped back, cocked his fist, and let loose with a haymaker. He turned to Joe Bishop.

"Too busy pulling your daughter out of the car."

What's better than nirvana? Sylvia Sanchez knew. She squealed like she'd just reached the third peak of a triple-crested climax. The fabled hat trick. A climax lover's dream. She pointed her microphone at Brady.

"Are you the mystery man who saved little Sarah Bishop?"

Before he could answer, Junior elbowed his way in front of the cameras and waved Devon Marshall's photograph again. Gordy stepped behind Brady and stared over his shoulder at the picture.

Sylvia shouted at him, and not in a friendly way. "Get out of the way, Junior."

Much pushing and shoving ensued. Curses laced the air. Watermelon head fell to the ground, his camera crashing on the concrete with an expensive-sounding thud. A newspaper photographer took a swing at a television videographer. Incendiary catchphrases waved wildly in the background. Brady watched the melee with growing alarm. Then Gordy leaned close and whispered in his ear.

"Boss, I gotta talk to you."

Gordy looked like a puppy that had just peed on the carpet. Brady knew instantly he had a problem. He grabbed his arm and pulled him inside the Shanty and closed the door.

"Talk to me."

Gordy grimaced and swayed, shuffled his feet, and hemmed and hawed, as much at a loss for words as Junior had been moments ago. His mouth finally kicked into gear.

"That guy in the picture…"

"Ugh," Brady groaned. Something bad was coming.

"…he was in here. I woulda told you but I didn't know it was the same guy in that accident."

Red rage erupted inside Brady. Gordy saw it and shrank back.

"How many times have I told you I don't want binge drinking here? How could you let him get that drunk? And then drive off?"

Gordy looked like he was going to cry. "I didn't, boss. I swear. He came in and ordered a shot of Jim Beam. Smelt like a barnyard. I poured his drink and walked away. Couldn't stand the stink. When I come back he wanted another. Then a third. Polished 'em off in three minutes flat. Bam, bam, bam. Like he was practicing to break the world speed-drinking record. I could see he was getting hammered. When he ordered another shot I cut him off. Refused to serve him. He started fussing at me like a baby bein' weaned from the tit. Screaming. Swearing. Ranting. Talking crazy. I asked him to pay his tab and leave. He threw a twenty on the bar and stumbled out. I watched him cross the street and figured he was going over to *Coconuts* looking for more whiskey. I promise, boss, he only drank three shots here. If his blood alcohol level was four times over the legal limit, he didn't get that way at the Shanty."

A minute ago, Brady had been ready to fire Gordy. Now he softened. Gordy had his flaws, but dishonesty wasn't one of them. If anything he was too honest. Brady had always wondered how he'd survived in the real estate business, then remembered. He hadn't.

"You're sure? Only three drinks?"

"Cross my heart."

Brady opened the door and walked back out onto the sidewalk. The brouhaha had subsided and the media people were regrouping. Sylvia Sanchez and watermelon man were leaning over their camera on the sidewalk, like priests administering Last Rites. Junior was off to the side giving a one-on-one interview to another reporter. Brady spoke over the chatter.

"Before you go, my bartender has just informed me that Mr. Marshall, the drunk driver, was in the Sea Shanty yesterday."

Junior abandoned the interview and rushed to the front of the crowd. Back in business. Smug smile plastered on his face.

"Ladies and gentlemen," he announced, "Mr. Brady now admits he was lying. I only wish he'd get his story straight. In the legal system there is a principle known as *'false in one, false in all.'* It means that if a man lies about one thing, you may disregard everything he says." He pointed a finger at Brady. "You can now ignore everything this man says."

Brady had an overwhelming urge to slap the smile off Junior's face. Just for old time's sake. He suppressed the emotion and turned back to the cameras.

"My bartender informs me that Mr. Marshall did come into the Sea Shanty yesterday. He consumed three drinks. Three shots of whiskey. Jim Beam, to be exact. In rapid succession. As I said before, we do not serve alcohol to patrons who are obviously inebriated. After three drinks, Mr. Marshall appeared to be feeling the effects. When he ordered a fourth shot my bartender refused him. He protested loudly and abusively. At that point he was asked to leave the premises. But, I repeat, he consumed only three drinks here. Not nearly enough to account for the blood alcohol level Mr. Ball alleges. If he was that intoxicated, he did not get that way in my bar."

Junior kept smiling, although he didn't look quite so smug anymore. Brady detected his confidence flag.

"I have a witness," Ball shouted. "He will verify everything I've alleged."

"Your witness is a liar too," Brady said. He faced the dead woman's husband. "Mr. Bishop, I am very sorry about your wife. I wish I could have done more for her. By the time I got to her it was too late. I'm just thankful we were able to get your daughter out of the car before it blew up. I hope she'll be okay."

Joe Bishop's face was etched in confusion. He didn't seem to know who or what to believe. Brady couldn't blame him. He was clearly still in shock. Who wouldn't be? Trying to make sense of the senselessness that had destroyed his family. Junior had given him a foil to vent his rage upon. Now even that was being taken away. Then his eyes hardened and his cheeks shook with rage.

"Sarah is not going to be okay. Her mother is dead. That man was drinking here, like Mr. Ball said. That makes you responsible."

The press moved in and began firing questions at Bishop. Junior stepped close to Brady and jabbed a forefinger into his chest.

"Been a long time, Max."

"Not long enough."

"Just like the good old days."

"Really? You still beating up weaklings? Still blinding defenseless animals?"

"My conscience is clear."

"Then your memory's lousy."

Ball looked him straight in the eyes, their noses almost touching.

"Are we having a staring contest?" Brady said.

"You always did push things."

"That's how I get my exercise, Junior. By the way, where were you two nights ago?"

Ball's face curled into another surly smile. He was asking to be slapped. "I heard that that fat fuck Ben Chance will have a marble slab sitting on his forehead for the next million years." Junior clapped Brady on the back. "Speaking of gravestones, you should tell your girlfriend she's playing a dangerous game."

Brady looked at him quizzically. "I have no idea what you're talking about. But that sounds like a threat?"

"Call it a prophecy. Tell her she needs to keep her nose out of my business."

"Speaking of noses." Brady pressed a finger against Junior's and pushed it to the side. His face followed. "Promise me you'll find a new mouthwash."

Ball backed away and snorted several times. It sounded like a coke sniffer's snort. He squeezed his nostrils back in place and curled his lip.

"Still the wiseass, Brady."

"Sweet of you to remember."

Et Tu Brady

Chapter Fifty-Nine

THE FORT LAUDERDALE City Commission was wrapping up another vexatious session dominated by lots of arm-twisting and hair-pulling about the budget crisis hanging over the city like a headsman's sword. They'd been at it since eight in the morning and even those with skin in the game – contractors, unions, lobbyists – had long since flown. Commissioners and staff members were tired and hungry and just wanted to end the depressing affair.

Mayor Liz Donnelly chewed on her fist trying to cover a yawn, then picked up her gavel. "I think we've kicked this dog until its fleas are dead. Do I hear a motion to adjourn?"

"Wait," Rose Becker blurted from the end of the commission table. The mayor dropped her gavel and fell back in her seat. Rose noticed several dozen jaundiced eyes firing daggers in her direction. "I'm sorry, I'm sorry. I know everybody wants to get out of here, Madame Mayor. I just need to ask one question."

Donnelly sighed and glanced at her watch. "I hesitate to ask what that might be, Commissioner Becker? But please be quick. I have a lunch date with my husband and I really need a good meal. I've been eating so many tuna sandwiches from the swill pits around here that I'm afraid my body contains more mercury than a thermometer."

"I understand, Liz. Sorry to drag this out." Rose looked down the table at Walter Dean. "The City Attorney was supposed to update us on those slip-and-fall lawsuits."

Dean's head dropped like a school kid whose teacher called for homework seconds before the bell rang. He looked at Rose. He was beginning to hate her as much as his hemorrhoids. Maybe worse. At least hemorrhoids didn't get you sent to prison.

Thank God Seymour Tate was out of the way. *The Lauderdale News* announced this morning it had suspended the prize winning reporter over a sordid incident involving a drug deal gone bad. His journalistic credibility was kaput. Even better, his exposé had been spiked.

Dean knew it was all bullshit. He remembered Junior Ball's words at the Titty Room. *"Tate's gonna wish he never heard my name."* Then he made a telephone call to someone named Darnell. That was about four o'clock. According to the newspaper account, Tate was assaulted three hours later. The lawyer deplored violence, but better some scumbag reporter goes down than him.

Dean's only worry now was the bewitching young woman at the far end of the table. He had expected the Dram Shop lawsuit to shut her up. Florida juries had been hitting bar owners hard on drunken driving cases. They would use the threat of a huge damage award against Commissioner Becker's boyfriend to muzzle her.

But the plan had spun horribly out of control when the young mother was killed. If police discovered the crash was staged at his suggestion, Dean would be finished forever. Last night he'd gotten drunk for the first time in years. While his wife and two daughters slept upstairs, he sat in his den with the lights out and contemplated sticking a pistol in his mouth.

At some point his telephone rang. His first thought was that it was the police. A courtesy call to the City Attorney. They were coming to arrest him. But it was Junior Ball. He had a plan to turn the tables. Do a double-reverse on the disaster. The tragedy, he explained, only made the case more compelling against the boyfriend.

"Max Brady," he said, spitting out the words.

Dean knew the name well. Brady was the guy responsible for his onetime political ally, Mayor David Grand, going to prison. Retribution would be sweet. Junior said he planned to hold a press conference in the morning and blame Brady for the fatal crash. Dean guessed the presser was still in progress at that very moment. Then they would put the squeeze on Rose Becker.

"If the bitch clams up about the slip-and-falls," Junior said, "we'll drop the Dram Shop action."

The City Attorney had to give Ball credit. He might be psychotic, but he had his moments. He'd sure as hell made Dean plenty of money. For now, though, his problem was staring at him from the opposite end of the table. Becker didn't know about the lawsuit yet. He only hoped they hadn't underestimated her.

"Walter?" she said with eyebrows raised." What can you tell us?"

"To be honest, Commissioner Becker," Dean said, realizing the irony of his words as they left his lips, "my staff has been swamped with budget issues. We just haven't had time to investigate thoroughly. Frankly, I think everyone's too tired and too hungry to consider that at the moment."

He saw Rose glance at the left side of the room where Dean's City Attorney staff encamped during Commission meetings. His chief assistant Phil Stone was sitting there. Marci Bennett, one of the office paralegals, was beside him. He was scribbling notes. She was chewing gum and sliding an emery board over the tips of long, garish fingernails.

Dean had known about their affair for months. He couldn't blame Stone. He wished he'd gotten to Marci first. She wasn't exactly pretty, but she was buxom. A chemical blonde with too much forehead and eyes set a little too close. Her mascara looked like it had been caked on by a stage door mortician. She tended to wear outfits two or three sizes too small, giving the impression of a bologna stuffed into a sausage skin. Marci oozed sexiness, though. She could undulate while sitting still. Dean stole peeks at her at every opportunity. Rose Becker seemed just as interested. She turned to Dean.

"Look, Mr. City Attorney, I'm starving too. I'd love a big Philly Cheesesteak right now."

Marci dropped her emery board.

"Maybe a nice Tastykake for dessert."

Phil Stone bolted upright like a man who'd sat in a scalding bath. He looked at Marci and they stared at each other, eyes wide, mouths open. Liz Donnelly spoke up.

"That sounds absolutely sinful."

"Trust me, Madame Mayor," said Rose, watching the secret lovers. "It absolutely is."

Marci abruptly scooped a stack of files off the desk and rushed from the room.

"I guess Ms. Bennett couldn't wait," the mayor said. She looked at Dean. "Come on, Walter. Tell us what you can so we can go feed."

Dean nodded. He took a fleeting glance at Phil Stone, wondering what had just happened. Then back to Rose. A prickly smile emerged on his face. He looked friendly as a porcupine.

"First of all, Madame Mayor, I feel it incumbent to inform you that Commissioner Becker may have a conflict of interest in this matter."

Rose's brow furrowed and she fixed her eyes on him, like her tolerance was wearing thin.

"Oh? And what conflict might that be?"

"I've been made aware that one of the attorneys you mentioned the other day has filed a lawsuit against a gentleman who I understand is a close associate of yours."

Rose folded her hands together and leaned forward. "I mentioned one lawyer. Austin Ball Jr. I have no idea who this close associate is you're talking about."

"I believe his name is Brady."

Rose blinked. Dean's smile turned priggish. He'd surprised her.

"I do know a Max Brady. I haven't got the foggiest idea about any lawsuit, though. If what you say is true, I find it quite a coincidence that Austin Ball would file an action against a close friend of mine after I mention his name. However, as a commissioner of the City of Fort Lauderdale, it is my responsibility to make sure taxpayer dollars are not being wasted – or worse. Thomas Jefferson said it two hundred some years ago. *'When a man assumes a public trust he should consider himself a public property.'* You and I are pubic property, Walter. And I assure you I intend to protect the public trust. Attempts to intimidate will not deter me. I will not back off. You can pass that along to Mr. Ball."

Dean felt his face turn crimson. "Are you implying…"

"No, Walter, you are implying. And isn't that ironic?"

"What's that, commissioner?"

"That *you* would accuse *me* of conflict of interest."

Dean squirmed like a snake had just been tossed in his lap.

"That's outrageous," he sputtered. "I don't know what you mean."

"Do you really want me to be specific, Walter? I can if you wish."

Liz Donnelly slammed her gavel.

"All right, you two. Obviously we're all hungry and tired. I'm going to cut this off for now. Walter, I know you're office is flooded with work. However, please have the information by our next meeting. And I suggest the next time you raise issues of conflict of interest by a City Commission member that you do so in a less officious manner."

The mayor wielded her gavel again and Walter Dean hurried for the door. As soon as he reached his office he picked up the telephone.

Et Tu Brady

Chapter Sixty

MAX BRADY HATED snakes. Always had. He wasn't sure why. Maybe it was the no arms thing. Or legs. Or that they looked slimy. Or that some are deadly. Or maybe it went all the way back to the Garden of Eden. Adam and Eve. Forbidden fruit. Satan as serpent. All that biblical fiction. Whatever the reason, he hated snakes.

That's why, as he drove away from the Sea Shanty, the vision in his head was so disturbing. It was a snake with a human face. That the face belonged to Junior Ball made it all the more disconcerting.

If there was one person Brady could have gone the rest of his life never seeing again, it was Junior. Every memory of him was loathsome. The newest one fit perfectly with everything he remembered from childhood. The bully who beat up Ben Chance. The sadist who blinded helpless alligators. The snitch who tipped Buck Foxx where he could find him delivering newspapers.

He'd always suspected Ball had set him up that morning of what became the worst day of his young life. The day that culminated in that horrific night when so many lives were destroyed. Brady had suppressed what happened for three decades. Now, after seeing Junior again, the memory was forcing its way into his consciousness.

After Buck drove off in the rain that morning, Max finished delivering his newspapers barefoot. Keeping constant vigil. Shivering all the while. His euphoria dissipated. The absurd thrill of being hunted like an animal vanished. Replaced by a stark awareness of how close he'd come to death. And that a very scary man was still out there and wanted to kill him. Haunted by a single thought.

What happened last night at Whiskey Creek?

By the time he tossed the last newspaper onto the last lawn, the rain had stopped. He made his way home in the wet morning mist, staying off the roads, darting through lawns, swimming across canals, trekking through woods. When he reached Eden he remained in stealth mode, not wanting his grandparents to see him, especially Grandma Kate. The oracle would know in a heartbeat that something bad had happened. Max slipped into the big red barn and ditched his saddlebag then tiptoed down the coquina foot path to the lagoon. He unraveled the Whaler's mooring line from its dock cleat, paddled into the river, and cranked the starter rope.

Thirty minutes later he swung into Whiskey Creek. The day remained ragged. Clouds the color of old nickels scudded across a spitty sky. A mournful wind blew off the ocean and moaned through the tall Australian pines that lined the creek, as if enticing him to his demise like the Sirens luring Ulysses.

The creek was deserted. Max steered past the mango-strewn beach where they had their war yesterday. Past the seagrape tree where he kissed Delray. Past the spot where he'd seen Duke and Buck bury whatever it was they were burying. He continued another hundred yards then coasted into the weeds and tied the Whaler to a branch.

The island was silent except for the tick of raindrops dripping off vegetation. He trudged barefoot up the bank and into the brush, his toes sinking into the spongy soil and releasing an earthy scent from loam blackened by centuries of decayed leaves.

He reached the center of the mangrove and felt near where he'd been last night. He was uncertain of the exact location and began walking in concentric circles, making a wide arc, shrinking the loop with each revolution, eyes on the ground like a squirrel hunting for the spot where it had buried its acorns. On his fifth go round he found it between a cypress and big buttonwood tree. A small notch with a plot of fresh-turned sand. White sand, like the beach, amidst black earth. He scanned the area for landmarks, trying to get his bearings. The Intracoastal Waterway was visible through a window in the vegetation. The channel was wide here. Deep gray water, heaving and inhospitable beneath the wind. On the far side was Port Everglades. A cargo ship was tied up at one of the docks a half mile away. A large blue crane was plucking tractor trailers off its deck and depositing them on forklifts to be carted away. In the distance, four giant candy canes pointed at the sky. Red-and-white striped smokestacks. The Florida Power & Light plant.

The magnet that had drawn him here, though, was at his feet. He had to know what Duke and Buck buried last night. And why Buck tried to kill him this morning. The answer was underneath the patch of white. Max dropped to his knees. The sand was soft. He began digging with his bare fingers. He made rapid progress. About a foot down he hit something and jerked back his hands like he'd touched a hot stove. Goosebumps broke out on his skin. The whole thing was too creepy. He spoke out loud.

"Do you really want to know what's down there?"

The boy stared at the hole. Duke and Buck had definitely buried something. Now he'd touched it. He asked himself again. Did he want to know? He didn't wait for an answer and plunged his hands back into the sand and dug faster. Within minutes he'd uncovered two rolls of white canvas, each about six feet long. The material looked like sailcloth. Both were tied at the ends and around the center with lengths of yellow nylon cord. Ski rope. The sign on the yellow Donzi said *Duke Manyon Ski School*.

He reached down to the roll nearest him and used the flat of his hand to brush sand off the canvas. The bundles had been secured with bowline knots, a versatile hitch favored by sailors that didn't slip or jam. Grandpa Zack taught him to tie a bowline when he was five years old, dangling a short length of rope from his thick, powerful fisherman's hands.

Max went through the steps in reverse order and dropped the rope ends on the sand. He took a breath, pulled back the canvas, and lurched backwards. His head slammed into the buttonwood. Stars. Blinding light. White pain. He heard Peanut's voice. *"Holy headache, Batman!"*

He rolled onto his hands and knees and puked in the sand just as a fresh cloudburst erupted. Plump raindrops spattered his back and head and ran down the sides of his face. He huddled there, eyes squeezed tight, and let the storm pelt him. He finally sat up and rested his back against the tree. He pulled a handkerchief from his back pocket and wiped vomit off his lips and chin before letting his eyes return to the hole. *You need to get out of here.* He cleared his throat, spit bile into the sand, and crawled back.

The woman was staring up. But not at him. Past him. Past everything. Her head was wrapped in clear plastic, like the bags the dry cleaner hung over Grandma Kate's best blue dress. She had flaming red hair. Her blue eyes were bugging out. And her tongue was black and swollen and distended from the side of her mouth. She didn't look very old, and wasn't going to get any older. Something about her seemed familiar.

He untied the second roll and peeled back the canvas. This one was blonde, her head encased in plastic, too. While rain pattered on the foliage, he knelt in the wet sand and studied them with morbid fascination. Max was no stranger to the face of death. He'd seen his mother and father in their caskets. But there was something about these women. The sight made him sad. Empty. As if he suddenly grasped the fragility of life. Despite their grotesque death masks, they had both been young and pretty. Now they'd ceased to exist – forever. The enormity of it was overwhelming. And Duke and Buck killed them. Now they wanted to kill him. At least Buck did.

Then it hit him like a bucket of freezing water. The redhead was the woman skiing with Duke behind the Donzi the other day. The one he'd sprayed. The one in the white bikini with the amazing body. Junior was drying her with a towel.

You need to get out of here, the voice said again.

This time he didn't ignore it. The rain had stopped but the wind still whistled its mournful requiem. Max began throwing sand back over the bodies, trying to decide what to do next. Should he call the police? Uncle Howard? His grandparents? Or do nothing. Just forget about it? Maybe Buck would forget about him.

Then he heard a boat. The Donzi? It had to be. He should have expected it. Duke and Buck left the bodies, planning to kill him. And probably bury him here with the women. When Buck failed they had to move the evidence.

His first instinct was to run to the far side of the island and swim across the Intracoastal. He looked at the water. It was rough and Port Everglades was a long way off. He could make it, but they would see the grave. They'd find the Whaler. And they'd find him before he got halfway to the other side. He'd be a sitting duck. Then a dead duck.

The boat motor died and he heard voices. He estimated they'd pulled up about a hundred feet away. Another squall struck, wind and rain, sudden and hard. Max made a split-second decision. He left the half-buried bodies and sprinted toward his boat. He took two steps and tripped over a fallen tree limb. He went down face-first in the mud. With his heart hammering inside his chest, he scrambled to his feet and began carving a path through the jungle. Then he had an idea.

He continued south, away from the grave, toward the Whaler. After about one hundred feet he slid down the embankment to the water and peeked through the brush. Thirty yards away, Duke was in the creek and Buck was just jumping in. He watched them wade to the bank and crawl up. When they disappeared into the undergrowth he sank beneath the surface and swam harder than he ever swam before to the Donzi. He unlashed its rope, clamped it between his teeth and began breast stroking toward the Whaler. He was halfway there when he heard a clamor. Angry voices. *They found the grave.* He stroked harder. Then he heard a splash and turned.

Duke was in the water, swimming straight for him. Buck was nowhere in sight. *He's coming on foot.* Max spit out the rope and swam back to the starboard side of the Donzi. He pulled himself up at the steering wheel. The key was still in the ignition. He yanked it out and threw it into the creek. When he looked back Duke was getting close. Max fell into the creek and raced for the Whaler.

Manyon was a strong swimmer, but the boy was faster. By the time he reached his boat, he'd doubled the distance between them. Max pulled himself over the low wall and fell into the Whaler. He freed the rope, pushed out of the weeds, and yanked the Evinrude's starter rope. It didn't catch. Duke was ten yards away. *Five seconds.* He pulled again. Nothing. Duke was just a few feet from him. *Two seconds.* He jerked the rope a third time. The engine throbbed to life. Duke reached for the transom just as Max hit the throttle and the boat surged. Duke stopped swimming and waded in the middle of the creek, watching him. Max raised his right middle finger in the air.

The Whaler was still picking up speed when Buck vaulted from the mangrove. Max saw him in midair. His face was red and his teeth bared like a wild animal. His hand hit the stern but he missed the boat and belly-flopped into the creek.

Max felt a burst of exhilaration. The same sensation he'd had hours ago hiding from Buck in the canal. He was smiling and about to flip Buck the finger, too, when he noticed the stern rope had fallen into the water. Buck had a death grip on it and was inching toward the Whaler as it dragged him in its wake. Max rammed the throttle all the way forward, but Buck kept coming. The boy laughed at him and shouted.

"You're not gonna get me, Mister Murderer."

That seemed to startle Buck. His eyes filled with confusion, followed by pure hatred. He grimaced and pulled harder, getting closer every second. Max searched for a weapon. The anchor was on the floor at the bow, out of reach. Buck's fingers curled over the edge of the transom. He was pulling his shoulders out of the water. Max grabbed a seat cushion and swatted his head, but he wasn't fazed. Buck wasn't going to be thwarted by a pillow. Then he looked down and spotted Grandpa Zack's bait bucket in the drainage well by the engine, the one he'd been using to sift for gold on Three Mile Reef.

Buck was acting as an anchor. His weight kept the Whaler from planing. His torso was half-in-and-half-out of the boat, but he was

416

caught in the vortex. While he fought against the drag, the water was sucking him back. His shoulder muscles looked like they were tearing through his skin. In another second he'd break the suction and catapult into the boat.

Max stood, held the wheel with his right hand, and swung the bait pail with his left. It caught Buck on the side of his face. He grunted and fell back into the creek.

Buck came up shaking his fist and screaming something Max couldn't decipher. Duke was floating thirty yards behind him, watching with a curious smile on his face. Max raised both arms this time and gave them single-finger salutes.

Et Tu Brady

Chapter Sixty-One

BRADY SHOOK OFF the memory of that distant day and steered the Jeep to the Fort Lauderdale Police Department. The same woman was installed behind the thick bulletproof glass at the lobby reception desk. He leaned his mouth close to the cluster of perforations and told her why he'd come. She picked up her telephone and pointed toward the row of green plastic chairs he and Delray sat in two days ago.

"Please have a seat."

He was too fidgety to sit and he paced to the far wall and inspected the smorgasbord of swindlers, smugglers, murderers, and terrorists on the FBI's most wanted poster, wondering if their mothers were proud. Osama Bin Laden was still dead. Sadly, so were the department's fourteen Fallen Heroes. He studied their names and faces again. Johnston, O'Neil, Kirby, Illyankoff, Conners, Petersen, Alexander, Bruce, Eddy, Dunlop, Mastrangelo, Brower, Peney, Diaz.

A tinny voice came from a speaker. The woman in the glass box.

"Mr. Brady, you can go up now. Second floor."

He turned back to the Fallen Heroes and saluted.

The Detective Bureau dedication was already underway. Several rows of folding chairs had been arranged in front of a small raised platform in the hallway outside the bureau. They were filled with police officers, politicians, and dignitaries. Brady suspected most were judges, lawyers, bondsmen and others who made their living off the department.

Mayor Liz Donnelly was at the podium when he slid into a seat in the back row. Howard Pickens was sitting behind the mayor. Police Chief Donald Begley sat to his right and Ron Register was beside the chief. To Brady's great surprise, seated to Pickens's left was none other than City Commissioner Rose Becker.

She was wearing a smart navy blue skirt and matching jacket, no jewelry, and her wild black Medusa locks had been tamed and pulled back behind her ears. He hadn't seen her since their blow-up at City Hall yesterday. It was the longest they'd been apart in months. He stared at her until her eyes met his. She rewarded him with a phosphorescent smile. It didn't linger long, but he'd never been so happy to see someone's teeth.

Mayor Donnelly delivered some glowing words about Pickens and his three decades of service to the City of Fort Lauderdale. Then she reached up and pulled a cord and undraped a gold-plated sign above the double doors. *Captain J. Howard Pickens Detective Bureau.*

Chief Begley followed with a brief statement of lukewarm praise delivered in a dull monotone. Brady remembered Uncle Howard saying he'd been pushed out of the department and sensed there was little love lost between the two men.

A procession of cops came to the microphone praising Pickens. The old man sat with his head bowed, clearly uncomfortable at the attention. A red-faced detective named Snuffy Smith greeted him with a karate chop salute.

"Captain Pickens was a supercop," he said. "We idolized him and everything he stood for."

Despite all the love, something about the ceremony didn't seem right. Brady realized Aunt Mo wasn't there. He wished she was still alive to see her husband honored. Something else was wrong, though. A tension in the air he couldn't put a finger on.

420

"Thanks to his brilliant police work, our community is a safer place," a captain was saying. "I give you Fort Lauderdale's finest. Captain John Howard Pickens."

He was greeted with a spirited standing ovation. Brady struggled to keep the tears from his eyes. With the aid of his cane, Uncle Howard labored to his feet and limped to the podium, a picture of dignity. For the next ten minutes he waxed nostalgic about his years at the department. How his special unit had taken a deep bite out of crime. Wistfully describing the break-up of cargo hijacking rings, violent home invasion gangs, and tracking down serial killers.

"My team wasn't big, but it was elite. We sailed a long way on a little wind. Every thief, every burglar, every confidence man knew that when they operated in this town they did so at their own peril. Despite criticism from defense lawyers, the press, and even some in this department – people I call *hitless wonders* – we locked up a lot of bad guys. Protect and serve was more than a motto for us. It was a way of life."

Pickens's voice broke when he spoke about Aunt Mo and how much he missed her. Brady wiped his eyes.

"Finally, I'd be remiss if I did not acknowledge someone who is not here. He was my best friend. Closer than a brother. I stand here today because of John Brady's valor. He saved my life and I dedicated my career to his memory. I'm grateful that John's son is here. Maximus Brady, my godson, was himself a police officer in New York City. Max?"

Brady half-stood to acknowledge the applause while Ron Register glared at him from the stage. Brady recalled Uncle Howard's words: *"Ron Register couldn't find the eye of a needle with a magnifying glass."* He smiled and nodded back.

When Pickens finished the crowd again rose to its feet in applause. Brady noted that Chief Begley and Ron Register did not join in. As soon as the ovation died Begley rushed off frozen-faced, a sullen Register at his heels. *Must be late for smiling practice,* Brady decided.

When the audience dispersed, he noticed Rose behind the stage huddled with the mayor and a small group of VIPs, including one or two judges and a county commissioner he'd met at political functions she'd dragged him to. Brady hopped onto the platform and hugged Pickens.

"I'm so proud of you, Uncle Howard. You truly deserve this."

Pickens misted up and his face wrinkled into a self-effacing smile. "That means more to me than you know, my boy."

"I'd almost forgotten what an amazing cop you were."

His eyebrows arched wryly. "That's what happens when you're gone. People forget what you did. Forget you were even there."

Brady pointed to the new sign. "They won't forget you now."

He held Uncle Howard's free hand as he grimaced off the stage and they retreated to a refreshment table. A big white cake sat in the middle trimmed with blue icing and a gold badge inscribed with Pickens's name and shield number. A large flaccid man was scooping a piece onto a paper plate. Judging by the crumbs sprinkled on the ample plateau of his upper belly, it wasn't his first. He layed down his plate and embraced Pickens.

"This was long overdue, captain. They should have named the whole damned building after you."

"Thank you, Walter," Uncle Howard said with a shy smile. "That's very kind but, please, my head's too big already. I might not be able to squeeze out the door to go home. Walter, I want you to meet Max Brady. Max, Walter was one of my wise men. Brilliant intelligence analyst. Of course, after I retired the geniuses moved him into the records department and put him in charge of paper shuffling."

Someone came up and congratulated Pickens and he was dragged away for another round of handshakes. The heavyset man threw out his hand.

"Lieutenant Walter Peebles. Pleasure. The captain spoke about you often. He was very proud of you."

Walter Peebles picked up his plate and gobbled the cake in a blink. He scraped white morsels off himself like a waiter cleaning crumbs off a table. While he did, his heavy-lidded eyes scanned the small crowd. He reached into his pocket and produced a business card and handed it to Brady.

"You ever need anything, call me."

"Thanks, lieutenant. I may do that."

"Anything for Pick. Just don't let the brain trust know. Well, back to the salt mines."

Rose was still nestled with the cluster of judges and politicians. Brady caught her attention and raised his eyebrows. She held up one finger. He took it to mean she would grant him an audience.

His stomach growled and his eyes were drawn to the cake. It dawned on him he hadn't eaten since before Ben's funeral yesterday. He wolfed down a slice while he watched Uncle Howard accepting well-deserved felicitations. Brady could see the gleam in his eyes. This was obviously a big day for him. Redemption Day. Pickens finally broke away and headed back to the table. When he reached Brady his face hardened. He reached out and squeezed his right shoulder.

"I saw the news about your old friend Richard Strong. What in God's name is going on, Max?"

"I wish I knew, Uncle Howard."

"I'm worried about you, my boy. You need to be extremely careful. Two of your friends dispatched. And all this tattoo business."

The remark startled Brady. He looked at Pickens. "How did you know about that?"

Uncle Howard smiled and winked. "Once a cop, always a cop. I still hear things." Then his face grew solemn again. "You should speak to Register about security. I'd say something, but that would guarantee you get no protection. What is he doing?"

"Still fixated on Delray. Convinced she murdered her brother. Wants to connect her to Peanut's killing, too. By the way, do you remember an intelligence guy used to work here? Furbush?"

"Fuzzy Furbush?"

"That's him."

"Used to work for me in Criminal Intel. In fact, he worked directly under Walt Peebles."

"Really?" Brady had come to the right place.

"Total flake. Run out of the department years ago. Too fond of nose candy and massage parlors."

"Hmmm." Brady thought back to his meeting with Furbush. "He is antsy. Maybe that explains why."

"Too bad. Fuzzy had the knack. Born snoop. Only reason he lasted as long as he did. Why do you ask?"

"Furbush is a P.I. now. Office in Plantation. Shortly before he died, Ben Chance began getting threats. He hired Fuzzy to investigate."

"Then he was murdered? Not exactly a ringing endorsement." Pickens reached into his pocket and pulled out an orange plastic vial. He nodded toward the food table. "Can you fetch me a cup of punch, my boy? Damned hip. Thank you, Max. Did Benjamin know who the threats were coming from?"

"He thought he did. A guy named Duke Manyon."

Uncle Howard popped a pill into his mouth, took a sip of punch, and swallowed with a harsh squint.

"Hate those damned things. New hip's being installed next week. Maybe I'll finally be free of this pain. Mansion, you say?"

"Manyon. Duke Manyon."

The old policeman's eyes narrowed and he got a faraway look, like he was trying to peer back in time. "Why does that name ring a bell?"

Brady told him what Furbush said about Duke being a suspect in a series of jewel heists.

"Ah, yes. Beach boy, as I recall. Lived on a boat. Had a surf shop."

"Ski school."

Pickens shook his head with a wan smile. "After all these years, my boy, the cases run together. Suspects, victims, witnesses. But isn't that good news for Benjamin's sister? If her brother was getting threatening phone calls from this Mansion fellow, that throws cold water on her culpability."

"It certainly creates uncertainty."

"Does that fool Register know?"

"He knows some things. I was going to tell him more, but he hightailed it out of here before I could get to him."

A mischievous grin crossed Uncle Howard's face. "Hope it wasn't something I said."

Rose walked up and planted an emphatic kiss on Brady's lips. A kiss of absolution, he hoped. He was tempted to throw her over his shoulder, smuggle her to the sloop, and shanghai her out to sea. Uncle Howard foiled his plot with a half-bow.

"Madame Commissioner, it was a high honor having you here today."

Rose hugged him. "The honor was mine, Captain Pickens."

"Please, call me Howard. Better yet, Uncle Howard. So at this rate, young lady, I estimate you should be our first lady president by age thirty."

"I probably should be, but unfortunately the Founding Fathers rigged it so you can't be president until the advanced age of thirty-five."

"Then you better slow down. Don't want to peak too soon. Now, if you two will excuse me. Max looks like he wants to carry you out of here."

Brady couldn't believe his ears. "How did you know, Uncle Howard? Don't tell me you're an oracle too, like Grandma Kate."

Pickens gave him a puzzled look. Then he laughed. "No, my boy. If that were the case I really would have been a super cop. But I do miss Kate and Zack. And John and Mary."

"And Aunt Mo," said Max.

He sighed. "I guess we'll just have to be grateful we had them as long as we did. Well, kids, I'll be on my way. Want to be off the road before my pill kicks in."

"I'll call you about that Heat game, Uncle Howard."

He waved his cane in the air. "Hopefully I won't need this thing by then," he said as he limped past the *Captain J. Howard Pickens Detective Bureau.*

Et Tu Brady

Chapter Sixty-Two

"HE'S SUCH A sweet man," Rose said watching Pickens recede down the hallway. "You're lucky to have an uncle like him, Brady."

"Technically, he's not my uncle."

"You're still lucky to have him."

"I'm not feeling so lucky."

"Why?"

"For one thing, the woman I'm crazy about wants to brain me."

Rose smirked. "Maybe you deserve to be brained."

"But if she knew how I felt about her."

"Why don't you tell her?" She stood on her tippy toes and kissed him. "Maybe she'll believe you."

"Brilliant! Why didn't I think of that?" He kissed her back. "Unfortunately, there's more."

He told her about Peanut and the *Et Tu Brady* tattoo on his forehead. And about being sued by a childhood acquaintance over the car accident.

"In fact, he mentioned you. Said you should keep your nose out of his business."

Rose's eyes grew wide. "You know Austin Ball?"

"We grew up together. Guy's been a menace all his life."

"He's a crook, too, Brady. I've got proof."

"What do you mean? What kind of proof?"

She looked up and down the hallway. No one was near. She stepped close to him and whispered in his ear. "I broke into Walter Dean's computer last night."

Now Brady's eyes were popping out. She told him about the slip-and-fall lawsuits and how Ball and Dean had been raking in millions. And about Seymour Tate being ambushed and police finding crystal meth in his pocket.

"*The Lauderdale News* suspended Seymour and killed his story."

"I'm not surprised. What's that got to do with you committing burglary?"

Rose's eyes were shining. She explained how Tate talked her into breaking into Dean's computer. She pulled a sheet of paper from her purse.

"Look what I found." The paper contained several columns of numbers and dates. "I slipped into Broward General this morning and showed them to Seymour." She pointed to the far left row. "He thinks they're case numbers for Austin Ball's slip-and-fall suits. This column next to it are settlement amounts. See how they're all between twenty five thousand and thirty five thousand dollars? Under the radar numbers that don't catch the eye." She moved her finger to a third column. "Seymour thinks it's a bank account number. Maybe an offshore bank where Walter deposits his cut. If he's right, Walter's been collecting seven-to-ten thousand dollars per case, depending on the size of the settlement. Multiply that by at least five hundred. Seymour says that's the number of lawsuits Ball and Dean have settled in the past few years."

"Why does that not surprise me?"

"Brady, I can't believe you know Austin Ball. Dean mentioned something about the lawsuit today at the commission meeting. I bet they're using you to try to shut me up?"

"Ya think?" Rose seemed quite proud of herself. "Congratulations, my sweet. You're first felony. And only twenty seven. Most politicians wait until their thirties or forties. Uncle Howard's right. You will go far in politics."

Her mouth turned down at the corners as a new reality set in.

"Your right. I'm a criminal. Just another crooked politician."

"Not in the customary sense. You didn't do it to line your own pockets. You're crime had a higher purpose."

The light had gone out of her eyes and her pale complexion had turned even whiter. "But I could go to jail, Brady."

"If you do I promise to come see you every weekend. Holidays too. Do you happen to know if Florida allows conjugal visits?"

Rose's lower lip jutted out. "Don't joke, Brady. It's not funny."

"Who's joking? I swear I'll visit." He said it with a straight face, then his expression darkened. "I'm more concerned about Junior Ball. He's a bully. Always has been. The attack on your reporter friend fits him to a T. You need to watch yourself."

Rose laughed. "He wouldn't dare mess with a City Commissioner."

"Just her boyfriend."

Rose frowned. "I'm sorry you got dragged into this. I guess that's the price you pay for canoodling a public servant – even a felonious one."

He kissed her again. "Just doing my civic duty, ma'am."

Chapter Sixty-Three

BRADY DROVE AWAY from the police department wondering why he was so attracted to bad girls. His old girlfriend was a suspected murderer. Now his new girlfriend turns out to be a break-in artist. He hadn't seen that coming. Girls like Rose had milk mustaches, not rap sheets. At least she'd forgiven him. He vowed to keep his promise and visit her every week in the slam. He made a mental note to check on that conjugal policy.

He followed Broward Boulevard east to the end, swung left onto Victoria Park Boulevard, and negotiated the maze until he reached Sunrise Boulevard then turned right. At the Atlantic Ocean he took another hard right and proceeded along the best beach in America. Three miles of white sand and blue sea populated by a parade of beautiful people – and some not so beautiful – many of them nearly naked. The only downside was pedestrians having to dodge distracted drivers.

He passed the dwindling number of small mom-and-pop hotels like the Seven Seas, Tropic Cay, and Jolly Roger, and the newer high-rise behemoths – including a Donald Trump albatross that had been sitting vacant for years and would probably never open. He continued past Las Olas, the Sea Shanty, Bahia Mar, and the Yankee

Clipper and turned right at Harbor Beach Parkway into the town's most exclusive neighborhood.

The entrance was blocked by a security gate and guard shack. Brady marveled at how the wealthy insulated themselves from the rabble by barricading public streets. He made another mental note to file a complaint with his City Canoodler, before she was packed off to the penitentiary. When he pulled up to the booth, though, there was no sentry on duty and the gate opened automatically. The road block was a ruse. If the commoners couldn't be stonewalled, maybe they could be hoodwinked.

The house was a three-story Mediterranean painted in avocados and golds with a chocolate barrel-tile roof and a dozen soaring royal palms standing watch. He steered around a circular cobblestone driveway and pulled up under the porte-cochère. A green Jaguar XK was parked outside the front door with a vanity plate that said *Futloos*. A white placard swung over the front door painted in gold-leaf letters identifying the manse as *Oceanbreeze*. He considered whether the well-heeled realized how pretentious it seemed to the proletariat that they named their cars and houses.

He pressed the doorbell. Muffled chimes rang inside the house like church bells at vespers. The door was opened by a handsome toffee-skinned woman wearing gray servant's livery and a white apron. *Mathilda*, according to the gold-plated name tag pinned over her left breast. *They even name the help!* He handed Mathilda his card.

"Of course, Mr. Brady," she said with a Caribbean inflection.

Mathilda led him to a glass-walled sun room flooded with daylight. A pleasant breeze was blowing in through large open doors. Décor was early Jimmy Buffett. White wood floors, pastel furniture, coral stone fireplace. The room looked out over a swimming pool with soft corners. Beyond was Lake Sylvia, a small bay off the Intracoastal lined with multi-million dollar homes. Parked at the dock was a white fifty-foot Carver with a tall flybridge and *S.S. Alimony* painted on the stern.

Her voice arrived before she did. She sounded merry. Maybe a little too merry.

432

"Can it really be?"

Ginger Brennan Ball entered the room in a glamorous rush. She wore a black bikini, a sheer black lace wrap, and black high heels and was radiating enough heat to cook a six course dinner. She threw her arms around his neck and kissed him on the lips. He seemed to be getting that a lot lately.

"My God! Max Brady! It's been soooo long."

"Too long. I wish I'd known you were here."

Ginger stepped back and posed, hands on hips, one foot in front of the other, like a contestant for Mrs. America. Radiocarbon dating couldn't have proven she was forty two years old. It was as if she'd been preserved in amber. She still had the tummy of a high school cheerleader. Her skin was as brown as her hair once had been, before it was platinum. A strand of diamonds as long as a stringbean twinkled from her navel. Her smooth forehead and apple-round cheeks were frozen in place. And her breasts, which were prominent in adolescence, now composed approximately twenty percent of her body mass. She looked like a poster girl for some fancy-pants Palm Beach cosmetic surgeon.

"Ginger, you look stunning."

Brady wasn't lying. He was stunned. She flashed a crop of blinding white teeth, exuding all the sincerity of a candidate's wife.

"Thank you soooo much for sayin' that, Max." Ginger had added a sugary drawl since childhood. Flatter consonants, vowels gliding into diphthongs, words drawn out just soooo. He wondered if the accent had been surgically implanted. "One of the perks of marryin' money. You can literally stop the incursion of time. But look at you, Max. You're positively gorgeous."

"Sold my soul to the devil. You should see my portrait in the attic." She looked at him, slightly baffled. Brady gazed out the window. Lauderdale Yacht Club was visible across the water. He remembered Ginger doing her Lolita act there, falling out of her Speedo by the swimming pool. He waved a hand.

"As I recall you were very popular over there once upon a time."

"Once upon a time I could crack walnuts with my butt cheeks," she said and laughed. He had to smile. It was the same big, lusty laugh from childhood. At least some things hadn't changed. "I guess my little titties did make those old men weak at the knees, didn't they?"

"I don't remember that."

She lit a cigarette. "Liar."

"I mean I don't remember them being little."

"Compared to what?" Ginger blew a plume of smoke down into her silicon valley. "Do you think they're too big?"

"If I say yes they'll revoke my man card."

Ginger cackled again. "We couldn't have that." She nodded in the direction of the yacht club. "I'm a member there now. Let me tell you, those Lotharios do more than look. Place is crawling with bottom pinchers. The wives hate me, especially since I'm single."

She was wearing a frisky smile. Ginger always did have a penchant for monkey business. Mathilda came in and set a tray on a small round teak table with three legs carved and painted to look like rainbow trout. It held a pitcher of icy-green liquid and two salt-encrusted glasses shaped like sombreros. Ginger motioned to a pair of peaches-and-cream-striped club chairs beside the table.

"I hope it's not too early for you, Max. I need my margarita in the afternoon." She stubbed her cigarette in a shiny silver ashtray and poured the concoction into both glasses, then lifted hers, a little too eagerly. Apparently she did need it. She tilted the rim to her lips, closed her eyes and took a long, slow swallow. "Oh! That's soooo good!"

Her tongue darted out like a pink eel behind a Chicklet fence and licked the salt off a pair of Botox-infused lips that would have made Angelina Jolie green. Brady tasted his drink and blanched. Too saccharine. Good tequila. El Tesoro Gold, he guessed. He favored white agave for margaritas, preferably Cazadores Blanco. But the secret to a great margarita was the other ingredients. Lemon rather than lime. And only the finest liqueur. This was mixed with Triple Sec, which accounted for its sugary character. Cointreau was expensive, but gave a dry, sharper edge. Ginger seemed to enjoy it, though. She made a low animal sound not uncommon among women during heavy petting.

"I heard you were back from the Big Apple, Max. What brought you home?"

"Did you know South Floridians have twenty percent more sex than New Yorkers?"

"Our most popular team sport. Somebody said you had a little bar on the beach. I've meant to pop in and surprise you."

"Why didn't you?"

"Something always stopped me."

"Your husband?"

Ginger gave him a small sad smile. She pulled her sheer wrap tight around her and crossed her shiny brown legs.

"Ex-husband."

"I don't want to offend you, Ginger." He knew she wasn't the type who offended easy. "But I was shocked to hear you married Junior. When we were kids you loathed the guy."

She lit another cigarette and took a drag while her right foot nonchalantly bounced a high heel. Ginger had always been multi-talented.

"Rich husbands don't grow on trees."

"So it's true? Money *can* buy love?"

"Let's just say Junior got a lot less loathsome after he inherited daddy's law firm and mommy's restaurant."

Surprise flitted across Brady's face. The memory was incredibly vivid, even after so many years. He'd seen the television commercial a thousand times as a kid. Junior Ball's mother, slim and attractive, wearing a grass skirt and flower garland, surrounded by a cast of hula girls and bare-chested male fire dancers, inviting everyone to visit her Polynesian Room, renowned for its South Pacific cuisine and *"world famous fruity rum drinks."* The report Fuzzy Furbush read to him yesterday mentioned that Duke Manyon had run the Polynesian's valet parking concession. He finally understood why Junior had been with Duke and Buck on the Intracoastal that day when Buck tried to run him down in the yellow Donzi.

"Ginger, did Junior ever mention the name Duke Manyon?"

Her brow nearly furrowed. She lowered her eyes and stared at something a long way off. After a time she nodded.

435

"Before we were married. But not Junior. I heard it from Austin Senior, his father. Right after Bobbi died. Austin's wife, Junior's mom. We were at T.M. Ralph's, the funeral home. Mr. Ball was drunk, as usual. Ranting about some guy. Threatening to kill him if he showed up. He worked himself into a real lather. Junior had to escort him from the room until he calmed down. Later I asked Junior about it. He said his mother had had an affair. Destroyed his parent's marriage, even though they stayed together. Of course, Austin was a shameless cad in his own right. I couldn't be in a room alone with him. Old drunk goosed me every chance he got. His own daughter-in-law! That's why I never really blamed Junior for his womanizing. Genetics. He couldn't help it. Anyway, this Casanova worked at the Polynesian. Can't remember if he was the chef or maître d'. No, wait. I think he ran the car park service. Yeah, that was it. He and Bobbi had been doing the horizontal hula. Then he just went away. Vanished into thin air. I never forgot the name. Recognized it the second you said it. Manyon. Duke Manyon."

"Junior didn't say where Duke went?"

"No. He was gone long before we got together. It all seemed very mysterious, though. I wondered if Austin had him whacked. But if he had I guess he wouldn't have been ranting about killing him." Ginger's eyes narrowed. She took a draw on her cigarette. "Why do you ask, Max?"

"Nothing important. Just a name. I still don't understand why you married him. He was such a jerk."

Ginger shrugged. "Junior's half Caligula, half Snidely Whiplash, and half Bernie Madoff. Nobody's perfect."

Brady smiled. "Including your arithmetic."

She showed him her teeth again. There was something sad about her eyes, though. They seemed washed out. He could almost see her faded dreams.

"Junior paid the bills and kept me in champagne." She held up her sombrero. "And tequila. When the time came to part, I kept the house, the yacht, and get a fat check every month. Who's complaining? Besides, we didn't have what you might call a traditional marriage. Junior always fancied himself a ladies man. Like father, like son. Like mother too."

Brady made a sympathetic sound without moving his lips. The benevolent ventriloquist.

She smiled. "Guess how he told me he wanted a divorce?"

"You want me to guess what Junior said? I'm the last person."

"He said: 'I must yield to the temptations I can no longer resist.'"

"Awww! He did not. That is pure poetry. I think from the Paleozoic Period."

She let loose another lusty laugh. "Frankly, I didn't care. You know me, Max. I always enjoyed the attentions of the male species. With him incapable of being monogamous, I had a few relationships of my own." She made quotation marks in the air with her fingers around *'relationships'.* "And I had them without suffering from that good old-fashioned Catholic school guilt."

"If Attila the Nun is dead she must be rolling over in her grave. And Ben Chance was one of those 'relationships.'" He added his own air quotes.

A kittenish smile broke out on Ginger's face. "My, my, my, Max Brady. What do you serve at that bar of yours? Steamy rumors, I suspect." A split second later a melancholy pout appeared. "Poor Benjamin. Such a shame. I hope they catch his killer."

"Right now they're convinced it was his sister."

Ginger's eyes widened. Brady didn't see any trace of wrinkles.

"Delray's back in town?"

"She arrived the day Ben was murdered. Found his body."

Ginger chewed on that tidbit for a while, along with a margarita-soaked ice cube. Brady tried to guess what was bouncing around beneath all that bleach and Botox. She regarded him with unlined eyes.

"What happened, Max?"

"To Ben?"

"No. To you. To all of you. When we were kids. Something happened. I remember. It was around the time that terrible thing happened to your grandparents. Delray and I were best friends. Then, out of the blue, she stopped talking to me. To anyone. Withdrew inside herself and got very strange. I thought she was sick. Then she was gone. I never heard from her again. You had already disappeared, as

I recall to live with an uncle out west. Even Benjamin and Peanut acted weird. Neither one of them would talk about it. God knows I tried to get it out of Benjamin. He wouldn't give up a thing, even years later. It was as if y'all had a secret pact. Mum's the word, as they say in the Mafia."

"I think that's *omerta*. Did you ever ask Peanut?"

She snorted a derisive laugh. "That guy has become such a loser. Total pothead. Even went to prison for a couple of years. So bitter. And jealous about me and Benjamin. I don't believe a word he says anymore."

"Ginger, Peanut's dead."

She stared at him for several seconds. Blank. Uncomprehending. Then the words seemed to sink in. She gasped and her chest heaved, like earth in an earthquake. Tears began pouring from her eyes. Peanut would have liked that.

"Oh, God, Max, no. When? How?"

"Last night. He was murdered."

She choked back a sob. "He was so harmless. Who would want to hurt him?"

"The same person who killed Ben. That's why I wanted to talk to you."

Ginger picked up her glass and drained the remains of her margarita then used the cocktail napkin to mop her cheeks.

"I hope you don't think I had anything to do with..." She was having difficulty speaking. "...Benjamin or Peanut dying?"

"No. The shock on your face told me that. Junior's another story, though."

Ginger folded her tanned arms over her synthetic breasts and hugged them, as if suddenly self-conscious.

"Why would Junior kill them?"

"I'm not saying he did. He's a bully and a fool, but I doubt even he's that stupid. The police are trying to pin Ben's murder on Delray, though. Maybe Peanut's too. They're wrong. I'm trying to suggest alternate suspects to them. Junior had motive."

"What motive?"

"No offense, Ginger, but you were screwing Ben. And Peanut has always wanted to screw you. You said Junior's father threatened to kill Duke Manyon for doing his wife. Maybe womanizing isn't the only chromosomal predilection in the Ball family DNA. Junior had a lot more motive than Delray."

Ginger filled her glass a third time and smiled at Brady over the rim. Her eyes were dry now, her grieving period for Peanut apparently over.

"Still got a thing for Del, do you, Max?" He didn't respond. "You two were soooo hot for each other back then. Not that you'd have gotten far with her in those days. Not with Miss Goody Two Shoes. Saint Delray. Patti Prude, she called herself. Soooo pure. Soooo perfect. But then you were too, weren't you Max, in your own bad boy way. Jumping off bridges. Fighting sharks. Standing up to Junior. Very ballsy. Very sexy. After that day in the schoolyard Delray couldn't stop talking about you. I'll never forget it either. Neither will Junior."

Brady shrugged. "Ancient history. Old as dinosaur bones. I hadn't seen her since we were thirteen. Until the other night."

She smiled like a cat with a key to the bird cage. "It doesn't take long to restoke a fire that never died."

Brady blanched. Rose had used almost the exact words.

"Look, Ginger, I'm trying to help Delray. She didn't murder anyone. I thought you might know something that could help her. You two used to be best friends."

"Help Delray by implicating my ex-husband? Or help you save yourself?"

"From?"

"I saw you and Junior sparring on the noon news today. Just like old times."

Brady downed the rest of his drink. "Not quite. I haven't beaten him yet. I will, though. But I'm guessing without your help."

Ginger licked more salt from the rim of her glass and looked him in the eyes.

"I was ditched on the courthouse steps after twenty squandered years. I have no warm spot in my heart for my ex-husband." She waved a hand at her surroundings. "But if he goes down, I lose all this. I'm not going to risk the little I've still got to help Delray. Or you, for that matter. Sorry Max."

Ginger lived inside a gold-plated bubble that came fully-equipped with splendid water views, midday margaritas, and plastic fantastic body parts. Life wasn't great, but it would get a whole lot worse if the bubble burst. She wasn't going to let that happen. Brady couldn't blame her. The truth was he felt sorry for her. He knew what was coming. Junior *was* going down. If not for murder, then the slip-and-fall scam.

"We're old friends, Ginger. I don't want to see you get hurt. You should know, though, Junior's got problems. And I don't mean Ben and Peanut."

He thought he detected a trace of alarm in her face, but he couldn't be sure considering the absence of moving parts. Her foot was bouncing faster, though. She tried to sound casual.

"What do you mean?"

He rose to his feet. "You'll know soon enough."

She lit another cigarette and stood. "You can't just drop something like that on me and walk away, Max."

"Junior's been a bad boy, Ginger. I'm afraid he's gonna take a fall." Brady looked out the window and nodded at the *S.S. Alimony*. "Ask him about it next time he drops off your check."

She didn't respond. Instead, she led him toward the front door. They walked past a table in the foyer lined with old photographs. Ginger as very young girl. Ginger as Lolita. Ginger as high school cheerleader. Ginger as bride – her groom nowhere to be seen. There was also a picture of a much younger girl. Something about her seemed familiar.

"My daughter Elizabeth. She was about ten there. Left home when she turned sixteen. Just like me. That was three years ago. We haven't spoken since."

"Sorry to hear that."

"These days our televisions are better adjusted than our kids. Elizabeth's going through a phase. I did the same thing. I screwed rock stars. Did you know I slept with Elvis?"

"I didn't. Congratulations." It was the best he could muster. He realized it may have been the highlight of her life.

Ginger smiled wistfully. "Just before he died. I was only four-teen, but I told him I was twenty." The wistful smile turned seduc-tive. "He had no reason to doubt me. By then Elvis was fat, of course. But, even on death's door, that man had more life in him than ninety nine percent of the slugs I've ever known." She nodded at the photo-graph. "I screwed real rock stars. Elizabeth screws phony vampires. Hopefully she'll wake up someday and marry a man with a big bank account. Just like momma."

She offered him a firm cheek. It was like kissing a honeydew melon.

"Good to see you, Ginger."

"Don't be such a stranger, Max Brady."

Et Tu Brady

Chapter Sixty-Four

THE INSTANT BRADY'S Jeep vanished from sight Ginger discarded her smile and retreated back into the house. She picked her cell phone off the fish leg table and pushed the speed dial. A voice answered after two rings.

"What in the name of Jesus fucking Christ have you done?" she hissed.

"What are you talking about?"

"Max Brady just left here. He says you're about to take a big fall. What have you done? If you jeopardize my alimony I will make your life miserable."

"Too late. You did that the day you said 'I do.'"

The line went dead. Ginger threw the phone down on the table and poured what remained of the icy green margarita into her glass.

Et Tu Brady

Chapter Sixty-Five

ON THE OTHER side of town, Junior Ball punched a number into his phone. He'd had all he could stand of Max Brady. And his girlfriend. Walter Dean called him this morning just after the press conference at the Sea Shanty. He sounded scared shitless.

"She knows something," he said.

"Calm down, Walter. She only knows what that drug-dealing reporter told her."

"You're wrong. I don't know how, but I think she knows a lot…"

"Are you on your office phone, Walter?"

"Yes."

"What's wrong with you? Haven't you ever heard of discretion?"

"I'm telling you, Junior, we've got a serious problem."

First Dean. Now Ginger. Goddamn Brady. Some assholes never change. The girlfriend was just as bad. He was finished playing games. Rose Becker was going the way of the dodo bird. His cell phone clicked. A voice croaked at the other end.

"Yeah?"

"I got another job for you."

Et Tu Brady

Chapter Sixty-Six

BRADY DROVE BACK through the faux security gate and turned onto the beach road and was heading toward the Sea Shanty when his cell phone rang.

"Max!" It was Delray. Her voice was frantic. "Come quickly!"

"What is it? What's the matter?"

"They're tearing my room apart. Hurry, Max."

When he pulled up to the Yankee Clipper, four blue-and-white police cruisers were parked in the front of the hotel with lights flashing. He tossed his keys to a valet, entered the lobby, and took the elevator to the fifth floor. The first thing he saw was Ron Register at the far end of the hallway leaning against the wall outside Delray's room.

"I've got bad news, Brady," he said.

"You haven't found Ben Chance's killer yet?"

"We're going to the grand jury tomorrow. I expect your client to be indicted for her brother's murder. And the Richard Strong homicide."

"You're making a big mistake, Register. Delray didn't kill her brother. And she sure as hell didn't kill Peanut."

"I'm not interested in denials. She's welcome to tell her story to the grand jury. We can't force her, but she's welcome."

They both knew that wasn't going to happen. Defense attorneys were not permitted in front of grand juries with their clients. Delray would be alone in a no holds barred interrogation. She was a smart woman, but a skilled prosecutor would twist her like Attila the Nun used to twist his earlobe.

"I'd be careful, Ron, or you're going to end up with egg on your face."

He left Register and ducked around the corner. A half-dozen uniformed and plain-clothed police officers were pillaging the suite. Delray was watching them from the calcified merlot couch. She was wearing a white blouse with pale yellow wide-leg trousers and matching yellow shoes, a stylish blonde outfit for an elegant blonde murder suspect. Her face was as ghostly white as her shirt. Her eyes were crowded with tears. One fell off an eyelash like a raindrop dripping from a leaf. He crossed the room.

"Max, I took a walk up the beach and when I got back they were here."

He reached down and took her by the arm.

"Come on, we're getting out of here."

She picked a white canvas shoulder bag off the onyx coffee table and they started to leave. Before they got to the door a large, well-dressed black man with a detective shield clipped to his jacket pocket blocked their path.

"I'm sorry, Mrs. Cross, you'll have to leave the bag."

"But my things…"

"We have to inspect everything. You can go. The bag stays."

Brady nodded. She handed him the bag and they walked into the hallway. Register was still propped against the wall. He was inspecting an orange plastic vial. He shook the ampule and it rattled like a maraca.

"Did you know, Brady, that Americans consume eighty percent of all the pain pills in the world?"

Something about the question rankled him. He realized that he didn't like someone encroaching on his monopoly for useless information.

448

"Is that a rhetorical question, Register?"

The policeman smiled, jangled the vial again, and held it up for Brady to inspect. It contained a few bluish pills. He read the label.

UniversityRx Inc.
BE7572957
>*Dr. Lefkowitz, Rada R. Md*
>*Rx 904401264*
>*Delray Cross*
>*66 Laurel Lane – Durham, NC 27705*
>*Take 1 tablet by mouth every 8 hours as needed*
>*QTY: 60 OxyContin Tablets*
>*Refills: 12*

"This prescription was filled six days ago at a pharmacy on the campus at Duke University. According to the label, she should have taken eighteen pills since then – maximum. That means there still should be forty two pills left. I count six."

Delray looked at Register with bewildered eyes, then to Brady.

"I suffer from a slipped disc in my back," she said. "It causes me a great deal of pain."

"Do you expect me to believe you've taken fifty four OxyContin pills in one week? Three times what the prescription calls for?"

"Don't answer that," Brady said.

"This stuff is like heroin," Register continued. "If you'd ingested that many pills you'd be dead or, at the very least, in La-La Land." He looked at Brady. "I haven't seen that. Have you, counselor? Did you tell your client her brother was doped up with this very same drug? We have good reason to believe Richard Strong was as well."

Delray gasped. "Peanut? Dead? When? How?"

She asked the same questions Ginger had, but her face cracked in ways that would not have been possible for her girlhood friend.

"Last night," Brady said. "He was murdered, Del." She let out a small sob. He put an arm around her shoulder and turned to Register. "You don't seriously believe she killed Peanut, too?"

"If she did her brother, she had to have done Strong. Not just the drugs. There's the tattoo. And let's not forget her husband."

"Husband?" Brady blurted.

Delray's pale face turned the color of tomato soup. Register chuckled softly. He gave Brady a quick account of Charles Cross's drowning death while scuba diving in Bonaire three years before.

"They found a very elevated level of oxycodone hydrochloride in his blood. Your client was sole beneficiary of his estate. Five million dollars. Add her brother's forty million and you represent a very wealthy lady. On the bright side, that should come in handy buying contraband at Lowell."

"Lowell?" Brady said.

"Correctional Center. Florida's Death Row for women."

Delray fell against Brady and buried her face in his chest. Register smiled. Brady felt his blood rise.

"I told you the other night it would take me ten minutes to win an acquittal. I don't hear anything to change that."

"No? Did I mention the car?"

"What car?"

"Ask Mrs. Cross. She forgot to tell us she rented a car the night of the murder. The minute she checked into the Clipper. Nice wheels. BMW, maroon, license plate AJC 319. We're impounding it at this very moment."

"Why?"

"My people checked the odometer the morning after Benjamin Chance died. Compared it to the mileage on the rental contract. Six miles had been put on the car. Chance's house is three miles from the Clipper. Six miles round trip."

"But, Max…" Delray said.

Brady stopped her before she could go on.

"That doesn't prove a thing. She could have taken a drive down the beach. I run that stretch every day. Its three miles from the Clipper to end of the beach road. Six miles back and forth."

Register chuckled again.

"I should mention we've been checking every day. Eight more miles were added to the odometer since yesterday morning. Guess the distance between this hotel and the Richard Strong murder scene?"

Brady groaned inside. "Four miles."

"Bingo. Eight miles round trip." He let the information sink in for a moment. "You're swimming against the tide on this, Brady."

"Yeah, well, I'm half salmon on my mother's side."

He tried to sound jaunty, but he was actually apprehensive. Delray had told him nothing about the car. Or the drugs. Or her husband's death. Brady knew he could convince a jury to look past some of the circumstantial evidence, however the police case was stacking up fast. Florida had more than four hundred inmates on Death Row and Brady knew presumptive proof based on circumstantial evidence had put more of them there than DNA data. Beyond that, Register was getting under his skin.

"If Mrs. Cross goes to trial, counselor, it's going to turn out bad."

"Yeah, and if fleas had money they could buy their own dog." Brady wasn't certain his riposte made sense, but gave silent credit to Busyman. "First you say Delray killed Ben for money? Now you say she killed her husband for money. Unless Peanut has a Swiss bank account we don't know about, she sure as hell didn't kill him for money. You're all over the map, Register. It's all bullshit."

"It's not bullshit. That's why I'm surprised State Attorney Volkey wants to offer Mrs. Cross a deal."

"What are you, Monty Hall?" Register didn't respond. The *Let's Make A Deal* allusion had apparently either gone over his head, or Brady had gotten the wrong host. Maybe it was Bob Barker. Or Howie Mandel. He couldn't remember. "What kind of deal?"

"A good one for your client. Too good, if you ask me. In my opinion we have an ironclad Murder One on Benjamin Chance's killing and a decent capital punishment case on the Strong homicide." He looked straight at Delray. "That means you're looking at the needle. Lethal injection. If a jury feels some sympathy for you and recommends against the death penalty, you still do a mandatory minimum of twenty five years in prison. That means you don't get out until you're at least sixty seven years old."

Delray covered her mouth with her hand and fresh tears filled her eyes.

"What's the deal?" Brady said.

"Volkey says he'll take a plea to second degree murder and recommend twenty years max. She'd be out in twelve or less, still a relatively young woman. So? Deal or no deal?"

Register *was* playing a different game. *Let's Make A Deal* was Monty Hall. *Deal Or No Deal* was Mandel's show.

"Take your deal and stick it, Howie."

Et Tu Brady

Chapter Sixty-Seven

IN THE LOBBY on their way out of the Yankee Clipper an offi-cious-looking man with a pasty face wearing a mustard jacket with a *Sheraton* patch on his pocket rushed up and informed Delray she was being evicted.

"You may stay the night, however we want you out by noon tomorrow."

Before they got out the door a heavyset woman with a flushed face wearing a wine jacket with a *Hertz* patch on her pocket stopped them. She informed Delray her BMW had been impounded. Police said it might not be returned for months. Delray would be respon-sible for the rental charge until then.

By the time they climbed into the Jeep she had the dazed expres-sion of someone who'd just escaped a terrorist bombing. Her world had fallen apart.

"Are you okay, Del?"

She stared at him from the passenger seat, wide-eyed and unsteady. Then she leaned over and kissed him on the mouth.

"I love you, Max. I know now I've always loved you."

Their cheeks were touching. She smelled of lilac but her lips tasted bittersweet, like the peel on an orange. He pulled away from her.

"Forget about you and me, Delray." He tried not to sound too harsh. "If Register gets his way, there won't be any you."

She recoiled against the door and was racked by a small shudder. Brady popped the clutch. The Jeep lurched onto the beach road and jostled through teeming traffic. Super Bowl mania had kicked into high gear. People were everywhere. He wanted to stop at the Shanty to see how Gordy was doing, but he needed to get Delray away from the crush. He needed answers. He turned left on Las Olas, crossed the bridge, and took a right on Siesta Lane to Victor Gruber's house.

"Follow me," he said.

They circled around back to the dock and boarded the Sea Ray. A warm winter sun was smiling down from its pastel perch. He navigated to the Intracoastal and they cruised wordlessly south. They passed the spot where Buck Foxx ran down young Max in the yellow Donzi. They passed the Bahia Mar Marina and dozens of lavish waterfront palaces. They passed the mouth of New River. They passed the Lauderdale Yacht Club. They passed beneath the new 17th St. Causeway Bridge that had replaced the span Max dove off as a boy. They both looked up reflexively, as if they expected to see the bridgetender up there shaking his fist. The Sea Ray negotiated the broad expanse of Port Everglades. An armada of giant ocean liners was moored there. Floating cities. Population approximately fifty thousand. Departure day. Smoke wafting from stacks. Decks lined with passengers.

A short distance past the port Brady steered left into a secluded tributary. Delray looked at him uncertainly. The water felt as familiar as the words to an old song. His eyes feasted on the snakelike ribbon. His lungs devoured its briny perfume. Warm memories washed over him. Water skiing. Mango wars. Rope swings. First kisses. Yet, the ambrosial recollections were quickly swamped by grim and threatful visions. Duke and Buck. The yellow Donzi. Ghastly faces. He hadn't been back since the day he found them and his eyes mechanically searched for the Donzi. About halfway down the deserted creek, Delray pointed to a seagrape tree on the east bank.

"Is that it, Max? Is that our spot?"

He didn't respond. He swung to port and beached the Sea Ray. A salty breeze was rolling in over the dune ridge and rustling through the tall pines. Delray sat in the passenger's seat watching him. He could see fear in her eyes. She spoke in scarcely a whisper.

"Why did you bring me here?"

He considered the question, not sure of the answer. Something had drawn him back. Maybe a need to return to the spot where it all began. The creek had spawned so much pain. So many nightmares. So many secrets. Now they were forcing their way to the surface like drowning victims after a spring thaw. The past had no place left to hide.

He looked her in the eyes and spoke in a flat tone bereft of cordiality.

"I need to tell you what's going to happen. You heard Register. Tomorrow the grand jury is going to indict you on one count of first degree murder. Possibly two. Register wants to be the next chief of police. He'll try to milk this for all the attention he can get. I don't want you paraded in handcuffs like a common criminal for an army of cameras. I will go with you to turn yourself in. You'll be booked into the Broward County Jail. All your possessions – jewelry, clothing, shoes, belt – will be inventoried and confiscated. They'll give you a disinfectant shower and an orange jumpsuit. You'll be fingerprinted and have your mug shot taken. Look as neutral as possible. Don't cry or scowl. That's the photograph the press will receive and the world will see. You'll be informed of the charges against you and then asked a series of questions. Are you ill or injured? Are you suicidal? You will be denied bail. That's standard in capital cases."

"What does that mean, Max?"

"It means you'll be incarcerated until your trial is over. You'll be vindicated in the end. I promise you. But it will take months. You need to be prepared for that."

Delray listened dry-eyed, betraying no outward emotion. Her blonde head was framed in a halo of yellow light. She was beautiful. Almost angelic. Despite everything Captain Register had said,

Brady could not accept it was the face of a killer. She lapsed into a meditative silence for several minutes before speaking again.

"I can't believe this is happening, Max. Why are they doing this to me? What am I going to do?"

"*We*, Del. What are *we* going to do? I'll be with you every step of the way. *We* are going to prove your innocence."

Delray swooned in the seat and then, without a word, removed her shoes and climbed over the Sea Ray's gunwale and jumped down onto the sand.

"Where are you going?"

She looked back at him with a melancholy smile. "That's a lot of information for a girl to digest. I need some time to think."

With that she scaled the dune bank and disappeared in the direction of the ocean.

Et Tu Brady

Chapter Sixty-Eight

BRADY LET DELRAY go. The days and months ahead were going to be torturous. Perhaps unbearable. He wondered if she was strong enough to withstand what was to come. And whether he was really capable of saving her.

Weariness descended on him. Three days of sleep deprivation had taken its toll. He closed his eyes and let the afternoon sun warm him like an open hearth. Within seconds he felt himself start to nod off. He needed something to stimulate his senses.

He stood and stretched and looked up and down the creek. Delray was nowhere in sight. He noticed the bank was still lined with seagrape trees. He hopped out of the boat. It took him ten minutes to find it. Their initials were still in the trunk. Weathered yellow pulp against brown bark. *MB + DC* surrounded by the crude outline of a heart. The night he carved the inscription he'd been a boy with an unblemished soul. Lovesick. Lighthearted. Deliriously happy. Within twenty four hours his life and the lives of his family and friends changed forever.

He wished he could go back in time. He gazed across the creek and wished the yellow Donzi had stopped a hundred yards short of where it did, or a hundred yards further on. He wished he'd remained hidden in the shadows, kissing Delray. He wished he hadn't followed Duke and Buck. He wished he hadn't returned and found the women's bodies.

Fatigue struck again and he felt like closing his eyes. Little wonder. It was exhausting being buried beneath so many layers of time. Three days since Ben Chance was murdered. Twenty nine years since *that night*. More than three hundred years since Michael Fury and Princess Nitcrosis may have walked along this very shore.

Brady shucked his T-shirt and dove into Whiskey Creek. The February water was chilly. It felt good. He was awake again. He waded for a time, his eyes drinking in his childhood playground. Trying to remember the golden days. Then he sank beneath the surface and swam in long potent strokes to the opposite side and pulled himself up the bank onto the mangrove island.

The undergrowth was denser than he remembered. Brady gingerly negotiated the brush. The ground no longer felt familiar to his feet. Maybe because his soles were no longer hard as leather. He picked his way through briars and over roots and sharp sticks to the center of the island. He felt close. He picked out three tall cypress trees about one hundred feet apart that formed a triangle and began a slow orbit around their perimeter, tapering his trajectory with each revolution. It took several circuits before he came upon a patch between a mango tree and a buttonwood. He stopped and stooped.

"Can this be it?"

He tried to revivify recollections buried beneath the sediment of time. He could see through an opening in the trees. Port Everglades was straight across the Intracoastal Waterway. Beyond it were four tall red-and-white striped smokestacks, the same Florida Power & Light chimneys he remembered seeing that day. He closed his eyes and smelled the air and was transported back in time. Back to that morning. The flinty sky. The chill rain. Wind moaning through the trees. Bare fingers clawing soft earth. Touching canvas. Yellow nylon rope. Ghastly frozen faces. The whirr of the Donzi. The hairsbreadth escape. Was this it? Was this the burial site? Was this the place where everything changed?

For young Max, the shock didn't set in right away. The adrenalin gushing through him had overpowered all other emotion. Barely out-swimming Duke in the creek. Buck flying out of the mangrove. Smashing him with the bait bucket. Leaving them in his wake. Raising fingers. Exultant. Cocky. Foolish.

He knew they would come for him again and spent the rest of that morning hiding in the intricate labyrinth of canals that crisscrossed Fort Lauderdale. He needed to lay low. Stay out of sight. Find time to think. Eventually he found himself on Middle River. Foreign water. Middle River was the money side of town. Coral Ridge, Bayview, Victoria Park. He was a New River kid. Many of his friends had boats, but none were rich. Their base was a narrow spit of white sand called Ski Beach that backed up to a dark, spooky wood. Middle River kids had George English Park, a pleasant, grassy sanctuary just off the Intracoastal. The park had a ski jump. He beached the Whaler and watched skiers take on the ramp. Some were good, flying through the air sixty, eighty, a hundred feet. But most crashed. The wipe-outs were spectacular. Some so gruesome Max wondered if the kids here harbored a secret death wish.

He knew he should ask himself the same question. It dawned on him that he was engaged in his own crazy death dance. He felt like a prisoner in a horrifying House of Mirrors. Oblivion stared at him everywhere he turned. Diving from the bridge. Fending off the shark. Buck running him down, first in a boat, then a car. The narrow escape at Whiskey Creek. Five near-death experiences in three days. His cat lives were getting used up way too fast. At this rate, his odds of reaching the ripe old age of fourteen were somewhere between zero and zilch. The most shocking part, though, was the exhilaration. He felt indestructible. Like he was playing a game he couldn't lose.

After a while all the thinking made him hungry. He left the Whaler at the park, crossed Sunrise Boulevard, and walked to the Gateway Center. Esposito's made the best pizza in town. He had a dollar in his pocket, enough for two slices of mushroom, a Coca Cola, and a quarter back in change. The food calmed him and he contemplated what to do next. Grandpa Zack always told him that every problem has a solution. He needed to find one now. His instinct was to call Uncle Howard and tell him to send the police to Whiskey Creek. But he knew the corpses would be gone. He considered calling his grandparents, then decided against it. He didn't want to scare them. Instead, he spent his last quarter on a third slice and did nothing.

Even though the rain had stopped the day remained ominous. He returned to the park and stretched out on the grass beneath a date palm and watched the ski jumpers again. The last thing he remembered was a flock of small green parrots chittering in the fronds above him. When he woke up the birds were gone. So were the skiers. The park was deserted and the summer sky was morphing into pinks and purples and dark blues. He estimated it was after seven o'clock.

The tide had receded and the Boston Whaler was half-in-and-half-out of the water. He had to push with all his might to float the boat. He fired the Evinrude and navigated to the Intracoastal then south to the mouth of New River. By the time he coasted up to the dock behind the Chance home day was dying like the last strains of a symphony. Ben and Delray came outside and met him.

"I have something to tell you guys," he said.

"Guys?" said Delray.

A silver smile broke out on her face. Max's remained dark. He stepped close between them and spoke in a covert voice.

"They're dead."

Ben and Delray stared at him with vacant eyes.

"Who's dead?" she said.

"What we saw last night. Those men in the boat. The rolls they unloaded. They were the bodies of two women. They were burying them."

The Chance twins watched him, still as salt pillars.

"How do you know?" Ben said.

He told them about Buck trying to run him down.

"He knew I had a paper route and right where to find me."

"Junior fucking Ball," said Ben.

"You might be right."

"I am right. That bastard."

He told them about going back to Whiskey Creek and digging up the bodies. They remembered the red-haired woman. He described narrowly escaping from Duke and Buck. Delray threw her arms around his neck.

"You could have been killed. If anything happened to you I'd die."

He felt a hot tear drip onto his neck and wrapped his arms around her.

"Nothing bad is gonna happen to me. Or you. I won't let it. I promise."

Delray turned her face up and kissed him. He tasted the salt of her tears. Then a jolt of electricity shot through him. Something was flicking his lips. Her tongue. He wasn't sure what to do. She thrust again. He parted his lips and received her. Soft. Warm. Probing. His heart was beating like a bass drum. He savored the taste of her. She was sweeter than peppermint ice cream. Things *were* moving fast. Yesterday their first kiss. Today their first French kiss. His mind reeled at what tomorrow might bring. But there were still things to do today. With herculean effort, he pulled away from her.

"I have to go home. I need to tell my grandparents what happened."

Ben was leaning against a dock piling, arms folded, his face painted in a bored expression.

"Tell them what? That you kissed a girl?"

"No, dummy. About the dead women. And Duke and Buck"

"You're not going anywhere without us," Delray said.

She kissed him with open mouth again, long and deep. Ben rolled his eyes.

Something distracted Brady from his remembrances. He looked up and realized it was late afternoon. He was still sitting on the fallen tree beside the spot which may or may not have once been the grave of two women. He listened and heard a splashing noise. He got up and made his way back through the mangrove to Whiskey Creek. He searched the water for some time before he found the source.

Someone was in the water. Swimming toward him. It took several seconds to sink in that it was Delray.

She crawled out of the water and scaled the bank and stood breathless before him wearing nothing but a smile. Her lips were blue and trembling and her skin was covered with gooseflesh. Before he could react she threw her arms around him and crushed his mouth with hers. Then she broke away and looked up with fevered eyes. *Crazy eyes.*

"Take me, Max. Before they lock me up. This is where our love was meant to be consummated. Take me. Right here. Right now."

Et Tu Brady

Chapter Sixty-Nine

JUNIOR BALL RUBBED a circle on the steamy bathroom mirror and examined his naked reflection, like Narcissus preening over a pond. Junior was not a man burdened by excessive soul-searching. He did like to keep tabs on his physique, though. What he saw did not please him. Perhaps because it was so fuzzy. He wasn't wearing his contact lenses and had to squint. It didn't improve the view. He had a golfer's tan. Face and forearms chocolate brown, upper arms and torso milky white. It seemed like just yesterday he'd been a splendid specimen of manhood. Tall and sinewy with a libido that never quit. He was still tall and randy. In the past couple of years, however, a hillock had developed around his equator that was fast maturing into a promontory. The wages, he knew, of a hedonistic lifestyle.

Junior sucked in the paunch, but could only hold the pose a few seconds. He vowed to cut down on the pasta and cream sauces at Martarano's. And the Cinnabon sweet rolls at breakfast. And the vodka martinis garnished with bleu cheese olives. He'd switch to gin and jalapeño olives. Only half the calories. If that didn't do the trick he might have to resort to doing sit-ups. Join a gym. Maybe that bitch commissioner's place. Walter Dean said she was gorgeous.

The thought made him smile. His new smile. He'd been working on it in the mirror for weeks. The one without the lip curl. More than one woman had told him that it made him look morally corrupt. Not that he wasn't. He just didn't want to advertise. He'd modeled his new smile after Donald Trump's. Top lip straight, drawn up over white teeth, eyes mere slits, crow's feet crinkling to their best effect. Guaranteed to make women weak at the knees. He planned to break it out for a test run tonight.

He brushed his hair forward, swooped it back, and applied lots of hairspray. Perfect. Had it been orange instead of black, people would surely mistake him for The Donald. What had Marla Maples said about his idol? *"Best sex ever."* He wouldn't mind hearing that line once or twice. He was admiring the face staring back at him when the doorbell rang downstairs.

Betty Jane Marshall was scheduled to arrive at eight. He checked his watch. Five minutes early. She was eager. Just the way he liked his women. Junior Ball – Conquering Male. It didn't matter that he paid for his female companionship these days. That just made good fiscal sense. He did the arithmetic after his divorce. Paid sex with a prostitute, he calculated, cost far less than free sex with a wife – at least if the wife was Ginger. He could rent the services of two or three new playmates every week for way less than she had cost him. Fresh young flesh. No alterations. No preservatives. And the anonymous promiscuity was priceless. Pay for a strumpet and, afterwards, forget her like a dream. Alimony was a nightmare that never ended.

Betty Jane had called him that afternoon to say she'd seen him on television outside the beach bar. After updating her on the case he mentioned that Dismas said she worked for an escort service.

"Yes," she said without hesitation. Bold, brazen, no trace of shame. He liked that.

"Do you take plastic?"

"Sure, but if it's American Express I gotta tack on an extra five percent."

The only sticking point was Dismas. He was Junior's primary recruiter. He haunted half the emergency rooms in Broward County hunting for clients. When that didn't work there were the deadbeats at his trailer park who were always willing to suffer a little pain for a payday. Dismas generated a lot of business. Junior did not want to risk losing his services. He considered the matter for somewhere between five and ten seconds before deciding. They made a date for eight. Now she was here early. Eager. Ready. He looked down and saw that he was ready too. He decided to greet her just the way he was.

The doorbell rang again. He took a deep breath, sucked in his tummy, and was halfway down the staircase when he heard the front door opening. He stopped and leaned back against the banister where the light was most flattering and switched on his new smile. When the door opened he was standing with hands on hips and his manhood on full display. A ten-point stag ready to rut. She walked in. Her face was blurry but there was no mistaking the slim young figure. Then a voice cried out.

"Oh, my God!"

Junior's golf tan fell off his face.

"Elizabeth?"

"You swine."

He made a fig leaf with his fingers.

"What are you doing here?"

She made a blindfold with her palms.

"No wonder mom divorced you! You are so disgusting!"

Junior turned and sprinted back up the staircase.

Et Tu Brady

Chapter Seventy

DEMONIKA HAD EXPECTED her father to be out with one of his trollops for the evening. She squeezed her eyes tight and tried to force the sight she'd just seen from her brain. There was no time to spare.

Less than twenty-four hours had passed since the big, brutal bald man broke in and beat Lazarus then left her violated and distraught. Distraught not so much because he raped her. That was over and done so fast she barely noticed. Lazarus – writhing in pain on the floor – didn't realize a thing, and she didn't tell him. The worst part was that the guy was so creepy. He reminded her of Uncle Fester from *The Addams Family* reruns. Gomez wouldn't have been so bad. A threesome with Gomez and Morticia might actually have been kinky fun. But fat old Fester grunting twice in her ear and leaving her face down on the bed with her panties around her ankles was going to be as impossible to erase from her memory bank as the image of her father posing on the staircase with a raging boner.

But Demonika's real agony was the ninety six thousand dollars they stole from Nudey Judy's house. Fester stole it back and killed their plans to split town for San Francisco. After she tended to Lazarus's bruised and battered ribs, they brainstormed.

"What if we go back and take it again?" Lazarus said.

They pondered the prospect and decided Judy would know it was them. Neither relished the thought of another visit from Uncle Fester. They kept thinking. Lazarus's fang and tattoo business was never going to make that kind of money. Nor was her cat and dog rental scam.

"I've got it," Demonika said finally.

After her father fled up the staircase, she moved into action. She hadn't been inside his house for months. The sight made her nauseous. Demonika hated her mother, but at least Ginger had a sense of style. Junior's house was a patchwork of what could only be described as vulgarian. From its *Gone With The Wind* staircase – Rhett Butler would never have greeted Bonnie Blue like that! – to its *Beverly Hillbillies* Fancy Eatin' Parlor, to its Louisiana whorehouse living room adorned in garish reds and purples, baroque furniture, and nude paintings. Designed to make his floozies feel at home, she guessed. Or maybe one of them had done the decorating.

The object of her desire was inside an ornate gold frame hanging on the wall above the fireplace. The rectangular gold name plate said: *Grover 100*. The *artwork* consisted of one hundred portraits of Grover Cleveland, the 22nd *and* 24th President of the United States. Grave and mustachioed, Grover's face graced the front of the one thousand dollar bill. Her father had seen a photograph in a men's magazine of a piece just like it and had an exact replica made – with genuine one thousand dollar bills. Daddy didn't know much about art, but he knew cold cash. Plus, his bimbos wouldn't have to strain to figure out his masterpiece was worth one hundred thousand dollars.

Demonika pushed a purple brocade bolster to the fireplace, stepped up, and removed the frame from the wall. She layed it on the floor and stomped the glass until it was shattered into bits, then dumped the shards and began peeling off the bills.

She stuffed the cash into a black canvas tote bag and ran for the door, desperate to make her getaway before her father returned. She never wanted to see him again. Ever. She jerked open the door and gasped.

468

A woman was standing there, her finger poised to push the doorbell. She was wearing a little black dress. She was thin, attractive, and youngish, although something about her eyes seemed old.

"You must be Mr. Ball's *next* date," Demonika said. "He's all warmed up. You'll find him upstairs."

Demonika rushed past the startled woman. A taxicab was backing out of the driveway. She ran down the street to the corner where she'd parked her lime green Honda Civic. She opened the door and threw the black bag inside and was about to follow when she noticed a white cargo van parked across the street. A shadowy figure was sitting behind the wheel. She saw the red ember of a burning cigarette, but couldn't make out the face behind it. A chill stole through her. *Fester?*

Et Tu Brady

Chapter Seventy-One

DISMAS BENVENUTI SAT in his van sucking on a Winston, wondering about the girl who just rushed out of Junior's house and sped off. A tortured expression wracked his face, like a man giving birth. But his thoughts were on death.

On the floor beside him lay his shotgun. A Stoeger twenty gauge side-by-side double barrel with a matte black finish and hardwood stock. He reached down and caressed its cold steel. Three inch shells were already chambered. One for his dogshit boss. The other for the woman he loved. Both of them in the big house together right now acting like a couple of animals. Not caring that they were tearing his heart out. Treating him like he was lower than dirt.

Yet, even as he fantasized about blowing them to smithereens, he knew he would never do it. He was a liar. And a con artist. And a thief. Hell, he'd been named after a thief. At least Dismas, though, was a Good Thief. Dismas Benvenuti was a lot of things, but he wasn't a cold-blooded killer. He had to do something. Murder, however, was not an option.

Like his great ancestor Billy Bowlegs, Dismas was a Seminole warrior. *What would Billy do?* He sat there smoking in the dark and thought about it. Three Winston's later he made a decision. Before the night was over he would prove to Betty Jane Marshall he was worthy of her love. He'd get that Seminole cash. He'd buy her a diamond ring. And a doublewide. And win her for all time.

Et Tu Brady

Chapter Seventy-Two

ROSE WORKED LATE in her office at City Hall. Scouring reams of bone-dry budget reports. Looking for places to slash spending. Trying to spill as little blood as possible. The city was staring into the abyss. She had no appetite for raising taxes on cash-strapped homeowners. Or for laying-off municipal workers and adding to the bloated ranks of the unemployed. But the city was on economic life support. She and her colleagues had to sharpen their scalpels and cut – hopefully without piercing any major arteries.

A hiring freeze was a given. So was a suspension in pay raises for city employees. Overtime would have to be reduced or eliminated – except for city commissioners, who didn't get any. Dozens of upper-and-mid level managers making six figure salaries were going to have to take pay cuts. Some might be encouraged to retire. At least one might leave in handcuffs. She thought of Walter Dean. The already paltry funding for libraries, museums, the Historical Commission, and other non-critical services would take hits. But she would fight to preserve essential programs like feeding children and the aged.

"This is not why I got into government," Rose said to herself.

She'd had enough. All she wanted to do now was find Brady. She wondered if he was still at the Sea Shanty. She ached to hear his voice. Wrap herself in his arms. Spirit him off to her rooftop greenhouse. She still felt awful about exploding at him yesterday. She realized now Delray Cross had initiated the kissing and hand holding. His crime was being too considerate to rebuff her. She was happy they'd patched things up at the police department ceremony. She decided to drive straight to the beach, drag Brady upstairs, and make him forget about Delray Cross amidst the perfume and butterflies of her magic garden.

She pushed the budget reports to the corner of her desk, did a quick scan of her e-mails, answered a couple, then turned out the lights and locked her office door. City Hall was deserted. Manny Gutierrez was at the night security desk watching a TV show on his new iPad. He got up and unlocked the door for her.

"Want me to walk you to your car, commissioner?"

"Thanks, Manny, but I'm a big girl. Have a good night."

The public parking lot was a fenced enclosure directly across Andrews Avenue. A ten story building loomed just beyond. Square lighted windows glowed from its east wall like a giant yellow checkerboard. Rose jaywalked across Andrews. The lot had been crowded when she parked her blue Miata hours ago. Now it was the lone car left. Three slots from the southwest corner. Ten yards from a large ficus tree.

Rose pulled out her keys. She was still thinking about Brady. If traffic wasn't too crazy, she'd be in his arms in ten minutes.

Et Tu Brady

Chapter Seventy-Three

HIDDEN IN THE dense shadow of the ficus, a hulking figure watched her approach. He was wearing a dark suit. A cigarette dangled from the corner of his mouth. Smoke curled up the sides of his pinched face. His left hand twitched. It was clutching a .22 caliber Ruger Mark III automatic pistol equipped with a silencer he built himself. Six inches of perforated aluminum pipe stuffed with steel wool attached to the barrel by three blunthead screws.

He had concocted a simple, ruthless plan. He would attack as she opened her car door. Walk up with the Ruger at his side. When she turned toward him he would raise the weapon and fire once at the center of her chest. A second shot to her forehead. Then a third tap to the chest. *Phffft-phffft-phffft!* Swift and clean. No emotion. No relish. No pity. No regret. Human life meant less to him than it did to a hangman on a scaffold. This was a job. No more. No less. He checked his breathing and pulse rate. Both were steady and slow.

She was ten feet from the little blue sports car when he stepped from the shadows. She saw him and stopped in her tracks. He took three steps toward her. She looked like she wanted to run, but she'd turned to ice. Before he could raise the pistol, though, a white van squealed into the parking lot and screeched to a halt at the Miata's back bumper. A man jumped out. He was clad in black and wore a ski mask.

She held her car key out like a weapon and backed away, her eyes shifting between the two men, not seeming to know which to defend against.

"Who are you?" she shouted at the masked man. "What do you want?"

He said nothing and didn't look at the other man. He lifted his arm, pointed a gun at her, and pulled the trigger. Wires shot out and struck her chest. The hulking figure watched her body stiffen. She began to shake. He knew what she was feeling. He'd been tazed many times. Fifty thousand volts were shooting through her body in five seconds intervals. Her skin felt like it was being stabbed by a million tiny needles. Every muscle was cramping. She couldn't breathe. Temporary paralysis was setting in. She would collapse any second.

He saw her legs give and watched the man in black rush in and catch her before she hit the ground. He opened the van's side door, lifted her inside, and climbed in behind her. Three seconds later they sped off. The big man took a drag on his cigarette and stepped back. He was swallowed by the shadows without having raised his gun.

Et Tu Brady

Chapter Seventy-Four

"THEY BRAINS AIN'T no bigger'n yer pinky finger," Dismas explained to Jimmy Jonas. "If we cain't outsmart one of 'em, what's that say 'bout us?"

They were in Dismas' aluminum flatbottom john boat puttering down a black canal on the eastern edge of the Everglades. The night was eerie and still. Dark clouds shrouded a crescent moon. The only sound was the low rumble of the twelve horsepower engine Dismas was steering from the stern. He was wearing a yellow hardhat with a flashlight taped to the top. A flood control levee was to their left. A sawgrass thicket covered the right bank. Jimmy was sitting on the bow.

"I don't like it here, Diz," he said. "Me with a busted arm. What am I supposed to do if we snag a big one?"

"Don't worry, Jimmy. Who got you that five thousand dollars?"

"What five thousand? You *said* I was gonna get five grand. I ain't seen it yet." He held up his cast-encased left arm. "All I got so far's this."

"Don't I take care of you?"

"I sure hope you take better care a me than you took of Devo."

"Shut up, Jimmy. The creatures is gonna hear ya."

It had been two hours since Dismas rushed from Junior Ball's house in a rage, his mind filled with visions of B.J. and Junior thrashing in bed. Hating him. Hating her. Hating himself. The time had arrived to prove to B.J. once and for all that he was deserving of her. Dismas vowed that tonight he would fulfill his destiny and become a Seminole warrior. He'd collect that Hard Rock casino money. He'd buy a new home for B.J. and her son Kenny. And she could quit being a whore.

He had rushed back to the Cloud Nine Trailer Park. Jimmy hadn't yet fallen into his nightly drug and/or alcohol induced stupor. They hitched his boat trailer to the van and drove west on Interstate 595 and then onto I-75 until they reached the edge of the River of Grass. They put in at a gravel ramp off Highway 27 and had been trolling for about an hour. Dismas raked his headlamp across the ebon water.

"Remember one thing, Jimmy," he said. "Gators only think about two things. Eatin' and survivin'. They's pretty dang good at both cause they been around since the dragons roamed Earth." He reached back and flipped a switch and the little motor went dead. "Looky! There's one. By the bank on the right?"

"I don't see nothin' 'cept two little red lights."

"That's him." Dismas switched the headlamp off-and-on. The red lights didn't move. "That's eye-shine. They got crazy eyes. Look at him floatin' there like a log. Just watchin' us. What's he thinkin' with that pinky brain?"

"How do ya know it's a he?"

Dismas rolled his eyes. He doubted Jimmy's brain was much bigger than a pinky finger. He stood and lifted a long metal pole from the floor, lowered it into the water, and began pushing the boat like a gondolier.

"Listen to me, Jimmy. We're gonna catch that feller, but ya gotta do what I say. Cause I guarantee ya he's gonna put up a fight."

"Jeez, I don't know, Diz."

"There's gonna be money in it fer ya, Jimmy."

"You said that about my arm."

"You'll get yer busted arm money. And when I'm done with the gator, you can have all the money from it. Gator hide's more valuable than mink. Gucci'll pay fifty bucks a foot to make them handbags and shoes and such. I bet you clear a thousand dollars easy just on the skin alone. Gator meat fetches fifteen bucks a pound down in Miami. Cubans love the shit. If he's big enough, you might get a few hundred pounds worth."

"Yer gonna give me all of it?"

"Soon as I get done showin' Billy Panther."

"Who's Billy Panther?"

Dismas kept pushing the pole in the water. They glided toward the red lights. The lights didn't move.

"Billy's my sponsor on the Seminole Tribal Council. He's seen my paperwork. Made me draw up a family tree an everything. Had to get a copy of my grandma's birth certificate. And my great grandma's."

"Did ya hire one of them gynecologists?"

Dismas nearly broke out laughing, but caught himself in time. He didn't want to scare the gator.

"You musta fell on yer head when you was a baby, Jimmy. A gynecologist's a vulva doctor."

"Vulva?"

"Ya know. Remember when you busted yer arm. That's the ulna. Vulva's the female privates. Yer talkin' 'bout geriologist, people who study family histories. I did it myself. Went to that big library downtown. You cain't believe all the books. I showed Billy how I'm rescinded from Billy Bowlegs, just like grandma always told me."

"Is all Indians named Billy?"

"Ever hear a Geronimo?" Dismas pushed. The red lights were getting larger. "Anyways, when Billy saw my paperwork he said he believed me. He said I'm real Seminole. He's gonna sponsor me to join the tribe. But first I gotta pass some tests. This is the big one. Catchin' a gator."

"Then ya get that casino money?'

"Sure. Now when I snag him keep yer hands away from his jaws. And don't stand up, else yer gonna end up in the water. That feller'll be sellin' yer meat to his pals 'stead a the other ways around."

Dismas layed the pole on the boat floor and picked up a fishing rod. A heavy-duty deep sea model rigged with forty-pound test line and a big three-pronged hook. He'd baited the hook with a smelly three-day-old chicken leg he'd saved from KFC. Extra crunchy. When the flatboat was ten feet from the reptile he stretched the rod out over the water and dangled the chicken leg just above the alligator's nose. For the longest time the creature didn't budge.

"Maybe he don't like chicken, Diz."

"Gators love chicken. Course, they love dog more."

"We coulda brought the carcass a that black mutt that's been layin' behind the dumpster."

"Stinks too bad to touch. I come back smellin' like dead dog and B.J.'s surely gonna walk out on me."

"Not if ya get that injun money."

The gator exploded, launching itself from the water, jaws wide, big jagged teeth exposed. The sheer size of it paralyzed the two men. It snapped the bait mid-air. Dismas lost his balance and the flashlight beam danced wildly in the pitch. The beast landed with a tremendous splash, soaking Dismas and Jimmy. Dismas jerked the rod and felt the hook set. He cranked the reel and the alligator went berserk, thrashing violently, throwing sheets of black water on Jimmy at the bow. Then it was gone.

"He's runnin'." Dismas stood at the center of the boat, legs wide, rod bent at a sharp angle. He set the drag, trying to slam on the brakes. The gator wouldn't be stopped, but it would expend energy trying to escape. He strained to turn the spinner. "I got him snagged good. Now he's like one of them blue marlins."

"Holy shit, Diz." Jimmy's voice was laced with fear and awe. "That things bigger'n the boat."

"Looks like about twelve feet. That's gonna mean lotsa money fer ya, Jimmy. Now we're gonna play him like a big fish. Let him keep runnin'. Pretty soon he's gonna tire hisself out and come to the surface, like that shark in *Jaws*."

"Then what?"

"My shotgun's there on the floor. When the time comes I'm gonna pull him over close to the boat and get a gig in him. Then I'm gonna lower his head about six inches underwater."

"Underwater?"

"You stick the muzzle into the water. Put it right between his eyes and pull the trigger. It's double barrel, so pull the right trigger first. If we need another shot, fire the left barrel."

"How come underwater?"

"Ain't so loud. Plus, you don't get sprayed with bone and blood and shit. Just make sure you don't shoot him on top of the head. They's skulls is hard as Sherman tanks. Blast'll bounce right off."

"Shit!" Jimmy said, sounding overwhelmed by the responsibility Dismas had assigned him.

For the next hour they battled the prehistoric creature. Reeling him close. The bull gator surging away. Back-and-forth. In-and-out of the light beam. Dismas felt the animal's primal power. He imagined its big black armored tail swinging furiously beneath the surface, propelling it like a powerful engine. It's sharp claws digging into the shallow canal bottom. It's puny brain doing what it had been programmed to do for a million years. Survive to eat again. Maybe try to eat him and Jimmy. Dismas wasn't going to let that happen. Not this night. He finally felt the monster's strength ebb.

"Here he comes, Jimmy. Remember what I said. Shoot him 'tween the eyes."

They were about twenty feet from a dense stand of sawgrass lining the bank opposite the levee. Dismas wanted to keep the gator from reaching the weeds where it could tangle itself in the reeds. They'd never get him out. And it might sever the line.

The creature broke the surface again, thrashing, but without the same resolve. Dismas kept reeling until it was five feet from the boat. He snatched a hard-toothed rake off the floor. Holding the fish pole in one hand, he leaned out and hooked the rake over the gator's midsection and pulled. It erupted again. Snapping its razor teeth. Whipping its muscular black tail. Flinging spray and vegetation on both men. Desperate to break free, it went into a final death roll. Dismas held tight and rode out the storm, determined to prove he was worthy of being a Seminole warrior. He'd prove it to Billy Panther. He'd prove it to Betty Jane Marshall. Most of all, he'd prove it to himself. The alligator finally stopped resisting.

"Okay, Jimmy, here we go. Switch off the safety on that shotgun and get ready."

Dismas dropped the rake and picked up an eight foot gaff with a sharp-tipped hook at the end. He leaned over and hooked the soft underside of the reptile's long snout and pulled it to the side of the flatboat. Jimmy stood up and aimed the gun.

"Not yet," Dismas said. "Wait till I got his head underwater."

But the gator flared again. Jimmy flinched like he'd been splattered with hot bacon grease and the shotgun went off. The blast hit the top of the creature's head. Bone fragments and bloody flesh flew like shrapnel. Jimmy dropped the gun and it discharged again. The explosion was deafening. He lost his balance and fell backwards out of the boat.

"Goddamn you, Jimmy," screamed Dismas. "Ain't you got no nothin'?"

The gator kept whipping the water. Dismas clutched the fishing pole in one hand and the gaff in the other while Jimmy flailed in the canal ten feet from the boat.

"Help, Diz, I cain't swim."

"Quit screaming, ya fool. Put yer feet down. It ain't but five feet deep. Get yerself over to that bank and I'll come git ya when I'm done."

Jimmy did as he was told and slogged toward the sawgrass, a human head drifting like a soccer ball on top of the water. Dismas cackled.

"Ya better hurry up before this feller's daddy comes alookin' fer him."

He dropped the gaff and reached down for the shotgun. He wedged the gun in the crook of his arm and snapped open the hinged barrel. He fished a 20-guage shell from his shirt pocket, jammed it into the right breech and cracked it shut again. He glanced at the canal's east bank. Jimmy was just reaching the sawgrass. The gator was placid again. Dismas lowered its head beneath the surface. He stuck the muzzle in the water, pressed it between the creature's eyes, and pulled the trigger. There was a muffled sound, more a thump than explosion, and the gator rolled over on its side and stopped moving.

Jimmy hollered from the bank. "Shit! This dang mud sucked my shoes right off my feet."

His eyes on the gator, Dismas yelled back. "I'll take ya down to Payless tomorrow and buy ya a new pair."

"Hurry up and come git me, Diz."

"Shut up, nitwit. I ain't gonna lose my hand cause you ain't got the brains of a dodo bird. Just cause this critters skull's been blown to bits don't mean it still ain't dangerous. If yer gonna be a Seminole ya gotta know when a gator's nerve system's still workin', even when it looks dead."

Dismas opened a gear box on the floor and retrieved a roll of black electrical tape. He lifted the animal's head out of the water and wound the adhesive around its snout ten times, fast, like a rodeo cowboy tying-down a roped calf. Then he reached into his boot and pulled out his ornate Indian-head dagger. He stabbed the blade through the tough hide at the back of the reptile's head and worked it between the vertebra. Using the palm of his hand, he pounded the hilt until the blade disappeared. Blood ran from the wound and the gator flinched. Its spine was severed. Now it was dead.

Dismas fell back on his haunches. Sweating. Exhausted. Triumphant. He'd done it. He'd completed his Rite of Passage. The U.S. Marines call it Baptism by Fire. Australian Aborigines call it a Walkabout. Christians call it Confirmation. Jews call it Bar Mitzvah. Some Native Americans call it Vision Quest. His great Seminole ancestor, Billy Bowlegs, drank a Black Drink to purify his body and spirit. Dismas had just imbibed his Black Drink. He was finally a man. A warrior. He'd proven himself worthy. To Billy Panther. To Betty Jane Marshall. To himself. Now his life would change forever.

He looked over at the bank. The sawgrass was rustling. Jimmy was cursing as he sloshed toward dry land.

483

Dismas shouted. "I got him, Jimmy. Let me tie him up. Lash him to the boat. Then I'll come git ya."

Jimmy screamed. It was the most hair-raising scream Dismas had ever heard. Like Jimmy's balls were being cut off with a dull knife. Dismas's blood ran cold.

"Jimmy? What happened? What's wrong?"

The caterwauling grew more high-pitched, more horrific. Frantic, Dismas wrapped a rope around the gator's right front paw and another around its torso and lashed it to the boat, belly facing outward. Jimmy's hideous shrieks continued. *What the hell's happenin'?* Dismas thought, terrified.

"I'm comin', Jimmy."

He reached for the engine rope and was about to crank when the screeching stopped.

"Jimmy? You okay?"

Nothing now. Complete silence. Dismas yanked the rope and pointed the boat toward to the sawgrass.

"I'm here, Jimmy!" he shouted. "Where are ya, Jimmy?"

Still nothing. He steered the blunt-nosed bow into the curtain of cattails and twisted the hand throttle. The boat pushed through. Beyond the tall grass there was several feet of open black water, then the canal bank. Dismas shined his flashlight up and down the bank several times before he stopped and inhaled sharply.

A giant Burmese python was curled up on the embankment. It was at least twenty feet long, maybe thirty, and as big around as a telephone pole. The Everglades was infested with the giant snakes, a product of exotic pet owners dumping them in the swamp. Since they were first discovered in the 1990s the estimated population had grown to two hundred thousand. The snakes were devastating native species, gobbling up everything from wrens and rodents to white-tailed deer. Dismas remembered seeing a photograph of a python that tore itself open swallowing a six foot alligator. The snake died with the gator's tail still sticking from its mouth. But, in his worst nightmare, Dismas never envisioned anything like this.

The serpent's long green body was coiled around Jimmy Jonas's torso. Jimmy wasn't moving anymore. The creature's reptilian jaws were hinged wide and had already swallowed Jimmy's head and shoulders. Now, inch by inch, it was slowly devouring the rest of him.

Et Tu Brady

Chapter Seventy-Five

GWENDOLYN DAILY ARRIVED for the graveyard shift at the Florida Fish & Wildlife Conservation Commission's Research Station in the Big Cypress Swamp. Daily was a short, round, thirtyish woman with dishwater brown hair and wire-rim glasses. She walked to the kitchen, put a turkey-and-avocado submarine sandwich in the refrigerator, and retreated to her laboratory.

A Fish & Wildlife biologist, Daily was the chief scientist on a project tracking the nocturnal migration patterns of the *alligator mississippiensis*. The American alligator had once been nearly extinct. After decades on the endangered list, though, its population had come back with a vengeance. Florida was now home to an estimated one-and-a-half million of the reptiles. Daily's job was to track their movement after the sun went down.

From the Florida Panhandle south to Florida Bay, FF&W had tagged about five hundred gators with Global Positioning Satellite transmitters. Daily kept a detailed chart on each of them, coming in every night and working until dawn. She didn't mind the hours. She was working on her doctorate at the University of Miami and the overnight shift allowed her to attend classes in Coral Gables during the daytime and sneak in a couple of hours of book study in the dead of night, on the state's dime.

Daily documented the locations of about two dozen gators a night. She typed each animal's GPS tracking number into her computer and the image of a state map popped onto the screen telling her the creature's exact whereabouts to within ten meters. She was studying her seventh or eighth alligator of the evening when she looked up at the screen and her jaw dropped. Daily watched with a practiced eye, then decided she must have made a dumb mistake. Another reason to be thankful she was alone. She cleared the screen and retyped the number. To her consternation the same image appeared.

"What the hell is going on?"

She picked up the telephone and dialed. A man answered.

"Florida Highway Patrol. Sgt. Longo."

"Hi, sergeant. This is Gwen Daily at Fish and Wildlife in Big Cypress."

"Hey, Gwen." Sgt. Longo sounded gratified to hear the genial voice of a fellow state worker. "Who'd you piss off?"

"What do you mean, sarge?"

"You must've pissed off somebody to be working dogwatch?"

"Actually, I happen to like these hours. But listen, I'm calling about something strange that's happening."

"Believe me, Gwen, you couldn't match some of the crazy stuff I hear. What's up?"

"I chart alligators that have been tagged with GPS monitors. At this very moment one of them is on Interstate 75."

Daily heard a low groan at the other end of the line.

"Damned thing must've crawled out of a canal," Longo said. "The chain link fence is supposed to keep them off the road. It must have found a hole and crawled under. Stupid critter's probably been run over. Surprised I ain't got a call before now. Give me a mile marker and I'll send a car."

"You don't understand, sergeant. This alligator hasn't been run over. It's moving. In fact it's traveling ninety miles per hour."

Et Tu Brady

Chapter Seventy-Six

THE SUPER BOWL Beach Bash was in full swing. Automobile traffic had been detoured off A1A and several thousand celebrants were packed shoulder-to-shoulder on the street and sidewalks and sand. Music was blaring everywhere. Alex Fox's flamenco guitar at Café del Mar. Slim & Sloppy playing rock at the Elbo Room. A gypsy quartet complete with belly dancers on the beach at Las Olas. On the sand opposite the Sea Shanty an anarchic heavy metal band was immolating the crowd with firebrand bedlam.

The party had passed the point of restraint. The night had become a pagan orgy of dance, music and libation – more *From Dusk Till Dawn* than *Where The Boys Are*. But that was Lauderdale Beach. Legend had it Ponce de Leon once took a break from his Fountain of Youth hunt to sip pina coladas and judge a wet T-shirt contest here.

The Sea Shanty was bursting at the seams. The place was a sea of laughing, chattering faces that filled the bar like floating balloons. John Mellencamp's *Authority Song* was blasting from the juke box while Brady and Gordy rushed non-stop to fill drink orders, working together as harmonious as synchronized swimmers. After three days of murder and mayhem, Brady welcomed the pandemonium.

The madness of his own existence had reached fever pitch a few hours earlier when Delray Cross emerged naked and glistening from Whiskey Creek, panting like an asthmatic, her eyes delirious, her face a portrait of animal lust.

"Take me," she had begged him. "This is where our love was meant to be consummated. I want you to take me. Right here. Right now."

Delray had come apart like the strands on an old wicker chair. She was so wanton. Brady had never felt such a clash between the erotic and the surreal. He thought she might have taken some kind of drug. More likely she was just plain crazy, finally pushed over the precipice. She pleaded and pawed. Trying to tear off his shorts. Until he grabbed her shoulders and shook her like a rag doll.

"Listen to me, Delray! We can't do this. Do you hear me? Whatever we had was a long time ago. It's over. I love Rose."

She knelt there in the dirt at the edge of the creek, blinking, gasping, her milk white breasts heaving. His words eventually sank in. Her face cracked and her body quaked and she crumbled face down on the ground. Brady fell to his knees and cradled her in his arms. He stroked her wet hair and let her weep. Whispering that everything would be okay. That he would never abandon her. That they were going to beat the murder charges. Finally she quieted and, in the time it took to flip a light switch, she slid from frenzy to a zombie-like state.

Brady sat her on the bank with her feet in the water and told her to stay put. He swam hard across the creek to the Sea Ray. When he returned Delray was listless and rubbery and he had to dress her the way one would dress a sleeping child. Then he lifted her into the boat. He navigated out of Whiskey Creek into the Intracoastal Waterway and headed toward Port Everglades.

The water was a beehive of activity. Fort Lauderdale had become the *Cruise Ship Capital of the World*. The port was the Times Square of the Seas. Some weekends one hundred thousand passengers sailed in and out. At the moment, more than a dozen giant luxury liners were in the process of shoving off from their berths and sailing into the Atlantic, most for weeklong voyages in the Caribbean.

A Coast Guard cutter sat at the mouth of the inlet, the center of chaos, its captain directing boats like a traffic cop. Brady got too close and an inflatable Coast Guard gunboat raced up to the Sea Ray. A young man in full battle dress armed with an automatic weapon was at the wheel. Another was holding a bullhorn. Behind them a female officer stood at a Browning M2 fifty caliber machine gun mounted on a revolving turret. She was aiming directly at Brady and didn't look like she was playing games. The guy lifted the bullhorn to his mouth.

"Halt immediately or you will be fired upon."

Brady pulled back the throttle and raised his arms in the air, signaling he was not a belligerent.

"Maintain your position until you get a signal to cross."

So they waited while the Allure of the Seas passed and headed toward the Atlantic. It was a breathtaking sight. The Allure was the largest ocean liner in the world. A floating metropolis. While it slowly nosed through the channel, Brady kept a close eye on Delray. Her face was going through changes faster than the color wheel on a Christmas display. Shame. Humiliation. Bewilderment. Resignation. Anger. Finally her blue eyes seemed bleached of energy. She grew still as a sleeping cat.

Brady docked the Sea Ray at Bahia Mar Marina behind the Bahia Cabana Hotel and escorted her across the street to the Yankee Clipper. She walked beside him, wordless, sphinxlike. Her suite was turned upside down. Ron Register and his team had torn the place apart and left without bothering to put it back together. The hotel hadn't either.

He layed Delray gently on the bed, as if she was a fragile piece of china. He covered her with a blanket and kissed her forehead. She stared up at him like a blind woman, her eyes vacant and devoid of emotion. Her face was immobile as a picture in a frame, like she'd fallen into a waking coma. He whispered.

"We'll get through this, Delray. Get a good night's sleep. I'll call you in the morning."

Hours later, even as he was engulfed in a maelstrom of sound and celebration, Brady could not shake the image. He was frightened for her. He blamed himself. With all the touching and kissing he should have seen it coming. His one consolation was he'd finally said what needed to be said. And proven his fidelity to Rose, even though it would be dicey explaining that to her. Especially the part about the beautiful, naked ex-girlfriend begging him to *take* her. Rose and Brady had vowed to keep no secrets from one another, but he decided to file this one under attorney-client privilege.

His problem now was how to save Delray from prison, or worse. One minute the puzzle pieces seemed to fit together in a coherent picture. The next instant he felt like he was trying to see through mud. Brady was adrift. He needed to regain his equilibrium. He'd constructed several theories of defense. Thus far, though, they'd each collapsed like houses of cards. At one point he thought Peanut might have murdered Ben – now Peanut was dead. Then Junior Ball – but even his childhood nemesis wasn't that stupid. Another contender was the Goth prince Lazarus. He did Latin tattoos. And looked like Duke Manyon's clone. But the connection was tenuous at best. Then there was Manyon himself, the pestilential phantom, lurking unseen. *Can he really be alive?* Brady knew that wasn't possible. But Ben and Peanut both believed he'd returned from the dead. Now they were dead. Even if they'd been right, even if Duke was alive, why would he come back and murder two people he hadn't seen in three decades? The gold? The dead strippers? And what about *Et Tu Brady*?

So, if Duke or Peanut or Junior or Lazarus didn't murder Ben, who did? Was it possible Delray was a psychopathic killer? Ron Register was convinced. And she was certainly acting bizarre. Regardless, he refused to believe she would kill her brother.

So many fragmented thoughts were bouncing around his brain. His skull felt like an atomic particle accelerator. He couldn't make heads nor tails of any of them.

Brady felt a vibration in his back pocket and fished out his cell phone. Ron Register's name was blinking on the screen. *Bad news.* He guessed Register was calling to tell him to where and when to deliver Delray tomorrow. He was in no mood to discuss that tonight and debated not answering. Then he pressed the talk button.

"Max, it's Ron Register." The homicide detective's voice sounded more conciliatory than usual. He took that as a good sign. "I'm afraid I've got troubling news."

He took that as a bad sign. "What else is new, Register?"

He was shouting over the music and the crowd and immediately regretted being so curt. A little good will might pay dividends for Delray down the line. Register's next words changed everything.

"Commissioner Becker has been kidnapped."

Time stood still. Brady felt his heart sink into his stomach. Then it bounced back up into his ribcage. Then it begin fluttering like a hummingbird. He was still behind the bar. The jukebox was booming and he was surrounded by a roomful of noisy, festive patrons.

"Hold on," he shouted. He pushed through the mob and rushed outside to the Sandbox, the open air sitting area outside the Sea Shanty. It had a beach sand floor, coral waterfall, coconut palms, and big twisty banyan tree wrapped in a garland of amber lights. "Talk to me, Ron."

"Commissioner Becker walked out of City Hall about thirty minutes ago. She crossed Andrews Avenue to the parking lot and was getting into her car. I'm told she drives a blue Miata?"

"What happened?"

Register told him what he knew. An ex-cop working the night security detail at City Hall was watching from the steps across the street. A white cargo van screeched up and blocked Rose's egress. A subject jumped from the van. The guard thought it was a man. It looked like he shot her with a stun gun and dragged her into the van. Gutierrez ran to help, but the van sped off before he got there. He didn't even get a tag number.

"Needless to say, Commission Becker's safety is our highest priority. We've put out an APB and have choppers in the air as we speak. The Broward Sheriff and Florida Highway Patrol are involved. The Florida Department of Law Enforcement is on the case too. The DMV is gathering a list of every white van registered in Broward County. And I've got two FBI agents in my office right now."

Brady felt like a small animal was crawling around inside his stomach. His head was in a tug-of-war between blind fury and outright panic. *Who would kidnap Rose?* He tried to force himself to think like a cop. He tried to pretend Register wasn't talking about the woman he loved.

"You got a description, captain? What did the kidnapper look like?"

"The guy – if it was a guy –was wearing black pants, a black shirt, and a ski mask, so Gutierrez, the guard, couldn't determine race. The van's windows were tinted. He couldn't see if there was a wheelman or anyone else in the vehicle."

This can't be happening, Brady told himself. He clamped his eyes shut, took a deep breath, and tried to gather his wits. *Think! Where could Rose be?* His mind was moving at full gallop. *Who would do this?* But he was drawing nothing but blanks.

"What else can you tell me?"

"I was hoping you could tell me something."

Brady told him Rose didn't have any enemies. Nobody from the gym. She'd never mentioned stalkers. He couldn't think of anyone at City Hall who would do something like this.

"It's possible," said Register, "that Commissioner Becker may have been in the wrong place at the wrong moment?"

That was the possibility that scared Brady most. Some random lunatic or anonymous predator was passing by and snatched her simply because the opportunity presented itself.

"We're working on it, Max. I'll call you when I have news."

The line went dead. Brady stood in the Sandbox for a long moment. Thousands of revelers surrounded him, dancing and rocking to ear-splitting music. He didn't see or hear a thing. Nothing but Rose whispering. *"Brady, where are you?"*

He knew one thing. He couldn't wait for the police. Her life was hanging in the balance. He had to act.

"I will find you, Rose," he said aloud.

He thought of his grandmother, Kate Brady. The one person in his life he had always been able to count on. *Please protect Rose, grandma.* She had never let him down. He hoped she heard him now. Just as he had heard her – that night.

Et Tu Brady

Chapter Seventy-Seven

YOUNG MAX'S INSTINCTS went on high alert the instant the Boston Whaler coasted into the lagoon behind Eden. He, Ben, and Delray had picked up Peanut at the Alligator Pit and cruised down New River to Zack and Kate Brady's. But something was wrong.

At this hour his grandmother should have been busy putting away the supper dishes. The kitchen was black, though, and the house was silent as a church. Max pushed open the back door and stepped inside. The white ceramic tiles felt cool against his naked soles. Normally when he missed dinner a warm plate would be waiting for him on the stove. Not tonight. There was no scent of food in the air.

The only illumination was coming from a swathe of light at the bottom of the door to the dining room. Max pushed with a finger and it yawned open. Muted sound was coming from a distant part of the house. It sounded like the television in his grandfather's den.

"Grandpa?" he called. "Grandma?"

No response.

"Maybe they went out to dinner," Delray said. "Do you see a note?"

Max flipped the light switch beside the door and scanned the kitchen. He shook his head. They slowly entered the darkened dining room, one after another, like four ducks in single file. Max turned on the light hanging over the long dark oak table. No sign of his grandparents. Rain thrummed against a windowpane. He shivered slightly. He felt like an actor in a scary movie. This was the moment the killer leaps from the shadows. They continued into the living room. He pulled the chain on a small lamp on an end table beside the couch. No sign of life there either. They followed the TV sounds into the den.

Zack and Kate Brady were sitting side-by-side on the couch with their backs to him. Max felt icewater in his veins. He circled around to the front of the couch. Their mouths were covered with strips of silver tape and their hands and ankles were bound. Grandma Kate's eyes were screaming at him.

"What the…"

Before he could finish the television clicked off and a voice came out of nowhere, sudden as a figment.

"Come on in, kids." Duke Manyon was sitting in grandpa's red leather winged-back reading chair in a darkened corner of the room. "Take a load off. If there's not enough space on the couch, sit on the floor by grandma and grandpa's feet."

Peanut was last in line and hadn't come into the room yet. He turned and started to dart toward the back door and crashed straight into Buck Foxx. Buck grabbed a fistful of curly red hair and dragged him into the den.

"Sit down, big boy," he said and shoved Peanut to the floor where Ben and Delray were already sitting.

Max silently cursed himself. Duke and Buck were deadly as Black Widow spiders. He'd led his friends and grandparents straight into their web. He looked down at Zack and Kate. They didn't seem to be injured, but grandpa was deathly pale and the light had gone out of his eyes. He looked old as Father Time. Grandma's white hair was a disheveled cobweb, but her blue eyes were alert and calculating.

"Untie them," Max demanded.

"Shut up, punk," Buck said. "Sit down before I knock you down."

He slapped the back of Max's head hard with an open palm. The blow propelled him forward. He tripped over a foot bolster and fell to the floor. Kate Brady let out a muted cry from behind the tape. Max looked up. Duke was standing over him, a pistol dangling from his fingers and a half-smile curling on his lips. The same smile he'd worn in the water that morning at Whiskey Creek. As if he knew what was to come.

"You're more trouble than a sniffer dog, young fella." He looked down at the elder Brady's. "You two give your grandson too much freedom. Kids his age get into trouble when they're left to their own devices."

"Let them go," Max pleaded. "They don't know anything. I'm the only person who saw…"

He stopped midsentence, knowing he'd gone too far.

"Saw what?" Duke said.

"I haven't told anybody. Let them go. I promise I won't say anything."

Manyon squeezed Max's shoulder with his free hand. "Do I look stupid to you, Max Brady?"

"No, sir."

"Then give some credit."

"They don't know anything.. Just let us go. Everything will be fine. You have nothing to worry about."

Buck pulled a revolver out of his belt and pointed the barrel at Delray.

"Do we look worried, punk? Everything *is* fine. And speakin' of fine…" He reached down and yanked Delray to her feet. "You got a fine little girlfriend here."

"Keep your hands off her," Max shouted.

He tried to stand but Duke put the sole of his shoe on his shoulder and pushed him back down.

"Relax, Sir Galahad. Do what I say and nobody gets hurt. Do you understand?"

The boy searched Duke's face for some sign he was telling the truth. His eyes were dark caverns.

"What do you want?"

"First and foremost – silence. What you saw at Whiskey Creek was a mirage. An invention of a very fertile imagination. There are no bodies there. There never were. Nobody's gonna be able to prove anything. You understand what I'm telling you?" Max nodded. "Bright boy. I bet you get straight A's."

"Max is the smartest kid in our school," Delray blurted.

Buck's fingers were wrapped around her arm. He pulled her closer. "A real wisenheimer, is he?" He touched Delray's face. "I'll give you one thing, tadpole. You do have an eye for the ladies. You are pretty as a picture, sweetheart. What's your name?"

"Delray Chance. My father's rich. He's got important friends. You hurt us and…" Buck twisted her arm and she squealed in pain. "Stop touching me." She turned to Duke. "Tell this big creep to stop."

"Keep your hands off her," Max said.

Buck cackled. Max looked at Duke and saw the outline of a smile on his cheeks.

"Here's the deal, young Einstein," Duke said. "If you or any of your friends say anything to the police, granddad and grandma here, and your little girlfriend, and these two swingin' dicks…" he waved his gun at Ben and Peanut "…are gonna have bullets planted in their brains. Got that?"

Max felt a surge of hope. The way Duke said it, he and Buck might leave without harming them. He was willing to do anything to protect them.

"Yes, sir. Your secret's safe. You don't have to worry about us. You can go now."

"Not yet. There's one more thing."

Max's heart fell. It was too good to be true. He should have known. These men were killers.

"What do you want?"

"The gold."

"What gold?"

"The Spanish coins."

Max was confused. *How does he know?* Had his grandparents told Duke about the gold coins? He couldn't imagine who else would. That didn't matter now, though. He'd trade the gold for their lives in a heartbeat. He reached into his pocket and fished out one of the ten coins they'd discovered.

"I've got four more in my bedroom. Ben and Peanut have five others between them. You can have them all."

Duke smiled and shook his head. "That's not what I mean. You're gonna take us to the spot where you found them."

Max nodded to the others. "Let them go and I'll take you to the reef first thing in the morning."

"Sorry. Can't wait. You're gonna take us right now."

"It's dark. We won't be able to see."

"A little birdy tells me you know the bottom of that ocean like the palm of your hand." Duke looked down at Grandpa Zack. "Must be in his blood, hey captain?" Max's grandfather glared up at Duke. He looked like he wanted to drive a harpoon through his heart. "We've got tanks and lights and everything you'll need. That reef'll be bright as day. Now get up."

Max pushed off the floor and stood face-to-chin with the taller man. He could smell the pleasant scent of Coppertone on Duke's skin. And his blue eyes were strangely benevolent.

"Free my friends and my grandparents and I'll go with you," he said, clutching at the vague hope Manyon wasn't the viper he seemed. Then Duke's mask slipped. His lips curled and his eyes narrowed to slits as thin as knife blades.

"Grandma and grandpa stay right where they are. You and your pals are coming with us."

Max looked at his grandmother. Tears were running down the wrinkled parchment of her face. He had never seen her cry, even when his father was killed in Vietnam. He didn't know she could cry. What he did know was that the clairvoyant had seen something cataclysmic. Despite the tape covering her mouth, he could hear her voice screaming to him.

"Maximus! These men plan to kill you. Save yourself and your friends."

The power of her telepathy stunned him. He leaned down and kissed her forehead.

"It's gonna be okay, grandma. Grandpa's right here. I'll be back to cut you loose."

He looked into her eyes and was hit with another silent portent, this one even more staggering.

"You must escape! It's your only chance."

Max nodded. "I'll be back." He gave her arm a tender squeeze. "I promise."

Duke pulled him away and thrust him toward the door.

Et Tu Brady

Chapter Seventy-Eight

BRADY WAS TWITCHING like a knife-thrower's assistant remembering that long ago night. In his life he had been shot, stabbed, beaten, and attacked by a shark, but he had never panicked. Not even that night. He had no explanation why. He didn't consider himself particularly brave or tough. He simply was someone who didn't panic. Until now. Rose's kidnapping had hit him like a rogue wave in the night. His composure wasn't just slipping. It was in free fall.

The Sandbox had become his own personal Gethsemane Garden. Bathed in sweat, he paced back and forth, leaning forward like a man scaling a steep hill into a mighty headwind. *Think!* Panic meant losing focus. He couldn't afford that. Rose's life hung in the balance. *What?* He flicked out his tongue to moisten his dry lips, but his tongue was as dry as his lips. Finally he collapsed in a chair beneath the banyan tree and went killer bee. Stinger out, emitting a Do Not Disturb signal.

The night around him had become uncontained. The Super Bowl Beach Bash was a decadent riot in full progress. Music blaring. Everyone drinking. Women screaming. Two college girls were locked in a passionate embrace on a sidewalk thirty feet away as a circle of party boys egged them on. They might as well have been background actors in a bad movie. Brady didn't notice a thing, including the men coming up behind him.

Without warning his right bicep exploded in pain. He felt like he'd been hit with a baseball bat. The blow deadened the muscle and turned him into a one-armed man. Then something struck the left side of his face. Another slam caught him square in the back and took his breath away. Fists began raining down like ice in a hail storm. He was defenseless as a piñata. He fell off the seat and landed on his back in the sand. The punches turned to kicks. A foot caught him in the ribs. His right thigh. His left ear. Through the fusillade he counted four attackers. Big men in bathing suits. Ballcaps turned backwards. Tattoos. Gold chains. Lance Jeffries and his posse, still on their pub crawl, had returned to make Brady crawl. The MVP kicked him in the side between his ribs and hip.

"How's it feel, old man?" he screamed.

"You can't do that to Lance Jeffries and get away with it, old dude," another voice snarled.

They sounded drunk. *Must be why they think I'm old.* The assault continued. Legs. Arms. Chest. He rolled onto his stomach and someone stomped his kidneys. It had become a field goal kicking contest with Brady playing the football. If he didn't get away fast they were going to kill him. There was a picnic table a few feet away. Cover. He began clawing the sand, using his elbows and toes to push himself. He was halfway there when a foot caught him in the right ear. He curled into a ball and went into turtle mode.

Gordy was still ministering to the merrymakers inside the Shanty. He'd been sticking his head out the side door every few minutes, checking on Brady. When he checked again he saw what was happening. He ran back inside and fetched the sawed-off Louisville Slugger Brady kept under the bar. He burst into the Sandbox swinging for the fences. The first shot caught Jeffries across the lower back and the MVP howled in agony. Gordy began playing Home Run Derby with his posse until they hastily backed away outside his strike zone. Gordy screamed at them.

"You sonsabitches better get the hell outa here or I'm gonna spill me some NFL brains."

The quarterback was propped against the banyan, bent over holding his lower back. He looked at Gordy.

"Tell your boss when he fucked with Lance Jeffries he fucked with the wrong guy."

Gordy raised the bat and stepped toward him. Jeffries retreated and he and his friends back-stepped out of the Sandbox onto the street and melted into the mob. Gordy dropped the bat and fell to his knees beside Brady.

"You alright, boss?"

He was balled up in the sand. Everything hurt.

"Should I call an ambulance? Or the police."

Brady shook his head and managed to croak out a *"No."* After a minute he uncurled from his fetal position. He sat up and leaned against the banyan.

"I'm okay," he groaned. "Nothing broken, I don't think."

He shimmied his back up the tree to standing position. He didn't have enough hands to massage all the spots he'd been kicked and punched. He fell into a chair and leaned forward, elbows on knees, chin cupped in his palms, still as stone, a statue to all outward appearances. Then he pushed himself to his feet and wobbled. Gordy held his arm until he stabilized.

"I gotta go."

"You're in no condition to drive, boss. Where do you need to go?"

He tried to answer but his mouth didn't work. He tasted blood on his lips. His ears were ringing. He took one step toward the street, staggered, and almost went down. Gordy helped him back into the chair. Brady found his tongue and told him about Rose. A horrified expression took possession of Gordy's face.

"My God, boss. What can I do?"

"Take care of business. I'm going to the police station."

The idea had come to him as he was speaking the words. He was relieved his mind was working again. Lance Jeffries and his hit squad had shattered the ice freezing his brain. He'd think better at the police station. He could brainstorm with Register. And if something broke he'd hear it there first. He regained his feet and leaned forward, stumbling toward the Jeep. Gordy called after him.

"What time should I close up shop, boss?"

Brady waved an arm in the air without turning around. He fell into the Jeep, cranked up the engine, and screeched off. Jamming the gearshift and grimacing at the harsh sound of grinding metal, he maneuvered onto Las Olas Boulevard and aimed west.

Traffic was insane. The number of cars on the planet was increasing three times faster than the population. They all seemed to have converged on Fort Lauderdale for the Super Bowl. He merged into an endless river of lights behind which sat an army of fun-seekers whose lives were at cross purposes with his own.

At that moment, the only thing he cared about was Rose. Her eyes stared at him through the windshield. Her reflection smiled at him from the dashboard lights. Her hand touched his as it worked the stickshift. They were mirages. Brady wondered if he'd ever see her again. If he'd ever touch her. He had just crossed the Intracoastal bridge when his cellphone rang. *Please be Rose.*

"Brady."

"Max," a voice said at the other end. "It's Billy."

"Billy?"

"Don't tell me you forgot."

Brady hadn't seen Billy Panther in years. After returning to Florida, he'd cruised up New River looking for him. The old Seminole Village was still there, but Billy was gone. Members told him he'd had become a tribal big shot.

"Can I call you back, Billy?" he said, holding his ribs. "I'm in the middle of an emergency."

"Sorry to hear it, old friend. I got a fellow here I think you need to talk to."

"Now's not the time, Billy. I'm sorry, but…"

"It's about your girlfriend."

Brady nearly drove off the road. He swerved the Jeep into a 7-Eleven parking lot and yanked the emergency brake. He jumped out and stood like a white shadow in the passing headlights.

"Rose?"

"That's the name. A few minutes ago this guy was telling me something about this Rose woman. Says she's some kind of politician. Then he mentions your name and my ears perk up. He don't know we go way back. So this fella's sitting here in my suite talking about you. Says this Rose is a commissioner or something. The TV's on while he's talking and all of a sudden I hear a news guy talking about a Lauderdale commissioner named Rose Becker. I can't believe what I'm hearing. I look up and they're showing her picture. Real pretty girl. Said she's been kidnapped, Max."

"What did this guy say?"

"He says he knows who grabbed her."

Et Tu Brady

Chapter Seventy-Nine

VENGEANCE HAD INFECTED Brady like a plague. If it meant saving Rose, he was ready to kill anyone who got in his way. Unfortunately thousands were in his way tonight. Super Bowl celebrations had broken out all over town and the traffic nightmare was only getting worse.

Las Olas was bumper-to-bumper as far ahead as he could see. The incessant cacophony of car horns was making him crazy. He made a violent right turn at Fifteenth and navigated a maze of back-streets, running stop signs, tires screeching on the hairpins, pushing the Jeep hard. He reached Broward Boulevard, which wasn't a whole lot better. Brady's insides were churning like a reactor core. He honked his horn and flashed his lights and weaved in-and-out of traffic all the way to Interstate 95. He headed south, slamming the accelerator to the floor, leaning forward over the steering wheel, hellbent on pushing the Jeep's speedometer to eighty. It would only reach seventy five.

Seminoles had occupied the same piece of land in present-day Hollywood for more than one hundred years. When Brady was a kid it had been a muddy cluster of huts on State Road 7 that catered to tourists who drove up in cars, unlike Billy Panther's village on New

River where sightseers came in tour boats. The overall impression driving past the reservation in those days was of dire poverty.

That was before the tribe began selling tax-free cigarettes. Then it discovered bingo, which was the seed that blossomed into a vast gambling empire. The marshy hamlet was now home to a sprawling entertainment complex. The Hard Rock Casino, a mammoth luxury hotel, bars, nightclubs, restaurants, theaters, comedy spots, and a dazzling Indian themed water-and-light show on the big lake fronting the property.

The Super Bowl crowd was as thick here as Lauderdale Beach. It took Brady forever to maneuver the Jeep to the valet stand. Billy lived in a penthouse atop the Hard Rock Hotel. He answered the door immediately.

His midsection was thicker and time had dusted his jet black hair the color of pencil lead, but he was the same short, sturdy man Brady remembered with such affection. The big difference was his surroundings. Billy's home had once been a humble concrete block house in the woods behind the river village. Now he lived in a lavish suite of rooms above a casino. The two men hugged. Brady attempted to smile, but couldn't quite pull it off.

"Looks like you hit the lottery, Billy."

"Good to be a Seminole these days, Max, and I don't mean the FSU kind." Billy led him through the opulent quarters. "We've gone from wrestling alligators to being a multi-billion dollar conglomerate. Living the Native American dream."

"Chief Osceola would be shocked."

"At least we didn't scalp any palefaces to get it. People spend more on gambling these days than music, movies, cruise ships, Disney World, and all the professional sports – combined. We've got more wampum than we know what to do with."

"You must be a popular guy."

Billy smiled and winked. "You have no idea, old friend. They elected me to the Tribal Council. We each get five million bucks a year to hand out to members, like redskin Santa's."

They entered a big room with a pool table, video games, three large-screen TVs and plush leather furniture. The room looked out over a patio with a private swimming pool.

"Can I get you a beer or something?" Billy said.

Brady wasn't listening. His eyes were trained on the far end of the room. A man was sitting at a long bar in front of a short glass filled with a liquid the color of teardrops. He was staring at the bottle it came from like a man searching a map for the exact spot his life had run off the road.

He strode straight to him. The man looked up with wide, shell-shocked eyes. His face was slick with sweat. He gave the impression of someone harrowed by a hellish vision. Brady noticed a sheathed knife hanging from his belt. It had a wooden handle with a silver pommel. He reached down and jerked it out. The blade was engraved with an Indian in full headdress. He recognized the dagger. Then he recognized the man.

"I know you. You pulled me out of that burning car yesterday."

The man blinked and his wide eyes popped halfway out of his head.

"You?" he said, incredulous. "You saved the little girl."

Brady examined the knife. It was coated with blood and gore. So were the man's hands and clothes. He felt his heart palpitate. Then a red curtain fell over his eyes. He pressed the blade to the man's throat and pushed until his skin looked like it was going to give.

"Whose blood is this?" he said through gritted teeth. "Where is Rose Becker?"

Billy stepped forward and touched his shoulder. "Max, this is Dismas Benvenuti. He's a friend of mine. Listen to what he's got to say."

Brady took a deep breath and steadied himself, but kept the knife to his throat.

"Talk."

"Dismas, this is Max Brady."

"Mr. Brady, I never 'spected nobody'd die."

"Die!" Brady felt the blood drain from his face. He pushed the blade harder. It pierced Dismas's skin. A red drop dripped down his throat. "Who's dead? Where's Rose?"

Despite the blade at his neck, Dismas picked up the glass and swallowed the clear liquid, then swiped the back of a filthy hand across his watery eyes.

"I promise you, sir, I never 'spected that woman'd get kilt."

"What woman? Where is Rose Becker?"

"I told Devo to drive his car into a tree, not another car."

"What?" It took Brady several seconds to grasp that he was talking about the wreck on Las Olas. "I don't mean the accident. Who's got Rose? Where is she? Tell me or I swear to God I'll cut your throat right where you sit."

He shoved the dagger harder. Dismas shuddered.

"I don't know nothin' fer certain, Mr. Brady. All I know is my boss wanted to mess up that Rose woman."

"Who's your boss?"

As soon as he heard the question Dismas's face took on a new cast, this one malignant. He looked like he wanted to hurt someone.

"Austin Ball."

Brady gasped audibly. "You work for Junior Ball?"

Billy's brown brow constricted. "Why does that name ring a bell?"

"Long time ago," Brady said, his eyes riveted on Dismas. "Red speedboat. The kid who blinded your gators." Then to Dismas. "Did Junior kidnap Rose?"

"I don't know fer sure. He don't do no dirty work hisself. If he was behind it he woulda had somebody else do it."

"What did Ball say? Why does he want to hurt Rose?"

"He said she was blowin' the cover on our injury cases. That's why he had me stage the wreck with Devo."

Brady's hand was shaking and his breathing erratic. Panic quaked inside him again.

"Are you telling me Ball ordered you to set up the wreck on Las Olas?"

Dismas tried to nod but the knife at his throat prevented him.

"Devo was supposed to get drunk in yer bar and bump into a tree so Junior could sue ya. When yer bartender kicked him out he called me and I brought him a bottle a Jack Daniels. I set there with him in the parkin' lot cross from yer bar whilst he drunk it. When he finished he drove off and headed west on Las Olas. I followed him. I saw him swerving all over the place. And he was goin' way too fast. I tried to catch up to him, but it was too late. I saw the whole thing happen. I just thank the Great Spirit you came along and saved that little girl. Mr. Brady, I never woulda done it if I knew people was gonna die. But I swear it was Junior's idea. "

Junior Ball. He'd certainly fulfilled his childhood promise and become a full-fledged dirtbag.

"What kind of car do you drive?"

"What?" Dismas said, confused.

"Your car. What do you drive?"

"I got a old Ford cargo van."

"White?"

"How'd you know?"

"Rose Becker was abducted tonight by a man in a white van. You drive a white van. You're bloody. Your knife is bloody. Your clothes are bloody. I'm finished screwing around. Where is she? And she better be safe."

Brady had the knife blade pressed against his jugular vein. Billy reached out and pulled away his arm.

"Dismas was out in the Glades tonight, Max. That blood's from a big bull gator he killed. The carcass is in his van. It's parked in one of my private spots in the garage. You can look if you want."

"And a python et Jimmy," Dismas volunteered.

"What?" Brady shook his head, wondering if he'd lost his mind. Or caught a case of the crazies from Delray. "What python? Who's Jimmy? What the hell are you talking about?"

Dismas sat wordless. He covered his face with his hands and kneaded like a man trying to mold a new identity. Billy took Brady by the arm and led him out onto the patio. A wall of noise was rising from the raucous Super Bowl festivities below. They stood on the balcony beside the swimming pool looking out at the water-and-light display of an Indian warrior firing arrows into the night sky. Billy explained how Dismas had come to him months before and asked to become a member of the *Unconquered People.*

"Who are they?

"We are they. The Seminole tribe in Florida. We never surrendered to General Andrew Jackson or the white devils." He swept his arm in the air over the Hard Rock complex. "We remain unconquered people."

"Why would somebody want to join your tribe?"

Billy rubbed his fingers together. *"Ka-nowee."*

"Ka-nowee?"

"That's Mikasuki for money."

"I thought you were Seminole?"

"Seminoles don't have our own language per se. In southern Florida we speak a dialect called Mikasuki, which grew from the Muskogee tongue. Ka-nowee means money. If you can prove you have one-quarter Seminole blood you will collect one hundred twenty thousand dollars a year. For the rest of your life. And that's been going up pretty much every year. That's why it's good to be a Seminole."

Billy explained that hundreds of people claim to be Seminole every year, but few can document their tribal heritage. Most are simply looking for a big score.

"I didn't believe Dismas any more than the others. So I toyed with him a little bit. Just for fun. Told him he'd have to pass some tests. Like living in the Everglades for a week with nothing but a knife. Wrestle a gator. Build a chickee. Make a pair of moccasins from the hide of a deer he killed. Finally, I told him he had to hunt and kill a bull gator at least ten feet long. That's what he was doing tonight when the friend he brought with him fell out of his boat and got swallowed by one of them Burmese pythons. Pretty gruesome. Dismas is in shock."

"Jesus, Billy," Brady said, bewildered at the story. "That doesn't sound like you. Playing the guy like that. Then his friend gets killed?"

Billy frowned and shook his head.

"Hell, Max, I didn't tell him to go out there by hisself. I was gonna go with him and teach him. Like I did when you were a kid. Remember?"

"Of course."

"Besides, it turns out Dismas is for real. He dug up his grandma's birth certificate. Even found one for his great grandmother. They were full-bloods. Tiger clan. Roots run all the way back to Billy Bowlegs hisself. Dismas's name is Benvenuti, but he's quarter-blood Seminole."

Brady turned away from Billy and walked back into the suite. Dismas had poured another drink. His haunted eyes were staring into middlespace, like he was seeing a ghost. Brady could only guess at the ghastly scene playing out in his head. He layed the knife on the bar and plucked the glass from Dismas's hand and slapped him hard across the face. His cheek reddened with four flog marks thick as Brady's fingers. Dismas shook his head and seemed to come out of his stupor. Brady pointed a finger in front of his nose.

"Listen to me, Dismas. You're in a shitload of trouble. You set up a crash on Las Olas that killed two people. That's double homicide. You could be looking at hard time. Now a friend of mine has been kidnapped and you're involved with that too. Tell me what you know or forget about your dream of collecting those Seminole dollars. You'll be too busy playing butt boy with your cellmate at Raiford."

Dismas's face crumpled and he started to cry. Big tears ran down his oily brown face. "Mr. Brady, Junior Ball ain't a nice man. Sonofabitch's screwin' my old lady right now – and I work for him. Thinks I don't know. But I know a lotta stuff about him. I heard him talkin' 'bout doin' something to you and that Rose lady. I don't know what he was plannin'. But if I had to bet who kidnapped yer friend, I'd put every penny I got on Junior."

Et Tu Brady

Chapter Eighty

FUZZY FURBUSH HEARD the hammer cock too late. He'd parked his car behind the Publix Supermarket and entered the breezeway and was fishing for his office key while he thought about Lilia Rodriguez. Wondering if he'd find her working at this late hour. Or if she was out having fun. With people her own age. With another guy. *Another guy!* What a joke. As if he was her guy. He doubted she thought about him at all. She had no idea how much he thought about her. To the point of obsession.

He wished he could stop, but he saw her everywhere he looked. Her heart-shaped face. Those eyes that shined like black diamonds. That caramel skin. The easy laugh. The stiletto-sharp mind.

He was fully aware that he was just another pathetic guy fixated on a much younger woman. Not sexually. His fantasies hadn't even gotten to sex. That was too much to hope for. He'd have been ecstatic just to hold her. Kiss her. Tell her how he felt.

"Don't sell yourself short," Max Brady had told him the other day. *"Some women appreciate men with seasoning. Miracles happen."*

Furbush liked Brady. Smart guy. Cagey, but. Knew a lot more than he let on. Knew about Duke Manyon. And Buck Foxx. And the missing strippers. Something happened way back when between Manyon and Foxx and Brady. It had to have something to do with the gold. Whatever it was, Ben Chance was still terrified of Manyon thirty years later. Apparently with good reason. Now he was dead. So was Richard Strong. Chance had called him Goober or something. They'd been thick as thieves as kids. Now two of them were murdered within days? What were the odds?

He regretted not sharing his file with Brady. The guy deserved to know what he had. He'd call him tomorrow. Maybe together they could find the killer. Maybe impress Lilia. *Maybe miracles do happen.*

Furbush inserted his door key and was turning it in the lock when he heard the gun cock. Fuzzy knew guns. He'd once been a firearms instructor. It sounded like a thirty-eight. Probably a Smith & Wesson. Probably a Chief's Special. Probably snub nose. Then he thought of Lilia.

Et Tu Brady

Chapter Eighty-One

A PURPLE RAGE consumed Brady. Mortar shells were going off inside his skull. If he'd stopped to think about it, he'd have realized he had never been so angry. By the time he pounded his fist against the door of the big house any semblance of self-control was gone.

"Open up!" he hollered.

Brady had rushed from the Hard Rock Casino forty five minutes before and fought through the omnipresent Super Bowl traffic all the way from Hollywood through the heart of Fort Lauderdale until he reached The Landings, an upper-crust section off the Intracoastal on the northeast side of town.

He punched the address Dismas gave him into the GPS program on his cell phone and it led him to a sumptuous two-story home on a large lot at the corner of Bayview and Fifty-Fifth Place.

A silver Mercedes Benz CLK with the price sticker still on the window was parked in the driveway. If the house had a price sticker it would have been seven numbers long, even in the current depressed real estate market. The façade was dramatic, but nowhere near as striking as the new home Brady planned to relocate its owner. That one was ringed with concertina wire and protected by guard dogs. He hammered on the door again.

"Open the goddamned door!"

The entry opened a crack. Brady lowered his left shoulder and rammed it. The door flew open and slammed into Junior Ball's face. He stumbled backwards and Brady shot into the foyer like a torpedo through a bow tube. He hit Ball in the solar plexus. Junior sprawled across the polished wood floor, legs splayed, black silk robe flying open revealing him to be naked beneath. When he stopped sliding he looked up.

"You?"

Brady grabbed the lapels of his robe and yanked him to his feet. The garment ripped off in his hand and Junior stood in his birthday suit. He was wearing a condom. Brady decided to start there and kicked him between the legs. Junior folded like a jackknife. Brady lifted his right knee and caught his face coming down. Junior stood up straight again. His nose had buckled forty five degrees to the left and was spurting blood. His face twisted with rage. He opened his mouth and looked like he was trying to scream, but no sound came out. Brady filled the void.

"Where is she? What did you do with her?"

Junior teetered like he was standing on prosthetic limbs. He lifted one hand to his blood-smeared face. Crimson seeped through his fingers. The other hand was cupped over his genitals, whether out of modesty or pain Brady didn't know, or care. A rush of images was firing through his brain. Ben Chance begging for mercy on the Great Lawn. Alligators with bleeding eyes. A young mother dead in the road. Junior blaming him on television for her death. Rose being kidnapped.

Brady feinted left, pistoned his right arm, and drove his fist far enough into Junior's doughy stomach to pick his back pocket, if he'd been wearing pants. Junior grunted once and toppled over like a timber tree. He landed hard and lay clutching his groin with both hands. His flabby, swollen lips were slobbering blood. He looked up and lisped.

"You crazy motherfucker! You need to be in a straitjacket!"

Brady stood over him and raised his foot.

"Tell me where she is, Junior, or I will stomp your head to mush right where you lay. I promise you I will."

Ball vomited. A gusher of red plasma spewed across the floor. Brady punted him in the ribs, much like Lance Jeffries had done to him two hours ago. Junior curled into fetal position.

"Where is she?"

Junior groaned. He kicked him again.

"What did you do with her?"

"*Her* who?"

Junior was pleading. His voice cracking. He was pathetic. Someone spoke from the top of the staircase.

"Mr. Ball?" Brady looked up. A woman wrapped in a towel was leaning over the bannister holding a cellphone. "Do you want me to call nine-one-one?"

Junior rolled onto his knees. He continued holding his testicles while he pulled off the condom.

"No!" he said to the woman. "There's been a misunderstanding."

He pushed himself off the floor. Brady picked up the robe and threw it in his face.

"Rose Becker was kidnapped tonight."

He watched Junior's eyes and saw surprise.

"That wasn't my doing."

"Like sending that drunk into my bar yesterday wasn't your doing?"

"Where the hell do you get that?"

"A little birdy tweeted in my ear."

"What birdy?"

"Name of Dismas."

The woman on the stairs inhaled sharply. Junior pulled the black robe around him.

"I don't believe you," he said.

Brady glanced up at the woman in the towel.

"He said you were screwing his girlfriend."

She covered her mouth with a hand. "Dismas knows I'm here?"

Junior scoffed. "That fool doesn't know shit. He's so dumb he'd flunk a moron test."

"Don't talk about Dismas like that."

Junior shook his head at her with disgust and turned to Brady. They eyed each other with malevolence. Junior touched his crooked proboscis.

"You broke my goddamn nose."

Brady cocked his right fist and stepped toward him. "Let me fix that for you."

Junior staggered backwards with palms extended. "You're barking up the wrong tree, Brady. I didn't kidnap your girlfriend. What the hell am I going to do with a city commissioner?"

A crushing despair crashed down on Brady. He wouldn't have trusted Junior if he told him up-is-up and down-is-down. But something in the way he spoke said he was telling the truth. Junior might have had Rose assaulted, or even killed. Abduction, though, didn't make sense, even for Ball. If *he* didn't, *who*? He racked his brain for the umpteenth time. *Who would harm her?* A political enemy? *She doesn't have any.* Lance Jeffries? *He got his pound of flesh.* Somebody from the gym? *None of it makes sense.*

Junior collapsed into a chair in the foyer and made a finger-tent over his nose. A black-and-white photograph hung on the wall over his shoulder. Junior's mother – Ginger called her Bobbi – standing in front of The Polynesian Room. Duke Manyon ran the parking concession there. Duke and Bobbi had an affair. Junior was with Manyon in the Donzi that day.

"Where's Duke?"

Ball glared up over his fingers. His eyes were strange. Pupils dilated to the size of dimes. *Cocaine eyes.* He looked at Brady like he was speaking Swahili

"You've always been a lunatic?" Junior said. "Now you're just plain crazy."

"What's the difference? Where's Duke?"

"Duke? You have lost your mind, Brady. Duke Manyon? Why would you even bring him up? I haven't seen him since I was a kid."

"Before Ben Chance was murdered he told people Duke was back in town."

"Why would Chance give a shit about Duke Manyon?"

Footsteps clattered on the staircase and they both looked up. The woman in the towel was coming down, now in a short black dress with black spiked heels. She marched up to Junior and held out her hand.

"Five hundred dollars, please, plus fifty for cab fare."

Junior gave her a savage look over his finger tent. "Five hundred for a half-baked blow job and dead-fish fuck? You should be paying me, bitch."

B.J. slapped his hands from his face and pinched his nose and he quacked like the Aflac duck. His robe fell away, exposing his privates. The stag was still ready to rut.

"Consider yourself fired," she said. "I'll find another lawyer to sue that bar."

Brady looked at her and then at Junior, who didn't look back. "That was your brother on Las Olas?"

She turned and faced him. Pretty woman, he thought. Her eyes looked like they once belonged to a sunny little girl. Now they held more shadow than light.

"Who are you?" she said.

"Don't talk to him," said Junior.

"Shut up. You're not my lawyer." She studied Brady. "Yes, Devon Marshall was my brother. He'd still be my brother if this bastard hadn't gotten him drunk and put him behind the wheel."

She turned and slapped Junior's nose again and he spontaneously ejaculated. B.J. dodged the discharge and slapped him one more time. He whimpered and more blood leaked from his nostrils.

"You are such a slime," she said.

She reached into her handbag and pulled out a picture of Grover Cleveland, grave and mustachioed and gazing from the face of a one thousand dollar bill.

"Forget the five hundred. I'll just keep this."

Junior's eyes grew wide and panicky. "Where did you get that?"

"Found it on the floor. That little Goth hussy dropped it on her way out. Now it's mine. Bitch!"

She stalked to the door and walked out. An appalled expression registered on Junior's face. Holding his nose, he leapt from the chair and ran into the living room, his black robe flapping behind him. A second later Brady heard a loud wail.

"She stole my money!"

He found Junior staring down at a shattered picture frame surrounded by a thousand shards of glass. He was choking with rage.

"A hundred goddamn grand!"

He grabbed a photograph off the fireplace mantle and smashed it on the larger frame. Then he moved to a small, ornate desk in the corner of the room. It looked French. Louis the Somethingth. He picked up the telephone and jabbed at the keys.

"Nine-one-one? I want to report a robbery."

Brady reached down and lifted the photograph off the floor. It was a teenage girl. He examined the face. She looked familiar. He'd seen her before. Pretty face. Very white skin. Black hair and lipstick. The photograph at Ginger's house. The same angelic little girl, about six years older. Her daughter. *"Elizabeth screws vampires,"* Ginger had said.

He'd seen her someplace else. The Slimelight. The girl stretched out in the chair with the Duke Manyon replicant. What had Lazarus called her? Dominique? No, darker than that. He stepped to the desk and jerked the telephone from Junior's hand.

"What are you doing, Brady?"

He held the photograph in front of his face.

"This girl is your daughter?"

"My daughter the thief."

"Where is she? Where do I find her?"

Junior looked up at him startled. "What the hell do you care about my daughter?"

Brady reached out and grabbed his nose. "Tell me where she lives or I'll make it point the other direction." Junior squealed like a little girl. He begged him to let go. Brady did and Junior bent over cupping his hands over his face. "Where does she live?"

"I don't know. We're not that close these days. All I know is she's living with some guy. I've never met him. They hang out at a creepy pseudo-vampire bar off Second Street." Tears were coming from his eyes. "You're insane. What the hell has happened to you, Brady?"

"We can catch up later, Junior. I'll come visit you in prison. For now, I've enjoyed about as much of you as I can stand."

Chapter Eighty-Two

BRADY RUSHED FROM the house and left Junior sitting there cradling his broken nose. He considered Brady's last words about prison. No way he was going to take a fall. Life was too good. The money, the big home, the thriving law practice, the Polynesian Room, golf three days a week, new women four nights a week. If Brady thought he was going to take that away and send him to prison he didn't know Austin Ball, Jr.

"Fuck him. And fuck h0is fucking girlfriend."

He looked down. There was blood on the floor. He realized it was coming from the soles of his feet. They'd been cut by the broken glass. The glass his daughter broke. *Elizabeth! Little bitch. Just like her mother. Money-grubbing sex maniac.*

Sex had to be at the root of her ridiculous vampire fetish All that blackness and gloom. And that phony boyfriend of hers. Junior had never met him, but he'd had him checked out. He knew about his business, the tattoos, the fangs, even the *Romeo of the Night* reputation. As far as he was concerned, the guy was a hustler in a tophat. Worse, he'd turned his daughter into a criminal. He could see them counting his money right now.

He sat there smoldering like meat on a frying pan thinking about what to do. He thought for thirty seconds then picked up the telephone again and dialed.

Et Tu Brady

Chapter Eighty-Three

BRADY BROKE EVERY traffic law between Junior Ball's house and the Slimelight Lounge. He came in the back way, twisting through a warren of narrow streets and alleys a block off Second Street. An unpaved parking lot behind the bar was half-filled with vehicles. He guessed most belonged to employees. Among them was a white cargo van.

Brady felt strangely light inside. His desolation had been replaced by a flicker of hope that he would find Rose here. He entered the club and slammed straight into a wall of sound. This wasn't the same NFL crowd kicking up its heels on the beach. This bunch looked more ZFL. One ersatz zombie wore a black football uniform complete with helmet, pads, and *666* emblazoned across his chest.

Brady pushed through the packed dance floor and past the bar and the anemic mixologist with the Mephistophelean goatee. At the rear of the big room he threw back the blanket-door to Lazarus's *world headquarters*. The space was empty. He was rushing out when someone grabbed his left arm in a steel-claw grip.

"Hello, handsome," a voice shouted in his ear. A deep voice. Basso profundo deep. Morbidia. She was wearing a black leather outfit with holes cut out exposing her breasts, which were flat and muscular and covered by a mat of black hair.

"Very sexy," Brady said.

"Did you come back to see me, Dr. Johnny Cash?"

Morbidia flashed a beguiling smile. He noticed she hadn't shaved her mustache since they'd last met.

"Actually, gorgeous, I'm looking for Lazarus. He was making me a set of fangs, but he's not in his lair." He showed his teeth and wrinkled his nose. "When I come back I'll be ready to play."

Morbidia showed off her own spiked incisors and hissed. "We'll play doctor, doctor."

Brady nodded toward Lazarus's room at the back of the bar. "Where can I find him when he's not working?"

"You never know. He does get around. A very naughty boy."

"*Romeo of the Night.*"

"You might find him in his apartment."

"Where?"

She jerked a thumb upward and rolled her eyes toward the ceiling.

A lone streetlamp cast mournful yellow light on the back of the building. The sullen beam crept halfway up a decrepit wooden staircase that left the top steps bathed in gloom. A red door stared down from the second floor landing. Brady stared up praying Rose was behind it, alive and well. The apartment looked deserted, though. A small window to the right of the door was dark. He heard music, but couldn't tell if it was the caustic Goth noise from the Slimelight or coming from the apartment. He tread lightly up the creaky stairs. They felt like they might disintegrate beneath him. The door at the top was dingy, it's red paint flaking. The wooden jamb around the deadlock was shattered. Music was coming from inside.

The window to the right was not covered. He edged to the corner of the frame and peeked in with his right eye. The room was small, no more than four hundred square feet. A single candle flickering atop a steerage trunk provided the only light. He could see the foot of a bed to the right and a door beyond that might have been a closet or bathroom. To the left was a small kitchen area, stove, refrigerator, and card table with two chairs covered in red vinyl. A ratty couch was pushed up against the far wall. Two people were sitting on it.

Lazarus was one of them. The other was the girl he saw layed out in his barber's chair last night. And in the photograph on her mother's credenza today. And in the smashed picture frame on her father's floor tonight. He remembered her name now. Lazarus had called her Demonika. Her parents called her Elizabeth. Rose was nowhere in sight.

They were counting money. *Junior's money.* Several stacks were piled on top of the trunk.

He tested the door. The knob twisted and he pushed. It opened a crack. He pushed further and slipped inside. Lazarus looked up. He dropped a wad of bills on the trunk and bolted from the couch. Brady closed the door just as the younger man lunged at him. He stepped aside like a matador waving his cape and Lazarus's momentum propelled him toward the door. Brady added his own impetus and slammed his face into the wood. *Romeo of the Night* grunted once and slid to his knees.

Demonika remained seated. Her big dark eyes were locked on Brady. So was the small black eyelet of the gun she was holding. Brady took two steps toward her and squared himself. He looked down and spoke in a loud imposing voice.

"Where is Rose Becker?"

The girl's eyes twitched left. He followed them. Rose was on the bed. Her ankles and wrists were bound with duct tape. Another strip was pasted across her mouth. But her eyes were open and smiling at him. He ignored Demonika and her gun and went straight to her. She mumbled something. He tore the tape from her mouth.

"Ouch."

"Sorry."

Brady leaned down and kissed her hard on her lips. They were sticky with adhesive. He unfettered her wrists and ankles and helped her off the bed. For a kidnap victim she seemed remarkably calm and collected.

"How did you find me, Brady?"

He nodded toward Demonika. She had risen from the couch and was helping Lazarus back across the room. His hand was cupped over his nose, reminiscent of Junior thirty minutes before.

"Her father's an old acquaintance. I think you've heard of him. Austin Ball, Jr."

Rose's eyes widened. "My, God. I had no idea."

"Did they hurt you?"

"No, no. Except for shooting me with a Taser. That hurt. Otherwise, they've been quite considerate – for kidnappers."

Lazarus collapsed onto the couch. Demonika stood over him caressing his face with her left hand, still holding the pistol in her right. In one swift motion, Brady snatched it and pushed her down next to her boyfriend. It was a forty five caliber Smith & Wesson double-action, black, scandium alloy frame, stainless steel cylinder, twenty eight ounces, two-and-a-half inch barrel. It felt strange in his hand and it occurred to him he hadn't held a firearm since he left NYPD more than a decade ago. He stuffed it in his back waistband then stepped to the window sill and switched off the music.

"Did your father put you up to this?" he said to Demonika.

She looked at Brady like he was a visitor from another planet. "Why would I kidnap somebody for that bastard?"

"Then why?"

Lazarus swiped the back of his bare right hand under his bloody nose and wiped it on his black shirt.

"I did it," he said. "For my mother."

"Your mother?"

"She was planning to whack your girlfriend. As in kill her. The only way to save her from prison was to remove Rose from harm's way."

He stared down at Lazarus and Demonika, then at Rose, trying to make sense of what he was hearing, but what he was hearing was too crazy. Rose shrugged her shoulders.

"He told me the same thing. That he kidnapped me to *save* me."

Brady shook his head in bewilderment.

"Who is your mother?"

"I am."

The apartment door swung open. Standing in the void holding a nickel-plated revolver was Delray Chance Cross. She stepped inside and kicked the door closed behind her. Her face was stony, her eyes devoid of warmth. For a woman who only hours ago had knelt naked at his feet begging him to take her, she was staring at Brady with eerie detachment. She waved the weapon toward one of the red vinyl kitchen chairs beside the small table. It looked like a thirty eight caliber Colt. The trigger was cocked.

"Please sit down, Max." Her voice was cold as stainless steel. She turned toward Rose and considered her like she was a stray animal. "You, on the bed."

Brady's mind was spinning. He wasn't sure what was happening, but he didn't like it. Not the least little bit. He stepped between Rose and Delray.

"What are you doing, Del? Put down the gun."

"Mother," said Lazarus, "do what he says before somebody gets hurt."

Delray kept her eyes on Brady, who was still trying to process what he was hearing.

"Why didn't you tell me you had a son?"

"I didn't tell you a lot of things," she said without emotion. She gazed at her son. "Lawrence, please take your vampy little girlfriend and go now."

Delray had undergone a startling transubstantiation. Her beautiful face was hard and haggard. The searing lust she'd displayed at Whiskey Creek had been replaced by icy dispassion. She looked mesmerized, as though someone had cast a spell over her.

"Why are you doing this, Delray?"

She didn't answer and waved the gun toward the chair again. Lazarus spoke to Brady as if she wasn't present.

"My mother is delusional. She's living in her own little fantasy world. She thinks you and her are going to get together and pick up where you left off when you were kids. Live happily ever after." He nodded at Rose. "But first she has to eliminate the competition."

"You know about us?" Brady said without taking his eyes off Delray.

531

"After your visit the other night I told my mother someone was nosing around about my uncle's murder."

"Ben Chance is your uncle. Of course."

"Was. Mother told me the whole story about you and her and what happened."

Delray took a step forward and pointed the gun at the center of Rose's chest.

"Not the whole story, Max. I said sit. I don't want to hurt you, but I will shoot the girl." She motioned to Rose. "On the bed. Now!"

Delray was a human hair-trigger. The hammer was cocked and her hands were trembling. Brady was afraid she was going to squeeze hard enough to fire, even by mistake. He stepped back into the firing line.

"At least uncock the gun, Del, before someone gets hurt. Please."

"You mean your precious Rose?"

Brady had always considered himself a keen judge of the human psyche. His training was extensive. Six weeks of behavioral psychology at the police academy and several years pouring beer and psycho-babble at the Sea Shanty. But at the moment he was silently cursing himself. Despite the flashing neon signs – the touches, the kisses, Whiskey Creek – he had not seen this coming. Or maybe he'd just turned a blind eye. Now he saw clearly. His diagnosis? Delray's condition had many names. The technical term was *dementia praecox* – paranoid schizophrenia. Also known as batty, barmy, cracked, cuckoo, deranged, loony, mad as a hatter, nutty as a fruitcake, and off her rocker. In short, she was batshit crazy.

"Delray," he said in a placid tone, "you know I care for you deeply. I don't want you hurt. But I cannot let you hurt Rose."

His words seemed to pierce the armor encasing her emotions. A light glimmered in her eyes and she stirred from her trance-like state. He needed her to lower the gun so he could disarm her like he'd pacified Demonika. Delray wasn't quite there yet.

"Can't you see, Max? We've always been meant for each other. Once your little plaything is out of the picture we can finally be together. Don't you want that? You can be the father Lawrence never had." She stepped around Brady, pointed the pistol at Rose again, and spoke in a frigid voice. "Now get on that bed."

Brady nodded to Rose. She hesitated, then crossed the room, Delray following her with the gun. She sat on the bed and looked back at him. Her eyes were brimming with terror. Brady tried to distract Delray's attention.

"What is this about, Del? What's going on? "

A tiny smile turned the corners of her mouth. There was something wicked about her now. Almost satanic.

"You have no idea, do you, Max?"

"No idea? About what?"

"Why I left when I was thirteen? Why my mother ripped me from our home? From my father? And my brother? And you? Why my family was destroyed? You never figured that out, did you?"

Brady shook his head.

"I'm confused, Del. What are you talking about?"

"Think about it, Max. You're smart. Very smart. Think about that night. Remember what happened. I'll never forget. I wish I could, but it changed my life forever. It's still changing. All our lives are. Think back, Max. It's all there."

Et Tu Brady

Chapter Eighty-Four

THE MEMORY WAS still as razor sharp as the blade on Max's old dive knife had once been. The four of them – him, Peanut, Ben, and Delray – stumbling from his grandparent's house. Buck and Duke prodding them with pistols into the Boston Whaler. Buck navigating out of the lagoon into the river and gunning the engine. A quarter-mile downstream pulling back the throttle and steering to the west bank.

The yellow Donzi was tied to a branch. Max realized that the men had walked through the thick woods that backed up to Eden. They must have scaled the tall wooden fence surrounding the property and surprised his grandparents. Zack and Kate never locked their doors. They coasted up to the Donzi. Duke pointed at Max.

"You come with me, kid."

Buck grabbed Delray by the wrist and spoke in a gravelly rasp.

"And you're with me, sweetie pie."

Duke clamped a hand on her forearm.

"Not so fast."

His voice was fraught with malice. Buck glared at him with venomous eyes. The two men engaged in a tug-a-war with Delray's arm while her face contorted in pain. Then Duke smiled.

"No playing with your food." He nodded at Ben and Peanut. "You take the slugs."

Buck bared his teeth. He looked like a feral animal in the darkness. Max could see daggers of hatred firing from his eyes. For an instant he thought they were going to fight over who got to keep Delray. Then Buck's eyelids fluttered and his savage sneer morphed into a harsh, unholy grin. He released her and scowled at the kids.

"Any of you little bastards try to escape and it'll be the last thing you do."

Delray stepped into the larger boat and promptly tumbled to the floor. Max jumped in after her. He saw that she'd tripped over two rolls of dirty canvas beside the gunwale. The same tarpaulins he'd unearthed that morning. Now they were bound by thick chains threaded through black barbell plates, like gruesome trimming on supine Christmas trees. He helped her to her feet. She gripped his arm like a vise and looked down at the rolls.

"What are those things?"

"Don't worry."

Duke jumped into the Donzi and pointed at the passenger seat to the left of the steering wheel.

"You two up front next to me."

The boat engines growled to life and the two vessels raced side-by-side down river. They passed the Seminole Village. Max wished there was some way to signal Billy Panther that his grandparents needed help.

The sky was a black tent, lightless except for a faint moonglow behind the clouds. The same moon that dappled their kisses only twenty four hours ago. It felt like a lifetime. They sat in the boat pressed together as close as they'd been beneath the seagrape tree. Delray seemed small and fragile and Max felt silent sobs wrack her body. He draped an arm around her trembling shoulders. She looked at him, in search of assurance. He whispered in her ear.

"It's gonna be okay. I promise."

The boats hurtled past Sailboat Bend and through downtown. It occurred to Max that he'd been hurtling toward this moment since…? That day in the schoolyard? The day they found the gold?

The day he sprayed Duke and Buck? Since last night when he saw them bury the bodies?

When all else was stripped away, though, he knew everything traced back to Delray. He had defended Ben because she was his sister. He found the gold coin showing off for her in the ocean. He was showboating when he sprayed Duke and Buck water skiing. And last night when he crossed Whiskey Creek. This was all happening because of him and his stupid juvenile bravado. He had put his friends and grandparents in a deadly fix.

They sped from New River into the Intracoastal Waterway and headed south until they made their way beneath the 17th Street Causeway Bridge. At the mouth of Port Everglades Manyon steered into the channel and didn't throttle back until they were beside the granite boulder jetties at the gateway to the Atlantic. Black thunderheads were galloping low over the horizon swollen with electricity. Atrocious sheets of lightning illuminated the whitecapped cauldron that was the sea. Duke turned to him.

"Okay, kid. You're up to bat. Navigate. Take me to the gold. And remember, if you want to see grandma and grandpa again, no games."

A wave crashed over the side and saltwater smashed their faces with the force of a fire hose. Max was blinded and rubbed his knuckles into his stinging eyes. When he reopened them lightning flashed and he saw the ocean rushing through the rocks, coming apart and merging again in short, violent surges, unseeing, unthinking, and as uncontrollable as the lethal vortex they were trapped in. His eyes scanned the skyline like a lighthouse beacon. When he'd gotten his bearings he pointed forty five degrees east-northeast. Duke jammed the throttle forward and they plunged toward Three Mile Reef.

The night belonged to the wind and rain and raging surf. The Donzi bucked through the mayhem like a rodeo bull. Max shielded Delray from the salty scalpels assaulting her face while his mind swam with questions.

How do they know so much about me?

They knew about the gold. His paper route. Where he lived. Grandpa Zack. Duke had called him *captain*. He had suspected

Junior. And maybe the information about Max's newspaper route did come from him. But he realized now the source was someone he had not considered. He thought back. *Was it only two days ago?* He and Peanut were in the Whaler on Sailboat Bend. They saw Buck in the yellow Donzi cruising in the opposite direction, heading where they had just come from. Matty Fitt's shack. Matty knew about his grandparents. Their address. The gold. Grandpa had warned him. *"You stay away from Matthew Fitt. That man is nothing but trouble."* He hadn't listened. Now Delray was crying beside him. He squeezed his arm tighter around her.

"Don't be afraid, Del."

Despite his comforting assurances, though, he held no illusions. Duke and Buck were cold-blooded killers. They murdered the two women wrapped in chains in the back of the boat. And they tried to kill him today – twice! Just as ominous was Grandma Kate's telepathic warning. *"These men plan to kill you. Save yourself and your friends."*

Max knew he could no more stop them than he could stop the rain. Once he led them to the gold he guessed they would throw him and his friends overboard. He doubted even he could survive the night three miles out in a stormy sea. There was no way the others could. They were beyond anyone's help.

Max had one advantage. The ocean was his domain. Other than Grandpa Zack, no one knew these waters better than he did. If they were to survive, he was going to have to save them. Somehow he needed to commandeer one of the boats. They could vanish into the night, into the storm. He considered his options. The list was short. One was to get his hand on a gun. Duke and Buck were each carrying one. The other was to get them out of the boats and into the water. A tall order. He was no match for them physically.

Delray's leg was trembling against his. He could feel the fear radiating from her. He leaned close to her ear.

"We have to get into the Whaler," he said over the roar of the engine. "When I tell you to jump, don't hesitate."

She nodded.

With the wind in their teeth, they bounded north and east away from land until the lights on shore were flyspecks. Max estimated they were about two miles out when Duke yanked back the throttle.

"This isn't it," he said. "We're not there yet."

Duke ignored him. He stood without speaking, pistol in hand. Alarm bells went off in Max's head. *They're going to shoot us right here!* The Whaler drew alongside. Ben and Peanut were curled together on the bow. They looked numb with fright. Buck growled at them to hold fast to the Donzi and, clutching his own gun, he climbed into the larger boat.

Max searched for a weapon. There was nothing. The only possibility was a small fire extinguisher hanging from a hook just to the right of the steering wheel. A feeble bludgeon against their guns and muscle. Buck and Duke were at the stern speaking in low tones with their backs to him. The moment had come.

He took a deep breath. He realized he was still composed and his mind nimble. The fear he'd felt before was gone. Delray was watching him, as if she could see his brain performing its calculations. Her fingers had a death grip on his forearm.

Out of nowhere, a mad plan popped into his head. He would grab the fire extinguisher, club Duke, and push him in the water. Then he'd rush Buck and knock him overboard. Buck might pull him into the water, but he'd take his chances. He had a good chance to make the two mile swim to shore. After all, he was half fish, and fish don't drown. He remembered Grandpa Zack's words. *Water is life.* The ocean was his salvation.

The important thing was that Delray jump into the Whaler and get away with Ben and Peanut. First, though, he had to take out Duke and Buck. He watched the scenario play out in his head. He assessed his odds of success at slightly better than playing Russian Roulette with a loaded gun. If he failed they were dead. But it was their only chance. Fight like a lion or be slaughtered like a lamb.

The wind was raging. The sky opened up and they were hit by a fresh burst of rain. Duke and Buck were still in muffled conversation, paying them no attention. Max unclasped Delray's fingers from his arm and nudged her legs aside. He had a clear path to the fire extinguisher. He whispered through the downpour.

"When I move, get into the Whaler and go." She opened her mouth to protest. He put a finger to her lips and shook his head. "Don't wait for me. Run it straight in to the beach and go find a cop. Send them to Eden."

"But…"

"I'll be okay."

Even in the dark and rain he could see she was weeping. She pressed her palms to his cheeks and kissed his lips.

"I love you, Max."

It was the first time a girl had ever said that to him. Things *were* moving fast!

"I love you too, Delray," he said and kissed her one last time. "Get ready."

It was now or never. He felt his heart throb inside his chest. Kate Brady's face flashed in his mind. *Help me grandma.* He moved toward the fire extinguisher. At the same instant he looked back and saw Duke and Buck bend over. *What are they doing?* Then they stood, each holding an end of one of the canvas rolls. They heaved the body over the side. As it splashed into the water, it hit him. They were in the Gulf Stream. The corpses, even weighted, would be swept north by the stream's swift current. If the fish didn't get them, they'd be off the Carolinas within days. No one would ever find them. The men lifted the second body and tossed it overboard.

"What are those things?" Delray whispered.

"I don't know," Max lied.

He fell back in the seat and relaxed, for the moment.

Ten minutes later the boats reached the approximate area of Three Mile Reef. Max had never been here at night. They trolled for another ten minutes, shining spotlights into the inky depths, peering through random torrents, until Buck spotted the pink coral formation. Duke threw an anchor overboard while Buck tethered the Whaler to the Donzi. Then Duke stood at the stern of his boat with the automatic pistol in his hand and called out over the wet and wind.

"Okay, boys and girl, here's what's gonna happen. Buck and young Max are gonna take a swim." He pointed his gun at Ben and Peanut, cowering in the Whaler. "I'm staying up top with you two losers and the little peach. Try anything funny and you'll be swimming home."

Their heads swiveled in unison. An infinity of black water lay between them and the now nearly imperceptible shoreline. Max looked at Ben and Peanut huddled together, paralyzed with dread. They'd never be able to protect Delray. He did not want to leave her with Manyon, but didn't seem to have a choice. Buck shoved a scuba tank into his arms.

"Wake up, kid. Mask and fins are under the seat."

By the time Max donned his gear, Buck was suited up and ready to go. Delray threw her arms around him and kissed his lips. Duke pulled her away.

"See what you got waiting for you, kid. After you show Buck the gold?"

"If you hurt her I'll kill you."

Max was shocked by his own words. He'd never threatened to kill anyone, but he meant it. Manyon smiled and wrapped an arm around Delray.

"Don't worry, tough guy." He squeezed her close to him. "She's in good hands."

Delray looked at Max with wet terrified eyes. Buck shoved a light at him.

"Let's go."

They perched on the boat wall, each with a hand over his mask. Max felt like he was walking the plank. They fell backwards. When the bubbles cleared he had the sensation of drowning in India ink. The sensory deprivation was almost total. He could hear his artificial lung gurgling but sight had abandoned him. He had absolutely no sense of up or down. It occurred to him that this was how a fetus must feel floating in its mother's amniotic fluid. Then a bayonet of light stabbed him in the eyes. He shielded his face with one hand and thrust out his other palm. Buck diverted his lampbeam and jabbed a finger at Max, signaling him to lead the way down.

Night-sea was unlike anything he had ever experienced. Eerie and exhilarating in the same instant. They descended forty feet to the coral ridge. Max couldn't believe his eyes. In daylight the reef teemed with fish. Now it was like the mall at Christmas. Barracuda, grouper, octopi, angel fish, snapper, and manta ray were everywhere. The colors were spectacular. The reef had come alive in the artificial light like he'd never seen. Vivid reds and blues, oranges and purples and yellows, like a night-blooming garden. It was hypnotic.

Something jarred him from behind. Buck was treading water without effort. Max was disheartened to see him so at ease. Through the window of his mask he could see the cold glare of Buck's eyes. He waved at Max to keep moving.

They drifted along the crest of the ridge until they reached the chasm. Max swam out over the hole and pointed bottomward. Buck followed and they let gravity draw them down the steep walls to the wide white sand floor. Again, Max was dazzled. The crater was crawling with crab and lobster. The crustaceans that spent their days cowering under rocks and in crannies were as nocturnal as bats and barn owls. Max pointed at the ground. He reached down and demonstrated to Buck how they'd sifted the bottom with their fingers.

For the next half hour they combed the fine white granules. Occasionally one of the spiny creatures would crawl up and watch like a nosy pedestrian at a construction site. While Max burrowed, his mind raced. He was certain of one thing. He had to get rid of Buck while it was just the two of them on the bottom. But there was no way he could overpower him. He had to find another way.

He was combing the sea bed with his fingers when he touched something metallic. He rooted around for several seconds until he pulled out a coin. It was gold, identical to the others. He looked up. Buck was watching him. And he was holding a speargun. He hadn't had a weapon when they left the boat. He looked closer and saw it was a Nemrod. *Ben's speargun!* The one he lost the day of the shark attack. The shiny silver sling was loaded, its black rubberband cocked, the spear ready to fire, its deadly barbed tip pointed directly at Max's chest.

Buck's eyes were smiling cruelly. He pointed the spear at the coin and gestured at Max to hand it over. The boy knew if he complied Buck would finish him right there. So this was it. In the next seconds one of them was going to die. And the odds were stacked in favor of Max being the dead one.

He stretched out his right hand. Buck was holding the spotlight in his left hand and speargun in the other. He transferred the light to his right hand and reached toward Max. Their fingers were almost touching when he dropped the coin. The gold disk fluttered downward, seesawing toward the sand, back and forth in slow motion, like an autumn leaf falling from a tree. Buck's eyes followed, malice replaced by sudden surprise. Reflexively, he released the gun and light and lunged his right hand for the coin.

His chance had come. Max thrust his spotlight at Buck's face. He reacted like he'd been shot in the eyes with tear gas. Blinded, Buck forgot the coin and pulled both hands up to shield his eyes. Max let go of his lamp and pushed off the bottom.

He shot to the top of the cave and dove over the reef ridge. The water was blacker than black. He descended the far side and made his way to the bottom like a sightless man, hands feeling the coral as though he was swimming by Braille. His heart was racing, but otherwise he felt extraordinarily calm. He had a several second lead. Once Buck recovered his vision he would have to retrieve his light and Ben's speargun. Or first he might sift the sand where the gold coin fell. Either way, Max had time to find a place to hide.

Feeling his way in the dark, it took him a minute to find a notch just large enough to wedge himself into. It was a perilous maneuver, considering all the sea urchins populating these rocks like venomous porcupines. He didn't even want to think about the dozens of razor-toothed moray eels. He only hoped he hadn't barged in on one. He pushed as far back into the cubbyhole as possible and waited, still as stone. Max knew Buck would be searching for his bubbles. He filled his lungs with air and held his breath.

Overhead he could barely make out the boats. Their white underbellies were floating side-by-side, as close as two front teeth. He prayed Delray and his friends had not been harmed. But they would have to wait. His immediate problem was somewhere here in the blackness. The moment had come to eliminate Buck. It was kill, or be killed. There were no other options. The weight of his task was crushing. He was thirteen years old, yet he *had* to destroy another human being – a grown man – or forfeit his own life. If he died Delray would die, too. And Ben. And Peanut. He could not let that happen. But how to stop it?

He pressed closer to the wall and kept his eyes trained on the top of the reef, taking as few breaths as possible. It was several minutes before he saw it. A giant grouper drifting lazily above him suddenly lit up. Seconds later a light came over the ridge. The glow brightened until a human outline came into view. Buck had the speargun in one hand and the spotlight in the other, fanning the beam across the reef and ocean floor.

Max reached down and touched the ground around him, searching for a rock or anything he could use as a weapon. He touched something and it moved. A manta ray the size of a boat cushion darted out from under a blanket of sand. The lightbeam caught the commotion and Buck plunged headlong toward the bottom. Max knew his cover had been blown and sprang from the fissure. He dashed away from his predator and swam low along the base of the formation.

He knew the contours of Three Mile Reef as well as he knew the twists and turns of Whiskey Creek. The bluff ran straight south fifty yards then doglegged sharp right and curled back around. On the far side of the bank was a wide, sandy canyon with coral walls twenty foot deep. Max disappeared around the bend. He ascended to the ridgetop and plunged over the crag and down the other side.

He flattened himself against the rocks again and was planning his next move when Buck surprised him. He came over the palisade waving his lamp. The lightbeam found Max and locked on him. Buck shot downward and stopped ten feet above the boy. He hovered and aimed the speargun. Max was trapped. He had nowhere to go. His only hope was that Buck would fire and miss or, if he didn't, the wound would not be lethal. Then Buck dropped down closer until the tip of Ben's spear was three feet from his heart.

With his back to the rocks, Max looked left and right. Nothing. No escape. To charge Buck would be suicidal. His only option was to turn his skinny frame sideways, his right shoulder toward speargun, and give him a narrow target. Buck smiled that ruthless smile and rose two feet until he was looking straight down on him. Death was too close to dodge now. His last thought was of Delray and how he'd let her down.

Then he saw it. Buck noticed Max's eyes. He turned to look, but too late. *Left Eye* swished over the ridge. Max's spear was still protruding from the right side of its winged head. The big fish lunged straight down, its mouth wide, and clamped its powerful jaws over Buck's head.

In the chaos that followed, Buck dropped the speargun and his light whirled in the black water like a strobe. Max watched in revulsion. The hammerhead thrashed violently, Buck attached to it like a remora. A cloud of blood spread through the water. The fray didn't last long. *Left Eye* worked fast. After a few seconds the shark stopped shaking and just swam away, ignoring Max as if he wasn't there.

The boy raced to the spotlight and pointed it upward. A gusher of bubbles was rushing toward the surface. He followed the trail back to its source. Floating in a crimson fog ten feet above him, the airhose to Buck's scuba tank writhed in the nightwater like a live electric wire. The mouthpiece to his regulator had been severed. Buck himself was drifting in the gentle current, his arms and legs spread wide and motionless. The bronco tattoo was still bucking on his chest, but something was missing. Then he realized. Jagged flesh waved in the water where only seconds ago Buck's head had been attached to his body. Now his head was gone. *Left Eye* had amputated it.

Max's first reaction was to vomit. The discharge filled his mouthpiece and he began to choke. He pulled out the regulator and forced himself not to inhale. He pushed the release valve and cleared the device with a rush of air and shoved it back into his mouth.

His next reaction was euphoria. Buck was the darkest demon he'd ever crossed paths with. Sister Mary Aloysius seemed like a saint by comparison. Buck being dead meant Max wasn't.

But blood was filling the water. He remembered Grandpa Zack telling him that hammerheads travel in schools. It wouldn't be long before *Left Eye* returned with his friends and family for the main course. Max started to swim away. Then he stopped and turned. He waved the light at the bottom until he found what he was looking for. The metallic tip of Ben's speargun was sticking out of the white sand.

Duke would be watching from above and Max hoped he hadn't been able to decipher what happened. Even so, Duke had to know something was wrong. He didn't need the lamp anymore and was about to switch it off when he had an idea. He swam to Buck's headless body and tied the light to his backpack and watched it float off.

He swam along the foot of the shoal and back around the dogleg to the outer edge of Three Mile Reef. Staying low to the sand, he held his breath to prevent creating air bubbles and stroked away from the rocks. He swam until he was beyond the boats, then began a slow ascent. *Toward what?* He could see no sign of Duke or his friends. *Is that good or bad?* He released the safety on the speargun and zeroed in on the needle nose of the Donzi. Ten feet from the surface he unlatched his weight belt and attached it to the backpack. He removed his tank, took a last lungful of air, and let it sink. He surfaced beneath the bow of the yellow boat.

A ferocious wind was raging. Waves slapped at the two hulls. The vessels rocked violently. He clasped a finger through the Donzi's trailer hook and held fast. Sounds were coming from above him. He thought he heard muffled sobs. *Delray?* He couldn't be certain in the wind. Then heavy footsteps. *Duke?* Max took a chance. Using the bow as cover, he edged closer to his Boston Whaler. He caught sight of Ben and Peanut. They'd moved to the back of the boat but were still bunched together. They seemed to be crying. He heard Duke, as if offstage. His voice was cruel.

"Shut up you little turds or I'll give you the same."

The same? Max estimated Duke was standing at the center of the Donzi. Too far to strike from his current position. Plus, the Donzi's windshield was between them. He had one spear. One shot. One chance to take out Duke. If he failed he and his friends would be shark food like Buck. From the sound of it, he didn't have much time.

Max checked his emotions. He'd just come within seconds of being murdered. He'd watched a man beheaded. A few feet away another man with a gun wanted to kill him. He should have been terrified. Somehow, though, he knew he wasn't going to die here tonight. *Water is life.* The rush of primal energy was back. The same feeling he'd had escaping Duke and Buck in the creek this morning. Maybe it was bloodlust. Maybe it was the advent of combat. Or maybe he'd just lost his mind. *A distinct possibility*, he thought, floating under the bow. *I'm not even sane enough to be scared.*

A new squall struck and the boats were engulfed by sheets of rain. Max's face was pelted by water pellets the size of pebbles. Between the rain and the lashing waves, he could barely open his mouth to breath. Hearing was impossible.

He needed to find a better angle of attack. The Donzi and Whaler were lashed together. There was no room between them to fire. He had one option. He sank three feet below the surface and swam down the Donzi's beam to the stern. Still submerged, he clutched the lower housing of the big Mercury engine just above the propeller and held fast.

Things began happening in microseconds. He looked up. Raindrops were distorting the water's surface. Max couldn't see. But he could hear better underwater. The sound of footsteps came through the boat floor. Then Duke's voice. Louder now. He couldn't decipher the words, but his anger seemed to be growing by the second.

As fast as it started, the deluge stopped. Max looked up again and his heart skipped. Illumined by the Donzi's running lights, Duke was standing directly above him leaning over the transom looking down into the water. The boy froze. Duke hadn't seen him yet, but if he shifted his eyes a few feet to the right they'd be staring straight at each other. Unbreathing, the boy followed his gaze down toward the reef. He saw a flash of light. Duke was fixated on the lamp dangling from Buck's body fifty feet below. There was no way to know he wasn't wearing his head anymore. When he looked up again Duke had his gun out. He was shouting something and waving the muzzle toward the stern of the Whaler. Max couldn't hear his words but his gesticulations were savage. Then he heard Ben and Peanut. They sounded like they were pleading.

Pleading for what? He couldn't take a chance. The sand had run from the hourglass. He was three feet down. He released his grip on the engine and descended another three feet. *This is it,* he thought for the third time tonight. He kicked his flippered feet with all the fury he could muster and shot out of the water waist-high into the air. He found his target and roared.

"Duke!"

Manyon turned. Max saw astonishment in his eyes. He started to raise his gun but before he could get off a shot Max fired the speargun. The recoil threw him onto his back as Duke pulled the trigger. He heard the discharge a split second before he sank back beneath the surface. He dropped the speargun and darted under the boat, expecting more shots to follow. Then he heard Delray scream. He knew he couldn't hide. He kicked off his fins, reached up, grabbed the transom and vaulted into the Donzi.

Duke was standing at the center of the boat. The spear had penetrated his chest just above the left nipple. The tip was sticking out his back. He'd dropped the pistol and was clutching at the gaff with his right hand. He seemed to be trying to figure out what had happened. He looked at Max and his face took on a savage cast. He bent over to pick up the gun, but a big wave struck the Donzi broadside. Saltwater drenched them and Duke stumbled backwards. The back of his knees hit the gunwale and he lost balance. He flailed his arms trying to right himself. Max stepped forward, lifted his right leg, and kicked him in the chest with the sole of his foot. Duke let out a low groan and tumbled into the sea.

Delray was curled like a fetus on the floor of the boat laying in several inches of water. Her wrists and ankles were bound with yellow nylon ski rope. And she was naked. In the faint illumination, Max could see the water beneath her was tinged red. A bolt of fear raced through him. *The bastard shot her!* Her shirt and shorts were sloshing in the red water. He picked them up. They'd been torn to shreds. He grabbed a wet towel off the boat seat and fell to his knees. He covered her then untied her arms and legs.

"Duke's gone, Del," he whispered. "You're safe now."

She stared up at him with wide eyes. Her breathing was ragged and she was weeping. She seemed to be in a state of shock.

"Did he shoot you?" She didn't respond. "Where did he hurt you?"

Delray just looked at him. He felt blindly beneath the towel, touching her with his fingers. Back, stomach, arms, legs. Searching for a wound or some source for the blood. He didn't find any. He looked at the Whaler. Ben and Peanut were still entwined at the stern.

"What happened?" he shouted. Neither answered. "What did he do to Delray?"

They shrank under his gaze. Something profound had changed in them. Their faces were pictures of horror, their eyes hollow, transfixed, as if their souls had been stolen. Max looked down.

"What happened, Delray?"

She sniffled and her eyes flickered sideways, then her face crumpled and her words came in a rush.

"I begged him. He wouldn't listen. He was like a...he, he, he..." She couldn't say anymore and wept again.

Max looked over at Ben and Peanut once more. They watched him with empty eyes. Ben began to shake. His tremors grew more intense until he erupted in sobs. Peanut covered his eyes with his hands, hiding from Max's glare.

"We couldn't do anything," he shouted. "He had his gun on us."

"Why are her clothes torn? Where did this blood come from?"

Peanut didn't answer. But he didn't have to. Perception finally flared in Max's brain.

The Donzi lurched and he heard sounds coming from the front of the boat. He scrambled to the bow. It was Duke thrashing in the water, still impaled by the spear. He was holding onto the boat with his right hand trying to pull himself up. Max leaped back over the console and searched for a weapon. The pistol was on the floor beside Delray. A wooden paddle was on a shelf against the port wall.

He grabbed the oar and scurried back. Duke had a grip on a deck cleat and had pulled himself halfway out of the water. He was straining to get his torso onto the boat, but the spear blocked him.

The clouds opened and they were inundated by another deluge. Duke squinted up through the downpour.

"Give me a hand, kid."

Max held the oar like a baseball bat. White lightning pitchforked in the black sky, illuminating him poised wild-eyed above Duke. Thunder rumbled across the water like a radiation wave from a nuclear blast. The boy felt as if he'd been speared by a firebolt. A primitive rage surged through him and he screamed down at Duke.

"What did you do to Delray?"

A lurid smile glimmered across Manyon's face.

"Help me up and I'll explain the facts of life to you."

Max was beyond restraint. He raised the oar over his head.

"Die you bastard!" he screamed and smashed the paddle down like an ax on a log.

The blow struck Duke on the skull with an audible thud. He grunted once but held on. Max swung again and again and again, with each blow roaring at Manyon to die. Until the wood finally shattered in his hands. Still Duke kept his grip. Max used what remained of the oar handle to smash the fingers holding the cleat. Duke looked up at him. His face was covered in blood, but he was wearing a peculiar smile. The same smile Max had seen that morning on Whiskey Creek. Then he let go. He fell back into the water and slid beneath the waves.

Max stood unsteadily on the bow, rocking with the sea, black rain lashing his face, his body still filled with fury, watching the water, waiting for Duke to resurface. But he didn't. And finally it hit him. Duke and Buck were dead!

Another bolt of lightning struck, this time so near the crack of thunder knocked him to his knees. Then, without warning, the bloodlust vanished and remorse washed over him. *What have I done?* What he'd done, he understood, was commit murder. Duke had been helpless. A spear was sticking through him. And they had his gun. He could never have overpowered them. They could have tied him up and taken him to the police. Instead, Max had murdered him. In cold blood. He would never be able to undo that. He was overwhelmed by the enormity of his crime. He knelt over the water and vomited as fat drops of rain raked his back.

After a moment he crawled off the bow. Delray was still curled under the towel, mewling like a small child having a bad dream. The puddle of blood had washed away in the rain. With his head turned away, he dressed her in the torn garments and pulled her to her feet. He helped her into the Whaler. Ben and Peanut hadn't budged. They seemed to be catatonic. Max yelled at them.

"Get up on the bow."

They obeyed him without a word. Max spread the towel on the floor, layed Delray down, and slipped a boat cushion beneath her head. Then he jumped back into the Donzi. He found Duke and Buck's guns and threw them overboard. He unhitched the anchor line, climbed into the Whaler, and set the yellow boat adrift.

Max looked toward shore. Lights were flickering on the horizon like votive candles in a dark church. He cranked the starter rope and the Evinrude belched to life. He had to shield his eyes from the blinding salt spray as the little boat crashed over storm waves. The sky was beginning to clear to the east and the moon and stars were rushing across the blackness as if blown by a celestial wind. It took nearly an hour to reach the granite jetties at the mouth of Port Everglades. He wheeled into the inlet and by the time they entered safe harbor the rain had stopped and the wind subsided and the water was finally calm. A foghorn moaned from the shadows. He navigated the little boat to the bottom of the 17th Street Causeway Bridge, to the same spot they'd tied up when he dived off the raised span. *Was that only three days ago?*

He switched off the engine and sat perfectly still. Breathing hard. His body pulsating. He was overcome by another attack of nausea and vomited over the side. Soothing yellow light from the Pier 66 Marina did a slow dance atop the water. The only sound was the occasional drone of car tires crossing the metal drawbridge. It felt to Max like it was past midnight.

Delray appeared to be asleep. He crawled beside her and stroked her wet disheveled hair. Her teeth were chattering like a patient with a high fever. Her eyes were open, but she was staring at nothing.

"Are you okay, Delray?"

"Uh-huh," she responded, her voice small and listless, almost serene.

Ben and Peanut were coiled up at the bow. The sight made Max's blood boil. He climbed over Delray. They turned their heads away in unison.

"You cowards," he said in a low threatening tone. "You didn't protect her." Hot tears spilled from his eyes. He slapped Ben's face with his open palm. "You let him do that to your sister?"

He raised a fist. Ben cowered and he held back. Peanut refused to look at him. Max turned back to Delray. Her eyes were dark and dry and shorn of emotion. She had retreated to someplace deep inside herself.

"You're safe now, Del. I'm going to get you to the beach hospital."

That brought her out of her stupor. She looked up at him and shook her head.

"No, no, no." Her voice was frail. "Take me home."

"But you're hurt. You need to see a doctor."

She reached up and grabbed his arm. Her fingers dug into him like talons.

"I said no." There was a sudden ferocity in her voice. "I don't want to go to the hospital. I don't want to see a doctor. Take me home. Do you hear me?"

Her dry eyes were filled with a vehemence Max had never seen in her before. He reached down and touched her cheek and she flinched.

"But Delray…"

"Take me home. *Now!*"

Et Tu Brady

Chapter Eighty-Five

THE ROOM WAS silent, except for a rumor of music coming through the floorboards from the Slimelight. Brady sat on the red chair, head in hands, deep inside himself. Lazarus and Demonika were on the couch, their mouths agape. On the bed, tears dripped from Rose's eyes. Delray still held the center of the room, her revolver trained on Rose. Brady looked up at her.

"I never understood," he said.

Delray gazed down at him. "What?"

"Why you didn't let me take you to the hospital. You hadn't done anything wrong. You were the victim."

"You didn't really know my mother and father." She spoke in a low, flat voice. Her eyes were as dry and emotionless as they'd been that night in the boat. "They were judgmental people. Very punitive. Somehow the fault would have been mine."

"You were a little girl, Delray. You were violated by a grown man. Nobody could have blamed you."

"That wasn't the entire reason. It was you. I was trying to protect you, Max."

"How were you protecting me?"

"I knew what you'd done to that bastard. He deserved to die. When you killed him I was happy. But then I saw how you reacted. How you realized that you'd murdered him. I didn't want you going to prison."

"Why didn't you tell me?"

"I never saw you again. Not after your grandparent's funeral. Then you were gone."

"Brady?" It was Rose. Her voice cracked with emotion. She glanced at Delray, then back at him. "We said no secrets. Tell me. Tell me what happened to your grandparents?"

He stared at the floor. All the talk about that night had unleashed a tsunami of images, old and new, coming at him so fast he was drowning in the flux. From a naked young girl curled up like a fetus on the floor of a boat, to a skinny young girl gyrating on a bar. He looked at Lazarus.

"What does the tattoo say?"

Lazarus gazed at him. "Huh?"

"That tattoo on your friend's leg. The Latin phrase. What does it say?"

Lazarus gave a confused shrug. *"Da mi basia mille, deinde centum, deinde mille altera."*

"But what does it mean?"

"I know," said Demonika. She was wearing a foul expression. She pulled up the hem of her short black dress and exposed the tattoo on the inside of her milky white thigh. "He inscribed the same little jingle on me." She shot Lazarus a dirty look. "He's got it too. *'Give me a thousand kisses, then a hundred, then another thousand.'*"

A laconic smile materialized on Lazarus's face. "I heard it once. Thought it was sexy. From some old Roman dude. Catullus somebody. Why do you ask?"

Brady shook his head and looked down at the floor. "I was thinking about Pandora."

"That little troll whore." Demonika spit out the words.

"Not that Pandora. The Pandora of Greek mythology. The very first woman, as the story goes. Molded from clay on orders from Zeus, who was pissed off at Prometheus for stealing the *secret fire* and giving it to humans. Pandora was created as retribution on humanity. She opened a box and released all the evils of mankind. War. Famine. Plague."

"So?" said Lazarus.

"Did you know Pandora's Box wasn't really a box?" The four of them watched him, waiting for the rest. "It was a *pithos*. A jar."

They kept watching and waiting, but there didn't seem to be any more.

"What are you talking about, Brady?" said Rose.

He spoke without looking up. "I'm talking about me. I'm Pandora. I opened the jar. I released the evil. Everything bad that happened was because of me. I found the gold coin. I taunted Duke and Buck. I saw them burying those women." He looked up at Delray. Her eyes were riveted on him. "I opened the jar, Del. But you paid the price. You and Ben and Peanut. And my grandparents."

"Tell me, Brady," Rose said.

His eyes went back to the floor. He was watching something far away. Something he'd buried long ago. Something he did not want to exhume.

"I did what Delray wanted. I took her home. And Ben. I dropped Peanut at the Alligator Pit. Then I went to Eden. When I got there my grandmother and grandfather were still sitting on the couch. Right where we left them. Hadn't moved. They were so still. At first I thought they were asleep. But that was wishful thinking. I saw their wrists and ankles. Still bound with tape. His mouth was covered. Hers wasn't."

He stopped speaking. Rose covered her mouth with a hand. He tried to get more words out, but faltered.

"Tell me, Brady?"

"I didn't see until I got close. Just a couple feet away. Little red circles, no larger than dimes. One on each of their temples. Like somebody had painted dots on them. I didn't know what they were. Or what to do. I said: *'Grandpa?'* He didn't move. *"Grandma?"* Nothing. I walked around the couch. The dots were entry wounds. Then I saw the other sides of their heads. I saw the exit wounds and…"

Words failed him again. Rose squeezed her eyes shut.

"I'm so sorry," she said, her voice trembling. "But who? Duke and his partner were dead."

Brady sighed. "Matty Fitt."

No one spoke. Brady didn't notice. He wasn't talking to them. He was in another time and place. Reliving a moment he realized had not been buried deep enough. The worst moment of the worst night of his life.

"Matty Fitt shot them. One bullet each. Then he went home and wrote a confession and blew out his own brains. I never saw the letter. Someone at the police department told me he claimed to be tormented by guilt. He said that during Prohibition he and my grandfather were running liquor into Whiskey Creek. One night they got caught by a federal Revenue agent. In his suicide letter Matty claimed my grandfather shot and killed him. He blamed Grandpa Zack for ruining his life. Accused him of stealing my grandmother and living a happy life while he wallowed in guilt. That he couldn't stand the pain anymore."

"But that all happened fifty years before," Rose said. "After all that time he suddenly decides to murder your grandparents? That doesn't make sense."

Brady cast a rueful smile her way.

"Like I said, I'm Pandora. I opened the jar and released the evil. Matty's letter said when I went to see him about the gold that day it opened up all the old wounds. He murdered my grandparents because of me."

No one argued. They seemed too stunned to speak.

"After the funeral I was sent to California to live with my great Uncle Buddy, my grandmother's brother. I hated it there. I ran away a couple of times and refused to go to school. It was a bad time. After a few months Uncle Howard and Aunt Mo arranged for me to come home and live with them." He looked at Delray. "By the time I got back you were gone. I tried to find you. I tried to contact Ben, but he wouldn't talk to me. Until I saw you again the other night, I had no idea what had become of you."

Delray stared back at him. Her face was bereft of emotion. Brady wondered if she'd gotten her hands on another prescription of OxyContin.

"You still don't get it do you, Max?" she said.

He looked at her, trying to understand what he was missing. Delray watched him, calm, detached, trancelike. Demonika was curled into the corner of the couch, small and scared, wary of the madwoman with the gun. Lazarus peered off into space, like he was watching a film made before he was born. Brady looked at him and then at Delray. *Before he was born!* And the pieces came together.

"Duke Manyon is Lazarus's father?"

Delray laughed mirthlessly. "Give that man a cigar."

They all turned their heads and peered at Lazarus. He looked at his mother. She looked back at him and seemed to thaw.

"He raped me on the boat that night, Lawrence. I was thirteen years old."

"I didn't know, Delray," said Brady. "I didn't understand."

"While you were in the water, Max, he tore off my clothes and bent me over the boat seat and…" Her voice broke and she fought to regain her composure. "I begged Benjamin and Peanut to help me, but they just sat their crying like babies. Neither lifted a finger."

Brady watched her.

"That's why you killed them?"

She ignored the question.

"I swore my brother to silence and didn't tell anyone what happened, especially not my mother and father. I was afraid. A few weeks later I started having dizzy spells and vomiting. My mother took me to our family doctor. He ran some tests. My parents went crazy. They demanded to know who'd done this to me."

"What did you say?"

"I told them it was yours."

"Mine?"

"I didn't know what else to say. I was so confused. How could I tell them I'd been raped? How could I tell them the boy I was in love with murdered the man who impregnated me?" A tear fell from her eye. She wiped it away and lowered the gun. "Maybe I just *wanted* you to be the father, Max. I wanted to believe someday we could be together. That we could be happy."

Brady sat reeling. "Why didn't you tell me?"

"You were gone. I had no one to turn to. My father insisted I have an abortion. My mother wouldn't hear of it. She was the hard-core Catholic of the family. They fought terribly. Our home became a house divided. Finally, she took me and left. We flew to New York. My grandparents lived in a little village, Highland Falls, an hour up the Hudson River from the city. I stayed at Ladycliffe, a convent overlooking the river." Delray looked at Lazarus. Tears were falling freely down her cheeks now. "I had just turned fourteen when you were born. A baby having a baby. They let me hold you for a few minutes. When they tried to take you away, I didn't want to let go. I wanted to keep you. They wouldn't let me. They told me they had a good family that was ready to adopt you."

Silence saturated the room. Brady's head was spinning. How could he have been so oblivious? He ached for Delray. He couldn't fathom the agony she must have endured.

"I didn't know," he said again.

The words seemed to snap everyone back into the moment. Rose stirred on the bed. Her face was wet. She looked at Delray. There was compassion in her eyes.

"How did the two of you find each other? You and your son?"

Delray tightened. Her jaw clenched and she raised the pistol at Rose again. Lazarus answered in a low voice.

"I was brought up by a family in Pennsylvania. Bethlehem, PA. When I was still young they told me I'd been adopted, but refused to tell me who my real parents were. When I was eighteen I broke into my father's, adoptive father's file cabinet and found some papers saying I'd been born in New York. It took me years to track down my mother. I finally found her at Duke University."

Delray lowered her gun again. "I was walking across the Quad carrying an armload of books and papers. I had just passed Allen Hall and was heading toward Chapel Drive when I noticed a student approach. The closer he got the more familiar he looked. Then

I dropped everything. I was terrified. I thought it was him. I really thought he was Duke Manyon. Then I realized."

Lazarus stayed in Durham, North Carolina for three months getting to know his mother.

"It was too weird, though. We had the same blood, but were total strangers. Now I understand why. Every time my mother looked at me she saw the man who defiled her."

Delray said she contacted Benjamin. They'd barely spoken in almost a quarter century. Their parents were dead and she thought he'd want to know his nephew. Lazarus moved to Fort Lauderdale and Ben set him up with an apartment and a job as an electrician's apprentice.

"That didn't last long," Lazarus said. "Uncle Ben was good to me, though. Gave me money when I needed it. Made sure I was okay. I bounced around until I fell into the Goth thing and started making money doing tattoos and fangs." He looked diagonally at Demonika. "And all the kinky girls."

"*Romeo of the Night*," said Max.

"Then I met Elizabeth."

She looked at him, with tenderness this time, and cupped her hand over his.

"We're going away," she said.

"What?" Delray blurted, startled. "When?"

"Tonight," Lazarus said. He nodded at Rose. "We'd be gone now if you hadn't told me about your plan. I grabbed her before you did something crazy."

They all turned to Rose, sitting alone on the bed. The insanity had subsided. Brady hoped the kumbaya moment would last. Delray's deadpan face, however, was frantic.

"You can't go," she said. "We're finally going to be together. You and me and Max. We're going to be a family."

Somewhere along the line, Brady realized, Delray had broken the bonds of gravity and spun off into her own orbit. Little wonder, considering the crown of thorns she'd been wearing most of her life. Brutally raped at thirteen. Mothering a child at fourteen. Then discovering her son was the reincarnation of the man who violated her. Delray had been forced to retreat to a parallel universe. Fantasy had become her reality. She had murdered her brother. And Peanut. And now, in a deranged act of love, she planned to eliminate Rose.

Brady couldn't let that happen. He got up from the red chair and stepped toward her. She turned the pistol on him.

"Stay back, Max."

He stopped three feet from her. He considered lunging for the weapon. If Delray was serious about pulling the trigger, he gauged his chances of taking away her gun without being shot at about fifty-fifty.

"Listen to me, Del. I should have protected you. I didn't. You've suffered more than I can imagine. I'm so sorry."

Something softened in her face. She spoke in a voice as frail and timorous as the frightened girl in the boat that night.

"I told you, Max, what happened wasn't your fault. You were just a boy. As it was you saved my life. You saved us all."

He took another step toward her.

"I can save you again, Delray. We'll beat this thing together. They can't prove you had anything to do with Ben or Peanut's murder. You can walk away. You and Lawrence can be together. I'll always be there for you."

Her shoulders sagged and she sighed deeply. Her sad eyes were filled with resignation, as though his words had exorcised her demons. For an instant the illusion of peace filled the room. He chanced another step. She didn't react. He stretched a hand toward her.

"Give me the gun, Delray. Too many innocent people have been hurt. Let's end that now."

She removed her finger from the trigger and was extending the automatic pistol to him. His fingers were inches from it when the door burst open and Junior Ball stepped into the room.

Et Tu Brady

Chapter Eighty-Six

JUNIOR HAD CHANGED from his black robe into gray slacks and a white shirt. His nose was still red and swollen and listing badly. But Brady saw the same bully's violence in his eyes he remembered so well from childhood.

Behind him loomed the silhouette of what looked like a distant mountain. It moved and through the door came the muzzle of a gun with a long silencer attached. An enormous man lumbered in behind it, mechanical, pestilent, like a low-budget movie monster. His weapon captured the attention of every eye in the room. Delray's pistol seemed like a toy by comparison. Brady reached behind him and pulled Demonika's gun from his waistband.

The big man scanned their faces from cavernous black eye sockets. He appeared placid, but Brady noticed his trigger finger twitch. His nostrils flared like a bull preparing to charge. A lethal situation that was seconds from resolution entered an infinitely more perilous phase.

The tiny room had become a geometric configuration of madness. The shadows of seven people and three guns flickered on the walls. The dread was palpable. Scientists have demonstrated that fear has its own scent. An ammonia odor. Brady could smell it. It was coming from him. That old boyhood bravado didn't exist anymore, no more than that boy still existed. That sense of exhilaration in the face of menace had been replaced by cold, stark fear. Something bad was about to happen and there was nothing he could do to stop it.

A tribal dirge was moaning up from The Slimelight. Brady looked at Rose on the bed across the room. Her eyes were large and watchful. She turned them toward him. He tried to send her a silent message. *If shooting starts get on the floor.* He didn't possess his grandmother's psychic powers, but hoped she could hear him. Junior pointed a condemning finger at her.

"Darnell, shoot that bitch."

The big man's black eyes followed Junior's finger and, like an automaton, he rotated his left arm toward Rose. Brady raised his gun and spoke through bared teeth.

"Don't even think about it."

Darnell swung back and grunted something unintelligible. Delray stood between them, not knowing which way to turn.

"I've got some bad news for you, big fella," Brady said. Darnell grunted again. "Did you know left-handed people live nine fewer years than normal people?"

"That's a myth," the behemoth croaked.

"Not for you."

For several long seconds they stared at each other. Brady felt like an undertaker was sizing him up for a box.

Junior's eyes were still on Rose. "I said kill her."

"Shut up, Ball," Brady said. His weapon stayed steady on Darnell. "Drop the gun. Now!"

Darnell peered at him through dark, soulless eyes. A smile curled on his lips. It reminded Brady of a rattlesnake rattling just before it strikes. He spoke in a trombone voice.

"Seems like we got us an old-fashioned Mexican stand-off."

He was right. They stood facing the business end of each other's pistols, locked and loaded and poised at the vertex of an appalling last act. Neither knew what to do next.

Lazarus was still sitting on the couch. It seemed to dawn on him who Darnell was. He pointed at him. "Hey, that's the bastard who robbed us."

Darnell's eyes stayed fixed on Brady.

"Shut up faggot or I'll kick the shit out of you and have my way with your little slut again."

Lazarus looked at Demonika. She was glaring at Darnell, invisible lightning bolts firing from her eyes. If the big man had been made of ice, he would have melted.

"Daddy," she said.

Junior looked down at his daughter, as though he hadn't noticed her before.

"Elizabeth?"

"Daddy, that man raped me."

He turned and looked at Darnell then back at Demonika with a bewildered expression.

"What are you talking about?"

"Him. He broke in here last night. He beat up Lazarus and took our money. Then he forced me down right there on the bed and he raped me." She vaulted screaming from the couch at Darnell. "You filthy *rapist*!"

Lazarus snatched her arm and pulled her back. Junior stared at his daughter, then turned slowly to his hired gun, his eyes wide with incredulity. Even in the faint light Brady could see his face was flushed.

"Is that true? You raped my daughter?" The threat of violence in his voice rose an octave with each word. "My daughter?"

Darnell stood stock still for what seemed like forever. His pistol was still pointed at Brady. The fingers of his gun hand were fidgeting faster now.

"How did I know she was your daughter? She's a thief. She stole somebody's money. I recovered it."

"You raped my daughter?"

"She paid a price. It was that or jail. She got off easy."

Junior charged straight at Darnell with his arms extended. He wrapped his hands around what there was of the gargantuan's throat

563

and tried to throttle him. Darnell's elbow jerked back and his gun went off. Two shots in rapid succession. *Phffft! Phffft!* Even muffled by the silencer, there was no mistaking the sound. Everything stopped. Junior stiffened, hands still around Darnell's throat. Then they slid down and he clutched his stomach. He stumbled backwards two steps and turned. His face was waxen and had taken on a puzzled expression. He pulled his hands away. They were covered in blood. A red circle the size of a beefsteak tomato was growing at the center of his white shirt. He groped at it like he was trying to pull the bullets out of his stomach. Junior looked across the room at his daughter and reached out to her. He took two robotic steps and dropped to his knees. His mouth opened. The others stared, waiting for him to speak, but no sound came out. He lifted one knee and tried to stand, then went limp, as if his bones turned to rubber. Without another word he fell face first onto the floor.

Demonika screamed and rushed to her father. Darnell turned his pistol on Rose.

Brady shouted. "Don't."

The shooter peered at him through the black holes, sneering at Brady's small gun. His finger tickled the trigger. He made a croaking noise that sounded like *"fuck yourself."* Brady fired.

Darnell's head snapped back then recoiled, his sneer replaced by a look of disbelief, like he suddenly remembered he forgot something. His face had a new black hole at the dead center of his forehead. A dark red tear trickled between his eyebrows and down the ridge of his nose. He staggered backward and fell against the closed door. The entire room vibrated. His legs buckled and he slid to the floor, slow, like cement oozing down a chute.

Delray watched without moving a muscle. Then she looked at Rose sitting on the bed. She hadn't received Brady's telepathic message to get on the floor. Delray lifted the gun and curled her finger around the trigger.

Lazarus shouted. "No! Mom! No!"

He leaped off the couch and lunged for Rose just as Delray fired. Brady saw the back of his head explode. Lazarus landed on top of Rose, trapping her with all his weight. Delray understood instantly what she'd done. She began to ululate like she'd been possessed by banshees. For several seconds she rocked back and forth emitting a high-pitched wail. Then she stopped and her despair turned to sudden rage. She cocked the hammer again and screamed at Rose.

"You bitch! Look what you made me do."

Brady yelled.

"Delray don't."

She turned and looked straight at him. Her eyes were wild and her face wet with tears. She spoke in a near whisper.

"I love you, Max."

Et Tu Brady

Chapter Eighty-Seven

A TELEVISION CRACKLED on the wall of the emergency room at Broward General Medical Center. The space was harshly lit and just a shade warmer than absolute zero. In one corner of the room a Latino man sat with his head bowed, running his fingers through thick black hair, impervious to three small children screeching and laughing as they climbed over and around him. Two policemen barged in dragging a rowdy, bloody-faced man in handcuffs. At the center of the room, a young female doctor with exotic features was informing a young couple that their eight-year-old son had broken his leg falling from a tree.

Max Brady was oblivious to all of it. He was too busy sitting there in his blood-stained clothes, staring at his blood-caked hands, looking like a slaughterhouse shift worker, waiting for Rose Becker to die.

Somewhere behind the blue swinging doors, Rose was laying on an operating table with her life hanging by the slenderest thread. An hour before, a young ER surgeon in blue scrubs had come through the doors and explained the situation.

"She's been shot in the heart. The bullet penetrated her right chest halfway between the breast and clavicle." He pointed to the spot on his own chest. "It entered her thoracic cavity between the second and third ribs and passed through her right lung, collapsing it. That alone isn't necessarily life threatening. Unfortunately the projectile ricocheted off an anterior rib and grazed her right ventricle before finally lodging beneath the scapula."

"Is she going to live?" Brady said in a wooden voice.

"My colleague, Dr. Singh, is performing an emergency resuscitative thoracotomy right now."

"What's that mean in English?"

"He's trying to suture Miss Becker's ventricle wound."

"I asked you if she is going to live."

The doctor didn't say anything for a few seconds. He chewed his lip while he evaluated Brady, deciding whether he was in any condition to hear the harsh cold truth.

"Look, Mr. Brady, I'm not going to soft soap you. Morbidity among cardiac gunshot victims exceeds eighty percent. The good news is she was still alive when we got her. We didn't have to revive her. She did not suffer cardiac arrest. That gives her a fighting chance. Her other advantage, and it's a big one, is that she is in superb condition. If anyone is going to survive it will be someone like Ms. Becker."

So Brady sat in the cruel light of the chill room, unconscious to the hospital smells, the cacophonous television, and unruly children, alone with his soul-crushing sadness, powerless as he waited for the young surgeon to return and tell him she was gone.

He should have known it would happen. That's what all the women he loved did to him. They died. They always had, and it looked like they always would. As if it was written in the stars. Clear as night. Max Brady goes on living his bleak, lonely life while the ghosts of everyone he'd ever loved swirl around him, invisible spirits he couldn't see or hear or touch. Ever again. Because they were not really there. He'd finally accepted that life after death was a sham. There were no happy endings. No Santa Claus. Never would be. Not for him. So he sat there. His only want now to be with her when she took her last breath. To be with her every second she had left.

He rubbed his red hands together and relived the bloodbath. Six shots. Four dead. A fifth soon to follow. He cursed Junior Ball for showing up just as Delray was about to surrender her gun. He damned himself for hesitating at the crucial instant, giving Delray time to pull her trigger a millisecond before he pulled his. His last image of Delray was her collapsing like the fallen angel she was, her mouth open in a silent scream, looking straight at him with those crazed, tragic eyes.

After that everything was a blur of sounds and smells. Sirens. Chaos. The mordant malodor of gunpowder. The coppery stench of just-spilled blood. The tiny room littered with four corpses. Delray, Lazarus, Junior, and Darnell Dent. Rose, her skin gray and cadaverous, barely alive, a candle guttering in the wind.

Brady pulled Lazarus's body off her and let it fall to the floor. He turned to Demonika. Her face was a Greek tragedy mask bathed in scarlet. She looked like she was crying blood. Babbling gibberish, crawling on her hands and knees back and forth between the lifeless bodies of her father and her lover. He grabbed her by the shoulders. She didn't respond. He slapped her face.

"Call nine-one-one. Now!"

He cradled Rose's head in the hollow of his arm. The human heart generates enough pressure to propel blood thirty feet in the air. A hot red spring was shooting from her chest. Brady bunched a bedsheet and pressed it hard into the wound, trying desperately to stanch the bleeding. Her eyes were open, watching him with a strange detachment, seemingly amused by his futility. Her lips moved, but her voice was less than a whisper. Then her eyes fluttered and closed. The flame expiring.

"Do not die! Rose!" Brady screamed from point blank range, as if the louder he said it the longer she'd live. "Please don't die!" Knowing she would.

There was a mad rush to the hospital. They wheeled Rose into the ER and a scrum of doctors and nurses surrounded her while Brady stood watching, impotent. Then they took her away from him. Perhaps forever.

Ron Register came to the hospital at two o'clock in the morning with Perry James, the large black detective with intelligent eyes and professional manner. They took his statement. He told them about Delray's twisted girlhood dream. And about her placing a bulls-eye on Rose to fulfill it. Register said he was closing the investigation. The record would show Benjamin Chance and Richard Strong were victims of Delray Chance Cross. Brady didn't argue.

"I let emotion cloud my judgment," he said. Hollow. Defeated.

"You're just guilty of trusting your friend," the captain said, more generous than kindness required. Brady would thank him for it someday. "In the end, she was the author of her own demise."

He nodded. Almost as an afterthought, he told Register about Junior Ball's connection to the fatal collision on Las Olas and gave him Dismas Benvenuti's name.

After they left, he spent the rest of the night watching the blue swinging doors. Or roaming the bare hospital corridors. At some point he noticed the astringent hospital scents. The nauseous smell of alcohol, antiseptics, and disinfectants. Sickness and death. Odors burned into his childhood recollection sitting in this very same hospital waiting for his mother to die. Now it was Rose's turn. He wished there was a drug to kill the part of him that felt.

Then, in the depth of night, his shoulders quaked and the tears came and he sat in the cold, bleak, noisy room and let go. The storm came in waves. He tried to be quiet. He covered his face with his hands to muffle the sobs. They went on for some time. The only person who seemed to notice was a heavyset nurse gawping at him from behind the E.R. reception desk.

After three, maybe four hours he got up and gave her his cell phone number and asked her to call when the doctor came out. She directed him to the hospital cafeteria. Kitchen workers were banging large metal trays of scrambled eggs, sausage, bacon, and grits. Several tables were occupied by hospital workers in green and blue and red scrubs, eating, gabbing, laughing, deaf and blind to the tragedy that was Max Brady's life.

He sat alone at a small table, staring hollow-eyed at the funnel of steam rising from his black coffee, watching again in slow motion as he and Delray fired their guns in unison. In a heartbeat he had killed the first girl he ever loved, who killed the last woman he ever loved. That had to be some kind of Guinness Book world record.

"Mr. Brady?" A voice jarred him from his contemplations. The young doctor in blue scrubs was standing beside his table, surgical cap covering his head, mask hanging from his chin. His shirt and pants were spattered with red spots. *Rose's blood.* He wanted to reach out and touch it. *Touch her.* The doctor was holding a cup of coffee in his hand. His face was inscrutable.

"Say it." Brady hardly recognized his own voice.

"She's still alive."

A sob erupted deep inside him. He tried to choke it back but it came anyway. The young doctor reached down and patted his shoulder and waited for it to pass.

"We lost her a couple of times. Less than a minute each time. Her heart flatlined, but we got it going again. Dr. Singh repaired the ventricle wound and reflated her collapsed lung. If she hadn't been in such fine physical condition she wouldn't have survived this long."

"She's a physical trainer," Brady said. His mind was reeling. Rose's heart stopped! Did that mean she was clinically dead? But she was alive. He'd take that for now. Nothing else mattered. "Can I see her?"

"I don't want to dash your hopes, Mr. Brady, but I have to be frank. The damage to Miss Becker's cardiopulmonary system is catastrophic. We've induced coma in the hope her body will repair itself. But very few people survive the kind of trauma she's suffered. I think you should be aware of that. You should go home and get some sleep. We'll call you in the event of…"

He didn't finish the sentence. He didn't need to.

Brady wouldn't leave. If Rose died he was going to be with her. He was going to cling to every precious second. The doctor escorted him to the Intensive Care Unit, a hushed and dimly lit wagon wheel with glass-walled rooms and a nurse's station at the hub. A television flickered silently on the wall of Rose's room. He collapsed into the only chair.

Her eyes were closed. He touched her. Her skin was clammy and several shades lighter than her normally pale complexion. Brady sat in the low chair holding her hand. Examining the confusion of tubes and wires attached to her. Listening to the monitors beep. The click-and-wheeze of the respirator. Staring at her still face. Searching for signs of life. A pursed lip. A fluttering eyelid. Anything. Rogue waves of emotion washed over him during the night. He hadn't felt so helpless since 9/11, searching for Victoria at Ground Zero, knowing she was somewhere in the rubble, knowing it was too late to save her.

"I'm here, Rose." He'd read somewhere that hearing was the last sense to go. "I'll never leave you. Please don't leave me."

She was twenty seven years old. During medieval times, twenty seven years had been the average lifespan of peasant women. Diet and healthcare were to blame then. In more recent times, twenty seven had been a notable tipping point for some, particularly the famous. Jimi Hendrix, Janis Joplin, Jim Morrison, and Kurt Cobain all died at that age. But they'd brought on their own ruin. Rose Becker was going to die because he hadn't protected her.

He thought he should pray, just in case he was wrong about afterlife. But to who? God? Who was God? What was God? Was he a he, or was he a she? Catholic? Muslim? Jew? Rastafari? Zoroastrian? It wasn't that he was atheist. He just believed the God he'd been taught about was more fantasy than fact. To know the ultimate truth you had to take the ultimate trip. He didn't see any way around it. Rose was too young to take that trip. And too good. So he prayed. Not to God, or Allah, or Jehovah, but to his Grandma Kate. To his mother Mary. To his wife Victoria. He prayed to the women he'd loved. He couldn't see or hear or touch them. But maybe they *were* there. Maybe they could hear him. If there was a higher power maybe they could put in a good word for Rose. Maybe they could save the one woman he loved who was still alive. She was the difference between everything and nothing. If she died, he didn't want to live. Though he knew he would.

He'd been awake almost three straight days and his eyelids were drooping. At some point he received sleep like a sacrament.

Corkscrewed like an adagio dancer in the small chair, he slipped into a restless trance-like state and dreamed about Rose. Making love to her in the butterfly garden. Her perfect face framed by those long black curls. Her pale eyes fluttering at the moment of abandon. Her soft trill as she cascaded over the precipice. Then, in an instant, bleeding on a bed in a room filled with gunsmoke. Those same violet eyes – serene, surreal – watching his desperate attempt to stem the tide of her lifeblood.

When the fog lifted his cheek was resting on the bed. He lay there for several seconds surrounded by darkness. Everything vague and strange. He heard the monitors beeping. The whoosh of the respirator, steady as an oil rig. And something else. What? His cell phone was ringing. Green iridescent letters on the caller ID glowed in the dark: Francis U. Furbush. He punched the talk button.

"Fuzzy?"

"Is this Mr. Max Brady?" a female said. He could hear tears in her voice. "This is Lilia Rodriguez."

The name didn't register.

"I'm sorry but…"

"I worked for Fuzzy Furbush."

"Worked?"

"Someone shot him last night. Fuzzy's dead."

Et Tu Brady

Chapter Eighty-Eight

FUZZY FURBUSH HAD lied about Lilia Rodriguez. She was more beautiful than he'd described. Like Rose, she was the kind of woman who demanded to be looked at without trying. Petite. Soft black hair. Green eyes. Perfect skin. Brady wondered why she had her sights set on the FBI. She should have been in the movies.

She arrived at Broward General just before noon. Rose was still deep in a coma. He'd kissed her forehead, one of the few patches of bare skin not blocked by the monitoring devices. He made the ICU head nurse promise to call him the instant anything changed.

Lilia was waiting in the main lobby. She wore a fawn cashmere dress and a tan calfskin handbag the size of a briefcase was hanging from her smooth brown shoulder. At the center of the room, a player-piano was tinkling out Scott Joplin's *The Entertainer* with the aid of a pneumatic music roll.

"I'm so sorry about your friend, Mr. Brady. They were talking about it on the radio. Have faith. Miracles happen every day."

"I hope you're right," he said without emotion. "My condolences about Fuzzy. He spoke very highly of you."

"He was like a father to me."

Brady had gotten the impression Fuzzy's feelings for Lilia went beyond paternal, but said nothing. They sat in a pair of soft chairs beside a planter filled with yellow silk sunflowers and green plastic ferns.

"What happened, Lilia?"

She looked at him when she spoke. Her green eyes were tinged with redness and her voice was tremulous. Plantation police called her around midnight. Fuzzy was found face down in the breeze-way outside his office. He'd been shot once in the head and once in the back of his neck. The detective she spoke to, Lieutenant Frank Velasquez, said it looked like the killer had been waiting in the shadows. The coroner estimated time of death at about nine o'clock.

"Do they have any suspects?"

Lilia sniffled. Brady handed her his handkerchief and she dabbed her eyes. "Detective Velasquez said Fuzzy hadn't been robbed. They found his wallet still on him and a couple of hundred dollars in his pockets. But the killer used his keys to open the office door. They had me come identify Fuzzy's body." She choked on a sob. "The file cabinets had been rifled. Papers were strewn everywhere."

"Any idea what the killer was after?"

"They asked me to go through Fuzzy's things to see if I noticed anything missing, but nothing stood out. Then I remembered this." Lilia reached into her bag again and pulled out a manila file folder about three inches thick. "Fuzzy gave this to me the day you came to the office. I must have just missed you. He liked you. He said you were smart. That's high praise from him. He told me to hang onto the file. He said if anything happened I should give it to you."

"Fuzzy thought someone might try to harm him?"

A sad smile crossed her face and she rolled her eyes.

"I thought he was just being melodramatic. The stories he told! Always so adventurous. Fuzzy always the hero. I never quite knew what to believe."

Brady was impressed by Lilia's insight. Maybe she would make a good FBI agent.

"Have you been through this?"

"Of course. Fuzzy made me read his old files and then quizzed me on my impressions and ways I would proceed. He said he'd read you a portion of the contents. But there's a lot in here you aren't aware of."

Lilia said she had to go make arrangements for Fuzzy's funeral. They stood and she hugged him and they held each other for a moment beside the silk and plastic garden. A pair of kindred souls. Sad survivors.

He returned to ICU and layed the file on the floor next to the chair. Rose's condition hadn't changed. Black hair surrounded her ashen face like funeral bunting. He stroked a wisp off her forehead.

"Miracles happen every day," he whispered.

He spent the rest of the day at her side. Holding her hand. Swabbing her skin with a cool damp cloth. Whispering to her.

"When you're better we'll stock the sloop. Get lost in the Bahamas. We can live on fruit and fish. Make love on deserted beaches. We can marry if you want. Have a fine wedding under a palm tree by the sea. Make a baby. Start a family. Would that make you happy, Rose?"

She didn't answer him.

Et Tu Brady

Chapter Eighty-Nine

RAIN FELL IN the afternoon. Brady watched the big drops patter against the window and water beads rindle down the glass. It was as if the whole world was crying. A bluejay sat in an oak tree outside the window, huddled beneath cerulean feathers, impassive, serene, waiting for the storm to pass. He wished he could be as stoic. He doubted his storm would ever pass. He caught his reflection in the glass. His jaw was peppered by a two day bristle and purple crescents punctuated his eyes. Below, traffic was backed up at the light at 17th Street and Andrews. Life went on unabated for everyone, it seemed, but he and Rose.

The young surgeon came in near dusk. Brady rubbed the stubble on his chin while the doctor checked Rose's vital signs and shined a penlight in her eyes. He announced he was mildly encouraged.

"If she remains stable her heart might have time to recuperate. She's got a shot. A very long shot. But remember, Mr. Brady, it's not always easy to die."

It was dark outside when Brady picked Fuzzy Furbush's file off the floor and walked to the cafeteria. He hadn't eaten since... he couldn't remember. He needed fuel. A few tables were occupied. One by the dark-haired Latino man and his three children from the

Emergency Room. The kids were subdued now, eating hamburgers and French fries while their father gazed into space. A large smiling woman behind the counter spoke with a Caribbean lilt.

"What can I get you, baby boy?"

"What do you recommend?"

"Depends on what you like, dear. Myself, I prefer oxtail stew with red beans, rice and plantains." She slid her hands down the sides of her bountiful body and laughed. "But you know what that does to my girlish figure."

Brady smiled and pointed. "Give me some of that."

"Chicken parmigiana? Excellent choice. I'll throw some extra sauce on your pasta."

The aroma made Brady realize how famished he was. He took a corner table and ate amidst the clatter of plates and silverware. He used a tablespoon to spool spaghetti onto his fork in the traditional Italian manner. While he ate he watched people at other tables. Three nurses were giggling at the center of the room. At another table an elderly doctor was sipping coffee and reading the sports page. The headline trumpeted the Super Bowl showdown. Brady had lost track of time. The big game was being played tomorrow. A bus boy pushed his cart through the room depositing dirty dishes in a square gray plastic tray and wiping off tables.

A copy of *The Lauderdale News* was lying on the cart. Brady grabbed it. The front page headline screamed at him. *Bloodbath: City Commissioner Near Death*. It was the type of scandalous, gossip mill barbarism that sent spasms of ecstasy through the bloodsucking press. Rose got most of the ink. The city commissioner shot in the heart by the other woman in a love triangle. The article detailed the victims. The prominent local attorney. The ex-Fort Lauderdale cop. The renowned economist. The Goth entrepreneur. Ron Register was quoted extensively. He officially declared that Delray had murdered her brother and a childhood friend. About two-thirds of the lengthy piece was accurate, which in Brady's experience was pretty standard. The rest was speculation and innuendo, including a comment by an anonymous source – Register, thought Brady – that Delray was a mentally disturbed college professor who had been sexually molested as an adolescent by Ben and Peanut. A small sidebar reported the murder of another former city policeman, Francis U. "Fuzzy" Furbush. No link was made between his murder and the shooting above the Slimelight.

Brady thought about Fuzzy. How bizarre that he was killed the same night Rose was shot. The same night Delray, Lazarus, Junior and Darnell Dent died violently. The world had gone crazy. He pushed his plate away, the chicken parm half-eaten, and opened Furbush's file.

For the next half hour he sat, chin in hand, examining the contents with a clinical efficiency befitting the hospital setting. The first page was a summary written twenty nine years ago by a detective named Kenneth Dunlop. *Dunlop?* The name felt familiar, but he wasn't sure why. The document was dated days before *that night.*

It was the same report Fuzzy read to him at his office detailing how Duke Manyon and Buck Foxx had been identified by confidential informants as the culprits in the *SunSplash* jewel heist. The file contained several statements. One from Harold S. Gomez, a security guard at *SunSplash*, the oceanfront estate owned by Jonathan Osgood Kimble III, the prominent citrus magnate and owner of *SunSplash Orange Juice*. At the time of the robbery he had been eighty years old. A notation said he was in the South of France with his thirty-two-year-old wife, Mandy Binghamton, an ex-Broadway dancer. Gomez had been the only person at *SunSplash* the night it was robbed.

The guard described walking in on two men in Kimble's second floor library at one o'clock in the morning. They were dressed in black and wore ski masks and had peeled back a large Persian rug that covered the center of the room. A floor safe hidden beneath the rug had been unlocked and its door was open. A lacquered wooden box approximately twelve inches long was on the floor beside the safe. Gomez said he pulled his service revolver.

One of the intruders rushed me and knocked me to the ground and I dropped my weapon. He sat on my chest and punched me several times in the face. The next thing I knew he was pressing the barrel of my gun between my eyes. I heard the hammer cock. I told my assailant I have a wife and four children and begged him not to shoot.

His response was: "Tough luck, chump."

I was certain I was going to die when his accomplice shouted 'No.' He grabbed my attackers arm and jerked it upward just as the gun went off. The explosion was so loud both intruders froze for a second. The gunman pushed his partner away and pointed the pistol at my head again. The second man slammed into him from behind and the gun discharged again, this time inches from my left ear. After that everything is hazy. My ears were ringing and the smell of the gunsmoke was burning my eyes and nostrils. My vague recollection is that the two intruders wrestled on the ground beside me for a brief time and then the lights went off. A second later a flashlight shined in my eyes.

"You're a lucky son of a bitch, mister," a voice said.

I will never forget the gunman's response.

"I'm telling you, Duke, we gotta ice this guy."

I clearly heard the name 'Duke.' The man called Duke seemed to be in charge. He snapped at his accomplice. 'Shut the fuck up.' He ordered the other man to tape my eyes, mouth, hands and feet and they dragged me into a closet and closed the door. I heard sounds for a few more minutes and then nothing. I remained in the closet until my relief came on duty at 8 A.M. I must add that if it had not been for the man called Duke, I believe I would be dead. I owe him my life.

Detective Dunlop's report stated that Jonathan Osgood Kimble III had been contacted in France. He told Dunlop he often bought expensive jewels for his wife and close friends. Kimble claimed the safe contained two-dozen diamonds ranging from two to seven carats, several sapphires, and some rare gold coins. Kimble estimated their value at more than one million dollars. He asked Dunlop to send him a copy of the police report so he could register a claim with Lloyd's of London.

Brady stared at the document. Somewhere in the recesses he had a vague recollection of the robbery. It had been big news when he was a kid. The details were vague though. He rifled through the file. Any question about Duke's identity was put to rest by a second affidavit written by Detective Dunlop. It contained the statement of a confidential informant identified as Mitzi Bloom. The report identified her as a *"striptease dancer"* at the Pink Pussycat Club on 17th Street Causeway.

Mitzi Bloom (MB), age 23, has been working as CI for this affiant for nine months (in return for plea deal arranged by affiant on drug and prostitution charges). On 7/23, the day following the SunSplash robbery, MB met this affiant at FLPD and reported that she and a friend, Veronica Salerno (VS), age 24, were present early on the morning of 7/22 aboard the Manta Ray, a sailboat docked at Bahia Mar Marina, Slip F-19.

Bloom told Detective Dunlop the boat was owned by Duke Manyon, who operated a water ski school on the Intracoastal and had the valet concession at the Polynesian Room restaurant on North Federal Highway. She said she and Veronica Salerno had been invited to the boat by Buck Foxx, who was a frequent patron at the Pink Pussycat. Neither Manyon nor Foxx were present when the women arrived at two in the morning. They waited on deck.

At approximately 3 A.M. Manyon and Foxx arrived in a yellow motor boat. MB says that upon seeing them suspect Manyon became visibly upset and ordered Foxx to 'get rid of the whores.' Foxx protested, saying the girls 'want to get naked and party.' While Manyon secured the motor boat, Foxx escorted MB and VS into the cabin and dumped the contents of a black velvet bag onto a table at the center of the room. MB said she was astonished. The walls were 'dancing with light' reflected by the pile of gemstones. At that point Manyon came in and saw them. MB said he became enraged and took she and VS roughly by their arms and yanked them out of the cabin. 'Get the hell out of here,' he said and pushed them off the boat onto the dock. MB says VS became upset and swung her bag at Manyon, narrowly missing his head. Manyon slapped VS in the face, which made her more angry. She began loudly accusing him of being a jewel thief. Manyon grabbed VS's face in his hand and squeezed hard. 'You got a big mouth, sweetie. If you want to live long enough to see those big tits of yours sag someday you better keep it shut.' MB said she was frightened and dragged VS away from the marina. 'I really thought he was going to kill us,' she told affiant.

Detective Dunlop stated that Mitzi Bloom called him the next day and said she was still afraid for her life and requested protection. He told her that if another threat occurred she should contact him immediately.

An addendum dated August 5th was stapled to the report.

It has been 12 days since affiant took statement of CI Mitzi Bloom (7/23) concerning SunSplash robbery suspects Wayne Peter 'Duke' Manyon and George David 'Buck' Foxx. Since then affiant has attempted to contact MB on several occasions without success. Today, Mike Rumsfeld, manager of the Pink Pussycat Club where Bloom and Veronica Salerno work as striptease dancers, filed missing person reports on MB and VS. Rumsfeld informed this affiant's partner that the women haven't been seen or heard from in over one week. He suspects they have gone to Las Vegas on holiday or to find work, but was not certain of that. He expressed concern because they hadn't informed him they were leaving town.

A third report was a verbatim transcript of a tape recorded statement from an unnamed confidential informant identified by the alias *Vic*. Detective Dunlop's report described him as a fence of stolen jewels who had been providing him reliable information for a number of years. The report didn't say why *Vic* was a snitch. Brady guessed it was not out of a sense of civic duty.

I read about the Kimble job in the newspaper. The next day I got a visit from Buck Foxx, who is Duke Manyon's partner. Buck is dumb as a skunk, a muscle head with a violent streak you gotta watch out for. He comes to my house by boat with a bag full of hot rocks, diamonds and sapphires and some 17th Century Spanish coins.

Buck's got a big mouth. Likes to brag. Typical of most guys who done time. The bigger and badder the other cons think of you, the better off you are in the joint. Buck said they were tipped to the job by Kimble's wife, who Duke Manyon had been giving water ski lessons. She used to be a Radio City Rockette or some shit and is apparently quite a piece of ass. Her husband is rich but older than dirt and Duke had been giving her more than ski lessons. She was the one who told him they were going to the French Riviera and about the box of jewels in the upstairs safe. She's not supposed to know the combination but does anyway.

My standard cut is ten percent off the top. Buck said he and Duke would take half what was left and the other half would go to the wife. She claimed the stones was worth half a million, but as soon as I seen them I knew they was twice that.

I got a guy in the Diamond District on 47th Street in Manhattan, one of them Hasidics with the black hat and corkscrew sideburns. Been doing business with him twenty years. Pays fifty cents on the dollar. That's a good rate. Most fences get a third. That's why Duke comes to me.

Vic told Buck that Mrs. Kimble was right. The jewels were worth a half million. At fifty percent, that meant two hundred fifty thousand. *Vic* would take twenty five grand off the top. The Rockette would get half of the rest and Duke and Buck would split the other half. *Vic* would actually get *"a shitload more, since the Hasidic's gonna pay a half mil."* Buck took the stones and told *Vic* to come to Bahia Mar the next night. If Duke gave his thumbs up, he'd be on the next flight to Gotham.

I gotta be honest. I was gonna do this deal and keep it to myself. I've given you fellas plenty and this was gonna be my nest egg. But when I get to the boat that night I find Buck sitting on the couch, slobbering drunk and crying like a baby. Two broads are stretched out on the floor with plastic bags over their heads. I lean over and look at them, hoping they're alive, but the second I seen their faces I knew. Eyes open wide, tongues sticking out their mouths like they was a couple of them gargoyles on churches.

I'm thinking one of them is Kimble's wife but Buck says they're strippers at that joint over next to Kim's Cabin, that barbecue restaurant on 17th that advertises they make the world's worst ribs, which I never understood. Buck was messed up. He says they saw the diamonds the night of the heist. Duke kicked them out but Buck says when he got to the boat he finds them tearing the cabin apart. Shit everywhere. The strippers say they know Buck and Duke did the SunSplash job and they want a piece of the action or they're going to the cops. Buck says wait till Duke gets back and they can talk about it. So they start snorting cocaine and doing tequila shots and after a while one of them, he called her Missy or something, stumbles into the head and he can hear her puking. The other one's passed out on the couch. He says he ties her wrists and ankles and tapes her mouth.

When Missy comes out she sees her friend and starts freaking out. Buck's afraid somebody's gonna hear the noise so he throws her on the floor and sits on her but she don't shut up. Buck grabs a plastic bag off the table and pulls it over her head until she shuts up. Then he does the same to the other broad. He said she woke up and started fighting but didn't last long.

He's telling me this shit and my brains doing somersaults. I don't want nothing to do with no murder. I tell Buck to find another fence. I'm heading out the door when Duke shows up. He sees the girls and goes ballistic. Grabs Buck by the shirt and starts beating the shit out of him. The two of them tripping over the dead broads. Buck's crying and begging Duke to stop.

Then Buck blurts out something that scares the piss out of me. 'Our guy called. He says the bitches was snitching.' I take that to mean they got somebody inside the police department telling them what's what. Duke looks at me like I ain't supposed to hear this shit. I'm blowing a gasket cause if they got a dirty cop telling them these whores are stoolies, maybe they know about me too.

I wanted to get out of there. I open the cabin door and Duke grabs me. He's usually a pretty cool customer but the look on his face was enough to make me piss myself. 'You better forget what you saw here,' he says. He shoves the bag of jewels at me. 'You got one week. Go to your Jew and come back with a quarter mil. Or I'll put your head in a bag too.

He pushes me out the door. Real rough. That's when I decided to come here. Those sonsabitches is crazy. I figure Duke don't suspect me or he ain't giving me no diamonds. But who knows tomorrow? They found out about them girls, they can find out about me. You can't let nobody know you're talking to me. They'll snuff me without batting an eye. Them dudes is bad medicine.

The file contained several manila envelopes. Brady opened one. It had diagrams of the *SunSplash* estate, photographs of the stolen jewels and coins, and a snapshot of Jonathan Osgood Kimble III and his young wife. Then he found pictures of the two strippers. Glossy black-and-whites from the Pink Pussycat Club. The girls were posing provocatively in skimpy costumes they presumably shed during their acts. Young, pretty, vivacious looking girls. Brady was catapulted back to that rainy day at Whiskey Creek twenty nine years before. The shallow grave. The same faces, but encased in plastic. Not pretty or vivacious anymore.

Et Tu Brady

Chapter Ninety

WHEN BRADY GOT back to ICU he saw activity in Rose's room. Two nurses were scurrying around. The young surgeon was working over her. *Rose is dead!* He started toward the room, but his legs wouldn't move. He felt dizzy. A nurse at the main station saw him stagger and grabbed him. The name on her scrubs said Barbara Bishop. She pulled a chair over and he collapsed into it.

"She's dead, isn't she?"

Bishop looked down at him with compassionate eyes.

"That's not my post, sir. Stay here. I'll check."

He watched her cross the floor. She stuck her head into the room and had a brief exchange with one of the nurses. The first nurse nodded and Brady could see her sigh. *She's gone.* He put his face in his hands and tried to conjure an image of Rose alive and happy, but all he saw was blackness. He felt dead.

"Mr. Brady," Barbara Bishop said. He didn't look up. "Can you walk?"

He shook his head. A hand touched his wrist and Nurse Bishop drew him to his feet. She led him like a child, a little boy again being taken to his mother's death bed. The surgeon and two nurses were bent over Rose's body with their backs to the door. Barbara Bishop steered him to the foot of the bed. He refused to look. He refused to see Rose dead. The surgeon looked up.

"Mr. Brady, I guess miracles really do happen."

He looked at Rose. Her eyes were open and a fragile smile adorned her face. Beads of perspiration sparkled on her brow like a diamond tiara. Brady couldn't speak. He rushed around the bed and fell to his knees. He buried his head at her side and wept without shame. Bishop pulled him to his feet.

"Miss Becker doesn't need any excitement right now, Mr. Brady," the doctor said. "I think the worst is over, but her heart has been severely traumatized. We don't want to elevate her pulse rate. You understand."

Brady nodded. He managed to thank the doctor and the nurses before he was wracked by another sob. Rose's eyes were wet too. He took her hand and squeezed.

"I thought I'd lost you."

She blinked at him and squeezed back, but he could barely feel the pressure. The doctor came around the bed.

"Say goodnight and let's let her rest. From the looks of it, you could use some shut-eye yourself. Go home and get a good night's sleep. Come back in the morning. Maybe that breathing tube will be out and you two can talk."

Brady didn't want to leave her. Not ever again. Doctor's orders, though. He wasn't going to argue. They had saved her life, against all odds. He kissed her forehead. Her skin was cool, the fever gone. She had knocked on Death's door, but Death hadn't answered. Rose smiled at him.

Et Tu Brady

Chapter Ninety-One

TIME BEGUILES RECOLLECTION. Absolves delusion. Casts shadows over perception. Until light expels deceit and lifts the veil on verity. Recollection swirled through the umbra of Max Brady's dream like ill-fitting pieces of a hypnagogic puzzle. Droopy gold coins. Flaming copper nooses. Soft lips. One-eyed monsters. Headless ogres. Bloody skewers. Sweet kisses. Statues on a couch.

Brady bolted upright like he'd awakened from a coma. Consumed by darkness, he felt like he was suffocating and sucked air greedily into his lungs, then exhaled gratefully. He was soaked in sweat. He rubbed his forehead, trying to force away the image of his grandparents in their death poses.

He rolled out of his bunk and stumbled naked to the deck of the *Victoria II*. In the predawn murk, still drunk with sleep, he plunged over the side into the inky canal. He lingered in the chill water only a few seconds before clambering up the small ladder at the stern. His skin tingling. His spirit soaring. He felt reborn. Rose was alive.

Brady resisted an urge to rush to the hospital. She'd be sleeping. He'd let her rest. Her recuperation was more important than slaking his thirst for her. Instead, he ducked down into the cabin and brewed a pot of strong coffee. He toasted two slices of bread and slathered them with apple butter and returned to the deck. The sun was rising and he sat in silence for a long time watching the new day arrive. Wondering what it would bring.

Maybe it was fruit from Rose's miraculous recovery, but his senses were incredibly keen. The coffee tasted earthy as potting soil. He savored the toast crunching between his teeth. The cinnamon tang of the apple butter. The brackish breath of the black canal. The soft sound of water lapping against the hull. The new sun casting diamonds from an untarnished cobalt sky. His entire being was on red alert.

At the speed of light, images began firing through his brain. Ben's body on the floor. Peanut on the morgue slab. Uncle Howard being lionized. Fuzzy Furbush pacing. Delray naked and primal. Junior trying to pluck bullets from his body. A red tear dripping down Darnell Dent's nose. Lazarus's head exploding. Rose's surreal smile.

The past three days had been the strangest of his life – at least the last twenty nine years of it.

He thought about Delray. Shiny. Golden. Luminous. Tortured. An angel with broken wings. Raped. Torn from her family. Torn from him. Torn from her newborn son. Devoured by darkness until she'd become a psychotic murderer. He had failed to protect her as a child, only to kill her as a woman.

Ben, Peanut, and Delray had been indelibly branded that stormy night. As had Brady himself. Each had lost their innocence out on that black sea. Delray by being violated. Ben and Peanut by being cowards. Him by murdering a helpless man. The others had paid the ultimate price. Now only he survived, alive but damaged.

His lone consolation was Rose. With Ben and Peanut's murders resolved, they could put the turmoil behind. When she was able, they would sail beyond the edge of the world. Vanish in the Bahamian archipelago. Let the sun and sea heal their wounds. Her heart. His head. Knowing that no amount of time would absolve his recollections.

One question still gnawed at him. Who killed Fuzzy Furbush? The very night of the bloodletting above the Slimelight? Brady didn't believe in coincidences. He calculated whether Delray had time to shoot Fuzzy that night before she came for Rose. Lilia Rodriguez said Furbush was shot at about nine o'clock. So it was possible. Why, though, would Delray kill Fuzzy? He had no answer.

Lilia. The file she gave him had two envelopes inside. He scooted down into the cabin and brought the paperwork on deck. Last night at the hospital he'd read about Duke Manyon, the jewel heist, and the strippers. He opened the second packet and was stunned by what he saw. The label identified it as the police investigation into *"the homicides of Zackary and Kathryn Brady."*

What was Fuzzy's interest in the murder of his grandparents? One person would know.

"I hope I didn't wake you," Brady said into his cell phone.

"I'm in my car on my way to class," Lilia Rodriguez said. "Last semester at Nova Southeastern. Then it's off to Gainesville. The University of Florida Law School."

"Go Gators! Just one warning. Beware of tequila served in wine sacks. But what about the FBI?"

"After I get my diploma. Fuzzy thought I'd make a good agent. I don't want to let him down. How is your friend?"

He filled her in on the good news then turned the conversation to the file.

"Why did Fuzzy have the records on my grandparent's murder?"

"Benjamin Chance told him that Duke Manyon had something to do with their deaths. He was very cryptic. He wouldn't explain how or why. Fuzzy has a good friend in the records department at Lauderdale PD."

"Walter Peebles?"

"You do get around, don't you, Mr. Brady."

"Just nosy by nature. And please call me Max."

"Lieutenant Peebles and Fuzzy go way back. The lieutenant dug the file out of the archives and slipped him a copy."

"Did you read it?"

"He showed me. I'm so sorry. I read that you discovered their bodies. It must have been incredibly painful, especially at such a young age."

"What did Fuzzy say?"

"He thought the whole case was all too tidy."

"What did he mean?"

"We didn't really have a chance to discuss it in detail." He thought he detected a quiver in Lilia's voice. "Fuzzy had good instincts. He taught me that every case has loose ends, even after it's been solved. He thought the investigation into your grandparents' deaths had been wrapped up too neatly. 'Something stinks,' he said. But he didn't say why. Anyway, gotta run. Class in five minutes. Call me if you have any more questions."

The first page of the police report was a short summary of the investigation. Brady breathed deep and told himself to think of the victims as strangers.

Subjects Zackary John Brady, age 74, and Kathryn Doyle Brady, age 72, shot execution style with .38 caliber handgun. Perpetrator Matthew Fitt committed suicide at his home same night or early next morning. Written confession found beside body. (See letter in file and related Case # 26-324 concerning homicide of U.S. Prohibition Agent Woodrow Dexter, 9/17/26.) Case closed.

The file was more than two hundred pages thick. It contained photographs and autopsy reports. Brady could not bring himself to look at them. He noted that Matty committed suicide by sticking a shotgun in his mouth. He'd murdered his grandparents with a thirty eight caliber pistol. That gun was never recovered. He envisioned it, still at the bottom of New River, buried beneath three decades of silt.

The report on Case #26-324 was handwritten. The ink was faded and the jagged letters resembled hieroglyphics. Brady had to squint to decipher that an agent with the Bureau of Internal Revenue's Prohibition Unit was shot to death by bootleggers. There were no eyewitnesses. The report speculated Agent Woodrow Dexter had come upon smugglers offloading a shipment of contraband at Whiskey Creek.

He felt his stomach tighten. He remembered Matty telling him that he and Grandpa Zack ran liquor from Bimini to the creek. Matty said they hadn't talked in almost fifty years. Not since a *"falling out."* Was their falling out over the murder of the federal agent?

The file contained a Xerox of a photograph of Agent Dexter. His date of birth had been July 22, 1901, which made him twenty five years old when he died. Ancient newspaper clippings blared *Smugglers Slay Prohibition Agent* and *Execution at Whiskey Creek.* The articles noted that the creek was notorious as a drop-off point for rumrunners and that Agent Dexter patrolled it on a routine basis.

News of the killing had been overwhelmed by the hurricane that struck the next day. The Big Blow of 1926. One of the most destructive storms ever to hit the United States. Three hundred fifty people dead. Massive destruction. Florida's Roaring Twenties land boom wiped out. The state economy wouldn't recover until after World War Two.

The file contained little actual data. Most of the physical evidence had been washed away by the storm. Agent Dexter's body was found floating face down in the creek just as the hurricane was coming ashore. Cause of death was a single shotgun blast to the chest. After 1926, no new information was entered into the file until a copy of Matty Fitt's suicide note almost five decades later. The confession was typed. Brady wondered why. Matty didn't seem like the typing type.

To Who It May Concern.

I have lived in remorse my entire adult life for a dibolical sin. It has been my Hell on Earth. I cannot tolorate the pain no longer. Tonight I evengd the murder of Agent Woodrow Dexter by executing his killer, Zack Brady. I am overcome by blackness for also ending the life of my childhood love, Katy Doyle, who chose my former friend over me, even thogh he committed the abomable crime against Agent Dexter. I never planned to harm Katy but after I shot Zack she said her life was not worth living without him and begged me to shoot her too. A rage came over me that the woman I had loved since yuth could instead love a cold-hearted murderer. Therfor I granted her wish.

I have confessed my sins to a priest and now hereby confess them to the world in the hope it may bring cumfort to Agent Dexter's family after so many years not knowing. We arrived at Whiskey Creek that night after sailing through mountanis seas carrying 100 cases of Havana rum and Canada whiskey from Alice Town Bimini. Are plan was to unload it at the creek onto a truck but when we got there no truck was to be found. Insted we were surprised by Agent Dexter. Zack pulled his shotgun from the cabin and shot the poor agent point blank. My only consolashun was that I tried to stop Zack, calling to him not to shoot. But to my everlasting regret he ignored my plee. We fled in the boat and navygated through the storm to Lighthouse Point and unloaded our cargo at Cap Knight's speakeasy. I did not want the blood money and refused to take it. Zack used it to buy a fishing boat and a peace of land up river. Do to his sudden wealth, Katy Doyle picked Zack over me. I never spoke to Zack or Katy again til this very night. They have lived in bliss while I have scraped and suffered aflicted by shame and gilt. On this night I have squared the ledger and killed the killer – and regretfully the woman who chose him. Now I pay for my part in the crime. May God have mercy on my soul.

    Matthew Francis Fitt

Brady gazed at the epistle, refusing to believe what he'd read. Not a word of it. He remembered Matty that day outside his shack when he said Grandpa Zack had been a bootlegger. He didn't seem to be the tortured soul described in the suicide note. Brady could still see Matty's cruel smile when he asked him about their falling out.

"That'd be me and Zack's little secret, wouldn't it?"

So this was their *little secret*? Grandpa Zack had murdered a federal agent? The same warm, kind, loving man who'd raised him was a cold-blooded killer? He'd never known a more decent man than his grandfather. Zack Brady went to Mass and took Communion every morning. Then again, maybe he did because he was plagued by guilt. Maybe he'd spent the rest of his life trying to atone for what happened on Whiskey Creek. No. Brady could not envision his grandfather intentionally harming another human, let alone committing murder. Then he thought about Delray. He couldn't imagine her murdering her own brother, either. Or Peanut. Or Rose. Everything was a crazy patchwork of contradictions. None of it made sense.

Brady threw down the papers and leaned back in the deck chair. A bird was trilling in a nearby tree. An unseen yardman cranked on a leaf blower and the warbler gave up its song. Then something happened. The new noise triggered a redirection of his thoughts. His mind began moving at computer speed, as if the stout coffee had been spiked with a cognitive enhancer. It came to him in a rush and he realized it had been hiding in plain sight the whole time. Everything had been a hodgepodge of random pieces, too fractured for him to see a coherent picture. Then, to his horror, it all came together in an instant and he didn't want to believe what he was seeing.

He hastened back down into the cabin and retrieved the rest of the file. On deck he pored over the reports again. The security guard's account of the *SunSplash* jewel theft. The confidential informant statements to Detective Dunlop, one by the stripper Mitzi Bloom, the other by the jewel fence known as *Vic*. Dunlop's follow-up memo about the disappearance of Bloom and her friend Veronica Salerno. He combed the papers once and felt sick to his stomach. He read them again and the scales slipped completely from his eyes.

He began to shake like a feverish man with the chills. He hugged his arms tight against his body and rocked back and forth.

"It can't be true."

Yet, he knew it was. Appalling beyond belief, but true. *Why didn't I see it?* Still, all the puzzle pieces were yet in place. The complete picture was still too sketchy to act upon. He sat on the deck for a long time staring out at the canal, oblivious to the rising sun's rays beginning to sear his skin. Every minute or so a fish leaped into the air and slapped back down onto the water. He watched the black concentric circles undulate outward, like the ripple of long ago events still reverberating today.

Cadaverous faces began swirling through his brain. His father – dead. His mother – dead. The strippers – dead. Buck – dead. Duke – dead. Grandpa Zack – dead. Grandma Kate – dead. Matty – dead. Victoria – dead. Ben – dead. Peanut – dead. The young mother in the street – dead. Devo – dead. Junior – dead. Darnell – dead. Lazarus – dead. Fuzzy – dead. Delray – dead.

Brady's ghosts. As though he was host to some biblical plague that killed everyone he touched, except him. And, thankfully, Rose. It had to end. After a time his plan took shape.

Et Tu Brady

Chapter Ninety-Two

BRADY TELEPHONED THE hospital and spoke to Nurse Bishop in ICU. Rose had been awake off-and-on through the night and early morning, but was now asleep. The young surgeon had come in twice and was encouraged by her progress. Brady asked her to tell Rose he'd be in later in the day.

He dressed and hopped in the Jeep and pointed it west toward Plantation. He called ahead to Benny Jefferson, an old friend from his NYPD days. These days Benny was deputy chief of the Plantation Police Department. When he arrived, Jefferson brought him to the video room and assigned a young technician named Bruce Hendricks to assist him. For the next two hours they sat in front of a bank of video monitors and watched recordings from two nights before taken by traffic cameras at several intersections along Broward Boulevard between State Road 7 and University Drive.

Hendricks was a techno whiz. His fingers danced over the control board like a concert pianist on a Steinway grand. He panned, stopped, zoomed, and decelerated images to super slo-mo. They examined cars. License plates. Vehicle occupants. It took more than an hour before Brady found what he was looking for.

"Stop," he said. "Can you back up?"

"Is the Pope Catholic?"

Video whirred across the screen in reverse.

"Stop there. Freeze that."

It was an Oldsmobile with dark paint. Black or navy blue. Stopped at a light westbound at the intersection of Broward and Country Club Circle. The time was 8:22 p.m.

"Can you push in?"

"Does a bear shit in the woods?"

Hendricks twisted a dial, punched some buttons, and jiggled a toggle switch until the car was boxed in a blue square. He pressed a key and enlarged the picture. They saw a lone figure behind the steering wheel. It appeared to be a man. The sun visor was pulled down blocking his face above the chin. Hendricks scrolled through the video frame by frame. Twenty eight frames per second. On the 560th frame – or twentieth second – the driver leaned forward.

"Can you push in once more?"

"Does a squirrel love its nuts?" Hendricks said. "Is that what you want?"

Brady stared at the screen for a long time. The face filled the frame. There was no mistaking it. He still didn't want to believe what he was seeing, but now he knew it was true.

"Can you make a print of that?"

"Does a wooden horse have a hickory dick?"

Et Tu Brady

Chapter Ninety-Three

BRADY LEFT PLANTATION and drove back eastward on Broward Boulevard. He dialed the Fort Lauderdale Police Department and asked to be put through to Walter Peebles.

"Lieutenant, you said I could call if I needed anything."

"Sure, Brady. Anything for Howard Pickens's godson."

Fifteen minutes later he turned into the police department parking lot. At the reception desk he told the female officer behind the perforated glass he had an appointment with Peebles. She picked up a telephone and punched four numbers and said something Brady couldn't hear.

"Lt. Peebles will be out in a moment. You can have a seat over there."

He was too antsy to sit and meandered around the lobby instead, hands jammed in pockets, mind reeling, trying to sort through the facts, searching for reasons not to believe what he now believed. Could he have been so incredibly wrong? Hoping he was wrong now.

He found himself perusing the *Wall of Fallen Heroes* again, scanning the faces of the departments slain. Johnston, O'Neil, Kirby,

Illyankoff, Conners, Petersen, Alexander, Bruce, Eddy, Dunlop, Mastrangelo…

Dunlop! Dunlop! I knew that name looked familiar.

He examined the photograph of Detective Kenneth A. Dunlop. He'd been a handsome, mustachioed, dark-haired man. The inscription said he died at age thirty five.

"Circumstances Surrounding Death – Fatally wounded in the line of duty. Assailant unknown."

Brady's eyes fixed on the date. Dunlop was shot to death two days after his grandparents were murdered. He was staring at the wall trying to make sense of what he was seeing when Walter Peebles waddled up. They shook hands and were buzzed through a heavy blue door into a long, stark, low-ceiling hallway.

The Records Department was on the first floor at the far end of the corridor. Peebles brought him into a small cluttered office. Slats of afternoon light glared through the window blinds. The lieutenant's chair groaned as he lowered himself into it. Brady sat across the desk from him.

"What can I do for you, Max?"

"I want to ask you about a file you slipped to Fuzzy Furbush."

A look of surprise flashed in the policeman's eyes. Followed by suspicion. Then resignation.

"Damn shame about Fuzzy. He was good people. Good cop. Got railroaded."

"Why?"

"The usual. Department politics."

"Not Fuzzy's appetite for massage parlors and cocaine?"

"All bullshit. Trumped up to get rid of him. He got fired for being too good at his job. Fuzzy pissed off the wrong people. Made them nervous."

"Like who?"

Peebles shook his head without answering. Brady pulled out his grandparents' murder file. The lieutenant nodded.

"After we met the other day, it dawned on me you were related to the victims."

Brady handed the papers across the desk.

"Take a look at this, lieutenant. Tell me if you notice anything suspicious?"

Peebles studied the file. Intent. Sober. Methodical. Flipping through the pages. Returning to the index. Back and forth for several minutes. Finally, he raised his eyes.

"Bates numbers."

"Bates numbers?"

"Before a document is entered into an investigation file it's stamped with a Bates number. Don't ask me why they call it Bates. Probably the guy who came up with the system. It's a reference number for identification and organization purposes. Helps document chain of evidence. This file has a gap."

"Good eye, lieutenant."

Peebles looked at him. "It's a gift."

"Three pages are missing."

"Correct. The numbers jump from one twenty four to one twenty eight."

"Could it be a mistake."

"Possible." He leafed through the pages again and shook his head. "Never seen it before, that I can recall. Like they say, though, anything's possible."

"Any way to determine if those pages ever existed?"

"These days after a document is stamped we scan it right onto a hard drive. This file's almost thirty years old. Back then they used microfilm and microfiche. I'm in the process right now of digitizing all that old film. I'm an intel guy. If I can't do the digging myself, at least I can make it easier for my old chums in Intelligence. We're working backwards in time. I think right now we're to around 1982. This file should still be on a film cassette. The question is whether those pages were photographed before they were removed. If they existed in the first place."

"Can we check?"

Peebles glanced at his wristwatch.

"I got a meeting in the chief's office. I can set you up in the microfilm room. Hardly anybody uses it anymore. You'll have plenty of privacy. Hope you find what you're looking for."

"Thanks, lieutenant. I hope I don't."

Et Tu Brady

Chapter Ninety-Four

IT WAS NEARLY DARK when Brady steered the Jeep onto Key Lime Drive. The street was part of the Citrus Isles, a string of waterfront cul-de-sacs on the east side of New River just south of the Davie Boulevard Bridge. The long fingers of canal homes were identical to Lauderdale Isles where Brady delivered newspapers as a kid. Tall sailboat masts jutted into the sky behind houses like limbless trees. At the end of the street he pulled into the driveway of a handsome little yellow ranch house built around the time Elvis recorded *Hound Dog*. Brady knew it well. It had once been his home.

The front door opened before he could knock. Howard Pickens stood at the threshold holding himself up with a walker. His was made from two aluminum *U's* turned upside-down and connected by a pair of bars. The front legs were equipped with small wheels and perforated tennis balls had been slipped on the back feet like a pair of shoes. Pickens seemed to have aged ten years since Brady saw him at his dedication ceremony two days before.

"Max, my boy," he said with a tired smile. "Come in, come in. This is a pleasant surprise. I hope you've come to reclaim your old room. When you went away to college your Aunt Mo insisted on keeping it just the way you left it, in case you ever wanted to return."

"Just dropping by."

"Wonderful. The Super Bowl is about to kick off. Can you stay and watch?"

The old man pushed the walker through a small neat living room that had changed little in the twenty-plus years since Brady went off to college, never to return. They proceeded to the Florida Room, an airy space at the back of the house with glass walls on three sides. It looked out over New River and the bridge was visible to the right. A large flat screen television was on. Gloria Estefan was singing the national anthem at the fifty yard line of the Miami Dolphins football stadium ten miles away. Pickens picked up a remote and muted the sound.

"Should be a good game. My money's on the Steelers. Can I get you a drink, Max? I might have a beer in the fridge. Or would you prefer coffee?"

"Coffee, thanks."

"I wish I could offer you some of your aunt's oatmeal cookies. One of the many things I miss since she's been gone. Have a seat, my boy. I hope you know this is still your home. Always will be. I'll put on a fresh pot."

Pickens shuffled off. He faltered once and had to steady himself on the door jamb before disappearing into the kitchen. Brady strolled around the room. He inspected the non-glass wall. It was covered with plaques and photographs, mostly mementoes from Uncle Howard's glory days at the Fort Lauderdale Police Department. Commendations from law enforcement and civic organizations. Pictures of him as a young uniformed patrolman. Later in plainclothes. Posing with mayors, governors, and assorted dignitaries. A portrait of Aunt Mo. A framed snapshot of Brady's mom and dad, impossibly young, in bathing suits on Lauderdale Beach, arms around each other, laughing, in love. A shot of Uncle Howard and John Brady in full battle gear somewhere in Vietnam, M-14s slung over their shoulders, smiles on their dirty faces. *"Closer than brothers,"* Pickens said at the dedication the other day.

At the center of the wall, hanging like a piece of artwork, was Uncle Howard's gold detective shield framed against a black background. Dangling from a peg just below it was a pair of silver handcuffs and a shoulder holster holding a service revolver. Pickens had told him once he'd worn the same gun his entire career. He called from the kitchen.

"You'll have to schlepp your own cup, Max. I can hardly function anymore pushing this damned thing."

Two heavy blue ceramic coffee mugs were steaming on the kitchen counter. Brady picked them up and they returned to the Florida Room. He deposited one on a small table beside a brown leather recliner positioned directly below Pickens's wall shrine. Uncle Howard grimaced as he sat in his chair. Brady took a seat across from him in a green suede armchair that faced away from the river. A glass top coffee table was equidistant between them.

The television was to his left. The Green Bay Packers were just kicking off. Brady reached behind him and pulled Fuzzy Furbush's envelope from the waistband of his pants and tossed it on the table. Uncle Howard looked at it, but said nothing.

"You heard what happened?" Brady said.

"I read about it, my boy. Terrible. Absolutely terrible. I was going to call, but I didn't want to bother you at a time like that. How is Rose?"

Brady filled him in on her condition. Uncle Howard watched him with somber eyes.

"I couldn't believe it," he said. "Junior Ball? I've known Darnell Dent since he was a recruit in the academy. And Delray Chance? My God! Such a tragedy. She must have suffered some kind of breakdown. To imagine her killing her own brother. And Richard Strong. It's unthinkable."

Brady listened silently. Then, without preamble, he asked the question he thought had been answered almost thirty years ago.

"Who murdered my grandparents?"

His voice was firm, commanding, prosecutorial. His eyes cold, piercing, adamant. Pickens blinked and his pale skin flushed. He gazed across the glass table, dumbstruck.

"What do you mean, my boy?" he said in a wooden voice. "Where does that question come from?"

"Who shot Zack and Kate?"

"That was a long time ago. My memory's not what it once was."

"We're talking about my grandparents. Your best friend's parents. The mother and father of the man who died saving your life."

"I do remember the murderer left a written confession and then committed suicide. His name eludes me, though."

"Matty Fitt. You had a partner at the time. Do you remember his name?"

"What is this about, Max?"

"Kenneth Dunlop was murdered two days after my grandparents. Ambushed late at night outside his house. Do you remember it? Thirteenth Terrace off Cordova Road. His killer was never caught. The day before he was shot, he wrote a memo saying he didn't believe Matty Fitt murdered my grandparents."

Uncle Howard inhaled and looked up at the ceiling. "My goodness, that has to be thirty years ago. I don't remember. Why are you asking me? After all this time?"

Brady leaned forward and picked the envelope off the glass table. He removed three pieces of paper and pushed them across the coffee table.

"Maybe this will refresh your recollection."

Pickens gazed at him. He didn't look happy. He slipped on a pair of reading glasses, picked up the pages and studied them. After a minute his face took on a pained guise. He put the papers down, reached over to the small table beside his chair and picked up an orange plastic vial sitting next to his mug. He tapped out a bluish pill, popped it in his mouth, and washed it down with hot coffee.

"I'll be so relieved when this hip is repaired. The pain is driving me out of my mind."

"What is that you're taking?"

"Oh, this stuff." He held up the vial and squinted at the label. "I can never remember."

"Oxycodone?"

"Yes. How did you know?"

"Ben and Peanut were drugged with oxy before they were murdered." Pickens didn't reply. His eyes drifted to the television set.

The Steelers had just scored a touchdown. Brady nodded to the papers on the glass table. "So does that ring a bell?"

Pickens shook his head. "I don't recall it, no."

Brady picked up the pages and began reading aloud. Dunlop requested that his memo be entered into the file on the Zackary and Kathryn Brady double homicide investigation. It described the murder scene and how, in his suicide note, Matthew Francis Fitt admitted killing the Brady's because of his guilt over a homicide he and Zack Brady were involved in as young men.

After examining the available evidence it is this affiant's professional opinion that Mr. Fitt did not write the suicide note found with his body. Affiant also believes Mr. Fitt did not take his own life, or that he was the perpetrator in the Brady homicides.

Dunlop wrote that Matty Fitt had been his confidential informant, code name *Vic*, and was providing information on the *SunSplash* jewel theft. The day before his alleged suicide, Fitt identified Wayne Peter "Duke" Manyon and George David "Buck" Foxx as the *SunSplash* thieves. Manyon and Foxx were also implicated by confidential informant Mitzi Bloom who claimed she and fellow *striptease dancer* Veronica Salerno saw gems on Manyon's sailboat matching those stolen from *SunSplash*. Bloom and Salerno had since disappeared and Dunlop believed them dead based on the eyewitness statement of Matty Fitt.

Mr. Fitt believed Manyon and Foxx have a source inside the police department who tipped them that Miss Bloom was an FLPD informant. He was afraid that if the same insider implicated him, Manyon and Foxx would not hesitate to terminate his life.

It is this affiant's belief that suspects Manyon and Foxx did in fact discover Matthew Fitt was working as a CI and murdered him, or had him killed, then staged his suicide.

Dunlop noted that Matty Fitt was not well-educated, yet his suicide note was written on a typewriter. The only typewriter found on Fitt's property was an old Olympic that did not contain a ribbon and did not appear to have been used in some time.

If this affiant is correct, one or more unidentified members of the Fort Lauderdale Police Department provided confidential information to Manyon and Foxx that led to the murders of Mr. Fitt, Miss Bloom, Miss Salerno, and likely Zackary and Kathryn Brady.

Brady looked up. Pickens's eyes were blank, his fingers templed in front of his lips. He looked like he was praying.

"You never saw this memo?" Brady said. He shook his head. "Detective Dunlop didn't tell you any of this?"

Uncle Howard lowered his hands and folded them in his lap. His attitude toward Brady had quickly turned cold as Alaskan ice.

"I'm not at all certain we were still partners at that point."

"I checked. You were. In fact, you gave the eulogy at his funeral."

Pickens cleared his throat and raised an eyebrow. "Where did you find that memo, my boy?"

"Your friend Walter Peebles." Brady saw a look of surprise ripple across Pickens's face. "Somebody removed it from the investigation file. Whoever did, though, forgot about the microfilm back-up. Walter let me look at it. *'Anything for Howard Pickens's godson,'* he said. So Matty Fitt was your partners' confidential informant. Was he your CI too?"

Uncle Howard's skin had turned ghostly white. His lower lip was trembling.

"My memory's not what it used to be, my boy."

"You don't remember that your confidential informant murdered my grandparents? Did Matty tell you he knew Zack and Kate? Did he tell you about killing the federal agent at Whiskey Creek?"

He shook his head again. Brady rose from the chair and stepped across the room. He reached over Pickens's head and pulled the gun from the belt hanging on the wall.

"Be careful with that, Max. I keep it loaded. We've had prowlers."

"Did you hear about Fuzzy Furbush?"

Pickens turned toward the television. Green Bay had the ball on Pittsburgh's twenty yard line.

"I saw it in the paper," he said with a vacant expression. "Too bad. Such a waste."

Brady inspected the weapon. Smith & Wesson Chief's Special, snub nose, thirty eight caliber.

"Fuzzy was shot with a thirty eight."

"Was he?"

"Where were you two nights ago?"

"I rarely go out at night anymore."

Uncle Howard picked up the remote and raised the volume. Brady reached into his shirt pocket and pulled out the photographs Bruce Hendricks had printed for him from the Plantation Police traffic camera. The date and times were coded in orange letters at the bottom. He threw them on the coffee table and they spread across the glass like a deck of cards. Trump cards.

"Big Brother was watching."

Pickens looked at them but made no move to pick them up.

The Packers quarterback threw a touchdown pass. Brady reached down and took the remote out of Pickens hand and hit the mute button. He picked up the photos and handed them to him.

"Look at these carefully."

Pickens looked up at him with stony eyes, then lowered them to the photographs. He glanced at the images for five seconds and tossed them back on the table and turned back to the television without speaking.

"They were taken on Broward Boulevard near Fuzzy's office shortly before he was shot. Recognize the face?"

Pickens spoke without looking at him. "I don't understand what you're getting at, my boy."

"I'm not your boy. I'm not even your nephew."

The older man's face reddened. He sat up straight in the recliner and finally looked at Brady.

"What the hell has gotten into you?"

Brady raised the cylinder of the gun to his nose and sniffed.

"Has this weapon been fired recently?"

Pickens exhaled audibly, as if exasperated. "I hope you're not implying I had something to do with Furbush's death."

Brady pointed the pistol at him. Uncle Howard's eyes grew wide.

"Are you stark raving mad?"

"Answer me."

Pickens cowered. "What has gotten into you, Max?" He was shouting, his voice frantic. "Stop that before you shoot me."

Brady kept the muzzle trained on him.

"How about Ben Chance?"

"That's enough. Stop."

"And Peanut?"

Pickens made a small whimpering noise.

"And Kenneth Dunlop?"

"Maximus Brady you should be ashamed,."

"I just accused you of murdering four people. Let's throw Matty Fitt in for good measure. And you haven't denied one of them."

"Put that gun down and leave my house right now."

Brady stretched his arm until the short barrel was three feet from Uncle Howard's head.

Pickens shrank back against the brown leather. "I didn't murder anyone."

"Lying time is over."

Brady pulled the trigger. A deafening explosion filled the room and Pickens tumbled onto the floor.

Et Tu Brady

Chapter Ninety-Five

BRADY LAYED THE gun on the glass table and walked into the kitchen. He returned to the Florida Room with a short, sharp carving knife and began digging at a splintery black hole in the wooden door jamb beside the reclining chair. Pickens stared up at him from the floor.

"You didn't shoot me."

"Why should I soil my conscience with your blood?"

"To send me to Hell?"

"I don't believe in Hell, although I kinda like the idea of Heaven. Be nice to see my family again someday. My wife. My mom. My dad. You remember my dad. The guy who died saving your pathetic life. And I know you remember my grandparents. If there is a Hell, you're going there, but not yet. First you've got a reservation at the Florida State Prison."

Pickens watched him gouge at the door frame.

"What are you doing?"

"Sealing your fate. You were the leak. You told Duke and Buck that Mitzi Bloom and Matty Fitt were snitching to your partner."

Pickens shook his head. "Don't be ridiculous."

Brady stopped and turned and stood over him.

"You were at Eden the night Duke and Buck kidnapped me and my friends," he said in a low growl. Pickens didn't respond. "After they took us away, you murdered my grandparents. You shot Zack and Kate in the head."

Pickens shook his head weakly.

"No," he said in a near whisper.

Brady turned back to the bullet. "Then you went to Matty's. He'd already told you about killing the Prohibition Agent. Matty shot him, but you concocted the fiction that my grandfather did it. You typed the suicide note. You forged Matty's signature." Still no response. "You blew his brains out with his shotgun and took the diamonds Duke and Buck had given him to fence. Then, when your partner Dunlop started connecting the dots, you whacked him."

Pickens lay on the floor looking up at Brady's back. He was quaking now.

"Lies! Lies! Lies! You've lost your mind."

"We'll find out. My grandparents were murdered with a thirty eight. So was Dunlop. And Fuzzy. Dollars-to-donuts ballistics matches the bullets that killed them to your gun."

Brady finished prying the slug from the door frame. He turned and held it out to Pickens. The old man was on his feet. Standing tall and steady now without his walker. He was holding his service revolver. It was pointed at Brady's chest.

"Sorry, my boy. I cannot let you do that." He flicked the wrist of his gun hand toward the green suede armchair. "Sit down."

Brady ignored him. "Why did you kill Ben and Peanut?"

"Sit down *now*."

His voice possessed a new power. Brady sat. Pickens stood over him without speaking. He looked like he was searching for the right words, but there were none.

"Put down the gun," Brady said. "You're finished."

"You're right, of course, my boy. I did build a house of cards. Frankly I'm amazed it stood for a day, let alone decades." He sighed. "I'm not going to try to justify my actions. Suffice to say I did what I had to. But I never stopped worrying. Never stopped being haunted. I doubt I've had a good night's sleep in thirty years."

Brady's brow contracted in an ironic smile. "Sorry to hear that. Take comfort that Zack and Kate have been sleeping soundly. So has your old partner Dunlop. And Matty. And Ben and Peanut. Not to mention Delray. Her death goes on your ledger too. So does her son's. And Junior's. And Darnell Dent's. You've run up quite a body count."

Pickens's shoulders stiffened. He stepped around the glass coffee table with no trace of a limp and squared himself to Brady.

"I took no pleasure in any of them. And I take none in this. You were always the one I feared most, Max. I fully expected you to figure things out at some point. But you seemed to have put it behind you and gotten on with your life. Then Walter Peebles told me Furbush was snooping around, asking about some old files."

"The jewel theft investigation. And my grandparents' murders."

"Walter thought I stayed in touch with him because I was a lonely old man. It was much more than that. I knew there were things in those files that could bring me down. I sanitized them the best I could, but they still contained enough to hang me if someone put the pieces together."

"Poor Uncle Howard. No wonder you couldn't sleep. Did you try warm milk?"

Pickens shook his head and smiled sadly. He held the thirty eight in both hands, caressing it, as if he hoped a magic genie would pop out the barrel and rebuild his house of cards.

"When Walter told me Benjamin Chance hired Fuzzy to help find the sunken gold, I knew the end was near. I came very close to eating one of my own bullets."

"I never told you about the gold."

"Matty did. He was my informant. I'd been milking him for years. I introduced him to Kenny Dunlop. Matty told me about bootlegging with your grandfather. And the Whiskey Creek shooting. He knew I'd never turn him in. He was far too valuable as a snitch. You're right, though. Matty shot the Prohibition agent, not Zack."

"My grandfather was no killer."

"I knew it was over when Furbush started digging. Fuzzy was a nosy pain in my ass."

"So you had Fuzzy drummed off the force?"

"I couldn't take a chance. Years ago he developed an unexplained obsession with the missing strippers."

"So the stuff about the cocaine and massage parlors?"

"The coke story was an easy sell. He was so high strung. As for the massage parlors, I'd had my thumb on Magic Fingers for years. It wasn't hard to get some of the girls to feed that story to Internal Affairs."

"Was Fuzzy that big a threat?"

"He made Ron Register look like Inspector Clouseau. Once he started pulling the thread on the strippers I knew the cover-up would unravel like a cheap blanket. I didn't breathe easy until Furbush was fired. That was ten years ago. When I heard Benjamin hired Fuzzy I tried to scare him off by raising the ghost of Duke Manyon. I knew he'd be terrified. But Fuzzy was too much of a bulldog. He'd never let it go. It was just a matter of time."

Brady sat staring up at a man he'd revered his entire life. The man who'd been like a father to him. The man whose career he'd emulated.

"So you murdered Ben. And Fuzzy. But why Peanut?

"He worked for Benjamin. You found the gold together. I had to assume Benjamin told him what Fuzzy was finding."

"And *Et Tu Brady*?"

Pickens shrugged. "I didn't want you tangled up in this thing, my boy. It was a very clumsy attempt to scare you off. I should have known better."

"Why kill my grandparents? They were no threat to you."

"Blame yourself. After you saw Duke and Buck burying the women at Whiskey Creek, Duke was determined to find you. I told him to stay away from Eden. He wouldn't listen. There was nothing I could do. If they'd gone down, I'd have gone with them."

"So the Super Cop was in bed with thieves and killers. You were a traitor. You sold out your own department to Duke Manyon."

"Duke proposed the arrangement. I would tip him to jobs. I had access to information on wealthy residents. Homeowner schedules, alarm systems, house lay-outs, security guards. Duke and I would pick out targets and plan the jobs meticulously. He'd pull the heist and we'd each take a cut. Two or three a year. It was quite lucrative for both of us. An opportunity to get ahead financially. Then he got involved with Foxx. I told him to stay away. Buck was trouble. Violent. Hothead. Duke ignored me. When Buck killed those strippers, I knew it was over. Then, of all people, you stumbled across them. I was distraught. But I knew it had to be done. We decided they would take care of you and your friends. I was left with Kate and Zack."

"Must have been painful for you."

Pickens blanched. "I don't expect any sympathy from you, my boy. I didn't want you or your grandparents harmed. It was a simple matter of survival. Me or you. I hated myself for what I had to do."

"What about your partner?"

"Kenny Dunlop was too smart to buy the Matty Fitt suicide story. I knew he suspected me. I had to do something." Pickens took a deep breath and let it out slowly. "I've tried to make up for my sins. I counsel wayward kids. Go to prisons to pray with convicts. I'm a deacon at the church. I do good deeds. I dedicated my life to God's work. Then Benjamin stirred the silt and the whole mess floated to the surface again."

"I guess they're going to need a new name for the Detective Bureau."

"That won't be necessary."

"So now you're going to finish the job by killing me."

"I'm afraid time for talk is over." He aimed at Brady's chest. "I'm so sorry, my boy."

Pickens pulled the trigger.

Et Tu Brady

Chapter Ninety-Six

THE GUN CLICKED. He pulled again. *Click.* Again. *Click.* Brady looked up at him with sad eyes and shook his head. He held out his left hand and uncurled his fingers. The snubbie holds five bullets. Four rested in his palm.

Pickens wilted. Brady rose from the chair and took the revolver from his hand. He led him by the arm to the recliner. Pickens didn't resist. He sat him down then reached up and removed the handcuffs from the wall display over the chair and lashed his right wrist to the armrest.

"I'm glad Aunt Mo didn't see this," Brady said.

He took out his cellphone and punched in the number for the Fort Lauderdale Police Department. When he asked for Ron Register, Pickens turned his head away.

After he hung up Brady left him in the chair and began a cursory search of the house. It was a small three bedroom concrete block, maybe eighteen hundred square feet. Built by Bob Gill, the king of Fort Lauderdale developers. During the boom years after World War II, Gill constructed thousands of homes, an average of one every day, as well as Lauderdale Beach's most iconic hotels, including the Yankee Clipper, Yankee Trader, Jolly Roger, and Escape. Pickens' kitchen was small. Stove, refrigerator, pantry, and serving counter that looked out on a dining room where Brady had consumed countless meals. He searched the drawers. Silverware, dish towels, pot holders, screwdriver, pliers, scissors, Scotch tape, flashlight, spare batteries, plug adapters.

Uncle Howard's bedroom was spartan. A queen-sized bed, two bedside tables, a dresser, an old tube television in the corner. Brady found nothing of significance there or in the adjoining bathroom or closet. He entered the bedroom he'd slept in for five years before going off to college. Pickens told the truth when he said Aunt Mo had left the room untouched. The walls were still covered with his old posters. Gerry Lopez surfing the Bonzai Pipeline. Young Bruce Springsteen with his E Street Band. Larry Csonka and Jim Kiick of the old Miami Dolphins flipping birds from the cover of Sports Illustrated. In the closet he found his Mickey Mantle signature baseball glove, his high school calculus textbook, and a Monopoly game. Way in the back, hidden under a stack of spare bed sheets, he found a black satchel. He pulled it down and set it on the bed. Inside was a roll of paper towels, a pair of black-smudged latex gloves, two bottles of black Kuro Sumi Tattoo Ink, and a box of Monster Point Tattoo Needles. He envisioned Uncle Howard branding Ben and Peanut's foreheads with *Et Tu Brady*.

He felt dizzy. He sat on the bed and buried his head in his hands. It occurred to him that Pickens was a monster on par with the worst serial killers. On the surface they are often respectable men, so woven into the fabric of their communities that no one notices them until it's too late. *How did I not see?*

Between the two bedrooms was an alcove. He remembered Pickens using it as his home office. It contained an easy chair and a small wooden desk. He rifled the top drawers. They held pens, pencils, paperclips, and a Swiss Army knife. The middle space was stuffed with telephone and electric bills, bank statements, and a checkbook. A monthly statement from a Fidelity Investments account showed a balance of four hundred thirty six thousand dollars. He thought of the *SunSplash* diamonds. Uncle Howard had invested his ill-gotten loot wisely. The bottom drawer held a stack of old greetings cards from Christmas's and birthday's yore. At the bottom of the pile he noticed a postcard with a picture of an idyllic palm-fringed beach at the foot of a verdant mountain. The legend read: *Greetings from Paradise!* A hand-written note was scrawled on the back. *Be cool! Be careful! – W*

The card was postmarked Roatan, Honduras. It had been mailed in early February, around the time Ben Chance began getting telephone calls telling him Duke Manyon was back. Brady walked into the Florida room and held the card in front of Pickens' face.

"W?"

Uncle Howard turned his head. Aloof. Cold. Insolent. Something snapped inside Brady. He picked up the Smith & Wesson, slid in a bullet, and spun the chamber.

"I should put you out of your misery."

"You'd be doing me a favor."

Brady jammed the barrel hard against Pickens' temple. He grimaced. Brady cocked the hammer and his finger caressed the trigger.

"Is this how you did it to them?"

"Who?"

"You know who," he screamed. "Did you stick this gun to their heads and fire? Did you tell them why? Did you apologize for your betrayal? Did you ask forgiveness? How did you do it, *Uncle Howard?*"

"Go ahead. Take your retribution."

Brady was seething. His body shaking. Blood pounding in his ears. The same rage he'd felt that long ago night when he was murdering Duke Manyon. His finger tightened. Pickens closed his eyes, like he was taking a nap. Brady pulled the trigger. The gun clicked. Pickens jerked and his eyes opened wide. The spell broke and Brady's fury subsided as fast as it had come.

"Your lucky day," he said, shaken at how close he'd come to killing another helpless man. He took a deep breath. "I want you alive for what's coming. The press will be foaming at the mouth. They'll savage your sterling reputation. *Hero Cop Psychotic Killer.* The great J. Howard Pickens is a fraud. A Benedict Arnold. I want you to enjoy that."

Pickens stared at the television. The Packers scored another touchdown. Brady dropped the weapon on the table and walked away. He didn't want to be in the same room. While he waited for the police to arrive he continued inspecting the house and didn't realize what had happened until the first squad car arrived. He met the patrolman at the front door and led him to the back room.

Pickens was slumped in the chair. Foam was bubbling from his mouth. His breathing was a death rattle. It sounded like his lungs were filled with milkshake. On the table next to him the orange vial lay on its side with the cap off. It was empty. The patrolman clicked his handheld radio and summoned EMS. But before help arrived Uncle Howard went into convulsions. By the time they rushed him to Broward General he was comatose. An hour later he was pronounced dead. Belinda Boulanos, the assistant Medical Examiner, estimated he'd ingested approximately fifty tablets of oxycodone.

Et Tu Brady

Chapter Ninety-Seven

"I CAN'T BELIEVE it," Rose rasped. "It's like a terrible dream."

She sounded like she was speaking through a mechanical voice box. It was the first time she'd spoken since doctors removed the breathing tube from her throat. She'd been moved from ICU to the Cardiac Care Unit. Even so, she still had more wires attached to her than a marionette.

The chair in her room was small, but more comfortable than the plastic seat in Intensive Care. He'd been sitting beside her bed describing how he deciphered Howard Pickens was the killer.

"Does he really qualify as a serial killer?"

"Zack and Kate, Matty, Kenneth Dunlop, Ben, Peanut, and Fuzzy. I'm not sure what the rules say, but seven bodies should get you into the club."

"He seemed like such a fine man.'

"He took the coward's way out."

Rose spent two weeks in the hospital. Brady remained by her side all the while. Feeding her. Bathing her. Reading to her.

"I'm glad you're alive," he said out of the blue one day.

It was a simple sentence, yet jarring in its profundity. That wasn't like Brady. She looked at him for a sign he was toying with her. His eyes were daydreamy, focused on nothing, as though he didn't real-ize he'd spoken.

"How nice of you to say so," she said. No need for excess pro-fundity. She thought for a moment then seemed to reach a conclu-sion. "I don't think I'd make a good dead person."

Now it was his turn. He searched her face for a hint of insincer-ity. Her eyes and lips and cheeks were still as a marble bust. He smiled at her.

"Maybe I'll sell the Sea Shanty."

Rose did a double-take on that one. He just blurted it out. No set up. No segue.

"Where did that come from?"

"Maybe Gordy will buy it. I could let him pay it off over time."

"What would you do?"

"We could sail away. Find an island. Lay in a hammock. Drink mojitos all day."

"I don't drink much."

"You can learn. We could buy a little inn. Get married if you want. Have a kid. Maybe two." He put his hand on hers. "How's that sound?"

"Um, where?"

"I've been thinking about Roatan."

Chapter Ninety-Eight

BRADY HUDDLED IN the bosky undergrowth of the green mountain slope. Rivulets of sweat trickled down the valley at the middle of his back. He breathed through clenched teeth, trying not to swallow the mosquitoes flying around his head. Night crawled over the ocean's edge, its shadow sharp as a scalpel, and cut across the island like a black plague. The blanket consumed the sea, the braid of alabaster beach at its fringe, the swaying palms beyond, and moved up onto a narrow table of grassland.

A long brunet spine cleaved the flat like a road to nowhere. At that moment it was a beehive of activity. A small company of toilers dressed in white was scurrying about as the ink crept up the lush mountain pitch. Brady was captured in sightlessness when the taciturn shadows erupted in clamorous converse. Red-lored parrots cawing, spider monkeys screeching, frogs ribbiting. Brady felt like he'd stepped into a Tarzan movie. He guessed this nocturnal jabberwocky had been in progress for eons and at that moment the night creatures were yakking about the intruder hidden in their midst.

From the leafy camouflage he heard the sound of generators belching to life below. That triggered a flurry of events. Two strings of white light transformed night to day. Within minutes a small

Gulfstream jet swooped in and touched down. The black strip was a clandestine runway. It glided to a halt at the end of the airstrip no more than one hundred meters from his position. The *narcoavioneta* had arrived.

For the next several minutes the scene resembled gasoline alley at Daytona Speedway. In the harsh glare a yellow truck backed up to the jet's cargo bay. A dozen armed men began offloading bundles from the vehicle and depositing them in the belly of the aircraft. A fuel truck pulled alongside and a hose was attached to the Gulfstream. The pilot hopped down onto the tarmac dressed in dark slacks and white long-sleeved shirt with epaulets. He was clutching a metallic silver attaché case. He monitored the activity, giving the pit crew instructions, inspecting the landing gear and wing flaps. Then an armed man summoned him to a small table that had been set up near the tail of the aircraft. The pilot sat down across from a man Brady hadn't noticed. He was older and dressed in a white guayabera and white pants that matched his cotton-colored hair and beard. The elder man poured from a tall bottle into two glasses. The men clicked and toasted. Brady could not hear what. The pilot layed the argent case on the table and the white-clad man flipped it open. He shuffled through the contents for several seconds then slammed it shut. Both men stood and shook hands.

A minute later the pilot was back in the cockpit and the fuselage door closed. The trucks pulled away and the Gulfstream taxied to the end of the runway, accelerated, and vanished into the black. Ten minutes after the light strings burst on, they were off again. The generators quieted, the airstrip was abandoned, and Brady was embraced once more by the jungle sounds.

He waited there in the darkness for thirty minutes before making his move. Staying low he slithered silent as a serpent through the trees making his way toward a big, brightly lit house atop the far slope.

He'd been staking out the property for four days and had detected only a small security contingent. The big house was surrounded by acres of neatly manicured lawn so that anyone approaching would be exposed. At night the guards worked in two-man shifts out of a small building near the main gate at the bottom of the hill. One sentry kept vigil at the entrance while another patrolled the perimeter in a golf cart. Both carried automatic weapons and seemed to perform their duties with casual vigilance, indicating they were not accustomed to gatecrashers.

The grassy area was ringed by white board fence, like something from Kentucky horse country. Brady made his way through the woods around the property line until he was above and behind the big house. He hunkered down behind a large prefabricated metal structure that smelled of oil and gasoline. He waited ten minutes for the border patrol to pass in his golf cart. When he was out of sight, Brady crossed a broad, unlit stretch of lawn to the well-appointed bungalow.

The white-haired, white-bearded man in the guayabera was sitting alone on the veranda facing down the mountain toward the wide black bay. He was smoking a cigar beside a half-empty bottle of Flor de Caña rum. The change was startling. For an instant, Brady thought he'd made a terrible mistake. He looked more like Papa Hemingway now than Clint Eastwood. The dashing cat burglar's lean, athletic frame had turned soft and doughy and his once-handsome face was etched with the lines and crevices of a man who smoked too many cigars and drank too much rum.

Brady stepped from the shadows.

"Remember me?"

Duke Manyon looked up through a cloud of blue smoke.

"A little birdy whispered to me there was a visitor in the neighborhood." He said it offhandedly, as one would discuss the weather. "Pickens warned me you might come someday."

"He's dead. So is your son."

"I don't have a son."

"Delray, the thirteen-year-old girl you raped, had a son. Your son."

Manyon took a drag on his stogie. He stuck out his tongue and picked off a speck of tobacco then blew out a billow of smoke.

"I didn't know. What'd he look like?"

"You."

"How'd he die?"

"Shot in the head."

"Police?"

"It's a long story. You don't have time."

"I hope you don't think you're taking me back."

"Who said anything about taking you back?"

Seeing Manyon was like discovering the boogeyman was more shadow than substance. One glimpse purged Brady of the nightmare that had terrorized his dreams for the largest part of his life. And the remorse that he'd committed cold-blooded murder. It turned out he'd murdered a man who hadn't died. He knew as soon as he found the postcard in Howard Pickens's desk.

Greetings from Paradise! Be cool! Be careful! – W.

W as in Wayne. *Wayne* as in Wayne Peter "Duke" Manyon.

A week after Rose was released from the hospital Brady boarded an American Airlines flight from Fort Lauderdale to Atlanta. From there he flew into Aeropuerto Internacional Golosón in La Ceiba on the north coast of Honduras. It turned out that Victor Gruber's freshman class roommate at Harvard was now *El Presidente de la República de Honduras*. One telephone call from Victor and Alberto Valenci Villegas ordered his National Police to put out discreet feelers on one Wayne Peters of Roatan. The response came fast. It seemed the government already had a complete dossier on Peters. Brady made his way to Tegucigalpa, the capital city, and met with Capitan Benicio Suazo Córdova of the National Police.

Córdova was about Brady's age, a swarthy man with an oily sheen to his skin. His English was polished and his manner elegant. He wore a hand-tailored suit that looked far too expensive for a civil servant. In that regard he reminded Brady of Ron Register. An exemplary Latin subcomandante. They sipped stout black coffee while the capitan gave Brady the standard tourist promotional pitch on Honduras.

The country was caught in the throes of a drug war raging throughout South and Central America. The Cocaine Trail led from Columbia through Venezuela. From there the narcotics were loaded onto small planes and flown into Honduras. They landed on covert airstrips in hamlets along the coast where they were offloaded and the planes often set afire before police or military arrived.

An entire industry had grown up around the *narcoavionetas*. Locals could earn five hundred U.S. dollars in one night preparing runways, off-and-on-loading aircraft, and providing food and shelter to pilots. In Honduras the drugs were placed on small jets and flown to remote islands in the Bahamas. There they were packed onto high-speed boats and smuggled into Florida for shipment north. The same route, Brady imagined, Grandpa Zack and Matty Fitt had taken seventy some years ago. But the profits were infinitely larger now. A kilo of raw coke that cost eight hundred dollars in Columbia fetched eighty thousand dollars after being cut and sold on the streets of New York City. Capitan Córdova said the government had documented more than fifty such flights already that year, which probably represented one-tenth the total activity. And it was only March.

"The situation has reached a tipping point for us here in Tegucigalpa, Señor Brady. Violence has taken over our streets. Our homicide rate is one of the highest in the world. Important cities such as San Pedro Sula have become the domain of the *maras*, drug gangs, which carry out ghastly beheadings, eye-gougings, and rapes with impunity. Last month our drug czar, Julian Aristides Gonzalez, was assassinated in front of his daughter's schoolhouse seconds after dropping her off."

"Where does Wayne Peters fit into the picture?"

"Your Señor Peters owns a large estate on the western end of Roatan. Several hundred hectares. He has constructed a five thousand foot road, straight and flat and wide, that comes from nowhere and goes to nowhere." Capitan Córdova smiled. "We have reason to believe he is allowing smugglers the use of it as an aircraft runway."

Córdova said Peters arrived in Roatan approximately twenty years before. Honduran intelligence documented that he had bounced around the Caribbean for several years, basing his operations for varying lengths of time on Grenada, Montserrat, and Trinidad and Tobago, before landing on Roatan. He bought a plantation near Coxen Hole where he maintained a sugar cane operation.

"Far too modest to generate an income sizable enough to bank-roll the profligate lifestyle he enjoys," said Córdova.

"Yet, he lives with immunity."

The capitan shrugged and rubbed his thumb and forefinger together. *Soborno* was clearly as alive-and-well among the *funcionario público* of Honduras as it was Florida's public servants. *Rose would have a field day down here!* Brady wondered if Wayne Peters' *soborno* had helped pay for Capitan Córdova's fine livery.

The next morning he bought a ticket on a high-speed ferry for the one hour jaunt to the long, scabbard-shaped island of Roatan. He landed at Dixon's Cove and traveled by taxi to Half Moon Bay at the western tip of the island. Posing as a *tourista,* he spent the next four days conducting his surveillance.

Now, twenty nine years after Brady thought he'd murdered him, Duke Manyon sat puffing a cigar and smiling up at him. He poured three fingers of brown rum into a clean glass.

"Have a drink, kid. You know, I knew it was you the minute I saw you."

"How so?"

"You look just like your old man."

Brady stared down at him with a flabbergasted expression. Duke laughed and coughed out smoke.

"You knew my father?"

"We served together. Bravo Company, 1st Battalion, 26th Marines." Manyon waved a hand at the chair opposite him. "Sit down and drink your drink."

Brady plopped down, still stunned, and kept staring.

"Why didn't you tell me that way back when?"

"Couldn't," he said, dragging on the stogie. "If you knew I served with your father you'd have known I served with Pickens. Couldn't afford to blow his cover. We were partners."

"You mean the sonofabitch who murdered the parents of the man who saved his life."

Duke blew out another cloud of fog. "You kill him?"

Brady shook his head. "Did it himself."

Manyon chuckled. "Howard the Coward. What we called him in Nam. You should know, though, your dad didn't die trying to save Pickens's life."

"What are you talking about?"

Duke took a slug of rum and a pull on his cigar. The jungle noises were almost deafening. A moth the size of a humming bird was dancing around the veranda light.

"Pickens was a spineless jellyfish. We all knew it. One of us would have fragged his ass if it hadn't been for Goody."

"Goody?"

"What we called your pop."

"Why?"

"After that Chuck Berry song. *Johnny B. Goode*. Fit him perfect. John Brady. *Johnny B*. A good man. Everybody recognized it. If he hadn't been Pickens' best friend, Howard the Coward woulda woke up with a live grenade in his tent long before what happened. As it was, he ended up getting your old man killed."

"You were there?"

"Sorry to say."

"Tell me what happened."

Manyon eyed him across the table. He didn't seem worried about his safety. Without speaking, he slowly scraped ash off his cigar, like he was scraping away the years and traveling back in time.

"It happened at Khe Sahn. Hill Six Two One A. We were patrolling about a click outside our fire base. Slogging through that slimy red mud. I can still feel that shit. Slippery as soap. The hills around us were crawling with VC and PAVN regulars. Me, Pickens, and Goody were holding the right flank.

"Our sergeant major was a big black fella out of Memphis by the name of Otis Starr. He signals that there's movement in the elephant grass. Next thing we know we're in the middle of a shit storm. Shells bursting everywhere. Bullets whistling over our heads. Guys screaming. Me and Goody jump in a crater and start returning fire. Then your father realizes Pickens ain't with us. We turn around and see he'd dropped his weapon and is running like a scared jackrabbit.

He's slipping in mud, tripping over kudzu, in a total panic. Starr's hollering at him to get back and fight before Charlie overruns our asses. Howard the Coward keeps going, like a sissy being chased by a mouse.

"Goody knew what would happen. Marines don't tolerate desertion under fire. He'd spend twenty years in Leavenworth, if he wasn't dragged in front of a firing squad first. Hell, Otis Starr mighta shot him right then and there, if he hadn't taken a round to the throat. So, with the air thick with gook tracers and incoming mortar, your daddy jumps out of the hole and tears after his sorry ass excuse for a friend. That man had some serious balls. He caught up with Pickens and was trying to drag him down from behind when the bullet caught him. Went through the center of his back and out his chest. Clipped Pickens' shoulder. Goody didn't die trying to save the sonofabitch's life. He was trying to save him from being court martialed for desertion."

Brady stared at Manyon, dumbfounded. His entire life he believed his father sacrificed his life to save Uncle Howard's life. Now this thief, this rapist, this murderer, was telling him that was fiction.

"Why should I believe a word you say?"

Manyon smiled and leaned back in his chair. He chewed on the end of his stogie and sloshed the rum in his glass. Then he returned Brady's stare.

"Believe what you want. Your dad was a hero. He took a bullet for his friend. With Starr dead, that left just me and Pickens. A brave man died because of that worthless piece of shit. I wanted to castrate him with my bayonet. Instead, I grabbed him by the scruff of the neck and dragged him back toward firebase, fully intending to turn him in for fleeing in the face of enemy fire. I was gonna testify against him. Hell, if they wanted to shoot the bastard I woulda gladly done the job myself. Then he starts crying and begging me to protect him. Said he lost his head. That he'd do anything for me. That he'd owe me for the rest of his life. He was so pathetic I let him go. We concocted the story about Goody being shot saving a wounded comrade. They gave your father the Medal of Honor. He deserved it. They even gave that cocksucker a Purple Heart."

"Why did you protect him?"

Manyon swallowed a mouthful of rum and replenished his glass.

"Nothing was gonna bring back Goody. I decided to let Pickens live with his guilt. Plus, he owed me after that. I was gonna make sure he made good. After I got discharged I bought a boat and made my way down the east coast to Fort Lauderdale. By then Pickens was a cop. The jewelry jobs were my idea. Your daddy and I were snipers. We could climb trees like a couple of monkeys. I thought I could put my talents to use climbing in and out of rich folk's windows. Especially if I had a plant in the police department pointing me to the best jobs. We came up with a plan. He'd help me identify targets and give me all the data I needed to pull off the heists. Then he'd end up investigating most of them. It was a sweet set up. Ran smooth as a Swiss watch for about three years. We were hitting a handful of marks a year. Making nice scores.

"The ski school was cover. So was the valet concession at the Polynesian. The future was bright. I was gonna do one or two more hits then get out of the business. But the dominoes started falling the wrong way. Pickens found out some whore stripper was ratting us out to his partner. He tells Buck to tell me. Before he does, Buck snuffs her and her friend. I almost killed the bastard myself. We bury the bodies, but you stick your nose in our business. I could not believe John Brady's kid was going to ruin me. What were the odds?"

"You deserved it. You were a thief and a murderer."

"Buck killed them girls. I did a shitload of gooks in Nam, just like your daddy. But I wasn't a murderer."

"Spare me, Manyon. You were a predator. You were going to feed me and my friends to the fish that night."

He sucked on his cigar and studied Brady in silence. Then he looked out over Half Moon Bay. A sliver of moon had waxed over the mountain. Its beam was surfing the faces of waves rolling ashore. He squinted through curls of smoke.

"Aren't you being a hypocrite, kid? You put a spear through me. I was defenseless. You had my gun. You could have turned me over to the police. Instead you whack me over the head and leave me for dead. That qualifies as cold-blooded murder."

Brady shrugged. Manyon was right. He did kill him, or thought he had. And spent most his life living with the guilt. But he wasn't going to give Duke the satisfaction of saying so.

"You deserved it. How is it you are alive?"

Manyon laughed. "I was under water waiting for my lungs to collapse, or some bull shark to pick up my scent. Ready to accept my fate. I'd done a lot of shit in my life. I probably did deserve what was coming. Then I hear that little boat of yours crank up and just take off. I come up and my boat's still floating there. You cut the anchor but didn't tow it away. I never did see Buck again. You spear him too?"

"Lost his head."

"Ah! Well, he did deserve it. More than me. Anyway, I managed to climb into the Donzi and get to shore. Pickens found a doctor who fixed me up then he helped me get out of town."

"What about the SunSplash diamonds?"

Manyon gave him a look of surprise. "You did your homework, kid. You sound like a cop."

"Ex-cop."

The older man nodded. "That explains a lot. We split the diamonds. I bummed around the islands for a few years. Laying low. Waiting for somebody to put out a warrant. Never happened. I ended up here. Been living the good life since."

There was a pause in the conversation. Brady didn't know what else to say. His mind was still trying to digest the news that his father and Manyon had been friends. And how his dad actually died. And the extent of Uncle Howard's betrayal.

"What now, kid?" Manyon said after a time. "I ain't going back. And there's no way you get me off this property alive, let alone this island. What's your plan?"

Brady reached behind him and pulled a twenty two caliber pistol from the waist band of his pants. Manyon looked at him with a bemused smile.

"I pour a lot of gravy on the National Police to keep people like you away from me. They're not gonna appreciate losing such a generous benefactor."

"Already arranged. I've got connections in high places."

"You pull that trigger and my men will cut you down before you get off this porch."

"Don't bet on it. But even if they do, you won't be around to find out. Not this time."

"I told you, kid, I didn't kill anybody. How can you justify shooting me."

"You would have killed me and my friends. And you raped a thirteen-year-old girl. Destroyed her life. Now she's dead. Her son, too. Your son."

Manyon poured more rum into both glasses, though Brady hadn't touched his.

"A dark side of myself I wish I'd never visited. I'm not sure what happened to me that night. I suppose I don't wanna know. I guess we're all capable of behavior we regret. But I'm no murderer. Or rapist. Just that once. I don't even patronize the little *putatistas* in Tegucigalpa."

"Admirable, Duke. Man of the Year stuff. But you did rape her. And planned to kill us. And my grandparents were murdered because of you. So was Matty Fitt. And Pickens' partner. A lot of people died because of you."

Manyon's chin dropped to his chest. There didn't seem to be much more to say.

"So, kid, what's your plan."

"Simple, Duke. I want a favor."

A trace of smile came out on his face.

"What can I do for you?"

"If you meet my father, tell him his son sent you."

Brady cocked the hammer and fired one shot into the center of Duke Manyon's chest.

Et Tu Brady

Chapter Ninety-Nine

"OCARINA."

"OUTRIGGER."

"OBELISK."

"Ophelimity."

"I need a definition, Brady."

"Ophelimity. The ability to please or satisfy."

"You're bragging again."

"Me?"

She smiled and kissed him. "Well, I guess you'd be well within your rights."

Max Brady wondered how he'd gotten to this place. Stretched out next to this woman, on the deck of his schooner, three miles off shore, both of them in their birthday suits, drinking wine, nibbling black cherries, the sun's rays warming their skin while they engaged in a war of *O*'s.

"Oblongata," she said. "As in medulla."

"Oenophile. As in wine lover."

"Obsequious. As in obedient."

"I like the sound of that."

"Shut up."

He held a cherry by its stem in the air.

"Come on. Roll over for a treat."

"I will not."

Three months had passed since Rose was shot in the heart. She'd returned from clinical death to near complete health. The lone remnant, a thin scar down the center of her chest that would remain with her the rest of her life. Rose wore it like a badge of honor.

"How many people can say they've taken a bullet to the heart?"

"You think you're pretty tough, don't you?"

"How many people can say they've been dead?"

"Come to think of it, you are pretty tough."

They'd left Victor Gruber's dock at dawn and sailed to Three Mile Reef. Now the *Victoria II* was anchored above the pink coral outcrop. The first time Brady had been back in three decades. Since that night. He brought scuba gear to take Rose down and show her where he'd found the pirate's gold. Her eyes brightened.

"Maybe we'll find the treasure."

"Doubtful."

"Says who?"

"Says Michael Fury."

"Who?"

Brady went down into the cabin and returned with Michael Fury's diary and gave her a quick primer, Ned Pike's gold, the Loxahatchee tribe, the beautiful Princess Nitcrosis, and the salvage of *The Nemesis*.

"They found the ship?"

"Half of it." Brady pointed down at the Three Mile Reef. "Sitting about fifteen feet from where we are right now. They'd nearly picked it clean before another storm hit and the ship was washed away."

He opened the diary and read aloud.

The tempest had been predicted for weeks by Lagartos Man, one of the village shamans who dressed in the skin of the lagartos.

"Lagartos?"

"What the natives called alligators."

After the storm the shaman announced he had had a vision of a new river created inland. Solac the Cacique took an expedition into the interior of the Floridas. It was me first venture away from the sea. After two days travel by canoe we discovered a crystalline river where, according to Solac, none had existed before. We followed it for days, traveling in the direction of the setting Sun. Eventually we found ourselves in the midst of a giant swamp teeming with life, including bear, panther, lagartos and all manner of bird. We hunted and filled our canoes with food and returned to Tonista. Along the way Solac named the water Himmarshee, which Nitcrosis explained meant New River.

When we got back to the village, Nitcrosis informed me she was with child. I was not surprised. Most girls her age had already borne fruit. We was very happy. With the blessing of her father, the Cacique, we married. I be'd sixteen years of age at the time. The Loxahatchees did not keep measure of their ages but Nitcrosis was near me own. She was very happy and often asked me to massage her belly. Over the following months her stomach swelled and her small breasts grew large and we was very happy and looked forward to the birth of our bairn.

It was the practice of tribal women gravid with child to drink a potion the Loxahatchees believed produced strong babes. When a member of the clan became sick, the shaman cut into their foreheads and sucked out the evil spirit. He spit the blood into a bowl and the dribbly phlegm was drunk by women ripe with child. The practice was repulsive to me and I urged Nitcrosis not to partake but she assured me it was safe and would bring us a healthy bairn.

Sadly, the day after Nitcrosis drank the shaman's potion she became terrifically ill. Her skin burned and she began to vomit and within hours she was dead. The shaman blamed her sudden demise on Nitcrosis carrying the child of a White Devil. The Loxahatchees hated Europeans. They believed the interlopers was systematically destroying all native tribesmen. They sacrificed every white-skinned man or woman they encountered. I had been spared because of Princess Nitcrosis. With her gone and the shaman blaming me for her demise, Solac's attitude toward me changed.

The night Nitcrosis died, I slipped away from Tonista. Over the next many weeks I made me way north along the coast moving by *night and hiding during the light hours. Eventually I reached the outpost at St. Augustine. When the Spanish discovered I was an escaped slave and had been held captive by the natives nigh three years, they took me in, fed me, and put me on a boat to Sevilla. From there I managed to reach the British Isles. In Liverpool I was hired onto the crew of a trade ship bound for the New World.*

Brady layed down the manuscript and stood. Rose looked up at him.

"Why are you stopping. There's more. I want to hear what happens."

"Patience, my sweet. Time for lunch."

He stepped to the rail and dove naked over the side. Three Mile Reef was smaller than he remembered. The fish weren't as plentiful and the colors not as prismatic as they existed in his mind's eye. Or maybe everything just seems larger and more vivid when you're a kid. Even so, he felt like he'd been reunited with a long lost friend. He hoped this reunion would turn out better than the last.

He swam down into the cistern where they'd discovered the gold coins. Two large conchs were sitting in the sand. He grabbed them and returned to the boat, pleased that his lungs still possessed a semblance of their former capacity.

Back on board he retreated to the galley while Rose remained on deck sunning herself. Conchs are sea snails that make their homes in beautiful shells, anchoring themselves by suctioning onto the pink insides of their spiral cubbyholes. Brady tapped the sharp tips of the two shells together, piercing them both, breaking their vacuum seals. With the tip of a carving knife, he extracted the snails and sliced the meat into small chunks. He diced a Habanero pepper, chopped a celery rib, onion, cucumber, green pepper, tomato, squeezed in lime juice, and tossed them together. He uncorked a cold bottle of Alsatian Pinot Gris, grabbed forks and wine glasses, and returned to deck.

Rose had donned her Papillon Gym T-shirt and was leaning against the mast reading Michael Fury's diary. Brady held up the fare.

"French wine and conch ceviche fresh from the sea."

He strung a canopy over them and they ate in the shade, caressed by a soft spring breeze. Hurricane season was still a month away and the Atlantic was docile and blue.

"This is delicious, Brady. You're gonna make some girl a great wife someday."

"It better be soon. My biological clock's ticking louder every day. Hey, how about I marry you?"

"Me? Sorry. I would have, when I thought you were gonna be a billionaire."

"You mean the gold?"

"I just read the last chapter."

"What does it say. Where's the treasure?"

She cast him a smug smile and adopted a professorial cast.

"As you may recall, Michael Fury found a new ship in London. It turned out the captain was a brutal man and after three months at sea the crew mutinied. Fury didn't participate but his crew mates knew he had sailed with the legendary Ned Pike, *Scourge of the Caribbean*. Despite his youth, they elected him their captain. Fury renamed the ship *The Scourge* and began rampaging Spanish gold ships. After a year of plundering, Fury found himself off the Floridas again. His crew was large and well-armed and he decided to return to the Loxahatchee village where he planned to relieve Solac of the cache of gold he'd taken off *The Nemesis*.

"It had been four years since his escape. Fury took two boats ashore with three dozen heavily armed men. They trekked to Tonista without encountering a single native. When they arrived they found a handful of tribal members, sick and barely alive. The Indians told Fury that, after his escape, Solac and his warriors captured a small party of European shipwreck victims. Not pirates. Civilian men, women, and children. They brought them back to the village and sacrificed them by beheading. But, in death, the Europeans gained their revenge. They were carrying an infectious disease that spread through the village like a sail on fire. Solac succumbed and within weeks all but a few Loxahatchees remained. Those that survived were no match for the pirates. Fury and his men unearthed the treasure buried beside Solac's hut.

"Rich beyond his wildest dreams, Michael Fury decided to retire from his piratical ways before he ended up like Ned Pike. He sailed to Barbados, reunited with the Lady Arianna Hightower, and sailed off with her to Ireland. Fury murdered the treacherous uncle who had betrayed his father and regained his family estate, where he and Arianna lived happily ever after, at least until Fury died at age forty nine."

Rose put down the diary and shook her head.

"Bottom line, Brady, Ned Pike's treasure is gone and your prospect of becoming a billionaire is approximately zilch."

Brady leaned over the side of the boat and looked down at the reef.

"Except that Fury's diary says the Indians only got half of Pike's gold. The bow end of *The Nemesis* was swept off and never found. It couldn't have gotten far. Another billion in gold is still down there someplace. I bet I can find it."

"Not so fast," said Rose. "Remember, your old friend *Left Eye* the hammerhead shark? He might still be swimming around."

"Hey, don't knock *Left Eye*. That fish saved my life. Besides, even if he is alive, he's probably lost his teeth. He'd have to gum me to death."

It was a perfect spring day. There were no boats for miles around. They finished the ceviche and wine and made love. Slow and soft. Luxuriating in the feel of each other. Stretching it out for more than an hour. Brady gently satisfying her until Rose finally made him stop.

"Remember, I have a delicate heart."

"Me too."

Afterwards, they swam then lay on the bow deck. He lathered sunscreen on her pale skin and they let the sun warm them while they talked. Brady told her everything. About his childhood. About his feelings for Delray. About killing Duke Manyon on this very spot twenty nine years before. Then again in Roatan. He told her about his agony as she lay dying.

Rose listened, the soft wind rustling her Medusa locks as puffy clouds sailed on the blue sky.

"Do you remember," she said, "asking me once who I thought the last person I'd think of before I died?"

"Sure. The morning after Ben Chance's murder. We were on the roof of The Papillon. You were wrapped in a blanket and I wasn't."

An enigmatic smile came onto her face.

"I know the answer. Dying is such a strange experience. The doctor said they lost me twice on the operating table that night. For all practical purposes, I was dead."

"He told me."

"He didn't have to tell me. I was there. I saw everything. My spirit, or something, was floating over the room. Like I was a spectator at my own death. I did not expect them to bring me back. The funny thing was, I wasn't afraid. I accepted that my earthly life was over. It seemed so natural. So normal. Almost pleasant. Like I was being seduced by Death. Not at all what I expected. But I was ready."

"I wasn't," Brady said.

Rose smiled at him again. "Then I thought of you and suddenly I didn't want to die. I didn't want to leave you. I couldn't bear the idea we wouldn't be together. So I fought Death. I refused to let him take me. And the next thing I knew I was back on the table and I could hear the doctors and nurses. They were giddy they'd brought me back. That was when I knew I wasn't going to die. I had something to live for, Brady. I had you. I don't ever want to leave you."

She leaned over and kissed him.

"And you never will," he said. "I won't let you."

She closed her eyes and lay flat with her face to the sun. Brady slathered more sunscreen on her pale skin. Then she lifted her head and looked at him.

"Well, there is one thing."

"Oh?"

"I've been asked to run for the state Senate. If I'm elected I'll be spending a lot of time in Tallahassee."

"That snakepit! You think Walter Dean was crooked. The vipers up there will sell their children's souls to the first lobbyist who stuffs enough money in their pockets."

"It probably doesn't matter. I doubt I could even get elected."

But they both knew that wasn't true. Since the shooting, Rose had become the most famous political officeholder in the State of Florida. The scandal over the slip-and-fall scam had burnished her reputation as a smart, honest, crusading young public servant. Junior Ball was dead. Walter Dean was under indictment. And the beautiful woman who nearly lost her life exposing them would be a virtual shoo-in.

"What do you say, Brady?"

"Senator, huh? I kind of like the sound of that. In fact, I'm beginning to think you could go far."

"Let's not get carried away."

"While you're in Tallahassee I can find the rest of Ned Pike's gold. Then I can buy you a few elections. Maybe I can get you elected the first female President of the United States."

"Give me a break, Brady."

"I'm very serious."

Rose rolled over and lay on top of him.

"You can't fool me, mister. You just want to be First Canoodler."

"Obviously."

"Good *O*-word."

"Shall we canoodle?"

"Olé."

About the Author

Joseph Collum is the recipient of more than 100 major journalism awards during his career as an investigative reporter, including the Alfred I. duPont-Columbia University Award, two George Polk Awards, five Investigative Reporters & Editors Awards and a dozen Emmy Awards.

His reports have led to a Congressional inquiry into elder care, saved the lives of people denied adequate medical care, prevented hundreds of low income homeowners from eviction, and resulted in the imprisonment of dozens of corrupt public officials. Collum was the first reporter in America to expose the widespread practice of racial profiling (the Oxford English Dictionary credits him with coining the term *"racial profiling"*). His final journalism assignment was at Ground Zero on September 11, 2001 and the days immediately following the collapse of the World Trade Towards. His account of the tragedy is excerpted in the book *Covering Catastrophe*.

After retiring from journalism following 9/11, Collum returned to his childhood roots in Fort Lauderdale, Florida to write books. His novel *Brady's Run*, a murder mystery set in Fort Lauderdale, was published in 2009. The sequel, *Et Tu Brady*, was published in 2013. *The Black Dragon: Racial Profiling Exposed*, the true story of the invention of racial profiling and the fight to end the practice, was published in 2010. His next novel, *A Bullet for Brady*, will be published in 2014.

Collum and his wife, Donna, are the parents of four sons, Peter, Simon, Spencer and James.

Visit Joseph Collum on the Web at www.josephcollum.com or contact him at josephcollum.author@yahoo.com.